and my
hero...
Best of
everything...
Don Ross
2015

TRAILS

A WESTERN SAGA

DON ROSS

LIGHT SWITCH
PRESS

Published by:
Light Switch Press
PO Box 272847
Fort Collins, CO 80527
www.lightswitchpress.com

ISBN: 978-1-939828-06-4
Printed in the United States of America

DEDICATION

Conceding that this may be the only dedication that a 70-plus year old author will produce, I have a list of those who mean a lot to me. This book is dedicated to…

Parents Robert and Marion

Brothers David and Mike

Joannie

Son and daughters Steve, Jody, Liz, Lauren and Ashley

Grandchildren Arthur, Alec, Ethan, Logan, Mitch, Christian, Brett, Kaleb, and Micah

Aunt Mina, Jim, Woody, Michele, Andy, Karina, and Joel

And to generations of students, colleagues, and friends
who have touched my life in many positive ways…

Special thanks to Joannie and Ashley, who put in long hours re-typing and formatting the manuscript: Steve, whose proofreading and suggestions contributions were massive; and to Bonnie Lee Lewis.

CHAPTER ONE
1830

The Choctaws had a name for Andrew Jackson: Hatak-haksi, "evil worker." To them, he was not the Great White Father. He was the instigator of a nefarious plan to rid them of their lands and to change their lives forever. It had been different when they fought alongside him against the British at the Battle of New Orleans, but as soon as he began his Presidency in 1829, he determined to remove all tribes east of the Mississippi River. They would be exiled to unsettled land in the West.

"…Ample lands will be guaranteed to the Indian Tribes as long as they shall occupy it," he told Congress.

Most of the Indians in the South were members of the so-called Five Civilized Tribes--Choctaws, Chickasaws, Seminoles, Cherokees, and Creeks--tribes who had peacefully assimilated into co-existence with whites. They were farmers for the most part, not warriors. They wore white man's clothing and inter-married with them, and plowed their fields with oxen.

Because of their numbers, and because of their predicted non-resistance, they were the initial targets for Jackson's shortsighted and morally bankrupt manifesto.

The Choctaws, the most numerous of the Five, were in the Presidential bulls-eye. Bribed, threatened and lied to by government agents, Choctaw chiefs signed the Treaty of Dancing Rabbit Creek in 1830, ceding 10.3 million acres in Mississippi for parcels in Oklahoma and Arkansas, some of which they already owned from previous treaties.

At every step, Jackson was challenged by the Supreme Court. He ignored them, as did Congress.

The Indian Removal Act of May, 1830, promised safe conveyance and set in motion the terms and times for the migration.

Isuba Kamassa-- Strong Horse-- stood on the banks of Chunky Creek in western Mississippi one afternoon in September of 1831. Behind him was his village, Chunky Chito, a neat collection of homes weaved with river cane and vines. A large cornfield in the distance had been exhausted for that year. What normally would have been a flurry of tribal activity to prepare for winter was confined now to a listless shuffling about while the village waited.

His ten-year old daughter, Pachallhppuwa Tuchena- Three Doves--broke his reverie.

"What is it, my father? You have been standing here a long time,"

"I am listening to our ancestors, my Dove. I am receiving blessings from them, and from the land." He answered her without turning around. She saw from his side that there were tears on his cheek.

"Is it for the journey?"

Her father was a respected member of the village, a man who, from past the midpoint of his life, saw things much more clearly than most men. And he was wrestling with prescient thoughts now which alarmed him.

"Are you worried, father?"

"The white chiefs have promised us fertile, unspoiled lands in a faraway place. We must trust them. We will make new lives, raise new crops."

"There are some in our village who say that the white chiefs are tricking us. Some who say that they will not take the journey."

"Such talk is foolish. We have made agreements. Our great Chief Mushalatubee signed the white man's papers. We will go."

"Is it a long journey?"

So many questions from this strong little girl, this little girl who played stickball with the tribe's boys, her dark hair dancing behind her, her dark eyes sparkling at the fun. There was much of the warrior in his daughter, maybe more than in his sons, Nitushi and Naskoba, who were much older and who were among the village's respected tillers of the land.

"It is a journey that we will take, my little Dove."

She realized that the conversation over, and danced away from him.

A military force arrived a few days later and began barking orders. The journey would begin that day. They brought wagons, not enough. Many of the tribespeople were startled at the suddenness and the brutish behavior. Most were not prepared; some would walk without shoes.

"My husband," Talking to Angels asked as the departure neared, "Where are Nitushi and Naskoba?"

Strong Horse knew, but he would never tell anyone, not even his wife. His sons had told him that they would stay in Mississippi, that they would run east and keep running until the removals were complete. As the soldiers approached, the two sprinted to the cornfield. By now they were hidden somewhere miles away.

Strong Horse found a spot in a wagon for Talking to Angels and for his feeble father, a tribe elder, Okshakla – Deep Water. He and Three Doves would walk.

As the villagers pulled away, many heads turned back to the huts. Leaving the green fields, the only home most of them had ever known, was more ominous than they had expected, especially in the light of this harsh treatment. Some of the soldiers had their guns trained on the marchers. More than a few doubters were born in those moments.

There were four delays as other villages joined the queue. By the start of the second day, the count of migrants was in the hundreds. Three Doves couldn't see the front or back of the line.

At first the few discomforts were overcome. Strong Horse walked stoically, looking straight ahead, while Three Doves skipped and bounced beside the wagon which carried her mother and grandfather. Walking ahead were her mother's brother, Hashuk Mali, and his family. Three Doves had never liked her uncle much. He chided her for trying to be a boy and seemed put off by her buoyant spirit. Her cousins were insular, removed from social contacts with others her age, distant, even unfriendly.

Several different routes were being used that week as thousands of Choctaws wended their ways toward the setting sun. Three Doves' people would cross the Mississippi River at Vicksburg and trek north to the Arkansas River, where steamboats would convey them farther west. They would then walk the remaining distance toward the Washita River in south central Oklahoma.

At "depots" along the way, the government had stocked supplies of pork, beef, and vegetables, but no clothing, blankets, or shoes. Both actions would prove fatal.

Torrential rains began on the fourth day, creating large areas of swampy bogs, through which Three Doves sloshed in knee deep pools. Then the October weather changed abruptly to cold drizzle. Among the walkers, those who became sick or weak were left behind.

One morning Talking to Angels told her husband that his father had died during the night. It had taken a while as he lay gasping for breath and delirious. There was no dignity and no honor in his passing. She had not summoned Strong Horse, because she wasn't sure where he was. There was no ceremony, no mourning. The family was given shovels and an order to "get it done quickly." Strong Horse gave the old man's blanket to Talking to Angels, and stuck an amulet from his father's neck into his own pocket.

Afterward, Strong Horse became more isolated and more troubled. He would not acknowledge his daughter's questions now. There was a vacant look in his eyes, and his mouth was tensed in a grim frown.

Talking to Angels gave up her wagon spot to a young girl. She would walk next to her husband for the rest of the journey.

The steamboats were a godsend, but only briefly. Flooding made the river dangerous, and the boats were considerably overcrowded. Then a prolonged blast of cold weather froze over parts of the waterway. The marchers were ordered off. This time there were fewer wagons.

One day, Talking to Angels complained of a temperature and extreme cramps, and kept falling behind the group. His wife's agony jarred Strong Horse from his stony demeanor. Soon she couldn't continue. Strong Horse would not leave her behind. He bargained for a wagon spot for her. It didn't matter. She died quickly from cholera, as did many others.

Brackish drinking water was the cause. In addition, most of the meat and vegetables, moved from old locations to new "depots," had spoiled. Over 100 Choctaws perished from eating tainted food.

Strong Horse was inconsolable. Worse, the soldiers wouldn't permit a burial until the scheduled stop that night. Friends from the village got out of a wagon so that Talking to Angels could be laid out, covered by Deep Water's blanket. Three Doves sat next to her, holding her mother's head in her lap.

That night Strong Horse sat on frozen ground next to his wife's grave, and made a decision. He was finished with this journey of misery. He would not move from this spot.

In the Choctaw culture, the most important influence in a child's life was considered to be a maternal uncle. That had not been the case with Three Doves and Hashuk Mali. Perhaps it was time. The next morning Strong Horse counseled with his brother-in-law, and then with his daughter. Three Doves was horrified.

"My father. You are my only family now. I am nothing without you."

"I must stay with your mother in this desolate place. I cannot leave her spirit here alone. You must go on. You will be the seed of the next generation in a new place. It is what your mother would want."

"Father…" She began to weep, and then sob, in paroxysms that shook her body.

He put his arms around her.

"Hashuk Male will take care of you. He gave his promise. You must do this now, for me…for your mother. My last thoughts will be of you, my little Dove."

Her last view of her father was of a solitary figure hunched over a mound of earth, growing smaller as the group began another day of arduous travel.

The journey took six months, a pathetic experiment which would not improve in repeated removals for the next nine years. Over a quarter of the Choctaws perished and were buried haphazardly along the long trail. Many more were left behind; they too were casualties. And the Promised Land was a treeless sunburned plain, an endless expanse of yellow and brown, barely arable or tillable, in south central portions of the Oklahoma Territory.

But the resourceful Choctaws persevered. Soon there were neat huts and fields of crops, grown through intense labor and constant struggle. The tribe made the reservation livable, if not lush. They traded for livestock and seeds, and for blankets and trinkets with the trappers from the Northwest, who were overjoyed that a new market existed, and would continue to grow.

All members of the reservation community were called upon to share the work. At the callow age of eleven, Three Doves was recruited for tending to the oxen, and to the small herds of mustangs and cattle. But her trademark vivacity had faded. As she grew into a woman's body, a beautiful sun-tanned teenager with large brown eyes, she withdrew more and more. Hashuk Mali and his family tended to her basic needs, food, a homeplace, but the nightmare of losing her family persisted, and the wretched half-year in purgatory was indelible, a darkness which tormented her endlessly. If others could forget the past with industry and hope, no such exorcism was possible for her.

She was sixteen when an unforeseen event changed the direction of her life, and gave her new nightmares.

A general commotion spread through the reservation one day in the spring of 1837. Big Hunter was back, with rum, knives, guns, ammunition, clothing, jewelry, and pelts. Big Hunter, Jean Luc Bernier, a Canadian-born trader-trapper from the Rocky Mountains, made the trip once a year, and returned home with buffalo robes and horses, plus whatever skins and pelts the Choctaws could summon from the barrenness around them. He was unique in several ways. He had charm that crossed the cultures, and dressed well. He was fair in the bartering process. He was reasonably young, and had rakish good looks that caused younger Choctaw women to giggle among themselves and hang around the fringes of the trading area. His hair was shiny, they noted, and his beard was immaculately trimmed. And if his nose was overlong, and his gray eyes somewhat expressionless, it didn't matter to them. His arrival in camp was an event, a celebration.

Bernier also had an eye on his admirers. One solemn looking girl caught his attention. He spotted her standing in the back of the crowd, a slim, attractive Choctaw maid, somewhat under twenty, he guessed. He conferred in broken words and phrases with the Indian next to him.

That evening, Hashuk Mali pulled Three Doves aside.

"Big Hunter leaves at sun up. You will go with him."

"Uncle, what do you mean?"

"Big Hunter has traded well for you. You belong to him."

"You traded me?"

"There is no time for making you his wife. He leaves tomorrow. He has promised to honor you."

"My father trusted you to guide me in the Choctaw way. He wanted me to build a Choctaw family here, to honor him and my mother."

She realized that she had taken a defiant position in front of him. She was talking loudly, disrespecting him. But she was surprised, angry, and scared.

"No more. It is done."

The next morning, she left, looking neither left nor right. She sat next to Big Hunter on the wagon seat. Strings of Indian ponies were tied behind the wagon. She heard voices from the village as the wagon left. "Ooooo. Big Hunter...Three Doves leaves with him...Three Doves will be cheerful now..."

The two didn't acknowledge each other for miles. That night, he threw a blanket on the ground next to the fire where she sat. He indicated with gestures that he wanted her to disrobe, but she sat adamantly, without moving. He sat next to her, smiling confidently, and began to undress her.

She didn't resist as he eased her back onto the blanket. His breath was next to her ear, and she was unsure of what to do, but his gentle ministrations guided her through long minutes of pain, then a sort of warm resignation. He stood above her as he pulled his pants up. He was still smiling, but he wasn't looking at her now; he was staring into the fire. She lay there undressed and waited until she heard him snoring on the blanket beside hers. She pulled her clothes on and fell asleep quickly. For whatever reason, that night, for the first time in five years, she slept soundly, untenanted by visions of her mother's grave or the lonely specter of her father on the frozen ground.

CHAPTER TWO

1836

Herkimer Grimes saw her first, a figure stumbling toward the Ranger camp, the image wavering from the rising heat.

She was more than 500 yards away, partially hidden behind a slope. It was a female; he saw the dress skirt. But maybe it wasn't. Maybe it was a Comanche trick to lure the company away from the Colorado River, to an ambush. He couldn't see much behind her, the configuration of land was such that it afforded wary eyes enough time to see an advancing enemy horde, but not much more.

He squinted hard against the Texas sun, trying to discern more. Instinct, more than anything, told him that it was a girl or lady in extreme duress, nothing more.

He ran to his horse, calling out to the other Rangers in the encampment, "Somebody in trouble out there!"

When he reined in, she was prone on the ground. She raised her head and looked at him, pleading. He pulled his pistol and rode to the top of a rise behind her to satisfy himself that there were no renegades hiding. In an instant he was joined by Captain John J. Tumlinson.

"She's in bad shape, Cap'n."

"Looks that way. What's she doin' out here?" He dismounted and moved to her side.

Lady…lady…you're OK now." He lifted her head and rolled her into his arms. "Lady, can you hear me?"

She answered through blistered lips, a whisper, "They're dead…my son…my son…help me…help me please...Hibbons…"

Tumlinson lifted her to Herk's saddle.

They put her in Tumlinson's tent. Herk looked at her as he lowered her onto a blanket.

"Thirty to forty years old, I'd guess. Somebody worked her over pretty good. Had to be Comanch."

"They wouldn't just turn her loose or leave her out here, Herkimer. If anything, she's escaped from them somehow," Tumlinson asserted. "Must mean they're close by somewhere."

Flapjack Bailey entered the tent, and stared at her. "Oh my word. My word. Pore lady. Pore, pore lady."

"Flap, quit standin' there lookin' stupid. Bring her some water, dammit." Tumlinson glowered at him. The rotund Ranger turned on his heels and returned with a canteen. Grimes left the tent to scan the horizon again. Calling out to his companions, "Comanch in the area!" he remounted and rode out again. Bailey soon caught up.

They rode west, away from the river and the camp thirty miles northwest of the Ranger capitol at Austin.

At the age of 27, Herk was the youngest, tallest, and most promising in his company. Tumlinson counted on him in many ways. He was the group's unofficial second-in-command. The company had no scout; he served that purpose. In skirmishes with the Comanche, he had proved to be most fearless and best shot among the company's men, which normally numbered thirty-three. Some of the force had been diverted to the south, where they were destroying supplies behind Mexican army's lines.

Without being asked now, Herk rode in a wide semi-circle in the direction the woman had come from, looking for any signs of what had stranded her in this no-man's land.

Jack Bailey particularly looked up to him. The corpulent Bailey was nearing forty, and was short in guile, intelligence, and stature, but in battles, he was dependable, and nearly as valuable as Herk.

"What are you lookin' for, Mr. Grimes?"

"Smoke. Bent grass. Horse droppings. Anything."

They criss-crossed the area in silence for over an hour. Bailey was quiet out of deference to the scouting skill of his young companion. He watched Grimes intently. Herk grabbed his canteen and took a long draught, then wiped his bushy black moustache with the back of his hand.

"Flap, circle over that range of hills to the left. I'll meet you back here in an hour."

He jerked his horses head to the right, and trotted away.

Bailey was waiting when Herk galloped back later. It was mid-afternoon.

"Find anythin', Mr. Grimes?"

"Found plenty. Let's get back to camp."

Tumlinson stood outside of this tent. "Well?"

"Raiding party camped maybe ten miles from here. Less than twenty braves. Had a young white boy with them."

"The woman told me her story while you were gone. Name's Hibbons. Seems she and her family was on the move ahead of the Mexican army, clearin' out. They was attacked by the Comanche. They killed her husband and brother, and took her, her young son, and a baby with 'em."

Herk was quiet.

"They camp, and the baby starts cryin'. One of the Comanches grabbed it by the feet and smashed its head against a tree. She passed out, and they left her alone. She run away early this morning'."

"She OK?"

"Seems to be. So, what do you think, Herkimer?"

When he was serious, Herk's voice dropped an octave and became an assertive mumble.

"Gotta rescue that boy, Cap'n."

"Twenty Comanches. Sixteen of us. Seems like a fair fight to me," Tumlinson smiled.

"Surprise them tonight, it'll even the odds."

"Nope. Gotta do it now. They'll prob'ly be on the move tomorrow. Might be gone now."

Tumlinson called to the other Rangers, and Herk began drawing a map in the dirt in front of the captain's tent with a stick.

"This here's the camp. Top of a small ridge. This side's flat for a long ways. Can't sneak up there, too far. I'd say we get above them here, and come up from below them here."

"See any lookouts?"

"Nope. Pretty quiet."

Tumlinson took the stick from him. "We'll look it over when we get there. Flap, Gurney, and Big Head'll ride with you. If this is a good map, the four of you can spread out above them, ride into camp, and get their attention. Grab the boy too, if you can. Big Head, you find the ponies and scare 'em away. The rest of us'll come at the camp from here. Gonna have to make every shot count. Flap, don't shoot any of us."

"Aw, Cap'n…Hey, what if they ain't there?"

"We'll stay with 'em. Better to fight now when there's only twenty. Nother thing… we ain't aimin' to scare 'em away or take prisoners. They killed a baby and two other folks."

He turned to enter his tent. "Spect I better tell her to sit tight."

As the sun withdrew from the Texas plains, they separated a mile from the Comanche camp.

"Give you 30 minutes to get behind 'em. We'll stay clear till you commence firing. Gonna be almost dark, so be sure what you're firing at," Tumlinson cautioned.

Herk's group circled right at a slow trot, to minimize noise. Minutes later, they were looking down at the renegades from the cover of high grass and several thin trees. Two campfires threw a kaleidoscope of images across the camp area. The chattering of a cowbird broke the stillness.

"Anybody see the boy?" Herk whispered.

"Ain't that him 'bout twenty feet from the fire on the right, lyin down? Two bucks sittin' by him?" Gurney answered.

"Yep, that be him," Bailey affirmed. "Little fella."

"I'll ride at them two. Gurney, you and Flap ride toward that second fire. Seems to be a bunch of them over that way. Big Head, you see the ponies?"

"Yeah. I see 'em Herkimer. Clear over by them trees."

"Should be thirty minutes by now. Don't be in a hurry till you see me start to gallop."

"Sure hope the Cap'n shows up quick. It's gonna be lonely down there for a while,"

Gurney said.

The four started down the slope, pistols drawn. After the first pistol shots, they would dismount and use their muskets. Each had three shots from his weapons until he'd have to reload. By then Tumlinson would spill into the area from the other side.

This is odd, Herk thought. No lookouts. Comanche weren't this careless. The whole scenario was odd. Why were they still camped here? Probably preparing for a raid, maybe on Austin. How lucky was Mrs. Hibbons, stumbling around distraught, to have chanced on the Ranger camp.

Now he was at a gallop. Peripherally he noticed Flap and Gurney galloping in tandem to his left. The two braves at the campfire jumped up, startled. Herk's first shot hit one somewhere, and he fell heavily to the ground. The other one drew a knife and moved toward the young boy. He's going to slit his throat, Herk thought. He reined up forty feet away and fired. The shot hit the Comanche in the face. He dropped the knife as soon as he was hit. Herk heard scores from Gurney and Flapjack to the left, and almost immediately a volley of shots from the other side of the camp. He dismounted and ran to the boy, grabbing his musket. The first brave was on his feet whooping and snarling, seemingly weaponless. Grimes swung his musket like a club, and the brave went down again, for good. Herk hovered over the boy, and fired his musket toward the group charging Gurney and Bailey. A scream told him that he had hit his target.

From there, reloading, he saw a brave rush from behind Gurney, who had also dismounted. He could do nothing as a tomahawk flashed in the firelight and crashed into Gurney's head.

Across the area, Tumlinson and his men were effective and efficient. Then Big Head, having scared off the ponies, appeared on the far right, and dispatched a brave trying to run away. In seconds it was over.

"Seems there were only fifteen of 'em, Herkimer. Gonna have to work on your countin'," Tumlinson said.

"We lose Gurney?"

Tumlinson nodded. "How's the boy?"

"Scared. Cryin'. Seems to be OK though."

As the company rode back to camp, cradling the young boy and carefully leading Gurney's horse and its burden, they had no inkling that the Hibbons Rescue would be inscribed in Ranger lore for years.

Nor did they know yet that seventy miles to the south two days before-March 6, 1836--Mexicans had overrun the mission at San Antonio. All American defenders had died at the Alamo, including a small company of Texas Rangers.

CHAPTER THREE
1838

For as far as the eye could see, tents, lean-tos, and tepees stretched along the Wind River. The Rendezvous of 1838 was sited in Wyoming, and as usual since its inception in 1825, hundreds of fur trappers and mountain men and thousands of Indians showed up for several weeks of socializing, contests, horse racing, wrestling, shooting, trading, and debauchery. The Rendezvous gatherings were sponsored by the Rocky Mountain Fur Company; previous to the event, trappers had to make a thousand-mile trek to St. Louis with pelts and hides to do business with the Rocky Mountain group and the Hudson's Bay Company. The Rendezvous brought the business to them.

One notice promoted the 1838 event with the wording, "Come the Wind River for white women and likker."

Jean Luc Bernier had attended the past eight years. As an independent trapper, he was somewhat of a maverick. Most of the trappers were casual employees of the two fur company giants, who vied contentiously for hides, notably beaver pelts used to make fashionable, popular hats. The two companies had staked out sections of the Rocky Mountains for their exclusive use. Jean Luc trapped where he wanted, and concentrated in buffer areas between the unofficial reserved lands.

Trappers did their work in the fall and winter of each year, and were ready in the spring to trade their collections for money, or provisions to get through another trapping season. It was not a lucrative undertaking. The company men were hard-nosed in trading sessions. Most of the trappers were in debt to the Rocky Mountain Fur Company.

Not Jean Luc. He bartered with tribes and with individuals and only rarely crossed paths with the fur companies and their minions. He was at Wind River for the social activity and for the whiskey, which flowed freely along the mile of tents and tepees. He was among the very few that had bucked the system and thrived. He not only trapped, but he also hunted, and his cache included skins and pelts of buffalo, elk, deer, grizzly, and mountain lion.

Three Doves understood the significance of the gathering as the two made their way down the gauntlet of temporary homes. To that point, she wasn't sure why Big Hunter had brought her in the long journey from their modest cabin in the Rocky Mountains. He had packed most of her possessions. They were moving to a new home, she guessed. She was on a saddle horse, trailing behind Jean Luc, who pulled a string of pack animals.

The past eight months had been a mix of confusion and resignation, tempered with occasional moments of contentment, if not joy. The language that passed between them was mostly gestures and phrases; neither spoke the language of the other. During the days Big Hunter was tolerant of her, sometimes kind. On some nights he was attentive and gentle. All too often, he was gone to hunt or check his traps. At first, she didn't understand his absences, and she languished in loneliness and fear until he returned, his pack horses laden with skins. Had she wanted to run away, to escape, she would have faced an unknown, wild landscape and no idea of how to leave it, and there was no conveyance; Jean Luc had the horses with him.

Recently, he had devised a system. "I go…" he would say, holding up a number of fingers to indicate how many days he'd be away.

Her loneliness during his absences was palpable, overwhelming at times. The cabin, a simple one-room log building, was confining and claustrophobic. Some days she would walk the mountains, taking care not to stray farther than she could easily return. She busied herself around the cabin, cleaning and rearranging.

Life was neither bad nor good. A child would give her company, occupy her time, and if that was what life would be, it was acceptable. Jean Luc provided for her, and although they were not husband and wife, there was an element of satisfaction. Recently his lovemaking had become rougher and more dispassionate, but those were still moments she anticipated, even on the nights when whiskey dictated his actions.

Jean Luc selected a spot somewhere near the middle of the 100-acre Rendezvous string, a temporary community, and pitched a large, impressive tent, the same one he had set up back in Oklahoma. The first night, he had her sit on the ground at the tent's front flap, while he greeted innumerable acquaintances a few yards away. She noticed that most of them looked at her while Jean Luc talked. That night, roaring drunk, he had passed out in the tent.

He was away most of the next day. She briefly walked the tent line, until she sensed that she was drawing too many comments, too many stares. She had hoped to run into some tribesman that she could talk to, a Chickasaw perhaps. She returned to the tent.

Shortly after dark, she thought that she heard Jean Luc's voice outside the tent. Suddenly, the front flap opened, but it wasn't Big Hunter. An enormous, dirty, drunk mountain man abruptly lurched into the candlelight, grabbed her, and threw her down on a pile of blankets. Then he was pawing her, pulling up her skirt, touching her, and finally pinning her while he pushed off his boots and pants. It happened so fast that she was defenseless. Then she felt the unbearable pain of his penetration.

"Keyu! Keyu!" she screamed. "No! No!"

Over the shoulder of the panting, smelly, frantic monster above her, she saw Jean Luc open the flap, a lantern in his hand. She would be saved.

But Jean Luc looked at the coupling, smiled and left.

Suddenly, she understood.

Three Doves suffered through a seemingly endless procession of visitors that night. Before the second one entered, a skinny, toothless trapper who sodomized her, she resolved to fight back.

She kicked at the man, grabbed him by his matted hair, and elbowed him across his wizened face. He responded with a wild punch to her nose. She fell back dazed, and succumbed.

She lost count. Throughout the unspeakable torture, through the searing pain, she heard Big Hunter's voice outside the tent, often laughing. She was conscious of his entering the tent just before daybreak. By then she was sitting in the dark, numb, her body aching.

She couldn't summon the strength to move, but her mind became active that morning. In some way, she would run to a tepee. Her own kind would protect her.

Jean Luc jostled her, grabbed her by an arm, and hustled her down to the Wind River near midday. He virtually threw her into the water. The cool flow was soothing to places which seemed raw. Several trappers were bathing nearby. Jean Luc yelled to them, and pointed to her. Minutes later, he ordered her out, and as she emerged, snarling at him, he slapped her to the ground. He then dragged her back to the tent, soaking wet. As she sat in there during the day, drying off, she knew that he had prepared her for another horrible night.

He brought in a tin plate of food during the afternoon. She noticed that he was looking at her with obvious disdain. A fixed sneer, a look of unmistakable repugnance, was fixed on his bearded face. Late that afternoon, he re-entered the tent accompanied by a chubby, giggling white woman of indeterminate age, with frizzy hair and too much make-up. The two undressed and made noisy love. Jean Luc looked at Three Doves throughout the rutting. The woman tittered and sighed, and screamed at the end, a wide smile on her face. When she left, Jean Luc patted her ample backside and gave her something. He then stared at Three Doves. The lesson was obvious to her. This was the way he wanted her to act later.

Before the tent flap opened that night, she resolved to lie motionless and quiet when the attacks began. She would give no man the pleasure of a squirming, active partner. Early the next day, she would find a tepee and a kindred soul. That plan was destroyed when the visits began. Many rapists on this night were Indians. She tried to ask for help in her language. The Indians neither responded nor acknowledged her protests and pleas. Race and culture were ignored as they groveled and manhandled her. There would be no escape.

For four nights the visits continued. She had not experienced such pain or humiliation in her seventeen years. She was beyond resistance, emotionally and physically. She knew that she would soon die. She began praying to her parents.

On the afternoon of the fifth day, Jean Luc walked in with a length of rope, threw her clothes at her, and motioned for her to get dressed. He then bound her unresisting arms in front of her and pulled her outside. Standing there was the skinny man who had hit her the first night. The two lifted her onto the back of a skinny mule, and tied her hands to the saddle's pommel. Jean Luc secured her bundle of clothes behind her. The skinny man crawled onto a horse, grabbed the reins of her mount, and rode away from the Rendezvous.

The ride was painful, but thankfully short. After two days, he led her up to a shabby small building among a collection of boulders at the foot of a mountain. Along the way she had memorized landmarks, although there was no clear purpose to it. Several times, he rode alongside her, pointed to himself and said "Rafe," his name, she was sure. She was repulsed by the man whose leer revealed just a few yellowed teeth. Once he had reached over to fondle her breast, grabbed his own crotch, and began to chortle at her, one eyebrow raised. She leaned away and shrugged. He wasn't pleased.

He pulled her off of the mule roughly and shoved her through the front door of the house. Dust had settled on a few wooden chairs and a long, stained table. The pungent odor of rotten food permeated the room. A pile of rags, or clothes, was stacked shoulder high in one corner. She noticed a collection of firearms in another corner below a cabinet.

When he closed the front door, the room got suddenly dark. There was only one window, and it was covered with a blanket. He struck a match, and lit two lanterns and a long candle, watching her. In the light, the place looked worse.

He reached behind him and pulled out a knife, and walked toward her. The knife was large, a skinning tool. As he got close, he raised it and pointed it at her face, cackling and smirking. He had her cornered, but her mind was racing. She'd have to act fast, but she'd get only one opportunity. He was obviously stalking her for sex, and after that he'd tie her up again. He grabbed her crotch as he set the point of the knife against her throat. She whimpered, and he moved the knifepoint enough to nick her.

He grabbed a handful of her clothes, and swiped at them with the knife, stepping back. As part of her shirt fell open, he indicated that she should undress. She shivered as she stood there naked. He stared at her breasts and set the knife down while he unbuckled his pants, and let them drop. The knife was on the table, too far away for her to reach. His erection disgusted her.

He shuffled over to pick up the knife, his pants still around his ankles. Then he was against her, the knifepoint at her waist, his left hand on her shoulder, forcing her to her knees. No! She'd die before she'd do that. She began stroking his upper thigh and his grip on her loosened until she could stand again. She edged slowly toward the table, and bent over it, looking back at him with as much of a smile as she could muster. He was quickly on her. His hands rested for balance on the table on each side of her, his right hand still tightly clasping the knife. He began, thrusting violently against her so hard that each movement caused the table to lurch.

Her eyes were fixed on his right hand and the knife. Soon now, she thought. She began to encourage him, moving against him. As the thrusts became faster, she said his name, "Rafe!" and audibly moaned. Then she heard his breath quicken and stop, and then a gasp, and at that moment, his knife hand opened and trembled.

With incredible swiftness, she grabbed the knife from him, spun around and drove it into his neck almost to the hilt. His eyes bulged, a hoarse rasp forced itself from his damaged throat, and he fell backward, stumbling for a few feet against the resistance of the pants at his ankles. Blood spurted from the wound, covering the knife and pooling onto the floor. His legs kicked twice and stopped. He didn't move.

She stood there unmoving for an eternity, debating whether to retrieve the knife and stab again, just to make sure he was dead. It became clear that it wouldn't be necessary.

Three Doves was methodical in the next hour. She sorted through the cabin and made a pile of things she'd take. A handgun and musket, ammunition-although she had never used a firearm-the large knife, several faded shirts, a pair of boots, a blanket, a collection of foodstuffs from the meager choice in his cabinet, a bag of coins, and two pairs of dirty pants from the pile in the corner. She stuffed all of it into the saddlebags on the mule. She then went back inside, took the candle, and lit the pile of clothes. A fire roared throughout the cabin quickly, flames eagerly consuming the contents and leaping against the walls and ceiling.

She didn't see it. She was on the horse leading the mule away from the hell behind her, testing her memory to see how many of the landmarks she remembered.

As she had hoped, the Rendezvous was still going strong, as it would for several weeks. She had ridden to the Wind River, tethered her horse and mule, and proceeded along the riverbank until she saw the outlying tents in the distance. It was getting dark. She could do no more until early morning. This was dangerous. She would need stealth and good fortune from this point on. She returned to the animals, and slept fitfully.

Well before down, rain started. Perfect. The rain would reduce the chances of anyone seeing her. The rain would keep trappers in their tents. That it was soaking her made no difference. She was totally focused on a mission. She could dry off later that day.

She reached into a saddlebag and pulled out an object, and then began running in a crouch back toward the tents. She stayed close to the river to avoid the main thoroughfare of the event. This was the time. She knew that most revelers were exhausted or unconscious. She recognized the back of Jean Luc's tent. There was a soft glow emanating, which meant that a lantern was still burning, a strong sign that Big Hunter has passed out after another night of carousing and drinking, and had not shut down the lantern. She slowly and carefully lifted the tent flap. He was lying on his back, fully clothed, his arms behind his head, snoring loudly.

She crept inside, and stood briefly looking at him. A great anger rose in her. She crossed the tent and sat astraddle him. He didn't budge. She didn't want it that way. She slapped his face with a full swing of her arm. His eyes fluttered and opened slightly, and there was a hint that he recognized her. At that moment she buried Rafe's knife into the area below his chest with two hands, in an overhead movement that delivered all of the strength she had.

It was over that quickly. He hadn't made a sound. Before she got up, she spat on his face. She couldn't pull the knife out. Jean Luc's body was discovered at noon the next day. He had been stabbed to death. Nobody had seen or heard anything. There were no suspects.

She rode east, back toward Oklahoma, though she knew that she couldn't return to the reservation. Several weeks later, she rode into Bent's Fort in southeastern Colorado.

Two brothers, William and Charles Bent, had built the fort north of the Arkansas River in 1833, to trade with trappers and Plain Indians. It consisted of adobe buildings surrounded by a wall 100 feet to a side, and it soon became a stop on the Sante Fe Trail.

More, it was a center of a trade empire that attracted trappers, soldiers, adventurers, and tribes of Indians, many of whom set up villages outside of its walls.

Anything was possible at the fort. Blacksmiths set up shop, as did wagon craftsmen, scouts, trappers, and other merchants. A steady flow of explorers and pioneers guaranteed business. It was a hub of activity surrounded by hundreds of miles of plains and desert wilderness. A large turret was built above the main gate. Cannons poked out from second floor windows. Nothing short of a barrage of cannon fire could dent its thick walls, and attacking cannons were unlikely out there. Even warring Indian tribes, notably Comanche, recognized the fort's impregnable status, and wisely refrained from assaults on the complex.

Three Doves hitched her mount and the mule, and walked through a nondescript door. She was dressed in clothes she had salvaged at Rafe's, baggy trousers, boots, and a checkered shirt, all of which she had soaked in a mountain stream and dried days before. She had a small amount of money stuffed into her pockets, found just before she burned the cabin. She wasn't sure what it would buy, but she was hungry. She'd have to trust the merchant to help. She had no appropriate language.

Her tired eyes adjusted to the light. She was amazed as she took in the contents of the room. On one long shelf were blankets, bolts of different materials, tinware, coffee mills, and cans of gunpowder. In the back of the room were several shelves of clothing, shirts, pants, hats, gloves, and handkerchiefs. A case in the corner contained a large selection of knives. On top of the case were bars of soap. Boots, shoes, and moccasins were visible in opened boxes.

Food. That's what mattered most now. She glanced to the left at stacks of cans, labeled in words she couldn't read. Some held coffee, maybe, and beans, and jerky, flour. Next to them was a stack of muskets and traps and horse gear, lariats, and three large plowshares.

A portly, balding man with glasses on the tip of his nose looked up as she walked in. He was middle-aged and somewhat short with a slight paunch and kindly face. The clerk smiled at her.

"Good afternoon, Miss. How can I help you?" He walked behind a counter. She was quiet, puzzled by what to do next. She put her hands out, palms up, shook her head from side to side.

"Don't understand me… Well, I know some Cheyenne…" He tried several phrases, and knew immediately that she didn't recognize what he was saying. Now he was puzzled.

She reached in her pocket, and grabbed a handful of coins. Then she swung her arm in a slow arc around the store, trying to make him understand that she was there to buy something. A wide-brimmed black hat was on top of a stack of headwear. She picked it up, and walked to him, the hand with the coins open.

"Well Miss," he looked at her earnest face, pretty, young. "If you want that hat, it'll take up just about all of those coins." He pointed toward the shelves of foodstuffs, and raised his eyebrows. "That? You need any of that?"

She was having trouble focusing on him. Sparks began to dance in front of her, and she felt an annoying tingle in the back of her head. She put both hands on the counter for balance and lowered her head. His voice seemed to be moving away from her. A week of physical torture, too little food, riding in the sun for days, the emotional expense as she got her revenge, it all had collected at this moment. She realized that she was about to pass out. Not here, she thought. As she turned away, she slumped to the floor.

Three Doves opened her eyes, and realized that she was in a bed, a soft bed, with her head against a pillow, and a sheet pulled up to her neck. The room was neat and clean, she noticed immediately, with several chairs, a wash basin and two large windows open to the desert air. It took several seconds before she could explain it, then she remembered trying to make the clerk understand her. With sudden panic, she checked what she was wearing, a long white gown of some type. Underneath that, nothing. Where was she? How had she gotten here? Who had undressed her? The clerk? Had he violated her?

She looked at the small table next to her. On it were a pitcher of water, a glass, and the black wide-brimmed hat.

As if cued, the door opened, and the clerk walked into the room, smiling broadly.

"Well hello, Miss. You gave me a scare. Didn't think we'd get you back again. You've been under for three days."

She didn't understand any of it, but his voice was gentle. She didn't feel threatened.

He continued to babble, even though he knew she had no idea of what he was saying. "Been feeding you soup and tea. Gave you a couple of baths and changed your clothes, but I didn't molest you. Nothing inappropriate, mind you. I was worried about you."

He pulled a chair next to the bed.

"My name's Stephen Butler. Stephen....Butler." His voice was deep, resonant, seemingly at odds with his slightness and demeanor.

She gave him a wan smile and repeated the words. "Ste-pan But-lerk."

"Yeah, yeah. Close enough. Stephan Butler. You?"

She pointed to herself. "Pachallhppuwa Tuchena."

He began to chuckle. "That's a big name for a little girl. Pacckaloopah…"

"Pachallhppuwa Tuchena." Now she was smiling. She began to weakly flap her arms.

"Bird? Your name means Bird?"

He poured water into the glass, lifted her head, and gave her a drink.

She lay back and got drowsy. The last thing she felt before sleep was his gently patting her hand.

The next day, she was on her feet to use a slop jar, but considerably weak. She retreated to the bed, but she was awake for the next bath. He didn't take the nightgown off of her, didn't move her from the bed, and averted his eyes when he washed her. It was apparent to her that he was more embarrassed than she was.

One morning she woke up to find a new white shirt and a pair of expensive-looking pants at the foot of the bed. There was also a small stack of undergarments. She hadn't touched any of it when he knocked on the door and entered. She saw her coins placed neatly on the bedside table, picked up a few, and pointed to the clothes, shaking her head.

"No, Miss Bird. Those are gifts. No charge. No money," he said as he folded her hand closed over the coins. He shook his head no, took the coins from her, and put them back on the stack. She noticed immediately that none was missing.

He spent a long time at her bedside the next day, teaching and learning words from the two languages. "Horse," he would say, pointing to a picture from a book. "Isuba," she would answer. Toward evening, she leaned on him as he helped her walk to another room, one with a table with a candle and several plates of food. They laughed as he showed her how to use utensils.

Soon her strength returned. She got up daily, dressed herself in clothes he had left for her, and joined him in the store, a floor down from the bedroom. The language lessons resumed, but now they consisted of numbers from price tags, and addition and subtraction. Over time, it was she who learned the language, English. He was the teacher all of the time. The Choctaw lessons were forgotten.

Those who patronized the store noticed her, but said nothing; Indians from the village outside the walls frequented the various stores. Many had affected white man's clothing.

She could have left at any time. He had taken care of her horse and mule, and they were healthy and groomed, but she was taken by this man who was both parent and friend. Gratitude and affection welled in her. She owed him her life, but he had asked nothing from her. One night she walked naked to his bed outside of her bedroom and crawled in beside him. He was clearly unnerved, and didn't move after an initial utterance, "Bird?"

She led him through the love-making that night, and after a while, he participated eagerly. She fell asleep in his arms. He kissed her on the cheek and was soon snoring beside her.

That night was not mentioned the next day. There was no awkwardness between them, but there was a new intimacy, a comfortable equality that transcended the first few weeks. Those nights together occurred only at irregular intervals, always initiated by Three Doves. On nights that her gratitude was at its strongest, the merchant got physical workouts of great intensity and duration.

Her grasp of English progressed quickly. He gave her odd jobs in the store. Soon she was greeting buyers, and helping them with purchases. "Help you?" she would ask. "What you need?"

This new visibility bothered her. Bent's Fort was far from the site of the Rendezvous, but many men had seen her then. What if they showed up here, in this store?

One morning, she took scissors and cut off her hair to shoulder-length. She always dressed in men's clothing now. She looked different enough, more mature, more worldly that the young girl who had been savaged at the Wind River.

On some evenings, she went for rides with Butler. He didn't sit a horse particularly well, and, in riding clothes topped with a dented gray hat, he looked almost comical. Often they rode to the Indian village, where she saw a variety of tribesmen, Cheyenne, Arapaho, and to her delight, a small group of Chickasaws. The Chickasaw and Choctaw languages were similar. There were kindred souls in the encampment.

On nights when Butler didn't accompany her on rides to the village, she would dismount, look for Chickasaws, and engage them in conversation. After a while, she brought them gifts from the store. There were perhaps ten families, possibly thirty-some Chickasaws, who had left the stifling heat and control of their Oklahoma reservation. They were looking for new grounds, but had stalled here.

She began to notice a young man, older than her, who never responded to her visits. He sat alone in front of a tepee, usually with his head down. One night she asked about him.

"That is Rides With Fire. He had a fall while riding away from a prairie fire years ago, and the pony fell on him. He cannot walk. He should be a warrior or a farmer now. But he cannot walk. His arms move him around in a sitting position."

"He seems so sad."

"Rides With Fire is mad. He talks to no one. He will not share his tepee or his soul."

"You have tried with him?"

"It does no good. He doesn't want our talk or our sympathy."

"He had no family?"

"None. He lost them in the Great Move."

"Why is he here?"

"Rides With Fire has no home. He must be somewhere."

"How did he get here?"

"He can ride in wagon, can drive a wagon. Can sit a horse if someone helps. But cannot walk."

"And he won't let anyone help…"

"No one. He will talk to small children. Will not smile at anyone."

"How does he live?"

"Others here take him scraps from food. He trades with trappers. But he has used much of what he brought from the reservation. Sometimes he goes on hunts, but cannot get on or off horse without help."

I will find a way to reach him, Three Doves resolved. His pain must be greater than mine.

One afternoon she returned, with a handsome range hat. She had found an eagle feather in Butler's store, stuck it in the hatband, and spent many of her coins on the two objects. The merchant had told her to take them without paying, but she insisted. "It is a gift for a friend," she explained.

She approached him warily. He was in his usual spot, sitting in front of his tepee.

"My name is Three Doves," she began, in Choctaw. "Your friends call you Rides With Fire?"

He turned his head slightly toward her, then looked away.

He was a good-looking young man, in truth badly in need of a bath, but strong-featured and muscled in his upper body. She noted that his legs were shriveled, and that the foot on one was severely mangled.

"I have a hat for you. The sun is hot," she said, holding the hat out to him. He didn't move.

She lay the hat next to him. "My life has had much sadness. I need a friend," she continued.

He looked at her and replied in an emotionless voice, "Everyone has much sadness."

"Yes, I know. It is good to talk about such things."

"Talking doesn't change those things that have happened."

She sat down, well away from him.

"I too lost my family in the Great Move."

"Many families were lost."

She pulled a handful of brown grass from a spot next to her, and busied herself looking at it. He watched her. We're talking, she thought, even if it's not going well.

"You are Three Doves?" He had initiated a comment.

"My mother gave me the name.. The morning I was born, she heard birds singing all around her. I never changed it. My friend Stephen just calls me Bird."

"Stephen is not an Indian name."

"Stephen is a white man. I live with him."

"Why would you live with a white man? They are evil."

"Stephen is a kind man. He saved my life."

"He saved you?"

"When I had no hope, nothing to live for, nothing to rejoice about and was dying inside and out, he became my friend and protector. Stephen is a good man."

She realized that she had made a point to him. That first part of her thought also described Rides With Fire.

Soon after, she rose to leave.

"I've enjoyed talking to you, Rides With Fire. May I visit you again?"

He didn't answer. She began to walk away.

"Three Doves," he said. "Thanks…for the hat."

She kept walking, and smiling.

She was fond of Stephan Butler. Because of him she had a home and peace in her life. She had become friendly with Charles and William Bent, and with their partner in the Bent's Fort enterprise, Ceran St. Vrain. It was St. Vrain she like the best, even though he spent most of his time at the company's Taos trading center. He had been born in St. Louis in 1802, the descendant of French aristocrats who had fled that country during the French Revolution.

He was the personality, the charm behind the success of the Bent enterprise and similar locations in Taos, Santa Fe, and Old Fort Saint Vrain on the South Platte River. He called her "Little Bird," and several times when visiting trappers had tried to test the possibility of intimacy with her, St. Vrain had dissuaded them, forcefully but diplomatically.

Charles Bent was also only occasionally at the fort. His home was in Taos, where he directed the Sante Fe trade, but he visited his brother William often, and on those stays, he enjoyed bantering with Butler and his Indian ward.

William was the full-time manager at the fort. A serious expression belied a kindness and compassion that earned him the affection of trappers and Cheyenne alike. He combed his dark hair back from his forehead, giving him the appearance of premature baldness, and bushy eyebrows shaded his eyes. At first, Three Doves had felt uncomfortable when he was around, but she gradually noticed the deference in Butler when William Bent came by. Then she saw William smile, and she was taken by the fact that he always seemed to be dressed up. He was definitely in charge.

William was the driving force in the Bent-St. Vrain partnership, and the reason for its existence. Years before while he was trapping, he had saved two Cheyenne from an attack by Comanches. Because of the reverence the Cheyenne had for him, the fort he established flourished, and was protected by Cheyenne vigilance. In 1835, he married Owl Woman, a Cheyenne, and they were raising two children in Bent's Fort. By 1840, the fort was a major merchandise center.

"Good morning, Bird!" he would call to her daily. "This is a good day!" When she ventured outside the fort on her pony, he would shout to her. "Don't stay away too long, Bird. We need you here!"

There were hired interpreters at Bent's, and when they freed themselves from work, they sought her out to trade languages, Cheyenne for Choctaw.

So she was surrounded by people that she mattered to. But she also knew that there was a tenuousness to all of it. Butler was much older than she, and he was the center of her purpose here.

One night he explained things that she should know.

"You don't know much about my earlier life. Nothing really to talk about, or be happy about. I have no close relatives. You are my family. Everything I have is yours when I die. I really don't own much except for the horses and wagons, the furniture, and a little of the stock in this trade room. The property, all of the rest, belongs to the Bents."

She lowered her eyes. His dying was not something she wanted to think about.

"I've talked to William. When I die, he will make sure that what is mine becomes yours."

What had started as a project was now a friendship. She had broken the sullen barrier Rides With Fire had built over the years. One angry afternoon, she lectured him severely about feeling sorry for himself.

"Don't you understand that after a while no one cares about your problems? Your entire life is centered on how unfair life has been to you. When you do nothing to overcome the problems, you isolate yourself more. The pity stops except in your own mind."

"What do you know about pain and suffering and legs that won't let you be a man?"

"You don't need to know the pain in my life. There have been moments that I wanted to die. I was on the verge of losing my mind. I think that I did for a while. My problems were more than grief. They were also physical, and some took away my respect for myself. That's all I'm going to say. I don't want to have a friend whose spirit is crippled. Goodbye."

She left, and didn't return to the village for several weeks. A noticeable change greeted her. Rides With Fire was dressed in clean buckskin. Her black hat with the feather stuck in the hatband sat jauntily on his head. He smiled at her as she approached. He was in the fire circle in the middle of the village propped against a log.

"My friend, Three Doves…"

"My friend, Rides With Fire."

"I have missed you."

"You look nice today, Rides With Fire."

The next time she visited, she brought Butler's wagon, and strapped him into the driver's perch next to her. They went for a ride that lasted for hours, bumping across the Colorado plains, talking, and more important, she thought, laughing.

Stephen Butler died in the autumn of 1843. One morning Three Doves went to check on him. He always got up before she did. He was lying on the floor next to his bed. When she saw him, she knew.

Things happened fast. William Bent helped her bury him in a shady spot outside of the fort walls. He assembled a large group of mourners from fort personnel and tribes camping nearby and gave a eulogy at the gravesite, and Three Doves added a prayer she remembered in Choctaw. His wife, Owl Woman, prepared meals for her for several days.

One morning, Bird was overwhelmed by emotions that she had suppressed, and rode to the tepee of Rides With Fire. Sobbing, she told him. "Stephen. My friend Stephen. He's dead…"

He held her quietly as she wept, stroking her hair. She wondered later about it. Do you move toward one you love in a crisis?

"I cannot stay here longer. Mr. William Bent. The memories make me sad. I need to find another home, another place."

She had tried for several months. She felt like an intruder. She continued to live above the trade room at Bent's insistence, but the new merchant, a humorless spare man, paid little attention to her. There were no meaningful conversations and many awkward interactions during the days. She was spending more time at the tepee of Rides With Fire.

"Where will you go, Bird?"

"I would follow the sunset, but I know little of those lands."

"Will you go alone? I know that you have friend over in the village."

"Rides With Fire. I will ask him to go."

"OK. Here's a suggestion. My brother Charles and St. Vrain are over in Taos. That is the territory of Mexicans, but it's beautiful land. They would help you get settled, probably find something for you to do. Stephen left you an amount of money that will give you choices after you get there."

"Taos…?"

"Easy to get to. You just follow the trail, the Sante Fe Trail. You could take the wagon. We'll fill it with things you'll need. Hitch the horses behind. You could get there in two weeks or so. If you decide to go, I'll send a message to Charles. We'll miss you here."

CHAPTER FOUR
1840

Bartram and Alice Brody of Natchez, Mississippi had settled into late middle-age without worry. They felt fortunate, and even a dispassionate observer would have agreed. They owned one of the most prosperous and successful cotton farms in an area which was the cotton-growing center of the growing country.

They had done it their way, using poor white folks and freed blacks as their labor force. Bartram abhorred slavery. His hands were allowed to come and go as they wished. All were salaried. He provided on-site homes-- comfortable cabins, and three meals a day for those who opted to live at the farm. His methods were despised by his cotton-growing neighbors. Slavery was an accepted way of life, they argued. Except the renegade was producing more and better crops, and selling at top price across the South.

The business end of the operation was handled by their son, Eli Whitney Brody, named after the inventor of the cotton gin, a smallish, aggressive thirty-year old who was so good at what he did that his parents could afford to be distracted by other facets of life. Called "Whit" by everyone who knew him, including his parents, he was their only son. Two daughters, Mary and Frances, were both living in Natchez. Mary had two children with her husband William, who managed operations on the waterfront of the Mississippi. Frances was betrothed to a flatboat captain.

Someday, Whit would inherit the farm, and his only problem would be to find someone to replace himself, someone as honest, as hard-working, and as thorough.

On the morning of May 7, 1840, Whit was upriver, to seal yet another sale. He had left the previous Monday. Bartram and Alice slept late on this Thursday, taking advantage of a morning breeze which would probably precede a humid and hot spring day. There had been a rain overnight, a furious little storm which had dumped over three inches of rain.

Bartram sat up in bed, saying to no one in particular, "Heard the rain last night.. We needed a good rain." That was his mantra; most days began with a weather-related utterance. After thirty-six years of marriage, Alice expected it, and had become inured to it. "Yes, dear, rain."

"Better check the field. Some'll be too wet to plant today, I suppose."

"Let's have a bite first, Bartram. If it's too wet, your overseer will make that decision."

By late morning, Whit was already doing what he did best, closing a cotton sale. He sat across a polished wood desk from the buyer in the business district of Vicksburg.

"Mr. Slocum, I promise you that you'll get the best product on the market. If you have any problems, we'll take the cotton back, and you'll get your money back."

"And you deliver, Mr. Brody?"

"We deliver. We'll put the entire lot on your back porch, if you want."

"Mr. Brody, the warehouse will be fine," the buyer grinned. This sincere little cotton-seller would be as good as his word, Slocum knew. His reputation for fairness was well-known along the Mississippi River.

"You know, Mr. Brody, that we rarely buy cotton without seeing the product. Most sellers from around here wagon it in to us, and we decide once we see it. Asking us to commit when the crop is still five months away, this is highly unusual."

"We can do that for you, Mr. Slocum, We can bring you wagons in October. No problem for us. But I have to tell you that we fill a lot of orders from buyers, sight unseen. We take care of them first. Lots of folks'll have their cotton by then."

"So you're telling me that if we have you show it to us first, we'll have to wait a while after it's picked."

Slocum knew that the bulk he wanted, early in the harvest season, and at the fairest price in the South, was worth a small risk.

"Yessir."

"You're asking me to speculate here, Mr. Brody?"

"Yessir."

"Mr. Brody, let's sign the papers."

Bartram was out on his land by 9am that morning, checking out the latest plantings. His holdings were so vast, and the business so good, that his workers began planting his early fields in March, and usually finished his late fields by mid-May. His picking began in September, and lasted for over a month. Then the cotton was systematically shipped to buyers. Drought and boll weevils were the forces that could interfere with his success, but the Natchez area was blessed with a temperate, moist climate, and the demon insects never made much of an impact.

There was limited activity this day. The rain from the previous night had flooded most of the fields. There were two on higher ground which had drained, and a reduced force was there planting. Just before noon, Bartram noticed thunderheads moving in from the southwest. Lightning began to flash, and steady rolls of thunder began to shake the air.

"Move into the buildings!" he called to his overseer. The entire work force began to abandon the fields. Bartram grumped. There was such a thing as too much rain. He rode back to the house, and reined in just as the rain began to fall in large drops. He put his mare into the barn, and trotted to the house.

As he reached his front porch, a pain began to grow in his left shoulder. "Damnation. That pain again. What is it?" He massaged the area with a gnarled hand. He was sixty years old, and recently time seemed to be catching up to him. He entered his kitchen door.

"Well Dear, looks like you'll get more rain. Bartram…what is it?"

"That pain again, Alice. That damn pain again."

"You're scaring me, Bartram. Here, let me rub it down for you."

He sat on a chair at the kitchen table. She began to gently knead the afflicted area.

Several miles to the southwest, somewhere near Concordia, the large storm escalated. A rolling effect caused by warm, moist air tumbling over cool, dry air caused a spinning effect into a vertical position in the lower atmosphere, creating a violent, rotating column of air.

A gentle rumbling became a roar as the column grew in force and size, and began to digest clouds of dust and objects on the ground. Water vapor and inhaled dirt made the condensation tunnel visible, and as it moved to the northeast, it fed off of the intensity of the storm which spawned it, growing and picking up speed.

The monster smashed into the Mississippi River valley and turned north to follow the river bed seven miles south of the city.

The largest, most dangerous tornado in the history of the continent was moving toward Natchez.

Natchez was built into the landscape in two tiers. The Under-the-Hill portion was on the river, a busy port and trading center where steamboats, ferry boats, and cargo-laden flatboats plied the water and filled excessive wharves. On any day, at any time, it was a buzzing, populous area, which also included stores and hotels. Travelers from all over the eastern United States passed through or debarked from this section of the Mississippi.

Upper Natchez was where the plantations, homes and churches were built. There was a theater, a newspaper, and showplace mansions. For miles around, from Concordia to Vadalia, rolling hills hosted over 60,000 acres of cotton, corn, and oats. Almost 50,000 bales of cotton were produced annually, and picked by hundreds of slaves. The lumber industry was thriving.

"Bartram, look at that sky. It's turning green. Never saw a storm do that before."

"Yep. This is a another good storm. Yeah, right there. That feels good, Alice."

"Must be letting up. The rain's slowed down."

"Wait a minute. You hear it?"

"Hear what, Bartram? Sounds quiet to me."

"That's what I mean. It just of a sudden got completely quiet."

As he spoke, a surge of wind carried in large pellets of hail.

"Don't like this. It only hails in real bad weather. Those are the size of small lemons. Listen to them beat up the roof."

She stopped rubbing his shoulder to watch the hail bounce off of their yard. "That'll be doing some damage. Hope none of the workers are out there, or the animals."

He looked up, and then stood up quickly.

"Listen! Listen!"

They both heard it, a loud whooshing sound as the view and the room became dark.

He went to the window, and looked to the side of it, toward the southwest. What he saw stunned him. No more than a mile away, a dark wall of debris was moving toward them, an immense force of nature destroying trees and buildings.

"It's a twister, Alice! We got to get to the fruit cellar! Now!"

As he spoke the last word, and turned to her, he felt a terrible ache in his chest. He grabbed at it, looked at her quizzically, and slumped to the floor.

"Bartram! Bart! What is it, Honey?" She leaned over him.

He managed a whisper. "Alice…run to the cellar…Forget me…"

"Oh God! Oh God!" She covered his body with hers, and looked at his closed eyes, and spittle at the side of his mouth. "Bartram! Bartram!"

At that instant the house exploded.

The twister devastated Under-the-Hill, flattening or dislodging every building, and hurtling boats against each other, or flinging them hundreds of feet through the air. In Upper Natchez, hundreds of buildings were toppled, whole fields of crops were smashed, and the great trees of surrounding forests were uprooted; some were carried for miles before they crashed out of the wind.

Vicksburg received the dying remnants of the storm, still nuisance enough to send residents scurrying for protection, ducking hail, and hiding from excessive blasts of wind. Whit Brody knew that the storm had come from the south, and suspected that it had probably played havoc with the farm. The hail had probably destroyed some of the crop, maybe battered a building or two. As the rain ended, he mounted a horse and rode for home.

A few hours into his journey, he passed a rider. "Mister, I wouldn't ride south if I were you. There's nuthin' left down there. Twister. Bad one. Really bad one."

"Natchez?"

"Don't know 'bout that. Seen what it did about twenty miles north of there. Real bad."

Whit pushed his horse. He could be home by early the next day if he rose early and rode hard.

He continued at daybreak, after fitfully tossing and turning throughout the night. He passed a wagon in mid-morning.

"Where you all from?" he asked the driver. He was looking at an ashen-faced man, disheveled and obviously distraught. Behind him in the wagon's bed, several women were weeping. One stared at him with expressionless eyes, not really seeing him.

"Jes' north of Natchez. Nuthin' left. People dead, missing. Boats stacked up in the river. Steamboats aground. Houses gone. Goin' upriver a piece to stay with family. Won't go back for a spell. Gotta get away. Nuthin' but death back there."

He rode harder. Several miles north of Natchez, he began to see the horrific details. The landscape was bare of houses and trees. He rode past a flatboat, which had been tossed and carried two miles from the river. Detritus was scattered everywhere.

He guessed the worst before he turned up the lane toward the farm. He saw two large barns still standing, miraculously, but in all the scope of the farm, there was nothing else left. The house was down. Trees were felled clear to the horizon. He galloped toward a small group of people standing near where the house had been. As he rode up, he noticed several objects on the ground, covered by blankets. He reined in. The gathered group was farm workers. He knew what was under the blankets.

"My mother? My father?"

"Mistuh Whit. They gone. Twister hit the house full force. They there on de groun' under dem blankets."

Whit Brody lost most of his family in the tornado. Among the 317 reported dead or missing were both of his sisters, Frances' fiancé, and a niece. Mary's husband left town one day with his remaining child. Whit never knew where they went. He buried his parents on the farm.

He analyzed his options. He would not rebuild. There was still cotton in the fields, and deals that would have to be forfeited, money returned. He had no thought of staying beyond those dealings. Natchez was not home anymore. It was a wasteland.

After all business transactions had been completed, he sold the entire property. One afternoon, he stopped at his parent's graves one last time. Then he left Mississippi forever. He would go to Pine Bluff, Arkansas.

****

Herkimer Grimes rested against a lacey oak tree a half-mile from Austin. As usual, his sleep was troubled and light, but it was also necessary. For the past few days he had been in the saddle, trying to make sense of what seemed a migration of Comanches from the north across the plains. They were heading southeast, for what purpose he wasn't sure.

Buffalo Hump had a party of what might have been 1,000 braves, women and children. Herk didn't understand, but he didn't trust Buffalo Hump. What seemed like an orderly march, ostensibly to establish a new camp, might have been disguising something more sinister. With Comanches, you couldn't believe what you saw. With Buffalo Hump, you couldn't assume anything. He galloped back to Ranger headquarters with the news, and then rode out of the city to be alone.

Moreover, all of Texas was on the alert after what had become known as the Council House Fight in March of that year. Herk hated the Comanches--he had seen too many atrocities in past years—and he distrusted all Indians, but he was forced to admit that Texans had made tragic mistakes in that event, which was supposed to exact a peace treaty.

Numerous Republic of Texas officials and thirty-three members of the Comanche peace delegation had met in San Antonio on March 19. The Texans asked for white hostages to be released. The Comanches wanted guaranteed boundaries on their lands.

The Comanche party, which numbered sixty-five and included women and children, brought with them one disheveled, emaciated woman, captured years before. The Texans asked about other hostages, but the Comanche indicated that they would only release more if the white men gave them great quantities of blankets and ammunition.

Militiamen entered the room. The Texans then announced that they would hold all Comanche present as hostages.

Herk had heard different versions of what happened next. In the aftermath of the pitched battle which followed, seven Texans were killed, some caught in the crossfire of their own weapons, and ten were wounded.

Thirty-five of the Comanches were killed, and twenty-seven were taken prisoner.

Soon, word reached the Texans that the Comanche had executed thirteen of their hostages back on the plains. Most were roasted to death over a fire.

So instead of a treaty, or even a truce, both sides wanted revenge. Peace was impossible. Each side waited for a provocation or an opportunity. That is what had caused Herk to ride far from Austin to check on Comanche actions. That was when he saw the great march.

The summer of 1840 was coming to an end, but it seemed unwilling to relinquish a cauldron of heat to the calendar. Before he lay down, Herk unbuttoned his shirt, and peeled off his boots. What did he want most, a bath, a meal, a change of clothes, a soft bed? The solitary nap, away from the confusion of town, away from the tomfoolery at the Ranger bunkhouse, and away from the incessant pestering of Flap Bailey, won easily.

He started awake at the fluttering of a small flock of birds, reaching for his pistol. He gazed at his long legs, too thin, stretched out in front of him. Sitting up, he peeled the crusted socks from his feet, and laid them in the sun beside the tree. He ignored the pain in his lower back, and walked a few feet to the small stream, decimated in the August heat. He sat on a large rock at the water, and put his feet in the tepid flow. After a few minutes, he retreated to the tree and shade, and sat again against the trunk. A breeze from nowhere blew across him and lured him back to sleep.

He didn't know how long he had slept when he woke again, but the sun was in a vastly different position. He came slowly out of the fog of another bad dream, a collection of images of shooting, of dodging arrows, of huge Indians in Mexican army uniforms stalking him, of trying to run away on legs that didn't work, of firing a pistol with no ammunition.

He was thirty-one years old, but he felt older. His back ached constantly from hours in the saddle. He was gaunt and graying. Moreover, he was disenchanted with his entire life. His only meaningful contact with another human had recently ended badly. Maria, a pretty young Hispanic with whom he often shared a bed, had left Austin weeks ago with a Mexican man, leaving him a terse note in fractured English that described her life as too lonely. He had been away with the Rangers on an extended foray, one of many over the past years. He didn't blame her, but he missed her.

He often questioned his Ranger membership. He had been dedicated as a young man. He felt that the group had an elevated mission, bringing peace and humanity to a volatile country. He was appreciated and trusted and lauded by the Ranger hierarchy. It was apparent to him over the past two years that very little of substance was being accomplished, however. The Comanche were persistent and increasingly bold in harassing white settlers. As a Ranger colleague told him, "You shoot two of them over here, and there's four more even meaner takin' their place over there."

Then too, there was the fragile situation with Mexico. The war with them had depleted Ranger manpower. Surveillance was necessary now, as powers in Washington tried to solve problems here, 2,000 mile away. He was certain that there'd be another, more terrible war in the near future. Once again he'd be taking orders from military commanders who didn't understand subtleties such as diplomacy and inventive warfare, and careful planning and human nature.

He had to leave this life, but for what? What could he do besides scout and shoot? Too often these days he had misgivings about his life, and more about his future.

As he reached for his socks--too late he knew he should have soaked them in the stream and dried them in the sun next to him as slept--he heard it.

The bell. The damn Ranger bell, calling for assembly. That was a signal for general assembly, immediately, all companies. He knew before he rode into Austin what was up. The party of Comanches he had been tracking earlier were on a mission. Somewhere they were wreaking havoc.

John J. Tumlinson addressed the body of Rangers, perhaps a hundred, with a grave face.

"We've got trouble, boys. Big trouble," he shouted.

"Grimes spotted a large party of Comanches, Buffalo Hump's party, headin' toward the coast. Well, we just got word. They routed Victoria. Took some prisoners, burned some of the outskirts, stole a lot of livestock, killed some folks. There's more than a thousand of them. Worse, they're headin' toward the coast now, toward Linnville. We probably can't get there to help them folks, but we can waylay them red devils in good time. We're ridin' out in thirty minutes. Be back here soon as you can."

"Grimes, Bailey, Big Head. Need you up here!"

The three made their ways through the crowd, now dispersing.

"You three leave now. Grimes, get to the coast quick as you can. See what's goin' on. Take Big Head with you. Flap, you get to Gonzales; find McCullough, and round up a group of militia. Find us out there before you do anything. If we get Buffalo Hump this time and take out some warriors...maybe we can end this Comanche thing for good."

Flapjack Bailey had doubts. Thousand Comanches, couple hundred of us. Outnumbered again. What he didn't know was that all of central and eastern Texas was mobilizing at the outrage. Adam Zumbalt gathered a gang of Texicans and rode east; so did Clark Owen. Colonel Edward Burleson's militia force was on its way, accompanied by Tonkawa scouts. Bailey himself would ride back toward the confrontation with 117 men, led by Captain Matthew Caldwell and Captain James Bird. Jack Hays led a company of soldiers from Bezar. More soldiers rode from Port Lavaca; General Felix Houston was on his way with another company.

The middle-aged couple watched the shore from the safety of a ship moored well out from Linnville. Children and women were being abused, accompanied by war whoops and screams. Over this the couple saw their town on fire.

There had been little warning. A rider had spotted the advancing horde while they were still miles away and had galloped into Linnville shouting as alarm. Defense, he said, was impossible. There were hundreds of Comanches. Escape routes were limited, almost non-existent. What then? The boats in the bay. Maybe the townspeople could defend themselves out there. Maybe the Comanches would leave them alone if they were on the water. The plan worked, for the ones who made it to the boats

The woman gasped as she recognized a man struggling on the shore with a group of marauders. Her son. The young man was scalped in full view of the boats.

The woman fainted into the arms of her sobbing husband.

In the heart of the city, Buffalo Hump was frustrated. The plan had been to loot the storehouses, set fire to the town, and steal horses. He knew that Rangers, militia, and soldiers would soon descend on the area. Several times he tried to rally his forces, to command them to the storehouses, and then to a quick departure. No good. They were looting every house, taking too much time.

There were too many raiders, scattered over too much territory. The squaws added to the frenzy, ransacking the stores. He had brought them only as a diversion, to mask the intent of the journey south, to confuse anyone who saw entire families on the march.

After several hours the warehouses and storerooms were stripped bare. As last his tribe was ready for the return to the plains.

An enormous procession left the city. Toward the middle were hundreds of horses and mules, many weighted down by booty. At the end were several captive women and children, walking. Scattered along a queue which was miles long were the warriors, many adorned with blankets, jewelry, and clothing, particularly hats. Mixed in were the Indian woman and children, most on foot; they began to lose touch with the rest of the Comanches, who were now in a decided hurry.

Herk Grimes watched the Comanche nation leave Linnville. He and Big head had reached the unfortunate city just as Buffalo Hump began to lead his tribesmen out.

"Christ Almighty!" Big Head exclaimed as he saw the raider army. "They done destroyed Linnville."

That was a filibuster for Big Head. The large man didn't much like to talk. Most of the Rangers knew that he was a half-breed. More than that, they only knew that he was a fierce fighter, who didn't seem to fear anything. He obeyed orders, and no assignment seemed to intimidate him. Herk always felt confident when he was paired with Big Head.

Everything about the man was oversized. A large nose extended prominently from his sunburned face. Long dark hair didn't hide his outsized ears. His arms were as big as a man's legs, and they terminated in meaty hands, too big for gloves. Nobody knew what became of Big Head between assignments. He just seemed to disappear into Austin, to materialize again when he was summoned.

Conversation with the man was difficult. His answers to questions were grunts, sometimes a "yep" or a "nope." Yet, except for those moments in battle when he was dark and effective, he was not a sinister presence. Sometimes Herk would catch him grinning at some memory or at some Ranger's attempt at humor.

He wasn't aware of the man's real name, although he'd heard Tumlinson call him "Franklin" once. Whether that was a surname or a given name, he didn't know. Herk usually just called him "Big."

"Too many of them for Tumlinson to attack head-on or surround. We're going to have to ambush them somewhere," he murmured. "Pears so," Big Head answered.

"Let's find the captain," Herk said, jumping back into his saddle, and pushing his horse to a full gallop.

Within an hour, they were well in front of the parade of Comanches and bearing down on a large company of Rangers and soldiers.

Tumlinson's and McCullough's forces had met up a few hours before. Surveying the assemblage, Herk reined in beside Tumlinson.

"This it, Cap'n?"

"For now. We've got word that there are volunteers and even some soldiers on the way. The Comanch coming?"

"Yeah, they're coming, hundreds of them. Women and children too. They've got captives and horses traveling behind. Probably be close to maybe three, four hours behind us."

"Linnville?'

"Pretty much destroyed by what we seen. On fire. Some dead folks."

McCullough rode up beside them, an intense, humorless man with a high forehead and a square jaw.

"What's the story, John?"

"We're considerable outnumbered. They're on the warpath. Can't go head on with 'em."

"Suggestion, Cap'n?"

"Go ahead, Herkimer. One plan's good as any."

"Well, if more guns are on the way, I'd say we harass them till we get help. Hit them and ride away. Then again, just before we get to the Casa Blanca River crossing, we break off and take a stand there."

"That'll work. Let's get goin'. Them red devils got a lickin' comin'," McCullough said.

"Ben, we gotta be careful here. We could lose a lot of men," Tumlinson answered.

"Them Comanch just killed white folks. We be too careful, and they'll get back to the plains and scatter, just like ever' other raid."

The two Indian fighters formulated a plan quickly. They would keep in touch with the march, make threatening runs toward it, set little ambushes to within ten or twelve miles of the Casa Blanca River, then break off to take defensive positions ahead of the warriors along the banks of the river crossing.

"Don't matter much if we kill any of them before the river. We won't get close enough for them to get us. But if we can slow them a bit till we get reinforcements, there'll be plenty of killin'," Tumlinson stated.

Herk was again impressed with his captain. Tumlison had an uncanny sense for appropriate battle. McCullough was a great leader too, but sometimes impulsive. He hated the Comanche, and had a reputation for success against them over the years, but Herk knew that caution was their only course for the next few hours, maybe longer.

"Time's a-wastin'," McCullough said.

"Let's go. Organize the men. We'll ride out in five minutes. Herk, you go find 'em for us. Flapjack, don't shoot any of us."

"Oh, dammit, Cap'n," Bailey muttered.

The groups converged two hours later. The Rangers effectively threw diversions at the army, and to some extent, it worked. The line of Comanches would rein up, whoop, but they made no advances from their long line.

Herk reined in beside Tumlinson.

"Cap'n. They're actin' mighty strange. Don't seem like they want to fight."

"Trying' to get that booty to the plains, I reckon," Tumlinson answered.

Herk noticed that a large group of braves broke off and rode back down the line, to protect the captives and the stolen horses and goods, he guessed.

The ranger party rode away toward the river at the designated departure site. There was still no sign of the reinforcements. They reached the far bank, and hurriedly dug small fortifications. Then they waited.

"What if they don't cross here, Cap'n?" Bailey asked.

"They will. They have to. They try anywhere else, they'll never get across with all them walkers and horses."

An hour later, they came into view, wending their way toward the river cautiously. Herk had seen a small party of scouts a while before. The Comanche knew what was waiting for them.

A large group of warriors rode toward the river, only to be driven back by a fusillade of fire. Minutes later, they tried again, with the same results.

"This ain't getting' it!" McCullough called out to Tumlinson.

"Sure it is. They ain't across. We're gaining time. Final battle won't be here anyway."

"What! We got 'em here in one place. Best time and place is here!"

Herk watched Tumlison shake his head. The captain knew that a concentrated charge would get the Comanches across the river, and wipe out his men. The Rangers were outnumbered ten to one.

"Here they come again. More of 'em!"

Each attempt seemed to be bolder. Just before dark, a Comanche shot and killed a defender named Morris.

Tumlinson huddled with McCullough.

"When the sun comes up in the morning, we'll be gone," Tumlinson said.

"Gone! That's crazy, John! We're holdin' em off. Ain't no time to run."

"They'll come at us full force at daylight. Probably throw seven hundred of the devils at us. They're getting' impatient, mad. We'll withdraw, and wait for 'em up the trail somewhere. They've still got a couple of days before they're back in familiar territory."

"I'm against it, John."

"Don't matter. Go along with me on this."

When Buffalo Hump threw the full force of his army across the river, just as the sun broke the horizon, there was no resistance. There were no Rangers.

"White man runs away like a woman," he heard a war chief call out.

"Rangers are gone from this place. They are not gone from our journey," he shouted.

The Rangers rode north until Herk spotted a cloud of dust on the horizon late in the day. Colonel Edward Burleson's militia had arrived.

Burleson told Tumlinson that Plum Creek was the strategic target. The battle would occur there, farther north. He promised that there would be a large army of volunteers and Rangers waiting for them there.

As promised, one hundred seventeen men were at the creek the next day, already waiting for the Comanches. They were the Gonzalez group, led by Caldwell and Captain Bird.

The odds are improving, Herk noted.

In short order fighters arrived from Port Lavaca and Bezar. The Bezar militia numbered two hundred. General Felix Houston's company rode in two hours later, and Houston took command of the entire fighting unit.

Houston's first thought after listening to reports form Tumlinson, McCullough, and Herk was that the next encounter would be a charge by his assembled troops. The Comanche behavior was erratic, and they were fresh off of several days of white resistance which was more of a nuisance than episodes of warfare.

Herk waited for a chance to talk to his captain alone.

"Somethin' on your mind, Herkimer?"

"Cap'n, there's white folks in that party. We gonna' try and get them out?"

"Houston wants to charge the Comanche when they ride up here. We'll clear them captives out then."

"Them Comanch'll start killin' the captives if it gets hot. Same thing for the horses."

"Well, Herkimer...what do you want? You wanna go in and rescue them yourself?"

"Give me about twenty men. Gotta at least try."

"Twenty men? You'd get swallowed by them devils. Suicide, Herkimer."

"Don't think so. We'd be at the back of the line. That's where them pore white folk are."

"What if the whole bunch turns on you? I don't think you can do this thing. And I don't want to lose you."

The two men stood facing each other. The face-off became awkward. Tumlinson took of his hat and peered to the horizon, as if the discussion was over. Herk rubbed his moustache. He didn't budge.

Tumlinson knew that Herk wouldn't back down. The thought brought a hint of a smile to his face.

"Ok, dammit, ok…I'll go to Houston and tell him. How you figger to do this?"

"Ride back the trail a piece. Hide. Wait till the shootoing starts from the front. Hit 'em from the back."

"Now listen to me, Herkimer. You're goin' to have to clear them out in a hurry. That whole bunch might retreat, scatter, or back off. That'll put em' in your lap."

"Have to take that chance. I'll take twenty men and Big Head."

Jesus, Tumlison thought, who's the captain here?

The Comanche advance had slowed dramatically since the skirmishes at the Casa Blanca River. That had occurred on August 9. August 12 dawned, and the great group of militia still waited for Buffalo Hump.

Herk Grimes, Big Head, and twenty Rangers had ridden out early yesterday, and were somewhere in position out there, Tumlinson knew.

A cloud of dust far to the south signaled the arrival of the warriors, just after a Tonkawa scout rode into the lines to alert Houston that he had spotted them slowly wending their way toward Plum Creek. The line had condensed, he said. A great body of warriors was now clustered at the front of the march. The captives and horses had been moved up to the point where the Comanche women and children dawdled. The small group driving the stolen horses was in front of them. Buffalo Hump knew what awaited him. Houston had lost any ambush aspect, but that mattered little. His attack plan was all he needed, he reasoned.

The various militias and volunteers were in a huge funnel formation, as well hidden as they could manage. They would let the marchers ride inside the funnel, and then collapse it, attacking them from three sides.

They were in sight. Then the front phalanx was only a hundred yards away. A command to "fire!" was screamed, and a growing thunder of gunshots rolled up and down the formation. Braves fell from their ponies, and for a moment the Comanches froze. Then quickly they were mobilized and charging toward the enemy's main formation.

A second round of gunfire drove them back again, and more bodies littered the hard ground, newly-acquired top hats and flop hats rolling around under the panicked hooves of the ponies. Houston ordered a full charge.

The would-be rescuers waited until the first shots were fired. They mounted and rode toward the end of the marchers' line. To properly conceal themselves, they had hidden at some distance, but even from there, Herk could see the human tragedy, slumped shoulders of the Linnville women, some carrying children, being jostled by the ponies of the braves who were herding them. Herk saw a small figure sag to the ground, and a Comanche guard ride intentionally back and forth over it. A woman toward the end of the captive group was half-running, and ducking a spear-like object that a guard beat her with, ferocious blows to her back and head. Finally she lay still on the ground.

Herk was tempted to rush in to stop the atrocities he saw from far away, but if the rescuers acted prematurely, it would adversely affect Houston's plan.

Now, after the army ahead had opened a salvo, they were in full gallop, the Ranger group, toward the guard detachment, which had just reacted to the gunfire by riding forward ahead of the captives. Good, Herk thought, they're separating themselves from the body of captives. That was fortuitous because the twenty-one now rode into position between the two groups.

There were perhaps fifteen guards, mostly boys and older men, and they were little match for the enraged Texans. Eight Comanches fell; the rest fled.

Herk dismounted. "Big, take five or six men. Ride up and free some mules! Bring 'em back here."

The Comanche women became a problem. They were protecting their captives, screaming Comanche invectives. A Ranger to Herk's left shot a squaw who was charging him. It happened again in front of him. Those incidents turned the tide. The Indian women began to run or ride from the scene, toward the gunfire they heard in front of them.

Herk surveyed the motley collection of Linnville survivors. He knew that he had to move them to high ground, to the relative safety of distance, and that had to happen immediately.

He shouted above the wailing and screaming.

"Listen. You're all safe for now. But we got to move fast. If you can run a little bit, we'll be safe in mebbe twenty, thirty minutes. If you can ride, there'll be mules here in about ten minutes. That shootin' you hear is a huge posse, takin' care of the Comanch."

Most of the rescued were in shock, bedraggled, dispirited. They had trotted and walked for four days. They probably didn't understand completely what was happening, but a survival instinct and the thrill of possible freedom quieted the pathetic moans. They were easy for Herk to control.

The Ranger mounted next to Herk groaned and fell from his saddle. Three Comanches were bearing down on the group, and their first shot had hit a mark. Herk swung his horse around, unholstered both guns, and let the reins fall onto the horse's neck.

Crazy Comanch, he thought, three of them charging twelve of us. He spurred his mount and rode straight for the invaders. One brave rolled his pony, and was down. Herk saw why. Big Head was riding up behind them. He had shot the pony.

Herk's hat flew off. He waited until he couldn't miss. The two remaining warriors, sandwiched between the two charging Rangers, reined in. Herk got off a pistol shot that felled one of the braves. The other rode out of the sandwich and turned to gallop back toward the battle at the front of the line.

"Where'd they come from, Big? They slip past you?"

"Dunno."

"You got mules comin'?"

"Yeah."

Herk rode back to his fallen comrade. The shot had burrowed into his upper arm.

"Mount up. One of these women will tend to you when we get them out of here."

"Think it went clear through, Herk. Should be alright. Bunch of blood.."

The snarling warrior who had lost his horse stood in the middle of mounted Rangers, whooping, knife drawn.

"Somebody put a rope on him. He's the captive now. Drag him over to the white ladies."

A string of mules wandered into view, most still carrying loads from the raid.

"Mount up if you can. Strip the packs off of the mules," Herk yelled.

Off to the side, he noticed that several captive women had the captured Comanche on the ground. Unable to defend himself because of his bonds, he had fallen. The women were quickly on him, kicking him, pulling his hair, spitting at him, smashing fists into his face, shouting. Herk rode up and looked into the eyes of the battered Indian. He understood. "Clear away!" he ordered. As the women backed off, Herk pulled his pistol and shot the man in the forehead.

From the horseback he began reloading his pistols. "We're movin' out!"

Up in the main battle, the Comanche were losing warriors and losing ground. Buffalo Hump sensed disaster. Already some of the Comanches had broken off and were riding away. The area in front of the main Ranger surge was carnage. Wave after wave of Texans kept breaking through his lines along a wide area. To his left, a large body of warriors had thrown down their weapons and dismounted with their arms raised. They were circled by a throng of Texans, some of whom kept firing at the defenseless Indians.

It was over, he knew. The only course now was to ride en masse through the Ranger attackers at some point, and ride away. He knew they'd be followed, knew that many more might die before they reached the plains. But that was the only option left.

"So, what's the story, John?" McCullough asked, a high soprano betraying his emotion.

"We lost some men. We got a lot of wounded. Looks like the Comanch lost 80 to a hundred. We've captured a lot of them. Squaws too. Got most of the mules and horses."

"Seen Grimes?"

"Yeah. I see him now," he answered, pointing to the south.

There they saw a group walking toward them, a somewhat motley crew on mules and on foot, being led by a thin man on a gray horse. The Herkimer Grimes legend was about to grow again.

CHAPTER FIVE

1841

Hank Rosbottom made a good living. The slight, sandy-haired, Georgia-born son of a dirt farmer was a musician. He plied his trade in bars and on riverboats, mainly playing a fiddle. He has also saved his money from years of menial labor to afford a Boucher banjo made in Baltimore, Maryland.

He was thirty-two years old in 1837 when his life changed. He had been well-known along the southern Mississippi River. For years, if there was fiddle or banjo tournament in the area, Rosbottom was the likely winner. He had learned to play the fiddle as a youngster by watching a slave play a crude model. Then had mastered the mandolin too, a bowl-backed Neapolitan instrument he had heard in New Orleans in the mid-1830's.

He had collected a repertoire of slave songs and popular songs and ballads of the era. He would start a performance with "Old Rosin, the Beau," and end it with "Bonaparte's Retreat," a frantic rush of fiddle sounds that usually had listeners clapping spontaneously during the song. In between, he usually hammered out "Zip Coon," and "Crazy Jane" and "Yankee Doodle," and "Our Old Tom Cat," on the banjo, although his complete repertoire consisted of hundreds of songs on all three of his instruments.

It was his enthusiasm that captured his audiences. Throughout a song, he would rock on a chair, playing with his right foot keeping time on the floor, and a wide smile. If a song needed vocals, he supplied them with a loud and clear, earnest, if unpolished voice. He always wore a derby, a clean white shirt, and a red vest. It was the vest that identified him, so much that he was once billed as Red Vest Rosbottom.

In every show, he tamed his performance for one song, "My Cher, Angeline," a song he had written for the love of his life, a Cajun girl named Angeline Chiasson that he had met six years ago, in 1835.

You came into my life
And the dawn spoke your name
And the sunsets forever
Will all do the same
Lazy days on the bayou
And the nights in between
They speak of your beauty
My angel, Angeline
And I can't live without you
My cher, Angeline
Gentle child of the river,

The first breath of spring
I adore you my angel,
My cher, Angeline

Theirs was such a bond of reliance and affection that they were rarely apart. Angeline Chiasson was raven-haired and notably beautiful, and she had only made it to the age of 29 unattached because of a physical deformity. Angeline's right leg had been severely deformed since her birth. She could walk only with the aid of a crutch.

She had despaired of ever meeting a soul mate until the thin musician with an unkempt beard and an amazing wealth of optimism and tenderness bumped into her one day outside of a New Orleans market.

He was leaving the building in the French Quarter in a hurry, his arms full of purchases. As he cleared the door to start up the boardwalk, he had a quick sense of a body in the spot, then a collision knocked the fruit from his arms, and he spun around to keep from falling.

"Damn!" he had said, and then wished that he could retract it. On her back, her skirt up to her knees, was a girl. Next to her was a crutch. Her eyes were closed in a grimace. Long locks of shiny black hair half-covered her face.

"Oh, God, ma'am, I'm so sorry. So sorry."

She squinted at him.

"You alright ma'am? I'm so sorry."

"You said dat." She said, and the hint of a smile creased her tan face.

"Here, let me help you. I'm…sorry." He retrieved the crutch and offered a hand to help her to her feet.

She pushed her skirt down just as he noticed that her right leg was shriveled. She grabbed his arm and he lifted her. She balanced herself against him, bounced once on her good leg, and put the crutch under her right arm. She is so beautiful, he thought.

"Ga lee. Must have bumped ma head. Dizzy."

He helped her to a long bench in front of the store's window.

"Let's sit here a minute. Can I fetch you water? Something?"

"Non…No."

He sat down a respectful distance from her.

"I'm Hank Rosbottom. Ma'am. I shoulda been more careful."

She answered without looking at him. "Angeline Chiasson."

She had said "Chee-aw-so." Even so, he knew the name.

"Chaisson? That it? Played music once with a fiddler, Louie Chiasson."

She looked at him, and her eyes brightened.. "Dat is ma nonc…ma uncle."

"Yeah a fiddler, a good one. Big guy. Believe he was from up near the lake."

"Dat's it. Still lives there. Dat was my home too."

"Called himself the Ponchartain Toulooloo."

She giggled. "Dat means crab. Fiddler crab. You understand dis?"

"What I remember is that he made that fiddle smoke. He could play faster than anyone I ever heard. Never missed a note."

"What you play?"

"Mostly fiddle, not as well as your uncle though. Banjo. Mandolin."

"You live in New Orleans?"

"Right around the corner here. You're in Jefferson Parish?"

"Non. Used to live dere a while. Born west of here. Settlement called Picotville. My parents moved here when I was eleven, after a year on da Maiterie, near Uncle Louie. Dey sell at the magasin. Probably sold you dose bananas."

They looked at the bananas and oranges scattered over the boardwalk.

"Suppose I'd better collect them. Liable to make someone trip and fall. They might even make some clumsy oaf run over someone." He watched her smile turn into a grin. He was taken with her looks, her face, a beacon when she smiled, sultry and dark when he had helped her up. But her eyes hadn't once lost their sparkle in the ten minutes they'd been together.

She studied him as he collected the fruit. His hair was wheat-colored and somewhat combed back, and his beard short, barely covering a square jaw and even white teeth. His eyes were deep-set and light, green she thought. His shoulders were a bit too broad for the rest of his body, and his forearms seemed taut and muscled. He had done labor of some sort, she guessed, probably a lot of it. His hands fascinated her, small and somewhat delicate, a musician's hands. All in all, she thought him handsome, and to that point certainly interesting.

"So, Angeline…" He shrugged a bit to return to the conversation. Sometimes the simplest things were difficult for him. He could play the fiddle in front of hundreds of people without flinching. But away from the stage, from his music, he was hesitant, even shy. Not that he was inexperienced with women. More than a few had flirted with him, offered themselves to him. He had often responded, but he knew those were frail relationships, built solely on his prowess with musical instruments.

She rescued him. "You play music for a living?"

"I do."

"Where you play?" Her voice hinted at interest in him. But he knew she wasn't like the others.

"Mostly all over. Canal boats. Here in New Orleans. Weddings. Mardi Gras. The resort on the lake. Competitions. Fais-do-dos. Even played a funeral once."

"You must be good."

He simply grunted, and muttered, "Dunno," shaking his head somberly.

"What you do when you're not playing music?"

"A lot of fishing. Love to fish." He realized that he was becoming uncomfortable. The conversation was only about him now. He leaned back against the bench, and crossed his legs in front of him, a tactic to stall for a new direction. "What do you do, Angeline Chiasson?"

She grinned again. "Mostly help my parents here at da magasin. Go to stage plays. I paint too."

"Pictures?" he asked, and then hated the stupidity of the question.

She rescued him again, treating the question as a serious expression of interest. "I paint landscapes, scenes of da Maiterie. Some of de western bayous, some here."

"What do you do with them?"

"Sell dem," she said matter-of-factly, nodding her head as she spoke. Hank didn't realize at the time that he was talking to a well-known Cajun artist, one whose oil and sketches of Cajun life were displayed and sold in galleries all over the city.

"You must be good," he chuckled.

She mimicked him, "Dunno…" complete with the somber shake of the head.

This time he laughed a natural belly laugh with an intensity that made her laugh too.

The conversation ebbed and flowed for over an hour. The two were oblivious to passersby, to the hubbub of wagons, and to the increasing heat and humidity. He told her of his humble beginnings, how his father had died in the fields when Hank was twelve, after a lifetime of trying to extract life from unyielding soil.

"Daddy took me fishin'. Didn't get to do much else with him though. He was always workin', even in winter."

"Dat was a big loss to you, yes?"

"It was too much for Ma. My older brothers, two of them, took to workin' at plantations in the area, just to support the family. They weren't much more than slaves; did the same kind of work. Older sister got married; she was only fifteen. Other sister was sent to live with mom's brother in Atlanta. Left home myself coupla years later."

"You were young too?"

"Barely sixteen. Had some relatives near Savannah. Never did find them. Took jobs anywhere I could find them." The memories returned. He sat silently for a while. She reached over and patted his arm.

"Lived for a while in an abandoned shack outside of Savannah, barely had a roof. I'd get into town everyday to find odd jobs and food."

"How you survive? So young."

"Just knew there was somethin' better. Once I was takin' care of horses on a farm in the area. Fellow name of Lipscomb hired me. Let me sleep in the stables. Ate with the slaves, five of them."

"So things were not getting better?"

"Strange. That's when they turned around. Old slave there named Ike played a fiddle; not a real good one. Made it himself. He showed me how to play. Made one for me. A few months later, we was playin' together. Kinda knew then what I wanted to do. Found a real one in Augusta soon after. Saved up and bought it. Taught myself. Pretty soon I was playing" for money. Started on street corners. I'm boring you?"

"Non. Non. Go on, please."

"Came to New Orleans when I was twenty-three, 1828. Heard there was music here."

She spoke of her dream of owning an art business, an expansive area where she could paint extensively and sell her work, all in one place.

"Been savin' too. Not quite there. Papa said he'd help out, but I do it myself. Someday."

"That's great, I spose everyone needs a dream to keep goin'."

"You have dreams, Hank?"

"A family. Never met the right person to do that. And I'd like to get to the place where I don't need to play music all of the time...where I can take time off, take my sons fishing whenever I want."

"Dat is a dream you can do."

"Yeah, except I don't have a lot of extra money...and I don't have any sons," he laughed.

"Your parents here during the Battle?" he asked.

"Non. Dey move here two years later, 1817. Went first to spend a year wid Uncle Louie, den move down here."

"You already told me that, didn't you," Hank said sheepishly.

"You bet. Already tol' you dat. C'mon Hank. I show my parents to you. Dat sound good to you?"

"You bet."

He wanted to help her rise, but she obviously didn't need help. Adroitly she hopped up and balanced herself on the crutch. He followed her back into the market.

Her parents stood behind a counter. Her father had a trace of a pot belly, white hair to his shoulders, a face creased with wrinkles, and a friendly expression which altered slightly when he saw his daughter with a man. Her mother was a tall woman who looked amazingly like her daughter. She had waited on Hank earlier.

"Mama, Papa. Dis is Hank. He played with Uncle Louie."

"Mais. A musician?" her mother said. "I am Yvonne Chiasson. Dis my husban' Maurice."

"Pleased to meet you. I was in here a while ago. When I left, I ran over your daughter."

"You play wid Louie?" the father asked. He was still not sure about the young man.

"Several years ago. Downtown. He probably doesn't remember me."

"Louie, he don' forget a good player. If you good, he remember you." The comment was curt, and more than a little accusing.

The father was sizing him up. He noticed Angeline looking at her father quizzically. There was silence. This was awkward.

"Well, I've got a lot to do this afternoon. Glad to meet y'all. Angline, mo chagren... is that how you say it? I'm sorry?"

He took her hand. She was looking straight into his eyes. "Maybe, sometime soon, you pass by again?"

"Yeah. I will. I sure will."

Then he was gone. But he felt three pairs of eyes following him, and he heard Angeline's voice back in the market.

"Coooh! Mama..."

A full ten days later, Maurice Chiasson saw his brother and immediately spoke of the thing that was bothering him.

"Louie, ma Angeline, she meet dis boy say he play music wid you. Dis boy, he don' come back ta see her, ya know. She coo-yon over dat boy. Tink he may go ro-day on her."

Louie Chiasson was larger than his older brother, stoop shouldered, and balding. He squinted at Maurice. "Played the music wit many udders. What his name?"

"Hank. Hank Rockbottom, I tink."

"Slim boy, light hair, nice face?"

"Dat be him."

Louie started to laugh. "Rosbottom. Dat be him. He make dat fiddle go 'Choooh!' you know."

"Nice boy?"

"I tink he make nice man for Angeline. Don' see him for a long time. Was a good, hones' boy"

"Mais, she boude'd a long time now, since he don' pass by."

"In two weeks, we have a boucherie at da lake. Satiday. Big fais-do-do. You bring him to dat. Tell him tuh bring dat fiddle. Mebbe banjo too. He play dat."

"If I see him."

Hank was not avoiding the Chiassons. For over a week, he had played daily on a canal boat, exhausting himself because of the long days, which sometimes ran from nine in the morning until dark. For the last three days of those performances, he hadn't sung. His voice was hoarse from overwork. The money was excellent, but he kept to himself, harboring the notion that he would go back to that store to see the girl again. He tried to remember details about her. She had the easiest smile he'd ever seen, which forced dimples onto both of her cheeks. Her black hair was shiny, down past her shoulders, framing her oval face. When she smiled, her dark eyes retreated to a playful squint. He loved her somewhat refined Cajun accent, a mixture of dialect and Southern drawl.

Yep, he'd go back to the market. He'd take the fiddle this time. Maybe he could earn some respect from Maurice Chiasson.

Hank Rosbottom enjoyed himself. The previous five days had passed quickly. First, he had gone back to the market, where he had been warmly greeted by the Chiassons. "Ya pass by tomorrow 'round late afternoon, Angeline be here." The father had said. He did, and she was, looking beautiful. Under her left arm, she had a bundle.

"Dis is for you," she had said, handing him a package which contained a canvas. The picture was an oil of a solitary old man from the back, a fishing pole visible, bait in the water, an extraordinary sunset in front of him reflected in the calm water, and surrounded by the lush vegetation of the bayou. A pirogue was beached beside him.

"Did dat several years ago. Wanted to give it to you."

"Angeline. This is wonderful. This is jes' wonderful. Thank you." He was sincere, and he was impressed. She could easily see that. He stared at it a long time. She studied him. He was in a starched white shirt with a rumpled waist jacket and dark dress pants. The light beard was neatly trimmed and his hair neatly tousled. He wants to be here, she thought. He is cute.

"Will you take a walk with me, Angeline? Can I leave the picture here till we get back?"

Maurice and Yvonne pretended to be busy, but both periodically looked up to watch the scenario several feet away. As the young couple walked away, Maurice winked at his wife.

Outside, Hank was hesitant.

"Mebbe kinda unfeeling for me to suggest a walk. Don't know if it'll be hard for you or not."

"I walk all da time. I'm a pret' good walker. Forget dis crutch. Where we goin?"

He led her to the old Absinth Bar, several blocks away on Bourbon Street.

"You can go in here?" he asked.

"You bet, Hank. Dis is New Orleans," she answered.

They sat in the corner of the nearly empty bar, and ordered white wine.

"Didn't tink I'd see you again, cher," she said.

"Got real busy. Been workin' for two weeks or more ever' day. Finally just decided to take some time off. Took it off…jes' to see you."

"Yes?"

Maybe he had stretched too far with that statement. He started to apologize. "Sorry. That was a bit too bold."

"Why you say dat? Wanted you to pass by again. Wanted to see you too."

He took that pack off of his back. "Brought my fiddle. Thought I'd play somethin' for your father. Seemed like he didn't believe me." He laid it on the small table.

You jes' put it dere? Not goin' to play it?"

"Why not." He pulled the instrument out of its case. "Here's one you probly know."

He began a rousing version of "Allons a Lafayette," many years old. She leaned forward, eyes on him, buoyed by his energy and the uplifting music. Waiters came onto the room to listen and stood a few feet away, keeping time with their feet. The few patrons listened intently. Strollers outside peeked through the front door to find the source of the spirited music. When he finished, she led the applause. "Play again, cher."

"One more. Too many people interruptin" us here."

He slowed the pace, playing a traditional Acadian song "J'ai Passe Devant ta Porte," dropping the fiddle to the crook of his arm and singing along, "I passed by your front door…" alternately in Georgia English and Louisiana Cajun.

Five days passed. He had seen her every day, mostly in the afternoon. On Friday, she had taken him to her studio, a modest building attached to her parents' house. He finally understood the scope of her talent. He posed with his arms folded while she sketched him.

Then he had gone with the Chiassons to the boucherie at Uncle Louie's small house on the lake, where he was greeted with much fanfare, and invited to play music with Louie Chiasson and a brace of other musicians for most of the afternoon. "Aaaaaayeeees" echoed across the shore, couples danced around the yard. It seemed to Hank, that a healthy portion of Jefferson Parish had come. Long tables were filled with crawfish pie, jambalya, tasso etoufee, endouille, beignets, and pitchers of beer. Tables off to the side overflowed with pots and mounds of vegetables and fruits.

Louie was the host and the star. Tirelessly, he coaxed sounds from his fiddle, nodding at Hank to pick up riffs. Much of the music was new to Hank, but his ear for music, and the rush he felt playing with the legendary "Toulooloo" forced him to improvisations that took the music to new levels.

When the band quit playing, Hank strolled to the lake with Angeline.

"You are wonderful, mon cher," she had said.

"Maybe, but here I am, makin' you walk again."

She looked at him without speaking. When he turned, he saw her eyebrow arched, and a serious expression, which he correctly identified as anger.

"What's the matter Angeline?"

"Don' see me as a cripple. Don' tink of me as fragile. Can do anythin' most folks do."

He stopped. She kept walking.

"Hey, I don' see that crutch anymore. I see a beautiful woman that I want to take care of."

"You ask other woman can she walk?"

"Yeah…no…you're right."

"You gonna catch up to me?"

Later, he took her face in his hands and kissed her gently. As he pulled away, she grabbed him and kissed him, much longer, and with more ardor.

As they returned to New Orleans, Angeline sandwiched in the carriage between her parents, and Hank riding an old dapple that he had borrowed from his landlord, he couldn't keep his eyes off of her. More than once, she turned in her seat to look at him. Once she winked at him.

They would return to the lake in the summer of 1836 to be married. Louie Chiasson was his best man; Hank had played in Louie's new band, *Bon Temps*, for eight months, and it was the most venerated collection of musicians in three states.

Together the newlyweds bought a large building up the street from his in-laws with his carefully saved wages from band appearances and the ongoing sales of paintings. He had it remodeled. "Art by Angeline" an arts emporium, consumed the front half of the large ground floor. The back half was Angelines's studio, and he had it outfitted with every imaginable art supply. They lived on the second floor, up a set of stairs that Hank had commanded from carpenters that featured wide, short steps and a sturdy banister.

The walls upstairs were covered with pictures. Above their bed was the fishing picture she had given him. They afforded adequate furnishings, and a carriage and horse stabled behind the building.

In 1837, he left *Bon Temps* and returned to solo work. He could control performance frequency, and maximize time with her.

Every corner of their life was perfect, except one. Angeline couldn't conceive, even though the two tried almost daily. Hank was privately disappointed, but in the bigger picture, he had more than he deserved, he reasoned: a beautiful soul mate whom he loved more each day, a comfortable home, his music. In lieu of a son, he often took her fishing. She accompanied him on every play date.

Late in 1837, white scales appeared on Angeline's arms and hands, followed by rashes and bumps on her legs. Neither of them was overly concerned, some skin malady that would eventually disappear. By May, he was alarmed. She was experiencing areas of numbness, and the fingers on her right hand sometimes pulled into a claw that made painting difficult.

"Angeline, it's time to see a doctor," he told her.

"Cher, it's nuttin', Usin' ma crutch too much, ya know."

But he persisted. They found a doctor in the French Quarter, near Jackson Square. His diagnosis was quick. He escorted Hank into his office, away from her.

"Sir, you'd better sit down. I have some grave news."

What is it, Doc? What is it?"

Mr. Rosbottom…your wife has leprosy."

Hank was stunned. For a moment he knew that he would pass out. The feeling subsided. He struggled with a reaction.

"Leprosy? Doc, that's a disease from the Bible…from foreign places. It can't be. It can't be…"

"There is no question. And it is a disease that we see here every so often. Seems to appear in those of Acadian descent most frequently."

"But why? How would she get it?"

"We don't know. We suspect that it's contact with another leper. Maybe something else. We just don't know much about it."

"Doc. What can we do? Is this thing goin' to take her?"

"Maybe someday. We're not sure of that either. Little by little though, her condition will get worse. She'll become disfigured. Her hands and feet will become useless. She'll need care."

Hank's jaw set. "Any chance you're mistaken here?"

"None. It is leprosy, I'm sorry."

"Anything you can give her? Anything make it easier?"

"Medicine has no cure. And no treatment."

"Then I'll just take care of her."

"Well, Mr. Rosbottom, that brings up another point. She will need to be hospitalized, away from other people."

"No, Doc. I'd never do that to her. She'll stay with me. I'll take care of her."

"No sir. That is not possible. Leprosy can be spread to other people. There is that danger. I'm afraid you have no choice. You have to put her in an institution, a hospital of some sort."

"No, Doc. I will take care of her. You said that there is no treatment."

"You must understand that I have to report this to health authorities. They will insist that you commit her."

"To a place where they shut her up away from other people? Where even the doctors are afraid of her? No sir! Dammit, No sir!"

"As I said, I will have to report this. Sadly there is no facility which treats it. But she will be cared for. She must be kept away from other people," he continued.

"No," Hank replied. "No. I will not do that! Well, Doc, I guess our business is over."

"I could summon the authorities right now, sir, if you try to leave with her. It is my duty."

"Doc, if you try to stop me, I will knock you cold, right here… and if the authorities come after her, anybody, I'll be back to put a bullet in you."

Hank was surprised at his own anger. The doctor realized that he could not stop the belligerent and stubborn man. Fear and shock had created a formidable opponent.

He found he in the carriage, weeping. They had told her too.

"My darlin', this don't matter much. I'll stay with you. We'll fight it together. I'll never leave you. We'll do our best, I promise you."

He clicked the horse. She was soon sobbing.

"It ain't fair, Angeline, but I'll make it easy for you. This thing's not gonna separate us…never."

"Not cryin' for me, cher. I feel bad I do dis to you."

"My God, Angeline…I love you, my angel." He pulled on the reins, and held her, and kissed her face repeatedly.

Her parents were shocked. Yvonne hugged her daughter. Maurice slammed his fist into a shelf and growled in fury. But no one had time to mourn the news, or to curse the gods.

"Mr. Chiasson. Doctor told me that they'll come for her. Put her in a hospital. Got to leave New Orleans. Got to take her away. Somewhere."

"He can find you?"

"Had to fill out information when we walked in. Address is on there."

"You tink dat doctor, he really send folks for her? Never hear such a ting."

"Can't take a chance that he won't. Sides, I don't want her to be around people that are disgusted by her, afraid of her."

"Where you go?"

"Dunno. Someplace away from folks. I'll take care of her myself. Don't have any idea where, but gotta do it fast."

Yvonne spoke up. "Maurice, the ol' place. You know, cher. Outside Picotville."

Angeline looked up. "The house on the bayou. I remember dat."

"Dat's it. Dat's it!" Maurice clapped his hands once.

"The old place?" Hank asked.

"Yvonne and I one time live in a old house 'bout ten miles east of Picotville. Iberia Parish, sout' of Lafayette 'bout twenny mile. Dat be sumtin' over twenny years ago. Angeline was a little girl dere. Moved into Picotville settlement later, when she still little. Da house is on da Bayou Embarrass, surrounded by swamp and da marshes. Ain't no neighbors for miles, clear to da settlement. Went to live in da town, and lef' the place dere. Jes' left. Didn't own much lan' with it. Jes dis ol' house. Took half a day jes' to get to Picotville."

"Somebody else there now? That's a long time ago."

"Don't tink so. It be all by itself out dere. Hard to get to. Lotsa cypress trees, lotsa water. Lotsa bebettes…mosquitoes. House in not much. Coupla rooms. Tried to sell it, give it away."

"Can you tell me how to get there? How far?"

"Hunnerd mile from here. Can put you on da front porch, you bet. Angeline remember too, I bet."

"By now, some fisherman or somebody could have moved in."

"Tink in twenty-some years, it not be much to look at. Take lotsa work."

"Have to deed you our house. You can sell it later, or live in it. Buy a large wagon, coupla horses. Put everything we can into that wagon. Need food to start on. Take clothes, some furniture, tools, Angeline's art supplies, some paintings to sell. Try to do that all in two days."

Maurice led Hank to the door, and lowered his voice.

"Hank, you want to do dis ting?"

"Yessir. It's the only way."

"Jes' tinkin'. You be sure to get dis leprosy too, ya know."

"Maybe not. And if I do, so what. I don't want to be apart from her. An isolated hospital room somewhere would break her spirit."

Maurice's eyes filled with tears. "You pretty special, Hank. My Angeline, she a lucky girl."

They left New Orleans at night under a quarter-moon. Perfect, Hank thought. No one would see them leave. They had filled the wagon in an area behind their building near the stable, out of sight of the street. Preparing to leave had taken four tense days. Maurice and Yvonne had taken turns, stationed up the street watching for the arrival of anyone who might be a "health authority."

There were quick good-byes, with the Chiassons promising to follow the couple in a few months. For several miles, neither spoke.

"You tink dis is a mistake, cher?"

"No, Angeline. Never been so sure of somethin'."

"You know we be alone on da bayou. You know da music stop."

"No, Angeline. The music is you. Don't matter if I never play again."

"You know da fishing picture? Dat ole man fishing?"

"Yeah. The one you gave me. That is what the bayou looks like?"

"Dat is the bayou. Da place we're goin'. Painted it from memory."

The farther they got from New Orleans, the closer to their new life, the more buoyant she became. For the first time since the diagnosis, they were laughing again.

It took almost five full days to reach the old house. The last one, they spent lost. Maurice's landmarks had changed. Almost by accident, they found the spot at dusk on the fifth day. For several miles the wagon had bumped and jolted over marshy terrain which looked as if they were the first to see it. More than once, Hank had to leave the wagon to remove debris from a trail that wasn't really a trail. They were suddenly in front of the old house.

"Your father was right. This does need some work."

The house was in severe disrepair, overgrown with weeds. A front porch had pulled away and crumpled. Vines circled the house and entered every window and door. A fallen tree had crushed the roof in the back.

"Chooooh, cher. Dis be worse dan da leprosy," she laughed.

"Well, we won't have to worry 'bout gettin' bored. Enough here to keep us busy for a while, ya know?"

"What you tink? We got a chance?"

He was at the front door, then inside, testing floor boards, knocking on the walls.

"Pretty doggone solid. Won't have to rebuild much. Maybe we can get by with just straightenin' it up a bit." On his next step, the floor gave way. He jumped back from the rotted spot. "Maybe not." He grinned at her. She was laughing. She is so beautiful, he thought.

So, on this day in 1841, he reflected on their last four years. The disease was progressing, but slowly. She had a few more numb spots, mostly on her feet, but the leprosy had not reached her face nor her arms. Her right hand had clawed a little more, but she could still paint, although the finished products took somewhat longer. She was slower on her crutch, but refused to concede any small victory to the disease. A uniformed visitor would not have suspected that she battling an insidious malady.

Of course, there were no visitors. His in-laws came once each summer. On their first trip, Maurice had wagoned in a load of more tools, fresh-cut lumber, and building skills that he had accrued when he had lived in the house. He also brought a bundle of money, from the sale of the art studio and home.

The house was Hank's pride. He had re-built the front porch and re-attached it to the building. Then he had added a back porch. He painstakingly cut and carted away the dead tree which had fallen into the house, laid a new floor with Maurice's gift of lumber, and put on a new roof of shingles. Last year he had added two rooms to the side of the house, doubling its size, and providing a work room and storage room for his wife. Angeline was by his side through much of the renovation, putting in long hours hammering, measuring, and carrying small items to him.

More importantly, she had reclaimed the yard, nurturing or clearing away the overgrowth from twenty years of neglect, and maintaining a garden in a sunny spot 200 yards behind their dock. On early evenings, they would brave the mosquitoes, and sit on chairs on the dock, fishing and talking until darkness forced them in to bed. Sometimes he took his fiddle down and they both sang. Often they created new lyrics or new songs.

"Try dis, cher… 'da alligator, he not welcome here…"

Hank would pick it up.

"Ate ol' Hank with Cajun beer…"

"Saddest thing you ever seen…"

She would finish: "Den he ate poor Angeline…"

She would hum some tune, and he would repeat it on the fiddle.. Together they fashioned a melody that Hank dubbed, "Our Bayou Home."

On both sides of their plot, the land gave way to marshes, in effect nearly surrounding them with water, and on rare occasions, men in pirogues floated by, nearly all calling out to Hank, "Aallo!" He ignored them, mindful that if he seemed unfriendly, they wouldn't dock for conversation.

He never tired of looking at the splashes of sun on the quiet water, nor the canopy of green above. He loved the quiet during the days, and cacophony of critter noises at night.

The worst times for Hank were the two days every other month that he left her alone to wagon into Pirotville. He would try to sell her paintings, under the guise that he was "A Chiasson." He would buy seeds and lamp oil, clothes, and other necessities, and start back to his Angeline. Sometimes , he did business farther away, in Lafayette, a larger community, and he frequently carried a bundle of letters, from Angeline to her parents and often returned with letters from them, mailed to "H. Rosbottom, Lafayette, Louisiana."

Yesterday, he had begun to hollow out a tree he had felled, so that the Rosbottoms would have a pirogue.

Their affection for each other, their joy at being together, never wavered. She was doing so well that the disease was never mentioned.

CHAPTER SIX

1842

The Redlands of east Texas were untamed and volatile, especially in the areas of Harrison and Shelby counties. A long-standing feud in that area, which had begun in 1839 and festered for three years, had become a war by 1842, a conflict that even the President of the Republic of Texas, Sam Houston, couldn't control.

It had begun in what was known as the Neutral Ground, a lawless swath of land between the American and Mexican borders. Its inception was due to rampant land-swindling and cattle rustling, and the genesis event was a dispute between Sheriff Alfred George and a settler named Joseph Goodbread. George hired Charles Jackson to quiet Goodbread. The former riverboat captain from Louisiana, a wanted man, shot Goodbread at Shelbyville in 1840.

Jackson, aware that he would probably have to answer for his action, organized a gang which he called "The Regulators," whose aim, he declared, was to protect the area from cattle rustlers and other law-breakers. This high-minded purpose, he thought, would impress any who wanted him punished for shooting Goodbread. The Regulators were vigilantes who would suppress the waves of crime in the Redlands, he said.

Their concept of law enforcement was beatings, murder, and arson, and it seemed that no one was immune from their crime-stopping charade.

Hastily, Edward Merchant organized another group, the Moderators, to combat the Regulators. Numbers on both sides grew, but at that point there had been no open hostilities.

There was, however, a public outcry for justice in the Goodbread shooting, brought to bear by the Moderators. Jackson was "arrested" by Sheriff George, and a trial date was set for July 12 of 1841 before Judge Hansford in Marshall, Texas. Hansford was a supporter of the Moderators.

On the trial day, Jackson marched into court carrying a rifle. Tagging along was George. Behind him were 150 armed Regulators. They filled the room.

Judge Hansford was livid. "Why," he shouted, "is Mr. Jackson carrying a rifle? This is my courtroom!"

Then he addressed Jackson, pointing a finger accusingly, "You, sir, will be fined for this!"

Jackson walked up to the judge's bench, pulled over a chair, laid his rifle in front of the judge, sat down, and took off his boots.

"Let this trial begin," he boomed. He glared at the flustered judge.

Hansford looked back, and melted. "Ahem…court is adjourned until nine tomorrow morning." The co-leader of the Regulators, Charles Moorman, led the assembled group in laughter. The judge quickly left the room. That night the celebrating Regulators burned the home of the Moderator McFadden family.

The trial never was held. Jackson was ambushed and killed, along with a man named Lauer, who just happened to be with him. The Moderator McFaddens were the ringleaders.

Moorman assumed command and led a party to find the assassins. The McFaddens were caught, and tried in October. All were hanged except the youngest son.

The Regulators then extended the terror into Panola and Harrison counties, hanging Moderators and their sympathizers. The Regulator numbers grew so large that Moorman talked about overthrowing the Texas government.

In the midst of this, the Moderators started proceedings to impeach Judge Hansford for his inaction against Jackson. Hansford quickly left office and retired to a farm near Joneville, where he would be shot and killed two years later.

The Regulators stepped up their efforts. Seventeen Shelby County Moderators were killed. The Moderators retaliated by systematically ambushing Regulators at their homes, on city streets, and even in the hallowed confines of churches.

Vigilante justice, in effect no justice, was spinning out of control. To combat the growing numbers of the Regulators, the Moderators turned west, to Austin. Their plan was to recruit Texas Rangers to the fray, to encourage them to leave the force to take up guns for them for better wages. It was a modest success. Several of the Rangers were siphoned off. When the Moderators noted the plan, they too began to pursue the Rangers.

It was perfect timing. There was discontent in Austin. Sam Houston was using Rangers as couriers, scouts, and soldiers. Peacekeeping and control of Indians were forgotten pieces of their purview. Pay was minimal. Some left the group. Others were enticed west, to the Redlands.

Flapjack Bailey and Big Head were among the early defections, to the Regulators. Bailey tried to convince Herk Grimes to join them.

"Not for me. Ain't goin' to be a hired gun for vigilantes," Grimes responded.

"But, Mr. Grimes, ain't you doin' that anyways, for the Rangers?"

"Good luck to you, Flap. I'm stayin'."

But increasingly, Herk's loyalty was being tested. A few months later, he heard rumors that the Rangers would soon disband.

"Don't think so, Herkimer," Tumlinson had counseled. "That there's just talk. The Comanch are still out there, ya know."

In spite of the Captain's words, Herk sensed that the tide was turning. Maybe it was time to follow another trail. He met with a Moderator, Judge S.F. Lester, in an Austin saloon.

"Mr. Grimes, we need a man of your stature in the Moderators. You'll be well-paid for your efforts for us."

"If you want me to go around ambushin' people, our talk is over now."

"No. No. No. We feel like your very presence will end this dispute once and for all."

"One man?"

"Yes, if you're that man. The whole state of Texas knows about you, respects you."

"So what do you have in mind?"

"We'd want you to find some ways to stop things, or at least slow them down."

"Why work for the Moderators? Why shouldn't I work for the Regulators? Don't seem there's much difference to me.

"Mr. Grimes, we were formed to control the Regulators. They were the ones burning and killing. We are the good guys, if you will."

"Don't know much about that area. Don't know where I'd stay."

"We will get you a boarding house room near Pulaski. No cost to you."

"So who would I report to? Who'd I work for?"

"Mr. Edward Merchant. Mr. John Bradley."

"Tell me this now, or we got no deal. Those fellers aren't goin' to send me out to kill people, are they? Cause if I'm to be a hired gun, I ain't leavin' Austin."

"Mr. Grimes, this is a war. We will pay you for your ability to use a gun. You will be a soldier, so to speak. So in that respect you will be a hired gun. There's no hiding that fact. You will have to unholster those guns, but it will be in the cause of justice, I promise you."

Herk had misgivings, but he agreed to follow Lester back to Shelbyville after he resigned from the Rangers. "Give me two weeks. Tell me where you want me."

Fourteen days later, he was across a table from Lester and John Bradley.

Bradley was an innocuous-looking man, probably in his forties. He had a facial tic which occasionally winked one eye, and drew up the corner of his mouth. He was well-dressed and well-spoken. He seemed delighted to be in the company of a Ranger legend.

"Mr. Grimes. I finally think that we can slow down the terror, now that you're here. For a while now, we've been outnumbered and outfought."

"You asked for help from the Republic?'

"Mr. Sam Houston wants nothing to do with this war. He suggested that these counties leave the republic and fight it out until the thing's settled."

"What's next?"

"Well sir, I know that you don't cotton to killing unless it's necessary. It's necessary."

"Killing? Necessary?"

"The Regulators have a stable of enforcers. Those men have no mercy, show no mercy. They're in this fight to eliminate the Moderators by whatever means."

"Gunfighters?"

"Some. They're effective. Most Moderators can't fight them, not on even terms. Besides, they work by surprise. Ambushes, outnumbering us."

"Lot of Texas Rangers came this way. Any of them involved."

"You'll see. A few of them on both sides."

"Killers or peacekeepers?"

"There are not many peacekeepers. This has divided entire towns and counties. Seems like everyone's a target. Everyone's an enforcer. Most of the fighters on both sides are just citizens of Texas, rugged men who believe in a cause."

"Names?"

"A lot of them we don't know by name. We've had reports of Regulators with names like Fats, the Rat, Rattlesnake, Frank, Scar…ambushing our followers, killing innocent citizens. We know descriptions and we know the ringleaders, but you do realize that there are hundreds of partisans on both sides."

"Don't sound much too attractive," Herk offered, standing to leave.

"Well, Mr. Grimes, you're here. Maybe this entire thing will even out a bit."

"Can't do this by myself."

"Won't have to. We'll give you the names of Moderators in Panola County. You'll have a group of them at your disposal all of the time."

Herk was frustrated. After four months, there had been no appreciable action, and very little communication with Bradley or Merchant. He was operating in a vacuum. He did collect his promised pay via courier, but he had no clear idea of what was expected of him, nor of how to utilize the somewhat ragtag collection of Moderators in Panola County.

There was James Lewis, a good man, tall and quiet and friendly, probably nice to have on your side. And there was Spook Stryker, who was a mystery and an enigma. He was always heavily armed, a very pale man with snow white, stringy hair, and a sneer that spoke of a potential for evil effectiveness. His gray eyes were expressionless. Herk could only guess at his past, but mayhem was surely part of it. Beyond that, Herk had a constantly changing cast of farmers, a few professional men, even some teen-agers, more of a dysfunctional posse than anything.

He had few diversions. One was alcohol. He had started drinking, something he'd never done while a Ranger. Not much at first, but he had used it more and more recently.

The other diversion was one that bothered him, Loretta Lewis, wife of his fellow Moderator, and proprietress of his boarding house, a large home with roses and a picket fence outside, and spartan furnishings inside.

That was how he thought of her, external beauty of sorts, but an internal vacancy of mind and purpose. She had come on to him immediately upon his arrival. She wore too much makeup, low cut bodices, and had cultivated a walk which featured exaggerated swaying hips.

He guessed that she was in her mid-thirties somewhere, childless, stuck on a frontier which didn't appreciate her.

One day, she had crossed the line. It was a cool morning, and he had risen early to sit on the back steps of the house, thinking that he'd ride to Shelbyville. She came out with a basket to collect eggs, and purposely brushed against him as she started down the steps.

"Mr. Herk, I'm sorry. I just get all flustered around handsome men like yourself."

"Mornin', ma'am."

"Cool today, but it'll be hot later. Sometimes I think the only way to be comfortable in Texas is not to wear anything at all."

He didn't answer.

"James had to go to Nagagdoches this morning. Said he wouldn't be back til late tonight."

He nodded at her, but didn't speak.

She was comely, voluptuous even, with dark hair pulled back severely, two ringlets carefully combed to fall in front of her ears, and a round, expressive face. She had thin lips and a wide mouth, not her best features.

"Something I've been wanting to ask you, Herkimer. Do you have a big gun?"

"Ma'am?"

"A big gun. I'll bet you use a real big gun."

The conversation had turned awkward. Herk squirmed, and stood up to leave.

But thirty minutes later, he was wrestling her around on the large mattress in her bedroom, in a marathon which lasted until early afternoon.

That had repeated itself a week later. Herk had avoided her since, not an easy maneuver since they were in the same house, and she was the cook and the maid for roomers. He was safest when James was around, which was much of the time. Recognizing that, he began to develop a friendship with the husband. He rose early, and returned late to his room, filling the hours with solitary rides into the pine woods, and long evenings in the dilapidated saloons of Panola County.

Then all hell broke loose.

A man named Stanfield killed a Moderator named Hall in Shelbyville, accusing him of hog theft. Hall's friends asked the Moderators for revenge. Stanfield was arrested, but escaped from jail, and sought refuge in the home of a Regulator named Runnels. Moderators under John Bradley arrived, killed Runnels, and re-captured Stanfield.

The faction leaders were hauled into separate courtrooms. Regulator judge John Ingram dismissed charges against Moorman. Moderator judge S.F. Lester dismissed charges against Hall and Bradley. A Hall relative was shot and killed on his farm. The battle was on again.

Regulators led by "Fats," it was reported, killed a Moderator in front of his farmhouse and burned the building while firing continuous rounds into it. No one in the Moderator's family escaped the conflagration.

The Regulator gunfighter named "Scar" was shot in the back by Spook Stryker. Stryker then gunned down a doctor who was returning to Shelbyville after tending to a Regulator family.

"Stryker is crazy. He may be one of ours, but that man is dangerous," James Lewis commented to Herk.

"Settin' himself up as a target. Settin' us up too," Herk replied.

In a period of ten weeks, Herk captured or drove off Regulators in four separate incidents. In none did he have to fire a shot. What frustrated him, however, were the light sentences meted out. They were either slaps-on-the-hand from the Moderator-inclined magistrates fearful of retribution, or complete exonerations from Regulator judges.

The word got around that Herk was dogged, fair, and effective, but he saw little progress in stopping hostilities. He was also bothered by the fact that he was no more than a bounty hunter. He had no official title, no legal job description, no sanction from the laws of the Republic.

A mob of Regulators rode into Center and terrorized the town for hours, raping a young girl. They forced several males to strip, and then bull-whipped them in front of the cowering populace. One died.

Herk, Lewis, and seven Panola Moderators rode into Center the next day.

"Find out anything you can. Talk to the people. Get back to me," Herk directed.

Lewis quickly returned. "Just talked to the family of the girl they raped. One of the Regs told her if she wanted more, they'd be at the Stamper ranch."

"Where is that?"

"Bout 10-15 mile south on the Old Trail."

"Stamper a Regulator?"

"Dunno. You figger they was braggin' or tryin' to lure us down there?"

"Don't much matter. We're goin'."

The nine took the dusty trail, an ill-defined, meandering route between hillocks covered with boulders and sagebrush.

Herk reined in after a half-hour. "Find some shade. Check your weapons. I'll be back directly."

"Herkimer, you fixin' to go in alone?"

"Nope. Just havin' a look-see."

"Mighty dangerous."

"Ranger work. Did this for years. Regs are not as bad as the Comanch."

Herk then rode a zigzag path, watching for lookouts, checking for hoofprints. What he saw told him that the Center mob had come that way. He counted eleven sets of prints. He pulled up just as the Stamper spread came into view. Several buildings sat in a long valley. He counted horses in the corral. Fourteen. Ten saddled.

Surprising the raiders would be impossible. Any approach to the ranch house would expose his men for a long distance. A night attack would work, but with his untrained little army, attacking at night would be a disaster. Too much going on at night. A Ranger company would have handled it, excelled at it.

His Moderators would have to ride in from different directions, the group with him riding up with much dust and noise to distract the Regulators. Surround the house.

"Won't be easy," he told his posse sometime later. "But we ain't goin' in there to kill people. Gotta make sure them's the ones. There might be some killing, but we're takin' back captives for justice. Don't any of us shoot first, less'n they pull guns. If you shoot, shoot to wound. Defend yourselves, but don't get loco."

Herk and three untested men rode toward the house. A stooped man carrying a bucket saw them coming, and turned to yell at the house. Several other men appeared on the front stoop.

Herk pulled up. "Who are you?" he yelled to the man with the bucket.

"Uriah Stamper. Who are you?"

"This your place?"

"It is. Whut's yore bizness here?"

"Seems that you've got a lot of company today. Get them all out here."

"Don't much like someone orderin' me. This be all of us," the man answered, sweeping his free arm toward the stoop.

"Don't think so. Lots of horses with saddles over there."

"You're damn Moderators, aincha."

"Don't matter. We're here to round up some scum. Killed a man. Hurt a little girl."

"You ain't the law!"

"We're here to act for the law. Get everybody out here. Want to have a talk with them."

Herk saw a man on the porch move quickly to his left, away from a window. A rifle shot from the window glanced off of the ground, well in front of Herk. He noticed Lewis and two Moderators riding up behind the house, and two more closing in on the right.

Stamper was leveling a pistol at him, the bucket spilled on the ground.

He spurred his horse toward the porch, low in the saddle. His first shot knocked Stamper to the ground. A shot from somewhere tore into the chest of a man near the door. The man who had moved from the window was felled by Lewis as he tried to get off a shot; he catapulted off of the porch. Herk's group circled back to reload. Herk saw a Moderator on the right fire into a window from close range. A man from the house broke for the corral. Lewis stopped him with a rifle shot.

There was a lull in gunfire. Herk called out, "The rest of you throw your guns out now! We'll burn the building with you inside!"

The four men on the porch seemed undecided, but they were not soldiers. The crazy man on horseback seemingly had gunmen everywhere. Their decision was made for them when the front door eased open, and six men filed out with their hands in the air.

Herk ordered them to take off their shirts, pants, and boots. Eight Moderators kept guns trained on them as Lewis tied them together with the lengths of several lariats.

"Now, we're goin' to take a walk. Any of you try anything or don't keep up, I'll shoot you in the legs, and the men tied to you will have to carry you back, 'less you bleed to death first," Herk shouted.

Stamper was dead. So were three other Regulators. Herk ordered three Moderators to round up the horses, and to take them back to town.

"Herk, we burying them dead men?" Lewis asked.

"No time. Carry them inside, and set fire to the house. Least the buzzards won't get them."

The incident was celebrated by the Moderators, and by the law. To return from a mission with no casualties, and with live captives, was unusual. Though some Moderators groused that all of the Regulators should have been killed on site, the general reaction to the act was positive. This time, justice of sorts prevailed. The abused girl identified three men who were among her attackers, but didn't seem certain about others. A family pointed to another Regulator as the one who had wielded the whip which had killed their father. The four were hanged. The others were set free.

Herk was lionized, perhaps too much. He sought out Lewis.

"I'm going to have to move out of your house. The Regs will be comin' after me soon. Don't want you or your wife to be caught in the crossfire."

"Too bad, Herkimer. I always felt safe with you there." Lewis paused. "There is another thing..."

Lewis didn't finish the sentence. Herk looked at him, waiting.

"Don't think you know that I was shot up in the Mexican War. Can't be a husband to Loretta. I think that I keep her happy, but it ain't a pleasant thing for her, no kids and all. Was hopin' you could help us out with that some day. You know, the children part. We admire you a lot, Herkimer."

"Don't know what to say."

"God forgive me for bringin' that up. It's a touchy kind of thing. Figure she'll leave me some day, with no kids to mind." Lewis turned away so that Herk wouldn't see the emotion.

"Lewis, thanks for tellin' me. The problem now is my bein' out there with you."

The conversation had rattled Herk. He suddenly understood a lot of things.

The war settled down again, except for an occasional Regulator ambush organized by "Fats." There was usually a gruesome response somewhere, courtesy of Spook Stryker.

In mid-1844 the Moderators met at Bells Springs, and re-named themselves the Reformers. They also dismissed Bradley as their leader, and elected James Cravens. There had been votes for Herkimer Grimes.

Herk had not attended the session. He knew nothing about Cravens, but he suspected that Reformers were about to launch serious warfare again. His lesson to both sides –moderate revenge involving the law, protecting the lives of even your enemies—was probably lost.

One August morning he was intercepted on the streets of Shelbyville by a young boy.

"Mr. Grimes. Mr. James Lewis sent me to find you. Somebody shot up his house last night. Nobody hurt, but he's left to find them. Said he's meet you by the big bend in the Sabine River."

"Why didn't he come for me?"

"Don't think he knew exactly where you was, Mr. Grimes."

A gruesome discovery was waiting at the river. James Lewis was staked to the ground, almost naked. Bullet holes were evident on every part of his body. He had been shot in both eyes. A heavy rain was falling, so pursuit of the attackers was impossible. Herk covered Lewis with a blanket, and loaded him on the horse.

Later, he made his way to the boarding house. He didn't want to do it, and he was heavily fortified with alcohol. As he dismounted, he noticed that several windows were missing, obviously from the attack the night before. He knocked on the door.

She answered. In her hand was a pistol.

"Herkimer. Thank God you're here. We was attacked last night."

"I know."

"What's the matter? You look terrible."

"Loretta. James was ambushed this morning. He's dead."

"What's that? James dead?"

"Found him by the Sabine. You don't want to know the details."

She stepped back, and fell heavily onto the sofa.

"No. No. No. Can't be...James."

"Seen him myself. Brought him back. Body's in Shelbyville. Take you there tomorrow morning, if you want."

He sat on a chair in the corner. The alcohol was hampering clear thought, and he couldn't focus adequately on her. She was sobbing. She needed to be consoled. He wasn't capable of that. He was aware when she retreated to the bedroom. He crossed the room to the sofa, and fell asleep.

The next thing he knew, sunlight was creeping across the floor. His head was clear, but something had awakened him.

"Herkimer?"

She was standing by the sofa, naked. She gently stroked the hair off of his forehead.

"Herkimer. I need you."

"No, Loretta. No."

"Please. Please."

She led him to the bedroom. This time the love-making was gentle. Nothing was said between them. Her eyes were closed the entire time. When he left the house, she was crying. She didn't want to see the body, she said. She asked him to bring James back, so that she could have him buried on the property.

When he reached Shelbyville, commotion and confusion reigned. Craven had sent out word for all Reformers to meet. They would ride out 200 strong, and they would clean out several counties of Regulators. Herk was furious. He tried to find Cravens, and instead found an underling, a man named Elliott.

"What is this you're plannin'?"

"Mr. Grimes, we're goin' to end this war tomorrow. You better get your gear."

"You aim to kill folks?"

"Yessir. As I understand, we do. We're goin' to drive them Regulators out of Texas. Them we don't kill."

"Don't have to kill. There's other ways."

"No, there ain't. Ranger ways? You tried them. Too slow. We've been told to get ready to ride."

"Nobody got word about this to me."

"Tried. Nobody knew where you was."

"I ain't goin' with you. Fact is, you can tell Cravens I'm through."

"Your decision, Mr. Grimes. You ain't with us. Mebbe you're against us. Better watch your back from now on."

Herk glared at Elliott. "Don't much like it here anyways. Won't be here if you run out of other people to kill."

The Reformer turned away.

Herk was preparing to return to his hotel, to pack up, to leave the nightmare, when a rider approached Elliott.

"Bout two miles west. I seen it ! Spook Styker's been killed. Strung up!"

"Don't have time for that now. Deal with it later," Elliott dismissed him.

Herk's curiosity had been raised. Stryker dead. He had to see. He would leave east Texas after he checked out the story. He left the hotel and rode west, circling for an hour, looking for the reported scene. He dismounted at a convergence of tracks, and walked his horse to the top of a rise. Below was a small grove of scrub trees. There was a solitary horse grazing nearby. A few yards into the grove he saw Stryker, hanging by his feet from a high limb. His head was nearly separated from his body, dangling inches from the ground. His shirt and vest had been torn off. Strips of skin fell from his neck and chest. He had been scalped.

Instantly, Herk knew. This looked like Comanche torture, but there were no tribesmen close to the Redlands. The torture had been done by someone who had seen the results of Comanche warfare. A Ranger. Fats.

"Turn around real slow," a voice commanded from behind him.

"Flapjack Bailey," Herk muttered.

He had been waiting nearby, hiding behind a rockfall. Herk had not been alert enough. Distracted. He cursed, and turned around.

"Thought it might be you, Flap. You're Fats."

He was surprised by the large figure behind the former Ranger. Big Head. Big Head Franklin. "Frank." Both had guns trained on him.

"Been wondering where you two were. Thought you'd moved on before I got here."

"Mr. Grimes, we been here long afore you. Over two years now. Kinda avoided you."

"Regulators, huh."

"They pay us well, Mr. Grimes. Put your hands up."

"Ain't a very happy reunion, is it?" Herk raised his hands.

"Regulators wouldn't let us take you out. Afeared that Houston would take an interest. We coulda kilt you a hunnert times."

"You that good, Flap?"

"Tired of all the noise about how good you are. You taught me a lot 'bout trackin' and other things. But you chose the wrong side over here. I was a good Ranger, but you was Tumlinson's boy."

"Came to jealousy, didja?"

Big Head had not spoken.

"Don't matter, Mr. Grimes. In a few minutes won't be any need for jealousy, nuthin' like that. Mr. Herkimer Grimes be as dead as that white-haired friend of yours over there."

"Gonna kill me, Flap?"

"Gonna kill the Ranger legend. Be a big bonus for us. Stryker and the great Mr. Grimes, the same day."

Herk was looking for an advantage. There was none. Both Bailey and Big Head were too far away to rush, too close to run from.

"Take off your pistols, Mr. Grimes. One at a time. If you make any funny move, we'll kill you right now."

"Sounds like that don't matter much. You're fixin' to kill me anyway."

"Take off your pistols!"

"Go to hell."

"Take off your pistols, Mr. Grimes!"

"Flap, you're a joke."

"Don't mess with me! Do what I say!"

"Don't get excited, Flap. You might wet your pants. Be just like you. You're a coward."

He wasn't sure of what he was doing, but it was having an effect. Bailey was red-faced, furious. He'll make a mistake here soon, Herk thought. I'll draw down on him. But I can't handle Big too.

Bailey fired a shot at his feet, and quickly changed pistols.

"Careful, Flap. You'll shoot yourself."

"Damn you! Damn you! Damn you!"

Bailey took a step forward. His pistol was pointing at Herk's head.

"Good-bye, Mr. Grimes." Flapjack spit.

There was a shot. Flapjack's eyes grew wide and his hand opened. His gun fell to the ground. He slumped, stumbled, and fell heavily. Behind him Big Head's pistol was smoking.

"Never did like that little bastard. Went crazy."

They stood for a moment, watching Flapjack Bailey die.

"Now what, Big?"

"Dunno."

"Well, if you aim to shoot me, you'd better get to it. Cause I'm goin' to draw on you."

"Not gonna shoot you. Save your bullets."

"Kinda surprised at you, Big. You never was a killer."

"Hated this war. Wasn't me ambushin' folks. Just got in a few gunfights."

"You didn't ride with Flapjack?"

"Not in two years. Until today. Them was my orders."

"Well, Big, I'll tell you what. I'm getting' on my horse and ridin' out of Texas. You do what you want. Tell them Regulators you killed me, if you want. I been in Texas too long."

"Don't have the stomach to do this no more. Think I'll ride out too."

"I'm going alone. Don't want company."

"Fine with me."

Herk turned his horse's head toward the north. "Adios, Big. Thanks for what you did here."

Big Head didn't answer. He just nodded his head and watched Herkimer Grimes ride away from Texas forever.

CHAPTER SEVEN
1846

Hank Rosbottom's life had changed dramatically in the past few months. His wife's leprosy was raging. Her face was swollen. Her legs and arms were covered with sores. She had lost energy and appetite. He often found her, pensive and quiet in a dark corner of the house, or under a cypress tree staring straight ahead. He had to help her get around. He dressed her every morning, carried her into the sunlight, sang to her.

She still told him that she loved him every day, still listened to his music with a smile, but it was evident to him that she was losing ground rapidly. He was losing her.

Frantically he pored through the books and medical papers and journals that Maurice had been bringing him every summer and winter. In the past five years, the Chiassons had made the trip twice a year, bringing clothes and food, art supplies and books.

During their latest visit, in December, Maurice had noticed that his daughter was much thinner, much less optimistic. He had maneuvered Hank into a private conversation.

"Dis is hard on you, Hank. Do you tink Angeline is worse?"

"I'm noticin' differences. I dunno. I just dunno."

"Time to talk about dis, Hank. If da worse ever happens, Yvonne and I agree dat you should bury Angeline here. She's been happiest here wid you. You do what you tink is bes', but we will be fine if ya do dat."

When Hank had exhausted the treatises on leprosy, he devoured other medical subjects, hoping that he would find a connection, something that would ease her pain or stop the progression. He concocted salves and ointments. He posted medical information on nails around the house. He held her at night when she couldn't sleep. He treated the sores and bathed her several times a day, gently ministering to her. Both of her hands were useless. He massaged them tenderly, endlessly.

During the colder months, he would wrap her in clothes and blankets, and take her to Picotville or Lafayette with him. Those visits seemed to revive her. She would sit, covered, in the wagon while he attended to matters. No one paid attention to her.

On one trip, four years earlier, he had paid a man $2 for a young dog, a large female mutt with liquid brown eyes. They named her Lady Lafayette after the town where she was purchased. The dog adopted Angeline, seemed to sense that she needed company. Until Angeline's condition deteriorated, Lady would lie peacefully near while Angeline painted or gardened. If there was even the slightest threat to Angeline's safety, if a large flock of birds suddenly burst from the cypress, Lady would snarl and bark until Angeline settled her. Hank felt more secure if he had to go to Picotville alone.

Now Angeline had lost weight, but more crucial to her condition, she seemed to have lost hope.

One morning, she had told him, "Wish I could die, cher. I'm such a burden to you."

He stammered a reply, “No, Darlin’. No. If you die, my life is over too.” He then went down to the water, away from her, and wept.

He had gotten her ready for bed one night, and when he crawled in next to her, she was watching him.

“Cher, we’ve had a wonderful life. Yes?”

“Eleven years of joy, Angeline. We’ve been lucky, in spite of…” He couldn’t finish.

“Dat first day at the magasin ? You really got my attention,” she giggled.

It was the first genuine laugh he had heard from her in months.

“Yep. I was in too much of a hurry. But if I hadn’t run into you, we might never have talked, or met. Pays to be clumsy sometimes.”

“Never really tol’ you. I fell for you at once, in more ways den one.”

“Country boy in too much of a hurry. Don’t know why I got so lucky.”

“And such a hero, cher. Dat carpenter when we were re-doing da house in da city? You defended ma honor.” She giggled again.

He remembered. One of the carpenters had playfully grabbed her posterior one day as she passed him. She had barely gotten “Hey!” spoken when Hank rushed past her, grabbed the offender by both shoulders, and threw him to the floor. “Get your tools and get out of here now,” Hank had commanded, “or I’ll use a hammer on you!” The carpenter scrambled to his feet and fled the house.

“Remember too…after da wedding? We didn’t get outta bed for a week.”

“Not much of a honeymoon was it?”

“It was da best ! Da best ! Never really ended.”

He pulled her to him, and nestled her in his arms. “We were good at that, my angel.” He instantly regretted using the word “were.” She didn’t seem to notice.

“I remember da firs’ time in da pirogue. Miles from da house, an’ you saw a leak. Den you lose da pole.”

He chuckled. “Ugliest part of the whole bayou, open swamp water, nothin’ but reeds and scrub. Had to get in the water with gators and snakes. Then we got lost. Tryin’ to forget that part.”

“Distracted a bit, cher. Dat’s all. We saw our house in good time.”

“Yeah. Good time. Maybe four hours later.”

“You were scared, cher?” she teased.

“Well, I had a leakin’ boat, and I was…distracted…in miles of water with the same lookin’ trees. Yeah, I was terrified.”

“Our guardian angel, same one who gave us happiness here, she was watching over us.”

“Our guardian angel is a she?”

“You bet.”

“Nope. Couldn’t be. That would be two female angels here.”

“Hank, you an angel too, my love. Took two of us to keep you from runnin’ away. An’ we have Lady. She’s an angel too, an’ the child I never have for you.”

“Outnumbered all these years, and I didn’t know it.”

“You are a saint, my husband. I have such love for you.”

“My Angeline.” He kissed her forehead.

"Dat leprosy. It change our life, but how many people spen' so much time together? Alone. Wouldn't change these ten years."

He cleared his throat. "You've become a better fisherman than me."

"Dat's because I talk to da fish."

He laughed. "What do you say?"

"Chooh, fish. I got dis perfect man. Want to feed him. Can you help me out?"

He laughed harder. "If I were a fish, I'd find your hook. I'd try to get caught by you."

"What you do when I'm not here, cher?"

"Don't. Don't ask that. Won't even think about that."

"Have to. You go back to New Orleans. Play music again. Fin' a nice woman. You still a young man."

"There is no other woman on earth. I got the best one."

She changed her position. Her weight was nothing. She is so frail, he thought.

"Jes' feel so weak. So useless. So tired."

"I know. I've been reading. Tryin' to find out if maybe there's another illness involved. Somethin' we can treat."

"You know as much as da doctors, Hank. You'd make a good doctor. So kind, so caring."

"Dr. Rosbottom. I kinda like the sound of that."

She didn't answer. She was already asleep. He was thankful for this respite from suffering. They had just spent minutes together like so many a few months ago. He kissed the top of her head, gently patted her cheek, and was soon asleep too.

Sometime during the night she passed on. He knew it immediately when he awoke.

"Lady," he whispered. "She's gone."

He continued to hold her for a long time, then carefully extracted himself from her, and began to get dressed.

He returned to their bedroom later, and held her until the afternoon. The conversation the night before, the brief re-awakening of her spirit, and the reflections on their life together, it was almost as if she knew that she would die that night.

He buried her in a box nailed with wood from the headboard of their bed, in the sunlight near her garden. He fashioned a headstone from the only boulder he could find, and carefully scratched out letters with a knife.

Angeline Chiasson Rosbottom
October 12, 1806 – May 22, 1846
God's Angel, My Angeline

He buried her in the best clothes from her closet, with a scribbled copy of "Our Bayou Home," a rag toy that she had made for Lady, and the sketch of him that she had done so many years before. Then he sat by her grave for two days, Lady at his feet, her front paws and head resting on him, her eyes full of sadness.

He would have to load the wagon, travel to New Orleans, and tell her parents. After that, he didn't know. He didn't care.

CHAPTER EIGHT
1847

Peace and great happiness found Three Doves. She had taken the advice of William Bent in 1843, and her proposal to Rides With Fire to accompany her to Taos was met with a huge smile.

"Yes, Three Doves, my friend. I will go with you."

The relationship raced past friendship in short order. On the third night out, a great starry night with a light breeze, she discovered that Rides With Fire was capable of all male responses despite his crippled condition. Through the night, in a tangle of bodies and enthusiasm that robbed them of sleep, they romped without inhibition or pause, whispering endearments and caressing each other for hours. That continued nightly for the next two weeks into Taos. Long before that, Three Doves realized that she was in love for the first time in her young life.

During the days, bouncing in Butler's wagon, with the horses tied behind, and their meager possessions taking up only a fraction of the wagon bed which also contained foodstuffs and sundries from Bent's Fort, they talked about whatever was waiting for them in Taos, what they expected, what they wanted, and what they feared.

"Three Doves, for the first time in many moons, I feel that I have worth."

"My love, you are more of a man than any other I have known."

"I want to care for you, protect you. I have questioned whether I can do that."

"We will do what we can do. Being with you is important to me. We will take care of each other."

"How will we live in Taos?"

"Mr. William Bent wrote to his brother and St. Vrain that we would leave for there. Mr. Charles Bent sent a letter back that our arrival would make him happy. He promised to find me work at his trading post. He will find us a room there."

"And what of me?"

"We will be together. I will insist."

The wagon was quiet for several miles.

"I must find a way to become a provider. I must find work."

"We will make that happen."

"Three Doves, I am only half a man. I do not know the white man's language."

"Rides With Fire, I will teach you. And you have great strength in your arms and back. You are wise. You can still ride a horse and drive a wagon. There will be work."

Even as she spoke the words, Three Doves was not sure. Somehow, she would have to nurture this man, encourage him, teach him, and help him reach some level of pride in himself. There would be other requirements of her too. Each morning, each night on the journey to Taos, the two exerted considerable effort to get him into and out of the wagon. His strong arms and her dogged pushing or pulling succeeded. That was as it should be, she thought. Their life would be a partnership in many ways.

Taos was a refreshing change for the two. Mountains, often snow-capped, formed a backdrop for the collection of buildings built on a small plateau. A cosmopolitan populace included Texans, Mexican families, and a large group of Indians, mostly from the Taos culture. At elevation, the setting seemed more hospitable, the sun less intense, the vistas less austere than those of the Colorado plains.

Charles Bent was true to his word. He welcomed the couple, and installed Three Doves as a clerk in the Taos Post. Then, as if tuned in the young brave's determination and the apprehension that both felt, he asked Rides With Fire to drive supply wagons to and from Simeon Turley's Mill in Arroyo Hondo, several miles from Taos.

One day several months after their arrival, they were stunned when Bent delivered to their room, at the end of the line of adobe buildings, a large crate which contained a wheelchair.

"Heard about this thing. Never saw one before. Had some friends on the coast look into it. They had this shipped from England. Took a while to get here."

Bent carried Rides With Fire to the chair, and sat him in it.

"I've seen you two struggle getting him around. Almost more than Bird can handle, Rides With Fire struggling, crawling and all. This should make life a little easier."

Three Doves pushed Rides With Fire around the room, then watched as he worked the chair himself. Both began laughing. Three Doves hugged Bent, tears rolling down her cheeks.

"Seems to be a little stiff. Might have to use some muscle power to move it on the ground."

"Thank you, Mr. Charles Bent. Thank you."

Rides With Fire wheeled over and shook his hand. "Tank yo," he whispered. English lessons with Three Doves were showing an early return.

"Mr. Charles Bent. I have something to tell. Rides With Fire and I will soon be parents."

"Parents, you say? Well I'll be. When, Bird?"

"Several moons yet. Maybe four. Maybe five."

"Well, that is wonderful. Wonderful. I'll let everyone in on that."

"Don't know. We are not man and wife."

"That's a small detail. That baby is going to have great parents whatever. I'm happy for you."

"And we are happy, Mr. Charles Bent."

Three Doves gave birth to a boy in April, a robust, dark-haired bawler. She named him Chula Humma, "Red Fox," and with maternal care dependent on instinct more than observation, raised him in the Taos Trading Post.

Rides With Fire was a proud father. She often walked into their room after work, and found father and son in the wheelchair, Rides With Fire gently rocking back and forth, Chula asleep on his chest. He alone had assisted in the birth, even though Charles Bent had offered the services of his slave/cook Charlotte.

"You are a good father, my love."

"And you are a good mother, my little Bird." He would smile at her. He smiled often, she noticed.

Much of that was attributable to the peace that they felt, but some was due to the fact that Charles Bent and his brother George were trusting Rides With Fire with more responsibility. He had recently made a wagon trip to Santa Fe, accompanied by a translator and a guide. His twice-weekly trips to Turley's Mill continued; sometimes he made them alone. Mill workers would unload the wagon loads, and re-load the wagon with whiskey, flour, and furs for the trading post. They called Rides With Fire "Chief," and as his English improved, so did the badinage with the mill hands and trappers.

"Three Doves. What does 'goddammit' mean? Mr. Thomas Tobin says that I should say the word often."

Bird began laughing, but stopped when she saw his expression change to confusion and possibly hurt.

"It is a word of anger which offends many people. It speaks of the Great Spirit as an angry god. It is used when one cannot control his feelings. It would be wise never to use the word. Mr. Thomas Tobin is having fun with you."

Rides With Fire understood, and smiled. "Maybe I should teach him the Chickasaw word for the droppings of buffalo."

****

By 1846, there was unrest in the territory. Unhappy with the annexation of the Texas territory, which included Nuevo Mexico, as a United States territory, the Hispanic population and the Taos tribe populations began to threaten violence.

In 1845, President James K. Polk had sent diplomat John Slidell to Mexico to purchase all of the Mexican holdings north of the Rio Grande, and also parts of California. The Mexican government refused to see him. Polk became angry, and asked Congress for a return to hostilities with Mexico. Just prior to that, Polk had sent troops under General Zachary Taylor to territory which was claimed by both Texas and Mexico. Taylor marched his charges all of the way to the Rio Grande River. Mexican troops subsequently attacked one of the American detachments.

War was declared on May 13, 1846.

Taos was seemingly out of the line of fire, but there was worry in the town.

"The situation is ugly. Most of the fighting will be far south of here, but what concerns me is the emotion of many people here. They feel that the Americans are too heavy-handed. These people don't want change," Charles Bent explained to Three Doves one afternoon, soon after the news of war reached Taos.

"Should we leave?" Three Doves asked.

"Only if the fighting moves this way. We're a community here. It's difficult to imagine a rebellion or uprising occurring. If you like it here, I'd stick it out. I'm not moving my family."

In August, worry was set aside. Stephen Kearney led a large force of soldiers into Santa Fe, and took control of the region without firing a shot. His orders were to then proceed to California. Before leaving, Kearney left a command under Colonel Sterling Price to oversee the area from Santa Fe.

He then appointed Charles Bent as the first governor of the territory. Bent would govern from the relative safety of Taos.

Bent moved into governor's quarters, leaving the management of trade to his brother George.

Some suspected that the peace which followed was tenuous, even with the large force of Colonel Price monitoring the area, but as months passed, there were no incidents, no reason to suspect discontent strong enough to spark violence. Bent could deal with other parts of the territory which were on the brink of open warfare. Taos, at least, seemed stable.

Just before Christmas, a small group of Mexican women from Santa Fe appeared at the governor's headquarters, part of a house that Bent and his family used in Taos.

Through an interpreter, Bent listened to a story that alarmed him. The unrest in the territory was about to explode in rebellion. The women told of a plot to take Santa Fe, an armed revolt involving hundreds of Mexicans and the Taos Indians. Whites, particularly those in power, were to be targeted for arrest, and some said, execution. It would occur on Christmas Day, the women said.

Bent acted quickly, summoning Colonel Price.

"What do you think, Sterling? Can this thing happen?"

"Yes Sir, I think it can. What worries me is that it's been quiet since Kearney left. Before that there was definite agitation. Then suddenly it seemed to disappear. Sometimes you have to worry most when it seems there is nothing to worry about."

"Supposing that there is an uprising. What chance do you have?"

"I'd guess it to be good. We'd be armed better with more participants. We can get reinforcements in a couple of days."

"You think there might be trouble here too? We're not really protected up here."

"Unlikely. We'll stop them in Santa Fe."

"Just be ready. We're fortunate that we got a heads-up."

"Best thing is, they don't know that we know."

Price was wrong. Word of the woman's trip to Bent got back to the leaders of the malcontents, Pablo Montoya and a Taos Indian named Tomasito. The plot was postponed.

It was not cancelled.

Christmas Day 1846 was quiet.

Rides With Fire had bundled up for the journey. Funny, he thought, as the wagon creaked along toward the narrow arroyo pass that led to the mill, a few years ago, he had hated white men. Now he dressed like one, spoke their language, and worked for them. And one in particular had somewhat adopted his family.

A thin coating of snow had dusted the landscape this 19th day of January 1847. A morning sun was beginning to insure a good day for the trip. That was good. His fear was to someday get snowbound at Turley's Mill and have to spend days away from Bird and his son Fox. Worse, and he couldn't think about it, was a scenario in which he'd be caught out here in the mountains in a bad storm, for even though he had become admirably independent, the wagon was his lifeline, the horses his legs. Of course, if he didn't appear back at the trading post on the night of a trip, Bird and George Bent would send help.

George Bent had told him once that when he became more literate in the English language, another job would be his, perhaps as a clerk, or as a liaison with the tribes for his brother Charles.

Turley had also promised him steady work as an overseer at the mill, noting that his employees and the trappers who frequented the mill had a fondness for the crippled man who was always smiling.

From the abyss of self-pity and hopelessness of five years ago, he had transformed into a confident, competent young man, a family man who was trying to increase his offspring. Bird had not become pregnant again after Fox, but they kept trying, and hoping.

As he clucked the horse team up a small rise between outcroppings of rock, a group of men jumped into the path ahead of him. He slowed, then stopped the wagon, using his strong left arm to apply the brake. The number of men increased. He was looking at over fifty of them. Many had long rifles trained on him. A few had bows with arrows at the ready. More arrived.

He didn't recognize any of them, although he understood immediately that their numbers consisted mainly of Mexicans and Taos Indians.

He tried his faulty English on the group. "Good morning. What I can do for you?"

The men conversed in Spanish. A bandy-legged, swarthy man with a ragged moustache motioned for him to get down from the wagon. At first he didn't understand, but he definitely felt threatened. He thought about snapping the reins and trying to charge through the group. Foolish, he decided. Too many of them, and he was surrounded. That would be suicide. He hesitated.

The man motioned him down again, this time yelling. Obviously he couldn't get down without help. He pointed to his legs and held out his arms in supplication. "No. Can't do."

An arrow was loosed from his left and buried itself in his chest, surging through layers of clothing. He gasped and grabbed the arrow's shaft to pull it out. Another arrow struck him in the back. He toppled from the wagon and struck the hard ground. He tried to turn over, to plead with these men. Before he could do that, the swarthy man put his pistol against the prone man's head and pulled the trigger.

The insurgents stood above the inert body.

"Why'd you do that, Pablo? This is an Indian. Looks like he was a cripple."

"The Taos got him first. I just put him out of his misery."

"Why did they shoot him?"

"Took him for a white man, I guess. Doesn't matter. He works for Bent. Good riddance."

Montoya kicked the body into a shallow ravine next to the trail. A rebel got on the wagon, released the brake, and drove toward Taos. The army followed.

Charles Bent was at his desk when he heard the commotion at the front door, voices yelling, stomping, a crash, a scream. He stood quickly and was striding toward his pistol when the door to his office flew open.

Before he could react, the room was swarming with Taos Indians, and they filled his body with arrows.

He was already dead when the rebels dragged his wife and children into the room and made them watch as they scalped the governor.

The family was shunted to a windowless room in the house, and locked inside. The revolutionaries, bloodthirsty now, would decide what to do with the family later. They had other targets in Taos. Santa Fe would come later.

Their numbers increased, and in short order, they murdered Sheriff Stephen Lee, Probate Judge Cornelio Vigil, Circuit Attorney J. W. Leal, and Narcisse Beaubien.

Unwatched, the Bent family dug through the adobe wall of their prison and ran to safety.

The next day the mob made their way to Turley's Mill, laid siege to it, and eventually killed eight Americans there. Later in the day, they killed seven traders near Mora.

In Santa Fe, Colonel Price received word about the Taos uprising from Charles Autobees, who had seen the mob advancing on Turley's Mill. Price and 300 soldiers, Ceran St. Vrain, and 65 volunteers rode to the area. They attacked and defeated 1,500 insurgents at Santa Cruz de la Canada and Embudo Pass, in large part because they used cannons to even the odds.

The remaining rebels retreated to an adobe church in Taos Pueblo, where American cannons again won the day in short order. The soldiers killed 150 rebels there, and captured over 400.

The revolt was over.

Three days after the uprising, a mountain man found the body of Rides With Fire, and took it to the trading post. Bird knew, even before the trapper, hat in hand, walked up to her adobe hut. When word had reached the post of the events at the Bent household, the trading post was secured. No one was permitted to enter or to leave. Perhaps he can't get back, she thought. He's probably still at the mill. When word of the slaughter at Turley's reached her, her thoughts had no place else to go. He's dead. Rides With Fire is dead.

She would bury him in the mountains, above the now-quiet Taos, where they had evolved into a loving family, where Chula was born, where Fire had won back his self-esteem and his zest for life.

She made two promises to him at the gravesite. She would honor him forever by raising their son to be like his father, and she would never give her heart to another man.

CHAPTER NINE

1848

The Dooley sons and daughters grew up in a family devoid of affection. The two-room shack at the foot of Wild Boar Mountain in the forests of eastern Tennessee cradled nine uneducated, feral youngsters, offspring of Tay and Nella.

He was a brutish man with no ambition. Unkempt and crude, he fostered a tangled beard, a fetid odor, and terrible outbursts of anger. She was a tiny woman grown old and exasperated by a brood she couldn't manage, and a repulsive husband who used her in disgusting and depraved ways. She had married him when she was thirteen, anxious to escape a dominant, over-zealous evangelist father.

"Nella, I forbid you to marry that man. He is a heathen! No good can come of of it. It isn't God's will." He was screaming. He always screamed.

"Daddy, I will marry him."

"Off with you, Jezebel! Leave this house! Until God truly lives in your soul, you are dead to us!"

He had punctuated that declaration with a slap at her face, a precursor of what she'd endure for the next quarter-century.

Her life with Tay was as barren of joy as she was fertile at producing offspring. She gave birth to nine children in twelve years, knowing that she could not provide for them, powerless to stop getting pregnant. Tay lost interest in her soon after the last conception, except for rare sadistic instances, within hearing of her children, that made her feel dirty for weeks. Much of the time her face was bruised and swollen. She stopped crying, and she stopped caring.

Over the years, the two oldest sons, Lester and J.T., took on their father's sloth, and his loathing for anyone who was not a Dooley.

At early ages, they became proficient at stealing merchandise from a small general store near Johnson's Depot, five miles across the mountains. Encouraged by their father, who distracted the clerk with inane conversation, the two filled their pockets and baggy pants with all manners of food and other items.

After a time they went by themselves. Lester, the older, would enter the store first with a cheery greeting and a wide, crooked smile.

"Hi. How's it goin'?"

He'd ramble on about raccoons and rain while J.T. emptied the shelves.

If the clerks were aware of it, they didn't let on. Tay Dooley was feared throughout the county.

For more substantial possessions, the two ransacked cabins in a wide area, taking whatever they could carry, particularly muskets and handguns. Over time, the Dooley clan amassed an impressive arsenal, which Lester and J.T. used on stray dogs, boars, and the farm animals of their far-flung neighbors.

J.T., I been wonderin' what it be like to shoot a man," Lester allowed one afternoon in his sixteenth year.

"Dunno. Bet it be good. Bet his eyes be all bugged out like them dogs," the brother answered.

Both were tall and gawky, with none of their father's porcine qualities. Lester's straw-colored hair was tousled and a smirk played constantly on his sunburned face. J.T. was freckled, and seemed incapable of original thought. He parroted both his brother's mannerisms and his opinions, and rarely showed emotion.

As the family grew, the older Dooley children were sent to live in the ramshackle barn until they left home. Three girls married and left in their early teens. A son left to explore the world beyond the mountain and never came back. Nella privately rejoiced when Lester and J.T. moved their possessions to the barn. Her husband sickened her, but her two oldest sons scared her.

She was torn between relief at ridding herself of her own children as they moved away, and the thought that someday, she would be left alone with a man she hated.

But the two oldest sons didn't leave. Sometimes they disappeared for a few days to visit the daughters of settlers near the North Carolina border, she reasoned, or to steal someone's prize horse.

But they always came back.

In 1848 the two--by then 25 and 24--were discovered raiding a home near Kingsport, on the Holston River. The owner walked into his front room to find two scruffy men pulling drawers from an old chest.

"Hey! How's it goin'?" Lester called out.

"What the hell…!" Those were the owner's last words. Lester fired on him from ten feet away, a direct hit into the man's chest.

The brothers stood over the body, smoke circling from the dark vest, blood spreading in a wide pool.

"Didja see that? Purty good, I'd say! Ya see that shot! Yessir! Yessir!" Lester crowed.

"Yep. Purty good, Lester. Purty good."

"Why doncha take a shot at him. J.T.?"

"But he's already daid."

"Don't matter. Give him another eye. You scared?"

J.T. put the barrel against the man's forehead and pulled the trigger. The man jerked upward, the roar of the shot reverberated in the small room.

"Gawd… Gawd! Ya see that?"

"C'mon J.T. Someone coulda heared them shots. Let's git."

Someone did hear the shots, and saw the two galloping away. The witness had seen Tay and the brothers a year earlier near Johnson Depot. "Ya see them three," his companion had said, "Tay Dooley and his whelps from over to Wild Boar Mountain. Stay clear of them. The laws know they be robbin' folks 'round here, but nobody wants to go into the forest to look for 'em."

Three men did this time. Sullivan County Sheriff "Hanging" Boone Carver, Washington County Sheriff Wilbur Erwin, and deputy Zeke Williams rode through thickets and jumped the wash-outs around Wild Boar until they came to a cabin against a bluff, surrounded by weeds and undergrowth. They saw three young adults in ragged clothes, still teenagers probably, throwing knives against a barn door.

"That's not them. If they're here, they're prob'ly in the cabin," Carver guessed.

The three lawmen drew their pistols and walked their horses to within 100 feet of the front door.

"We'd best stop here. We got a bit of protection if they come out shootin'," Erwin suggested.

They were in front of a grove of trees opposite the barn.

"Zeke, go over to the barn and get the drop on those kids over there. Be ready to get back here, if we need you. Careful. Them two might be in the barn," Carver said. He was beginning to feel uneasy. He wished that he had brought more of a posse.

The massed Tennessee clouds began to drizzle rain.

"Hallo the house! Come out with your hands up!" Carver yelled.

The front door creaked open. A burly, rumpled bear of a man stepped into the mist.

"Who you be? Get off this propity!"

"You Tay Dooley?" Carver called out.

"Maybe. What you want?"

"We're here to arrest the murderers of James Bush of Sullivan County."

"Don't know nuthin' 'bout that."

"Your sons do, Mr. Dooley. Where are your oldest sons?"

"Dunno. Ain't seen them for days."

"Anybody else in the house?"

"Just the missus."

"Tell her to step out here."

Dooley hesitated a moment.

Something was wrong.

"Woman! Get out here!"

The rain fell heavily now, helping to mask the sound of a snapped twig behind the sheriffs.

Near the barn, Williams saw a blur behind Erwin and Carver. "Sheriff! Look out! Behind you!"

Carver spun around in time to see a grinning blond-haired man pointing a gun at him from twenty feet away. Lester's gun roared. Carver fell.

A red-haired man sprinted out of the cabin, running toward Erwin with a pointed rifle, yelling in a eerie growl. Erwin didn't have time to decide which man to face. He got off a shot toward the house, which buried itself in the ample mid-section of Tay Dooley.

"Damn!" the father shrieked, "I been gut-shot!"

J.T.'s rifle silenced Erwin.

Williams jumped for the barn door. Too late. Lester Dooley shot him from behind; the shot pierced his right thigh. He stumbled and fell; his gun skidded across the mud. Lester walked toward him.

"Hey, how's it goin'?"

He emptied his pistol into Zeke Williams.

"Will ya look at that! Look at what we done!" Lester squealed.

"Lester walked over to his father, who had stopped breathing.

"Nuthin' here no more. We'll take the law's horses. Get some guns and ammo from the barn. Anythin' else you think we need. Nobody here's goin' to need nuthin' from here on out."

In a few minutes, without a word to their mother or siblings, they rode away from Wild Boar Mountain. They would ride west to lose themselves in the anonymity of the Western frontier.

Even before the rain stopped, the younger children were directed by their mother to dig a grave for their father. Nella didn't help, but she enthusiastically helped to throw dirt onto his body after they rolled him into the grave. She chortled the entire time.

Tomorrow she'd walk to Johnson Depot, and tell somebody there to come get the dead lawmen out of her yard. They had been killed, she would say, by her sons, Lester and J.T. Dooley.

CHAPTER TEN

1849

He was restless and depressed. He had tried, tried to return to some semblance of life in New Orleans, tried to play music, tried to socialize, all to no avail. He couldn't shake the great melancholy, couldn't focus on relationships, even with his in-laws.

Yvonne had scolded him with little effect. "Hank Rosbottom, it's been mos' tree years now. Angeline would hate to see you dis way. Can't keep grievin' over her, cher. You still a young man, you know."

"No use. Nothin' matters."

"Well, wat you gonna do, den? You drinkin' your life away."

"Dunno. Just dunno."

He did know. He had to leave New Orleans. He was reminded of her every day, in a hundred ways, in numerous places. He would tell them.

"I'm dyin' here," he said one day, after rehearsing it for hours, "suffocatin'. I love you two, but I can't do anything here. Just can't. I'll be leavin' tomorrow morning. Hopin' you'll watch over Lady for me."

The Chiassons stood watching him, trying to formulate some quick plan, some combination of words which would change his mind.

Maurice spoke first. "Hank, you be like our son. We love you. Lost our Angeline. Now we lose you?"

"Ain't nothin' gonna change if I stay here. If I look around for a spell…I dunno."

Yvonne walked up to him. "You gonna go, Hank. Where you go?"

"North. Just start out on the Military Road, maybe the old trail from Natchez."

"We never see you again."

"Maybe. Maybe not. I have to do this."

He left early the next day in a wagon sparsely packed. He took several of her paintings, including the one she had first given him, the old man fishing in the bayou. He had packed his musical instruments, with little thought that he'd ever use them to earn a living again.

He didn't look back, giving the Chiassons a perfunctory wave. He also didn't want to see the sad-eyed dog sitting at their feet.

****

At the beginning of the Nineteenth Century, the Natchez Trace was known as the Columbian Highway, and was an undeveloped stretch of commerce between Nashville, Tennessee and Natchez, Mississippi, a 440-mile stretch of territory inhabited by tribes of the Chickasaw and Choctaw nations. They had crudely carved out the trail for inter-tribal trading.

At the urging of Thomas Jefferson, the military began to develop it as a roadway in 1801. By 1809 it was a major trail, complete with inns and trading posts at numerous locations called "stands." Communities appeared, Washington and Port Gibson among them. The expansive route provided easy travel for any mode of transportation, even though it traversed topography from mountain passes to swamps.

All manners of travelers used the trail, from "Kaintucks"—the general name for all ruffians who brought goods to Natchez from the north—to migrant residents, bandits, and bushwackers. Itinerant preachers frequented the area, looking for converts. The highwaymen became more than a nuisance; they organized into gangs that terrorized the entire length of the highway.

The development of Jackson's Military Road in 1816, coupled with increased steamboat travel on the Mississippi River, conspired to lessen the use of the Trace, and by 1830, it was largely abandoned and neglected. The forests began to grow together over the area.

Occasional travelers still found it the least costly and most efficient method for commerce, so it still saw some traffic, although that was substantially reduced.

Joseph Tyler continued to use it. Several times a year, he would load wagons with produce, animal skins, smoked meats, and crudely-fashioned furniture from his farm south of Florence, Alabama, and travel southwest on the vestiges of the Natchez Trace. His teen-aged sons drove two wagons, he drove a third, as they made their way toward the busy port of Natchez through ruts and tangles.

When the small queue reached the area of Jackson, the trail widened and improved somewhat, and the miles in from Port Gibson to Washington to Natchez were still easily managed, as those stretches of the Trace, shaded by cypress trees and Southern oaks, recalled the glory days of the trail.

His sum total of profits from the loads of goods might approach $200, if he sold everything. But even if he realized only $75 or $100, the amount would feed and clothe his family for months. The market was good in Natchez. That was why he made this unwieldy trip, long after most others had abandoned the route.

The procession rounded a bend, and Joseph saw a hundred feet ahead two riders in the middle of the pathway. He slowed his team and turned to see that Buford and Joey were doing the same. As he got closer, he scanned the faces of the two ahead. Both were smiling.

Pleasant sorts, he thought. One was bare-headed, red haired. The other rode up to him.

"Hey, how's it goin'?"

"Not bad. Takin' a load of goods to Natchez. Where you headed?"

"Goin' the other way. Hey, looks like some good stuff in them wagons, J. T."

"Looks like mighty good stuff, Lester."

Too late, Joseph recognized danger. He reached for his rifle under the seat. A moment later, Lester Dooley's shotgun barked twice, and buckshot tore into Joseph's right arm and upper chest, knocking him from the wagon. Buford, in the last wagon, died quickly as J. T. charged him, yelling, and shot him in the stomach from ten feet.

Joey was trapped. His wagon, in the middle, had no place to go. He jumped from the seat and ran toward the thick forest. Lester galloped up from behind and ran him down, and as he lay on the ground, Lester calmly shot him in the head.

"Spunky fella, ain'tcha," Lester muttered.

"What now, Lester ? We got three wagons of junk."

"Somebody will buy it. We'll take what we need in two wagons. That last one, forget it. Nuthin' but ugly tables and chairs. Junk."

"We leavin' the bodies here?"

"Hell no, J.T. We take them in to Natchez and sell them too. Of course we leave them here, you big dummy."

"We ain't gonna hide them?"

"Nobody be through here for days, mebbe weeks. Bodies be picked clean by then. Don't matter nohow. Nobody know who done this."

"Lester, the old man's not daid. Seen him move."

"Don't matter, J. T. Bastard drew down on me. Let him suffer. He be bleedin' out here purty soon."

Soon they were on the way to Natchez, each driving a wagon with his horse tied behind. They would sell what they could tomorrow, including the wagons, and spend it gambling or whoring in the seamy areas of town.

When the money ran out, they would find more, whether it involved cheating or stealing or murder.

CHAPTER ELEVEN
1850

Jonah Brooks didn't look like a minister, except perhaps for the black garments he wore. He had the visage of a sailor, a creased face which had weathered too many storms, crow's feet at the corners of green eyes, broad shoulders, and large, rough hands which surely had secured masts or stowed cargo.

And to watch him tend to his flock would have given one pause. He was not a fire-and-brimstone clergyman. He converted souls with gentle logic, and a soft voice which left back-pew occupants leaning forward to hear the message. His sermons were pointed, intelligent discourses on humility and compassion. His raspy voice led congregants through a cappella hymns which were sincere, if not melodic. He appeared at the bedsides of those who were ill or terminal, held their hands, and talked the poor souls into the next world in a soft voice of empathy which exacted beatific smiles from the unfortunates as they expired.

Jonah's simple home was as humble as his demeanor, and far less complicated. He shared it with Shag, a furry mutt with over-sized ears, who lay contented thirty feet away from Jonah's Sunday morning sermons, and who greeted his returns home with much commotion, barking and swinging his large tail furiously until Jonah stroked his head. For years Jonah had no other close companions. There was a failed romance years ago. His ministry produced adulation, not friendships. When he was invited to a parishioner's home for Sunday lunch, he was treated with reverence, but not intimacy. His flock regarded him with awe and trust, but his business was saving their souls, they reasoned, not quaffing ale or engaging in frivolous repartee.

Loneliness was not part of his existence, however. He often rode out of Syracuse into the wilderness with Shag trailing, and camped beside a lake or stream to fish or to read, or to practice with his pistol, a fascination that would have alarmed his congregation. With his shirt sleeves rolled up to his elbows, and his boots caked with mud, he resembled a lumberjack more than a man of God. He scribbled sermons below tall evergreens, bathed in the bracing stream water, and took long hikes through the underbrush. These frequent getaways renewed him, intellectually and spiritually.

He could be stirred to action, to a version of anger, by what he considered inequity, some abomination of God's will, or actions which did not hold to equality or to love. That had made him a participant in hiding and transporting escaped slaves from the South to and through Syracuse, New York, where he had pastored since he was thirty-one, some ten years ago.

There was the time a few years before, when he was secreting two runaways, a young man named Simon and an older woman named Charity, toward a lonely bungalow on the road to Oswego. The owner of the house was another Unitarian minister.

That man would take them the final ten miles to the Oswego home of John B. Edwards the next night. Edwards would load them on a boat to cross Lake Ontario to Kingston, Ontario. How many times had Jonah done this? It didn't matter. Numbers were for historians and census takers.

A loud voice out of the darkness interrupted the journey two miles or so from the house.

"Who's there? Identify yourself!"

A bounty hunter perhaps. Law officers usually got involved during the day. Bounty hunters seemingly never slept.

"Church members. On our way to a meeting tomorrow," Jonah called back.

Two riders, one with a lantern, rode slowly toward them. Jonah pulled his hat low and whispered to his companions. "Stay on that horse, whatever happens. I'll handle this. Don't be afraid. Don't say anything."

The lantern-holder trotted closer. "They's three of 'em, Hobie. I'd say we found some runaways."

The other man rode up to Jonah's side. Jonah didn't look at him.

"Well, well, well. This here fella's sneaking' these runaways toward the lake, I figure."

Jonah's voice was emotionless as he answered. "There's no funny business here. We're going to a church meeting. These two are freed slaves." God will forgive all of this lying, Jonah thought.

"No, that ain't right. Them two are ridin' double, and look at them shabby clothes they be wearin'."

"I've got their freedom papers here," Jonah was stalling, waiting for the right moment.

"Get off that horse. You two stay where you are. Micah, have a look at them papers."

Both men had drawn their pistols.

Jonah dismounted, and felt inside his shirt pocket for a paper that he had used for scribbled notes for Sunday's sermon. The bounty hunters also got off their horses. The man called Micah walked toward him, his right arm extended with the lantern. Hobie kept his pistol trained on the runaways.

"Let's have a look at them manumission papers."

Jonah extended his hand with the scribbled notes. Micah holstered his gun, and reached for it. Jonah waited until the man grabbed it, and swung his other arm in an arc, knocking the lantern from the man's hand. It shattered as it hit the ground.

"Damn you!" Micah shouted, mere seconds before Jonah's fist exploded into his face.

It was dark and the advantage changed. Hobie fired a wild shot. "Micah! Where you at?"

Jonah was on him quickly. Hobie was no match for the minister. They rolled once on the ground, and as Jonah took the top, he knocked Hobie cold with two punches.

"Guess I'll have to find another route home tomorrow," Jonah said as he lifted the woman onto Micah's horse. He shooed off Hobie's mount, and the three rode away.

The Underground Railroad, as it eventually came to be known, had existed for over a century. All over the eastern half of the country, slaves were assisted to freedom by free blacks, religious groups, abolitionists, and sympathizers. The journey most often ended in Canada, where slavery had been outlawed through several legislative actions. The Act Against Slavery ended bondage in several Canadian areas in 1793. In 1803, Chief Justice William Osgood ruled slavery "incompatible with British law." In 1834, the British Parliament passed the Slavery Abolition Act, outlawing it completely in all British holdings.

Many times the runaways found new homes and safety in northern American cities, where they blended into the population.

Some runaways stowed away on boats along the Eastern seaboard. The greater number made months-long journeys on foot, usually traveling at night, and hiding in the homes or outbuildings of a variety of "conductors" or safe-house owners during the days. They braved weather conditions, pursuers, bounty hunters, geographical barriers, and starvation on the grueling trail, following the North Star, the "Drinking Gourd," on a lonely, perilous quest.

The system was unorganized, and that contributed to its success. None of the participants knew--or wanted to know--much about the others who were helping.

Jonah Brooks had willingly taken a role that had grown during his decade in Syracuse. None in his congregation knew of his activity, although his denomination was on record as opposing the practice of slavery. Bounty hunters and law officers had pestered the Syracuse area for years because it had won a reputation as a magnet area for escaping slaves.

The freedom trail activity took him to an October 4 meeting in 1850, a collection of over 500 citizens, including the mayor of Syracuse, Alfred Hovey. He had been invited by an old friend, who had rapped on his door late one night in September. Congress had just passed the Fugitive Slave Law of 1850, a document which provided stringent penalties for any person who aided the runaways in their flights to Canadian freedom.

In truth, a personal invitation to speak, had come from the friend.

"Reverend Brooks…"

"Mr. Loguen, I'm honored. Come in."

Jermain Loguen chose not to step inside. Jonah was not insulted; his respect for the man was immense, but his spartan abode was perhaps inappropriate to host this eminent citizen tonight, given the solemn tones of the speaker.

"My business must be quick. On the fourth of October at seven in the evening, a meeting will be held to address the Slave Law enacted by our President. We see it as a heathen law, a danger to all of us who are doing the work we are doing."

"I will be there."

"Another thing, Reverend Brooks. Mr. Samuel May and myself will address the crowd. We invite you to speak also."

"I am complimented. Why me?"

"You are venerated by the white community. We on the other side look up to you. You are perhaps the most suitable person in Syracuse to educate us, and to lead our thoughts and actions in this matter."

"Mr. Loguen, you flatter me far beyond the facts." Jonah grinned. "Your words describe you more than they do me."

Now Loguen was smiling. "It appears that there is mutual admiration here. You'll speak?"

"I'll say a few words."

"God bless you. Good night, Reverend Brooks."

"I was a slave. I knew danger and pain. What was life to me if I was a slave in Tennessee?

"My friends and neighbors, I have lived beside you for many years. My home is here. My children were born here. Do you know that I can be taken from you and my wife and my children and be a slave again in Tennessee?

"Some good friends advise me to leave this country and stay in Canada until this has all passed. But my thought is that their advice comes with good intentions, but from a lack of knowledge of the matters at hand."

He had the attention of every man in the large room. He was a handsome, powerfully-built man, a young 37-year old who had endured years of tribulation because of his race and his parentage. His mother was a slave girl named Cherry. His father was her owner, a man named David Logue from Davidson County, Tennessee, who didn't acknowledge Jermain as any more than another chattel. He had stolen a horse from his father when he was twenty-one, and ridden to freedom in Canada.

Jonah knew that Loguen had added the final "n" to his name to reject his paternal legacy, had learned to read in Canada, and had studied at the Oneida Institute in Whitesboro. In his thirties, he had opened schools for his race for children of upper New York state. More than anyone else, Jermain Loguen was the face and guiding force of the abolitionist movement in the Northeast.

"The time has come," Loguen continued in a rising voice, " to change the tones of submission into tones of defiance. I owe my freedom to the God who made me. I will not consent that anyone else shall force the claims of a vulgar despot to my soul, to my body.

"I have no chains, and am in no prison. I received my freedom from Heaven, and with it the mandate to defend my title to it.

"I don't respect this law. I don't fear it. I will not obey it! I despise it and the men who will enforce it. I will never be a slave again. Never! And if force is used against me, I shall make preparations to meet the crisis as a man.

"Your decision to be here tonight in favor of resistance will give life to the spirit of liberty. Heaven knows that an act of noble daring will break out somewhere, and may God grant that Syracuse be that spot, where it shall send earthquake voices throughout the land."

The room erupted in applause. Jonah was next, and his comments were like his sermons, brief and to the point.

"My fellow citizens," he began, clearing the gravel out of his voice with the words, "Sometimes we must break men's laws in deference to God's laws. In doing so now, we could not follow a more exalted path. We must be prepared to stand defiantly and resolutely until all men are treated fairly and equally.

"Whether we take up arms or extend hands of compromise, the glory will be in doing the right thing.

"Soon you will be asked to make choices, choices that may jeopardize your lives and your freedom. Ultimately, your only choice should be on the side of true justice, not on the side of these pretentious and self-serving laws of politicians and scoundrels."

He continued for several minutes, interrupted occasionally by shouts of assent and agreement.

"With guidance from the Almighty, and commitments from you, we will ignore, reject, and resist the Fugitive Slave Law. We will persist. We will continue to pursue the path of righteousness and the shining premise that all men are created equal, that all men are the children of a God who means for all of us to be partners in freedom."

A low rumble from the crowd, from faces both black and white, swelled into acclamation as Jonah sat down impassively.

It was rare to leave such a gathering motivated, inspired, and jubilant in the notion of unanimity. Those feelings came over Jonah Brooks, to the extent that he almost shouted as the group filed out the doors.

There will be trouble, he thought. So be it.

Sometime later, Daniel Webster himself made an appearance in Syracuse, and from a platform in the public square, he issued a stern warning.

"The Fugitive Slave Law will be executed in Syracuse, and if groups meet here to refute it, those groups will soon witness it in action. For those who oppose it are committing treason…treason…treason!"

In Springfield, Massachusetts, militant abolitionist John Brown founded an anti-slavery group that year, the League of Gileadites. He left soon after to a new home in the Midwest.

CHAPTER TWELVE

1851

Robert Gerdon approached the office of his magazine's owner/editor with some trepidation. He knew that he had a good idea. He wasn't sure that he could sell it. The thin, bookish Gerdon was twenty-seven, and stuck, he thought, as a proofreader. He wanted to write, and he did possess those skills, at least in his own mind. He couldn't abide his lot as the caretaker of other men's writing products, however.

His boss, D.F. Sawyer, had started *The Easterner* in 1837 in this same building, an old brick edifice in Manhattan with a view of the East River. It had always been a modest success, combined with the publication of some novels, and the output of a stable of writers well-paid by Sawyer.

Gerdon knocked timidly on the glass pane of Sawyer's office.

"Come in, Gerdon," Sawyer called.

Gerdon walked into the spacious room, and approached the massive oak desk of the mogul. Sawyer had his bald head bent over something on the desk, pince-nez glasses on the very tip of a somewhat bulbous nose. He was working in his shirt sleeves again, a situation noted and admired by his employees. The boss continued to take an active role in the publication of the magazine. As each edition of *The Easterner* progressed, he was constantly in motion, bustling from desk to desk, making suggestions, ordering changes. Nothing of substance eluded him. He even directed the artwork. He was in charge.

Gerdon stood nervously, shifting his weight. He felt beads of perspiration on his forehead, and a small lump in his throat. Sawyer had not yet looked up.

"Sit down, Gerdon, for God's sake."

The proofreader sat in a large, soft chair facing Sawyer. He crossed his legs, then re-crossed them.

"What is it, Gerdon? What do you want?"

"An idea, sir. I have an idea."

"An idea, you say? This have to do with proofreading?"

"No, sir. I've got an idea for a series of stories, maybe even a book."

"I'm willing to listen. Tell me."

Sawyer leaned back in his chair. He was looking at Robert Gerdon with a raised eyebrow. Gerdon noticed. This wasn't going to be an easy sell.

"The frontier, sir. It's about the West."

"The West? You mean the territories?"

"Yes. The lands beyond the Mississippi River."

"Go on."

"I got the idea from reading James Fenimore Cooper. He wrote *The Prairie.*"

"I'm familiar with Mr. Cooper, Gerdon."

"Then I read a book by Samuel Parker, written a few years ago. He called it *A Journey of an Exploring Tour.* It was about a scout and mountain man named Kit Carson. Then I went to the library and found a book by Samuel Metcalfe from years ago. It was about Daniel Boone."

"So?"

"It struck me that there are great stories and heroes out there. So I went looking for one. Late last year, I wrote letters to newspapers in Kansas City, St. Louis, Austin, and Independence. I had folks out there mail me newspaper articles. This is my collection," he said as he laid a pile of neatly folded papers on the large desk.

"Gerdon, I don't have time to read all of that."

"I'll summarize, sir. I found a man, a gunfighter, Indian fighter, Texas Ranger."

"So what are you proposing to do?"

"Write a book, Mr. Sawyer. Or start a set of articles in *The Easterner.*"

"You'd write facts?"

"Mostly. But I may have to embellish it some."

"Make things up?" Sawyer thundered, "No, not in my magazine!"

"That would mostly do with small things like characters' names, people whose names are lost or forgotten, but whose presence is necessary to tell the story. Exact dates get lost too. I would be faithful to the import of the stories."

"Perhaps it's a book. Can't see it contributing much to the magazine."

"Yes, sir. Good idea. Maybe a book previewed by articles in *The Easterner.*"

Sawyer was quiet. Gerdon had some hope. Maybe the silence was grudging acceptance.

Sawyer continued a fixed stare toward Gerdon's pile of collected research.

"That stuff there. All facts?"

"Yes, sir, all facts and quotations."

"Such as?"

"This man was on Fremont's second expedition with Kit Carson back in '43. He was sheriff of Weaverville, California during the gold rush. He rescued captives from Indians several times. Been in several gunfights; won them all."

"This is how we'll do this. Prepare your story, but not during workdays. Bring that to me. We'll see."

"The story's already written, Mr. Sawyer."

"I suppose you've got it with you."

"Yes, sir. Right here." Gerdon handed over a stack of papers. Sawyer could see from the cover that the collection was legibly, probably painstakingly, written.

"I'll look it over."

Gerdon rose to leave. Sawyer was already back to work, head down. Gerdon walked across to the door.

"Mr. Gerdon?"

"Yes, sir?"

"What is the name of this hero of yours?"

"Grimes, sir. Herkimer Grimes."

****

The slavery issue in Syracuse, New York came to a head on October 1, 1851, when the New York State Liberty Party convened in Syracuse. Timed to that event, federal marshals from Rochester, Auburn, and Canandaigua descended on Syracuse, determined to ferret out any escaped slaves living in the area. The motive was clear: a crackdown on abolitionists and runaways at the time and place that a noted anti-slavery group was in convention.

The marshals accosted William Henry, also known as "Jerry," at his workplace, a barrel-making business.

"You are being arrested under the Fugitive Slave Law. You will be tried, and returned to slavery."

"That is not right," Henry responded, "I am a free man!"

He struggled as he was manacled, but he was subdued and taken to the office of Commissioner Sabine for arraignment.

At that moment, church bells rang from several points in the city. The Vigilance Committee was aware of the marshals, and the bells signaled that those deputies had begun their work.

Reverend Jonah Brooks grabbed his pistol, hoping that it would not be needed, and his Bible, and rode to a pre-arranged meeting spot to find out details. Apprised of Henry's arrest, Jonah pressed on to Sabine's office. He reined in, just ahead of a crowd of sympathizers, and walked into the office, shoulder to shoulder with a large iron worker named James Clappe.

"Release this man," he said, in an emotionless, curt voice, which caused the marshals to unholster their pistols.

"This man is an escaped slave. He will be held accountable," a marshal responded.

"This man is a human being. I demand that you release him."

"Under what authority?"

Jonah held up the Bible. "Under God's authority, and the will of all of us."

Jonah felt the room fill up behind him. Dozens of sympathizers had arrived, and were crowding into the room.

The marshals quickly formed a semi-circle around Henry.

"Now see here. This is doing you no good. Disperse immediately!" a marshal ordered.

Jonah saw an opportunity. He jostled the nearest marshal, knocking the man into another deputy. The crowd pressed in, there was shouting, and the confusion worked. The protestors were too packed in for the marshals to use their firearms.

"Go," he yelled at Henry. Henry was passed from man to man, and out the door. But there was no organized help outside. Henry tried to run, but hampered by the confining irons, made it only to the bridge over the Erie Canal before a marshal bounced out of the door and caught up to him.

"Halt! One more step and I'll fire on you!" Henry stopped. Further flight was impossible. He was dragged back to the building.

"We're going in. Any of you get in the way, and I'll shoot this man," the marshal warned.

Inside, the law was again in control. "I order you all out of here. Anyone who doesn't leave now will be arrested!"

The effort was lost. The townspeople left the building. Henry was escorted into a back room, once more confined and controlled.

In the street, Jonah rallied the crowd. "Don't leave! We'll get another chance!"

"We need more help here," a man yelled.

Jermaine Loguen rode up. Soon the crowd doubled, and then tripled. The certainty increased that the number would support another attack of some kind.

"They moved him back somewhere. We don't know where his is in there," a man told Loguen.

"We'll find him."

Marshals appeared at the windows. Rifles and pistols poked out.

"Getting dangerous now, Mr. Loguen," Jonah said. "We don't want anyone to get hurt."

"There are too many of us, Reverend Brooks. I don't think that they'll chance a riot by shooting anyone."

A small group carried a makeshift battering ram to the front door. A few shots were fired from the windows, all into the air. The street was filled with humanity, over 2,000 shouting, irate citizens.

Clappe burst through the door first. "Where is he?"

Another shot was fired by the defenders, into the ceiling. Clappe, undeterred, charged past the lawmen and down a hallway.

Outside, a pistol shot was fired from the crowd. It ricocheted off of the building. "Hold your fire!" Jonah yelled from the doorway.

Loguen appeared beside him. ""Put your guns away!"

The crowd surged forward.

Inside, Clappe was throwing open doors. The surge behind him prevented the lawmen from getting any advantage. The marshals dispersed. Daunted by the numbers against them, they scattered and disappeared. One was heard yelling over his shoulder as he hurried away, "This ain't over! You folks are in trouble!"

Clappe opened a door in the back of the building, and there was Henry, sitting on the floor in the corner, a deputy with a gun trained on him. The deputy was uncertain.

"Give it up, man," Clappe said. "There's too many of us."

The deputy hesitated briefly, then laid his gun on the floor, and quickly exited through a rear door.

"C'mon. You're a free man again," Clappe said to Henry, helping him to his feet.

"Thank you, sir. Thank you."

Loguen embraced Henry as he entered the main office, still shackled.

"Mighty grateful, Mr. Loguen."

"You've got a lot of friends, Jerry," Loguen answered.

"Mr. Loguen," Jonah interrupted, "he's free for now, but he can't stay here in Syracuse."

"No, he can't. There will be recrimination. We've got to move him."

"Best thing is to do it now. I'll see him to the lake tonight."

"They'll be all over the roads tonight," Loguen replied. "We'll need to hide him somewhere for a while, and spread a story that he's already in Canada."

"We could take him to a crossing farther east."

"You understand, Reverend Brooks, that we're going to be the targets of some legal reprisals. Any of us who can be identified. Several of us, you included, are going to be watched closely, perhaps arrested. Somebody else will have to manage the escape."

Henry was listening closely to the conversation. "Suppose my life here is over?"

"For now, yes," Loguen answered, putting his arm around Henry's shoulders. "None of this should have happened to you. There will be a time that you can live anywhere in peace. For now the best place is Canada."

Henry looked at the floor as he exhaled audibly. "Yes sir."

"We need a place to hide him. Mr. Clappe, any ideas?" Jonah asked.

"My brother-in-law's outside. He's got a place on the north side. Got him a house with several hiding rooms. Neighbors are all sympathizers. 'Spect that'd be a good place."

"Your relative ever move a runaway to the border?"

"Well, yes," Clappe grinned. "I spose that's happened a few times."

"Mr. Henry, change clothes with this man. Take my hat and pull it down on your head. Mr. Clappe, go find your brother-in-law." Jonah said.

"I'll go out and talk to the crowd. If we can keep them around until we're ready to move Jerry, any of the other side won't be able to spot what we're doing," Loguen suggested.

Minutes later, Jonah heard the stentorian tones of Loguen addressing the crowd.

"Congratulations, my brothers. Tonight you struck a mighty blow for freedom. You risked your freedom so that Mr. Henry could have his. We will move Mr. Henry to Canada tonight."

A loud cheer pierced the night.

CHAPTER THIRTEEN
1852

The side-wheeler steamboat *Saluda* chugged into the wharves of Lexington, Missouri in April of 1852.

It was almost halfway to St. Joseph on a 750-mile journey, fully laden with passengers and assorted goods, traveling on the muddy, icy Missouri River, which even in the heart of summer presented numerous challenges to boat pilots in the form of strong currents, sandbars, snags, and hidden logs.

On the passenger log were 110 Mormons form Europe on a leg of a journey to Utah, part of a large group that had departed Europe months before.

The *Saluda* had a checkered past. Built in Cincinnati in 1847, it had already survived an accident which had sunk it on the Missouri. It was eventually refloated and salvaged, re-equipped, and was back on the river soon after. Given the short life spans of steamboats, it was approaching relic status.

But it new co-owner and captain was attuned to the fortunes which could be amassed with a steamboat on the commercially-clogged Missouri River. Migration to the West was at a peak. On any given day, eight to ten steamboats were moored at Lexington, picking up or dropping off passengers, undergoing repairs, loading goods. The *Saluda* made regular runs between St. Louis and St. Joseph.

This run had left St. Louis at the end of March, a shaky time for travel due to chunks of ice and unpredictable currents, but having secured over 200 passengers, the captain decided that it was a risk worth taking. Besides, there were many other steamboats plying the waters that early spring.

As the *Saluda* tried to leave Lexington, the pilot encountered Lexington Bend, a narrow channel with strong currents. It was a stretch detested by every pilot on the Missouri, and on this April day, it was particularly unforgiving. There had been numerous accidents in the strip over the years. The pilot couldn't get enough power to get through the channel. He tried all morning to get through, weaving, hugging the shoreline, and criss-crossing the space. He finally pulled into the north shore.

The next day was a repeat. The pilot couldn't *force* the *Saluda* through the passage. The captain ordered attempts for most of the day, and then conceded that perhaps his steamboat needed work. The pilot directed it to the south shore. He would turn it over to experts for as much of an overhaul as they deemed necessary. Too, one of the two side-wheels had been damaged from repeated collisions with ice.

Some of the passengers, irked at the delays, left the *Saluda* to look for other modes of travel to St. Joseph. The others scattered around town looking for inns and hotels.

When Hank Rosbottom pulled into town, there was no place to stay. He finally found a flophouse near the wharves, which was so run-down that none of the boat passengers, however desperate, deigned to stay in it.

Hank was on his way to Kansas City. He had tried Memphis for two years, and St. Louis for one, and he was as directionless as when he had left New Orleans. Cities were beginning to bother him. Whereas his needs encompassed little more than good whiskey, a bed of some sort, and an occasional meal, he had grown nervous and bitter in surroundings where people flourished and where interaction was impossible to avoid. The whiskey helped him sleep, and sleep helped him forget, except on those nights when he dreamed of her.

He had worked at odd jobs, and one night in St. Louis, he had pulled his banjo out of the back of the wagon, tuned it, and sat in with a group in a tavern. It was no good. He had lost his fondness for making music, for causing joy, for receiving acclaim. He found it difficult to converse, and consequently avoided it. He was looking now for quiet, a routine which would ask nothing of him. The frontier offered that. He would look things over in Kansas City, and probably wander farther west.

The captain was impatient, and angry. The delay stretched to four days. He told the pilot and the rest of his crew to be ready on Friday. They would attack the channel again, and this time they would make it. At least the ice had cleared away. The passengers were alerted. Several new ones had signed on. The passenger list was again over two hundred.

Good Friday of 1852 was sunny, and warmer than it had been since the previous autumn. As the *Saluda* prepared to leave, a small crowd gathered on both banks, curious as to whether the steamboat would gather enough momentum and enough power to slip through the channel. The pilot backed the *Saluda* into the river, and turned it toward the bend. The captain ordered full steam, and the steamboat lurched forward.

It had gone thirty feet toward the bend when it exploded, a horrifying, violent, concussive blast so extreme that the steamboat basically disintegrated.

Bodies were thrown into the air and some were hurled against the bluffs on the north side. A thousand shattered pieces of the boat were airborne, many driven into the watching crowds. The river was instantly littered with cargo and screaming passengers.

The blast shook the entire wharf area, and jolted Hank Rosbottom out of the fogginess of another hangover.

He opened his window and yelled to a crowd running toward the river. "What is it? Something blow up?"

"Explosion. Steamboat exploded! Terrible! Terrible!"

He dressed quickly, and bolted toward the river too. Then he had a thought, retreated to his room, and grabbed a half-empty bottle of whiskey.

Before he reached the wharves, he heard the wailing. He wasn't ready for the sight that greeted him. The great Missouri was stained red for hundreds of feet, the remaining shell of the back portion of the steamboat rested crookedly on the bank, people cluttered the river, some floating face down, others floundering, some trying to make shore, pandemonium, as the people of Lexington tried to help.

He ran toward the docking area with the most activity and passed a child, its body distorted. Dead. He checked on a man whose clothes were virtually ripped off. Dead. A confused man was placing a groaning woman on the wharf ahead of him. A metal piece had pierced her back. Hank stopped, pulled the jagged metal out, ripped the woman's bodice off and poured whiskey on the wound. There was little blood. She'll be OK, he thought.

He skirted the crowd and found a man turning gray, his arm missing from the elbow down. He tore off the man's shirt and tied it tightly above the mangled remnants of his arm. Before leaving, he gave the man a gulp from the whiskey bottle. A teenaged boy was sitting, dazed, holding a badly twisted arm. Broken, Hank knew. A pile of discarded lumber was stacked twenty feet away. Hank found two short pieces, and fashioned a makeshift cast, tying the pieces tightly to hold the arm immobile. As he finished, a breathless, small man with his white shirt rolled up to his elbows and carrying a bag, rushed past. He slowed to watch what Hank was doing.

"What's your name?" he asked between wheezes.

"Rosbottom," Hank replied tersely.

"You're a doctor aren't you? Don't know where you came from, but thank goodness you're here, Dr. Rosbottom."

Before Hank could respond, the little man interrupted. "Bring your bag. Dr. Rosbottom. Come with me. We're going to set up a hospital in that big warehouse on the shore. They'll bring the injured to us."

"Traveling to Kansas City. Don't have a bag. I'm not even a…"

Again the man interrupted him. "I'm Dr. Gleason. Sent some folks to my office to get laudanum and such. Let's go. We're going to get real busy."

Hank stood, and began to follow Gleason. The doctor was running, in the halting awkward manner of an elderly man years removed from youth and fluid motion.

He thinks I'm a doctor. I'll tell him the truth when I get time. As they approached the warehouse, Hank felt a surge of adrenaline. He had surprised himself back there. Whatever expertise he had just shown was attributable to the years of reading medical literature on the bayou. There was more to be done than Dr. Gleason could manage alone. As long as he could help, he'd play along.

"Told the folks on the river to bring bed sheets and blankets. We're going to have to work from the floor." Gleason said. "Sent two men out of town to fetch doctors Bowring and Gordon. They should be here to help in an hour or two.

A group of citizens rushed into the warehouse behind them, arms loaded. "This here stuff was locked up, Doc Gleason. Had to bust up your cabinet. Sorry," a man said as he dumped a pile of medical tools and some bottles on the floor.

"We're goin' to need lots of boiling water," Hank offered.

"Dr. Rosbottom is right. Tillie, can you do that for us?"

A plump woman nodded her head, grabbed the arm of the nearest man, and rushed out the door.

The first of the injured and the bed sheets arrived almost simultaneously. Immediately, Hank and Gleason were overwhelmed.

"Some of these aren't going to make it, Dr. Rosbottom. We'll do what we can for them, then put them in that corner. The ones that are dead, we'll lay at that end."

In short order, a system evolved. Gleason grabbed two women to assist him, and ordered a bewildered teen-aged boy to help Hank. At first the youth was worthless.

"What's your name, boy?"

"Aaron, sir," the boy answered.

"You feeling' a bit queasy, Aaron?"

"Yes sir."

"Well, look, Aaron. A lot of these folks are going to die, if we don't get to work. You can help by holdin' them down while I work on them. That OK?"

"Yes sir."

"Good boy."

The two summoned doctors arrived hours later, and the four worked will into the night. Candles and lanterns appeared. By that time, Hank and the boy had become an efficient team. Many of the injured were beyond help. Hank soothed them, administered laudanum. Towards dark, he had to amputate a leg, his only moment of hesitancy in the long day. He had probably botched it, he thought, but the tourniquet and the packing held, and the patient seemed to stabilize.

Early the next morning Gleason tapped him on the shoulder. "Dr. Rosbottom. We need a break. Come with me."

Hank followed him to a room off of the main warehouse.

"Here, Dr. Rosbottom. Do you drink?" Gleason said, as he proffered a bottle of whiskey. "Tillie brought this in. We probably need it as much as the injured."

Hank took a long swig while Gleason watched him.

"On your way to Kansas City, are you? Going to open a practice there?"

"Dunno."

"Going to buy medical equipment when you get there, I suppose."

Hank grunted. Maybe it was time to confess.

"Dr. Gleason, as to being a doctor…"

"You're a mighty fine one, Dr. Rosbottom. I was watching you. Got a good way with the patients. Took care of a lot of people. Didn't lose many."

"I was lucky."

"No, Dr. Rosbottom, you are good. Confident. Wondering if I could talk you into staying in Lexington a spell."

"Staying?"

"I'm not a young man. There's only three doctors in this whole area of the Missouri. Lot of business here. I'd be happy to take you on with me. You could work out of my office. Let you use my equipment until you get your own. You could stay in the room behind until you find a place. You think about it. We need a doctor like you."

"But I don't have formal training. I don't have papers."

"Dr. Rosbottom, this is the frontier. None of us do."

What had she said, her last words to him on the bayou?

"Hank, you'd make a good doctor."

Over a hundred people died in the explosion, including the captain and the pilot. Many more were claimed by the river, and their bodies were never found. Days later Lexington buried the dead. By that time, Lexington had a new doctor.

Hank had a new purpose.

CHAPTER FOURTEEN

1853

Riding back the half-mile lane from the rutted mountain road was like entering another reality. At the end of the forested entry was the farm of renowned educator Jeremiah Chase, a Doctor of Letters at the University of Vermont. A simple four room house had evolved over the years, as sons become old enough to help carpenter, into an expansive two-story abode, shaded by old maples and birches. The parcel of land was above Lake Champlain, but light years away from the bustle of activity from the shipping industry of the Burlington Harbor.

In the same way, an intellectual and sociological difference was also represented in that half-mile. The library of the house spilled over with books, and the raising of his sons included direct and implied daily lessons on the worth of human life, and the limitless boundaries of the mind and the spirit.

A meadow behind the large barn grew wildflowers for seven months a year, and fronted on a mountain stream that poured water into the valley below. The capacious barn itself held whatever livestock Jeremiah deemed appropriate, both for maintaining the farm, and for instructive purposes in raising three stalwart sons. There were stalls for a variety of horses, some expensive, exquisite equivalents to the boys, and others which had been rescued from less compassionate owners.

From their father, the sons inherited intelligence, curiosity, and an abiding love of the Green Mountains. From their mother, Molly, the sons acquired compassion, personality, wit, and great stamina. Her forebears were mountain people.

The lanky professor made a happy life for his brood, and instructed his sons in skills of survival, marksmanship, swimming, and literature, while conveying continuing lessons on what he considered more important: tolerance, humility, reverence, honesty, and courage.

Joshua, born in 1835, was an achiever, a young man capable of deep thoughts and incisive action who aspired to West Point. In philosophy and practice, he was most like his celebrated father. He seemed to always have his face in a book, and he faced crisis with equanimity and logic.

At the age of eleven, he had rescued his brother Jonathan from drowning in Lake Champlain. He had sized up the situation quickly, and outrun the adults to the water. He was 20 yards into the lake, swimming strongly before other onlookers put a toe in the water. Afterward, he had counseled his bedraggled brother about his lack of wisdom. Taking a canoe into rough water alone, and then abandoning it when it overturned, was not acceptable. For most of his childhood, he was more a third parent than a peer to his siblings. Unlike his brothers he was never known by an informal appellation. He was never "Josh." That didn't suit his personality nor his maturity, even as a youth.

Two years younger, Jonathan was the adventurer, the errant canoeist, an irrepressible charmer who attracted a host of Burlington young ladies. He in turn was attracted by danger and new experience. He resembled his mother in appearance, more blond and fair-skinned than his brothers, more compact, and stronger.

This adventurous Chase walked away from home as a five-year old. Dr. Chase found him after a frantic search, three miles from home, happily exploring a rock outcropping thirty feet above a ravine. "That boy," Molly laughed to her husband, "has nine lives. And he's already used up seven or eight of them."

"That boy," the professor answered, "better understand that he has limits."

Privately, Jeremiah reveled in the audacity of his middle son, and enjoyed the misadventure that seem to follow him, because Jonathan had proved that he was a survivor. What could life confront him with that was any more tenuous than a rock ledge over a dangerous chasm?

A composite of his parents, Jefferson was 18 months younger than Jonathan. Lithe, well over six feet by the time he was sixteen, he was fascinated by the outdoors, and bonded with animals easily, notably horses.

A replica of his mother's wide smile flashed white against the contrast of skin which seemed perpetually tanned, even in Vermont winters. "He studies clouds and dreams of rainbows," was Jeremiah's description of his youngest. He alone camped out on many frigid northern nights, reveling in the experience, while his older brothers opted for a hearth and warmth.

A lightning strike destroyed the family barn and four prize horses one summer night, and Jefferson had to be restrained from running into the inferno to lead the horses out. Afterwards he was disconsolate for months. Even a new barn and replacement horses didn't relieve the melancholy. Jefferson excelled at almost everything he attempted, his parents noticed, but he had no ego about any of it.

Jeremiah once explained his sons to a colleague. "If faced with a dilemma, Joshua will solve it, Jon will ignore it, and Jeff will make friends with it."

The father nurtured and prodded, but he never showed favoritism, or allowed any of his offspring to gloat.

"Enough! 'Pride goeth before a fall.' The real truth is that none of you is as good at anything as you should be."

Molly smiled throughout that lecture. Mothers were allowed to be proud.

"So what are you reading now, Joshua?" the father would ask during a shared task, perhaps cleaning out a stall."

"Confessions of an English Opium Eater."

"Thomas De Quincy. What are you learning, Joshua?"

"Because of his weakness, he struggled throughout his life, and gradually deteriorated."

"What is the lesson?"

"It seems that if one searches too hard for ecstasy, he can end up in torment."

"And what of his writing?"

"Father, it seems a bit too overwritten. It seems scattered to me."

"Is that intentional?"

"Well, maybe it sort of mirrors his experience."

Nothing seemed too mundane for the professor to teach or to share. An expressed rule during hunting forays was that the musket be carried pointing upward or toward the ground. If a son inadvertently lifted the barrel, he was sent home after a stern reminder about safety.

Jefferson, the most gifted marksman, didn't accompany the others on many hunts. When he was eight, he told his father that he couldn't abide killing a creature.

"Jeffie, you won't hunt, but you'll eat the meat of the game we kill?"

"It's not the same, Father."

"Why do you say that?"

"When it's meat, it's already been killed, and I didn't do it."

Jeremiah walked away so that his son wouldn't hear him chuckling.

Molly's time with them was less imperious. She was a natural story-teller and dispenser of wisdom on a more ethereal level. "Respect your elders, and respect whatever lucky girls you fall in love with," was a standard piece of her advice. Until they outgrew them, she spun nightly stories at their bedsides, soaring tales of heroes, and lands of hope and beauty. Most were improvisational. She talked them through problems, allowing for the fact that they were not as perfect as her husband insisted they be. She was far more tolerant of imperfection and of occasional failure.

At an afternoon reception for Joshua in Burlington before he left for West Point, a gang of local toughs crashed the party to set upon Jonathan, whom one boy suspected was paying too much attention to a common female friend. Outnumbered four to one, the teen-aged Jonathan was barely holding his own until his brothers arrived. Joshua wrestled two to the ground at once. Fourteen-year old Jefferson jumped on the back of another, and rode him to the ground.

Arriving at the tangle of bodies in the dirt, Jeremiah began to separate his sons from the piles.

"Shame on all of you! We are not ruffians," Jeremiah scolded.

But as he drove the family carriage back to the Chase home later, a broad grin creased the professor's thin face.

For years the Chase brothers rode trails through Chittenden County, fished in the Winooski River, and romped on verdant mountain slopes. All three grew taller than their father while still in their teens, and grew accustomed to a household which entertained scholars and politicians and New England's social hierarchy.

Jeremiah Chase was approached to consider a run for Governor of Vermont. He was judged to have the best chance to ride intellect, image, and honesty to the Governor's office. He declined. He would not leave an ailing wife or his mountains for the statehouse in Montpelier.

Before that his sons had left the home place, Joshua to West Point in 1853 and Jonathan to the University of Virginia two years later. Jefferson opted for the New York School of Veterinary Surgeons in 1857.

They would all return home in 1859 for Molly's funeral.

Without the sons, the vitality had left the home. Molly contracted an undiagnosed disease and faded quickly.

****

In 1853, a wagon train of forty-some families, over fifty wagons, countless trailing horses, cattle and dogs, and over 150 dreamers of all ages left Independence, Missouri for California. Several weeks later, it had wended a slow descent onto rolling plains covered with tall grasses. Wildlife of every description was spotted daily, hourly, coyotes, antelope, black bears.

Whit Brody, a forty-three year old most recently from Arkansas, noticed with mounting interest.

One night he approached the wagon master, a bearded, heavy-set man known to the train as Cap'n Willis.

"This place," he asked, sweeping his arm in a wide arc, "what can you tell me about it?" His hands rested on his hips, and he thrust his face forward, an attitude he assumed whenever he was gathering information.

The wagon master spit tobacco juice toward his own feet.

"Wal, most of it is fer Injuns. Gov'ment moved 'em here mebbe twenty years back."

"Indians? We haven't seen any."

"Kanzas and Pottawattamie 'round here. Peaceable. Keep to their selves mostly. The bad uns are a few hundred mile ahead of us."

"We haven't seen any settlers." Brody stooped to grab a handful of dirt. "Look at this. Pretty good soil. Had a cotton farm in Mississippi some years ago. Good soil there, but this is maybe better. A fella could farm it, grow livestock. Don't understand why nobody's settling here. Lots easier to get here than to California or Oregon." He sifted the soil through his fingers, and let it trickle away.

"Two things I'd tell ya. 'Spect most folks through here already have their plans set for California. The other is, don't think a body can buy it."

"Seems odd to me that land like this is protected for tribes you don't even see. Seems to go on forever."

"Fella name of Leavenworth did start a settlement here a few years back. More of a fort though. Military fella. Kinda a safe place for wagon trains and such. Probly be some others. We was near that fort jus' after we left Independence, little south of it. Name for all of this is Kansas. Don't think it's a territory yet. Jest a lot of Injun land."

"Well, sir, I thank you for the information."

Back in his wagon, Whit checked on his sleeping wife, Margaret, and thought about waking her. Instead, he pulled off his boots, and propped himself against the sideboard. He fell asleep in that position several hours later, his hand resting on his eight-year old daughter, Rose.

When Margaret, a good-looking woman with lively blue eyes, several years younger than her husband, woke before dawn, Whit had already unhitched the horse from the wagon and saddled it.

"Maggie, there's something I've got to do today. I'll be gone most of the day. I talked to Travis; his boy'll drive our wagon today. I'll catch up at suppertime."

She was alarmed. "Whit, what is it? Where are you going?"

"Don't know for sure. Got something nagging me. Maybe it'll change our plans, and our life." He kissed her. "I love you, darlin' girl."

When he returned well after dark, he had an explanation.

"We're leaving the train tomorrow morning. I think I've found our new home."

Arguing the point, even a mild protest, was pointless. Her husband was stubborn; not that she minded. He had not made a mistake for them in ten years of marriage.

Born in 1810 in Natchez, Whit had made cotton his life. He had taken over supervisory details of his parents' large plantation when he was nineteen, neglecting many aspects of his personal life. He understood, and accepted, that he was crucial to the farm's success, but something, perhaps many things, was missing. Wanderlust was part of that, but more of it dealt with an urge to achieve something meaningful on his own. Something different.

His life had changed in May of 1840, when the immense tornado roared in from the southwest, blowing away the plantation and killing his parents.

He did not re-build. He sold the Brody cotton fields and moved to Pine Bluff, the eastern boundary of the coastal plain of Arkansas, where he bought a farm and livestock from a local family, and settled down.

Two years later he married Margaret, the widowed daughter of a neighbor. It was not a marriage of convenience, nor of whim. She won his heart with her sincerity, and with extraordinary amounts of ebullience and charm. She was fascinated by the bow-legged small man's hard work, his gentle nature, and his attentiveness to her. One night on her father's porch, he had sung to her. She was stunned by her subsequent feelings for him.

She remembered a cool night in 1845, sitting in their spacious house next to a crackling fireplace when he told her how important she was to him, how all of his dreams centered on her, how crucial it was to him to make her dreams come true. Counting back later, she guessed that was the night she conceived.

Margaret managed the delivery of Rose with difficulty. She and Whit discovered later that Rose would be their only child. Margaret had wanted five or six sons and daughters for him. Rose would suffice.

In 1852 an urge he couldn't explain began to take a hold of him.

"Maggie, we're doing good things here. But I've been hearing about California. There's land of all types and good weather. Seems a man…seems a man and his family…could do most anything out there. Sounds good to me. Sounds awful good to me. We've got plenty of money saved up, more than we can ever spend. Your parents have passed. What do you think?"

Margaret listened quietly. This wonderful man, the sunshine in her life, was dreaming again. If he wanted California, she would leave a comfortable life, and raise Rose in the West.

Within two months they had purchased the largest Conestoga wagon available and two teams of oxen, and were meeting with Cap'n Willis in Independence, Missouri.

At seven a.m., a single shot started the wagon train lurching again toward California, but a solitary wagon set off in the opposite direction, back to St. Joseph, Missouri, a closer destination than Independence. This would be home while Whit reasoned things out. And if this was errant speculation, they would join another wagon train in a year or two.

For over ten weeks, Margaret and Rose languished in St. Joseph while he made forays in all directions, some of which lasted days.

One afternoon he galloped back, covered with dust, bundled against the early autumn plains weather.

"Found it, Maggie," he announced, "I found it ! Followed a river till it ran into another river. Right there. Right at that spot. Best land I've ever seen. There it is, Darlin'. There it is."

It wasn't easy. A piece of luck became an ally, but also became a nuisance. A bill organizing the Kansas territory was passed that year. The former Indian lands in the eastern part of the territory were opened for settlement. Attracting homesteaders was the goal. Squatters from western Missouri invaded the land in droves, beating the deadline for claiming land, and often driving off bona fide settlers. Back east, several companies were formed to recruit settlers, the Massachusetts Emigrant Aid Company and the Emigrant Aid Company of New York and Connecticut among the most prominent. A tidal wave of families came to stake out their 160 acres.

Whit's chosen area was a bit west of the most heavily sought areas. He wasted little time, writing letters to government officials, in effect bidding for property by offering impressive sums of money.

I will develop a large ranch north of the Kaw River to become a stable influence on the area. It will become a source of sustenance for those who settle there. It will make the best possible use of the land, and I will be the best possible caretaker; I managed the Brody Plantation in Natchez, Mississippi before the 1840 tornado, he wrote in his missives.

There was resistance from those supervising the settlement. That was not the purpose of the bill, he was told. The object was to populate the area, to offer property to those who couldn't afford it. Whit's dream would ignore those intentions.

"Whit," Margaret asked, "can they change the intent of the bill?"

"There's language in there. They can do what they want."

He was persistent. As 1853 came to a close, a resolution was close. "I'll make one last offer for a few thousand acres," he told Margaret, "The government will make out quite nicely, if they accept it."

"Whit, what if they don't accept it?"

"Maggie, it's worth a try. That land is wonderful. But if they don't accept it, we'll move on to California in the spring."

No, she knew, he'd keep trying. California would probably never happen. The resistance to his plan was making him more determined to see it through.

CHAPTER FIFTEEN
1854

Whit Brody purchased 10,000 acres of Kansas plains in March of 1854. The parcel was north of the Kaw River by several miles, and was bordered on the west by the Solomon River.

He never explained the circumvention of a homesteader bill by the U.S. government to Margaret, but she did know the sum of their savings that was paid for the land. It was fully one-third of their accumulated monies left from the sales of the Natchez plantation and the Pine Bluff farm.

With spring fresh in the air, he left her for fourteen weeks, with three large wagons loaded with building materials, boxes of tools, provisions to last for several months, a couple of cows, and his mare. He would not take Margaret and Rose until the area was hospitable and reasonably comfortable.

He was accompanied by Lem Hacker, a young jack-of-all-trades; Lem's friend Cooper, and two black men from St. Joseph, Noah and Lige. He would feed them and pay them wages while they helped him build a home and some outbuildings.

Whit had chosen well. The four were diligent and efficient, and in a bit over three months, a 40' by 40' square cabin, with a porch and a fireplace made from river stones stood on high ground above the flood plain. Nearby was a smaller structure-- a temporary dwelling for his workers-- and a storage shed.

One afternoon as the group waited in the cabin for rainfall to lessen, Whit addressed them.

"I want to tell you this. Years ago, I had a cotton farm. Had a lot of workers on that farm. A lot of black workers. But there were no slaves. We paid everyone good wages. Some of them lived on the farm with us, some lived in town. They could all come and go as they pleased. I hate slavery. I would never own another man."

He looked at Noah and Lige as he continued.

"Made a lot of folks in Mississippi pretty mad, but that's the way it was."

The rain wasn't letting up.

"The reason that I'm telling you this is that I respect all you have done out here. I'm going to build a ranch here. Raise cattle and crops. Horses, too. There'll be work for good men. I'll pay you well. I'd like for all of you to consider staying here with me. What do you think?"

There was a long silence. Whit got up and walked to the open front door. He stood there for a moment, turned around, and walked back, searching the faces of the others.

Lem Hacker was the first to answer. He stroked the stubble on his chin. He was an earnest young man, but full of humor.

"Mr. Brody, I appreciate this work. You're a good boss. Thing is, there's things I haven't done or seen." He twirled his hat in his hands. "What I mean is, this is not the place for me right now. You understand?"

"Kinda figured you might say that. Do what you have to do."

There was an apologetic tone to the young man's response. "Feel bad sayin' that. I'll probly wander out here often to see how you're doin.' I will stay here until you have a barn."

"I couldn't have done this without you, Lem. How about you, Coop?"

Cooper wasn't the talkative sort. He had listened intently to Lem's response. Whit knew what he'd say.

"Spect I'll be goin' back too. Dunno."

"Noah, what are you thinking?"

Of the group, Noah had surprised him the most. He was surprisingly well-spoken. He had spoken once of a 'massuh,' and had even referred to Whit that way once. There was slavery in his background, Whit was certain. The vestiges of scars showed on the back of his neck above his work shirt. Whit had seen more on his back. He was probably a runaway, one who was looking for freedom and dignity on the fringes of the Western expansion. Whit guessed that he was nearing forty.

"Mistuh Whit, I'd like to work for you here. I'll stay. Thank you."

"You're a good man, Noah. I'll keep you busy. Lige, you staying or going?"

Lige looked at his massive hands, studying nothing. This quiet man of great strength was searching for words, something to express more than a "yes."

"I be proud to work here, mighty proud, Mistuh Whit."

He returned for Margaret and Rose in August, leaving the others at the site with two hunting rifles and the remaining provisions. Cooper would drive a second wagon.

"Listen, if things get tough out here, you all come on in. You take care of yourselves. Pick me a good site for a barn. We'll build the best barn in the West when I come back. I'll be back within a month, late summer, maybe sooner."

He gave each man an awkward hug before he clucked the wagon's oxen to a start.

They had come to love the small man. He had asked them all to call him "Whit" when Noah had called him "Massuh."

"Hey, we're doing something together here. I'm nobody's master."

But he was, in some ways. He was the provider, a crack shot with his rifle who kept fresh game at their meals. He was the cook, and the architect and the hardest worker they had ever seen. He asked for their ideas and opinions, but deferred to Lem on construction details. In a midday ritual, he would race them to the Solomon River, where they all splashed noisily until he said, "That's enough fun for now. Let's go build something."

He followed the Kaw River west in their Conestoga wagon when he moved Margaret and Rose there, and turned north when he reached the Solomon. "There'll be a trail out here someday," he said. He pointed out the boundaries of their holdings.

At that instant, Margaret spotted a hawk circling above them, and shortly a small group of antelopes feeding near the river. A warm breeze was moving the clouds in intricate patterns and pushing the tops of red and purple wildflowers.

Omens, Margaret thought. Good omens.

She saw the cabin on the horizon long before the wagon stopped. She saw a small garden near it.

He noticed that a good-sized barn was framed 100 feet away.

That night they sat on a tiny porch after Rose fell asleep, listening to the sound of the Solomon River and crickets. He arranged the chairs so that he could hold her hand.

"Already talked to the men. Lige and Noah want to stay with us here."

She looked at him adoringly. "Wonderful."

"Lem's young. Nothing happening out here for a while. He'll stay until the barn's up. Guess the rest of us will build the main house by ourselves."

He got quiet. She waited.

"Right now we got a Conestoga, two wagons, four oxen, two milk cows, a horse, two hands, Rosie, and each other. Not much, but we've got money left. We'll buy cattle as soon as we can, and hire some more help. Dig a well. Grow some crops too. What do you think, Darlin'?"

She was overwhelmed by all of it, especially by his timetable, this incredible plan.

"I love you, Whit."

"And, Maggie, there are several large ponds on our land, one as big as a small lake. Plenty of water, plus the river," he continued to enthuse.

"Yes, Whit. Several large ponds." She smiled at him.

CHAPTER SIXTEEN
1855

He watched his daughter Rose reading on the front porch of his house, a 10-year old cherub in that year of 1855, with his wife's good nature and his mother's delicate features.

Dimples creased her left cheek and her chin.

The ranch house had been completed scant weeks before, a project that had taken more than a year. A mild winter had helped. Lem had left before then, but at Whit's direction and with Whit's money, he had hired and sent out a small crew from St. Joseph with more materials and some building skills. Lem then followed an elusive destiny to the east, but returned chagrined some months later.

The building crew had left. Whit and Margaret and Rose, and the newly-hired cook, Caroline, had moved into the house. Lige, Noah, and the prodigal Lem moved into the cabin.

The white frame house was large enough to be seen from a distance, even though it lay in a low triangle formed by three hills. Margaret had picked the spot because a grove of trees surrounded the footprint, and because it was two-hundred yards from the other buildings, close enough to supervise, far away enough for a modicum of privacy. The lower rooms included a grand entrance hall, a main room, a library, a dining room, and a splendid kitchen. On the level above were five bedrooms. It was basically a well-planned rectangle, but that plain aspect had been countered by two balconies above, and the front porch.

Furnishings were sparse. The house had swallowed the tables and chairs and beds and utensils that had filled the smaller cabin. All in good time, he mused. Frontier living required patience.

As proud as Whit was of his home, the centers of his life were Margaret and this little girl. Rose romped on the large staircase, pored over books in sunlight filtered through the arched windows of the dining area, stole naps in front of the generous fireplace in the main room, and frolicked on the balcony outside of her bedroom.

She rode a horse soon after the big move. Margaret had left the new corral that day, certain that her daughter would be thrown and trampled.

Children had not been a part of his Grand Plan, but there she was, more important to him than his 500 head of cattle, more important than the wonderful isolation of his ranch.

Lem Hacker had drifted back in March of 1855.

"Was just out this way, wonderin' if you could use me. I'd like to come back, if you'll have me."

"What took you so long? You miss God's country, or me?"

"I missed what you're doin' out here."

"Of course, I'll have you. I need help with the house; so much going on, I can't seem to finish it. We'll need a bunkhouse soon. I want to hire more hands. We get a little bigger, you'll make a good foreman. But you know, it can get lonely out here."

"There'll be too many people in the area soon enough, Mr. Whit."

"Yes. I suppose that's true."

"I brought your wagon back, the oxen too. Dumb animals."

"They're still yours, if you leave again. I'll pay you $15 a week. That seem fair?"

Weeks earlier he had hired Simeon Whittaker, a toothless, grizzled man who played a battered old fiddle. A former trapper, he had an untamed shock of prematurely white hair, and he moved in a permanent stoop, looking up to speak through eyes squinted by too much sun and too much hardship.

Whit didn't consider it charity. The strange man didn't have much to say, but he understood the land, and he could oversee the fields of crops. More important, Whit liked him.

So, in October of 1855, he had four ranch hands and a cook. Within two years he'd have some 2,000 cattle, and another 500 acres. That was the plan. Trail drives to St. Louis would require more help, temporary employees. Even now, the day-to-day operation of the ranch required more help.

The sound of hooves brought him onto his porch early one morning in October. Riding up to him were a dark-haired woman dressed like a man, and a boy. She was driving a wagon pulled by two underfed horses, and the boy was on a small pinto, riding without a saddle, Whit noticed. She stopped the wagon and jumped down with surprising agility.

She was pretty in a rugged sort of way, with dusky hair hanging loose and a wide-brimmed hat pulled down to her eyebrows. She was taller than him by several inches, and markedly slim.

"You Brody?"

"I am. Who are you?"

"Bird. You need help here?"

"Well, Bird, we have a cook."

"I'm not a cook," she said with mild annoyance, "I tame horses and brand cattle and mend fences. I can cowboy better than most men."

She was a full-blooded Indian of some heritage, and there was just a hint of accent in her English. When she spoke, she looked at him directly.

"That boy there," Whit nodded, "what's his name?"

"Fox. He's twelve or thereabouts. He can help out around here for free."

He did need help. If this didn't work, he could let her go.

"There's a lot of hard work here. I'd expect you to do your share."

She waited, looking at him without answering, expecting more. He saw a smile start, then disappear.

"Put your stuff in that small building near the cabin up there," he pointed. "Used to be a storage building until we built the barn. It isn't much more than a room with a small fireplace, but you and the boy'll have it to yourselves. We plan to build a bunkhouse directly. If you stay, you could probably have the cabin someday. If the tool shack doesn't suit you, we'll move you into the big house for a spell. I'll pay you $15 a week, the boy half of that if he does some work. That fair?"

He knew that it was probably top-dollar, but it seemed that he never got an answer to that question.

"You can take your meals with the other hands, in the house twice a day, seven in the morning, six at night."

"Thank you." She turned back to the wagon.

"Your wagon and your horses can go in the barn. Plenty big. If you don't mind my asking, how did you know we were out here?"

"Asked some questions in Topeka. They told me."

"I may have made a mistake," he reported to Margaret. "I just hired an Indian woman and a little boy."

"To help Caroline?"

"Nope. She says she's a cowboy."

"Whit..." There was really no response she could think of.

Within two weeks, Bird had assisted in the delivery of several calves. She made daily perimeter checks of the wandering herd on a mustang Whit had given her, tracking strays and returning them to the Brody herd. She cut timber on the ranch's northeastern border with Lige and hauled it back to the area where Lem was making fence posts.

One day, Whit asked Lige, "How's she doing ? Bird?"

"Mistuh Whit, she don' tire out. Worked all day wif her. She never stopped." That convinced him. Lige, who had first come to the area as a callow twenty-some year old, had thrived on ranch life. He had become an immense man who carried barn poles by himself, and whose energy never flagged.

The boy, Fox, attached himself to Lem. The first day, he had hung around tentatively, as if he had been assigned to a job, but was too shy to begin. Lem noticed his resemblance to his mother, thin and fine-featured, expressionless, with overlarge brown eyes.

"What's your name, boy?"

"Fox."

"Fox? That all?"

The boy nodded.

"That all of your name?"

The boy nodded again.

"Heard your mother call you 'Charlie'."

The boy responded meekly, "No. Chula. Means fox."

"Chula, huh. Sounds like 'Charlie' to me. Everybody need two names. How 'bout I call you Charlie Fox. That sound right?"

The boy nodded again. This time he smiled.

"Hey, Charlie Fox. You can help me make fence posts."

Caroline the cook regarded the brood she cooked for. There was a strange, middle-aged drifter, two illiterate black men, an Indian woman, a boy, and a nice young cowboy with acceptable good looks, if one discounted a weak chin.

This is what her life had come to, and she was comfortable with it. She had first met Margaret at the St. Joseph boarding house while Whit was exploring the plains. She was the cook there, a plumpish woman with remnants of what once might have been modest beauty. She was years past that at forty. Hints of gray had appeared in her auburn hair, which she pulled back severely. For years she had bumped around the edges of the frontier, looking for something that she couldn't explain, or find. Her expertise was in the kitchen, and that had earned her jobs at every stop. She had no family, no close friends, and no idea of what she was looking for. Years ago, she had despaired of ever finding a husband, or even a good male friend.

She felt that she had dead-ended in St. Joseph. When Margaret, a very nice woman she thought, had shared with her the Grand Plan out on the plains, she was intrigued. Going beyond safe limits, taking chances, forging into the unknown, building something, maybe those things defined her quest.

When the Brodys moved into the main house, Margaret had Whit contact her on one of his buying trips. He invited her to join them on the river as cook and housekeeper. She fed the family three times a day, and cooked two expansive meals for the ranch hands, which she served on a long table in the kitchen. Margaret helped in every circumstance.

"We'll pay you $15 a week. Is that fair?" Whit had asked.

Margaret had given her free rein in the kitchen, and a large bedroom at the back of the second floor, accessible from the kitchen. It was a room that she invited Lem to share once or twice a week.

Caroline knew that the assignations didn't constitute a romance, but she loved the bawdiness and the company, while Lem, ten years younger, was grateful for lusty and energetic feminine attention.

"I don't know much about you. What is your story?" she asked him one night as they lay in the dark. His arm was around her.

"Not much to tell, I reckon. My father taught me how to build things. Then he left us when I was thirteen, or so."

"He died?"

"No. He just saddled up one day and never came back."

"You miss him?"

"Sure." There was silence in the room.

She changed positions so that she was facing him, then crossed her leg over the top of his. She reached up and gently stroked the hair on the back of his head.

"You know that I'm old enough to be your mother…well, almost," she said.

"Miss Caroline, those are numbers. You're a fine woman. You give me lots of pleasure."

"You know, we can be friends like this, until you get tired of me."

"Don't reckon that's going to happen anytime soon."

"It will, some day."

"Some days. Can't count on them. I've always had the feeling that my some days aren't going to be there very long anyway. Something about my life that makes me think that I'll never get to be an old man."

He stretched his long legs, and turned to her. Their bodies were touching full length, their faces close together.

"There's something about life out here," she said. "Every day's the same, but it's exciting. The Brodys are fine folks. Probably as close to family as I've ever had."

"Yep."

His short answer and the change she felt in his body told her the conversation was over. He was ready again. So was she.

If Whit or Margaret knew of the liaisons, they never let on, nor did the three men in the cabin on the nights when there was an empty bunk.

In time, the disparate group did resemble an odd family. At Margaret's insistence, Whit gave all hands Sunday off, with only the most necessary work ordered. Lem fished with Charlie Fox. Whit took groups on all-day hunting trips to fill the ranch's larders.

On a trip to Topeka, Whit bought four shirts, two pairs of pants, rain gear, a winter coat, new hats, a box of underclothes, and shoes for each of his hands, including Charlie Fox. He had guessed at sizes, not too well. Lige's shirts were stretched taut across his broad back, and his pants barely reached his ankles. Charlie Fox made do by rolling up his pants legs several times. Caroline and Margaret made alterations for weeks.

Caroline was also a beneficiary of his generosity. Brand new pots and pans and coffee cups filled the kitchen shelves.

Getting supplies was much easier. Years before, two Indian sisters had started a ferry service across the Kaw 70 miles east of the ranch. Their husbands sold moonshine. In 1854 the Topeka Town Association was formed at that spot by nine settlers, to encourage commerce and settlement. Steamboats carrying meat, lumber, flour, and all manners of other products began docking at the landing, and carried away the crops of new settlers. It was two days closer to the ranch than St. Joseph.

CHAPTER SEVENTEEN
1856

Less than 100 miles from the Brody Ranch, to the southeast, Kansas was becoming the epicenter of violence and bloodshed.

The Kansas-Nebraska Act of 1854 had created the territories of Kansas and Nebraska, and had enabled residents in those areas to decide whether slavery would be permitted within each territory. It had supplanted the Missouri Compromise of 1820, which had banned slavery in the Kansas territory.

Pro-slavery settlers came mostly from Missouri. Pro- and anti-slavery, thus had a battleground for a festering war of philosophies.

In 1855, abolitionist John Brown had received letters from two of his sons, who resided in Kansas. Like their father, they were staunch abolitionists. They told him that the pro-slavery factions in Kansas were becoming militant. They feared for the safety of their families.

John Brown promptly moved to Kansas, in a wagon loaded with firearms.

He was spurred to action by two occurrences early in 1856.

Newspaper writer Benjamin Franklin Stringfellow published articles which extolled and celebrated the use of pro-slavery violence, and predicted that Kansas would soon become a pro-slavery territory. Secondly, a large pro-slavery posse —later known as the Border Ruffians— attacked Lawrence, Kansas, destroying homes and a large hotel.

Brown went into action on May 23. John, four of his sons, and two friends left on a mission. They journeyed to Pottawatomie Creek in Franklin County, and the next day, they approached the home of John Doyle, a member of the Law and Order Party.

They took Doyle and his two adult sons to a nearby field well after dark, and hacked them to death with broad swords.

They next stopped at the cabin of Allen Wilkinson; he too was slashed to death. They continued up the Pottawatomie and similarly executed William Sherman.

Soon after, a force of Missouri men led by Captain Henry Pate captured two of John Brown's sons and destroyed the Brown home.

Brown raised a small army and subsequently defended the Free State settlement of Palmyra, Kansas, taking Pate and twenty-two of his men prisoner. Brown then forced Pate to agree to a treaty, in effect trading the captured twenty-three for the release and absolution of his sons.

Hostilities increased. A company of 300 Missourians crossed into Kansas, ransacked the Free State town of Osawatomie, and killed Brown's son Frederick. Brown retaliated by ambushing the Missourian army, but his men were outnumbered, and were forced to scatter. The Missourians looted and burned Osawatomie.

All of Kansas was nervous, lest these incidents spread. To that point, the turmoil had occurred relatively close to the Kansas-Missouri border, but as the population swelled westward, so did the possibility that the areas of atrocity would too.

****

Jack Bertrand, Margaret's nephew, arrived unannounced at the Brody ranch in July. He was nineteen, an educated and refined Arkansas native, who wanted to test his mettle as a pioneer with his aunt and uncle. He had ridden solo from Little Rock. Margaret was thrilled, the first family member she had seen in three years. Whit offered him a job. Margaret offered him a bedroom in the main house. He gladly welcomed the job offer, but told his aunt no thanks. He'd stay in the new bunkhouse with the other cowboys.

Barely a week before, a chunky redhead with a perpetually flushed face, a refugee from an Illinois orphanage named Elon Pack, had arrived at the ranch one afternoon, stuttering and flustered by the ranch owner he was addressing, nervous about what he wanted to ask.

"M-M-Mr. Brody…" He shook his head as if trying to rid himself of the affliction. "C-c-can I work for you?"

"Well, son. What can you do?" Whit was amused by the markedly anxious youngster, probably in his early twenties.

"Worked with a b-b-b-blacksmith for four years."

"Can you ride? Rope?"

"Spect so. I can shoe horses, take care of them." He didn't seem to be impressing the rancher.

"Can you clean house? Cook?" Whit noticed the crestfallen look. "Son, I'm kidding you. What's your name?"

"Elon Quincy Pack."

"Mr. Pack, when can you start?"

The boy looked surprised and was briefly quiet. "N-n-n-now?"

For the past four years, Whit learned later, Elon Pack had apprenticed with a blacksmith in St. Louis, after fleeing the orphanage. Tiring of the tedium and his martinet boss, he became fascinated by cowboy life as he watched great herds of cattle arriving in St. Louis, driven by men who would soon collect paychecks. He wandered west with his feelers out, until a chance conversation brought up Kansas and the Brody Ranch.

Elon, with few possessions, and Jack Bertrand, oldest son of Margaret's sister, moved into the new, spacious bunkhouse, already inhabited by Lem, Lige, and Noah. They had left the cabin happily as soon as the bunkhouse was completed. "Never did cotton much to housework," Lem had explained. Bird and Charlie Fox took the cabin, after sitting out a frigid winter in a bedroom in the main house.

Wednesday, December 3, 1856 began with ominous dark clouds swirling in the southwest sky and rolling toward the Kansas plains, a mile high wall of tumbling weather. Snow began falling heavily before daybreak in front of the advance, and noises from restless cattle woke Whit. He got up quietly. Margaret hadn't been feeling well the previous night, and it would be another hour until Caroline's breakfast. He pulled on a pair of pants and a shirt, and walked through the darkness down the staircase.

The day before he, Bird, and Charlie Fox had ridden the property's short side up the Solomon River, collecting some of the 1,200 Brody cattle, and herding them back toward a saucer of land just east of the main house. Numerous strays had begun grazing far past the Brody tract, in spite of Bird's best efforts. Lem, Noah, and Lige were sent to the long angle of property farthest from the house, a two day task of collecting and herding which also included the northern boundary. Jack Bertrand and Elon Pack were assigned to follow the southern boundary down to the Kaw River. They had returned last night. Collecting the herd was necessary due to a lack of fencing on the spread; too, it would provide a tentative head count before the spring drive to St. Louis. Most important, Whit didn't want to lose cattle to a harsh winter. He'd keep them close to scattered forage and an illimitable supply of oats and feed. Many would wander away again, but it seemed necessary, this ritual.

Whit was peering out of a front window, trying to sense what the wind and the snow portended, when he heard the insistent rapping at the back of the house. He heard Caroline scolding the intruder.

"Simeon! What are you doing here, making that racket? It's too early for breakfast."

"Gotta talk to Mr. Whit. Mighty important."

Whit entered the kitchen.

"Bad weather comin' Mr. Whit. Mighty bad weather. Seen it afore. We gonna have snow up to our arses. Gonna get frightful cold. Dangerous cold. Already startin'. Lissen to them cattle."

The territory was part of a large target triggered when an errant high pressure ridge wrapped itself around a low pressure front from the southwest. The abrupt collision created a "white hurricane," a cataclysmic explosion of winter weather. Before its 15-hour life ended, heavy snowfall would be borne on rages of wind, the temperature would plummet to dangerous levels, and downdrafts would cause whiteouts so absolute that orientation, seeing beyond 15 feet ahead, would be impossible. Snow drifts would collect at levels higher than prairie homes.

Simeon knew all of that would occur. He had survived several blizzards.

"Too cold out there now. We gonna get some cows froze to death. Thinkin' 'bout them other fellas. They'se still out there. It still be dark."

The day before had been almost springlike, cooling off just slightly at dusk, with no hint of an impending storm, no indication of this mounting apocalypse. Whit was sure that none of the three had taken any more than jackets and rain gear. The dramatic temperature swing just before dawn had occurred so swiftly that even if they had left immediately for the ranch, they would still have to battle the cold and the snow for most of the ride. Knowing them, they were probably trying to bring the cattle too.

"Simeon. Go tell all of the hands to come to this house immediately. Everybody! I don't want anyone to leave here. Build some fires in the fireplaces."

Whit hurried back upstairs, quickly dressed in two layers of bulky clothes, and rushed back past Caroline. He had strapped a pistol on his hip.

"Tell Mrs. Brody that I'll be back around midday," he called.

The wind had stiffened and snow was flying haphazardly, accompanied by stinging sleet. He grabbed a pair of snowshoes off of the barn wall and secured them on the rump of the hastily saddled Hank, the largest and strongest horse in his stables. He tied a bandanna over the top of his hat, and another over the lower half of his face, pulled on heavy gloves, and raced into the weather. Ice began to batter him. The frightful cold quickly penetrated layers of clothing and his heavy coat.

It was mid-morning when he reached what he thought was the eastern boundary. It was just a guess. Landmarks were already covered by snow. His vision was faulty. The snow was thick and swirling. If that was the easternmost point of his property, it usually took only an hour at a canter to reach. He turned north to make his way up the long east side, fearing that his men wouldn't be close to his line of travel. Even if they were, he could easily pass within shouting distance and not even know it, because of the wind's howl and the damnable wall of snow.

"C'mon Hank. C'mon boy," he encouraged the horse, aware that Hank might balk at any time. If so, Whit would dismount and pull him, or shoot him and proceed on snowshoes. He wouldn't leave him out there to suffer. The snow was already up to the horse's forelocks, and drifting high on any barrier it encountered, trees, hills, boulders. Hank continued to trot.

He was brushing snow from his eyes when he saw gray figures ahead, indistinct hulks in the colorless landscape. Lige and Noah. Their horses were turning in tight circles. A few cattle, stalled, stood huddled together nearby. He saw a larger group in the white distance.

"Can't get them cows moving!" Noah shouted at him.

"Forget the damn cows! Get back to the ranch ! Where's Lem?"

"Went chasin' some strays thataway!" Noah pointed toward the northeast. "Toward the woods! Ain't seen him since!"

"I'll look for him! Ride to the Kaw, that way ! Follow it to the Solomon, then home!"

"We'll stay with you!" Noah yelled above the din.

"No! You're not dressed for it! Go!"

The storm, already unspeakable, intensified even more as they left him.

He tried to keep Hank moving at a trot, but that was getting more difficult as the snow continued to collect and Hank lowered his head against the gale. He couldn't remember ever being this cold. He had been in the storm for four or five hours, and he realized that he would be in extreme jeopardy if he didn't turn back soon.

But he had a ranch hand out there somewhere.

A painful eternity later, he saw the dim silhouette of the woods. Some of it had been cut in the past three years for firewood, building materials, and fence posts, but most of it remained to provide some kind of shelter, if Lem had gotten on the leeward side of trees. Perhaps he could have dug some sort of snow cave.

He began to circle the perimeter. Hank's hoof prints were disappearing as soon as he left them, so there would be no trace of any left by Lem.

The wind quartered him, blowing ferociously from his left side. When it gusted, he could feel Hank waver. The backs of two cows appeared on his right, the only parts of their frozen bodies not buried. Maybe they were two of the strays Lem had chased.

He completed a half-circle of the forest area, keeping the trees on his left, and turned into the storm as he reached the northernmost part. The storm attacked him head-on.

He surmised that well over a foot of snow had fallen, a guess, because the incessant wind continued to alter the depth. Hank was slowing measurably.

He rode through the woods, using them as a partial wind breaker as he moved south, and almost rode by Lem. The white form he was passing could have been a large rock or a bush. A flash of red, from a saddle blanket, made him edge closer. Lem was slouched against a tree, his lifeless eyes open, staring at nothing. His face was crusted with ice. Whit knew that he was dead before he dismounted. His horse was nowhere in sight.

Whit was stunned by the discovery, but he had no time to mourn the young man who had been so much a part of his Kansas life.

"Got lost, did you?" he muttered. "Kind of gave up? Don't know how I'll manage this, my friend, but I'm going to take you home."

Bracing against another tree, Whit put on the snowshoes. Hank could not carry double in those conditions. With near superhuman effort, he lifted the cowboy and propped him against the horse. He crouched between Lem's legs and lifted him across the saddle, then secured him with his stiff, frozen lariat.

The ranch was over five miles away, if he didn't get disoriented. He couldn't retrace to the river, the route taken by Lige and Noah, because that would almost double the distance. The odds against him were huge. He might freeze to death out here, but he would not leave Lem to the wolves or to further ravages of the blizzard. He would walk until he couldn't walk any more.

He pulled on the reins of his snorting horse, and started on a diagonal through the woods, picking spots twenty feet ahead and walking to them. The snowshoes helped considerably, but Hank, with his burden, was lagging badly. Both were expending energy quickly, he pulling on the horse to keep him moving, Hank, picking up his feet to continue moving as the snow got deeper. He stopped several times to catch his breath, and to whisper endearments to the horse, which was confronting snow drifts which hid his knees.

Clear of the woods, he traversed slopes away from the wind which lessened its force, and when he walked across the tops of windswept hills stripped of heavy accumulation, he got momentary respites from the snow, but the wind buffeted him relentlessly.

He wrapped the reins around his wrist. His hands were numb, useless.

If his diagonal took him away from a beeline to the ranch, one of two rivers would guide him to their confluence, where he could get oriented. The ranch was north of that, if he could last that long. His breath, behind the bandanna that covered the lower half of his face, was condensing and freezing on the cloth. The unsecured front brim of his hat flapped and changed shapes, constantly exposing his eyes, which stung and were blurring his vision.

If only he could sit down for a few minutes.

He continued to lean into the storm, and understood through a growing mental fogginess that he wasn't walking to spots any more. He had a brief, lucid moment. How long had he been out here? How soon until darkness made all of this impossible? He was surrounded by a gloomy grayness. It might be dark in minutes.

The whiteout spun away temporarily, and he thought that he saw ranch buildings. It was a mirage, he was sure. A few steps later, his knees buckled and he fell forward into the snow. I'll crawl the rest of the way, he thought.

But he couldn't get up.

Strong arms jerked him to his feet, and he was conscious of Lige's voice. "Mr. Whit, it be alright now."

He heard other voices. "We've got you, Uncle Whit. You made it." And he heard Noah speak faintly behind him, "Easy, Hank. You be easy, big horse."

"Take care of Lem. He's passed," he muttered to the faceless voices. "Get a blanket on Hank."

They had to peel the clothing from his shivering body. They laid him in front of the fire in the front room hearth and massaged his arms and legs. Margaret cradled his head in her arms while Caroline dripped hot tea into his mouth. Bird covered him with blankets from several beds.

"He'll make it. You'll see," Simeon offered. Rose sat in a chair in the corner, crying softly.

He continued to shiver for an hour.

Noah struggled to the barn, brushed the ice from Hank's body, covered him with horse blankets, and forked hay around him. Jack, Lige, and Elon wrapped Lem's body in a blanket, and carried him to an unused upstairs bedroom.

At first light, after the storm ended, Jack and Lige carried Lem to a twenty-foot drift against the barn, dug a hole, and laid him inside. There'd be no burial until the weather changed, until the ground thawed.

Bird found her son alone in a bedroom upstairs that morning, his head down on his arms at a small table. Charlie Fox's good friend was gone, a male influence lost from his life. That had happened often, to her.

CHAPTER EIGHTEEN

1858

Anna Louise was freed in 1851, when she was six years old. She and her mother, Ollie, were beneficiaries of the death of Thaddeus Moore, a plantation owner of Savannah, Georgia. His will stipulated that the two, from among a coterie of over 60 slaves that he owned, were to be given an award of $200 and immediate emancipation.

That was appropriate. Thaddeus was Anna Louise's father.

Nor was that the only untoward incident in her lineage. Her mother, Ollie, had been the love child of a slave girl named Belle, and her master Phineas Henry from north Georgia, another wealthy plantation owner, in 1824.

Henry, harassed by his wife, had eventually sold sixteen-year old Ollie to Moore, a bachelor farmer who immediately made her his bedmate-on-call. Four years later, Ollie gave birth to Anna Louise, unattended, in a dirty shack on the west end of the plantation. In succeeding years, there were two more pregnancies. Both children, boys, died in infancy.

Anna Louise was a wondrous child, with little sign of her African heritage. She was pretty and precocious, a cheerful sprite with huge brown eyes, and her father's aquiline nose and high forehead. She had Ollie's full lips and dark hair, albeit straight. She could easily have passed for the white daughter of a white plantation owner. But she was a slave. Too soon, Ollie knew, Anna Louise would be a paramour herself, either to Moore, or even more frightening, to another white man on another plantation.

Often, Ollie thought of escaping, but she would not go without Anna Louise. She would wait until her daughter was capable of long nights of running and days of hiding. Then she would follow the Drinking Gourd, the North Star, to freedom in the North, maybe to a place that other slaves called "Canada," with reverence.

Moore's death was not widely mourned among the slave population of Fairview, his plantation. He was a taskmaster who had succeeded on the backs and hard work of his chattels. There were whippings and long days in the cotton fields under an unrelenting sun. Those who had tried to escape from Fairview were caught, taken away somewhere, and never seen again.

After he died-some said he choked on a piece of meat, his bulbous face turning bright red then blue as several house slaves watched dispassionately-- the balance of the Fairview slaves were sold at auction by a nephew heir who divested himself of the entire farm at great profit.

Ollie and Anna Louse bought train tickets and traveled north.

Ollie was fearful throughout the journey. She could not read. Years of servitude had produced in her an inability to look white people in the eyes. Her first few expenditures had produced travel clothes for the two, modest and mismatched. While Anna

Louise beamed in the first new dress and shoes she had ever owned, Ollie privately had doubts, which grew each time the train slowed or stopped, each time she saw a white face looking at her.

It was during the train adventure that Anna Louise realized that she was somehow different. The two were put into the last passenger car with others of African descent. None from that car were permitted in other cars, including the dining car. There were no meal provisions for her group, nor other comfort facilities. When the two changed trains to board for Cincinnati, they were shown the end of the line, harshly questioned, and forced to show their papers of manumission, which were scrutinized at great length.

"Mamma, I don't like that man in the blue shirt. He keeps looking at me. He looks angry."

"You hush, girl. Best not to look at white folks. Jes' like on the plantation."

"Why, Mamma? We're free now. Can do anything we want."

"Not so. May be more to fret about now than before."

"Why, Mamma?"

"Hush, Anna Louise. People be starin' at us."

A strange designation on their manumission documents affected both for the rest of their lives. Moore's will had named "Miz Olli Moore and her daughter AnnaLuis" as the beneficiaries of freedom papers. Those were erroneously transferred to "Missy Ollimore" and "Annalise Ollimore" and registered that way. Those would be their legal names henceforth. On sets of hastily prepared papers, the two were described as "Mulatto, aged around 25," and "Mulatto, female child, five or six." A southern lawyer had explained that to Ollie.

"We going to change our names in Cincinnati," she told her daughter. "You be 'Annalise' from now on. Can't forget that. Your new name is Annalise Ollimore. No more Anna Louise. Can't forget that, chile."

Cincinnati had been casually recommended by an attorney who had executed the will. The two alighted from the train, walked some distance, and took a ferry across the wide Ohio River, asking for directions from members of their race along the way. When they finally arrived on the northern bank of the river, the awesome complexities of what she was doing descended on Ollie. Now what? What should I do first? Where should I go?

She approached the first black man she saw, an old gentleman with a cane.

"S'cuse me, Suh. Lookin' for a place to stay. Kin you help me?"

He directed her to a rundown hotel two blocks away. The man at the desk, an unfriendly type with a pocked face, looked at her suspiciously.

"Gotta show me some money. This ain't no charity place," he growled.

"Yes, I have money. Jes' need a place to stay for a few days."

She took out a few bills. Instinct told her not to show him the entire roll.

He counted out what he said was $45.

"This'll get you a room. But four days from now, you gotta get out. Don't want no trouble from you. Got that?"

"Could you kindly tell me, is there a food place close?"

"You can't go into restaurants 'round here. Spect you oughtta buy some food from a grocery. One of them on the corner."

He showed her to a room in a long, dark hallway. A fetid, stank odor permeated the building. She saw bugs of some sort cavorting on the floor. The room was tiny. A single, unmade bed stood in the middle. There was one chair, a broken desk, and a dingy, uncovered window.

"Remember, four nights. Then you gonna leave."

That night, Annalise fell asleep immediately in her mother's arms.

Missy wept quietly until morning.

The next morning providence smiled on her.

Exiting the hotel holding the hand of her daughter, she saw another young black woman with a child. She approached the woman cautiously.

"Don't mean to bother you, Missus. Lookin' for work. Don't know how to find it."

The woman hesitated. "You free?"

"Yes'm. Free. We's both free?"

"Listen. Don't know if you be free or not. But you gots to see Mr. Coffin."

"Mr. Coffin…?"

"Mr. Levi Coffin. He got a store several blocks from here. Tell you how to get there. You tell him what you need."

Thirty minutes later she was in the store looking at a tall, thin, middle-aged white man.

"Mistuh Coffin, suh?" she said in a tentative voice.

"May I help you with something," he asked. There was something comforting about his manner, his soft voice.

Levi Coffin ran a free store in Cincinnati, an establishment selling goods made by freed slaves, mostly cotton merchandise. The store also sold produce, sugar, and spices.

Coffin had moved to Cincinnati from Newport, Indiana in 1847. There was much more to this Quaker than just storekeeping. He was called "The President of the Underground Railroad," a name bestowed on him by frustrated bounty hunters who knew his was the main safe house in southwestern Ohio, but couldn't catch him in the act of hiding or transporting runaway slaves. Thousands of runaways were protected by the man over the years, in both Cincinnati and Indiana.

He stared at the two in front of him, a young woman, pretty, with downcast eyes and a sad demeanor, obviously ill-at-ease, and the youngster, who stared at him with huge eyes.

"Please, suh. Got the freedom papers here."

Coffin glanced at the manumissions. It didn't matter; he would help her. But her freedom would make it easier for him.

"Tell me about yourself," he said as he led her to a room behind the store.

"Fum Georgia. Belonged to Mastuh Moore. Been free a short while. Jus'took some trains an' a boat here. Need help now. Need work." She still hadn't looked at him.

He checked the papers again. "Missy Ollimore. What did you do for Mr. Moore?"

She was embarrassed, and turned away as she answered. "Was his bed girl."

"I'm sorry, Missy. That was none of my business. I just thought that, if you had a skill, I could find you a job easier."

"I will do anythin', long as I not a slave no more."

Coffin liked her. What courage, he thought, to travel in areas so foreign to her, and the sweet little girl holding her hand. He would find something that would improve her life, something that she could be proud of.

"This is what we'll do. You get your possessions and come back here this afternoon. You and the girl can stay with my wife and myself until I can find a place for you."

There was little work. For three days Coffin worked his acquaintances, and finally scored a lead. The family of a professor at the Medical College of Ohio on the campus of Cincinnati College was looking for a housekeeper.

After a visit to the family, during which he described two desperate and beautiful former slaves, Coffin drove the two to the home in his buggy. There would not be an interview. The professor and his wife knew well the name of Levi Coffin. If he felt that Missy would be an appropriate employee, they would hire her sight unseen.

The family consisted of Dr. Herman O'Neill, his wife Maribel Chase O'Neill, and two teen-aged daughters named Deidre and Portia, who found Annalise irresistibly cute. The family home was a large dwelling on one of the Seven Hills. Ollie and Annalise stayed in the guest house, a quaint cottage at the rear of a backyard garden.

Missy was a dedicated housekeeper, but she was even more dedicated to her daughter's upbringing. Freedom was a gift from God. She would make sure that her daughter would enjoy all of the benefits of freedom, and none of the hostilities that plagued her race.

Cincinnati was a dichotomy, bordered on the south by slave state Kentucky, and by the Ohio River, which was a much-crossed waterway on the road to Canada for runaway slaves. The city was one of the first in the nation to provide schools for black children; those schools had their own boards of education. But there were also race riots. An early abolitionist paper, *The Philanthropist,* was driven out of town by mob violence, and forced to re-locate in the Quaker village of Springboro, thirty miles to the north.

There were Cincinnati stalwarts in the fight for equal rights. Author Harriett Beecher Stowe grew up in a house on the east side which gave refuge to runaways. There was Levi Coffin. There was newspaper editor Achilles Pugh.

There were also scores of lurking bounty hunters on the prowl for possible financial rewards by locating, apprehending, and returning to the South those runaways not wrapped in the safe arms of the Underground Railroad.

But the cream-colored mother with the elegant neck and the ample bosom played upon the positives, working for a respectable family which detested slavery, and loved her and her daughter. She enrolled Annalise in one of the finest black schools in the city, less than a mile from the O'Neill house. Missy would walk Annalise to school each morning, and return for her in the afternoon. If the weather was foul, Herman

O'Neill would drive the child to her school in a carriage. Maribel O'Neill, for her part, bought Annalise clothes and school books.

Annalise inhaled books and knowledge. It became apparent to her instructors that the little light-skinned freed slave was highly intelligent and remarkably social. At home, Annalise borrowed textbooks from the O'Neill daughters, and as if by osmosis, picked up a vocabulary, reading skills, and attitudes far more mature than her peers.

Soon the daughter was teaching the mother.

"Mamma, see this map in my book. This is Georgia, and this is where we are now."

"Such a big country, little girl."

"Mamma, "Cincinnati" has three "n's"

"That so?"

"Yes. We never have to go back to Georgia, will we, Mamma?"

"No. We finished with Georgia. We through with mean white people."

Missy had picked up the rudiments of house-keeping quickly, and soon expanded her responsibilities to cook, under Maribel's tutelage. She valued the evenings in the cottage with her daughter, who endlessly shared what she was learning. In time, the daughter taught the mother to read.

As the years passed, both thrived. The O'Neills were benevolent employers. When the older daughter married, 10-year old Annalise was the flower girl. Missy sat with the family, and wept when she saw her beautiful daughter in a white dress, beaming as she walked down the aisle.

One day in 1858, after Annalise turned thirteen, Missy disappeared.

She had walked her daughter to school, and didn't return to the O'Neill home. Initial worry turned to fear as Maribel realized that her housekeeper must be in trouble. Missy had walked that route for seven years. She wouldn't have gotten lost. That evening, Herman picked up the girl at school. The family contacted the police and Levi Coffin. There was no trace of Missy.

Weeks passed, then years. The realization settled in that Missy was gone for good, foul play probably, and that they would never see her again.

****

It was a question that he too had been pondering, somewhat fearful of the truth. It was posed by Margaret one evening in front of the fireplace, with Jack Bertrand sitting on the floor nearby, boots off, the soles of his feet turned to the fire.

"Whit, are we safe out here?"

"Sure, Darlin'. Unless we get another bad blizzard, or another wind storm. Don't you feel safe here?"

Jack had a sense of both the pertinence of the question, and of his uncle evading a relevant reply.

The room got quiet as each of the three considered what to say next, the only sound the noise of the firewood spitting and crackling.

"Whit, don't you know what I'm asking? I think we need to talk about it.," she said, her comment interrupted several times as she paused to fold clothes.

"Yes, Maggie dear, I know what you're asking…how soon before the slavery warfare reaches us." He paused and got up. "Now where did I put my pipe?"

"It's in your front pants pocket. You put it there five minutes ago."

He extracted the shiny pipe and a wadded bag of tobacco from his pocket, took his time tamping a new load, and stuck a kindling stick into the fire to get a light. He began talking between puffs as the pipe lit.

"Well, I'm not sure…to be honest. I haven't followed…the news very closely. Almost out of tobacco."

"Uncle Whit, you've told me about the war on the border, about Lawrence and Osawatomie. I picked up some more on my way out here two years ago. So far the battles and raids have either been in Missouri, or right across the border here in Kansas. That could expand, maybe this way. There are a lot of people involved," Jack offered.

"Well, let me ask you this. Why would either side come out here to cause trouble? We're ninety miles or so from the battlefront, if that's what it is. No pro-slavery or Free State people out here. Just us and the cows."

"This whole territory might explode someday soon. If I ride in here, Uncle Whit, I see free men succeeding in a large way, indications that we are on the anti-slavery side. Good sign for an anti-slaver. Might irritate me if I'm a pro-slavery man."

"Most of the raids have occurred in the larger settlements near the border, or close. Don't think anybody is going to travel three days to harass 12 people on a farm."

"Whit, do you know more than you're telling? You were in the Topeka settlement last week. Was there any news?"

"You mean anything to calm you down, Maggie?"

"I'm serious. You know that I trust everything you tell me, if you're telling me everything."

"Think of it this way. When all of this was starting, the territory was begging people to settle here. They still are. Don't think they'd be attracting people to a battlefield."

"From what I've heard, Aunt Margaret, they'd be attracting people to join one of the two sides."

Whit scowled at him, nodded toward Margaret, and shook his head from side to side.

Jack continued, "Of course, sometimes I get the wrong impression."

"You two can continue the debate," Margaret said, patting the stack of the small stack of laundry, "I'm going to bed." She rose to move next to Whit, and kissed the top of his head. He looked up and kissed her on the mouth.

"I'll be up in a while, Maggie."

After he heard the bedroom door close upstairs, Jack addressed the issue again.

"Aren't you really worried, Uncle Whit?"

"Of course, I'm worried. There aren't many people out here, but we stick out. Biggest ranch in western Kansas. But, near as I can tell, most of the homesteaders near us are no more than good people trying to make do. There's no reason for either side of the slavery issue to come after them. Some of the leaders of the violence have moved on, anyway. Heard that the John Brown fella from Pottawotamie Creek moved back east some time ago."

"You think the hostilities are over?"

"No. If this territory ever gets statehood, or if there's any reason for a vote on the slavery issue, or –Heaven forbid—if this country ever fights a war against itself, it'll be much worse. So far, unless I've missed something, the worst incidents in the last three years have been the Wakarusa War, Pottawatomie, Osawatomie, several incidents in Lawrence, and lots of skirmishes along the border. We'll have to pay attention, and that's tough way out here. If any of this moves inland, we'll have to be on guard. Anyway, nothing lasts forever. This is our land. If wc have to leave it for a while, so be it. We'll come back later and start over."

Jack could tell that it was difficult for Whit to speak the last two sentences.

"The Wakarusa War? Don't know about that one," Jack said.

"That happened before you came out, '55, I believe. It started with a killing, and then the Missourians came in and laid siege to Lawrence. John Brown had just come to Kansas, and he raised an army and defended the city. The Missourians were 1,500 strong by that time, and they had cannons, stolen from an Arsenal back in Missouri. Turned into a lot of posturing and bluffing. A treaty of peace was signed, and everyone went home. One man killed. The scary part was the number of pro-slavery men raised by their side, and the fact that they had cannons. It showed everyone that the issue had reached new levels."

"What about cattle drives ? We have to go toward the border every year."

"Nobody will interfere with that. Kansas City is safe, near as I can tell. Nobody will try to take on cowpunchers."

Both men stared into the dying fire for several minutes. Jack got up to return to the bunkhouse. Whit sat alone, trying unsuccessfully to re-light his pipe.

CHAPTER NINETEEN

1859

More than half of the New England foliage had fallen by mid-October, leaving a reduced collection of yellows, browns, and oranges on the Burlington hillsides.

The afternoon sun burned the cool autumn air as a string of carriages, wagons, and horses lined the lane to the Chase house, and the shuffling of many footsteps crunched the fallen leaves.

Inside the house, a procession of mourners filed past the seated Jeremiah Chase for hours, commiserating with the professor over the loss of Molly, his wife of over 30 years. She had succumbed a week earlier, the culmination of several years of failing health. The gradual decline did not prepare Jeremiah for the finality of the past seven days. The anguish was only multiplied by the well-intentioned friends from all over the Northeast, who visited on this Sunday to offer condolences. Among the group were old friends, legislators, much of academe, former students, and virtually the entire population of Burlington.

The spacious house seemed suddenly too small, but the entire scenario was presided over and orchestrated by the professor's sons, together again for the first time in over a year. Joshua, an officer in the Army Corps of Engineers, stood next to his father for the entire ordeal, shaking hands, making small talk, and deftly keeping the line moving past his grieving father. Jonathan worked the room, keeping plates full, introducing people to each other, and answering questions about his recent life in Virginia. Jefferson was stationed on the porch greeting newcomers and listening to myriad stories about his parents from those who weren't ready to leave.

A full moon shone on the last mourners to depart. Jeremiah excused himself to his sons and retreated to the privacy of his bedroom, weeping audibly as he left them in the living room.

"Let's take a walk," Joshua suggested to his brothers.

"Joshua, this house is a mess. Maybe we ought to start cleaning it," Jonathan said.

"No, later. We need to walk some things off."

The three strolled past the stables. No one had spoken yet.

"You know this may be that last time the three of us walk this farm together," Jefferson offered.

"Jeff, we'll be here often. If Father's here, we'll be back," Jonathan corrected.

"No. Jeff's right, Jon. Father won't stay here long. Too many memories. Too much loneliness. The two of them made this a home."

"I think that's why he buried her in town, instead of on a hill out here," Jefferson added.

"Father is failing too. There is more going on with him than grieving. The farm would be a burden. Much better to preserve good thoughts about it by leaving it," Joshua said.

"It'll be difficult to think of anywhere else he goes as home."

"Either of you interested in buying this from him, or inheriting it?" Joshua asked.

"I'm going to move back here until he's settled. Two years, at most. Long term? No," Jefferson answered.

"My life is in Virginia now. You, Joshua?"

"I love this place. But the timing is terrible. I wasn't going to make the military a career, but I think we're on the verge of a civil war."

"A war? Over slavery?"

"That and other things, Jeff. States' rights. Economic concerns. Ways of life. There's a rift now, and frankly, I don't see any way to avoid conflict," Joshua asserted.

"Now listen. The southern states aren't unreasonable. If the Northern states modify their philosophies somewhat, there can be a workable truce," Jonathan asserted.

"An uneasy truce at best, Jon. In my humble opinion, any alteration of philosophies has to start in the South. There's an unhealthy attitude down there that compromise won't solve," Joshua stated. He was looking at Jonathan, and a hint of a smile had disappeared.

"That's an attitude too. You have no idea about anything south of the Vermont state line," Jonathan countered. He glared at his brother. They had stopped walking.

"Sounds as if living in the South had clouded your normally astute mind," Joshua retorted.

"Wait a minute, Joshua. You are the epitome of a Northerner…pompous, and more than a little self-serving. Compromise is impossible with you people."

"Hey. We just buried a woman who thought you two were the most incredible adults she knew. Why don't we change the subject?" Jefferson stood between his brothers.

The other two looked at him and smiled.

"Jeffie, why are you always avoiding conflict?" Jonathon asked.

Jefferson grinned. The banter had turned to him. The discussion had dropped away before it became heated beyond repair. "It takes a cool head to keep you hotheads in line," he said.

Jonathan resumed walking. "I'm going to miss her. Father was our inspiration. She was our rock."

"We got the best of both of them. She had a huge heart, but ironically, it was not a strong one," Joshua added.

"I heard a lot of stories about them today. Did you know that Father was engaged to an actress before he met Mother," Jefferson asked.

"An actress? You mean an heiress?"

"Actress. He was in Boston for two years after he was graduated from the university. He fell in love with an actress named Dreama Lively. He came here to teach, met Mother, and broke off the engagement."

"Dreama Lively?" Jonathan said.

"That's the story. Also heard that Mother's family was related to Ethan Allen. She never mentioned that."

"Of course not," Joshua offered, "That would have been about her. She was all about us."

"After Mother and Father got married, they were supposed to go on a two-month honeymoon, a cruise to Europe, or something. Instead they sneaked to the farm and honeymooned here. They wanted to be alone. Nobody knew they were in Vermont," Jefferson laughed.

"A neighbor of hers from the early years told me today that she was the most beautiful girl in Vermont. I thanked him for the comment, and he got a bit angry. Told me it was true. 'Ask anybody' he said." Jonathan added.

"Speaking of beautiful girls, we missed your wife this week."

"Well…I suppose it's time for an announcement." Jonathan had hitherto been evasive about Catharine's absence.

"Yeah…? Do we need to prepare for this?" Jefferson asked.

"Sure. You've never been uncles before."

"Uncles? Catharine's pregnant," Joshua said.

"Due in four months. Her doctor didn't want her traveling."

"That's great, Jon, great," Jefferson enthused.

"Why so secretive about it?" Joshua asked.

"We had to be sure. Then we had to get used to it. This week it's secondary. We all needed to think about Mother this week."

"When will you tell Father?"

"In time. He's going to be distracted for a while. Too much emotion now."

"I'm thrilled for you, Jon," Joshua grabbed his brother in a hug which lasted several moments.

"Uncle Jeff…I like it." Jefferson wrapped his brother in another celebratory hug.

"I'm on a streak of luck... I'm married to an incredible lady, we're both doing meaningful work, and now this."

"Catherine had been good for you."

"She's just short of amazing. Intelligent, well-read, personable, gorgeous."

"That's great, Jon. You deserve the best. Don't know what she's thinking though," Joshua teased.

The three walked silently again, stopping at the brook, which was shielded from the moonlight by the thick woods. The gurgling of the stream was the only sound for a while. They turned without speaking and started back.

"Race you to the house!" Jefferson blurted.

"Jeff, that's a half-mile," Jonathan protested, continuing to walk. Then suddenly he broke into a full sprint.

Joshua was soon only steps behind him, and Jefferson's long legs soon caught up.

The race was not without peril. The three ducked branches and jumped logs barely visible in the darkness. Jefferson stumbled into a rut, rolled, and was back on his feet, abreast of the others, who had slowed to laugh at their floundering brother. They arrived at the porch together, kicking dirt onto its floor as they abruptly stopped.

"You…OK…Jeff?" Joshua gasped.

"Sure…I almost…beat you...with…a broken...leg," he wheezed back.

"Guess we'll… have to…shoot you," Jonathan said, bending over to recover.

"You two…run pretty well…for old…guys."

"You've grown up… in the past two years, little brother," Joshua said.

It was true, he noted, as he sat on the top porch step. Jefferson was noticeably taller than his brothers and broad-shouldered, a formidable young man. Again, there were minutes of silence.

"How long can you stay, Jon?"

"A couple of days. Jeff will be here for Father. I need to get back to Catharine."

Jefferson sat on the bottom step, stretching his legs in front of him. "Joshua, we've been here four days. I haven't heard you mention a girl's name."

"There are a few names I could say, but with little conviction. It hasn't happened for me yet." He glanced up at the autumn moon.

"Why?"

"I haven't met a young lady who compares to Mother. More important, a relationship with any of them wouldn't match the one I watched growing up."

"Out of all of the lessons they taught us, that was the most important. Love and respect. Family," Jonathan said.

"Without an anchor here, there is a strong possibility that the three of us will grow apart. We can't let that happen, whatever life, geography…or political beliefs have planned for us," Joshua looked at Jonathan as he finished the thought.

"It already has to some extent. We're in three different states in totally different circumstances," Jonathon offered.

"Father always told us to follow our own stars, but we'll always be brothers, whatever happens," Jefferson interjected.

"True. The world will change dramatically in the next decade, and men will be tested in many ways."

"We going to discuss imminent war again?" Jonathan asked.

"I guess I'm a fatalist. Sorry. Jeff, what star are you following now?"

"Veterinary medicine wasn't right for me. The science is underdeveloped and more rigid than I envisioned. That's why I'll come back here for a while. I need time to pick another star."

Jonathan chuckled. "Jeff, you'll stay here. Your star has always been this farm, this land."

"Not necessarily. It's a big country. There are some interesting things happening on the frontier."

"Father would approve of that thought," Joshua said, "new frontiers excited him more than anything, except his family."

They sat quietly for a few minutes, each with his own thoughts, but all silently reminiscing about life on the farm, and about the old man asleep inside.

CHAPTER TWENTY
1860

At the age of fifty-one, Jonah Brooks had not slowed down. In fact, his life had accelerated. His flock had grown exponentially as Syracuse itself grew. They had built a grand new church for him, a holy edifice with living quarters, a magnificent stage for his increasingly bold outbursts against slavery and the institutions which supported it.

He did not make as many trips toward the lake with runaways as he had a decade earlier, but he was in command of a vast network of brave souls who did. His name was bandied about on a national level, a champion of the oppressed, a holy man who fought for equality.

Former antagonists, like Daniel Webster, were either dead -- Webster fell from a horse and died soon thereafter in 1852-- or fearful of taking on a minister who was a formidable, popular opponent.

Some said that he should run for public office. That had little appeal for him. Others suggested that he broaden his geographical influence with public appearances all over the country.

He resisted the prodding, content to direct all of his passions from upper New York state. That is, until the receipt of a letter in 1860.

The letter had been posted in Washington, and in the upper left hand corner was the name *Albert B. Greenwood.* Underneath were four lines of wordy identification:

Commissioner of Indian Affairs; Bureau of Indian Affairs; Department of the Interior; Washington DC, USA.

He began reading the stilted language of bureaucracy.

My Dear Sir:

You have established an honorable name in your dealings with the downtrodden and the destitute. Your charity and equitable administration of difficulties involving those less fortunate have been brought to the attention of our President.

The Honorable James Buchanan has authorized me to offer you a position which will enable you to utilize your capable energies on behalf of a nation of Sioux Indians.

We endeavor to superintend relations with various tribes with non-discrimination and justice. The President believes that you would represent both the interests of government and the needs of tribesmen, with acumen and wisdom.

Currently there are two Indian agencies in the Great State of Minnesota. We would ask you to entertain the supervision of what is called the Upper Agency. The govern-

ment will pay you appropriately, and will reimburse you for costs incurred in moving to that area.

Policy to date has been to appoint military personnel or career diplomats to such positions. The President believes that the appointment of a gentleman with both a religious background and experience with those of special needs is a direction that our nation needs to explore.

I will be in Syracuse on 6 June, 1860, and will come on that afternoon to your place of worship. I will be honored to discuss this matter with you.

Respectfully, I Remain
Albert B. Greenwood

Not interested, Jonah thought. Completely not interested. There was still work to do in New York, and if his friends in politics had analyzed correctly, a war would soon be fought to end slavery in America. He felt momentary pride that he was known to the President. He would talk to Greenwood. He would listen to the Commissioner, but in the end he would tell him, "No thanks."

On the way back to Washington by rail, flushed with success, Albert Greenwood began to open up to his new aide, Benjamin DeWitt.

"President Buchanan will love this concept."

"Sir, I thought he had already agreed to it."

"Not yet. I invoked his name to sway Reverend Brooks."

"Why exactly is his appointment desirable?"

"We need an independent sort out there. We need a recognizable name. We need someone who will make decisions based on what is good for both sides. There is too much unrest out there."

"Sides, Sir?"

"You are new to all of this. The Indians are a nuisance, DeWitt. Perhaps too needy. Certainly too unpredictable. We need a strong hand. From what we know about Brooks, he's a no-nonsense individual. He will be kind to the Sioux, but he will also hold them responsible. He is fair. He will make the government look good."

"But he hasn't agreed to take the position."

"He didn't tell us 'no'. He was going to, but he listened, and more than that, he asked questions. I think we convinced him that the slavery issue will be settled directly, one way or another. The new concentration will be on the Indian problems."

Jonah decided to drive a wagon to Minnesota. He could take his time, fish and camp along the way. A series of goodbyes from his parishioners had worn him out, and truthfully, had kept him emotionally off balance. He would leave in July. They would expect him at the Yellow Medicine Agency by mid-August.

His talk with Greenwood had countered almost every objection he had about assuming the new responsibility.

"These people are gentle, peace-loving, and confused," Greenwood had explained. "They need mentors and advocates. They need to grow into valuable citizens. A man like yourself can make that happen.

"Without contributions by you, the tribe will die out, I guarantee it. The government can do only so much. It takes the personal touch of a man like you, a man they respect, to guide them to prosperity and happiness."

"Am I to force religion into their lives?"

"That is up to you, Sir, although that is certainly a consideration."

"I do not see that as a worthy objective. They have their own religion, their own beliefs."

"Fine, Reverend Brooks. But I do believe that many are willing to learn about our ways and our beliefs."

"And if I am not a good fit?"

"You can resign at any time, and return here. If, however, your experience with them is as valuable as I expect, you will be doing a great service to your country."

Privately, Jonah had begun to sift through the ramifications of the assignment after Greenwood left. The position as protector/missionary would continue those things that he was most qualified for, most passionate about. He would be returning to the wilderness, the venue he used to renew himself; the Syracuse area was growing, too fast. He would be too old to contribute to a soldier's role, if a war between the states did begin, so he would have no meaningful role in that eventuality. This would be a contribution to the evolution of his country. He began to lean toward accepting. First, he would have to talk to Loguen.

Jonah's route took him along the shores of Lake Ontario and Lake Erie, across the southern tip of Michigan, and around Lake Michigan. It was a revitalizing journey, fraught with rolling landscapes and interesting small towns. As he struck out across Wisconsin, the wilderness increased, and the endless forests of evergreens were suffused with lakes of all sizes.

He skirted the larger cities, and somctimes set up camp in the early afternoon to take full advantage of fishing opportunities. He was well past any regrets or misgivings about his new calling. They had evaporated early in the weeks-long trip to the northland, lost in the profusion of experiences that he most treasured.

The Indian Agencies of Minnesota were awash in ineptitude, and were pointedly questionable. As with other agencies across the country, there was mismanagement, and carelessness and apathy. The two in Minnesota were pitiable stretches of land, 20 miles wide, and seventy miles long, in the southwest portion of the state, hard by the upper Minnesota River. The Lower Agency was across the river from Fort Ridgely, which had the primary responsibility for the reservation, and within ten miles of New Ulm.

The Upper Agency was forty miles to the north, just above the Yellow Medicine River, and somewhat isolated. Hutchinson was the nearest community, and it was a hard day's ride to the east. The large Big Stone Lake formed the northeast boundary. This was the charge waiting for the Reverend Jonah Brooks.

He had tried to research the area and its history, and had mailed numerous questions to Washington. The answers he got were circumspect, uninformative, but he had learned that over 7,000 Dakota Sioux were sequestered on the thin swatch of land.

He might have questioned his choice if more information had been available. He didn't discover until he arrived that the tribe had hatred for white men, the product of broken promises and cruelty.

Two treaties in 1851 ceded large chunks of Indian land to the government. In return, the tribe was promised money, and goods of all descriptions, in perpetuity.

Most of the promised money never reached the tribe, stolen or misappropriated by shady employees of the Bureau of Indian Affairs. Corruption also consumed annuity payments guaranteed to the Dakota. Settlers flocked to the ceded land and commenced to clear the land for agriculture. Logging and farming destroyed forests and prairies, and virtually eliminated game which the Indians used for food and the sales of furs to trappers.

Their farming, hunting, and fishing in jeopardy, the Sioux tried to make the most of reservation land, but much of that land was prone to flooding or not arable. Crop failure led to food shortages, and then to famine, and then to angry discontent.

Their nominal leader, Little Crow, an ineffectual chief at best, made a trip to Washington to complain. The government laughed at him. Disgraced and mocked, he slinked back to his tribesmen.

On the brink of a civil war, the U.S. government could not be distracted by events on a reservation. It would be better to employ men of no-nonsense, men of stature and proven integrity, to control the mess. Men of God could stabilize the unrest, and in the process, possibly convert the heathen tendencies to upstanding Christian tenets.

That theory resulted in the recruiting of Jonah Brooks. He could provide stability in the Upper Agency. The Lower Agency was overseen by Minnesota State Senator Thomas Galbraith.

Jonah neared the end of his journey, thoroughly refreshed and focused. He cut across the state from St. Paul and Minneapolis, and then headed southwest to check in at Fort Ridgely. He was led into the office of Thomas Galbraith.

"Reverend Brooks, I'm glad you're here. I've been expecting you."

Jonah was invited to sit by the reedy man, who smiled broadly at him. Galbraith was dressed in a suit and a starched shirt with a precisely-tied cravat. Jonah noticed his highly polished shoes. Not an outdoor type, he guessed.

"Can I get you something, sir?" Galbraith asked. He even smiled when he talked.

"A glass of water, maybe. I'm a bit surprised that you're here at the fort. This is your headquarters?"

"Yes, Reverend Brooks. The Lower Agency is close by. I can manage affairs from here, a little less lonely, with conveniences."

"I was told that I'd have accommodations on the reservation land."

"And you will, sir. But the Upper Agency is miles from here. I'll give you directions before you leave. It should take maybe two days."

The smile was making Jonah nervous, and he surmised that it was a politician's smile, a vote gathering smile.

"What should I know before I head up there?"

"We're having some trouble with the Indians. They have a couple of real firebrands. Up your way are the Sissetowan and Wahpeton camps. They're relatively quiet. Down here we have the Mdewakantons and the Wahpekutes. And we've got Little Crow, the chief. You've heard of him? I don't trust the man."

"What kind of trouble?"

"So far just attitude. Nothing major yet. What the Indians do is conduct business with the trappers, and run up debts. Then they don't pay them. But they still expect money from us. We take their government money and pay off their debts. They don't much like that."

"So the trappers sell them things without collecting payment?"

"They do. If they didn't, the Indians couldn't buy what they do."

"But I was told that the government's treaty money was generous."

For the first time, the smile disappeared. "The tribe doesn't understand money. They squander it, misuse it. The government will not coddle them."

"Seems to me that the government has a responsibility to coddle them. We've changed their lives and their livelihood."

"Reverend Brooks, you'll soon see what I'm talking about. You'll see for yourself."

"I'm not fluent in their language. Is that a problem?"

"We've got help for you up there, an interpreter named Cleetus Wilburn. Odd little fellow. Quiet. Lives right at the agency. Has an Indian wife, Bear Woman, more white than Indian by now. Her English is as good as his Sioux. You'll have two interpreters, if you need them."

"So, my job is to make friends, disperse money, interact with trappers, and distribute goods?"

"Yes, except that I distribute the goods and most of the money for both agencies from here. And you should know, Reverend Brooks, that I have the ultimate say on any dispute."

"With the Indians? Or with me?"

"Both, sir, although I will consult with you frequently. Now, let's find you a place to clean up. I suppose that you'll be leaving at daylight."

Pompous. Too slick. Jonah suspected that he would have more trouble with Galbraith than with the Sioux.

A bumpy ride under a gray sky took Jonah to a clearing just beyond a forest of second-growth pine trees. He saw a long wooden building, dilapidated rather than sturdy, with broken windows and a scrawled sign that announced "Indian Agency, BIA, USA."

Beyond was a cluster of three modest log cabins in a semi-circle. The one on the right was separated from the other two, and on the warm afternoon, the front door was open. He heard a woman's voice singing from the inside. He moved his wagon toward that cabin.

A woman stepped onto the front porch, wiping her hands on her apron. She was dressed in a red, blousy shirt and a faded blue skirt, and her shiny hair was pulled back and plaited in a single braid. She was buxom, pleasant-looking, with round cheeks and a dimpled chin.The hands on her apron were large, and had obviously chopped firewood and skinned animals for years. She was agreeable to look at, even attractive, younger than he'd imagined.

"Good afternoon. You be the Reverend Brooks?"

"I am. You'd be Bear Woman."

"My Sioux name in your language. Never like it much. My husband call me 'Bea'. You can call me Bea too. Bea Wilburn."

"You can call me Jonah. Never liked it much either."

He liked her instantly. Some sixth sense told him that she was gentle, kind, dependable.

"Is Mr. Wilburn around?"

"Fishing for supper. He back in a coupla hours. We don't expect you yet."

"One of these cabins is mine?"

"Next one. Bed made. Clean. Food and coffee on shelves. Firewood in back for winter. Plenty cold here."

"I'm used to the cold. That last cabin?"

"Yours too. Do what you want. You a minister. Make a good church."

"I'll take a look around. Is there a place for the horses?"

"Cleetus build a small barn, down that path. Big enough for wagon too."

"Thank you. I'll be back when your husband returns."

"Yes, you will. You will eat with us tonight?"

"I'd like that."

"Water down that path too. A spring. Always running. Always cold."

"I'll see you later, Bea Wilburn."

She smiled warmly at him.

His cabin was spotless. Curtains of a calico material covered three small windows. It was good-sized, carefully pointed so that no air seeped in between walls; the adz marks were barely visible. A heavy blanket of red and yellow was nailed to one wall. Furniture, obviously crafted on site, included a wide bed, a desk, a wash stand, a long table with benches, and three chairs arranged around a fireplace large enough to cook from. On the wall next to the door was a bearskin, stretched and clean. A simple bureau was next to the bed. Jonah was impressed.

The headquarters building was another story. It was bare and dusty. It had obviously not been used for some time. A shadow appeared on the floor next to him.

"Pardon me. I am Cleetus Wilburn."

He turned to face a man of African descent, a dark and muscular little man with a barrel chest. He stood no taller than Jonah's shoulders. A scar ran from his left eyebrow to his chin, and his left eye was squinted, probably from that injury. Otherwise, he had a refined look, ruggedly handsome, with gray-flecked stubble from several days of not shaving.

Jonah offered his hand, and noticed that the man's eyes never left his during the firm handshake.

"Mr. Wilburn. How are you?"

"Well."

"I've heard that we'll be working together, Mr. Wilburn."

Wilburn nodded, but said nothing.

"What do you do besides interpret?"

"Arrange meetings. Carry messages. Build things. Repair things. Stack firewood." The last item was accompanied by the hint of a smile. It disappeared immediately.

"You are on the government payroll? They pay you?"

"Some. Not what you'd call generous."

"I understand that you work for both agencies, but report to me. That it?"

Wilburn nodded again.

"This building's not very promising."

"I let it go. It's never been used. I plan to use the materials to build other things."

"My cabin is good, very nice."

"Mrs. Wilburn."

"Mr. Wilburn, will you show me around tomorrow?"

"Where?"

"Show me anything you think that I should see within ten miles of here. I'll meet you here in the morning, maybe an hour after sunrise."

"You have a horse?"

"I'll saddle up one of the wagon's horses. I've done it before."

"Mrs. Wilburn said to tell you that we'll eat at dusk. Nothing fancy."

"Thank you. I'll be there."

Had it not been for Bear Woman, the meal would have been awkward. Cleetus was still sizing him up, Jonah guessed. She carried the conversation, lively and animated.

"You are a man of God. You will hold services for the Sioux?"

"Only if they want me to. I'm not here to promote religion, just to see that everyone gets a fair shake."

"Cleetus and I, we believe in God. Your God. Too many good things happen for us not to."

"That's a nice way to look at it."

Jonah tried to rouse Cleetus. "I know you were fishing today. That's one of my favorite things to do. Would you show me some good spots?"

"Yes, I'll do that."

"Hunting too. I haven't done much of that, however."

Cleetus was quiet. Bear Woman jumped in. "Not good here. Settlers drive away most of the game. Or kill it."

"Really?"

"Cleetus is good hunter, good provider," Bear Woman said, glancing fondly at her husband. "He brings meat for us, and many times takes deer or bear to villages."

"I'm guessing that you two get along well with the Sioux."

She waited for Cleetus to answer. When that seemed unlikely, she responded. "The Sioux are my people. They look on Cleetus with kind eyes, because he is fair to them, and because he makes me happy."

As the meal ended, Bear Woman stood up. "You go on porch. Talk a while. I clean up here."

Jonah didn't want to continue the awkwardness on the porch. There'd be ample time the next day to try to draw out the interpreter. "I think I'll turn in," he said.

"Thank you for the meal, Mrs. Wilburn. Mr. Wilburn, I'll see you in the morning."

The wife smiled.

Cleetus nodded, but said nothing.

The two followed a meandering trail for four hours, stopping briefly at two villages, and skirting several holy sites. Cleetus identified them as burial grounds. They stopped at the Yellow Medicine River to water the horses.

"Good fishing, just west of here, off of the reservation," Cleetus offered, the first conversation initiative from him to that point.

"Cleetus, we'll be working together. Tell me about yourself."

"Not much to tell." He looked away, upriver.

During the silence that followed, Jonah was giving up. What had Galbraith called him, an "odd little fellow"?

Cleetus looked directly at him, then looked away. In a low voice, he said, "I was a slave. Still am, I guess."

"A slave?"

"In Tennessee, a long time ago."

"How'd you end up in Minnesota?"

"Ran away. I was just short of 30. Ran from a family called Spalding. Took too many beatings. Almost lost an eye. Got up here with a lot of help from good folks."

"When did this happen?"

"About ten years ago. Made it up here. Could either go to Canada, or stay up here somewhere. This was wilderness back then, a good place to hide."

Jonah dropped the reins from his horse, which waded into knee-deep water to drink. He moved back onto the bank and sat down. "You're still hiding?"

"You have to know that I could still be caught. Could still be returned to slavery. Found out who I can trust. Been avoiding everyone else."

"So you hid here."

"In the wilderness mostly. I wasn't really prepared for that. Stole some things to survive over at the trading post at Shakopee. I'm not proud of that. Worked for a while at Fort Snelling for the army, tending animals. When Minneapolis started to get crowded, I followed the Minnesota River west. They were building Fort Ridgely. Went to find work and ended up joining the army."

Jonah stayed quiet during the little man's soliloquy. When Cleetus paused, Jonah prompted him, "Go on please."

"I stayed with them almost five years. Wasn't much to do over there." Cleetus too walked to the bank and sat. "Sergeant named Oliver more or less adopted me; learned a lot from him. I met Bear Woman there back in 1855. She was a widow. Her husband drowned. She was staying at the fort. I loved her manner. Thought she was beautiful."

"She is beautiful, Cleetus."

For the first time in two days, Cleetus smiled.

"We were married at the fort four years ago. Best thing I ever did."

"So you brought her out here."

"When I asked out of the army, they wanted me to come up here, and watch over things on the reservation. Built the three cabins, one each year. Bear Woman helped. Been here ever since."

"You happy here?"

"Mostly. I love Bea and I love the wilderness. Little rugged here in the winter. Don't much like what's happening to the Sioux."

"I got one story from Galbraith. Yours different?"

"Traders come in with fancy prices for goods. Tell the Sioux they can pay later. They can't; they end up owing more than their allotment."

"But don't they get deliveries of goods free? That was in the treaty."

"No. Not until they pay their other bills."

"Don't the Indian agents, or the Bureau, see what's happening?"

"They don't seem to care much. Myrick, the trader's man, is worthless."

Jonah felt an anger rising, the same feeling he had reacted to so many times in Syracuse.

"Thanks for the information. I'll go back over to Fort Ridgely tomorrow. Be gone a few days. I've got to get a better understanding of this. Thanks too for telling me about yourself. For many years I tried to assist runaway slaves."

"I know that."

"You know that?"

"You are well-known here. The Sioux call you 'God's Eye' because you watched over runaway slaves."

" 'God's Eye.' Be difficult to live up to that."

Jonah rose early, and was short-cutting behind the Wilburn cabin to the path which led to the barn when he saw a sight which not only startled him, but also troubled him for weeks.

There, just a few feet from the back door of the interpreter's cabin, angled away from view from the other cabins, was Bear Woman, unclothed, bathing from a large bowl of water. She had the bowl above her head, pouring a torrent of water onto her face and hair, which hung behind her. Her back was arched; her eyes were closed.

Jonah looked away immediately, but in that brief instant he had gotten several impressions. She was slimmer than she looked in clothing, and considerably endowed. He bolted toward the path, snapping fallen twigs in his haste. He hoped that she hadn't seen him. He was sure that she had.

He was appalled at this misfortune. She would think that he was spying on her. He had violated her privacy. And he had just forged a semblance of trust with Cleetus the day before. That was probably in jeopardy too. He cursed the encounter. It would haunt him for a long time, and affect his camaraderie with the couple.

He had no idea that Bear Woman had giggled at the intrusion. She had recognized by his frantic scurrying that he had stumbled onto her ritual by accident, and that he was profoundly embarrassed. She'd tell Cleetus.

Or maybe she wouldn't.

****

His fist crunched against her face again and she tasted blood. She dared to open her eyes to see if he would deliver another punch, but he was caught in the moment before orgasm, his head back, his face distorted, his eyes squeezed shut.

Then he began pumping again, brutally pushing against her in rapid movements, and then it was over.

She had survived another terrible moment with this smelly, brutal man. He withdrew, and got up snorting, and she curled into a ball, and turned from him, burying her face in the soiled pillow.

She turned her head slightly and again opened her eyes and realized that her left eye was swelling shut. This time there would be bruises all over her body, and she knew there would be more before these healed. When this happened, sometimes twice a week, she thought of her daughter.

That thought alone kept her alive, kept her from fighting back or trying a foolhardy escape. Somehow she would survive this. Some day she would see Annalise again. She would plan a workable escape, or maybe someone would find her. The latter was improbable; she had no idea where she was.

She had been on her way to see Levi Coffin so many months ago, when two men stopped their carriage to offer her a ride. When she ignored them, one jumped from the seat and clubbed her to the ground. In the following days, she was beaten senseless any time she tried to resist or to protest. They hadn't forced themselves on her, but the next three men had, taking turns with her for two terrible nights. She had a vague memory of being carried onto a steamship with others of her race and of two of them jumping overboard into the river. She had the notion that she would jump too, but she didn't get the chance. There was a long journey without food. One of the men brought her water in a pan. During the day, she was left alone, chained to the bed in a small stateroom. At night the three returned to rape her, and then the journey ended.

She was taken off of the boat to a noisy building, and shoved into a room where two more men pawed her, sneered at her. She heard the details of a sale.

Then there was another journey on land, and finally a cabin. There was a plantation, and slaves friendly to her. But nightly for weeks, she was summoned to the big house to be a bed warmer for two of the men who had brought her here. At times, she tried to hide or to feign sickness. Each time she was beaten.

That seemed to be her assigned responsibility. Little else had been required of her. Lately, other women and young slave girls had been sharing her terror-filled lot. Her hope for survival rose with her reduced status. Some time ago, she had to submit at least three nights a week; most recently it had become two. She was much less desirable now, thin, spiritless, battered. Soon they would tire of her. Then what? Undoubtedly she would be sent to the fields with the other slaves. She had to outlast these men.

Across the room, he was breathing heavily. He had been staring at her naked body, and was preparing himself for another go. She wouldn't resist at all this time. She would give in meekly, and even encourage him with movements and whispered words. That would end it more quickly.

Abruptly he was at the bed, and roughly turned her over, face down, holding her head against the pillow. Then he entered her from the rear, and the pain made her gasp, then scream.

"Shut up, bitch!" he snarled, and grabbed her hair and pulled her backwards until her body was arched in an awkward position. He violently thrust against her. Excruciating pain made her teeth gnash, and she realized that she was crying.

It will be over soon, she thought. Then his hands were around her neck, squeezing, and she fought for air. As he neared climax, his hands increased their pressure. She was losing consciousness. I won't let this happen, she thought. I will live through this for my daughter.

Then Missy Ollimore blacked out.

CHAPTER TWENTY-ONE

1861

South Carolina had seceded from the Union in December of 1860. Six other states followed suit. The seven formed the Confederate States of America.

On April 12 of 1861, Confederate batteries began to shell Fort Sumter, a Union-held fort in Charleston Harbor. The attack lasted for over 30 hours.

Union commander Major Robert Anderson surrendered Sumter on April 13, and his small army was evacuated.

The American Civil War had begun.

****

The rocking had worked. Little Jeremiah Ethan Chase lay on his father's chest fast asleep, a pout on his face. Jonathan was so fond of his son, and of Catharine, that he was having misgivings about what he had done the previous day.

Catharine watched them from the hallway, just out of sight of her husband. She had been crying, and was composing herself before entering the bedroom. He had never seen her cry. She had matched his carefree attitude and resolute stubbornness since their wedding, and before that.

She glanced into the hallway mirror, and fluffed her auburn hair. Why was this thing interfering with her life, her happiness? Damn this war that Jonathan felt so strongly about, a conflict that had already positioned him at odds with his family.

A few days before she had railed at Michael, a friend of Jonathan's, at a gathering in Scottsville. Michael had challenged Jonathon, questioning his loyalty to his adopted home. "How can you live here, enjoying all of the benefits of the South, when our way of life is threatened? Are you going to sit out this war? I enlisted last Thursday."

Jonathan didn't take the bait. Catharine did.

"How dare you question my husband's loyalty or his courage!" Her voice rose, turning heads. "He is grateful for his life here. He loves Virginia. He has more courage than all of you preening peacocks put together. He has more authentic feeling for this state than any of you. You go off and get killed for some cause that you can't even define. Nobody will miss you!"

Jonathan strode to her, put his arm around her waist, and began leading her away from a chastised and stricken Michael. "Catharine…"

She wasn't finished. She spun out of Jonathan's grasp, and hurried back to Michael. "It's his decision and mine, whatever he does. Keep your damn aristocratic snooty nose out of our business!"

Jonathan had led her to her coat, and they left without looking at the stunned guests. He lifted her onto the carriage.

"Well, Catharine, honey, that was…interesting."

"I'm sorry. Jonathan. I can't abide those pretentious, snobbish bastards." She settled somewhat as they rode. She put her hand tentatively on his knee. He looked at her and winked. She was also obstinate, fiercely protective, and capable of emotions that sometimes boiled over. Most of the time that was good. She was more passionate and cheerful and perhaps humorously vulgar than anyone he'd ever known. But there were dark moments too. She didn't back down, nor did she tolerate any attack, real or imagined, on anyone she loved. She had an intuitive savvy, which instantly identified those who were not genuine, those who would browbeat or con or patronize. She did not suffer fools.

"Catharine…"

"Jonathan, are you about to lecture me?" she asked playfully.

"What can I tell a person who knows everything?" he answered.

"True. True."

"At some point, we need to discuss this war. It's going to be long and it's going to be awful. It could also come to Scottsville. Who knows where the battlefields will be, who will be affected, or who will survive. I owe it to our family --to you and our son, to your parents, to our friends-- to make a commitment."

"A commitment. Soldiering? Why don't we just move? We could even go back to your home, Vermont. That's a commitment."

"No, it's not. That's an escape."

"So, you're telling me that you're going to enlist."

"No, I'm asking you to help me sort this out."

"We are going to reach a decision tonight?"

"No. But time is running out."

"Well, how about…I show you tonight what you'll be missing, if you run off to war." She began stroking his leg.

"Problem-solving suddenly interests me."

Now, mere days later, the decision had been reached.

Jonathan had enlisted in the 42nd Virginia infantry the day before.

She thoroughly composed herself and walked into the room.

"You got him to sleep."

"I spent some time telling him how much I loved him and his mother. Probably bored him."

"I hope the war ends before he forgets you."

"Catharine…"

"I'm sorry. I won't bring up the war again. You know, I do admire you for what you're doing. It's selfish of me to question it or refuse to accept it. I'm completely behind this decision. Completely."

She turned and left the room, hopeful that she had been convincing. He held his son a bit tighter.

Catharine Dexter had been graduated from Hollins Institute for Women in Roanoke, Virginia at the somewhat advanced age of 24. Her degree, earned with persistence and no small amount of intelligence, was the result of six interrupted years. Two years of college followed two years of indecision at home, which was followed by other scattered terms of attendance.

She was prepared for nothing of interest to her, a fact that had consistently interrupted her motivation and her momentum. But the periodic episodes of ennui away from the college campus had a far-reaching benefit. Her mother had taught her to sew, a sedentary activity completely at odds with her energy and hyperactive nature.

After graduating, she opened a dress shop in a small building in Scottsville. It was a perfect fit for her. By her twenty-sixth birthday, she was a favorite designer of ladies in nearby Charlottesville. She had five employees and a healthy income.

She was "The Belle of Scottsville," the name of her shoppe, and would have been in her life too if she had not displayed a fiery personality and a reluctance to commit to relationships with local men. Her attitude was equal parts elitism and an exacting demand that made escorts attain unreasonably elevated levels of acumen, wit, and accomplishment.

"You're too finicky, dear," her mother had advised more than once, mindful that her spoiled and unpredictable daughter would probably plummet into spinsterhood.

"Men bore me, Mother, except for Father."

Scottsville gossips credited her with hilarious episodes of embarrassing potential swains who had the temerity to ask if they could court her, or worse, if they touched her inappropriately or tried to woo her with money or acts of overt sexism. A black eye on a young man was commonly explained as "He must have tried to kiss Catharine Dexter." At least once, that assessment was accurate.

Her priorities changed one summer day in 1858 when a reckless young man, cantering on a Scottsville street, splashed through a large puddle, hurling mud all over the stylish young lady waiting to cross the street.

"Damn you!" Catharine shouted at the offender.

Jonathan Chase reined in and dismounted. "Ma'am, I'm so sorry. That was careless of me."

Jonathan's apology was earnest, but it disappeared in laughter was he looked at the pretty lady. Her bonnet was askew, muddy streaks of foul water ran down both cheeks, and the front of her dress was covered with lumps of sludge.

"What are you laughing at?" Catharine snapped.

"I'm sorry, ma'am, but you're a mess."

For some inexplicable reason which surprised her, she chose drollness over fury and mortification.

"Is this how you meet ladies?" she asked, feigning anger even as the hint of a grin contradicted it.

"One way. Is it working?"

"No. Not at all."

"What can I do to make you understand that I'm really an exceptional fellow, if a bit overenthusiastic on horseback?"

"Very little. As a matter of fact, nothing."

"C'mon now. How about this?" Turning quickly, he sat in the puddle that had splashed her.

She stared incredulously at him for an instant, and then began laughing, a loud, excessive giggle that disrupted the neighborhood.

They spent the afternoon in a pub, despite her initial protestations that "My mother told me that nice girls don't frequent establishments like this." It reflected some uneasiness, but she spoke it in a tone that mocked the thought. In a spate of conversation between two bedraggled and mud-covered young people, she learned that he was four years younger than she, a fact that Catharine dismissed quickly. He spoke of the Vermont Green Mountains and his desire to get a fledgling law career underway. He listened attentively as she explained her theories of business success.

They wed four months later, an extravagant event celebrated both privately and openly by her parents, who found the young man irresistible and irrepressible, a male counterpart of their Catharine. They settled into a cottage on the road to Charlottesville. He practiced law in a converted barber shop, and his client list grew, along with a reputation for courtroom success.

Her parents suspected that they were taming each other. Her anger and insolence had dissolved into devotion to him. He stowed his bachelor habits. The young couple enjoyed insatiable couplings, staged at all hours of day and night, wherever they happened to be, in a rocking canoe, in his office, in their back yard or attic or carriage, or on the front porch under the stars.

Little Jeremiah was born in 1860. Jonathan wanted four or five more. Catharine had answered, "Why stop there?"

Slavery and state's rights intruded on the idyll.

In the rocking chair, cradling his son, Jonathan remembered the heated debate with Joshua at their mother's funeral in 1859. After this war, after the Southern states proved their point and preserved their way of life, he would not rub it in to Joshua.

****

Back in 1859, two prospectors had been mining an area near Six Mile Canyon in Nevada. Peter O'Reilly and Patrick McLaughlin had no real direction in life, just a mindless quest to strike gold, or something which would change their lives. One observer, a casual acquaintance of the two, mentioned one day, "Hope them two never find anything. It'd ruin their fun."

They were working an area formerly mined by the Brosh brothers, who had died under mysterious circumstances two years before.

They had no extensive equipment, a few pans, a couple of pick axes, a couple of sledges, two mangy mules. Recently in this area, they had chinked out scattered nuggets of gold, small pieces which had done no more than pay for supplies for other attempts. There were stories of successful efforts in western Nevada, although none so far which would bring a torrent of opportunists.

"O'Reilly, come up here!" McLaughlin called one afternoon. He was perched on the side of a large outcropping halfway up a small mountain. O'Reilly, several hundred feet below, dropped his pan, and scrabbled up the mountain. "Better be good. Damn tough climb," O'Reilly complained.

"Look at this." McLaughlin pointed at his feet, where he had assembled several large chunks of glittering gold-flecked rock.

"Hey, looks good. Looks promising," O'Reilly enthused.

"No, you ain't seen nothing. Look in here."

"My God! My God! My God!" O'Reilly was looking into a small opening that McLauglin had painstakingly carved into the face of the mountain, into the blue clay. Inside, creased on the sides and top of the hole, were veins of something embedded in the clay which caught the sunlight and sparkled brilliantly.

"Know what you're seein' O'Reilly?"

"Yessir, yessir, I do. Ain't gold. It's goddamned silver!"

The two worked feverishly until dark. Whichever direction they expanded the hole, there was blue clay. It grew from streaks to full sides of the walls of the small area.

"This whole mountain is silver, O'Reilly! This whole mountain!"

"I'm a sonnuvabitch! It is!"

The two could not conceal their good fortune. They filled bags, which they sent to California to be assayed. The results were mailed to them with the notation that the silver was of the highest quality. In a few weeks, the news had spread, and the country immediately filled with prospectors and hundreds of people with questionable character.

One day, the pair was visited by a failed prospector and sheepherder named Henry "Old Pancake" Comstock, who seized opportunity with a bluff and a threat.

"You are trespassing on my land!" he shouted to O'Reilly and McLaughlin.

"Your land?" McLaughlin answered. "This is our claim."

"No! It is not! I live in a cabin near here, use'ta belong to the Brosh famly," Comstock yelled. "You get your asses off of my property!"

"There ain't no claim to this here mountain," O'Reilly countered.

"You are wrong! You are claim-jumpers. This is my land!"

The two miners backed off. If Comstock was telling the truth, they were in trouble, the kind that was usually followed by a lynching or a shooting.

"Plenty here for all of us, it looks like," McLaughlin meekly suggested.

"No! Get off of my land. Take the bags you have packed, and get the hell off of my land!"

O'Reilly and McLaughlin were in a bind. If the enraged man did own the property, they were trespassing, trying to get rich off of what was his. Too, he had said that they could keep the dozen bags they had collected in the past few weeks. The sacks contained more value than they could soon spend anyway. Maybe it was time to collect what they had already assembled, and leave the area. After all, they couldn't prove him wrong. They packed quickly.

"Listen. No hard feelings. You're bein' generous to us. We 'preciate it. What's your handle, mister?"

"Comstock," the man harrumphed.

"If'n anyone asks us 'bout this when we cash in, we'll tell them that we found it on private proppity, with your permission. We'll tell 'em it's the Comstock Lode," O'Reilly huffed, as he strapped the last bag to the mule.

Comstock didn't smile until they were out of sight. That was easy, he thought. I'm now the owner of a silver mine.

A drunk named James Finney smashed his bottle onto the ground a few miles from Six Mile Canyon, in the middle of a collection of shacks and lean-tos.

"This here place, I'm namin' Ole Virginny Town," he proclaimed, a christening highlighted by the bottle smashing and breaking at his feet. No matter that the bottle had been used and emptied.

Onlookers accepted the ceremony as legal enough. The boom town had a name, which was actually the nickname of the christener. "Ole Virginny" Finney had immigrated along with a motley group of miners, gamblers, swindlers, and prostitutes, to the ugly slum they had created on the side of a mountain high in the Washoe Range near the Sierra Nevadas. The slum now had an identity.

Upon the arrival of less inebriated and more worldly persons, the growing community near the Comstock Lode was officially named "Virginia City."

Land-grabbers and bankers and high-rollers of all kinds settled. Numerous cultures and races came, many to serve as laborers. Opium dens appeared.

The growth was unprecedented anywhere on the planet. In less than two years, 7,000 people of all social stations called it home. All with any connection to the mining of silver became astonishingly wealthy. The shacks were joined by fancy homes and places of business, including a six-story hotel with the West's first elevator. The Savage Mining Company erected a headquarters building with multiple sides and a surrounding porch.

The silver veins extended for miles in every direction. The enormous wealth would build flamboyant structures in San Francisco, and finance the Union cause in the Civil War.

In 1860, the momentum had been disturbed. Paiute Indians, pushed off of the land, killed 66 whites on May 12. Many Virginia City men joined a retaliatory force, and on Jun 2, the Paiutes surrendered, after losing 46 warriors in one fierce battle.

Virginia City returned to the business of silver.

There were many in the area who did not want to bother with the arduous labor of mining or the process of assaying or the drudgery of retailing. They took short cuts to wealth, holding up pack trains, robbing mining sites, and strong-arming citizens. It was time for Virginia City in the Nevada Territory to find a man who would neutralize the lawlessness.

In 1861, they turned to Herkimer Grimes.

CHAPTER TWENTY-TWO

1862

The mellifluous voice of Bear Woman rose a cappella on Sundays in 1862. Reverend Jonah Brooks held his weekly service in the third cabin in the grove, and Bear Woman supplied the hymns, many lyrics converted to the Dakota Sioux language by the second verse and chorus. Around her richly-delivered offerings, which of late had become tentative sing-alongs for the parishioners, Jonah talked, rather than preached, to the assembled Indians. He spoke of hope, of charity, of compassion, in a calm, sincere voice, which had none of the zeal or theatrics of many of his contemporaries. Cleetus translated in the same calm manner.

God was mentioned only peripherally, and no Sunday was devoted to a conversion of the Sioux to Christianity. Jonah was instilling trust and determination, and love for all peoples, and due to that tact, the gatherings had grown from a handful of curious tribesmen, basically ordered by Cleetus to attend the early sessions, to crowds numbering eighty to a hundred. The six rows of benches built by Jonah and Cleetus barely contained the attendees. Every Sunday, even those in the harsh winter of 1861, saw queues of the Dakota of all ages and genders traipsing to the grove.

Every other Sunday in warm weather, Bear Woman rose well before dawn and began cooking, with Cleetus and Jonah at her elbows, helping to prepare a meal for the church-goers. If they attended services, they could stay for the meal, and games, and afternoon naps beneath the evergreens. One Sunday a brave named Iron Shield had playfully challenged Jonah to an arm-wrestling contest. The brave had seriously underestimated the middle-aged preacher. It was no match. As fit as he had been as a young man, Jonah twisted Iron Shield's hand to the table in brief seconds. Realizing that his own stature had grown from that encounter, but that Iron Shield's was suffering, Jonah proposed a shooting match with an old musket, and deliberately missed the makeshift targets by wide margins, while Iron Shield hit a modest amount. Iron Shield's manhood was restored. He gave Jonah a bear hug.

The camaraderie was important because the Sioux were getting impatient and progressively angrier as missing annuity payments decreased and virtually disappeared. The payments were going to the traders, demanded by them to counter the mounting credit debts that they were owed. As July waned, Joshua feared trouble. There was scattered talk of revolt.

"Unfair. The traders are tricking the tribesmen into running up debt, and then taking their government monies. Many of the Dakota have no obligation, but they are without food and money because it is all being withheld or diverted. If we are to protect these people, we owe them their promised monies and the right to manage their own finances without the trader influence. It is part of the treaties," Jonah wrote Washington.

"And in addition, the money for their lands promised to them in 1851, has instead been stolen, probably by the Bureau of Indian Affairs," he continued.

His aggressive stance had earned him enemies. Andrew Myrick, the trader's representative, was particularly vocal, demanding that Thomas Galbraith silence "that damn preacher." Myrick owned a store on the Minnesota River in the Lower Sioux Agency.

"The Sioux are starving. Have you no mercy?" Jonah demanded of Myrick one day.

"The Sioux owe me money," Myrick countered.

"You are stealing their money. Probably more than they owe you," Joshua had answered. His eyes, piercing and squinted, made Myrick turn away.

"We'll see about that," was his response as he walked away.

"Yessir. We will," Jonah said to himself.

Jonah demanded a meeting of Dakota leaders, traders, personnel of both agencies, and representatives from the Bureau of Indian Affairs. Galbraith, uncharacteristically intimidated, arranged it for August 4 at the Lower Agency.

Jonah and Cleetus personally visited Little Crow to invite him.

The beleaguered chief was unimpressed. There was no humor in his eyes or his words those days. His posture was slumped. He was gaunt. He was hungry too.

"Will do no good, God's Eye," Cleetus translated. "The White Fathers would destroy us. Meeting is a waste of time."

"Little Crow, I will sit with you. I will express your will. I will argue for fairness."

"I know you will, God's Eye. My people trust you."

"We will try. If, as you say, nothing will change, then we will try something else."

"God's Eye, if nothing changes, my people will decide the next action."

"You are a wise man, a good chief. We must work together. We do not want war."

"The white man is now fighting a great war with his own people. If we are to fight him now, he will not call down large numbers on us."

"Because the white man is fighting elsewhere, he is not paying attention to injustice here. We will get his attention with words, with the truth."

"The truth will not feed my people."

The Lower Agency was everything that the Upper Agency was not. Thomas Galbraith had a two-story building in Fort Ridgely with a staff which included interpreters, a superintendent of agriculture and an agency physician. He was administrative, and had little contact with the Sioux, except in matters such as this.

He entered the meeting room, late, with his usual bluster, and immediately sensed the tension, the serious attitudes of everyone in the room.

Sitting to his left were Jonah Brooks, Cleetus Wilburn, Little Crow, principal chiefs Red Middle Voice and Shakopee, and a group of tribal leaders, including old Pay-Pay, Taopi, Other Day, and Wa-con-ta. Standing around the room were traders like Philander Prescott, Francois La Bathe, and Myrick, and agency staff members George Divoll and A.H. Wagner. A representative from the Bureau began immediately without introducing himself.

"Gentlemen, we will resolve this problem today. As I understand it, food is being withheld from the Indians," he said, in a voice so tiny that Jonah guessed that the official would not long control the meeting.

Jonah stood. "I'm speaking on behalf of the Dakota. The tribe is starving. The government is failing them. They cannot grow their own food in this dry summer. Mr. Galbraith is releasing their entitled money to other people. The traders refuse to give the Sioux additional credit, and have been the beneficiaries of the money from Mr. Galbraith."

There was mumbling from the traders. "We have a right to do business the way we see fit. We cannot continue to lose money because of a bunch of deadbeats," a red-faced Myrick interrupted.

"You, sir, are the reason they have incurred debt. You have overcharged them, taken advantage of their limited knowledge of finance, and attracted them into a position where you own them," Jonah responded.

"Damn you, man. You may know religion. You don't know business. Or Indians."

Galbraith interrupted. "What you're asking, Reverend Brooks, is unreasonable. You would ask the storeowners and traders to support malingerers."

"No!" Jonah rejoined, a bit too fierce, too loud. "I'm asking that someone show human kindness, that someone realize that we keep pushing them farther into corners. We have a responsibility to them, and all that the traders and administrators do is exploit them and ignore them. We are the interlopers here."

"This is not the forum for personal attacks, Brooks," Galbraith responded, intentionally omitting all but Jonah's last name.

"I ask that you listen now to the principal chief of the Lakota, Little Crow."

As Little Crow spoke, Jonah noticed the lack of respect in the room. Myrick walked to the window and gazed outside. The other traders talked among themselves. Galbraith fumbled with papers in front of him.

Little Crow was not eloquent, but he effectively stated his case with examples of starving within his tribe, of children going for days without nourishment, of elders giving up, of braves refusing their food so that little ones could eat, of braves eating their horses.

When he finished, Galbraith stood and began quoting numbers, citing examples of brutish behavior by braves in the Lower Agency, listing examples of non-payment.

Jonah started to respond, but the Bureau man suddenly became an ally. "In any society, Mr. Galbraith, there are miscreants," he stated, "and from what I see, these are honorable people. They badly need food, and the means to purchase it. I would ask the traders to consider that. These people need to eat."

"Let them eat grass, or their own dung!" Myrick exploded.

The room got quiet. Jonah fought to control his anger, and saw the shock on the faces of the warriors around him as the comment was translated.

The Bureau man cleared his throat. "That is an unfortunate remark, Mr. Myrick. It helps me make this decision. Mr. Galbraith, you will receive a large shipment of food from the government within a week. You will distribute it immediately. Until a resolution is reached from further meetings, that is the way we'll conduct business. When that supply is exhausted, the government will send more. You will immediately distribute whatever stores you have on hand, at once. We will attend to these starving people while the Bureau decides what to do next. The government will continue to forward treaty payments, which will go to the Sioux directly. I would again ask the traders to consider ways to reach a workable resolution. This meeting is over."

Cleetus leaned over to whisper to Jonah. "The traders will never give in. That remark by Myrick will stir up trouble with the tribespeople."

"At least they'll have food for a while," Jonah answered.

Jonah had a respectful affection for Cleetus and Bear Woman. She forever surprised him, positive and eager to please. The Sunday services were successful in large part because of her contributions. The Sioux had come to be with one of their own, joyous and gracious, sympathetic and hopeful. Her music helped, but the force of her personality was undeniable.

Once or twice a month she visited Jonah in his dreams, an unwelcome experience in which he again saw her bathing, with her raven hair falling against her full hips, an early sun sparkling on her moist body. He woke sweating, ashamed of the implied lust, wishing that he had not taken that short cut the year before.

Cleetus had become a valued companion in more than just the affairs of the agency. Jonah and he fished together weekly. Jonah had given him two split bamboo rods, a brass reel, a few lures, and several spools of oiled silk lines from his own collection, and had taught him the basics of casting and of fly-fishing. Prior to that, Cleetus had used primitive homemade equipment, and was a "dappler," dropping his lines baited with live insects into a pool and waiting for fish to get interested. They casted the rivers and lakes for miles around, and when Cleetus showed him a cold, rushing stream one day, the two began to fish for trout.

Both men had opened up during those outings; the excursions provided hours of conversation. Cleetus had become comfortable dropping the word "Reverend," and was calling his new friend "Jonah." The seminal incident had probably occurred when Jonah was demonstrating how to wade into a stream and fish from knee-high depth. He had lost his footing and flopped backwards into the water, disappearing except for the pole, which he had protectively held high over his head. When he sputtered to his feet again, Cleetus was doubled over with laughter, rolling on the bank, convulsed in delight. To that point, a smile was unusual for the little man. Jonah had laughed too, tentatively, and then he too was braying loudly. "If you're taking notes…forget that part of it," he had mumbled, which caused more laughter from Cleetus.

When the two weren't off visiting villages, Jonah prepared supper, and hosted the couple twice a week. Fish was usually on the menu. On other nights, they invited him to their cabin. He respected their privacy enough to forego their company three or four nights a week. On those nights, he missed them.

The government moved quickly as the Bureau man had promised. On August 16, treaty payments arrived in St. Paul, and were sent on to Fort Ridgely the next day.

Too late.

On August 15, a contingent of Sioux from the Lower Agency had met at Fort Ridgely to collect stored foodstuffs. Galbraith, pressured by the traders, had refused to release it.

On August 17, four braves, on a desperate hunting trip, instead broke into a settler's cabin in Acton Township to steal food. When they met resistance, they killed the five residents.

Little Crow received the news with mixed feelings. Whatever gains they had obtained from the August 4 meeting would be nullified. On the other hand, he was through begging. A war against the whites to drive them from the territory would, if successful, restore some of his lost luster among his peoples. He convened a council of war.

"It is time, my brothers, to take back what is ours. We will make war against the white man for miles around, as far as a man can ride in five days. We will destroy the settler families, and we will punish those who have punished us."

Not all of the Dakota factions were in attendance. Those that were, all from the Lower Agency, loudly supported Little Crow's vision.

"It is decided. Kill all of those who have lied to us and cheated us. Kill all of those whose skin color is not Dakota. Attack the white villages. Burn them!"

There were more whoops.

"Spread the word to all of our Sioux brothers. This will be our time!"

The commotion settled as the chiefs began to leave.

"Understand this, my brothers. No harm is to come to God's Eye, or to the black man and his woman. Whoever harms them will be sent from our tribes forever. Make this known to all of our warriors."

The next day Little Crow led a war party against the Lower Agency. They surrounded the buildings and attacked.

Andrew Myrick was among the first killed as he tried to escape from a second-story window. The Sioux stuffed grass into the mouth of the corpse.

Family members of the agency staff were led away as captives as the Dakota murdered ten of the staff, including Divoli, LaBathe, the trader Prescott, the agency physician, and James Lynd, a young clerk at the agency store. Alerted, forty soldiers from Fort Ridgely rode to the rescue. The Sioux were gone.

All along the Minnesota River Valley that day, Dakota war parties savaged settlements, killing settlers at Milford, Leavenworth, and Sacred Heart and burning all three to the ground. The next day, combined Dakota forces attacked New Ulm, murdering scores of settlers along the way.

Captain John Marsh rode to the rescue with the Minnesota Militia, but the soldiers were ambushed near Redwood Ferry. Twenty-four soldiers were killed, including Marsh. The others retreated.

Iron Shield brought the grim news to Jonah.

"Are all of the tribes at war?"

"No, God's Eye," Cleetus translated, "the northern tribes are split. The Mdewakanton refuse to go to war. Their leaders are trying to change the mind of Little Crow. He will not listen. He is on a path of revenge."

"Cleetus, you and Bear Woman must leave. Load my wagon. Go north. Circle to Mankato or St. Paul."

"I will take Bear Woman, then come back. I will not leave you alone with this, Jonah."

Iron Shield was talking excitedly again. "Little Crow has said that no harm will come to God's Eye or the man Cleetus or his wife, under penalty of death or banishment."

"That settles it. We're staying," Cleetus stated.

"I don't know if I'm comfortable with that. Iron Shield, who is resisting Little Crow?"

"I know of John Other Day, Wa-kin-yon-to-wa, Taopi, Wa-con-ta. Shakopi, I think."

"Cleetus, you and Iron Shield ride north. Warn the settlers to leave for Fort Abercrombie. They'll be safe there. I'll see you back here in a week. I'm going to find Little Crow."

The Dakota war parties were scattered throughout Minnesota by that time. New Ulm had successfully defended itself against the assault and a brief siege, but now the Sioux attacked to the north, destroying stagecoach stops and trading companies and the sparsely settled area between Canada and St. Paul.

Another body of warriors attacked Fort Ridgely, unsuccessfully, although many of the defenders lost their lives. A detachment of 150 soldiers was sent out after the attack to rescue survivors and locate the war parties, but they were ambushed fifteen miles from the fort. Thirteen soldiers were killed, and fifty wounded. Only the arrival of another detachment from the fort prevented a complete massacre.

Scouts told Little Crow of a mass exodus of settlers to Fort Abercrombie. He redirected his forces to mass an attack against that garrison, and to leave no survivors.

Sometime in the next few days, he received a message. Jonah was looking for him.

"Tell God's Eye that I have no time for him. Tell him I will leave a message for him at his agency. He is safe from harm unless he tries to interfere. It he tries, he will be as dead as anyone else." Little Crow was clearly enjoying himself.

****

With the publication of the fifth book in the series *Herk Grimes, Texas Ranger,* this one called *Revenge On The Comanche,* Robert Gerdon had become almost as famous as his character. All five novels had been re-printed several times, the first three also serialized and published by his former employer, D.F. Sawyer, in *The Easterner.*

A decade before, Sawyer had grudgingly used an article written by Gerdon in his magazine. It was titled, "A Western Hero," and was splashed over four pages, accompanied by an inauthentic drawing by a staff artist depicting a mustachioed man shooting a near-naked Indian at close range.

That had earned Robert Gerdon brief notoriety, but no raise and no promotion from his inhibiting duties as a proof-reader. Frustrated, he had quit his job and moved out of the city to upstate New York, where he was hired by a local newspaper as a reporter.

Gerdon felt that he was on the cusp of a new trend in literature, but he wasn't sure how to pursue it. On nights in his hotel room, he wrote, and put the products in neat stacks in a corner of the room. Over eight years passed. At thirty-six, balding, and in a creative vacuum, he continued to fantasize about his elusive literary concept.

In June of 1860, a publisher named Erastus Beadle of Buffalo had printed a novel entitled *Malaeska, the Indian Wife of the White Hunter,* written by Mrs. Ann S. Stephens. It was a sensational best-seller, and it led Beadle to believe that the genre of Western adventure novels could make him wealthy. He hired a full staff of writers to produce Western literature, writing continuously for weeks at a time. None of the authors had a working knowledge of the frontier; few facts accompanied the resultant books, but to Beadle, that was inconsequential. "Half the work done in the world is to make things appear what they are not," he said.

That philosophy was making him a rich man. His books, usually less than 150 pages, sold for ten cents apiece. He mass-produced them and they sold out. Some critics decried their lack of facts, their overly unrealistic plots, and their unwavering depiction of their heroes as unfailingly young, modest, and handsome.

D.F. Sawyer himself said that the books would be "the ruination of the American written word,"

At the same time he had conducted a search for Robert Gerdon, his former employee. This time Gerdon dictated the terms. He had just gotten his first novel published, *Herk Grimes, Texas Ranger. Rescue of the Captives.* He would continue to write and publish independently. Sawyer was welcome to serialize his books, for a substantial fee. Sawyer agreed.

This fifth book, circa 1862, was total fiction. The few facts that Gerdon had accumulated about his Texas Ranger hero had exhausted long ago. He had been on a creative roll, conjuring up exploits and locations that didn't exist. That would continue. Gerdon looked for new directions.

Maybe, Herk Grimes as a hired gunfighter. Gerdon knew that Herk had left the Rangers for the Regulator-Moderator War. So what would make someone hire him to help them win a range war? He was a crack shot. Gerdon had established that in the Texas Ranger series. Perhaps he never missed, and could unholster and shoot faster than any other man alive. Maybe he only shot to wound, unless a coquettish heroine was in danger.

The Regulator-Moderator affair was too murky, too fraught with evil on both sides. No, this Herk Grimes, the hired gun, would clean up Western towns, protect settlers, defend the honor of oppressed people. He would ride around the frontier to battle deviltry and transgression.

He would ride a mighty stallion named "Revenge." The possibilities were endless.

Soon after, in the middle of 1862, he submitted another novel, *Herk Grimes, Frontier Gunfighter, The Rancher's Daughter.* In mere weeks, he had another best-seller.

A year before, Virginia City had noted the exploits of Herkimer Grimes from the Gerdon dime novels. They needed a lawman. They would find him, wherever he was.

****

September of 1862 was quiet in Lexington, Missouri, as July and August had been. That was from a doctor's perspective, and not related to the persistent activity on the wharves down on the Missouri River. The little port town bristled with activity. Goods and people were still moving around in the West, even as the Civil War raged.

Dr. Hank Rosbottom slept late again and woke to a roaring headache. Last night had joined myriad others as a background for hours of drinking. He had passed sobriety many years before, haunted by the death of his Angeline, by the quirk of fate which had labeled him a doctor, and by the emptiness of his life.

He was fifty-eight years old, and he himself had predicted that he would not see sixty. Of course, he never let his patients see his weakness, never miss-performed as a doctor, and numbered legions of area residents who owed their lives to him. He was a good doctor, if a tormented man. His partner, Dr. Gleason, the one who had persuaded him to become a medical associate after the *Saluda* tragedy, had passed on four years ago, and had left Hank with the large frame building which was both his office and residence, along with boxes of journals and his medical equipment.

He had been in Lexington for a decade, and as long as he had emergencies to handle, patients to treat, he functioned well. The previous September, the Civil War had briefly come to Lexington. Over 3,500 Union soldiers had been trapped in the city, and surrounded by 12,000 Confederates, led by Major-General Sterling Price. During the resultant siege and final assault by the Rebels, 120 wounded soldiers and a large number of sick ones required medical attention. Hank and a Dr. Cooley had handled all of those cases in a makeshift hospital. The two worked without sleep for three days until the Union commander surrendered.

Recently, his caseload had dwindled, particularly in the areas of taking care of expectant mothers and delivering babies. With many of the young men of the area on faraway battlefields, the composition of his practice had changed. He still treated older patients, congestive problems, childhood maladies, and an occasional injury, but a dearth of complicated or challenging medical treatments, staying busy, was annoying. Worse, it was giving him more opportunity to drink, alone, in his apartment above the office.

His red hair had disappeared, replaced ten years ago by dull white. He was underweight and haggard. As long as a small number of people counted on him, he would press on.

He had tried several times to court local ladies, all of whom were impressed by his standing in the community, but confused by his reluctance to engage in meaningful conversation. None had lasted more than a few dates. He was relieved when each ended, as if they had betrayed his memories of his Cajun wife. It had been years since he had unpacked his fiddle or his banjo.

At mid-afternoon, he heard the jangling of the doorbell above his office door. A young couple waited for him. Leonard, the young man, was blind in one eye, a condition which had disqualified him for the army. His wife, Edna, was in her early twenties, and significantly pregnant.

Edna was enduring her first pregnancy, and it had not been easy for her. She had almost lost the child twice, and most recently had been experiencing severe back pain. She wondered if she were about to go into labor. Hank examined her. As he lay his stethoscope aside, he couldn't hide a frown.

"Doc Rosbottom. What is it? Sumthin' the matter?" Edna asked.

"Mrs. Edna, you're not ready yet. But there may be a small problem here. The baby's heartbeat is not quite where I expected it. Seems to me the baby has turned. Think it's called the breach position."

"I've heared 'bout that, Doc Rosbottom. Dangerous, ain't it?" Her large eyes looked to him for comfort.

"It can be, ma'am. I've delivered a few of those though. While you're giving birth, any day now, I'll try to turn the baby around."

"She be alright, Doc? Mebbe the baby turn itself around?"

"Maybe it will, Leonard. The important thing is that you've got to come for me, first sign of labor. Her water will break, and she'll start having spasms, cramps. You folks don't live far from town. There will be time. That happens, you come and get me, anytime, day or night. These things are painful and dangerous, but we'll get through it."

"Yessir, Doc. My mum is stayin' with us 'til this is over. She can stay with Edna. I will come and get you."

The couple left relieved, but without paying. That happened a lot in Lexington.

In late September, Edna's water broke in the middle of the night. Jolted awake, Leonard kissed her on the forehead, woke his mother, and grabbed a jacket. "I'll be back with the doc in fifteen minutes or so. The horse is already saddled. Don't worry, Edna, Honey." He bolted for the stable, heard her screams as he left, and rode hard to town.

At Hank's office, he pounded on the door. There was no response. He yelled at the upstairs window. A faint light was shining through one of those windows. He ran to the back door, calling, "Doc! Doc! I need you! Baby's a comin'!"

The back door was unlocked. He's a heavy sleeper, Leonard thought. Leonard entered the unlit room, still calling out. He bounced off of a table, unseen in the stygian darkness, and made out the outline of steps to the second floor. He took them two at a time, yelling. "Doc! Hey, Doc!"

Light was escaping under a door to a room on his left. He opened the door.

Dr. Rosbottom was sitting crookedly in a chair next to a flickering candle. "Oh no! Oh, no, he's daid!" Leonard blurted out.

Then he saw the whiskey bottle, still in Hank's hand, tilted and empty. Another smaller one was on the table next to the candle. The smell of alcohol was heavy. A stain covered the front of Hank's shirt.

Drunk. Passed out drunk.

****

For Jonah Brooks, it had been a frustrating month. He had returned to the North Agency in August after Little Crow refused to see him. Riding up, he noticed the long Agency building burned to the ground. The cabins were still intact, but that didn't worry him. He hurried to the grove. "Bear Woman! Bea!" he called out. She rushed out of the door of the Wilburn cabin as he dismounted.

"Jonah, Oh…Jonah," she said as she rushed to embrace him.

"What happened here? Are you alright?"

She held onto him tightly. "Little Crow come two days ago. Burned the agency. Left the cabins be. Me too. All he want was to burn the agency building."

That was the message that he had promised Jonah. You are our friends, but if you interfere with us as an Indian agent, we will harm more than the building here.

"Cleetus?"

"Don't know. No word. Nothing," she answered, relaxing the hug.

"Ok. We'll wait for him. He isn't due back for two or three days. After that, I don't know yet."

"You will stay with me until he returns"

"I will. We shouldn't have left you here alone."

"Not scared for me. Worried about you and Cleetus."

Cleetus and Iron Shield rode up five days later. The two had been trapped at Fort Abercrombie after escorting several dozen settlers to safety. The Sioux had attacked the fort, but had been repulsed. After they left, Cleetus and Iron Shield joined an army company assisting hundreds of refugees from the fort to St. Cloud.

Little Crow expanded his target areas, and aggressively attacked scouting parties and military units sent to stop him. Inflated by his successes to date, he re-attacked Fort Ridgely and Fort Abercrombie.

Finally attentive to pleas from Minnesota, Abraham Lincoln ordered General John Pope to command three large troop companies to stop the bloodshed. For days, the military chased the Dakotas around Minnesota. Jonah volunteered to help the troops on September 16. Maybe he would still get an opportunity to accost Little Crow, or at least to slow down whatever vengeance the military would seek. For days before, he had ridden futilely in a large circle, looking for survivors who might need help. What he saw sickened him. Horribly abused bodies littered the settlements. Young children were hung from trees or stacked on the top of mutilated bodies. Limbs and heads were scattered far from their bodies.

Any sympathy he harbored for Little Crow vanished. This war must end. And it must end with the total defeat of the Dakota.

Little Crow reacted to the military threat by mobilizing his forces. The scattered attacks stopped, but the great danger was that the consolidated Sioux might be sufficient to withstand the military action. Lincoln could spare no more troops.

The Dakota War ended on September 26 of 1862. Most of the Sioux fighting force was trapped in a ravine near Wood Lake. Three units of the Minnesota infantry, using advantageous position and a six-pounder cannon, blasted the warriors into submission.

The action at Wood Lake was decisive, and Little Crow retreated to Canada with large numbers of his tribesmen, most of whom were the most guilty of the horrendous acts of the preceding five weeks. Three hundred Dakota surrendered. Two hundred sixty-nine captives of the Sioux were freed at Wood Lake.

The government acted quickly.

Sixteen hundred Dakota women, old men, and children were sent to an internment camp on Pike Island. Disease and starvation killed 300 of them before the end of 1862.

Military trials began in November, such as they were. Some trials lasted a few minutes. The Sioux had no legal representation, and there was no explanation of the charges leveled at individuals. All 303 captured warriors were convicted of murder and rape. The tribunals sentenced them to death.

The Episcopal Bishop of Minnesota, Henry Whipple voiced his outrage at the proceedings and at the sentence.

They are victims of the system, he wrote to Abraham Lincoln. "Debaucherers and whiskey sellers were selected to guide a heathen people. We left them without government; treaties were destroyed or ignored. Traders and agencies saw them as pliant and sold them firewater on bad credit. Please proceed with leniency."

Both Whopple and Jonah tirelessly lobbied lawmakers, drumming up support for a review off the hasty, barely legal justice. The incarcerated Sioux called them "God's Eye," and "Straight Tongue."

Abraham Lincoln responded, personally reviewing the trial of each defendant, the evidence, and the pleas of the two men of the cloth. He commuted the sentences of 264 of the prisoners, and granted another a full reprieve. Thirty-eight would be hanged, he decided.

Those who had escaped execution by the Presidential commutation would be taken to Federal prisons at Davenport, Iowa and Rock Island, Illinois, along with other Dakota deemed dangerous.

"Reverend Whipple, justice was denied those condemned to hang. Perhaps we should petition for new trials," Jonah suggested on one of the few times the liberators were together after Lincoln's order.

The thin ascetic replied, "No, Reverend Brooks. It wouldn't change anything now. The government can't go beyond the heinous acts committed during the uprising. You witnessed the horror yourself. The President is being criticized as it is for being too lenient. This may be as close as possible to an appropriate conclusion."

"So these thirty-eight become martyrs. Little Crow and the others will go free because of national boundaries."

"It would seem so. Canada is their salvation. I think our path is clear. We should assure that whatever Dakota stay here are protected and left alone."

"A mass execution. Unthinkable. Mainly to satisfy the vengeance of the people who either caused or ignored the problems."

The execution occurred on December 26 on a long scaffold constructed in Mankato. The bodies were dumped into a single trench near a riverbank.

Four months later, the United States Congress abolished the reservation and nullified all previous treaties with the Dakota people. A bounty was placed on any Sioux of any age or gender found in the state of Minnesota. All remaining Dakotas were loaded onto steamboats and taken to the sere Dakota Territory on Crow Creek, a barely habitable location.

Hundreds of settlers who had survived the uprising left Minnesota forever.

Jonah would leave Minnesota in June of 1863. He broke the news to Cleetus a week before.

"Except for you and Bear Woman, and the fishing waters, there's no reason for me to stay."

"Where will you go, Jonah?"

"West. To the edge of the frontier somewhere. There are people out there who need guidance. It's time to open another ministry."

"But the war rages beyond the Mississippi River."

"I'll go beyond that somewhere. Perhaps a mining town."

The next day, Cleetus and Bear Woman came to his cabin where Jonah was filling crates with the collected items of the past two years.

"Jonah. We've talked it over. Bear Woman cannot stay in this place. It has too many bad memories. It's dangerous for any Sioux now. We wonder if you'd consider us going along with you, at least for a while.

"You'd be welcome. You're like family to me. But you understand that there's little guarantee of what lies ahead. I have a vision, but not much of a plan."

"Our whole lives have been like that," Cleetus said. Bear Woman smiled.

****

The barrage began in the stillness of pre-dawn December 11, 1862, bullets splashing into the Rappahannock and thudding into support boats.

Lieutenant Joshua Chase of the Union Corps of Engineers was both startled and dismayed by the suddenness and intensity of fire. The cold fog and darkness had been allies, a shroud of security, for over a half- hour.

The enemy couldn't see targets. In desperation, the Confederates, massed on the yards and riverfront windows of Fredericksburg, poured incessant gunfire toward the unseen engineers.

Screams of pain and curses and the soft plunks of bullets entering flesh accompanied the somewhat muffled sound of the staccato firing 200 feet away. Chance alone directed bullets to humans, but the volume was enough to elevate chance to numerous casualties.

What had started as a possible clandestine success had turned to chaos.

From somewhere behind Joshua on the partially completed bridge, a voice called, "back to shore!" He couldn't be certain if it was on order-- he hadn't ordered anything-- or a frenzied reaction from an engineer. Splinters from a board at his feet kicked against his leg.

In short minutes, the first glow of dawn revealed the predicament. Scores of his battalion lay on the pontoon span or floated in the shallow water behind him. The remaining engineers were becoming visible targets. Retreat to the Stafford Heights bank was not an option; it was a necessity, a safety imperative. The fusillade increased.

Joshua grabbed a crawling pontoon builder under the shoulders, and hustled him toward safety. Other engineers were scrambling up the steep banks or pressing against the ground at the water's edge. Some jumped into the support boats.

Joshua reached the shore and carefully laid the wounded man behind a barrier afforded by the pontoon boat in the first position.

No sooner had he fallen to the ground than he was back on his feet, racing onto the bridge. Another man was agonizingly crawling, and the surface around him was being pocked by a multitude of near misses.

He heard only peripherally the exhortations from the shore, a chorus of admiration and hope.

"C'mon, Lieutenant!"

"Stay low!"

"Run man, run!"

Seemingly his entire life had prepared him for this run. His long legs propelled him quickly across the expanse, much the same as they had done in his childhood, racing his brothers across the foothills of Vermont. His cap blew off in the early morning breeze, and his long dark hair flattened against his head.

"That boy scares me," his father had said once, years ago, "He never does anything wrong." He was like his father in many ways, tall and thin, handsome, and eminently educated.

He reached his fallen comrade. A Minie ball had destroyed the man's right knee, and what was below that was only loosely attached to the rest of leg. The man looked up, silently pleading, his eyes huge, agony on his twisted face. Joshua jerked the man up effortlessly and secured him on his shoulder.

Running back to the Stafford Heights shore, he realized that he was the only target for the Confederate sharpshooters. The pings of errant shots surrounded him.

He made it, to raucous cheering.

Lying in the mud, Joshua knew too well the series of blunders and bureaucracy that had already labeled this mission as star-crossed.

General Ambrose Burnside had taken control of the Union army from Joe Hooker in early November of 1862. Abraham Lincoln, tired of what he considered indecision and confusion at the top of his command, had directed Burnside to be aggressive and to secure immediate and decisive Northern victories, all too infrequent in the war to that point. Burnside immediately targeted an assault on Richmond, the Confederate capital. He would shift over 100,000 soldiers to Fredericksburg, a stepping stone to Richmond. His army would cross the Rappahannock River, gain control of the high ground, and then plan for Richmond, before Robert E. Lee was aware of any of it.

He'd have to race to the area, construct and cross pontoon bridges across the river, and storm the city. Speed and efficiency were essential to success.

Neither materialized.

Burnside sent word to Henry Halleck, commander of the Engineer Corps which was camped near Harper's Ferry, to have that battalion meet him at Stafford Heights with pontoon bridges on November 17. When the Army of the Potomac arrived on the appointed date, the bridges were not there. The cumbersome pontoon wagon train was stalled in Washington, where components of the bridge-building process were still being assembled for the 50-mile overland trek to Fredericksburg. The operation was floundering. Halleck had delayed ordering the engineers to move. His late notification to Daniel Woodbury of the Engineer Brigade took another few days to be delivered.

Woodbury tried to catch up. He divided his equipment into two sections, sending one by land. That train encountered heavy rain, and then reached the flooded Oceoquan River. They had to stop, assemble a bridge from their materials, cross the river, and then dissemble the bridge. The "land train" arrived at the Rappahannock on November 24.

The train sent by water routes, led by Major J.A. McGruder with Joshua Chase as an officer, arrived after running aground on a sandbar on November 18.

Alerted, Lee and his Confederate army marched into Fredericksburg on November 19.

For two weeks, the armies watched each other across the broad river. Lee, unsure about a target area, deployed his army along a 20-mile line of defense.

Burnside saw that as an advantage. He could pick several crossing areas, and get to the Fredericksburg shore and to the heights behind the town before Lee could muster enough men to those points. It all depended on a quick spanning of the river.

Mississippi Confederates heard the process begin on December 11 at 3 am. They were the sharpshooters who had disrupted, and then halted, the bridge construction.

Joshua saw a line of Union sharpshooters on the bluffs behind him open fire on the town. A withering explosion of covering fire soon had an effect. The Confederate firing slackened, then stopped. The engineers were ordered back onto the bridges.

Almost immediately the Southern snipers revived. Again, but with more accuracy in the morning hour, they picked off the bridge builders. Casualties mounted. Joshua ordered another retreat.

The covering fire was increased. Again it seemed to be successful. Again the order came to continue the construction. Sensing indecision and growing fear among his men, Joshua led the charge back onto the bridge. At the other four bridge sites, there was more of a delay.

Joshua reached the farthest completed section and turned to organize the scramble behind him. As he did, a "whomp" battered his lower back, knocking him to his knees. He struggled to his feet, intense pain accompanying the effort. He stood, unsteady, and realized that he couldn't force sound from his throat. He became dizzy.

He lost consciousness as he fell into the river.

CHAPTER TWENTY-THREE

1863

The sergeant stood in front of the tent, waiting for a response.

"Lieutenant Chase, Sir?"

"Sergeant Tillis. What time is it?"

"Bout midnight, I'd guess. Sorry, Sir, but this is important. Big news."

Jefferson knew that his cavalry unit was not moving out. News like that didn't come from sergeants. He opened the tent flap, and moved into the yard, buttoning his pants.

"Go on, Sergeant."

"Well, Sir. Me and some of the boys was over talkin', playin' cards with them New York boys. They started makin' a fuss about their townball team, braggin' and such. Well, Sir, we couldn't take it no more. Told them the First Vermont could take anybody in the whole damn war. Maybe even their Zouaves."

"Sergeant Tillis, you woke me up to tell me about bragging?" Jefferson's grin covered the minor anger he felt.

"No Sir. That ain't it. Set up a big game. This Sattiday, on the parade grounds."

"You arranged a game with the Thirty-eighth?"

"No, Sir. Them Zouaves. They's bivouacked over there too. We gonna play the 165th New York, them ballplayin' boys!"

Jefferson was quiet. He ran his hand through mussed hair, and shook his head.

"You playin', ain't you, Sir? Can't beat 'em without you."

Jefferson nodded. "Yes, Sergeant Tillis, I'll play. Goodnight." He turned without waiting for a salute, and returned to his cot.

"Yes, Sir. Thank you, Sir," Tillis hooted, and did a little jump step.

Before he fell asleep, Jefferson reflected on the game itself, and its impact on the war. Relatively new, at least to the Vermont soldiers, it was being played in camps on both sides, between battles, after battles, in prison camps, on leave. A story he had heard was of a game somewhere when a Union game was interrupted by a Confederate attack. The ball players had scattered for their weapons. When the skirmishers were driven off, there was horror in the Union camp. The rebels had taken their middle-fielder captive.

The game was evolving even as the war continued. It was now called "baseball," and several companies in the Northeast were making official equipment, bats three feet long fashioned from hickory and ash, tapered, and weighing an "official"48 ounces. Harwood and Sons in Natick, Massachusetts, made balls with India cork centers, tightly wound in string, and sewn together with a covering of leather. Some enterprising companies were selling gloves -- protective, oversized work gloves-- for catchers and first basemen.

One challenge game in a South Carolina camp had drawn thousands of spectators, mostly soldiers. The Zouaves had won that game, defeating an "all-star" team of men from several regiments.

The Vermont cavalry troops had learned the game before they were first deployed from Washington. Many of the men in the First were soon devoted players. Tillis was one. The stocky sergeant was overweight and slow, but he wielded a mighty bat. He was a catcher. He had an extensive collection of bats and balls, which he treated better than his rifle. He carefully packed them in a supply wagon when the unit left on a campaign.

A thin private named Taylor Reed was the pitcher. He had mastered throwing side-armed, almost underhanded, with a whiplike motion. A friend of Jefferson's from Burlington, Spalding Rooker, was perhaps the fastest man in the Vermont cavalry, and it was almost impossible to strike him out.

The most athletic of the Vermont group was Jefferson Chase. He was strong, with an uncanny batting eye, a strong throwing arm, and sure hands. He was the only ranking officer among the players, and the regiment was duly impressed. He privately credited the endless competition with two older brothers as he grew up, for developing whatever skills he had.

The Vermont Cavalry needed a distraction. Their first year as a mounted unit was consumed with irregular service, fifteen encounters with the enemy, some severe and costly, mixed with periods of inactivity, while military leaders decided what to do with them. The various Union cavalries were being used to scout, or as complementary soldiers in an infantry war. The Union cavalry, after two years of the conflict, had no crucial role. The Southern cavalry units under Jeb Stuart were a main force in the Confederate effort.

After the Second Battle of Bull Run on the 30th of August of the previous year, Vermont One was on stand-by for almost a month until a foray at Ashley's Gap in Virginia. Leaders changed. Then there was a six-month hiatus marked only by uneventful raids. Then came another minor fracas in Broad Run, Virginia on April 1. They were in bivouac again, and May was receding. They didn't know that they were on the cusp of a furious skein of 28 major battles in the next year, and another twenty-five in the six months after that.

The latter portions of 1863 would become a period when they became major players in an effort which would slowly turn a Union advantage. The Vermont group would be paired with cavalry groups from Michigan and New York to form a formidable fighting unit. The war would swing on horseback, but this was May, and Vermont One was restless.

So there was baseball to be played.

Soldier spectators stood or sat five deep in a large circle around the playing field, which had been laid out in crude fashion at one end of a parade ground, next to a large stand of trees. The several thousand had claimed spots primarily to watch the legendary Zouaves, whose roster included men who had played on club teams before the war, and several who would become professional baseball players seven years after the war. In particular, they wanted to watch the New York pitcher, a big man named Pronto Kelly, who sported bushy sideburns down to his chin, and who threw harder than anyone else they'd ever see. The Vermont opponent was only an upstart group of mountain men who hadn't even played the sport until mere months ago. The result would be a travesty, a rout, they figured, but it was the main attraction on that Saturday.

Vermont was surprised and intimidated by the cocky attitudes of their opponents. Before the first pitch, the Zouaves yelled insults and filled the air with obscenities. Pronto Kelly was aloof, a permanent sneer on his face as he analyzed members of the cavalry team. Tillis won the coin toss to determine the home team. "That's the last thing you'll win today, horse-minder," the New York captain said. The Zouaves even had uniforms of sorts, white long-sleeved shirts, tight black trousers, and round hats, which they perched jauntily on the backs of their heads. Vermont One wore combat shirts with rolled-up sleeves, baggy issue pants, and whatever shoes were in a condition to sustain running.

It didn't go well. With first-bats, the Zouaves easily solved the pitching of Taylor Reed. It seemed that every Zouave hit the ball harder and farther than the previous batter. When the Vermonters came to bat, the score was already 9-0.

Rooker singled to left after nearly striking out, forcing a late swing to bloop the ball to right field. Tillis managed a ground ball which sneaked to the outfield. Jefferson Chase came to bat.

The first pitch from Pronto Kelly was past him before he could react. The umpire, stationed behind the pitcher called it, "First strike!"

The second pitch Jefferson drove on a long, high arc over the heads of spectators in left field into a row of trees. There was a series of gasps, of silent awe, and then the entire assemblage roared approval. By the time the Zouaves retrieved the ball, the three Vermont men had tallied. The next three struck out.

New York got the three runs back in the next inning, but Taylor Reed seemed to be pitching better. A running one-handed catch by Jefferson ended the half inning with three men left on the pegged bases. 12-3.

The score stood until Jefferson came to bat again an inning later. Kelly Rooker had struck out, but scrambled to first base when the ball eluded the catcher. Pronto Kelly flung his first pitch at Jefferson's head. Jefferson sat quickly, and the umpire behind Kelly yelled. "Here, here, Sir. We'll have none of that! First ball." There was a chorus of boos from the Vermont men.

Once again, Jefferson drilled the second pitch, this time on a line into the group assembled behind middle field, which scattered as the ball screamed into their midst. 12-5.

A brilliant barehanded catch by Spalding Rooker ended Zouave attempts to score in the next inning, and two Vermont men scored on errors by the New Yorkers in the bottom of the frame. 12-7.

The Zouaves asserted themselves and scored three times in the top of the fifth.

Tillis was on second when Jefferson lined the ball down the left field foul line, and the squat little catcher lumbered home. On third, Jefferson scored when the Zouave catcher couldn't handle a wild pitch from Kelly. 15-9.

The entertainment factor was high, and gradually the bulk of the crowd began to root for the underdog cavalry men, but it wasn't to be. The Zouaves scored six more times, the Vermont men four, thanks to another shot off of the bat of Jefferson Chase, which got lost in the tree line. The final score was 21-13, a respectable defeat. The squads shook hands at the end.

"Don't know who you are, mister, but you oughta be playing ball; pleasure to share a field with you," Kelly said to Jefferson.

Less than three weeks later, Kelly was killed at Gettysburg.

****

On June 9, 1863, the Vermont First Cavalry was rousted early, and was already riding by 3:30 am. They would help make history on this day, but trotting through the fog as part of a cavalry force of over 11,000 men, they were not aware of the destination nor of the purpose.

Major-General Alfred Pleasanton moved his large force toward Culpeper, Virginia, obeying an order from Major-General Joseph Hooker, commander of the Union Army of the Potomac. Hooker knew of a strong presence of Confederate cavalry somewhere near the Rappahannock River. Jeb Stuart's men were probably about to reconnoiter with Robert E. Lee's main army, which had won victory at Chancellorsville several weeks before, or perhaps they were organizing for a major raid.

"Conduct a reconnaissance-in-force," Hooker had ordered. "Find the Southern cavalry, engage them, and locate the main Confederate force. Disperse and destroy."

To the side of the advancing Union force rode the 18th Pennsylvania, the Second New York, and the First Vermont in three columns of 1,000 men. It was slow-going on the flank, which forced a route through heavy oak forests and along a railroad bed.

Two fighting units had been organized, one under Brigadier-General John Buford, the other commanded by Brigadier-General David Gregg.

Buford's division crossed the Rappahannock at Beverly's Ford at 4:30 am and caught a Confederate brigade by surprise. It was barely daylight. The Confederates scattered and fled, but the gunfire had alerted Stuart, who sent riders to summon his far-flung cavalry to the scene of attack. Before they could fully assemble, Buford had stormed through on the right flank, and was charging toward Fleetwood Hill, Stuart's headquarters. At that moment, the Virginia 12th regrouped and intercepted the Buford charge. Fierce fighting ensued, so hectic that the horsemen could not dismount. Sabers flashed in the air. Pistols were fired at the enemy, mere feet away on rearing horses.

The Confederates stalled the charge, but a contingent of Gregg's army arrived, and the combined forces drove the Southern army off of the hill. That division had detoured, and had reached the hill by late morning, just in time to support Buford.

Artillery units from both sides set up, and thundered volleys on enemy positions.

Meanwhile, the Vermont One and its sister units under Colonel Judson Kilpatrick swept in a great circle around Brandy Station on the east and attacked south of Fleetwood Hill.

Jefferson Chase remembered later that often during the hours-long battle, it was impossible to determine an army's line, impossible to determine who was winning, impossible to sense battle objectives. The two armies were intermingled. Waves of soldiers re-attacked whatever ground they had just lost, and then they were swallowed up by a force of the other army, which then lost its position momentarily. He always had a sense of what was going on all around him, but in the turmoil, he didn't know what color uniform those behind wore.

He saw Tillis fall from his horse. The sergeant jumped to his feet and raised his saber. A Confederate drove his saber through Tillis' back. The Sergeant stared ahead for an instant, and then fell, mortally wounded.

Reloading became an unmanageable chore for a long time. Six revolver shots and the weapon was useless. The saber became the weapon of choice. Hand-to-hand combat- fist- fighting-- was everywhere, even from horseback. Jefferson's horse was shot out from under him in the second hour, and he fought from the ground until he saw Tillis' Morgan horse wandering through the melee.

Artillery support, so crucial to cavalry warfare, was non-existent; the two armies were too integrated all over the battlefield. The mass of humanity swept back and forth across the hill. Jefferson pulled the rifle from Tillis' saddle holster, grabbed the barrel, and began swinging it like a club. He rode into a mass of soldiers fighting on the ground and clubbed two Confederates on the backs of their heads. Another Confederate took a wild thrust with his saber. It ripped through the front of Jefferson's pants, and he saw blood. He turned his horse sharply and rode into the man.

Jefferson saw Spalding Rooker leaning against a tree, head down, one hand clutched at his midsection. A Confederate soldier was stalking him. Jefferson jumped to the ground, picked up a errant saber, and plunged it into the rebel. He carried Rooker to Tillis's horse and threw him across the saddle, swatted the horse's rump, and it cantered out of the body of fighters toward the fringe of the action. For minutes, he stood over a fallen soldier from Michigan, who was groaning and trying to raise himself onto his elbows, surrounded by cursing Southerners. He continued to brandish the saber, and the rebels pulled away to other targets and other attackers. He fought his way toward a clearing.

Suddenly there was separation between the armies, defined lines. The Confederates were back atop the hill, and over a wide vista, the Union was neutralized. A New York Light Artillery unit moved into position to support the cavalry, but got too close to the rebel line. Thirty of them were killed instantly, before their big guns could fire.

The word spread along the Union lines, "Fall back. Fall back now!"

Pleasanton had seen a large dust cloud on the horizon, and guessed that the South's infantry was rushing toward the fray. Jefferson leaped onto another riderless horse. The North pulled back. The cavalry encounter was almost over. George Custer led the Michigan cavalry on a dash into town to confront the advancing infantry, but his horse was lost, so he mounted double with a comrade, and rode away. The Northern army left the area.

In a battle which had lasted almost ten hours, the Army of the Potomac lost 900 men; 480 of those were missing or captured. The South counted 523 casualties.

But it was a significant battle for both armies. Stuart had held the ground, and so claimed victory. The North, however, had utilized its cavalry in a meaningful fashion for the first time in the war, and they had performed brilliantly. It was a precursor of cavalry importance for the duration of the war.

"You OK, Lieutenant Chase?" Gregg himself questioned the large bandage on Jefferson's thigh early the next day.

Jefferson looked up. The appearance of a Brigadier-General in a hospital tent was noteworthy. Somehow Gregg knew his name.

"Yes sir. Flesh wound, lots of blood. I'm fine sir."

"Heard your name a lot this morning, Lieutenant. You are a hero to a large number of men."

Jefferson was struggling with the events of the previous day. All semblance of logic and sanity was missing yesterday. It had been a brawl, a hours-long fight for survival, an incongruous, even absurd encounter. Luck, more than fighting skill, had determined who lived, and who didn't. Tillis was dead. Rooker was missing. Bodies had been strewn all over Fleetwood Hill. His horse had been shot, and Jefferson still heard that scream. He was not a hero.

"Thank you, sir."

Jefferson Chase rode the short distance from the campsite of Vermont One, crossing several hillocks toward a vale emitting plumes of smoke. He knew his destination, but not its purpose. He was stopped by a sentry who didn't honor his rank or his obvious Union loyalty.

"Who are you? Where you think you're goin'?"

The answer brought immediate respect. The sentry snapped to attention and bade Jefferson to continue, followed by an extra-audible "Sir!"

The Michigan camp teemed with activity, marked by late afternoon campfires, music from harmonicas and Jew's harps, group drilling, and the hum of conversation and laughter.

Jefferson dismounted as he crossed the outer perimeter of the camp, and was immediately approached by a young man with no discernible rank.

"Your business, Sir?"

"I'm Lieutenant Chase from the Vermont One. Captain Custer is expecting me."

"Yessir. I figgered you was him. The Cap'n tole me to greet you. Private Hawkins, Sir. Tie yer horse to that there tree, and foller me."

Jefferson was soon standing near an officer's tent with all of its flaps down.

"Cap'n Custer, Sir. Lieutenant Chase is here."

A voice from inside called back. "Come in, Lieutenant."

Jefferson pulled back a flap and entered a grayness, lit only by heavily filtered sunlight through the tent walls, and a barely flickering lantern in a corner. Custer had been napping, he suspected. The silhouette of a slim man moved toward the barely visible lamp, and it soon grew to a bright glow.

"I get about one nap a month, Lieutenant. It's a luxury. This seemed like a good time. Didn't know when to expect you."

The light revealed a man familiar to Jefferson, a serious young officer with a thick moustache and shoulder-length blond hair. He had seen Custer before, usually leading a brigade of Michigan men in concert with the Vermonters, sometimes orchestrating a reckless charge against retreating Confederates, in a wide-rimmed hat. Jefferson noted that without the hat, George Custer had a high forehead and a receding hairline. He stood behind a table littered with maps.

"Lieutenant Chase, I am Captain George Armstrong Custer."

"Yes, Sir," Jefferson saluted. "Lieutenant Jefferson Chase of the Vermont One."

"I know you well, Lieutenant, although I've never met you. I've heard praise for your leadership and your actions on the battlefield. The Vermont One describes you as an authentic hero. I wanted to meet you."

"The Vermont One is exaggerating," Jefferson replied. "Their officers and yours are the heroes."

"The real heroes are the men on horseback." Custer asserted. "I've been informed that you were wounded at Brandy Station."

"It was nothing, Sir. A minor annoyance."

"What are your impressions of our encounter there?"

Custer moved to a chair behind the map table, and gestured for Jefferson to sit in a folding chair on the other side. The captain leaned forward, resting his forearms on the table, and looked directly at Jefferson.

"I'm proud of what our cavalry accomplished. I'm still overcome by the chaos and the intensity, trying to fight in close quarters in all four directions," Jefferson offered.

"It would seem that you made a good target out there, with your size and rank," Custer said. "What is your opinion of this great war?"

Jefferson was mindful of the intrusiveness of Custer's stare. The captain's eyes, squinted under furrowed brows, seemed at once both curious and withering, a mixture that challenged their target to respond with pertinence and alacrity. For some reason, Custer was evaluating him.

"It has lasted longer than I expected, or hoped. A clear outcome probably won't occur soon."

"And how would you change that?"

"Captain Custer, my opinion isn't based on a military background, nor am I privy to all of the circumstances, but I feel that the Union cavalry has been underutilized," Jefferson said.

"How would you use them?"

"More reconnaissance. Directly addressing Jeb Stuart's cavalry, surprise attacks, forays behind enemy lines. It seems that we've been an afterthought, serving mainly as support for the infantry."

"That's an astute observation, Lieutenant. Just out of curiosity, is that thought based on a desire for more action?"

"Only if it will hasten the end of the war. I don't like any part of this war. Killing other men will haunt me forever, however noble our cause. When I was a boy, I wouldn't even go squirrel hunting."

Custer briefly grinned. "Your boyhood. You grew up in Vermont. And your brother is Joshua Chase?"

Jefferson was taken aback. "Yes, Sir."

"Your brother was an instructor at West Point while I was there. He was a mentor to me. Gave me some of the best advice I ever got about honor and responsibility. He is a fair and highly intelligent man. I suspected that you were related, both from Vermont. That was another reason that I wanted to meet you."

"Joshua was wounded at Fredericksburg. I don't know anything else, except that he is recuperating."

"I'm glad that he's still with us. Any other siblings?"

"A brother, Jonathan. He's fighting with the Confereracy."

Custer raised his eyebrows. "A rebel? Why does a Vermont boy have Southern sympathies?"

"He earned a law degree from the University of Virginia and married a Virginia girl. He's made his home in Virginia for several years."

"Is he one of Jeb Stuart's boys?"

"No, Sir. Infantry."

Jefferson turned the conversation around. "You, Sir. You're from Michigan?"

For the first time, Custer looked away as he spoke. "Born in Ohio, raised in Michigan. I don't know how that has contributed to my military career."

"Obviously some past experience has served you well," Jefferson said.

"When this war is over, I would hope that historians will record that I was gallant and resourceful, and that I loved my men."

"I would hope that they will record that you survived it, Sir."

"Good point. I will survive. Great tragedies spawn great men. I am confident that opportunities await me."

"We're both young men. Sometimes, wars don't consider that."

"Lieutenant, I believe in taking the battle to the enemy. Dictate the outcome by acting first. When one has a reputation for being consistent and persistent, that alone can guarantee survival of some sort." He leaned back in his chair and crossed his legs. He continued. "If that attitude prevailed throughout the Union hierarchy, this war would be over in a month. Too often, our decision makers overestimate the enemy. I will never do that." He paused briefly. "Nor will I ever underestimate an enemy."

He was not finished. "Twenty minutes after a battle is joined, I can predict the winner. One has to exercise judgment as to whether to press an advantage or to moderate. When there is doubt, you attack."

Jefferson felt the need to nod. He wouldn't contribute to the topic.

"What will you do after the war, Captain Custer?"

"If we achieve victory, I will continue my military service. If we lose, I will endeavor to do the same. And you, Lieutenant Chase?"

"I will probably raise and train horses."

"Your heroism marks you as special. You don't aspire to greater glory?"

"Such as?"

"Politics perhaps. Some undertaking which will verify your status as a remarkable man."

"My father is remarkable. He was a college professor. My mother was remarkable as a wife and mother."

"Well said. My parents were remarkable too. Devout Methodists. My mother made me a soldier's uniform when I was four years old."

"Good memories," Jefferson offered.

"I hated schoolwork, yet for a while I was a schoolteacher, not a very good one. I was destined to be a soldier. I'll let you in on this, Lieutenant. I've seen new orders, new directions for our cavalry. You will have many opportunities for heroism, and for advancing in the ranks."

"I'm pleased with promotions already. Being a lieutenant is an honor."

"These are not common times. The war has seen many officer casualties, and the scope of conflict is so large, that ongoing officer promotions are a necessity. You, Lieutenant, will be a cavalry brevet-colonel before this war is over."

"With due respect, Sir, that's unlikely. My entire military experience is two years."

"But you are a leader. Your two years have not gone unnoticed. You have good instincts. Right now this is an old man's war, conducted by men who are too cautious and too patient. By necessity, the cream, the young cream will rise to the top. That will be particularly true in the cavalry."

"Captain Custer, you are deserving of advancement. It is not a priority of mine, however."

"This brings up another reason for our meeting today. This is confidential. I have received word that I am being considered for a brevet promotion to brevet Brigadier-General. I will soon after begin a process to name you as brevet-colonel. There are those in important positions who respond to me."

Jefferson was silent.

"You understand that the brevet designation is only a reward to you, if it occurs. There is little or no addition of responsibility or of pay. However, until these hostilities end, you will be addressed as Colonel Chase. Your rank will then revert to your rank when named. It will signal our gratitude to you. If you leave the service, the brevet rank will identify you. It is all only symbolic, but it does signify special recognition. "

"Thank you, Sir."

"The one thing I would add today is that a good soldier understands sacrifice. I am not the best soldier in our army, but I do understand sacrifice, dedication, physical and mental, to a resolution of conflict. Whatever it takes."

"Captain, forgive me for sounding impertinent, but do you have something to balance this war, something to escape the daily horror?"

"Some would resort to liquid spirits, but I gave that up years ago. A lady named Libby is very important to me. In my darkest hours, thoughts of her calm me."

Fifteen minutes later, Jefferson remounted for the ride back to the Vermont camp.

What was that all about, he wondered, an officer from another unit praising him, honoring him? Perhaps Custer was repaying some perceived debt to Joshua. Maybe it was a tribute to another young officer in "an old man's war."

Conceited, brash, unpredictable, pompous. Those were descriptions that he had heard whenever the subject of Custer had come up. He had evidence of some of that now, but the young captain had impressed him in that brief meeting. Custer was obviously attuned to personal success and adulation, but much of that had translated to Union success and Union image. He led his men, and as perilous and impetuous as that leadership sometimes appeared, it had marked him as special.

Brevet Brigadier-General. At the age of 24. Incredible.

****

For years, Herkimer Grimes had drifted in and out of diversions and occupations, many of which held little interest for him or no relevance to his abilities, which realistically were limited to using a gun, horsemanship, and herding cattle. He had been a bouncer in a brothel, a ranch hand in three states, a shotgun guard for a mining company, a bounty hunter, and for one depressing year, a bartender.

The last months had been comfortable. He had been hired in 1862 as the sheriff of Virginia City, Nevada, in no small part attributable to his expanding fame. Author Robert Gerdon had created a legend from his New York desk, and in the process had become splendidly wealthy.

The Herkimer Grimes dime novel series had been outsold in its genre only by missives on Kit Carson. They had inundated the East and then permeated the territories.

Gerdon had tried to contact him, but had been pointedly ignored by his illusory celebrity. The notoriety bothered Herk, partly because the circumstances were contrived, imaginary ramblings by a greenhorn who had limited knowledge of his subject and his protagonist. The other objection dealt with the image that he carried wherever he went. Too often he had to answer the question, "You the real Herk Grimes?" Several years earlier, he had broken a whiskey bottle over the head of a drunken cowboy who had challenged him in a saloon. "Herk Grimes?" You don't look so tough to me. You ain't nuthin' but a barkeep." He leaned over, his foul breath inches from Herk. Herk knocked him cold with a full whiskey bottle just as the man's gun started to clear its holster.

"Have a drink on me," Herk had mumbled.

More than once he had changed his name. As "Slim Smith," he drove cattle in Missouri. He had been "Waco Johnson" for a while. In each case, his identity had eventually surfaced, and he subsequently moved on.

It was his reputation which drew the interest of a Virginia City group which wanted to reform their city, however. After a somewhat lengthy search, they located him in Nebraska, again herding cattle.

It was an easy sell. They would pay him the astounding amount of $1,000 a year to keep order in their booming silver city. He could choose his own deputies. They would build him a jail and an impressive office. They would pay for a permanent room in a hotel.

Herk took the job with no reluctance. Two decades earlier he had been a peace officer, a Texas Ranger, and that had suited him well. He was fifty-two years old. It was time to settle into some sort of permanence in his life.

By the time he rode into Virginia City a month later, the jail had already been constructed, not as nice as the group had promised him, but still serviceable and well-built. A sign-painter had already brushed "Herkimer Grimes, Sheriff, Virginia City" onto a wooden sign to the left of the entrance to the office which fronted the jail area. As news of his arrival spread through the city, small crowds assembled on the planks outside, young boys peered in his window. A legend was in town.

"Mr. Grimes, welcome. Any trouble finding us?" The spokesman for city officials was Theodore Wisecap, a mining company owner, a successful entrepreneur from California, already wealthy when he moved the main concentration of his business to Virginia City.

"None."

"Settle in, Mr. Grimes. I'll show you around tomorrow."

Initially, Herk's only problem was finding deputies.

To him, the populace of Virginia City seemed to fall into three categories: the hardscrabble types with names like "Scruffy," and "Ole Virginny" and "Mosquito Moe," who were barely literate and frequently drunk; the stuffed shirts like Wisecap—citizens named "Philby" and "Ronald" and "Zachary," who understood silver ore and money, but were mystified by firearms; and the criminal element, obvious ne'er-do-wells who hung in the shadows waiting for a score of some kind.

It seemed to him that the meanest, toughest resident was Madame Lil, the owner of a local whorehouse, which he sometimes utilized, to the consternation of the city fathers. She had bitten the nose off of a recalcitrant once, and fired buckshot into the posterior of another, who had refused to pay. The thought of deputizing her amused him.

Scores of new residents arrived weekly. The town was growing at an alarming rate, and he alone was the sentinel against mischief. It hadn't mattered much for a while. Rising early one morning to walk the main street, he noticed a flickering light in Wisecap's building, and saw a sliver of wood missing from the area around the front door lock. He pressed against the wall next to the door, and when a slapdash man crept out carrying several bags, Herk pressed the barrel of his pistol against the man's nose.

"Drop them bags and lie down, or you'll be breathing out of a hole in your face," Herk growled. The man complied meekly.

A few days later, he had closed down a potential gunfight in front of a saloon. "Go ahead and draw. I'll shoot down the one who wins." The two combatants ceased hostilities and skulked away.

A favorite Herkimer moment to the citizenry concerned the afternoon when he had intercepted a notorious gunfighter on his way into Virginia City. Herk had been alerted by an anxious miner who rushed into his office around noon.

"I seed him, Sheriff. Ben Abrams, the Cyclone. He were out at our camp tryin' to set up some poker playin.' Told my buddies he's comin' here to run you out of town."

"Cyclone Abrams? Never heard of him."

"Wal sir, he's a comin' for yeh. Should be right behin' me."

When Abrams rode up to the city limits, Herk was sitting on his horse at the end of Union Street waiting for him.

Instantly Herk understood that the man was a sham. He was pathetically thin, wearing a stained dress shirt with garters on the sleeves, large jewel-encrusted holsters on his hips, and a flop hat with a rattlesnake skin headband. He had nervous eyes, a feature that Herk had noticed often in men who bluffed their ways to unsavory reputations. He's a gambler, Herk reasoned, not a gunfighter.

"Hold it. You the famous Cyclone?"

The man stopped. His horse continued to paw. "Who wants to know?"

"Grimes. Heard that you're lookin' for me."

"Mebbe."

"Well?"

Abrams looked away and licked his lips. He looked back at the badge on Herk's chest. "Let me pass. Ain't lookin' for trouble."

"Well, you found it anyway. Don't want you in Virginia City, Mr. Cyclone."

"You can't do that. Can't keep a man outta town." His tone had changed. He was now pleading.

"Heard you threatened me. Don't much want you around."

"Well, I'm goin' to ride in."

"One more step and you'll be dead before you get a gun out of them fancy holsters. Then I'll shoot that horse, and we'll bury you both in the same grave." Herk put his hand on the butt of his pistol.

"Damnation!" Abrams groused. He turned his horse's head and galloped away.

Those who witnessed the incident soon spun the tale of Herk's facing down a ruthless killer and driving him off.

At the end of three months, the town was calm. Herk had not yet fired a shot, but three or four jail cells were inhabited almost every night. The drunks and miscreants he freed after a few days. The hard cases he kept for the district court.

Then an improbable arrival in Virgina City altered his workload.

He noticed a weary-looking horse plodding slowly past his office. On its swayed back was a large man, weighing perhaps over three-hundred pounds. Disordered gray hair flopped on his shoulders, and a gray beard lolled on his chest.

There was no mistaking the profile and the outsized ears.

Herk stepped to the front of the porch. "Big?" he called out.

The man walked his horse over. "That you, Herkimer?"

"Big. You been eatin' well?"

"Reckon so."

"Christ, man. You're as big as a house. Near didn't recognize you."

"Yeah. You look old."

Herk smiled. "What you doin' here?"

"Nuthin.' You the law?" he nodded at the badge.

"That worry you?"

"Ain't done nuthin' wrong. Don't aim to."

"You just passin' through?"

"Dunno. Lookin' for a reason to settle somewhere."

"Lookin' for work?"

"Mebbe."

"I need a deputy. Pays well."

Big was quiet. Herk persisted.

"You were a good Texas Ranger, Big. This'd be a lot like that. Protectin' people. Keepin' the law. Lot less travelin. Lot more money."

"Spect so."

"You had a bath this month?"

"Dunno. What month is it?"

"Your last haircut?"

"Can't 'member. Few years back."

"I'm gonna deputize you. Then we'll buy you another shirt, and then get the dust washed off. Get you a haircut over to William Bird's. Buy you a big meal. I expect you're hungry."

"I could eat," Herk sensed that the giant was smiling. With the beard overwhelming the round face, he couldn't tell.

For the next few months, Herk Grimes and Big Head Franklin kept the peace in Virginia City. Incidents were dealt with promptly.

One morning, Herk was standing in front of the office on C Street when he saw Big Head walking up the plank sidewalk a block away. The deputy had two men draped over his shoulders, both apparently unconscious. As strollers on the plank boards greeted him, he acknowledged them.

"Mawning, deputy."

"Mawnin."

"Good day to you, Mr. Big Head."

"Mawnin' son."

"Nice day, Mr. Franklin."

"Mawnin'."

"Drunks, Herkimer. Passed out on the street. This un' he nodded his head to the left, "came to, pulled a gun. Smacked him down."

"Lookin' to put them down somewhere?"

"Ain't gonna tote them around all day, Herkimer. 'Sides, this'un smells a little ripe."

Mark Twain, a young writer at the *Territorial Enterprise,* the city's newspaper, described the scene as "…Samson in spurs delivering the Phillistines."

July 8 of 1863 began with ominous news delivered by a courier. A half-week earlier, a terrible three-day battle had been fought in the War Between the States, an epic encounter in Gettysburg, Pennsylvania. The news described it as a standoff, a melee with no clear winner, but with an appalling loss of human lives.

For years, Herk had witnessed the worst of the human condition. He questioned the motivations, the capacity for evil, and the endless malevolence of mankind. He had seemingly been hardened by the atrocities of the Comanche and the Mexicans, and by the participants in the Regulator-Moderator War so many years ago. But his imperturbable demeanor and his willingness to rise above chaos was beginning to crumble. He felt disgust. He felt sadness. He felt despair.

The diminished value of the two lawmen probably began with an official visit from Theodore Wisecap, eighteen months into Herk's employment.

"Mr. Grimes, we are pleased with your service to us, but…" He paused, and he had Herk's full attention. "We do not support your patronage of the establishment run by Madame Lil. It speaks of immorality. Such places are contrary to God's plan."

"Mr. Wisecap, I been in a lot of towns. Them that have whorehouses are settled. Men with things to do don't sit around and plan bank robberies."

"That may well be. But you, sir, represent the law."

"They are not illegal."

"I will not debate this. We are advising you to refrain from going there."

Herk was bothered only by the man's haughty attitude. Wisecap had probably cheated miners on a regular basis, and now he was preaching morality. It didn't matter much. If he wanted company in the future, Herk could always ask Lil to send a companion to his hotel room.

"If that's an order, I'll abide by it." Herk's response was spoken in a monotone. As he finished, he turned away from Wisecap and began to shuffle through a stack of papers on his desk.

"Very well," Wisecap muttered as he opened the door to leave.

Around that time, Herk was troubled by a set of recurring incidents. A pimple-faced teenaged boy began to follow him around. That accelerated. The boy would startle him by junping into his path from between buildings, pointing his finger to simulate a pistol, and clamping down his thumb as if he had just fired at Herk. Then he would fix Herk with a sneer and shout "Bang!" The first few times it had happened, Herk came close to drawing down on him.

"Big, that kid bothers me. I'm afraid I'm goin' to shoot him down someday."

"Yell at him."

"Can't. He runs away."

"Shoot him in the foot."

"If I knew who he is, I'd speak to his folks."

"He's the son of Whistlin' Annie, over to Lil's place."

Herk didn't question his deputy about how he knew that. He unhitched his horse from the post in front of his office, mounted, and rode to Lil's on the east side of town, R Street, which meandered up the mountain.

She was away from the main red light district, and worlds apart from the squalor in most of those houses. The building looked like a small hotel, clean, ornate, and perfumed inside.

Lil answered his knock. She was years past actively participating in the intimate components of her trade. She was probably Hank's age, maybe older, with flabby arms and a fleshy countenance which always glowed with too much make-up. Her no-nonsense demeanor was the force behind the success of her house. Her girls didn't leave her. They were well paid, well fed, and pampered.

"Sheriff, kinda early to jump on a girl, ain't it?"

"Not here for that. Need to talk to Annie."

"She in some kind of trouble?"

"No. Just need to have a word."

"Probably still abed. Had a good night. Lots of customers. I'll fetch her."

Hank settled on a red divan in a corner of the parlor. If he appeared relaxed when Annie came down, his presence wouldn't alarm her or give her the wrong idea. The house was unnaturally quiet. Middle of the night for these people, he thought.

Minutes later, a slim brunette with sad eyes walked into the parlor. Hank knew her well; he had spent several nights with her in the past. He had never seen her like this. Without makeup, she had evident wrinkles in the corners of her eyes and her mouth. She looked quite ordinary, even a bit haggard. Among the most popular of Lil's dozen, she was missing a bottom tooth, and had gotten her nickname from the whistle sound when she pronounced an "s."

"Sheriff, didn't have time to purty up. Too early. All the same, I'll make you happy." She pulled away her negligee, revealing a well-turned leg.

"Not here for that. Need to talk to you about your boy."

"Sonny Joe? What's he gone and done?"

"Nothing serious. More of a problem."

Herk explained the repeated harassing.

"He's growin' too fast," she offered. "Sixteen years old. Walks around this house like a rooster. Gets what he wants from the girls. Ain't really afeared of nobody, 'cept Lil. She wants him to move out. He ain't real smart, but he ain't never come up agin the law before."

"Maybe you should put him to work around here."

"Tried that. He stays up all night in his room. Gets one of the girls, or they get him, at closin' time most nights. Then sleeps to noon. Been doin' that since he was twelve years old."

"The girls don't mind that?"

"Some of them like that. Figure he's pretty good at pleasurin' by now. They tell me he's as big as a horse."

"Where is he now?"

"Asleep. Bedded Mae all mornin'."

Mae? Herk paused. She was the star of the house, a rounded, rambunctious redhead of surpassing beauty, the most requested and expensive whore on the property.

"Sheriff, what d'ya want me to do?"

"Tell him I've had enough. I'm either goin' to shoot him or arrest him."

"Lately, he been talkin' bout getting' a gun. Asked me once what killin' be like."

"What did you tell him?"

"Don't know. Never killed nobody."

"Gonna go now." Herk stood up. "Tell your boy what I said."

"Sheriff, want some foolin' around? Won't cost you nothin'."

She gave him her most lasvicious look. Herk understood that she was offering him an apology in the only way she knew.

"No, ma'am. I'm working."

He was seen leaving the house. It was 10 am.

Bullets were fired around a saloon one night. Big Head was on duty. Alerted by several shots, he grabbed a shotgun from the rack, checked that it was loaded, and hurried to the scene. He pushed open the swinging doors and eased into the room. A wild-looking man was in the center of the saloon, the other patrons huddled in the corners. The man's right arm dangled loosely, a pistol in his hand. He was stumbling and twisting in circles next to several overturned tables.

"I'm the meanest sonuvabitch in this here town. Anybody argue with that?"

Big Head leveled the shotgun. "It's over, mister, drop the gun!"

The obscenely inebriated man turned to face him.

"Oh, looka here. The big ugly depitty. Whatcha gonna do, depitty?"

"Drop the gun, now!"

Out of the corner of his eye, Big Head saw a man move toward him on the left at the same time that the drunk lifted his pistol.

Big Head threw a blind punch with his left fist, connecting with the attacker's nose. His shotgun roared, obliterating the drunk's face. Pellets ripped across the room, one ricocheting off of the bar and piercing the eye of the bartender, a gentle sort named Cyrus.

The barroom was still for an instant.

"Look, he done shot Cyrus! Jesus, depitty!"

The incident would resonate for weeks. Herk defended and praised his deputy, but was also quoted in the*Territorial Enterprise* as saying, "He was attacked on both sides by men who were armed and dangerous. Too damn bad if someone else got shot."

"Bad move by me, Big. I was getting' tired of the story that you fired a wild shot, killin' a man who was too drunk to fight, and accidentally shooting Cyrus too. Shoulda said something good about the barkeep."

Once again, Herk was visited by Wisecap.

He began a tirade even before the door closed behind him. "Now see here, Grimes. We're paying you to keep the peace, not destroy it. Did you hear that word, peace?"

"Mr. Wisecap, there was not even a hearing. The witnesses supported Big's story, most of them."

"Well, we've got a dead man and another blind in one eye for life."

"What do you want us to do? Keep peace with a hickory stick?"

"No. we want you to protect this town, not wipe it out. In addition, you were seen at Madame Lil's after we told you to stop patronizing it." Spittle was forming at the corner of his mouth.

"Who is this 'we' you keep talkin' about? All I ever see is your fat ass."

"Mr. Grimes!"

"You ain't even the mayor. Somebody with authority wants us gone, we'll leave tomorrow. How about you keepin' your mouth shut, and let us do our job."

Wisecap, chastened and silenced, turned to leave. Herk wasn't finished.

"You get a chance, check the crime in this town for the last two years. We are protecting it."

"Spect you feel better now," Big Head said.

"You know somethin', Big? Things have changed here. Keepin' the law is almost too big for just two of us. Sometime, this territory will become a state. That happens, these ole boys will cast us off, and hire a police force with fifteen men, with a policeman in charge, from a big Eastern city. Doesn't matter much who we offend now. Another year, maybe two, they'll be finished with us."

"Wal, don't matter none. I was lookin' for a job when I came here. Just start lookin' again."

Over the winter months, the city was relatively peaceful, and its growth slowed temporarily.

Still the peacekeepers were occasionally challenged. One man accosted Herk on C Street in a playful manner one cool afternoon.

"Ah, the great Herkimer Grimes. Read all your books. Ain't nobody that good."

"They ain't my books."

"Kinda uppity, ain'y you?"

"Mister, you got a problem, spit it out. Otherwise, keep movin'."

"They say you outrassled a crazy mountain man. You too puny to do that, aincha?"

"Probably so," Herk answered as he brushed past the man.

The man was offended. He took the encounter to the next plateau. "Not only puny. You're a coward too, I'd wager."

Ahead, Herk saw the boy, Annie's son, pointing an imaginary gun at him. It was the second time that day that the boy had surprised him. Annie hadn't talked to him, Herk guessed, or else he doesn't care. He would corner the boy now, and properly scare him.

He was stopped by the man, who grabbed his arm.

"I can take you with one arm, hero."

"You're welcome to try," Herk said, pulling away. "Your ass will sit in jail for a week."

"You're an old man, an old man," the man answered, taking a roundhouse punch at Herk, who swung his elbow, catching the man in the temple. The man fell backwards and sat in a light dusting of snow, rubbing his head.

"Ooops," Herk said, and looked up the street. The boy was gone.

He looked back at the man, who was regarding him with a dazed expression. He then turned and walked back down C Street, mumbling to himself, "Damn you, Robert Gerdon."

Whistlin' Annie watched her son from a second floor window of Lil's House. He was in the large vacant area behind the house, shooting his pistol again. The pistol was a new model, a leftover from some patron who had not come back to claim it, he told her.

Over and over, he crouched, practicing a quick draw, firing, and stopping only to reload. She didn't want to know where he had gotten an illimitable supply of ammunition. Better if she didn't know. Took it off Lil's patrons, maybe, or stole it from some merchant in town, most likely. There was too much about him she didn't know.

She did recognize that he was changing, a transformation which now included insolence and volatility, and had recently taken the form of abuse. Mae appeared one morning, after a particularly noisy rut with him, with makeup caked over a discolored eye, and bruises on her neck.

Lil had been quick to respond, attacking him with a riding crop, and threatening to remove his manhood if he ever treated another girl in that way. She had turned her fury to Annie. "Get him out of this house afore he turns seventeen, or I'll kick you out too!"

Earlier, Annie had tried to talk to him about Herk's complaint. He had sneered, laughed, and left the room before she finished. In a perverse act to control her, to show his indifference to her, he tried to mount her, his own mother, the next morning. He achieved penetration before she fought him off, scratching his face in the process. She couldn't tell anyone, especially Lil. Under his bed, she found a copy of Robert Gerdon's *Herk Grimes Tames a Town.* Each page had been dog-eared as if he had read it over and over. Sonny Joe's reading skills were seriously deficient. He must have struggled through the narrative, or maybe the girls had read it to him.

She didn't want to leave Lil's. It was all she knew. She had been introduced to whoring in California when she was fifteen, and in a desperate time. A year later she was pregnant. Of course, she had no idea of the identity of the father. Sonny Joe was born. Somehow she had managed to continue her life as a prostitute, despite her son. She was thirty-three in 1863, but looked considerably older.

She only had four or five years of earning left. But she had a plan. Over the years she had stashed as much money as she could in a box on the floor of her closet. Every few months, she took it out and counted it in private. Her last tally showed over two thousand dollars. When she left the profession, she would start a whorehouse of her own, or better yet, find a nice house in San Francisco, and settle down in comfort. Maybe both. By that time, Sonny Joe would be gone and forgotten. Good riddance, she thought, without a trace of guilt.

For his part, Sonny Joe was ready to leave, and he had a plan too, a grand design for his life, for becoming famous, and ultimately wealthy.

He prepared for that every day behind the whorehouse. Again and again he drew and fired, each shot chunking into the stump of a tree the size of a human torso.

Theodore Wisecap excelled at meetings. As the financial leader of Virginia City, he usually ascended to the chairmanship or advisor capacity of any gathering. He was unfailingly self-appointed to those positions. Wisecap had a bluster, unrestricted brazenness, and a healthy ego.

He convened an informal meeting in the late weeks of 1863. Present were the other high rollers of the city, George Hearst, Lemuel Bowers, William Morris Stewart, and three bankers who had built an unsavory but unprovable reputation for bilking prospectors. No matter how they achieved that status, William Sharon, William Ralston, and Darius Ogden Mills were rich, so to Wisecap's mind, they were important. These men had monetary control of Virginia City. In most other ways, they were unremarkable.

"Gentlemen," Wisecap began, "it's time we consider other law enforcement possibilities for our city."

"Theodore," Bowers interrupted, "you talking about firing Grimes?" He seemed astonished at that suggestion.

"Consider this if you will," Wisecap continued, "We have one sheriff and one deputy. In two years, we may have a population of fifteen or twenty thousand. We will be very large."

"Why not hire more deputies?" Stewart asked.

"No. What we need to consider is a police force, a trained staff which can supervise the business of controlling crime."

"With Grimes in charge?" Bowers questioned.

"Absolutely not. The man is not an organizer or supervisor. He has no background which would be helpful. He is a lawman only by opportunity. In the future we cannot rely on audacity and ammunition to manage a city which may spread for miles."

"Have you talked to Grimes about this?" Miles queried.

"Yes," Wisecap lied, "He agrees that the job has outgrown his capabilities."

"I don't know," Bowers stated, "he's done a fine job here."

"There are varied opinions on that. In his time here, he has frequented Lil's whorehouse, wounded an innocent citizen, assaulted another citizen in broad daylight, and has been disrespectful of authority consistently."

"Sounds like a good sheriff to me," Ralston joked, "He leaves us alone."

Wisecap ignored the comment. "This is what we need to do. With your permission, we will actively look for new personnel. I've got an envoy in Chicago as we speak, looking for candidates, another in San Francisco. We can attract many of their number for our force, organize precincts."

"Is the mayor aware of this?"

"Sometimes we need to help him out. As to Grimes, he will find employment in some cow town that needs a gunfighter to keep order. That is all, gentlemen."

As the group filed out, Wisecap smirked. Fat ass, indeed.

The end was near for Herk, with a codicil. An official city contingent visited him. thanked him for his service, and told him that he was dismissed. But, they continued, if he would agree to stay on until a police supervisor was hired, they would double his salary for that time.

He agreed. He was not particularly offended or annoyed. He had recently begun reflecting to the halcyon days as a cowpuncher, on horseback, alone with herds of cattle, or mingling with cowboys who were unimpressed or unaware of his legend.

Early in January of 1864, a visitor to the sheriff's office announced his presence with a knock. That's odd, Herk thought, nobody ever knocked before entering his office. "Come in," he called, anxious to see who had the extreme manners or temerity to announce themselves with a rap. He had a brief thought that he ought to get his pistol ready.

"Good day to you, Sheriff." The man was nicely dressed, even to a cravat. He was young, with a bushy head of black hair and a brushy moustache that matched it.

"I am Samuel Clemens of the *Territorial Enterprise.* I write under the name of Mark Twain."

"What do you need, Mr. Clemens?"

'Well, I thought I'd be writing about a crime this week, a kidnapping. It turned out to be a prank by some acquaintances of mine. So, instead, I would like to write a story about you. I'd like to have a conversation with you, Mr. Grimes. May I sit down?"

"I suppose."

Clemens sat in the chair across from Herk, and extracted a pencil from his coat pocket. "Are you busy?"

"Not so much. What do you want to talk about?"

"You. We ran a story a while ago about your dismissal. We understand progress, but we also need to honor you for the exceptional work you've done here. I'd like to write a two-piece or three-piece story on you, on your life."

"Ain't going to happen, Mr. Clemens."

"Why, Sir?"

"Seems people have been writing about me for years, stuff that ain't true. Brought a lot of misery, caused some bad times for me. To be honest, I don't trust writers." Herk didn't smile after he spoke.

"That may be, Mr. Grimes, but I'd only print the truth, whatever you feel comfortable with. You have seen history. You have made history."

"Mr. Clemens, if I was gonna let somebody write about me, it would be you. But all that I want to do when I leave here is to get lost somewhere. Don't want no crowds lining up to shake my hand, or to shoot me."

"You don't want me to set the stories straight?"

"Wouldn't do any good. Just call attention to me again."

"Let's leave it this way. If you change your mind at all, if there's anything you want to say, you get a hold of me. I promise you that I will stick to facts, and that I will let you read whatever I write before it's printed. I will be most fair to you, Sir."

"Fair enough."

"One more thing, Mr. Grimes. May I shake your hand?"

Herk stood and walked around the desk, extending his hand.

"And may I say, Mr. Grimes, that I think you're a remarkable man."

****

As 1863 came to a close, Cecil "Bravo" Wright was ensconced in a barren area of Texas.

Cecil Wright had been born on the third day of 1824 in Cooper County, Missouri Territory, a husky 9-pound screamer, the first child of his parents, Mann and Ida Wright, itinerant farmers in their late thirties. Ida produced twin sons the next year, and died as they were born. Mann could not find a way to raise three young sons, so he gave them to a second cousin, and they were raised, neglected, in a large, unruly household with no discipline.

The twins left home one day in 1849, and were never heard from again. Cecil, husky and unschooled, stayed in the Spartan surroundings for two more years, and then fled to the Mississippi River for sustenance. He caught the eye of a gambler, who immediately employed him as a shill and bodyguard. Soon his specialty became rolling drunks on the waterfront, taking from them anything of value, and leaving behind beaten and broken bodies. Those monies staked the gambler to many poker games, and being of more than ordinary skill with advanced techniques of cheating, he supported the two of them with his winnings.

Cecil learned much in his five years with the gambler, not so much about card-playing as about bullying, taking advantage of people, and breaking all moral and ethical parameters if it benefitted him.

He married briefly, to a teen-aged girl whom he beat up on their wedding night. She left him a week later, disappearing into the crowds along the St. Louis waterfront. For the next decade he worked the river towns, always a step ahead of the law. During that time, he killed his first two men, one in a brawl, the other after the man had the audacity to fight back while Cecil was divesting him of his wallet.

At the age of 34, he was burly, strong, and unremittingly evil, but still directionless. In spite of his errant ways, he had not spent a minute in jail, or been arrested on any charge. Well aware of that good fortune, he accelerated his activities. For three years, he broke into businesses in three states and held up payroll wagons from gold and silver camps.

Then, in 1861, back in Missouri, he met William Clarke Quantrill.

Quantrill, 24 years old, was a charismatic Ohioan with a checkered past. He had been in his young life, a schoolteacher, a gambler, a horse thief, a murderer, and a soldier. Born into a Unionist family, he had changed philosophies during time spent in Utah. When the Civil War started, he had enlisted in the Confederate army. Deciding that regular army was too indecisive and plodding, he organized a guerilla band of a dozen men, and began staging raids on pro-Union forces across the border in Kansas. He was a persuasive recruiter, and Cecil Wright was at a point in his life where he wanted to make a statement, to freely engage in any activity which would test his mettle and fill his pockets.

"Mr. Wright, you will not only be doing a service to your country, but you will also be exposed, let's say, to opportunities for becoming a rich man."

"I ain't no soldier. Couldn't take orders from some prissy-assed officer."

"This is not a normal army. We will operate with their approval, but they can't tell us what to do, where to go, or who to kill. That's the beauty of this for a man like you. Whatever we do will be legal," the well groomed young man asserted, repeating for emphasis, "Whatever we do."

The guerilla strength grew rapidly. By the summer of 1862, more than fifty hardcases and former soldiers had joined the group. Quantrill had changed his tactics from harassing and looting to murder and destruction. Cecil Wright had found a home. Ruthless in his participation, he was by then called "Bravo," killer. He had shot numerous Unionists, soldiers, and sympathizers, many in execution style. The so-called "Bushwhackers" had turned brutal, and Bravo Wright was among the most inhuman. Amazingly, he noted, the raiders were heroes throughout Missouri. That fact doubled the size of the crude army, then doubled it again. By 1863, William Quantrill had a force of over 400 men, including a young man from Clay County, Missouri named Frank James.

On the Kansas side, Senator James Lane organized his own guerilla army, the Jayhawkers, and soon that group and federal forces were making forays into Missouri.

Around that time, a 23-year old psychopath named Bill Anderson joined the Quantrill forces, motivated by his father's murder by pro-Northern neighbors in Agnes City, Kansas. While he was earning his spurs and eventually rising to Quantrill's lieutenant, an occurrence in Kansas City, Kansas provoked one of the most heinous incidents in guerilla history.

The Union army imprisoned a group of female relatives of known members of the Bushwhackers. The ladies were held in a rundown building in Kansas City. The building collapsed onto the hapless group. Bill Anderson's sister Josephine was killed.

Another of his sisters was crippled for life. Bill Anderson wanted revenge. Quantrill knew how to get it for him.

Lawrence, Kansas was virtually unprotected. It shouldn't have been. It was the epicenter of anti-slavery activity for the entire area. It was the home of Senator James Lane. It had already endured several raids and attacks, and a brief siege. One of the raids had been the burning of the Free-State hotel, back in 1856, which in turn provoked the John Brown massacre on Pottawatomie Creek.

Kansas City was too spread out, too close to troops, too neutral to become a site for vengeance. Lawrence, however, was a ripe target.

On the morning of August 21, 1863, William Quantrill and over 400 men galloped into Lawrence soon after dawn. Pausing briefly on the outskirts, he had given the order, "Kill every man and boy you find. Burn every building."

There was no advance warning, and no hiding. An overwhelming force of misfits and killers rode into Lawrence shooting, led by a well-dressed, cultured-looking leader, and a brutish lieutenant.

In an outrageous two hours, the Bushwhackers murdered over 180 men and boys, some in their early teens, others innocuous senior citizens. Bill Anderson left a macabre trail. He would break down a front door, force all residents outside, and then shoot the males in the head at close range while the rest of the family cowered and screamed. Bravo Wright followed him, shooting each body, dead or not, several times. When Anderson stopped to reload, Wright delivered death.

Senator James Lane escaped by hiding in a corn field, still in his pajamas. A large collection of men died together on Lawrence's main street, herded there by Quantrill for maximum effect. Bloodlust increased. Some of the invaders were cutting off the heads of the corpses. Quantrill noticed Anderson with a grim, purposeful, angry scowl on his face, his clothes stained with blood. Bravo Wright was smiling.

Gunfire was incessant for over an hour. Then the guerillas began looting and burning. At around 9 am, they rode away, leaving the apocalypse behind.

Quantrill led them south to Texas. They would lay low for a while.

As 1863 waned, Bravo Wright was restless. The inactivity bothered him. He wanted more. More killing. More looting.

CHAPTER TWENTY-FOUR

1864

Professor Jeremiah Chase sat in the rocking chair next to the window most of the day.

New snow was falling heavily, adding fresh layers to a cover which had reached a foot since December.

His world was bleak and gray, not so much from the Vermont weather, as from his perspective. He was a shell of the man who had been such a dynamic component of his family and of his university community. There was the weight loss, he wasn't used to eating alone, and there was perpetual worry, and for years he hadn't been in control of much beyond the spiritless lessons he prepared for the classes he still taught. Old friends were dying or moving on. His darling Molly had been gone for four years, and his three sons were scattered on various battlegrounds in a war that he didn't fully understand.

The letter had arrived in the university mail of the previous day.

The address was scribbled to "Professor Chase, University of Vermont, Burlington, Vermont," and in the upper left hand corner of the envelope was a name that he couldn't discern.

"SGT."... he could read that part too well. *Martini* or *Mortens* maybe, or *Marlin*. No matter. None of those names meant anything to him. It was the CSA under the name that bothered him the most. The crumpled letter was at the end of a tough journey, evidenced by the smudges and creases. The postmarks were the word "Steamship" and a fancy rendering of a locomotive.

He had already guessed at the content. He stared at it for a brief time, and then flipped it onto a table unopened.

Another letter. His life had been defined by letters the past three years.

He remembered a letter from his middle son, Jonathan, from three years before. It had been a prelude to a life spinning away from him.

My Dear Father,

I enlisted today, and I am confident that you will not be surprised by the details.

I have been in Virginia for over five years. In that time I have grown fond of the mores and tenets of the people of the South.

I am distressed that Southern traditions are now being threatened by a Federal government which has required states to adhere to prescribed standards of subsistence, That will not stand.

As you know your only grandson and namesake is a Virginian. Catharine and I have been blessed with little Jeremiah. Catharine's dressmaking business and my law practice have given us a rewarding life, and that has been magnified by our son, our joy.

Catharine's parents do not own slaves, nor do we or our friends. I do not see slavery as the causative circumstance for this conflict. No, the cause is a threat to our way of life, a threat to our state's right to decide how its citizens shall live. That is the centric factor.

Today, I enlisted in the Virginia 42nd Infantry. I pray to God that you will understand, and God willing, I will not face Joshua or Jeff in action.

Catharine sends her love,
I remain,
Your loving son, Jonathan.

"Impulsive!" Jeremiah had snorted when he read that letter.

His middle son was lost again, on another outcropping high above another ravine.

He waited days before the anger and hurt subsided. Then he wrote to Joshua, by then an instructor at West Point, who was waiting with the Corps of Engineers for assignment as the war gathered momentum. In a rare display of barely controlled emotion, he complained to his oldest son that Jonathan had lost equilibrium, had become wayward in his loyalty.

His anger was somewhat mollified when he got an immediate response.

...You always taught us to be faithful to our convictions, and to be stubborn in tending to them. You taught us well, Father.

While we may be disappointed in Jonathan's decision, we must pray that the battle is soon over. We must honor his commitment even as we fight against his beliefs. We will be reunited sometime soon...

Jeremiah thought about the transformation of his middle son. Jonathan had attended the University of Virginia; he had chosen to be educated at the college founded by Thomas Jefferson, additionally attracted by new experiences and new geography. He continued to explore life.

He had graduated with honors in three years, married Catharine Dexter, the winsome and intelligent only child of Scottsville, Virginia natives, and then enrolled in Virginia's Washington Law School.

In 1860, he celebrated the birth of a son, and the law shingle he hung outside his home.

Seven months later, he enlisted.

Another letter, this one from his youngest son, Jefferson, gave the father more reason to retreat from his anger at Jonathan.

...All of us are in equal danger, Father. We have always sought your counsel and your blessings, and those are crucial to the three of us now.

What a man believes doesn't diminish the man, if he has taken a position based on his head and his heart...

Much later he composed a letter to his renegade son and sent it. He hoped that it had reached him, but he never knew. Up to yesterday, the day the crumpled letter arrived, he had not heard from Jonathan.

In his mind, he reviewed the missive that he had sent to Jonathan.

My Son,

I continue to be disappointed in your choice, but your endeavor is worthy. Your decision is the best one for you. May your life as a soldier be fulfilling and safe.

The loyalties a man chooses in this war are complex. I have faith that you gave this matter thought that would make your mother and me proud.

You are never out of my thoughts. Persevere.

May God be your rock and your compass.

Your loving father

Then there was a letter from Jonathan's wife, in a perfumed envelope, which had arrived in February of 1863.

My Beloved Father-in-Law,

The days weigh heavily on me without my husband. I have not heard from him in some time, but I have faith that he is too busy to write.

I know that he has disappointed you, but you must be proud of a son so committed, so capable, and so strong. He regales me with tales of his childhood, and I feel as if I have been to Vermont. His affection for you, for his late mother, and for his brothers shines through each memory he shares.

You must meet your grandson when this terrible war has passed. He is so smart. He looks and acts like Jonathan.

The war rages around us for miles, but it has not come to Charlottesville or Scottsville. We fear that it will. I am concerned for my parents and my son. This war spares neither the elderly nor the innocent.

Someday soon, there will again be laughter and music and peace. We must all survive this terrible time.

With affection,

Catharine Dexter Chase.

Letters. He feared them, but he depended on them. He remembered the official-looking letter, the one with the eagle stamp that had been delivered by special courier, just a few days after Catharine's had arrived. He had been frightened then. He had taken a deep breath and whispered to his dead wife, "One of our sons is in trouble. Please help me through this, my love."

He had ripped off the end of the envelope, and slowly unfolded the enclosure with shaky hands.

He scanned, rather than read.

Sorry to inform you...Joshua...wounded in action...Fredericksburg...medical facility...prognosis good for a complete recovery...Washington...heroic action...gratitude...

He had then sat down heavily on his rocking chair and wept.

This newest letter. He couldn't procrastinate. That wouldn't change the content. He would read it. Oddly, as he adjusted his glasses, he was calm. It was as if he had already read it, so confident was he of the information it contained. The page had been folded many times. A set of fortunate occurrences had transported it across enemy lines to him. In some spots, the words wavered and ran together.

My Dear Sir,

It is with much regret that I report to you some bad news. Before I relate that, I must tell you that your son Jonathan was the best man I ever soldiered with. He was a leader and a gentleman. "Was..." Jeremiah noted.

It happened at Chickamauga on 20 September last year. I believe the Cherokees named the river that. It means bloody river according to some.

I served with your son. I am a Virginian. He was always afraid that if something happened to him. the Confederate army wouldn't get the information to a Northern location. He told me often of your work at the University of Vermont. So I addressed the letter there.

We was in a strange fight, a lot of skirmishing, and no daily orders. You'd stumble around in the thickets, and if you ran into the enemy, you just fought right there, usually hand to hand.

Anyways, he and I was in a group separated from our main unit, and of a sudden, four bluecoats jumped him from out of nowhere, maybe from the trees. I couldn't see.

Four opponents. Jeremiah was reminded of another afternoon a decade ago when Jonathon had been attacked by four young men. His brothers weren't with him this time.

I was too far away to get a shot, and there was too many trees between us anyways. One of them Union soldiers put a bayonet in his back. He kept fighting, your son, and we was trying to get there when we was attacked too. He pistol shot two of them. Then there was another shot just before we got there and run them off. We found him lying against a tree. He was gone.

He was a good soldier and a good man.

Don't know what came of his body after we carried him in. Expect he's buried near the river. The fighting increased in the next few days.

Jasper Martin, Sgt, CSA

"Molly, Molly, Molly…our dear Jonathan has used up his nine lives," Jeremiah mumbled.

He'd have to write to Catharine. He'd have to write to his other sons. He'd have to visit his grandson.

All of that could wait. He was almost beyond grief. He was just tired. So tired.

****

The day began with a passing shower. By mid-morning, a full sun had shrunk the puddles and sponged out the mud.

"Think I'll ride out east for a while. You be OK here?" Herk asked Big.

"Yup. Nobody in the cells today. I'll sit out front for a spell."

Herk slumped out and stretched, trying to shake off his physical and emotional lethargy. There was little movement on the streets. He walked off of the boardwalk into the street, preparing to cross to the stable. Virginia City had a new police administrator. Herk finally was in his last week as sheriff.

A loud voice, somewhere between a bellow and a shriek, stopped him short. He turned to look at the source of the sound, a pathetic, "Hey, gunfighter!"

"Are you kidding me?" He whispered.

He was dumbfounded. Sonny Joe was in a crouch forty feet away. Herk almost laughed at the sight. The kid had a large white hat on his head, much too big, with a tall crown and wide brim which pushed out his ears. He was wearing comical lamb's wool chaps and polished boots and an expensive looking black duster which still had the fold marks on front from its display in some store.

Behind him stood an impressive white horse, restless at the hitching post, with a saddle and a chest cinch which seemed to reflect gold. Herk quickly processed information. The kid was wearing fancy holsters, and had his hands resting on pistol butts. His face was tensed, his eyes heavy-lidded.

"Say your prayers, gunfighter!" Sonny Joe squealed. God, Herk thought, he must have read that in a book somewhere. It was obvious, the kid had dressed up, ludicrous as he looked, to shoot him.

"What's on your mind?"

"Don't it look like what it is? I'm gonna gun you down, Herkimer Grimes!"

"Why?" Herk was stalling for a way out the situation He didn't want to shoot a sixteen-year old boy. "For what purpose? You're a joke son."

"Ain't gonna be a joke when word gets 'round that I gunned down the famous gunfighter."

"You're way in over your head, I'll put a bullet in you before you unloose them fancy guns."

Herk sensed a body coming up behind him.

"Herk?"

"Don't shoot him, Big. Don't threaten him. I'll handle this."

"If'n he draws, I'm agoin' to fire this shotgun."

Sonny Joe interrupted. "You need that depitty, gunfighter?"

"Don't need nothing. He'll stay out of this."

"He better. He be dead too."

"You'd better think it over, boy. This'll end one of two ways. I'll shoot you down, or you'll get lucky and shoot me, and hang next week."

"Ain't nobody gonna hang me. Won't be around, leastways. Gonna outdraw you. If'n you don't draw, don't mean nuthin' to me."

"You think this is goin' to make you famous?"

"Yes, Herkimer Grimes. I be known all over the West…the man who shot down the great gunfighter."

"The man? You ain't nothin' but a snot-nosed, stupid little boy."

"No! No! I ain't. I know whut I'm doin!"

Thc boy was getting rattled.

"You lay them guns on the ground slowly, get on that fancy horse, and get out of town. Don't ever come back to Virginia City. Takes a man to live here, not some sissy who can't wipe his own ass."

The kid crouched again. It wasn't working. Someone was going to get shot.

Herk whispered to Big. "I'm gonna let him draw. Don't shoot him."

"On three, gunfighter? One, two, THREE!"

Sonny Joe's right hand was pulling a pistol awkwardly, Herk noted. Herk pulled his gun and hesitated.

The boy's gun barked, a wild shot, as Herk had suspected. There was a "thunk" beside Herk. He saw Big Head slump to the ground.

Sonny Joe fired again, kicking up dust ten feet in front of Herk.

"Damn you boy!" Herk said. He leveled his pistol, and shot the boy in the belly. The force of the impact bumped the boy backwards. His hat flew off and rolled away.

A strange look came over Sonny Joe's face. He dropped his pistol, and clutched at his midsection with both hands. A soprano howl rolled out of his mouth and gurgled as it mixed with blood.

Herk was going to shoot again, but decided that it wouldn't be necessary. The boy fell to his knees blubbering, shook his head slowly, and pitched face first to the ground.

Herk turned and bent over Big Head, lying on his back and grimacing.

"Big! You hit bad, man?"

"Shoulder, Herk. Mighta gone clear through. Hurts like hell."

"Sorry, Big. I shoulda just gunned him down. Didn't want to shoot a kid."

"I know, Herkimer. I know."

At almost the same time, a terrible thought had impelled Whistling Annie to uncover the box of money in her closet. She opened it. She was right, Sonny Boy had been stealing, alright. From her! There were only a few bills in it, maybe forty dollars. Sonny Joe had financed his fantasy with her savings. She was virtually wiped out.

The next day, Herk took off his badge and left it on the desk with a scrawled note, barely legible: *"Give my money to Big Head. I won't be back. H. Grimes."*

Before riding away, he went to the doctor's office where Big Head was abed.

"Leavin' Big. Just came to say goodbye."

"Figgered you'd do that."

"You gonna pull through?"

"Doc says I lost a lot of blood. Says I gotta stay here a week or so. Might not use my left arm so good from now on."

"Big, you was a good deputy, a good friend."

"Yeah."

"May not see you again,"

"Where you headed?"

"East. Thought I'd try Kansas. Get lost on a ranch somewheres."

"Bad things ahappenin' there, hear tell."

Herk nodded. "Slavery and such. The war. I'll stay clear of that." He walked to the door. "Get back in the saddle soon, friend."

Big smiled.

As he left Virginia City, Herk dropped off the white horse and saddle at Lil's. Maybe Annie could sell them and recoup some money, he explained to Lil. He didn't want to see Annie.

****

The argument had begun with the restlessness of Bill Anderson, who felt that time was wasting. The Quantrill band had been in Texas for some time, and there was no sign that their leader had an immediate plan to change that.

"Been thinkin' it's time to get back to the war in Missouri. We been holed up here too long."

"Well, Mr. Anderson, you're too impatient. The War will last for years. There will be plenty of action for us. Right now, every federal army west of St. Louis is looking for us. This is the safest course at present."

"This is a coward's course."

"Mr. Anderson, this is not the regular army. You can go when you wish."

Several nights later, the dispute arose again, this time within earshot of a large group of the Bushwhackers.

"Mr. Anderson, I've been told that you've been riling up the men. I will not tolerate that."

"Ain't happy 'bout what you're doin'. Not a little bit."

"You're a good soldier. It's a shame that you don't understand war." That much was true. Quantrill looked at his adversary of the moment, the tall young man with a rolled up hat brim and fierce eyes. The man was not schooled nor was he clever enough to hide his feelings. Anderson viewed the Bushwhackers as avengers, not the army unit that he, Quantrill, wanted them to be. Working within the boundaries of the Confederate army, the group could function untethered throughout the West. But crossing those lines would classify them as outlaws to everyone. The Lawrence raid had probably tested the tolerance of Rebel authorities. After it was over, Quantrill had reasoned that there would be no more similar massacres.

Still, in any level of warfare, Bloody Bill Anderson was a good ally. He feared no one, no battle circumstances, and he seem impervious to personal danger. He had ascended to his stature as Quantrill's lieutenant because he was so intent on destroying

Union soldiers and sympathizers. He was guileless and bloodthirsty, but he had been loyal until recently.

Anderson paced before Quantrill, nervous energy propelling him back and forth. Occasionally, he would glance at Quantrill, eyeing him with what appeared to be contempt, or at best disgust at his leader's inaction. He was heroic-looking, with a rage of whiskers, long, curly black hair, and clothing of impressive design and material.

Quantrill was also as close to impeccable as hours in the saddle would permit. He looked younger than his actual age; he grew a moustache to look older. Several changes of clothing, neatly wrapped in his bedroll, maintained the image that he had of himself, a benevolent leader freelancing a group of determined warriors through a hideous war against a nefarious foe. He needed to dress that part. His concept of morality didn't mesh, however, with his checkered past, which included murder and deceit well before the war. Several times he had served settlements as a schoolteacher. Those incursions into normal life had given him an intelligent shrewdness and a confidence in directing the activities of his uncivilized bunch.

"Quantrill, I'm going to leave you."

"As you wish, Mr. Anderson. Leave as soon as possible."

"I will take some men with me."

"Fine. I'd like all of you out of here before dawn."

Quantrill awoke the next morning to assess the damage. Anderson was gone. So was Bravo Wright. Gone too were Frank James, the Younger brothers, and Clell Miller. Scores of his former army, sixty or seventy men, had departed. Also gone, of course, was the young Texas bride Anderson had recently met and married.

Bill Anderson led his army back to the battlefront. For a brief time had he settled on a small ranch with his wife. He sent a letter to a Missouri newspaper defending what he had done and was about to do. He was biding his time, and it didn't last long.

He recruited additional soldiers including a murderous small man named Archie Clement, and a sixteen-year old whose brother was already riding with him, Jesse James.

The Border Ruffians were the scourge of western Missouri and eastern Kansas. They disrupted railroad systems and burned towns along the Missouri and Grand rivers. One signature trademark of the gang was the appearance of scalps tied to the bridles of their horses. The three horses with the most scalps belonged to Anderson, Clement, and Bravo Wright.

Wright refused any responsibility in the gang's hierarchy. Anderson had wanted him to be his lieutenant, but Bravo turned him down. "Ask Archie," he said, "he'll be a good leader for you." So the diabolical Clement, slight and round-faced and not even five feet tall, became second in command.

Bravo Wright was forty years old. He was healthy, happily overweight, and balding, and his zeal for the rampages had not subsided. There was always alcohol, and women. But he didn't envision guerilla life at fifty, and from what he knew, the war could go on forever. His stake in the war effort was secondary, anyway, to his determination to become a wealthy and feared citizen of the West. He relished forcing men at the point of his pistol to beg for their lives. At those times, his will alone determined what happened next. What happened next was always a bullet into their brains.

On September 27 of 1864, Anderson led his men into Centralia, Missouri, but his planned raid was postponed when some of his men stopped a train, and reported to him that there were Union troops on board, all of whom were going home on furlough.

"Get them off of the train. Tell them to take off all of their clothes," Anderson ordered.

Twenty nude young men waited next to the train as he rode up, laughing. "Well, look at this. Look at all the little peckers. Ain't no women gonna miss them. Kill them all, save that fella on the end. Get him out of here."

The designated soldier was led away. He would be a hostage, kept until he was needed for an exchange of prisoners or some favor.

The others were summarily slaughtered. Shot, toyed with, sliced with knives, scalped alive, many had their noses cut off before the final shots ended their torment. Laughter and lewd comments accompanied the mayhem. One adamant young man kicked and fought back.

"Break every bone in his body before you kill him," Anderson ordered. "Start with his fingers."

The maniacal, high-pitched voice of Archie Clement was a constant factor, louder even than the screams of the victims. After an hour, Anderson ordered his men away from the scene.

The 39th Missouri Mounted Infantry, a company of Union soldiers, arrived on the scene, so gruesome that many coughed up their breakfasts. A strong force of 150, they determined to chase Bloody Bill, and end his grisly reign.

They rode hard, and knew that they were gaining on the Border Ruffians. Crossing a large field, the pursuers sensed that Bloody Bill was near.

Too near. From the forest that surrounded the field on three sides, the guerilla army fired a salvo of shots which cut down many in the Union force. Then, screaming, the Rebels burst from the trees in a pincer maneuver which confounded the Northerners. Anderson led one of the charges, Clement another, and Cole Younger the third.

From the open side, Bravo Wright and thirty men who had acted as decoys rode back into the midst of the enemy, guns blazing. In a frenzy of rearing horses and cramped quarters, the Union troops could not even get off telling shots. In a short time, the Northerners lost their manpower advantage, then they were desperately trying just to maintain, then they were looking for escape routes.

One hundred-twenty Union soldiers died that day, with very few Border Ruffian casualties. Anderson's men began to decapitate the bodies. Archie Clement added a new twist. He began to cut off and save the ears of the vanquished, stuffing them into a large duffel.

As they rode away, Bravo Wright found himself next to Jesse James, the teenager.

"Ain't this fun, son? Ain't this the best time?"

"You bet, Mr. Wright. The best!"

General Sterling Price had a command of 12,000 Confederate troops and he had been assigned to the border states to control the Union guerilla activity. He had also been ordered to locate and talk to Bloody Bill Anderson. Anderson was becoming an embarrassment to his own cause. The Centralia massacre, following the Lawrence raid, had evoked outrage from those on both sides.

Price sent emissaries to find the guerillas and Anderson agreed to a meeting. He brought Clement, Wright, and Frank James to the rebel camp. Anderson suspected that he'd be feted, and was mildly disturbed by the conversation with General Price.

"Captain Anderson, I want you and your men to join us. We've got a lot of work to do."

"Join you? Why would I want to do that?"

"I need men like yours, proven in battle."

"General, you fight battles against big armies. My men and me, we're weeding out the nuisances, causing disturbances, stealing supplies, punishing people. It ain't the same thing."

"We can use some of those skills."

"Nah. My men wouldn't take orders from nobody else."

"Captain Anderson, I would first remind you that you are not officially a part of the Army of Virginia. You are independent in this war. As such, you have no official role. Whenever you act, you are doing it as an outlaw would."

Anderson twirled his hat on his knee, looked at Clement, and smiled. "Seems like you're mighty ungrateful, General."

"No, Sir. That's not it. We want you on the same course of action as we are. Our orders start with President Davis and General Lee. Yours must do the same."

"I'm going to refuse your offer, General. You can do whatever you're told to do. We're going to do what I think is necessary."

"Then I can't be responsible for what happens to you and your men. To the Union, you are outlaws. If they capture you, you'll be treated as such. There will be no consideration of your being soldiers carrying out orders."

"If they catch us, it don't matter what they call us. They're still going to kill us. But you see, General, they ain't going to catch us."

"You have been going far beyond the bounds of decency."

"How you figure? We're killing soldiers and Union men. We ain't killing kids and women."

"You are looting and plundering, Mr. Anderson," Price said, intentionally dropping the reference to rank.

Anderson leaned forward in his chair, a look of disgust on his face. "And so are your armies, Price."

The General was temporarily speechless before the withering gaze and lack of military respect. He cleared his throat. "We do not scalp or mutilate. We take only what we need."

"Who you kidding?"

The three men with Anderson guffawed.

"So, you refuse the government's wishes?"

Anderson was now playing to his men. "We not only refuse. We laugh at it. We'll stay north of the river. You keep your damn army out of our way."

"If that is your decision, Captain, our meeting is over."

As they rode away, Anderson complained to his subordinates. "Ungrateful. When this war is over, and people are looking back at why the Confederate states won, we'll be the heroes. Not General Sterling Price. Probably not General Lee either."

"Yessir, Captain. You told him off real good," Clement asserted.

On October 26, 1864, the Border Ruffians were camped in Ray County, Missouri, with Bill Anderson about to receive a notice of his mortality.

The Union army looked at the various Southern guerilla bands as unpredictable irritants, not worthy of committing a full army unit to, but deadly enough to warrant action.

Bill Anderson and William Quantrill, recently returned to Missouri with his army, were leaders of the two most prominent guerilla groups. To protect Union sympathizers, who lived with the intense fear that they would become victims, a measure of regulation was enacted.

Samuel Cox, a young officer, was given a command of 300 soldiers, and a directive: find the Border Ruffians, then the Bushwhackers, and eliminate them. Take prisoners if you can, but otherwise find them and destroy them.

Anderson was not difficult to find. Lately, he had been near the northern edge of the border between Missouri and Kansas. Subduing him was another matter. Bloody Bill had an uncanny sense of the tactics of warfare, and his men were reckless, near suicidal, in battle. They were proficient in the art of ambush, almost never in a position to be cornered themselves.

Cox had 300 men. He feared that he would need double that amount. He got a break. Scouts reported that the Border Ruffians were camped in an area where they were subject to a surprise attack. Good, Cox decided, we will use one of their own tactics on them.

Cox sent a group of fifty men toward the guerilla camp, where they opened a salvo of gunfire, wounding several of the outlaws. Anderson was furious at the effrontery, and yelled to his men to follow him as he rode out to confront the attackers. Every man in camp responded, and the force, guns ablaze, chased after Cox's decoys, who turned and rode away.

Too late, Anderson understood. Before a shot had been fired by the large hidden Northern army, he knew. He had ridden into a field where any ambushers would be protected, and he and his men were in the open. A volley of shots from hidden guns suddenly decimated his guerillas. There was only one course.

Shooting wildly, he charged the flank of his enemy. Clement followed, so did Bravo Wright and Clell Miller. Many of his men at the end of the queue turned and retreated.

Clell Miller fell first, shot in the shoulder. He would be taken prisoner by Cox. Bravo Wright pulled alongside Anderson, and was within five feet of his captain when a Union shot raised Bloody Bill out of his saddle. Then Wright was in the clear, through the lines, with Archie Clement close behind.

Several miles ahead, the two stopped.

"Ain't no one behind us, Archie. They's prob'ly satisfied they got Bill."

"Gotta go back, Bravo. Gotta try to rescue the captain."

"Won't do no good. He's daid."

"You don't know that!"

"Yep. I do. Seen his eyes before he fell. Shots killed him. No life in them eyes. Seen that look before."

"My God! My God! The bastards kilt him! What we gonna do?"

"We're savin' ourselves first. We'll talk later," Wright answered, and pushed his horse to a gallop.

CHAPTER TWENTY-FIVE
1865

Jefferson Chase stood on the lawn in front of the two-story brick house. The past three days had been a blur, and now he was a witness to history. Well, sort of a witness. A monumental event was occurring in the house behind him.

It had started with a march to this area, and was followed by a day-long battle yesterday, in which his cavalry unit, under the leadership of Brevet-General George Custer, had fought valiantly in heavy underbrush. The three cavalry units, from New York, Michigan, and Vermont, were still partnered after 18 months of successes, part of the larger command of General Phil Sheridan, a huge contingent, which had harassed and fought with Robert E. Lee's Army of Virginia across Virginia.

Custer's group had captured and burned three supply trains yesterday, in the midst of encounters with the Confederate forces, which now numbered in the thousands and were on a desperate move west.

Earlier, on this day, Lee had made an effort to break through the Union lines, suspecting that only cavalry stood in his way. However, innumerable infantry troops had hastened to the battleground, and were by then supporting the Northern effort. Lee was stymied. Then he was surrounded.

Just before noon, a message was delivered to Jefferson from General Custer, an invitation of sorts. "The General will be attending a meeting of surrender between Generals Grant and Lee this very afternoon," the young courier recited. "He has been invited to the meeting by General Sheridan. He is asking you to go along, if you wish."

Custer had formed a friendship with Jefferson before Jefferson's promotion to Brevet-Colonel. Jefferson was outranked, but the young brevet from Michigan found him not only intelligent, but also also a competent sounding board for his own views on many topics. He often sent for Jefferson from an adjoining camp, to join him in conversations and reminiscences.

The meeting would be held in the McLean house, a structure near the crossroad village of Appomattox Courthouse. Jefferson joined the group of Northern officers in the short journey. Upon their arrival at the site, an aide rushed up to Grant. "General Lee is here already, Sir."

As the Union staff dismounted, General Sheridan called over to Jefferson. "Colonel, will you help look after the horses?" Grant went in to meet Lee alone, and then later called in his entire staff, including Custer. Jefferson milled among the horses with the orderlies watching them. He spotted a great white horse, and inquired, "Is this beautiful horse General Lee's?"

The somber orderly replied, "Yes, Colonel. He calls the horse Traveler." Jefferson patted the neck of the horse, which was looking at him with one wary eye.

He walked over to the shade of a tree in the front yard, and noticed a stout man nearby. The man was a civilian, middle-aged, with a beard which covered his chin. He looked nervous.

"Sir, I am Jefferson Chase."

"Good afternoon, Colonel. My name is Wilmer McLean." McLean knew his rank. Former military, Jefferson guessed. McLean had noticed his stripes.

"This is your house?"

The man nodded. "General Lee contacted me about using it for a palaver. I figure that they're in there talking surrender."

"One can hope that's the case."

"Colonel Chase, my sympathies are with the Confederacy. I was a major in the Virginia Militia before this war."

"Those on both sides should welcome an end to it."

"And I will, if that's the case. My family has been through a lot of misery."

"It touched everyone's lives, Mr. McLean."

"Mine more than most. We were living in Manassas when the war started. Our house took a cannonball. A year later, we're next to the battle again, Second Manassas. It was too much. I moved down here for my family's protection. Yesterday and this morning, we're next to a battlefield again."

"That's quite a story."

"Yessir. Do you realize that if Lee is surrendering in there, the war started in my front yard, and it will end in my front parlor."

"How would a surrender affect you?"

"It'll ruin me. My wealth is tied up in Confederate money. Don't figure that will be worth anything now."

"What did you do? Maybe you can do it again."

"I was a grocer. Lately, I've been a sugar broker, supplying the Confederates with sugar."

"I'm truly sorry for your bad luck, Mr. McLean. I hope things work out for you."

Jefferson shook his hand, and was walking away when the front door opened.

Out onto the porch stepped Generals Lee and Grant. By looking at the Virginian, Jefferson knew what had just happened. Lee looked shocked, and obviously saddened.

The two men presented more than one contrast. Grant was short, stooped, and dressed in combat fatigues, suspenders, and muddy boots. Lee was somewhat taller, standing erect in full dress grays. He seemed older than Jefferson had imagined, with a silver beard.

Lee waited for Traveler to be brought to the porch, mounted, and rode away. Grant stood in the front yard, took off his hat, and waved it at the old warrior. The entire Union staff, including Jefferson Chase, did the same.

It was April 9, 1865.

On June 2, 1865, General Edmund Smith, Commander of Confederate forces west of the Mississippi River, signed surrender papers for his command. The last Confederate army was finished.

June thus brought some hope and renewal. The War Between the States had exhausted and horrified both sides for four long years, and the country and its territories began to recover, minus many sons and frightened of reactive days ahead. The optimists spoke of unity, opportunity, and equality. Others struggled to rationalize defeat and losses which could never be recouped. Pockets of hatred and rebellion could not be eradicated with the signings of surrender, nor with conciliatory actions. It was a new start for everyone, for better or for worse.

The news of Smith's surrender reached Kansas quickly, and on the sprawling Brody ranch, which had prospered during the war years, a decision was made, one that would impact the family forever.

In late June on a balmy evening on the front porch, Margaret broached a subject.

"Whit, now that the war's over, Rosie needs to think about her future, you know?"

"In what way?"

"Well, what kind of future will that be? She lives way out here, isolated from people her age, away from things that will stretch her mind and her life."

"We've done a good job of raising her, don't you think?"

"Whit, she's remarkable, and we made her that way. But will she meet a husband worthy of her out here? Will she learn how to appreciate fine things like art, theater, and music?"

"You want to send her away?" It was a question, and an accusation.

"Whit, we can't keep her forever. She's twenty years old."

"Darlin', you took her to St. Louis before the war. We all went to New Orleans."

She was smiling. "And we gave her good books, and an extraordinary life on the ranch, but is that all we're going to do for her?"

He was quiet for a few moments. "Well, what are you suggesting? Finishing school in the East? Something like that? We'll lose her forever," he harrumphed.

"There are other possibilities. How about a university?"

"University? There aren't any that'll take women, except in the East. Maggie, you're most worried about a husband. Yes?"

"Of course I am. The only eligible man for miles is her own cousin."

"What do you think she'll say about all of this?"

"Whit, she brought it up."

The next evening, all three sat on the porch. Rose responded quickly when asked for an opinion. "A university. Do you realize that I've dreamed about that since I was twelve?"

"You know, Rosie, that most of them don't take women."

"Papa, the State University of Iowa does, and it isn't that far away."

He was startled by the quickness of the response. "So how did you find out about that?"

"I read a story in one of those papers you brought back from Kansas City."

"What will you study, Rosie?"

"History, maybe. Science, maybe. I don't know yet."

"Men, maybe?" He raised an eyebrow.

"Papa!"

"Listen. You want to do this thing?"

"Yes, Papa. I most certainly do."

And so, Whit began writing letters to Iowa, to the State University. A quick exchange produced an acceptance. Rose could enroll in September.

In September the family traveled by coach, railroad, and riverboat to Davenport and then on to Iowa City. A new phase of her life would begin. "You will write, Rosie?" He extracted a promise, and returned, somewhat depressed, to the ranch.

The ranch consumed most waking hours. Whit assessed his operation, which had transitioned by trial and error into an admirable spread. Bird was an excellent choice as foreman; he knew she would be. A fence enclosed most of three sides of his property. The fourth side was the Solomon River and some land beyond. But there was a flaw in the system. He was seriously understaffed. He needed more farm hands. He could not hire just any applicant, however. This group was like a family. In fact, the spring round-up, the trail drive, and the most severe winter months were like family reunions. He could not interfere with the camaraderie, the production, by hiring just anyone. His crew was not seasonal, not lazy, nor of questionable character.

Still, he was fast approaching a critical point. During the war, he had purchased many more acres on the other side of the Solomon, and on his north side. He had added unclaimed land, or that abandoned by homesteaders. The herds kept growing. The boundaries kept expanding. In the most critical times, Rose had helped out. She was a two-time veteran of cattle drives, and she could break horses almost as well as her cousin. Now she was gone.

One afternoon, after he returned from a trip to Topeka, Margaret had a message for him.

"Whit, Bird says a man, gray haired and saddle worn was how she described him, has been here two days in a row, looking for you. We didn't know when you'd be back."

"Did he leave his name, Maggie? Or say what he wants?"

"Talk to her. He told her that he'd be back Friday."

"Tomorrow. I'll be here."

The incident slipped his mind, and Margaret's and Bird's. Late Friday morning, a rider approached the ranch house. Whit stepped onto the porch. Bird's description of him had been accurate. The rider had a gray, unkempt moustache which hid his mouth, and waves of gray in his hair, which flopped to his shoulders. He was tall and lanky, and obviously the beneficiary of a hard life, a cowboy of indeterminate age riding a horse with a worn saddle. He tipped his hat to Whit before he dismounted.

"Morning."

"Howdy. You Brody?"

"I am."

"Mr. Brody, I'm lookin' for work."

"What's your name?"

"Grimes." His voice was a low mumble.

The name, the physicality, there was something familiar about this man, even though Whit was sure that he's never seen him before.

"You a good worker, Mr. Grimes?"

"I will be."

"Not running from the law, are you?"

A smirk was barely visible under the ungroomed moustache. "Nope. Spent some time on the side of the law."

"Yes you did. I know you now. I've heard about you. You Herkimer Grimes?"

Quiet. "Yes."

"Mr. Grimes, I'm honored to meet you, but I have to tell you, I have no idea as to why you'd want a job here."

"You don't need help here?"

"Didn't say that. I just wouldn't be interested in someone who'd be here two weeks, and then ride away."

"Wouldn't do that. Asked some people about the best ranches, the biggest ranches, the most successful ranches in Kansas. Your name kept comin' up."

"Texas Ranger. Lawman. You want to herd cattle out here, miles from anything."

"It's the only thing I want to do now. I'll work hard for you, if everyone leaves me alone."

"Won't get rich."

"Don't matter."

""We've got a hard-working group out here. Good people. Like a family. Wouldn't want your being here to change that."

"I understand."

"You won't need guns out here."

"Good."

"One more thing, Mr. Grimes. You fought Indians. Might dislike them. The foreman out here, the best I've ever seen, is an Indian."

Grimes winced, and hoped that Brody didn't notice. "Don't matter."

"And a woman…"

"Indian woman gives orders to men?"

"Yessir."

"They take 'em?"

"Yes. Anybody doesn't get on with her will be out of here."

"Mr. Brody, I hate Indians, all savages…men, women, and children. Seen too much. But she'll never know that. I'll work as hard as your best man."

"Mr. Grimes, we'll try it. If it doesn't work, I'll let you go."

"Fair enough."

"When do you want to start?"

"How's this afternoon?"

"Got your stuff with you?"

"Don't have much."

"The bunkhouse is up on that hill."

"Got any other place?"

"Got the old shack. One room. One window. Pot-bellied stove. Some stuff we'll have to move out. I can put a bed and a table in there, and a couple of chairs. Used to have hands livin' there. It's pretty rough though."

"It'll work for me."

"What should I call you, introducing you and such."

"Herkimer is good enough. They'll forget who I am in a few weeks, anyways."

"One more thing, Mr. Grimes. You healthy? How old are you?"

"Fifty-six, I believe. Plan on living a while."

In November, Whit again reviewed the state of business on the ranch. As content as he was, Whit had reason to question the future. In addition to the aging Simeon—somewhere in his sixties-- Herkimer was fifty-six, Noah 51, Caroline the cook was also fifty-one. The indefatigable Bird was in her early forties. Each was well-fed and pampered, but within a reasonable amount of time, he would have to find replacements. He himself was fifty-five and in remarkable fettle, but the spectre of new help was a concern. He knew that he would house and feed his hands long after they could perform. The ranch had become home to all of them. He couldn't let them go at any time, however much they declined in health or value.

The best direction, he decided, was to enjoy the status quo. He and Margaret were comfortable, and he had achieved his dream. Life was good. He missed his daughter.

Jack Bertrand had grown into a good-looking man. At the age of twenty-nine, he had succeeded on the frontier. He had arrived at the Brody ranch untested and callow, and was thrown into the harshness of the ranch owned by his aunt and uncle. Perhaps the descriptions of intelligence and social deprivation that they used for their daughter Rose could apply to him too. Someday, his Uncle Whit knew, Jack would have his own ranch, farther west probably. He wore wire-rimmed glasses, a necessity, and they belied a ruggedness and masculine competence evident in his enthusiasm for hard work and a liberal amount of endurance.

A modest amount of randiness, of stretching his masculinity, was satisfied each November when Whit sent Elon Pack and him to Kansas City for the month. There were no outlets for feminine intimacy on the ranch, although Caroline watched him intently as he ate her meals, and imagined sharing a bed with him. At her advancing years, that would have required more effort, and more desirability, than she possessed, and so more by more she had developed maternal feelings toward him.

Jack was of average height, but breaking horses and heavy work had sculpted his former slim body into hard sinew. He had meager skill with firearms, disliking them, avoiding them, but he was a magician with a lasso in the training corral. He and Elon had become close friends.

His Mississippi upbringing had stuck. He still came to the ranch hands dinner table bathed and dressed up, sitting erect, using the proper utensils, excusing himself politely, in stark contrast to the primitive manners of his tablemates.

The tablemates didn't include Herkimer Grimes. He ate alone in his small shack, collecting a plate of food from Caroline before meals, and returning cleaned plates and cups afterwards. After a workday, he would sit in front of his shack on a chair propped back against the front door, hat pulled down to his eyes. He may have been taking a nap, but more than likely, he was hiding. Whit had seen books on the table in his small room, but none of the *Herkimer Grimes, Texas Ranger* series. Whit stopped by frequently, joining Herk by his front door before dinner. Their conversations had changed from terse to a level of respectful comfort over the months.

"Want some company, Herkimer?" The November wind was cold, but Herk rarely invited Whit inside.

"Yep. Have a seat."

"Blowing in some bad weather. We'll bring the cattle in next week. Have to talk to Bird."

"Yep."

"You doing alright? It'll get frigid in there this winter. You got firewood? Take all you need from the stack near the house."

"I'll be just fine."

"Don't get lonely working here, do you?"

"Nope. Pretty much content. Fact is, I ain't never been lonely by myself. Time was, people wouldn't leave me alone."

"When those books came out, I expect."

"Them damn books ruined my life."

"I haven't read them. What were they, lies?"

"They was all made up. Never did most of them things. Fella that wrote them tried to find me. For a while there, I was movin' around just to stay clear of him."

"You did fight Indians for a spell."

"Did that. Hated 'em. Still do."

"You ever think that there may be some good ones. The ones here in Kansas don't hurt anybody. They just try to get along."

Herk fixed him with a stare, a mixture of doubt and irritation. "You talkin' about the two here?"

"Partly. Mostly, the ones that were pushed off of their lands, marched away from quiet lives. I saw that happen in Mississippi years ago."

"You ever see a baby with his head smashed? Or a woman ravaged so much that she bled out? Or a man scalped and tied to the ground for the ants?"

"No, Herk. That is terrible. But some of the troops did similar things in the war, to people of their own kind."

"Spect that's so."

"So, what do you think about our two?"

"Boy's quiet. Strange. She's interestin'. In control. Kinda avoids me."

"How about the others."

"Your nephew's a good boy. Sometimes talks too much. Ain't worked with the blacksmith yet. The cook takes good care of me."

"You know that they'd like it if you ate with them."

"You tellin' me to do that?"

"No sir. Just want you to be content. You do whatever feels right for you."

Jack had tried hard with Herk, and given up. Herk Grimes was not a talker. During days together in the corral and in the saddle, they had found no common ground. Jack suspected that Herkimer respected him, but wasn't looking for friendship of any kind.

"Looks like it'll be hot today, Mr. Grimes."

"Yep."

"We'll take a break this afternoon if it gets too hot."

"Yep."

"Don't want you passing out."

"Ain't gonna happen."

In any case, the celebrity status that had accompanied him when he had first hired on had disappeared. He was an enigma to the other hands, a hard worker who wouldn't let others in to a tormented nature, an asocial sort who didn't even know their names.

Bird wanted nothing to do with him. She gave orders to Jack; he carried them to Herkimer. Indian fighter? She hated the term. In her experience, that related to military types barking orders, to compliant peoples forced out of their homes, to atrocities, and to cowardly sorts who ambushed or rode into campsites to plunder and murder.

Gunfighter? That was just as bad. The man had spent his life killing others. He had no redeeming features that she could discern. He kept to himself, pointedly ignoring everyone else at the ranch. He was productive and dependable, but no more so than anyone else. She expected him to ride on sometime soon. She hoped that it would be sometime soon.

CHAPTER TWENTY-SIX
1866

Joshua Chase had been chosen by President Andrew Johnson for a special assignment, a somewhat delicate matter.

For three years Joshua had sat behind a desk in Washington, recovering from a severe wound suffered at the Battle of Fredericksburg, a ferocious encounter which had him accurately labeled as a hero, but had also forced his inaction through the rest of the Civil War. Superiors had marked admiration for the young Vermonter, however, and his intelligence and knowledge of his specialties, bridge-building and road-building, earned him a rank promotion and the title Special Advisor to the Army Corps of Engineers. Even when his wounds had healed, there was reluctance to return him to action. He was too much of an integral force in strategy and methods for the Corps. He was posted to Washington D.C., and served as the liaison between the Corps factions in the capital and at West Point. As such, he jumped a rank, from lieutenant-colonel to "full bird" colonel, an unusual promotion away from the field of combat.

He realized that he was serving an important function, as did many in Washington. His duties soon expanded, and he was often called to the White House to consult with Abraham Lincoln. Soon those visits involved more than his advice on battlefield techniques. He was called often to sit in on strategy sessions, and later, on personnel evaluation. But in many ways, he was unfulfilled, restless. His brother Jefferson was rising rapidly through the battlefield ranks, he was a colonel too, contributing where it counted. His brother Jonathan had made a difference before he was slain. As the war slowly ebbed toward a conclusion, he understood that he would not again take up arms, nor would he become a career soldier. Perhaps, someday, a politician, an undertaking that his father had rejected, but not a military lifer. He would conclude his commitment until mid- 1866, then he would explore other options somewhere.

The end of the war stirred him. The assassination of the President crushed him. But soon there was a joyous reunion with his brother, and late in 1865, he had settled back to finish his posting.

The new President, Andrew Johnson, summoned him to the White House. He was led into the President's chambers, and saw that whatever was afoot would concern only him and Johnson.

Johnson, already beleaguered by his unexpected ascendancy to the Presidency, welcomed him warmly, and asked him to sit.

"Thank you for coming today, Colonel Chase. I am going to ask you to do something which will ease a very awkward situation. I have an assignment for you."

"Mr. President. You honor me. I should inform you, Sir, that I will probably muster out of the service next year."

"So I've heard. That will be a loss to our Army. But this will be completed in advance of that."

"Yes, Sir."

"This is a situation which involves a large group of Sioux Indians. I trust you have heard of the massacre in Minnesota back in 1862."

"Yes, Sir. Very unfortunate occurrence. A lot of lives were lost."

"Correct. Well, I would tell you privately that governmental apathy brought it on. The Sioux were provoked, even though their resultant actions were barbaric, reprehensible."

Joshua looked at him without answering.

"You may also remember that when it was over, there was a public demand that the entire tribe be punished."

"As I recall, President Lincoln ordered that thirty-eight of the ringleaders be hanged."

"And they were. The President couldn't win that one. Some people wanted only exile as a punishment; others wanted the blood of all warriors who participated. Mr. Lincoln was never comfortable with the outcome."

"What happened to the rest of the warriors, Sir?"

"They were sent to Iowa. Davenport. Fort McClellan, now Fort Kearny, where they were imprisoned. They are still there. The problem is that the prison will soon be razed, as the fort was."

"What will happen to the prisoners?"

"You will determine that, Colonel."

Again, Joshua was silent, waiting for a further explanation.

"I am sending you there to evaluate possibilities, to work out solutions, and then advise me on how to handle this. It is important that we appear benevolent without being cruel. The attitude of the prisoners is important. We cannot release 200 men who still want to fight. You will have to evaluate their potential for trouble. We must arrive at solutions that we can live with, solutions that make the government look good while meeting the needs of the Sioux. You have been recommended to me as a fair man, an intelligent man, a clever man."

"I have no background in Indian affairs, Mr. President. Perhaps someone in the Bureau of Indian Affairs would be more appropriate."

"You are far more capable of solving this than the inept men who caused the massacre. I would ask that you leave for Iowa as soon as possible, and get answers to me by next spring, at which time we will terminate your army service immediately, if that is agreeable to you."

"Mr. President, I will try to live up to your faith in me. I'll make arrangements to leave next week."

"I have prepared papers for you that outline the things I need to know. There are directions, and also contact names included."

"Thank you, Sir."

"No. Thank you, Sir. Your country is grateful."

Before he left, Joshua researched stacks of papers which explained events leading to the massacre, outcomes, and names. He discovered that in April of 1863, 277 Sioux men, sixteen women, and two children were sent to the facility. They were the final pawns in an embarrassing saga which originally had sentenced 300 men to be hanged. Abraham Lincoln had pardoned all but 38. The prisoners had been loaded on the steamship *Favorite* and transported to the prison, which had been hastily converted to hold them. He read numerous accounts of the idyllic conditions at the prison, which fed and clothed the 295 Sioux. Those reports, he noticed, were supplied by officials on site, and not by observers or government supervisors.

The prison was described as roomy, accommodating. The prisoners were called "docile and cooperative." Their days were passed in "meaningful activity." Joshua was immediately suspicious. If they were "docile," why were they still imprisoned? What types of "meaningful activity" were possible in a prison? The President must have known more that he had told Joshua. As he prepared to leave for Davenport, he began to have misgivings. Why was he being given three months to reach conclusions? From reading documents, one would expect a quick and comfortable resolution. Maybe the President was being atypically cautious.

Joshua was uneasy as he was led through the prison facility. The landscape was barren and uninviting. A fire in 1865 had destroyed the headquarters building of the fort. The balance of the recruiting and training facility had been taken down. All that remained were four buildings consisting of two undersized barracks, a small, unmanned hospital, and a guard house. There was a wire fence around the buildings, and a large, cleared area immediately outside. He noticed a contingent of armed guards patrolling the perimeter.

A nervous officer was his tour guide. "The Injuns live and sleep in the barracks. They can come outside when they want. They eat in there too."

"Let's have a look inside," Joshua asked.

"Have to get a coupl'a guards."

Why, Joshua wondered. These prisoners are supposed to be docile.

He was scrutinized thoroughly as he walked into the first barracks. His uniform, he theorized. The building was smaller inside than it had looked from the outside.

"Where do these people sleep?"

"On the floor. That works for them."

Wherever he tried to make visual contact, he was met with turned heads. The odor was sour, permeating.

"How many prisoners here now?"

"Don't know for sure. Some of 'em died of old age, and other stuff."

"Other stuff?"

"Illness. They're sort of a sickly people."

"What happens when they die?"

"We bury them in a nice graveyard outside the walls."

"Might I see that?"

He was led to a field, obviously a graveyard from the neat rows of white headstones.

"These are all soldiers."

"Injuns are over there," he pointed to a weed-choked field.

"Where? I don't see any stones."

The officer was getting peeved, but he was intimidated by the tall young man who was asking infelicitous questions. "Ain't no stones. Couldn't spell them Injun names anyway."

"How do you know where they are? How do you know who's in there? I'd like to see your death records."

"Ain't any. Leastwise like you mean. We got duty records that tell when we buried them."

"Give me your best guess. How many are in there?"

"Hard to say. I know we buried twenty-five, mebbe thirty the first year."

"So how do you treat the sick ones?"

"At first, an army doc looked at them. He left and no one took his place. Of late, they kinda look after themselves."

"You supply medicine?"

"Hell, most of the bastards use a witch doctor or somethin' like that."

"This place is a disgrace, and so are you. Don't you ever use language like that in front of me again. If I'm stuck with you, you'd better treat this situation as if it's the most important issue in your life or I'll have you posted to some remote outpost in the most desolate part of the country. You'll be drinking water from a cactus. You understand?"

"Yes sir!" The "sir" was accented, a subtle, insolent response.

Joshua watched the man slink away after a half-hearted, awkward salute.

His fist report to the President would be lengthy and incriminating.

In January, Joshua received an invitation from the President of the State University of Iowa, the result he guessed of numerous newspaper articles that debated the denouement of the Sioux prisoner matter, and named him as the key element, a "war hero from Washington."

My Dear Colonel Chase,

I have sent this letter to the Davenport Daily Gazette offices hoping that they would forward it to you. I have employed this unorthodox method because I do not know how to contact you.

We have read with interest of your service in Davenport, and of your exemplary record in the War Between the States.

We are the State University of Iowa, a coeducational institution in Iowa City, forty miles from you. One of our proudest features is a history program which serves both men and women. It is our signature classroom experience.

Would you consider spending two or three days with us in the near future, both to lecture to our history students, and to contribute to our archives pertinent information on the great war that our country has survived? It would accelerate our curriculum, and expose our students to information which would help them avoid the centuries of mistakes that precipitated this conflict.

We would be honored to host you, and to avail ourselves of your knowledge and experiences. We would also provide you with accommodations, meals, and a stipend of your choice.

Please respond to me at the address below. We eagerly anticipate your response.

It was signed by Oliver Spencer.

Why not, Joshua thought. His father had delighted in his own career as a university educator, and Joshua had fond memories of childhood associations with academe. He needed a break from the Sioux matter, and was waiting for a response from Washington anyway.

I will be there, he responded. How about the second week in February? I expect no payment.

Joshua was cutting across a field on the way to a lecture room, stepping high due to the six inches of snow which had fallen the night before. This was his second day on the campus. The first had been consumed with the formalities, getting settled, a conference with Oliver Spencer, a reception at the President's home. Joshua had been feted, toasted and eulogized. It had verged on idolatry and he had been uncomfortable throughout the affair.

He had been squired around by a young male student from Illinois, and on the night ahead he would be accompanied to a faculty dinner and reception by a young lady named Rose, described to him as "our brightest and most competent young lady." He was also scheduled to speak again.

This morning his audience would consist of history scholars, learned professors from all disciplines, newspaper personnel, and several hundred young men and women.

He reviewed what he would talk about: the causes of the war, heroes and key victories by both sides, the horrible cost in lives, economic outcomes, mistakes and failed philosophies, and reconstruction. Ideas were jotted on a folded paper in his shirt pocket. How much should he talk about his current assignment? It would come up because there was local pertinence. Some was classified. Other facts were bothering him now. His recommendations to the White House had gone unanswered for weeks. A jaded citizenry had to rebuild confidence in its leaders and policies, and he had a duty to reinforce that condition. But he was struggling with his own confidence in them.

Rose Brody had immersed herself in college life, academically, and socially as much as the student code of conduct would permit. Female students were not permitted to be alone with male students without a chaperon. Rigidly enforced rules demanded that young ladies set aside each evening for study in their residences. Strict university adherence to the doctrine of *in loco parentis*-"in the place of a parent," guaranteed her safety, but severely limited her interactions with other students.

She was dating a young history professor named Theodore. That is, she had gone to dinner with him several times, and they had taken afternoon walks together, sojourns which had not required a chaperon. He had kissed her. She enjoyed his company and their conversation. He was well-read, polite, astute, and a bit stuffy. She could not imagine him roping calves or mending fences.

On this morning, she was engaged in real fun with numbers of girls from her living quarters. She had organized this snowball fight in front of their living quarters, preparatory to attending a lecture by a visiting soldier. It was raucous and noisy, and their chaperon watched from the front window.

Rose took a direct hit in her back from a giggly housemate, and scooping up a handful of snow into a perfect ball, she whirled and hurled it, and watched in horror as it splashed into the back of the head of a well-dressed soldier walking ten feet away. The snowball flipped the hat off of his head and smeared the dark hair which had received the impact.

"Oh no!" she exclaimed loudly. "Oh my god!"

The young man turned, a broad smile of his face. To her quick reference, he was unbelievably good-looking. To her immense relief, he seemed to be forgiving her. He bent over to retrieve his hat, never taking his eyes off of her, and said softly, "Nice shot, ma'am." Then he walked away.

That's him, she immediately understood. That's Colonel Chase! And I have to host him tonight!

The wall sconces and three large chandeliers burned brightly in the large room of the Old Capitol Building, and a chamber quartet struggled to be heard above the murmurings of the group assembled early for the evening.

A comely young lady with upswept blonde hair and swathed in billows of dark green was making her way toward Joshua in the reception line. He noticed her first when she was fourth or fifth in line, and she commanded his attention, even as he shook the hand of the chairman of the Ancient Language Department. He smiled as their eyes met. She looked away quickly, and he noticed that her cheeks flushed.

Then she was in front of him. Oliver Spencer placed his hand on her back and eased her into position in front of Joshua.

"Colonel, this is Rose Brody, one of our outstanding first-year students, from Kansas, I believe. She will host you tonight."

"Miss Brody, my pleasure," Joshua responded. She extended her gloved hand. He took it gently.

"Perhaps I should have worn armor tonight," he continued, a comment that perplexed Spencer, but evinced a grin from Rose.

"There is no snow in here, Colonel," she replied.

"Miss Brody, will you assist the colonel here in the line for a few minutes? I have to attend to several matters," Spencer said.

"Yes, President Spencer." She stepped in line next to Joshua, and shortly whispered, "I was hoping that you wouldn't recognize me."

"I never forget the face of an attacker," he whispered back.

"I am sorry, Colonel. That was a reckless thing to do."

"That wasn't my first time as a snowball target. I had two brothers who ambushed me regularly, and they were excellent marksmen."

For a half-hour, she managed the reception line expertly. Joshua was impressed that she knew most attendees, and most seemed to know her. When she didn't, she quickly gathered information before presenting the guest to Joshua. One young man eyed him suspiciously after being introduced as "Mr. Theodore Brouff, of our history department." Joshua knew immediately, boyfriend.

A lavish multi-course dinner followed. At the head table, Joshua directed his attention to her.

"You're from Kansas, Miss Brody?"

"Yes, Colonel. My parents own a ranch, miles from nowhere, west of Topeka."

"I'd guess that you're an expert rider in that case."

"Not really an expert, but I've been riding since I was a young girl."

"Your parents raise cattle? Horses?"

"Both. My father bought into the land soon after the territory was opened for settlement. He is a remarkable man. He's taken me on several cattle drives."

"And your mother?"

"She's taken me to St. Louis and Kansas City, and New Orleans."

"Three places I've never been. You must have had an extraordinary childhood."

"Where are you from, Colonel?"

"Upstate Vermont, near Burlington. Close to Lake Champlain. We lived in the country too, but nothing as exciting as the frontier."

"Your parents?"

"My father was a professor at the University of Vermont. My mother was the most remarkable person I've ever known."

"Are they still with you?"

"Mother passed away seven years ago. Father died during the war."

"As a result of the war?"

"In a way. One of my brothers was killed at Chickamauga. That, coupled with Mother's death, just consumed him."

"I'm so sorry."

"What are you studying here, Miss Brody?"

"History."

"For what purpose?"

"I'm not sure. I'm fascinated by history. The college experience is stimulating. Right now, learning is the most important thing."

"That's an admirable goal for an 18-year old." He was fishing for personal information. She understood, and was flattered.

"I got a late start here because of the war. I am a first-year student, but I'll soon be twenty-one."

Then a ploy of her own, not as subtle. "Is there anyone back in Davenport or Washington that's missing you while you're here in Iowa City?"

"Probably not. I've never married."

For several weeks, Rose basked in the afterglow of those three magical days. Colonel Joshua Chase was on her mind to the exclusion of everything else. She was more than smitten. She had elevated him past hero status, almost to sainthood. She revisited the things he had told her, the perfectly-chosen words in his speeches, his knowledge, and the interest he had shown in her. Of course, the latter may have been feigned; he was a national figure, a confidante of the country's leaders. She was a country girl, naïve, eight years younger.

Would their paths cross again? Highly unlikely. But at least she had the memories. Poor Theodore. He just didn't measure up. She lost interest in him, and felt bad about it. They drifted apart.

Then, in the middle of March, a letter arrived from Davenport. She saw the army insignia on the envelope, and the name "Chase" above it.

My Dear Miss Brody.

I wanted to express my gratitude for your attentions to me while I was on campus. You honor the university.

My work in Davenport is almost concluded. The resolution I sought in the Sioux matter had been modified by Washington. In April, I will accompany the warriors to a new home in Nebraska. The Sioux will not be adequately compensated for their travails of the past six years. That is sad.

I wish you the best in your academic endeavors, and in whatever direction you choose after graduation.

I will be posted back to Washington sometime toward the end of April. I look forward to life after the military.

Thank you again. Be well.

Respectfully,

Joshua Chase

She re-read the letter and analyzed it. He hadn't included his rank at the end, just his name. That was more personal. It also occurred to her that the reference to being re-assigned might have been intended to assure that a return letter to him would be appropriately directed. Maybe. Maybe not. Should she answer his letter? Of course.

She composed, rather than wrote, the letter. Several drafts were rejected. She changed words. I'm spending more time on this than on a research project, she thought. At last, it was finished and mailed.

Dear Colonel Chase,

I received your gracious letter, and read with great interest of your involvement in the Sioux matter. There are several tribes in north-central Kansas. My father has great respect for them. Two of his most valued ranch hands are from the Choctaw nation. One is his foreman, a women named Bird, a wonderful, loyal, hard-working lady.

Your visit here gave us insight into the courage and commitment of our military, and of our citizens. Hopefully we will never again find ourselves at war with our brothers and sisters.

What will you do after your service is complete? Will you return to Vermont? You indicated a fondness for it in our conversations.

We received another substantial snowfall yesterday. I'm sure that it reached Davenport too. Unfortunately there were no military personnel to use as snowball targets.

I thank you for sharing your experiences with our academic community and with me.

Sincerely,
Rose Brody

Then there was a letter from him in April, them another after he had transferred back to Washington. Three more arrived in May. Each one was more familiar. Each of her answering letters was easier to write. He had signed the last one, *With affection, Joshua.*

She had written her parents about him. In each letter to them, references to him increased in length and in language. Margaret guessed early.

"Rose is in love, Whit."

"Nonsense. She's taken by his uniform, the people he knows."

"No, I don't think so. It's more than that. I wonder how he feels about her."

"Maggie darling, he's just being nice."

"Probably. But if I'm counting right, he's sent her at least five letters in two months, maybe more."

"Be realistic. He's a shining star of America. She's just our little girl. Besides, he's too old for her."

"Love doesn't read calendars. Anyway, it's only eight years."

"So what do you suggest we do about it? Encourage her?"

"Whit Brody," she paused and smiled at him. "You're jealous."

"No. You're wrong, I just don't know what to think of a military hero paying attention to Rose. I wonder about his intentions."

Now Margaret was laughing at him. "His intentions? They're a thousand miles apart."

Then he was laughing too. "I guess I am a bit jealous. If this gets any more serious though, we'd better have a look at him. Invite him here for a visit. We'll see how he sits a horse. See if he can split firewood, herd cattle."

"The important things in life."

"You bet." They both laughed.

Rose was home for the summer months when the letter came. She had invited Josh to the Brody Ranch, unless he thought she was too bold in extending an invitation. Her mother had enclosed a separate letter, inviting him to come "anytime." Rose wanted him to meet her parents, she had penned, to give him a tour of the ranch holdings, to ride with him. On June 26, 1866, she opened a letter which caused her to gasp.

My Dear Rose,

Thank you so much for the invitation. I don't know when this letter will reach the ranch, but I'm leaving tomorrow, June 11, for Nebraska, sort of a journey of exploration and personal curiosity, to look over the Sioux accommodations that I suggested before I left the military. I should arrive at the fort before the end of June. When that is completed, I would be most happy to see you. I can find the ranch based on your letters, and some research that I've done.

I am anxious, both to see you, and to meet your parents, I will arrive on horseback sometime during the second week in July. If this does not work for your family, I will busy myself in eastern Kansas, or perhaps follow the Missouri River on west. My knowledge of the West is limited to Iowa and Nebraska at this point.

Please extend my best to your parents, and don't plan anything special for my visit. Seeing you will be special in itself.

Much love,

Joshua

She flew down the steps, almost stumbling, and raced into the kitchen, startling her mother and Caroline.

"Mother, he's coming! He's coming. He's already on the way!"

Sixteen days later, just before noon, Rose, who had studied the horizon tirelessly for the past six days, saw a rider trotting down an eastern hill into the saucer. She ran toward him. Joshua? Yes, she knew by his bearing, his size, his ease in the saddle. Joshua. He slowed as he neared her, and smiled broadly as he reined in.

"Hi, Rose."

"Joshua. I'm thrilled that you're here!"

He dismounted and walked to her, extending a hand.

Ignoring the hand, she kissed him, full on the lips.

****

Herk and Jack were on opposite sides of the tongue of the empty produce cart, turning it toward the harnessed work horse, to hitch it up for Simeon's daily trip to the gardens.

The cart buckled, and a wheel snapped off, dropping the side toward Herk violently, and driving a six-inch splinter into the back of his forearm.

"Damn!" he screamed as he jumped clear.

Half of the jagged spike of wood protruded from the arm, and Herk jerked it away, gritting his teeth.

"Herk, you OK?" Jack asked.

"Hell no! Damn thing. Some of it's still in there."

Jack looked at it closely. "Ugly. It'll have to be cut out of there. I can do it for you."

"I ain't no little girl. I'm OK."

"Don't be so darn stubborn. That's going to infect, bad. I'll heat up a kitchen knife. Pour some whiskey into the wound." He turned toward the house.

"It ain't a wound. I've had bullets and arrows in my body afore. This ain't nothin'. Besides, don't need some young pup makin' holes in me. Forget it."

"If you end up walking around here with one arm and a stub, it'll be what you deserve. Ought'ta hold you down, and scrape it clean."

"You ain't man enough."

Jack bristled as he walked away.

Dammit, Herk thought. I like that kid.

Two days later, Herk developed a fever. The next day he noticed a red streak from his forearm to his bicep. A day later he understood that he was really sick. His vision was blurred; he was chilling. The area around the wound was purple, and the displaced skin was dark and malodorous. Moving his fingers on that hand was painful. He couldn't lift the arm. He realized that he was hallucinating. He would go for help, but he was too dizzy to stand, and he was so cold. He pulled on his pants, and sat heavily at his small table. A thought fought its way through the haze. Dammit, I'm dying. This is it.

Outside, Bird noticed that he was missing, and the sun told her that it was nearing 10 a.m.

"Anybody seen Herkimer Grimes?" she called to a group near the corral.

"Ain't seen him this m-m-m-orning. Seemed a bit off his feed yesterday," Elon called back.

He's always a bit off his feed, she thought. Maybe he's sleeping off a drunk. Maybe he's left. Nope, his horse was still in the barn.

Jack came running up. "You looking for Herkimer?"

"Yeah. He seems to be missing."

"Bird, we'd better get over to this shack."

As they ran, she called ahead to him. "Jack, what's going on?"

"He's in major trouble, I'd guess. Charlie and Lige, over here!"

They reached the small cabin. The door was latched. "Grimes! You in there?"

No answer. Jack put his shoulder into the slatted door. It opened, letting shafts of sunlight illuminate a neatly-organized room. They saw him, sitting at his table, slumped over face down, shirtless. His right hand was curled around a revolver.

"Drunk?" she asked. Then she noticed a faint odor, and then the cause. His left arm hung limp at his side, grotesquely swollen from his fingers to just below his shoulder. He looked up at her through lidded eyes, sweat beading every inch of his face.

"So cold," he murmured, "so hot."

"He ran a large splinter into his arm a few days ago. I've asked him about it every day since. Wouldn't let me see it," Jack explained.

Charlie Fox entered the room, Lige lumbering behind. "Mother?"

"Charlie, go get Mr. Brody. Lige, help Jack get Mr. Grimes to the bed." Summoning sympathy for a man she disliked was not easy, but this man was in danger, and he was helpless. "What can we do, Jack?"

"I'd say we treat it like a snakebite. Open it up. Get the poison out. Pull out the splinter that's still in there."

Charlie ran back into the room. "Mr. Brody rode out this morning. Won't be back until tonight."

"Can't wait for that. Unless we do something quickly, he'll be dead by noon. You ever do anything like this, Jack?"

"Suppose I can learn on the job. I guess that I'll need a pan of boiling water, a sharp kitchen knife, some towels or clean cloths, a bottle of spirits, maybe a belt or rope, in case he starts to bleed out."

Charlie left in a sprint.

Bird leaned down to Herk's ear. "Mr. Grimes, where do you hide your whiskey?"

"Ain't you heard? Firewater and Injuns don't mix. You hankerin' for a swig?" Herk's reply was just above a whisper.

"Maybe I want it to smash over your head," she calmly replied.

In minutes the procedure began. Lige lay across Herk, immobilizing him. Bird pinned the infected arm to the bed. Charlie held the boiling water, and an open bottle of whiskey. Jack slit the arm, releasing a thick greenish fluid and a stench. Herk grimaced, but made no noise. This man is tough, Bird thought. "Give him a mouthful of whiskey, son."

Jack probed the area with the knife point, flicking out several shards of wood. He widened the slit, and began pressing on the arm from different angles. A trickle of blood replaced the infectious flow. Then he took the bottle of whiskey and poured it liberally into the gaping wound. Herk's eyes rolled back, and he lost consciousness. Bird wrapped the entire arm tightly with strips of the kitchen cloth.

"That's it for now," Bird said. "You think he'll make it?"

"I don't know," Jack answered. "This is all new to me. We probably should have taken the arm off, but we don't have the tools, and I didn't see much rotted flesh. We got a lot of poison out. If he lives, he's going to have an ugly scar."

"You did good, Jack," she patted him on his shoulder.

The next day, Herk was no better. He was still feverish, and hallucinating. Whit sensed that he was slipping. At midday, Bird returned with a gelatinous gray mixture, unwrapped the arm, and slathered the open wound with the substance.

Sitting by the bed, Whit questioned her. "What is that?"

"Combination of herbs, chopped-up roots, flour, and some wheel grease to make it thinker. I saw it used years ago in Oklahoma. Don't know if it'll work. I added some whiskey to the mixture. It smells awful. Have to do something."

"I've been debating this. I see any sign that he's losing ground, we'll bundle him in a blanket, throw him in a buckboard, and head for Topeka. See if there's a doctor that way."

"How will we know?" She began re-wrapping the arm with clean cloths.

"Well, that's what I've been debating. I suppose in the war, they've have taken the arm off and crossed their fingers."

"He is a tough man. And stubborn. Take a lot to finish him off."

"You feel like staying here a while?"

"I can do that."

"I'll get someone in here every two hours. Rose'll sit a spell. Margaret too. Jack. Caroline. If he doesn't make it, I don't want him to die alone. Shoudn't happen to anyone."

"I know," she said quietly.

Sometime that night, with Margaret holding his hand, the fever broke. Sometime later, he opened his eyes, groaned, and fell back to sleep, snoring loudly.

He tried to get up the next day. Too weak. Whit ordered him back to bed for several days. "Man, you almost died. You crazy? Stay in that bed until I tell you to get up."

On the third day, he was sitting, fully dressed when Bird brought a bowl of soup from the main house.

"You look much better today, Mr. Grimes."

"Hell. Nothing wrong with me. I'm getting sick of being babied."

"Well, Mr. Grimes, on behalf of everyone who's cared for you, who's worried about you, you're welcome." She pulled up the bedcovers, and fluffed his pillow.

"Didn't say I wasn't grateful. But everyone's been in here 'cept an Injun holy man."

"I don't think a holy man would want to get near you."

"You're pretty feisty."

"Why shouldn't I be? You're…" Her voice trailed off. It wasn't worth pursuing.

"Something bothering you?"

"Yes. You. I'm way past trying to be nice to you."

"Why's that?"

"You have shown your contempt for Charlie and me. Several times, you've told people that you hate Indians."

"Why shouldn't I? I've seen Indians rape little girls, decapitate babies, burn women alive, scalp and gut men. Heathens." He raised his voice with each word. "Why the hell shouldn't I hate them?"

"You hate all of us? I never scalped a man."

"Don't matter. There's something inhuman in all red folks. I should know."

Bird felt bile rising in her throat. "You don't know anything! I've seen worse that you can imagine, coming from white men."

"Like what?"

Should she do this? Yes. She looked squarely at him, and walked toward his chair.

"My tribe was thrown off of our ancestral land and forcibly marched over 1,000 miles to Oklahoma. My father, mother, and grandfather perished on the journey. I was a little girl. I was sold to a white trapper when I was sixteen, and I became his plaything. He took me to a Rendezvous and offered me to thirty men who abused me in every possible way for three nights. He gave me to another trapper, who raped me." She walked to the bed and sat on the corner.

"I was shown kindnesses at Bent's Fort by Stephen Butler, who became my lover and guardian, and by the Bent brothers and by Ceran St. Vrain. I went to Taos with Charlie's father, Rides With Fire. He was murdered there. I sold my love along the Mississippi River for a time, just so Charlie could eat. Many of the men refused to pay me, or beat me. I still have the scar from a Bowie knife on my shoulder. One morning I woke up naked and bleeding on the waterfront. The old woman who watched Charlie went to the authorities to take Charlie away from me." She paused to see if he was paying attention. He was. She stood again, and realized that decades of racial abuse, previously unspoken, were now gushing forth. Decades of hate were being poured over this pathetic gunslinger, an Indian fighter, and the truth was, he wasn't worth it.

But she wasn't finished. "I went into Missouri with Charlie to hide away, and ended up in a run-down hotel with a German immigrant, a dirty, violent man who could barely speak the language. He took us to a small ranch and he was hired as a cattle herder. It was there that I learned to brand, to cut cattle, to rope, to take care of horses. One night, he beat Charlie, and I smashed a bottle on his head. He tied me to the bed, where he did unspeakable things to me for several days. Charlie freed me, and we rode a stolen pony and Stephen Butler's buckboard wagon west. We came here."

She was finished, almost. She walked to the door. "You are not the only one who has seen murder and watched the dark side of other men. The difference between us is that your heart is closed to my people. And if you hate my son, then I hate you. I am alive today because of Stephen Butler, the Bents, St. Vrain, and Whit Brody. There are good people of all colors. Until you embrace that thought, you will be bitter and lonely, probably die that way, and no one will mourn you. I know that I won't!" She slammed the door behind her.

"Jesus." Herk muttered. He sat staring at the door for a long time.

****

Annalise checked the pouch for the two most important items she carried, the letters of identification written by Herman O'Neill and by Ohio Governor Jacob D. Cox. The letters identified her as Herman's daughter, and as an emissary from Governor Cox on a fact-finding mission. Neither was exactly true. She hadn't been adopted by the O'Neills, but she still stayed with them, still called them, "Mother Maribel" and "Daddy Herman." Herman hadn't written his letter; he could no longer hold a pen in his hand; Maribel had composed it, and signed his name. Governor Cox had willingly supplied his missive on impressive official parchment containing the state seal, fully aware that Annalise was determined to scour the South for news of her missing mother. Mutual Cincinnati friends of the Governor and Herman had encouraged him to write the document.

As soon as the War Between the States had ended, she had crossed the Ohio River to ask questions, visiting the farms and plantations of disgruntled and often hostile former slaveholders. She had courted danger on those missions, and several times had been threatened. Once, in a village in central Kentucky, a pinch-nosed sheriff with yellow teeth had ordered her out of town.

"Don't need your kind around here, lady, mindin' us of the old days."

"But I'm looking for a free woman, my mother."

"Don't care if'n you're lookin' for Pres-dent Johnson. Get your sweet little ass outa town in an hour, or by God, I'll put you in jail…or worse."

On this trip, she would venture into western Tennessee, and the newly-acquired letters would hopefully guarantee safe passage on some level. She had a hunch, nothing more, that if her mother had been kidnapped, the party would have gone south or west. There had been a surfeit of slaves in the Atlantic Coast states, little need for another. Her mother's beauty would attract buyers wherever she had been taken, if indeed that was what had happened to her.

On these endeavors, she sought others of her race, and wherever she found them, she engaged them in conversation.

"Did you ever know a slave woman named Missy?"

"Do you remember a tall pretty slave woman? She might have worked in a laundry or in the main house."

Annalise had changed in the eight years since her mother had disappeared. Not physically; she was still striking, still beautiful, and she had matured naturally into a women's body. But her essence was gone; she had lost her sprightliness, her lyricism. Her chase of knowledge, of new intellectual pursuits, had flagged noticeably. Her sanguine personality had been altered into a cheerless aspect that worried the O'Neills. She had fallen into a dark sulkiness that expressed itself in silence and contemplation.

"Don't worry. It's natural. She misses her mother. Time will soften the blow," Levi Coffin had told Maribel. It hadn't.

Annalise was consumed with the need to find her mother, or at least to discover the circumstances of her disappearance. Herman O'Neill knew that the chances of ever finding anything were small to non-existent. But he had devoted large chunks of his own life to that cause, often neglecting his teaching and mentoring. He hired investigators; searched for witnesses; counseled with Coffin, who asked questions of his Underground Railroad network; and journeyed into parts of Kentucky and Tennessee chasing a ghost.

"Daddy Herman, I want to go with you," she had begged when she turned sixteen.

"No Annalise. It is too dangerous. Not yet. Someday maybe."

Each time he returned, she greeted him with hope. "Nothing, dear," he had to report. Even as the War Between the States raged, he continued to look.

The trail was cold, and the mission took a toll on Herman. He became frail, and eventually resigned from academe. He suffered a series of seizures which eventually robbed him of the ability to speak and to stand.

Annalise had dropped out of school at sixteen, and she began taking jobs that Coffin found for her. She faithfully saved most of her wages, thinking that someday they would finance her search. Despite the upheaval in their lives, the O'Neills would have it no other way. She was their daughter, in theory, and they considered it their moral duty to support her. They reasoned that they had a huge stake in leading her to resolution, even if the commitment took years.

One spring afternoon, Maribel tested a subject that had gone unspoken for years.

"Your father, Annalise. Do you have any memory of him, Dear?"

"A few details. But I was so young when he died, they are only scattered images. Mamma never wanted to talk about him. She told me once that he wasn't cruel to her, but that she hated him for using her, and for ignoring me."

"You don't remember any kindness toward you?"

"He never even spoke to me. I was a slave girl; he was the Master. He wasn't pretty to look at, sort of round-faced. Didn't have any family, a couple of nephews. When he died, choked to death, I remember that, our friends--the other slaves-- quietly celebrated. Mamma was in a good mood after that. Then we were freed."

"You two were the only ones freed, according to what your mother told me."

"Mamma was surprised, but she didn't say much, because our friends would have to stay there, work for the nephews, I suppose. I do have a specific memory though, one that possibly foreshadowed his final kindness. He rode up to our shack one day. I was on the porch. He was on his white horse, and he usually dressed in white too. He stopped in front of me. I couldn't see his face; the sun was behind him, but I remember what he said to Mamma. 'Ollie, this is a beautiful child.' Then he rode off."

Maribel continued folding clothes. Perhaps the subject was exhausted. She did feel huge relief. Annalise had softened during the conversation, a rare occurrence recently.

"Mother Maribel. Thanks for caring."

"Annalise. I love you. Of course I care."

When the war ended, Annalise went into action. She was twenty, and old enough, she told the O'Neills. She left on her searches as she could afford to, sometimes staying away a week, sometimes two. She rode her mare, heavily laden with food and clothing, and ventured farther into Kentucky, and parts of Tennessee. With each fruitless journey, she seemed more determined.

Her plan this time was to ride her mare as far as Nashville, stay in a hotel, and then walk around questioning each black face she saw. When she had to extend the parameters, she would ride with saddlebags containing whatever she required to spend a few days out of the city. It was not a method guaranteed to blanket the area completely, but it kept her searching. She would follow trails back toward Louisville, and then home.

After she had left this time, Maribel could no longer quiet her frustration.

"Herman, if Missy were still alive, she'd be back here, you know?"

Herman nodded.

"I think Annalise knows that too," Maribel continued, "she had a need to understand what happened, to become convinced that her mother didn't desert her. That's what pulls her out there."

Again, Herman nodded.

"So sad. So very sad. She is squandering her life. She had no friends, no future, except for this incessant searching. God, I love that girl, but this is taking a toll on all of us."

Herman didn't nod at that. Maribel saw the tears in his eyes.

Although she wasn't aware of it, canvassing Tennessee would be particularly difficult. Nashville had a slave market before the war, she knew, and several notable plantations. What she didn't realize was that more than 75% of Tennessee slave owners had owned fewer than ten slaves. So there were no geographical shortcuts for her, no collection of former large plantations in clusters, where she could collect answers in a logical and quick manner. Two weeks into the process, she became frustrated by the sizable task before her, visiting countless sites of modest farms, and hundreds of small cemeteries.

Then she met Tyler Hall Garret, a tall, rakish sort with red hair, freckles, a big grin, and limitless charm.

Garrett presided at Little Scotland, the remnants of a large plantation fifty miles northeast of Nashville. He had grown up on the land, owned by his father, Rodney Garrett, Jr., the son of wealthy English immigrants who had established and grown Little Scotland into a formidable holding.

Annalise saw him first as she rode up to the manor house on the property, sent there by a former slave who knew of the place.

He was sitting on the porch of the main house when she trotted up.

As she dismounted, he walked off of the porch, dressed in white riding pants and a white shirt with the cuffs rolled, unbuttoned at the neck. He towered over her.

"Morning, ma'am. Can I help you? I'm the owner's son, Tyler."

She was a bit intimidated by the man, who was at least a foot taller. A shock of red hair washed across his forehead. She was aware of other features, dimples, broad shoulders, and huge hands which took hers gently in a handshake.

"Yes sir. I'm Annalise. I'm looking for news of my mother. She was a slave. I believe she was kidnapped just before the war."

"You think she was kidnapped by us? We were plenty good to our workers, ma'am."

Annalise responded quickly. "I'm not aware of what went on here. I grew up in Ohio. I'm just checking all possibilities."

"Who is your mother?"

"She was called Missy, or Ollie by some. Tall woman, educated, pretty."

"Well, that description doesn't fit any of the ladies who worked for us, at least in the last ten years. You think she may have ended up around here?'

"I don't know. I've been looking all over the South, looking for information. Anything." She was briefly pensive, and quiet. "I'm not even sure that she was kidnapped."

He listened, grim-faced, then smiled at her. "Listen, my manners are terrible. Can I get you a drink or something? I'd like to hear more."

"Yes, please. Water? I'd love a glass of water."

They sat on the front porch alone for several hours. He was attentive as she related details of her life and her quest. Midway through the conversation, she turned the conversation around, questioning him. He was a son of privilege who would someday inherit the vast holdings of his father. The war had not decimated the plantation by much, nor deprived them of a workforce. They had never 'owned' other humans, he explained. They paid wages to their workers, many of whom lived in neat little houses on the plantation, and were free to come and go as they pleased. His beliefs were conflicted in the war, which he nonetheless served in, rising to significant officer status for the Confederacy. The war had deprived him of over three years in which he could have started a family of own.

"Of couse, I've never met a lady that I'd spend my life with yet."

He had paused before the word "yet." She smiled at him, then hurriedly looked away. "Mr. Garrett, Thank you for your hospitality. I've got a ride back to my accommodations, and a full day tomorrow. I'll excuse myself now." She stood up.

"You're going all of the way back to Nashville?"

"No, no. I'm staying at a roadside inn a few miles from here."

"You'll continue your search tomorrow?"

"Yes. I'll ride due north of here, and ask some questions."

"That's a scattered area for farms. You know where you're going exactly?"

"I'm never sure of where I'm going."

"You want some company?"

She didn't answer right away. That was not a good idea. She didn't know this man.

"I'll be fine. Thanks for offering."

"It's a sincere offer. I promise to be a complete gentleman." He raised his right hand, as if taking an oath. "I know the location of every burg, every farm, within 100 miles of Nashville. I could shorten your journey."

"That would be an imposition, but thank you." She stepped off of the porch and took the reins of her horse from a wizened old man who smiled at her. She hadn't seen him before.

"That's Moe, ma'am. He's been with us since before I was born."

"Thank you, Moe." She smiled back at him. He lowered his head and nodded.

"Let's do this, ma'am. I'll call for you at your inn at daybreak. I'll get you started. If I get in your way, you just tell me, and I'll ride on back here. I think I can shorten your search."

She mounted and hesitated. He would make the next day easier. Maybe…

"The Old Rover Inn, ten miles west. You know it?"

"I know it. I'll see you bright and early."

The days stretched to two weeks. Annalise began to regret that it would soon end, even though the search had been devoid of any success. No leads. No helpful information. The mollifying factor was her new friend, a courteous, affable, and witty man, several years older than she. Their rapport was effortless and comfortable.

In two days Annalise would break off, and begin the trek to Louisville, and then home. Tyler would ride back toward Little Scotland.

After several days of his routine of picking her up at various locations each morning, and then riding back to Little Scotland, they had expanded the search. They were some distance from his plantation, and he had begun staying at the same inns where she stayed. They used separate rooms, even though Annalise wouldn't have protested sharing a room, to test her judgment as to what he'd do, what she'd permit. There was even a night of camping out under the stars at a location that he knew. True to his word, he was a gentleman. She owed him plenty.

He was a few miles out of his bailiwick at that point, but many people they encountered recognized the Garrett name. In one small village, a former overseer refused to answer their question, and terminated a brief conversation with "Get your asses outta here! Mister, take that wench with you!" Garrett approached the man and threw a punch, which lifted the man off of his feet. They rode away as the man rose to his elbows, rubbing his chin.

She felt safe with this man. More important, she was becoming fond of him. She had recognized signs lately that he was not exactly what he had first seemed to be. He was somewhat of an overgrown adolescent, certainly not naïve, but at least somewhat raw. More and more in the last week, she had caught him studying her, often sensed his eyes following her as she walked ahead of him. The previous week, as they had scoured a small slave cemetery, she stumbled over a hidden root. He caught her, his arm around her waist. She steadied, but his arm stayed around her. He leaned over, put his other arm behind her neck, and kissed her. She pulled away, a reflexive instinct. "I'm so clumsy," she giggled, and turned away.

She regretted that impulse later, and tried to compensate by brightening her attitude toward him for several days. She greeted him each morning with a kiss on his cheek, and found reasons to compliment him, to laugh at his jibes, and to force conversation to items about him.

"Tyler, you've got to get back to Little Scotland. Please don't feel as if you have to see this to the end. When you have to go, please go," she had said.

"Sounds like you're trying to get rid of me," he groused, raising an eyebrow. She couldn't tell if he was joking.

"No, of course not. You've been wonderful. You are truly my friend, and I'm grateful."

"Friend? I guess that's a good thing." He was smiling again, and she knew that he was watching her as she walked away. She didn't mind.

Dinner on their last night lasted late, as if each of them didn't want it to end.

"Our philosophy was why we survived the war," he was saying. "We're doing the same things now that we did before it started. We didn't have property. We had people."

"That's refreshing. And unusual."

"Yes, ma'am."

She was fascinated by him. He had distracted her from her purpose, but it had been a different kind of adventure. He was so good looking.

No sooner had her room door closed behind them, she was in his arms, an effort that they both seemed to initiate.

He held her gently, and his mouth covered hers, the first time in her life that she had been kissed that way. He bent down farther and kissed her neck, and she couldn't stifle the gasp that escaped her mouth.

"Annalise," he whispered, and he kissed her more insistently. She responded on her tiptoes, her arms around his neck. For several minutes, the two embraced, and her eyes closed, and she began to breathe noisily. A part of her mind was telling her to let it continue, whatever the outcome.

His hand dropped to her buttocks, and he began fondling her there aggressively. Then a hand moved to her breast, and then into her shirt, and she was startled by his sudden aggression. She pulled back.

"Tyler, please."

The quiet plea had no effect on him. He pulled at her collar, and her shirt fell open, a button falling to the wood floor. His left arm circled her waist, and his right hand began to forcefully massage her crotch through the riding pants. He bit at her lip, and he spun her around, and his hands returned to her breasts.

Too fast. Too rough. Too abrupt.

In that instant, she knew. His experiences with the opposite sex, and there had probably been many, were nurtured by his plantation experience. There were probably numerous slave girls, and he had groped and grabbed, and made the conquests quick and selfish. He may not have treated white ladies that way. The thought frightened her. Her mind racing, she knew that she could not allow more.

"Tyler, stop, please." She pushed at his chest with an elbow, and stepped back.

"What the hell's the matter?"

"I guess that I don't want to do this." She put a hand to her collar to pull the unbuttoned shirt closed.

"Came too far to stop now." His visage was suddenly dark, his eyes narrowed. She had not seen him that way, or imagined it, before.

She put up her other hand, and there was no mistaking her annoyance as she stammered, "This is not what I want. This way. It isn't going to happen this way."

"What'd you expect? Flowers?"

"No. I expect you to treat me like a lady."

"A lady? You been teasing me for two weeks."

"Teasing you? I didn't even want you to come along." Her anger matched his.

"You owe me. I've worked my ass off for a piece of you."

"This has all been an act? Just to do this?"

"No. Not all of it. You're too fine to crawl on without some effort."

"I'm sorry that you feel that way. "

He was livid. "I was bored. Why else would I go after a wench? Look at you! Won't be too many opportunities to get a white man in your bed!"

She was shocked. "What?"

"Only thing you can count on is rutting with some dumbass buck. I don't have to treat you like a lady."

"Get out. Get out now!"

She wasn't sure that he'd leave. She walked to the door and opened it. He picked up his hat, chuckled in her face as he passed her, and pulled the door behind him until it slammed.

Through her window, she saw him gallop away from the inn minutes later.

She was stunned. Maybe she'd skip Louisville, and head straight back to Cincinnati tomorrow.

****

Rose was awestruck by her beau, if that's what he was. Neither spoke of such things, but both understood that they were far past just being friends. For days their exchanges were laced with intimacy and easy banter. They held hands often, and she greeted him daily with a kiss.

On his first day, Rose had indeed shown him the ranch, on an all-day tour which included a picnic lunch. On the second day, Joshua began to ingratiate himself to the ranch hands by actively helping to brand maverick calves during the daylight hours. He worked at a feverish pace without a break, except for a brief lunch with Rose on the front porch of the main house. The next day he offered to break two wild horses, and by sunset, the two cayuses were meekly walking around the corral with Jack and Elon astride. Joshua explained away the expertise. "We had horses in Vermont."

"Papa," Rose had accosted Whit. "He was shot in the back during the war. Some days he can't touch his toes. You're making him do some pretty rugged work."

"Making him? Rosie, darlin', I couldn't slow him down if I wanted to."

Dinners were animated, brilliant with discussions of philosophy and national affairs, wide-ranging in topic and in opinion.

"Tell me about President Lincoln, son."

"A remarkable, lonely man, Mr. Brody. Humble and straightforward. Most don't know that he had a temper, especially when the war effort seemed to be lagging. He was fair to everyone, and if you pulled your weight, he was gracious and grateful. He suffered when he heard casualty numbers, for both sides. He was the most complex simple man I've ever met."

Margaret was impressed with his knowledge and his modesty, nor did she fail to notice the looks he and her daughter exchanged. She caught Rose winking at the officer more than once.

Caroline was impressed with him too, after he helped Rose and her bake pies one afternoon, adhering to his own mother's recipes and kitchen habits. He cleaned out horse stalls, mended fences with Bird, and overstayed one night in the bunkhouse, playing cards with the men of the ranch, the lone evening in his visit that he hadn't spent with Rose before they retired to separate bedrooms. In several afternoon sessions, he taught Lige how to read, although the result of that was still very unpolished.

"Son, how long can you stay?" Whit had asked one August evening.

"I have been here a while, Mr. Brody. I'm sorry."

"Sorry? Listen, Joshua, you're the best thing that's happened out here for years. You stay as long as you want. Forever, if you're of a mind. We all think highly of you. I'm embarrassed that I'm not paying you wages."

"I'm fond of everyone out here. Mr. Grimes is sort of a challenge though." He paused and smiled. "I haven't seen my brother Jefferson in some time. He's an attaché in Georgia, working with the reconstruction effort. I need to visit him sometime soon."

"You two are close?"

"Yes, Sir. He's all I have left."

"I have to ask this. You and Rose. Any plans?"

"That's something we need to discuss. Do I have your approval to have a serious talk with her?"

"Yes, Son. You do."

Joshua was being only partially faithful to what had occurred several days before. He and Rose had talked about a future, and he had said, "I love you, Rose," and she had wept.

"But I'm unsettled now," he had told her, "I don't know what I'll do next. Politics, maybe. I'm also somewhat bothered by our age difference, to be honest."

"Joshua, am I too old for you?" she had teased.

He had laughed and the subject was dropped.

In September, he announced that he had to go to Kansas City, military papers to sign, he had said. He'd return in a few days.

On the night of his return, he asked Whit to take a walk with him. He showed him the ring. "Do I have your permission to ask Rose to marry me?" he asked.

Whit had hugged him. "You do. Yep, you certainly do."

Back in the house Margaret was startled when Whit escorted her briskly back to the kitchen away from everyone, and suddenly whooped, "Wahoo!"

Joshua Chandler Chase and Rose Ellen Brody were married in October of 1866, in a lavish ceremony in her parents' front yard.

Some among the few wedding guests must have questioned the swiftness of the courtship, and the suddenness of the wedding. Most of the scattered settlers in the area, and those people from the small nearby settlement of Abilene were aware of the Brodys' houseguest, a tall, handsome war hero. Why was the wedding three months after his arrival? An arranged wedding? Was the Brodys' daughter with child? No matter. Whit Brody was smothering them with food and music.

Joshua was saddened when he received a letter two days before the wedding: Jefferson's regrets.

My Dearest Brother,

I'm disheartened to report that there's no way that I can come west for your wedding. There is too much that needs my attention here, in this hellhole of greed and slimy politicians. Nor can I get a leave.

I think of you constantly and am happy that you have found a lady worthy of you.

I promise that I will visit you when my duty is complete next year, regardless of where you are.

My heart is with you on your special day. I love you.

Your brother,

Jefferson

Joshua had secured the only preacher in the Abilene area, a grumpy, religious zealot sort from near Topeka, to conduct the services. Whit had hired four itinerant musicians from among residents of Abilene to provide music. Margaret and Caroline had sewn a wedding dress from fine materials, using Margaret's old wedding dress as the model and the starting point. Jack served as best man, with Charlie Fox and Elon Pack as groomsmen. Caroline was matron of honor. Bird and Rose's roommate from Iowa completed the party.

"Margaret and I now have a son. Our daughter has fallen in love with a hero, a remarkable young man. This is one of the happiest days of my life. I hope that you two will stay in love as long as Margaret and I have. Longer, maybe, because we got a late start. If you all look behind me to the house, you'll see Noah and Lige bringing in our wedding gift," Whit had toasted.

The gift was a magnificent carriage, which had been secreted away by Whit under a stack of hay near the river. It was drawn by two imposing black horses, both of which had been tamed by Joshua.

Joshua responded. "I was raised in a wondrous childhood a thousand miles from here by Jeremiah and Molly Chase, two of the most exceptional people I've ever known. Both are deceased, but I remember them now with gratitude and fondness. If they're watching today, and I like to think they are, they are wondering how their oldest son got so lucky, to find a wonderful, beautiful life mate with parents that match his own. I would tell my wife now, in front of you: I love you, adore you, my sweet Rose, and I will forever." As Joshua looked to Rose, the tears in her eyes and her angelic smile caused him to pause and clear his throat as he concluded.

The last guests left long after the bride and groom had retired to an upstairs bedroom, away from the celebrants' noise and the slightly atonal music from three fiddles and a guitar. Sometime after midnight, Whit and Margaret sat together on the porch. The night air was cool, refreshing, if a bit bracing.

"I got the musicians in the bunkhouse. I think they'll sleep well tonight," Whit said absently.

"I love you, Whit," Margaret answered.

"Preacher don't mind much, sleeping by the fireplace."

They sat without words for a while. "Doesn't seem possible, does it Whit? Our little girl is a married woman."

"Married to a fine young man. Where did the time go?"

They were quiet again. Whit took Margaret's hand. Then he noticed something over by the lone shack, a glow. Herk smoking. "I'll be right back, Maggie. Gonna talk to Herkimer."

"Missed you at the wedding, Herkimer."

"Parties ain't my thing," Grimes responded.

"You holed up the entire time? Missed some good food and music."

"No. I took a ride by myself. Just got back a spell ago. Ain't really hungry."

"Got to take exception to that. I consider you part of the family. Ranch family, anyway. Mrs. Brody was upset that you didn't come down for a while."

"Too many people. Too much noise. Came here for peace and quiet. I am happy for little Rose. He seems like a good man. Just don't like weddings and such."

"Suit yourself." Whit stretched and got up to leave.

"Whit?"

"Yeah."

"I consider you folks like family too. Don't show it often, but I'm happy here."

"Alright, Herkimer."

"Bird, was she at the wedding?"

Whit paused. Why was he asking that? "Yes. Stood up with Rosie. Looked mighty pretty. Danced a few times, with Joshua and her son. Some with Simeon. Once with Noah, I think."

"That's good."

"Good night, Herkimer."

"Night."

Why did he ask that, Whit wondered again.

****

The death of Bloody Bill Anderson in 1864 did not end the reign of terror he generated. Neither did the Civil War.

After Anderson was gunned down, Bravo Wright and Archie Clement assumed control of the Border Ruffians, and the atrocities continued.

"Can't give it up, Arch," Wright had insisted.

"Ain't never givin' up. Whether there be two of us or a hundred of us, we gonna keep on."

"You figger we'll get the army back to us? They be scattered over three states by now."

"Hell, yes. You watch. They'll come back to us. Won't hafta find 'em."

"One other thing, Arch. Don't want to be the leader. You'd be the man for that."

Over 100 former Ruffians found their ways back to the pair. The little Clement took command, and was as ruthless and single-minded as Anderson had been.

The war ended. The Border Ruffians didn't. Clement took the raids to a new level, bank robberies against institutions owned by Unionists. That, despite the government's intention to pardon all terrorists if they stopped their activities immediately.

In February of 1866, the Ruffians had robbed the Clay County Missouri Savings Bank, getting away with over $150,000. In the process, they killed an innocent bystander. In October they went after a bank in Lexington, Missouri, and netted $2,000.

On Election Day in 1866, Clement led 100 men into Lexington to intimidate those citizens who would vote Republican. Republicans lost every seat.

A platoon of state militia was sent to Lexington, under the premise that Clement, a stupid man, would return.

He did. He rode back into Lexington accompanied by a large number of his followers on December 13. The other Ruffians gradually rode away after an uneventful afternoon, but Clement went to a local tavern, where he was surrounded by soldiers.

He drew a pistol and began shooting wildly until a soldier shot him in the chest. Limping outside, he struggled to get onto his horse. Another soldier shot him down.

He died in the street.

Many of the Ruffians saw that as an ominous sign, and abandoned the group. They returned to their homes. Some would pursue bank robbery years later, particularly a small group led by Frank and Jesse James.

Bravo Wright was not ready to forfeit his dream. He enjoyed the mayhem of killing and of robbing banks.

With a core group of former Ruffians, he would continue the mission, this time as their leader.

CHAPTER TWENTY-SEVEN

1867

Abilene was a small settlement, barely, when Joseph McCoy visited it in 1867. It had been platted in 1861, and soon thereafter became the county seat, but it only consisted of a dozen log huts, one of which served as a saloon. Most of the huts were congregated on the east back of Mud Creek. To the west and northwest of Mud Creek were miles of grasslands, rife with buffalo, antelope, and wild turkey, perfect for a notion he had. And even in its relative isolation and desolation, there were other positives. It was already a station on the Overland Trail Stagecoach line, there were two major rivers in the vicinity, and several earlier cattle drives had used the area for staging before continuing their ways farther east.

Joseph McCoy was an Illinois cattle buyer who came west with the idea of finding a location for a great cattle center somewhere near the end of the Chisholm Trail, one that would surpass those in existence elsewhere, one that would serve the cattlemen who raised longhorn cattle.

Mc Coy was looking for an advantageous geographical location, north of, and accessible to, Texas. For the vaunted longhorn cattle of major cattle ranches in that state had recently come into disrepute. They spread disease, they overgrazed. Cattle towns and scattered stockyard areas discouraged them. McCoy's dream was to construct a stockyard near the Union Pacific railroad line, and open it to any cattle owner in the Midwest and Southwest.

Abilene was about to become a boom town.

Before the end of 1867, McCoy's Great Western Stockyards were already processing cattle. McCoy also built the Drover's Cottage, a 100 room hotel, whose "landlord," Mrs. Lou Gore, soon became noted for her kindness and hospitality.

There were problems at first. Rival stockyard locations sent emissaries to the fording points along the Arkansas and Little Arkansas rivers to persuade cattle drives en route to Abilene that they should detour. McCoy solved that by putting a glib young man named W.W. Sugg in charge of staffing those fords with personnel to extol the praises of the Kansas market. Then he spent $5,000 to publish advertisements in Western newspapers.

Meanwhile, the Osage tribe was causing trouble to the west. The summer of 1867 was plagued by a drought, causing prices to drop to accommodate underfed herds. The market stalled a bit, waiting for the Union Pacific Railroad to produce more cattle cars. Often, they had to hastily convert flatbed cars that they owned. McCoy had to scramble to circumvent the Texas Prohibitory Law, enacted quickly under the prodding of politicians from Ellsworth, Abilene's Kansas competitor for the cattle market.

But, in its first summer of existence, the little settlement grew dramatically. Businessmen, opportunists, gamblers, and ne'er-do-wells ballooned the population. Texas ranchers not only noticed it, but they also made it their destination of choice. Thirty-five thousand cattle were sold and shipped.

Abilene needed controls on the rabble that came, or used it as a place of wild celebration at the end of cattle drives. That wasn't forthcoming.

Several law officers managed the town in haphazard fashion. One had the temerity to post signs that guns were not permitted within the town limits. The signs were soon riddled with bullets.

There were people who cared, upstanding citizens who endured the rowdy nature of Abilene to build something better. The situation was tenuous. Houses of prostitution flourished north of the main settlement, past the railroad tracks, but too close to reputable homes and businesses. Saloons and dance halls dotted the townscape, and in the summer months emitted the uproar and bedlam of loud voices, bad music and frequent gun shots. Games of skill and chance proliferated, billiards and ten-pin alleys.

It was not Eden, but it had immense promise, and that was noticed by Joshua Chase, 15 miles to the west on the Brody ranch. One summer night he asked Whit to take a walk with him. Whit had an idea of what was coming. They sauntered slowly toward the corral. Whit cleared his voice.

"You're leaving, aren't you?"

"Maybe. But if we do, it will only be a few miles away."

"What direction, son?"

"Mr. Brody, I think of you as a father, a hero. I will always cherish the fact that you are Rose's father. I can't express how much the past year has meant to me. But, I am not a rancher."

"Joshua, you know that you and Rose will own all of this someday."

"That is a wonderful inheritance, but Rose and I have talked it out. We've come to a joint decision, as much hers as mine. We want to forge a different kind of life. We don't want to leave you, so we're going to try some options to stay close for a time."

"Options?"

"Eventually, we've settled on moving to Oregon. It's a growing state looking for an identity. There are different kinds of opportunities than here in Kansas."

"Mighty long way from here. I'd surely miss my grandchildren, when you have them."

Joshua grinned. "We've talked about that too."

"So what is the rest of the plan?"

"It's obvious that Abilene will soon be a small city of a couple of thousand people. What we want to do is to open a large merchandise store of some sort, a general store. Doing that will get us on the ground floor of the growth that's coming. If we've calculated correctly, a few years of that, and we'll be able to afford the move west easily, and whatever else we decide on."

"Well, I'm not as upset as you may think. The same kind of thoughts were on my mind back in the Fifties. Go to California or Oregon. Just got sidetracked here. I think you and I are alike in many ways."

"That's a compliment to me."

"Son, you always say the right thing. Think you'd be a good politician. Your father would have approved of that."

"Mr. Brody, your approval is the important thing now."

"So, you need some help to do this Abilene thing? Some money to buy land, build the store?"

"No, Sir. I…we can afford everything. I've been investigating a large lot on the southern part of town. Rose and I have been planning the building. It would be two stories. Our living quarters would be on the second floor."

"Tell me this. You have been happy here?"

"Yes. That's not our reason for the plans. We need to expand and grow. We need a family identity. "

"Ever done selling before?"

"I think that I'm doing that now, to you." Both men laughed. "I think we can learn. You used to sell cotton. We could use some advice from you."

"How long before you head west?"

"It won't be very soon, I'd guess."

"You should know this. I love this ranch. A lot of good people have sweated blood here over the years. A favorite of mine, Lem, is buried here. Old Hank too; the horse saved my life. I am also fond of the people here, Bird, Lige, and Noah, Jack, even Herkimer. I need to take care of them."

Joshua waited for the point.

"I'm still anxious to see what's out West too. Right now, it's pretty interesting here. If I did leave, I'd have to sell all of this, or give it to somebody who'd keep it as a ranch."

"I understand that."

"You know that I love and respect you. If you're settled on this plan, I'll support you. I know you well enough to know that you could be a success at anything you try. You could be the best cattleman and rancher this state has ever seen. I also know that you and Rose deserve to follow your own dreams."

Joshua reached to shake his hand, "Thank you, Sir."

Rose was propped up in bed when he returned, covers pulled up to her neck. "How did it go, Honey?"

"Good and not so good. He'll support whatever we do. But I think it hurt him, Rosie."

"Joshua, he's talking it over with Mother now. They're both agreeing that we need to break away."

He was still leaning against the door, his hand still on the door latch. "I hope so. This smacks somewhat of our ingratitude."

"Are you going to stand over there all night?" she asked. She pushed down the coverlet. She was naked.

She was not entirely right about her parents. Margaret was fast asleep when Whit entered their bedroom. He went to the window and looked out at the darkness for a long time. He retired and lay on his back, staring at nothing for most of the night.

One night, Annalise Ollimore sat up straight in bed, prompted by a thought intruding on another restless and troubled dream.

"A steamboat. Yes! The river!"

She rose early and made her way to the O'Neill kitchen. She was lost in thought when Maribel scuffled in, her burnished silver hair already in a bun.

"Good morning, dear. Another bad night?"

"Mother Maribel, what if Mamma was taken by Cincinnati by boat? And, if so, that would put her somewhere west or southwest of here, on port cities on the Mississippi River."

There was a hint of excitement in her voice, and Maribel noticed a spark in her eyes, rare since she had returned last year in a sullen state from a failed journey into Tennessee. Something had happened beyond the simple experience of another failed search. For months she had been near-uncommunicative, remote, pathetically sad. She hadn't really confided in either of the O'Neills, nor had Maribel pushed the issue. For a long time she seemed to have lost interest in finding her mother.

"Well, it's a thought. But that would really expand your search, Annalise."

"All of this time, we've been set on the thought that she was kidnapped by a bounty hunter, taken away, and sold in a 200-mile radius, by foot or by wagon, or by horseback. We've eliminated so many possibilities, and we haven't found any reason to hope. Was there any slave activity by boat? How much?"

"Well, dear, I certainly don't know that answer. Mr. Coffin would." Maribel began preparations for breakfast, conflicted by the thought that her daughter had emerged from her long pique, but was once again poised to resume a barren prospect.

Annalise wasted little time. At mid-morning, she was seated opposite Coffin at a work table in his store.

"Is it a possibility, Mr. Coffin? Was there much of a transport of slaves through here by boat?"

"Yes, it happened, but as far as I know, not very frequently. It's not an entirely new thought, Annalise. I think that I looked into that after your mother disappeared."

"It might be possible to trace a journey by boat. We can narrow down the time."

"Let's think about the problems involved. There has been traffic on the Ohio River for a long time. Not all of it has been logged. Passenger lists probably wouldn't help. Given the attitudes back then, manifests wouldn't have listed passengers as transported slaves. They'd be given unidentifiable names, listed as cooks or manservants. What you'd have to do, Miss Annalise, is to talk to people on the river, like clerks or dockworkers. Their memories would have to extend back for seven or eight years, and might not be reliable. Specifics would be difficult to find."

"Worth a try?"

Coffin looked away. This girl was so persistent. He'd give anything to find a way out of this for her. "Yes, my dear, worth a try. I'll get some people on it. Look into it myself."

Early the next morning, Annalise walked along the sloping Ohio River bank, the heart of trade and passenger activity. The area was choked with boats of every description, and a lively Wednesday morning crowd was already intent on individual pursuits. There were vendors and crewmen and passengers and a bustling crew of dock workers loading and moving crates and livestock. The compelling young lady drew attention, and several ugly comments. She stopped in front of an older man, struggling to maneuver a large box onto a tipped cart. The man was thickset with unkempt eyebrows which glistened with sweat.

"Good morning, sir. Have you worked here long?"

"Been here most of my life. What's it to you?" He wiped the perspiration with a meaty hand.

"This is important to me. Do you remember slaves being transported out of here on steamboats in the years before the war?"

"S'pose so. Never meant nothin' to me. Didn't give it no thought."

"Any of the other men here, think they might remember, maybe eight years ago?"

"Mebbe. Mebbe not. Don't rightly know."

"Could you point out anyone here that I should talk to?"

"Wal, there's Calvin over there." He pointed toward a young black man, dressed in a checked shirt. She guessed him to be around her age.

He's probably too young to remember anything from 1859."

"Don't know. He's been around since he was a pup."

"Thank you so much. What is your name?

"Pudge. Ever'body calls me that."

"Thank you, Mr. Pudge." She smiled broadly and patted him on his arm. He tried to smile back.

The young black man saw her walking toward him, and turned away quickly , busying himself.

"Excuse me, sir." There was reason for caution. He obviously was unnerved that she had singled him out for something. He didn't respond.

"Calvin? Mr. Pudge sent me over to ask you an important question."

He turned back slightly, not yet looking at her. "Ma'am?"

"I'm trying to gather information to help find my mother. She was a freed slave."

He faced her, a tall, slim young man with nice features, and an honest face.

"I weren't a slave. Don't know much 'bout it. Jist been here since I was fourteen, workin' for wages."

"May I call you Calvin?"

"Spect so."

"My mother was living here in Cincinnati, a free woman, when she disappeared in October of 1859. We think she was taken by bounty hunters."

"Yes ma'am."

"We also believe that could could have been taken from here by steamboat. Do you remember coffles…groups…of slaves boarding boats here in the past?"

"Happened a few times. Not many. Didn't see much. Didn't much know."

"Can you remember anything in particular? Anything that would have happened eight years ago?"

His face brightened. "October, 18 and 59, you say? Yes ma'am. Fust week on de job. One mawnin' dere was commotion down dere by the river. Coupla black folks, bof of dem menfolks, jump from a boat into da river, start swimmin' away toward the Kaintucky side. Coupla men, dey be yelling' from de boat. Dey yelling "Stop them! Stop them. Dey belongs to us!"

"What happened?"

"Ma'am, dey jist kep' swimmin'. Got to mid-river or so, turn back to look at the shore, den dey go under. Don't come up. Da white men on da boat be mad, yellin' sumtin ' bout lost money. Yellin' at us ot go get 'em."

"Nobody went out after them?"

"No ma'am. It be no use. Time we swim out dere, they be drownded. We might drown too."

"The bodies were never recovered?"

"Don't know."

"You're sure it was October of 1859?"

"Positive. It be my first week here. Thought maybe dem things happen a lot, but never happen again."

"Calvin, who else would have seen that? Anyone else here?"

"Yes, ma'am. There be Ray-Ray. He get me dis job. He be standing next to me dat day."

"Can you point him out to me?"

He pointed twenty feet away to a dumpy, stunted man with a broad head and a squashed nose.

"Calvin. You're wonderful. Thank you." She embraced him. He looked to the ground, and then turned back to his work.

Ray-Ray verified the month and the year, and remembered something else. "Dere be lots a dark ones, watchin' fum da boat. I think den dey might jump too."

"Passengers? Slaves?"

"Dunno. Jist a lot of pore folks like me. Looked that way leastwise."

He directed her to a greasy man named Beechwood, who repeated the story. A man named Congo verified everything.

"This wasn't in the newspapers," Annalise said, mostly to herself.

"Don't speck so. Jist a coupla slaves. Nobody care 'cept them white men losin' money," Congo offered.

"Nobody else remembers the boat, or where it was going. Do you?"

"Oh, yes. It be goin' to St. Louie. It be called da 'Lady of St. Louie.' See dat boat a lot around here. Den heard it wreck on a sandbar years ago. Never see it again."

St. Louis, Misouri. Annalise began devising a plan on the way home. She would collect her thoughts, and leave for St. Louis within a week.

Her plans were postponed when Herman's health took a setback. He lingered in a hospital in serious condition for two months. Either Maribel or Annalise was always by his side. The O'Neill daughters Portia and Deidre, came for extended stays, in case the old man didn't recover. In December, he rallied and passed the crisis. He was allowed to go home.

Then, a fierce Midwestern winter set in, and its icy tentacle paralyzed the waterways and most other ways of travel. The arctic shroud lasted through the end of the year.

Annalise resigned herself to the delay. She would leave for St. Louis in March or early April of 1868.

****

One could easily see where the Brody spread started. Neat fences outlined the area. But the scope of the ranch was a bit of a surprise.

Big Head Franklin rode for almost two hours on the worn trail, looking for a collection of buildings that would indicate the house of the owner or bunkhouses or barns. Finally, they all came into view from the top of a low rise, down into a depression that included a house, impressive even at a distance, and numerous buildings and barns. He clicked his horse into a slow trot toward the house. All around him, in haphazard array, cattle grazed on the hillside, well-fed, healthy cattle, he noted. There was activity all around the obvious work areas, a corral, a vegetable garden spread out on the rise behind the main house to its top, a long, low building that would be the bunkhouse, he knew. He noticed a smokehouse with puffs of white clouds drifting away, a neat log house on the western rise, and a series of large barns --he counted three.

A man emerged from one of the barns as he rode up, and walked toward him.

"Can I help you?"

Lookin' for Brody."

"I'm Whit Brody. What's your business with me?"

Whit gave the man a once-over. He was impressive because of his size, and the amount of hair on his face, and sticking out from under his battered hat. Otherwise, Whit's impression of him was as a drifter, somewhat intimidating in his ragamuffin aspect.

"Truth is, I'm lookin' for Grimes. Herkimer Grimes. He here?"

"Maybe he is. Maybe he isn't. Why?"

Whit was becoming uncomfortable. He knew that every reputation-seeker in the West saw Herkimer Grimes as a ticket to notoriety. The man had a pistol strapped to his waist.

"What's your name?"

"Folks call me Big Head."

Whit was unarmed, as he usually was. So was Herkimer. Whit had just left him in the barn. If this man was up to mischief, he had the upper hand.

"You'd better ride along. Herkimer Grimes is not here."

"You sure of that?" The man was scowling.

"Listen, I don't know your plan, but if you're here to cause trouble, I've got a bunch of hands here who are good with a gun."

"No. No trouble. Served with Grimes in the Rangers and Virginia City. Ain't seed him since."

A voice from behind Whit spoke up. “That you, Big? Seen you from the barn. Had to be you. No one else so big and ugly.”

“It’s me, Herkimer.”

“This a friend of yours, Herkimer?” Whit interrupted.

“Suppose so. Known him for a long time.”

“I guess you two want to visit a while. Take a break for a while, Herkimer.”

“Get on down from that horse, Big. God, he’s as ugly as you.” Herkimer was smiling.

The two former Rangers walked to Herk’s shack. “Where you been, Big?”

“Doin’ nuthin. Driftin’.”

“That shoulder heal up for you?”

“Painful now and again. Ain’t complainin’ about it.”

“How’d you find me?”

“Heard some talk in town that you was out here. Thought I’d look you up.”

“Any reason?”

“No.”

“Where you goin’ from here?”

“Dunno. Ain’t much call for a lawman what got fired. Thought I’d try trappin’. Mebbe hire on with the railroad doin’ somethin’.”

“Ever think about bein’ a cowboy? Workin’ on a ranch?”

“It workin’ for you?”

“Best thing I’ve done. Happy here as anyplace I’ve been.”

“Dunno.”

“Maybe I can put in a word for you to Brody. If I do, you better work your ass off. Don’t want him thinkin’ less of me.”

“He a fair man?”

“He’s a fair man. These folks here are near family, and they leave you alone. Pretty good wages. Time off. Plenty of work. Got a squaw for a foreman.”

“A squaw? What the hell.”

“Hard-workin’ lady. Smart.”

Whit wasn’t sure when Herkimer brought it up. He’d be adding a middle-aged man to a work force that was getting old anyway.

“You say that he’s trustworthy. You figure he’ll stay a while. Won’t run off some morning?”

“If he does, I’ll shoot him,” Herk replied with a fleeting smile.

“Well, Joshua’s in town most of the time now, so there is work to do. Bring this Big over to talk to me. I’ll give him a try. Is there any chance we can get him to clean up a bit?”

That afternoon, Big moved into the bunkhouse.

CHAPTER TWENTY-EIGHT
1868

Catharine Chase made the decision soon after her mother passed away.

The war had killed her, Catharine reasoned, just as sure as if a battle had been fought on her property. It had come close. Several skirmishes had been fought near Charlottesville, and her parents' small plantation had been raided twice, once by each side, as companies of soldiers foraged for meat and vegetables and horses and money.

Catharine and little Jeremiah had moved there soon after word came that Jonathan had been killed in battle.

So distraught that her parents had feared for her sanity, Catharine had never completely healed from her tragedy. She neglected Jeremiah for a time, locking herself in her room, refusing to eat or to talk to anyone in the house.

The raid by Union troops had occurred in early March of 1865, part of a raid and a three day occupation of the area by General Phil Sheridan's army. That had jolted Catharine out of her torpor. So angry was she at their effrontery, and so willing to blame any Union soldier for Jonathan's death, she had appeared on her parents' front porch with a shotgun, and had screamed at the raiders to leave.

They had looked at the disheveled, wild eyed young woman accosting them, and apparently had felt pity on some level. She overheard one say, "Pity, ain't it? Bet she used to be good to look at." Her companion had answered, "You want some of that? Man, you be hard up." So the raid was unenthusiastic, and that time, only a few chickens and some garden products were taken. Most of the important items--wagons, mules, furniture, food, blankets, gold jewelry--had been removed by confederate troops months before.

In that February of 1864 the Rebels took something else too, her father. He was furious at their bluster. After all, he raged, he had contributed sums of money to the Confederate cause. He had encouraged workers on his farm to take up arms. He had already lost a son-in-law. In the middle of his tantrum, a blood vessel in his brain burst. Her mother hadn't recovered from that shock. Catharine summoned her resourced briefly, and buried her father ingloriously in the field behind the barn. Then she returned to her emotional nightmare, augmented by the loss of a parent.

Tended to by neighbors for a spell, she recovered somewhat at the realization that her son needed attention, as did her grieving mother. She did what she could to find and beg food. The farm fell into ruin. When the Union raiders arrived, she had reached a profound manifestation of anger and emotional arousal that seemed to shake her into action and recovery.

Portions of her personality and spirit returned, but they were compromised when her mother passed. The plantation, dilapidated and unredeemable, was hers. For a while she tried to reclaim it, begging for help from town, teaching herself to plow and harvest. It was useless. The value declined until her only option was to sell the land to a speculator, at far less that its value.

She moved back to town in 1866, but there were too many memories of Jonathan. She had neither the ambition nor resources to re-open the dress shop, which she had abandoned and sold in 1863. She found work as a seamstress, but she was constantly looking for something else, someplace else.

An idea began to grow in January of 1868. For three years, she had been corresponding with her late husband's brothers. Joshua wrote regularly. Jefferson sent presents for Jeremiah.

Joshua's letters awoke an interest in her. He was married now, to a ranch owner's daughter, and owned a general merchandise store in Abilene, a suddenly burgeoning town in eastern Kansas. He wrote of the energy and opportunity in the growing community, fueled by the cattle market.

That would certainly be a change of scenery for her. Her next thought was more pertinent. Her family was gone. Except for some cousins in Georgia, Jeremiah's only close relatives were his uncles, one in Washington, and one in Abilene. Jefferson had not settled down yet; Joshua had.

She wrote to Joshua.

My Dear Brother-in-law,

I have recently been contemplating changing my residence. I have a thought that perhaps I should move Jeremiah closer to his only surviving relatives.

I need your advice. In your opinion, would a dress-making business succeed in the Abilene area?

Let me hasten to explain that if I moved there, I would not be a burden to you and Rose. I have the financial means to move, and to pay my way once there. I am certainly not wealthy, but I would afford housing and the start of a business.

My concern is my son. The first years of his life have been filled with confusion and sadness. He has very little sense of family, and no stability. I tell him of his wonderful uncles, and of his wonderful father, but those are just words.

I have only recently been thinking about this. I need your opinion and suggestions. Could Jeremiah and I acclimate to life in Abilene? I should tell you that I am very self-sufficient.

Perhaps, in a way, such a move would honor Jonathan. I eagerly await your thoughts.

Remember me to your wife.

Respectfully,

Catharine

A month later, she received a response.

My Dear Catharine,

I am both surprised and impressed by your idea.

I would like to see my nephew, and get to know both of you. Rose is also enthusiastic.

I must tell you this. At this time, Abilene has no identity. It is growing so fast that there are elements of lawlessness and disruption. Only recently have we begun to see an influx of civilized residents, of businesses which cater to refined individuals, and of women who would patronize your dress-making business.

You would have to accept a somewhat basic life. At this time, there is no school, although one is being planned. Too, Abilene leads the world in saloons and houses of ill repute. The latter have been recently exiled to a remote corner of the community. We have had difficulty in hiring law enforcement officers. The town is a collection of shacks and makeshift buildings, but that is changing.

There is also a notable lack of children.

If you decide to move here, I would suggest that you travel by steamboat. A stagecoach line also serves the area. You could send many of your personal items to us ahead of time, to travel lighter. The mail service is secure.

Abilene has a large hotel and several more are planned, if you are looking for a residence. You could stay with us, if you wish. Rose and I have plenty of room. We will help you secure a house, and a building for your dress shop. If it is affordable to you, you might consider opening a boarding house. That seems to be the greatest need in Abilene. Often, railroad personnel and cattle buyers arrive here in such numbers that there are no suitable accommodations.

Also, I would gladly hire you to work for us initially, or for the long term.

In conclusion, I will help you in any way possible. You should be aware, however, that life here is an adventure. It will probably be unlike any you have experienced.

I have recently heard from my brother Jefferson and he will arrive here sometime in the spring. He recently resigned his commission. So, if you do come to Abilene, it will complete somewhat of a family reunion.

Please keep me advised of your plans. Tell Jeremiah that his Uncle Joshua and Aunt Rose love him.

Fondly,
Joshua

It's not a glowing recommendation, Catharine thought, but he did indicate that he would welcome them, and there were options. Bless his heart, he didn't seem to realize that she had been through four years of utter hell. Or perhaps his line "unlike any you have experienced" was an honest appraisal, and she should prepare for something almost barbaric. Of course, there were cultured beings in the area. Joshua had spoken in complimentary terms of Whit and Margaret Brody, and of Rose's cousin Jack. Abilene had a doctor, a dentist, and several bankers. How bad could it be?

More importantly, with Jefferson's arrival, both of Jeremiah's uncles would be in one location.

Jeremiah needed doting relatives. So did she. She would leave immediately.

She wrote back the next day. Yes, we're coming, she said. If you could, find me a nice residence somewhat close to you. Cost is not a factor. The boarding house idea is a good one.

Catharine Chase had questioned her decision daily, hourly, in the past two weeks. She had come to a Godforsaken place, devoid of culture, hopelessly chaotic, lawless and noisy, and primitive. And the cattle drives had not even started.

Once she had made up her mind, bolstered by what Joshua had written, she moved fast. She arrived in Abilene in mid-March, purchased a large house built by a railroad executive, bought mismatched furnishings from local merchants, and opened a boarding house a week later, the Chase Place. It was on First Street, just west of Joshua's store, and it needed work. She would attend to that in time.

Her hope of fostering a relationship between little Jeremiah and his only living relatives was working. His Uncle Joshua and Aunt Rose had been extra attentive to him, and to her. Rose's father had entertained the boy twice at his large ranch, and had promised to teach him to fish in the spring.

Catharine had no regrets about the boy's experience on the frontier thus far, even though there was no school in the area. She could teach him at home. It was her life that lacked substance and variety. It didn't take much foresight to see that her lot wouldn't improve. The few good men she had encountered in her brief tenure were married railroad and cattle company personnel, or transients on their ways to prospects farther west.

Maybe there would be no more romance for her. Maybe that part of her life was over. She was still young, with a healthy libido and strong feelings, authored by her too-brief marriage to Jonathan Chase.

At least business was good. The boarding house had tenants. She had hired two men to subdivide four upstairs bedrooms. Moreover, her housekeeper/cook was efficient, a young black woman named Minnie, who had lost her husband in a construction accident during the expansion of the railroad lines. Minnie was not literate, not remotely sophisticated, but she was proving to be loyal and dependable. Still, she was not a candidate to become a friend or confidante to Catharine.

If anything, Minnie's plight was more untenable than hers. The daughter of slaves, Minnie had reacted to her husband's death with the realization that it made her a prisoner of Abilene. She had neither the money nor the resolve to leave. She worked for a time as a maid in the home of Jackson Stillwell, a contractor for the railroad, until he brutally raped her one night in a drunken stupor. It was an incident which she realized would never be prosecuted or punished. Desperate, she considered prostitution. At least she would be paid for her debasement. As a last resort, she showed up one morning on the front stoop of Catharine Chase's new boarding house.

"Got work, mum?" she had asked with her eyes fixed on the porch floor.

"Can you cook? Clean?"

"Yes, mum. Anythin' you need."

"Won't make much money at first, but I'll give you a room, and food. If business is good, I'll pay you what I can. When can you move in?"

"This mawnin', mum."

Catharine already depended on her, and she liked the shy maid, but she could count easily the number of times that Minnie's large, sad eyes had met hers.

Little Jeremiah formed an instant bond with her. She had overheard them one recent morning.

"Miss Minnie, I'm gonna go over to the creek."

"Kinda cold today, Massuh Jeremiah. You bundle up. Don't talk to no stranger. Tell yo' mamma you goin'."

"I'll bring you back a frog, Minnie."

"No. Don't do dat."

"Maybe a snake."

"Lawd, boy. You teasin' Minnie." They both laughed.

The day before, Minnie had a brief moment of false hope.

A handsome, somewhat older black man, squat and powerful-looking with a scar on his face, had stopped at the boarding house. He was inviting people to a church that he was helping to build, on the west side of town. The minister would be Mr. Jonah Brooks, he said, "a well-known champion of human rights, a man," he continued. "who doesn't see the color of a man's skin, but judges him by his heart." He and Reverend Brooks were building the church. It was under roof and waiting for celebrants "next Sunday at ten of the clock, come rain or shine."

Minnie couldn't take her eyes off of the man while he talked to Catharine, his hands fumbling with his hat. Then she heard words which dashed her interest.

"My wife, Bea," he said, "she sings music which will fill the church. We'd be pleased to see both of you ladies."

On the same morning, Jonah Brooks had entered the northern section of Abilene, across the railroad tracks. It was still waking from a night of debauchery. It was the infamous collection of bordellos and bawdy houses, moved to the semi-remote location by the city fathers a year before. It was a visual nightmare, irregular rows of shacks with crude, hastily painted signs advertising "Cheap Wimmin," and "Anythin You Want, $2." The area offered excesses of the flesh and of "alkyhol" and "Pleasuring." A few establishments were bigger than the rest, dilapidated two-story houses of pleasure, thrown up to entice the paychecks and pent-up desires of cowboys at the end of cattle drives, and the wages of railroad construction workers seeking to score big at poker or at carnal pleasures.

The streets were virtually empty, as Jonah knew they would be. He was not there to knock on doors. That would come later. He was there to offer salvation to lost souls sleeping off a drunk, or wandering aimlessly through the reeking alleys. He was also there out of curiosity.

He passed a small group of gaggling women, soiled doves, huddled together near a poorly defined side street. One chubby, unattractive woman called to him. "Hey Mister! Here a little early, aincha?" Another chortled, "You big all over, Mister?" The group cackled as he walked to them.

"Good morning, ladies. I'm Jonah Brooks. I'm a minister."

"Well, I'm damned. You fixin' to save us, preacher man?" The comment came from a woman with smeared makeup, her face dessicated with deep-set wrinkles, her eyes dull above bluish bags.

"No, ma'am. But I would invite you to come to a new church Sunday morning."

The group laughed together, except for a young girl, possibly sixteen or seventeen, Joshua guessed, on the group's perimeter.

"Sunday mornin' you say?" the obese woman wheezed. "Preacher man, whilst you have your services, I be sleepin' off a drunk, with a coupla cowboys passed out on top of me." Several of her companions laughed again. Jonah didn't change expression. The laughter stopped.

"The young girl spoke up, meekly. "What time, Reverend? Where?"

The obese woman chided her. "Myra, what the hell do you care?"

"Ma'am, services start at ten o'clock, above the creek, across town. You'll see it, a new log church. It sits on a hill."

"You funnin'? We be welcome, I'm sure. Trudgin' through town, sittin' in a church with uppity folks," the dumpy woman said.

"I'll welcome you."

The stench of cheap perfume mingled with the noisome hint of body odor. As Jonah walked away, he heard no resumption of conversation from the group he was leaving. Then he heard a voice behind him, directed toward the young girl, "Myra, what the hell."

The Blessed Salvation House of Worship almost hadn't happened. Jonah had recognized the need for spiritual guidance in Abilene when he, Cleetus, and Bear Woman arrived in 1867. The problem was that there was no affordable building to use for a church, and no property of appropriate size which they could purchase. Having heard the name Joseph McCoy, Jonah asked to meet with the tycoon.

"Mr. McCoy , you've got an interesting community here. It appears that you're missing a church, or churches, however. I was hoping that you could suggest a solution to my problem. I don't have sufficient funds to manage the location for one."

"Are you asking for a loan, Reverend Brooks?"

"No Sir, I am not. I am looking for counsel."

"Well, as you suggest, this is a somewhat Godless place, and I am worried about that. But I cannot order people to sell you a property for what you can afford. Have you no sponsor? No church organization behind you?"

"Not out here, Mr. McCoy."

"Well, unfortunately, I have no appropriate suggestion. I do hope you find a way to do this."

Jonah told Cleetus that they'd probably have to move on soon, not welcome news. The three had been on a gypsy experience for several years, through Nebraska, Missouri, and Kansas, looking for a place to best serve the Lord. They had exhausted most of their savings, government funds from their employment in Minnesota. To stay in

Abilene, all three would have to find employment, and turn those monies into religious experiences for the cattle town. That would take time.

On his own, without consulting Jonah, Cleetus also asked to meet with McCoy.

"Abilene needs this man," he advised. McCoy had not even asked him to sit. "Do you know that this man was the force behind the safety of escaped slaves in New York for years? He had a large church in Syracuse. Later, President Buchanan appointed him to manage an Indian Agency in Minnesota. The tribes there called him 'God's Eye.' He saved over 200 innocent Sioux from being hanged after an uprising there. He is known all over the East for his fairness and his service to needy people."

McCoy listened, and was duly impressed.

"Well, listen. I can't promise anything, but let me check with some people to verify what you've told me." Ten days later, McCoy summoned Jonah from a boarding house, an address left by Cleetus.

"Reverend Brooks. This is what I can do for you. There is a property on the west side of town. It has a broken down log cabin on it. There is room for a church and a cemetery. You may use it, and if you stay here two years or more, it will be deeded to you. Too, the Great Western Stockyards will give you $2,000 to use as you wish, for the construction of your church, or for your personal needs. Again, if you stay two years, it will not have to be repaid. I hope it is attractive to you. Otherwise, you are on your own, success or failure. Agreed?"

"Agreed, Mr. McCoy. Thank you."

Jonah never discovered the reason for McCoy's sudden generosity.

The resultant structure was on a knoll just beyond the western edge of Abilene, a simple one-story building fronted by a planked structure which extended above the height of the building, and bore a small cross. Five large windows graced each side. All work had been completed by Jonah and Cleetus in six months; they worked throughout a harsh winter. The log exterior had been fashioned from the woods at the rear of the property. Some items were begged from merchants in town, or discarded by others.

Behind the church at some distance was a log cabin, built and abandoned years before. The two reclaimed it from a crushed shell, and it provided a home for the Wilburns, decorated and made comfortable by Bear Woman. Cleetus was bookkeeper and custodian of the church, Bear Woman a sometime officiate and the source of Sunday music. She had suffused the bare lawns with wildflowers and creek rocks.

Jonah lived a mile to the west in another abandoned cabin, more rustic, but inhabitable and appropriately remote.

The inside of the House of Worship was plain. Ten benches with backs had been crafted by Jonah and Cleetus for each side of the building, forming a wide center aisle. The pulpit was set at floor level. Jonah didn't want a superior position in the room, but he did build a small raised platform at the rear for Bear Woman, and hoped-for choirs of the future. The interior was devoid of religious icons, save for a cross hewn out of oak suspended on the back wall. Jonah didn't want lavish accoutrements. His mission and his mantra would deal with simple aspects. He would emphasize life, and not the afterlife. He would preach compassion for all persons. He would promote an uncomplicated God, a Creator who loved and guided and forgave, a spiritual being of veracity and surpassing decency. He would not endorse an angry God, nor a vengeful one.

The inaugural services were a modest success. Jonah had estimated that a full house would be around 150 persons, if they squeezed in. The attendees on that day filled much more than half of the room. Several railroad families were there, along with various families from among Abilene's businessmen. There were a handful of Orientals, but no cowboys, Jonah noted, and few attendees from areas outside of the town. Bear Woman's lilting soprano began the service. As she finished, three women entered, and sat in the back row. Jonah recognized them with mild surprise: Myra, the young prostitute; the dumpy woman; and a haggard older woman that he hadn't seen the previous weekday morning.

Their presence made a significant difference in his approach. Rejecting his planned sermon, he improvised.

"Respect yourselves," he said, "and you will honor God. Do not wait for signs of his stewardship of you."

Then he raised his voice and slowed his words. "You make your own ways in this life. Reject temptation. Care about your fellow men. Avoid anything which belittles your existence. God will celebrate your happiness because He loves you. You will see a path to righteousness if you trust Him, if you talk to Him. Live your lives in decency, in honesty, in faith in Him and in yourselves."

He paused and made eye contact with each section of the room. He spoke of Mary Magdalene, and spoke of God's forgiveness of sinners in the Bible.

He finished. "Love God. Love each other. Love yourselves. It is never too late to change your lives or your direction. May God bless all of you."

As quietly as they had entered, the three ladies left, ahead of the other congregants.

****

Few noticed the rider making his way up the muddy street toward a Cincinnati suburb on the west side of the city. The rain was incessant, and the rider had his wide-brimmed hat pulled low on his forehead to deflect the downpour. A long, black great-coat kept him moderately dry, but a mid-afternoon chill had begun to course through his body. His mount, a great black roan, continued to slosh through the ankle-deep mud and the many rivulets, and the pack horse, heavily loaded, slogged dutifully behind, tethered to the saddle horn of the roan.

They crested a hill, and the rider looked for a cottage on his left, described to him in a letter sent weeks before. He dismounted and walked toward the front door of what he was sure was his destination, after wrapping his reins around a small tree in the front yard. A small sign was attached beside the front door: "O'Neill." He was at the right place. He knocked on the door, and briefly a stately, white-haired woman stood in the doorway.

"Aunt Maribel?" It's Jefferson."

"Jefferson! My word, you're so big! Come in! Come in!" Even before he removed the greatcoat, she had wrapped him in an embrace. "It is so wonderful to see you, Jeffie."

He grinned at his father's sister, a woman he had not seen since he was seven years old.

She continued to effuse, only slightly relaxing her embrace. "You look like your mother, Jeffie, but you're as tall as your father. We didn't know when to expect you. Thought that it might be June, or so. You must have left sometime in February." She stood back to look at him.

"Mid-February. Probably not too smart. I've been running into a lot of weather like this."

"Goodness. Take off that coat. Herman! Herman! It's Jeffie!" she called to her left. He took off the coat, and then his boots, and was led by his aunt into a small room with a fireplace crackling in the back. A man sat looking into the flames.

"As I wrote you, Herman's not well. He can't move the left side of his body, and he can't talk, but he understands everything." Jefferson went to the front of the chair and kneeled. He saw a flicker of recognition in the old man's eyes, and a tear forming. His uncle crookedly smiled at him.

"Uncle Herman. It's wonderful to see you. I'm the youngest son of Jeremiah and Molly. I'm so glad that I'm here. I love you." Jefferson awkwardly hugged him. He grasped the old man's hand, and felt the pressure returned.

"We've got to get you in dry clothes. Don't know what we have that will fit you though. You're a big boy," Maribel said.

"I've got some clothes in the pack outside. Is there someplace I can get the horses out of the rain?"

"The stable's in back, Jeffie. There's plenty of room, and feed."

"I'll go tend to them, and be right back."

"Annalise can help you." She called to the back of the house. "Annalise!"

Jefferson looked confused. His cousins were Portia and Deidre. Annalise was perhaps the maid, although in this humble cottage, and given the obvious good health of his aunt, he wondered at the need for a maid.

He wasn't prepared for the beautiful young girl with the dark eyes and luxuriant hair who suddenly appeared in the doorway. She was dressed in jodhpurs and a checked shirt open at the neck. "I'm here, Mother Maribel," she said as she glanced at the stranger.

"Annalise, this is our nephew, Jefferson Chase. You've heard me talk about him."

"Many times. It's my pleasure, Sir," she said as she grasped his hand. Her voice was rich, but emotionless, and he noticed a sadness about her. She hadn't smiled.

"Likewise, ma'am," he said, somewhat taken aback by what was happening.

Maribel jumped in. "Annalise is our daughter. I probably didn't explain in those notes I sent. I know that I kept your father up to date."

Jefferson searched his memory. He vaguely remembered something his father had mentioned before the war, about a slave girl. He'd let this work itself out. His aunt would tell him later.

He led the horses to the stable where the girl was arranging bales of hay. Puffs of her breath blew across the light from several lanterns.

"It's starting to get cold. Probably be pretty chilly tonight," he said.

"Probably," she said, without looking at him.

He removed the packs of his possessions from the horse, and then the saddle from the roan.

"What a beautiful animal," she said, an honest expression which evoked the first smile from her.

"His name's Storm. I've had him for almost ten years, since before the war. Smartest horse I've ever seen."

She stroked Storm's muzzle just below his eyes, which never looked away from her.

"He likes you. Maybe you can ride him tomorrow."

She was non-committal. "Nice saddle."

"Bought it with severance pay from the army."

She brought several blankets, while he glanced around the building. There was a carriage in one corner, and the dim light reflected off of the eyes of two horses in a back stall.

"You were a war hero."

"Don't know about that."

"Thank you." she said. The comment resonated with him. A nice thing to say. Then she was gone, back to the house.

"So sorry that we couldn't get back east for your parents' funerals. Your father and I were so close. That was a terrible shock to us. Poor Jeremiah."

Jefferson stopped chewing on a piece of meat, swallowed, then answered his aunt.

"After Mother passed, he never really recovered. Jonathan's death was tough on all of us too."

"Yours was a remarkable family. Very few sons grow up like you did."

"Your family was admirable too. Sometimes we envied you out here on the frontier."

Maribel laughed. "It wasn't that much of an adventure. Cincinnati was a bustling city when we got here in the Forties." She watched her nephew eat. He was poised and mindful of etiquette. Molly had raised him well. He seemed to fill the room, this young man with large forearms and an engaging smile.

"Father often regretted that you were so far away. But you really couldn't pass up the opportunity here."

"The Medical College made Herman a nice offer. Except for missing relatives, we've never thought twice about leaving the East. I wish we could have lured your family here."

"Vermont was in Father's blood. Mother's too. I don't think that they'd have budged for anything."

Maribel worked to involve the other two diners. She addressed Annalise.

"They had a beautiful farm in the country, in the mountains, surrounded by trees. Acres. And they were close to Lake Champlain. It was idyllic."

Annalise smiled, but said nothing.

Jefferson looked at the sad-eyed old man. "Uncle Herman, you were a legend in our family. Father always said that Aunt Maribel couldn't have picked a better man."

"He picked me, Jeffie," Maribel laughed, and reached to pat her husband's hand.

"You moved to this house several years ago?"

"We hated to leave the house in town. So many wonderful years there. But after Herman got sick, we just couldn't take care of it. After the illness, he couldn't keep his professorship, so we bought here. If it stops raining tomorrow, you'll be able to see most of the city from our hill."

"I don't know how long I can stay. I mailed Joshua that I'd be in Abilene sometime in the spring. But I had to see you and Uncle Herman, and the girls."

"Both of the girls moved north. Portia's in Cleveland with two daughters. Deidre moved to northern Pennsylvania. She married a railroad man, and has given us a grandson, named after your father. They can't get in to see you this trip."

"Jonathan named his son after Father too."

The conversation retreated a bit.

"Annalise prepared this meal. She's an amazing girl."

"Annalise, this is a great meal. Best one I've had in a long time. Thank you."

The girl across the table was studying him, and smiled at the compliment.

"So it's Kansas you're heading to?"

"Joshua has a general store there. He married a rancher's daughter, a girl named Rose. He met her in Iowa after the war. According to this letters, it's a boom town. A lot of opportunities, and it's on the edge of the frontier, if a man wants to go farther west.

"You'll settle there? Vermont is not in your blood?"

"Don't know, Aunt Maribel. But Joshua and I are the last of our family. I need to spend some time with him. I doubt that I'll ever see Vermont again."

"What will you do?"

"There's work at the Brody Ranch. He's Rose's father. That's about fifteen miles from Abilene. That will probably be temporary. Someday I'd like to own a ranch of some kind."

"Can you at least stay here a few days?"

"You bet. Can't beat the company. Or the food."

The girl smiled at him again, fleetingly, and then got up to clear the table.

The clock above the fireplace mantel struck ten. Maribel came into the room and sat next to Jefferson on a large divan.

"Herman's in bed. Annalise too. We can visit a while, unless you're tired."

He grabbed Maribel's hand in his two, and kissed the back of it.

"So, Aunt Maribel. Tell me about Annalise."

"Isn't she beautiful? I know that surprised you. She came to us sixteen years ago with her mother. They had just been freed from slavery."

"She was a slave?"

"Her father was white. So was her grandfather. Her mother was a remarkable woman. Levi Coffin, you may have heard of him, brought her to us as a housekeeper and cook."

"Levi Coffin. He helped escaped slaves to freedom."

"Yes. We called it the Underground Railroad. By that time, she was a free woman. Missy Ollimore. She was more than a housekeeper. She was part of the family."

"Where is she now?"

"We don't know. One day in the autumn of 1859 she walked Annalise to school. We never saw her again. Annalise was thirteen."

"No trace?"

"None. We scoured the city. Mr. Coffin helped. We looked everywhere. Talked to people all over southern Ohio. Your Uncle Herman spent every free hour and weekend for two years riding to farms in northern Kentucky, thinking that she may have been kidnapped."

"The authorities didn't help?"

"Not much, after the first few months. There was nothing to go on. No clues. No evidence. No witnesses."

"It must have been tough on Annalise."

"She's never recovered. When she was young, she was sunshine personified, a smart, happy little girl. I loved her as much as my own daughters." She paused. "Still do."

"You described her mother as remarkable."

"She was kind, a dependable worker, a wonderful mother. She was illiterate when she came to us. She and Annalise learned together. The two of them sparkled, and brought a lot of joy to us."

"With the war over, there is information available, more people answering questions."

Maribel nodded. "That's when Annalise got particularly obsessed. She'd leave for Kentucky or Tennessee, looking for cemeteries, talking to people."

"Dangerous for a young girl."

"Herman and I worry every time she goes. We try to help out, but she refuses our money. She'll take a job downtown, menial labor sometimes. She'll save for a few months, then leave. This is her home. She knows that, and she thinks of us as parents. But each time she comes back, more of the joy in her is gone."

"You adopted her?"

"Jeff, I'm sorry. This topic is dominating the conversation. I need to hear about you."

"No, Aunt Maribel. This is interesting. Sad. Please go on."

"No. We haven't adopted her. She cried when we offered. She said that she had to find out about her mother first. I think she feels guilty about perhaps causing Herman's health problems."

Maribel got up to stoke the fire. "She had such potential, Jeffie. She could have done anything with her life. In elementary school, she was far ahead of the other children."

She turned to look at him. "That brings something up. I don't quite know how to approach this."

"Aunt Maribel?"

"Last autumn, she went down to the river front. She had this idea about bounty hunters taking her mother away on a river boat, probably heading west. She started to talk to dock workers. They remembered an incident in October of 1859, just after Missy disappeared. Seems that two slaves from a coffle tried to escape from a departing boat, and drowned. The workers remember other slaves on board. The steamboat was headed to St. Louis."

"That's not much to go on."

"To her, it was a revelation. She's about to leave for St. Louis."

"She has no names. Nothing to chase except a notion."

"Right. There were no police reports about the drowning. Just the memories of dock workers."

"Does she have a plan?"

"Not really. That's never stopped her. She says that she'll find out the names of major pre-war plantations around St. Louis, and visit them all."

"That could take a while."

"There is an emphasis to her search that borders on passion, and it constantly threatens her safety. Bless her. She may never discover anything. Even if she uncovers something tragic, she could get on with her life. Not knowing is what keeps her going."

"I'm heading toward St. Louis, Aunt Maribel. I could check things out."

"Jeffie, I'm about to ask you to go there with her." She sat next to him again. "If you could help her look around for a few days, and then send her back home, I would rest easier. So much could go wrong for her out there. It is much more dangerous than trips she has made."

"What exactly are her plans to get there? I've got two horses to take care of."

"She ruled out going by coach. She feels that she'll need a horse. She has tried stagecoaches several times, and says that it inhibits her after she gets to her destination. She'll take Rags with her on a steamboat to St. Louis."

"Rags is her horse."

"Yes, a nice little mare. She can also take our carriage horse as a pack horse. Jeff, you have to know that I haven't been planning this. I didn't know when you'd get here, and she's leaving next week. Your arrival was a Godsend in so many ways. We can reimburse you for whatever it adds to your trip."

"Aunt Maribel, no. I have to go that way to get to Kansas, and I've got more money with me than I need. Father's estate, army pension, sale of some horses, savings. I'd be happy to do this for you. What will she think about it?"

Maribel laughed. "Apparently you didn't notice her sizing you up at supper. I mentioned it to her as an aside while we were preparing the meal. She's a brave girl, but I don't think she'll mind some company until she gets this out of her system."

"I'll buy the steamship tickets, and pay for hotel rooms in St. Louis."

"I don't think that she'll agree to that."

"She'll discover that I'm headstrong too," he smiled. He suddenly yawned, "Sorry. It's been a long day."

"Time to turn in. You should have a warm room tonight, if you don't mind sleeping on the divan."

"I don't think that I'll fit on the divan. The floor's fine with me. Right here, in front of the fire."

"I'll get some blankets. You're a special person, Jeffie."

"So are you, Aunt Maribel. I love you."

"And, Jeffie…"

"Yes?"

"Tomorrow we talk about you."

When she checked on him shortly before sunup, the blankets were folded and stacked in the corner. He was gone. Annalise was already in the small kitchen.

"Jefferson is up early. You too, Honey."

"He's out in the stable with the horses. I couldn't sleep."

Maribel busied herself, readying the kitchen fireplace. "Annalise?"

"Yes, ma'am."

"Jefferson will go to St. Louis with you."

"Yes, ma'am."

They rode in the morning sun, across the tops of Price Hill, and then west, on rutted trails still damp and puddled from the deluge the previous day. After a while the terrain leveled, and Annalise led across a field awakening from the ravages of winter, bright green already. She rode Storm easily and well, and he was on his best behavior. Jefferson followed them on Rags, a nice horse uncomfortable with carrying one hundred pounds more than usual. Jefferson coaxed her through the ride, patting her neck and whispering into her ear.

They came to a stream, swollen from the recent weather.

"We can't cross that. Let's stop for a while," Jefferson suggested.

"Maybe we ought to start back," Annalise answered.

"Let's give the horses a break. Rags has been working hard." He alighted and led Rags to the water, and into a shallow eddy. She lowered her head and drank. Annalise followed, leading the roan.

He sat on the bank.

"Is it wet there?" she asked.

"I hope not."

She sat too, a respectful distance away.

"Aunt Maribel wants me to accompany you to St. Louis."

"I know."

"How do you feel about that?"

"I can probably use the company. How do you feel about it?"

"I was going that way anyway. I'll be grateful for the company."

As he spoke, her mind was full of a name and a recent incident. Tyler Garrett. That would never happen again. "I can take care of myself."

"Yes, Annalise. I'm sure that you can."

"In fact, I'm leaving in a couple of days. If that's too soon for you, I'll go by myself."

She was backing off again, becoming impersonal. She's an enigma, he thought, a beautiful enigma.

"Hopefully you'll give me a few days to visit with my uncle and aunt."

"Oh, sure. I didn't mean to..."

"Let's start back," he interrupted.

There was much to like about this man, Annalise thought, as she watched him play chess with Herman. He is gentle. He is kind. But so was Tyler Garrett. She would not trust anyone, not get close to anyone, until she found her mother. If it took forever, so be it. That was her focus and her duty. She would feel a measure of safety with him accompanying her to St. Louis. She would be civil toward him. She would appreciate whatever he did, but she'd never let him think that she needed him.

"Uncle Herman. I don't stand a chance here. Take it easy on me."

His uncle smiled. He seemed to smile constantly when Jefferson was with him. Herman managed the game well. He still had complete use of his right side, and he still had the mental acuity that had propelled him to the top of his profession. This was the third afternoon that they had matched wits across a chess board. Each had a victory, so Jefferson had called this game "The World Championship; Herman the Legend versus Jefferson the Upstart." Herman chortled, a garbled laugh which was all that he could manage.

Tomorrow, Jefferson and Annalise would leave by steamboat, departure in the morning. Annalise would take Rags and a modest roll of clothes. She didn't see a need for a separate pack horse; Jefferson's would be enough. When he left for the West, she'd be coming back to Cincinnati anyway.

Maribel saw them off, with the horrible foreboding that she'd never see either again. As events proved, she was right.

The distance to St. Louis was 750 miles, a four-day trip. The steamboat *Necessity* would follow the current of the Ohio 540 miles to the Mississippi near Cairo, Illinois, and then steam north for the remainder , to the hub of Mississippi steamboat activity, the docks and levees of St. Louis.

The newly-commissioned *Necessity* was one of a recent spate of large crafts built in Cincinnati. It was designed for the luxury of its passengers, and was of substantial size to carry a full load of cargo and numerous livestock. In essence, it was a floating hotel, for which passengers paid $12 apiece for six meals and commodious state cabins; transporting horses was extra. An open deck surrounded the cabin level. Those unwilling to pay the full amount gave the company $4, which served meals, but directed them to sleep on the lower deck without privacy or comfort.

Jefferson had purchased two cabins at opposite ends of the ship, an acknowledgement that he had no designs on Annalise, in spite of the possible intimacy of their mission. He would have gladly bought a ticket on the lower level, to be near the horses, had he been traveling alone.

Meals were served in the saloon, a lavishly decorated area festooned with red drapes and gold accouterments. Small tables were scattered around the room, and at one end was a walnut bar, fully stocked with liquor for an extra fee.

Horses were penned in an enclosed area with transported chickens, sometimes pigs or small groups of cattle. Passengers were responsible for their animal travelers.

The *Necessity* left the Cincinnati waterfront at 1:30 pm, a half-hour late, and swept under the newly built Suspension Bridge, the first to cross the Ohio, which spanned the river to Covington, Kentucky.

Jefferson waited in the saloon past 6 p.m. for Annalise to join him. The dinner announcement had occurred minutes before when a stentorian voice had called from the door, "dinner is served!" He waited a few more minutes, and then sat at a table with a middle-aged couple from Kentucky, as they told him. The conversation was good. By the time dessert was cleared, they were calling him "Jeff," and he knew all about the grandchildren that awaited them in St. Louis.

At 8:00 he wandered out to the deck, leaned on the rail, and watched the dark silhouettes of middle America hills glide by. The night was starry and quiet; the boat was somewhere in the twisting Ohio River below Indiana. She had not made it to dinner, had not even excused herself to him. He went to the holding area on the bottom deck, and stroked each of the three animals that were accompanying him on this trip. "Better company than she is," he muttered to himself. Then he climbed up to his cabin and retired.

The next morning, as a red glow illuminated the docks at Owensboro, the *Necessity* prepared to stop. A few passengers would depart, some would board, and new cargo would be laded. Jefferson was feeding the horses, tending to the thought that new livestock might crowd in on them, and protecting their space.

A voice from behind startled him. "Good morning, Jefferson."

"Good morning, Annalise. I wondered about you. Couldn't find you last night."

"I just didn't have an appetite. I apologize for not informing you."

"It's alright. You missed a good meal."

"We're stopping."

"One of several in the next few days."

"I was wondering. Is there a place on board where we can talk today? I thought that we could share thoughts about what to do in St. Louis."

Even then, at dawn, hair mussed, she was attractive. Her eyes were still swollen with sleep, but there was depth to them, he thought, such brown allure.

"There are chairs on the second deck. Hopefully be a nice day, although the sky's red this morning."

"Should we wait until this afternoon?" she asked.

"Fine with me. I'll come and rap on your door."

"You won't have to. I'll be on deck."

"See you later."

She was gone.

By 10 am, he had washed, shaved, and eaten. He decided to check on the horses again. As he entered the pen area, he saw Annalise with Storm. Behind her was a large man in coveralls, a crew member he had seen several times, walking up to her. The man was rotund and tall, with greasy-looking black hair to his shoulders, and a beard which was scatted haphazardly across most of this face.

Jefferson watched as the man grabbed Annalise from behind. Instinctively and quickly she spun around and delivered her elbow hard to his face. He backed away holding his nose, and then stepped back to wrap her in a bear hug, emitting a squeal and pinning her against Storm. Jefferson covered the distance quickly. He grabbed the man by the collar of his shirt and the seat of his pants, and running him out the door sideways, threw the man over the short rail into the Ohio River.

"Man overboard!" he yelled, and winked at Annalise. The great steamboat lurched and slowed as Jefferson threw a tow rope over the side toward the floundering crew member. Immediately other crew members ran to the scene. As the paddles reversed, one of the crew began pulling the large man back to the boat. Two more dragged him over the side to the deck.

The boat's captain, a nervous type with a requisite beard, rushed up.

"Harley, what happened? How'd you fall overboard? You drunk, man?"

The large man glowered at Jefferson. "This man…" he paused. If he got into details, he knew that Jefferson and Annalise would tell their story. He could get fired. "this man throwed me a rope. I done got too close to the side. Lost my balance, Cap'n." He was a comic sight, soaking wet, with his shoulders slumped and his eyes cast to the deck.

"Dammit, man. You cost us time. Be more careful. Your nose is bleeding. Take care of it."

The captain addressed Jefferson, "Thank you, sir, for whatever you did."

"My pleasure, captain."

Annalise and Jefferson walked away grinning. "Thanks," she whispered.

They found seats on the cabin deck.

"This is beautiful country. Reminds me of parts of Vermont, the hills above the river mostly," he said.

"It is beautiful. The rivers in the South either run through flat lands or mountains. There is something serene about the Ohio."

"You OK?"

"Of course. I'm glad you showed up. He was a little more than I could handle."

"Well, I don't know about that. I think you broke his nose."

"He probably outweighs me by 150 pounds."

"And twenty of that is dirt."

She laughed, the first time he had heard it from her.

"Do you think we should have told the captain what happened?" she asked.

"No. They probably would have dropped him off at the next stop. Who knows, he might be supporting a family."

"Yeah, a mama bear and two cubs."

He laughed, so hard it made her laugh again.

"I just went down there to look after the horses. Their feedbags were empty. I was getting ready to fill them," she offered.

"I'll go take care of that now. I'll be back."

"I'll go with you."

Jefferson couldn't believe what he was seeing when they reached the bottom deck. There was Harley, still wet, with something in his hand, a stick of some sort. He was whacking Storm across the neck.

Again, Jefferson descended on the large man, picked him up, and deposited him in the river. This time he waited a while. "Man overboard!" he called, and this time he didn't cast a rope toward him.

The paddle reversed again. Other crew members arrived, and once again they dragged the sputtering man aboard.

The captain was livid, churning out invectives as he rushed to the scene.

"Harley, can't you stay on this goddamn boat!"

Harley couldn't answer. A mixture of blood and mucous ran from his nose. He looked at Jefferson, a plea for his silence. Jefferson glared at him.

"Captain, I'm speaking for the passengers. We'll never get to St. Louis if this man goes swimming every five minutes."

Annalise walked over to check on Storm, biting her lip to keep from laughing.

Harley was completely defeated and deflated. This young man was more than a match for him. There would be no more revenge. Jefferson recognized that, and walked to stand next to Harley, continuing to glare at him. Harley slinked a step away.

"Point taken. Harley, get to your bunk and stay there. You're screwing up this entire trip."

After lunch, they made a list.

"If someone bought Mama who used slaves, he was a farmer. Cotton. Wheat. Beans. He would have traded in St. Louis. A farmer's market. Cotton buyers," Annalise suggested.

"That is horse country too. Missouri is famous for its mules and cattle. Maybe we can get a lead from the military. Train records."

"Maybe he wasn't a farmer. Maybe he was just another slave trader. Missouri was a slave state. The auction houses are gone. If the Missouri buyer was a slave trader, we'll be at an impasse."

"The people who ran the auction houses are still around. That will take some time. Rides in the area to former plantations, Aunt Maribel mentioned that was your usual plan. We'll need some names."

"Almost ten years ago, A long time. And so much to investigate."

"Maybe we'll get lucky, Annalise. The steamship will be making stops throughout this trip. A trader could have unloaded before he got to St. Louis."

She was impressed with the way he was analyzing the task, even though the search, one that she had been so confident about, was reaching needle-in-a-haystack proportions.

"The trader could have gone overland from Missouri to some other state or territory, Jefferson."

"Unlikely. The territories didn't have much slavery. There were no slave states north, east, or west of Missouri."

"Good point. If the ones who bought her were from Mississippi or Texas, they would have been traveling a great distance, when there were slave auction houses much closer to them. We can eliminate them."

"Still, Missouri is a large state. Slave traders and bounty hunters moved around a lot," she said.

"A trader would have gone west, if he had a particular buyer that he was providing slaves for."

"You know, we can save time if we divide the work. I'm sure that you're anxious to get to Kansas."

"Let's do this. We'll check out newspapers first. We'll go together. They're a good source for information on plantations around St. Louis. We'll get some names and locations there. Later, I'll take the military post, Jefferson Barracks, south of town. I'll look for old auction houses. You take cotton buyers, the farmer's markets, and harbor records. "

"I'll take police records too," she offered.

"We'll meet back at the hotel each night to compare notes. If we get solid information, we'll look into it together the next day."

"Good. And thank you."

"Annalise, do you have a weapon? A gun?"

"No, Jefferson, but I told you, I can take care of myself."

"I won't debate that. Do you have a pistol?"

"No."

"Have you ever fired one?"

"No. Papa Herman was going to show me. Then he got sick."

"So you made those trips without protection?"

"I had my wits, and attitude, and a purpose."

"Well, this time you're going to carry a pocket pistol."

"Your gun?"

"One of three. I've got two single action revolvers issued near the middle of the war. I'm going to show you how to use a smaller pistol that you can conceal."

"Single-action? I'm afraid I don't..."

"We'll work it out."

Two days later the *Necessity* pulled into the pandemonium that was St. Louis. Steamboats, flatboats, and barges were line up for miles. A cacophony of noise greeted the arrivals, shouting voices, whistles, horns, the clatter of horses' hooves.

"What day is this, Jefferson? I've lost track."

"Wednesday. We'll find a hotel. Tomorrow morning, we'll start asking questions."

He noticed that she had tensed up considerably in the last day. She was getting somewhat close to a possible resolution, and she had so much hope invested in this journey. Conversation between the two stalled. He was concerned about her state of mind if this excursion proved fruitless. She would have few other options left to find her mother.

That night, in a hotel a mile from the river, he reminded her of the plan for the next day.

"I asked some questions downstairs. The papers with the most credibility are the *Herald,* the *Register,* and the *Dispatch.* We'll find them after breakfast."

They made only one stop, at the *Herald*, where they spent the morning in the office of the editor, who revealed early in their conversation that he was an avowed abolitionist who was forced to sit on stories before and during the Civil War.

"A lot of information came across this desk," he said, "Stories of atrocities, abuse, naming names. I would have lost my job, or hurt the paper, if I hadn't been discreet."

"We're interested in names that we can follow up on," Jefferson noted.

"St. Louis may have been the center of alleged atrocities. The name I heard the most was Corby Pitcock. He owned a farm north of the Missouri River. Still does. Probably the most successful around here, earned on the backs of chattel. He was active in the slave market. Heard that he bought a lot of young women and young boys, more than most. They say that tomfoolery got him that land in the first place. I don't know. There was a wholecommunity of slaves at his place, sort of isolated, away from the law.

He's still one of the wealthiest owners around."

"Without slaves?"

"Not even sure about that. Figure he's got a lot of them to stay by treating them special, or scaring them."

Annalise wrote down the name. "Anybody else?"

"Well, there was the Graham spread. Old Man Graham was a lunatic. Thing is the farm burned in '58, and he committed suicide. Then there was the Boatman farm, called Fair Acres. Thomas A. Boatman. He's still around, west of here. Never married; he used slave girls to take care of his needs, I was told. The other name I heard a lot was Alfie Myron. Nice sort of man, I suppose, but he hated blacks. There were stories that a graveyard on his property was filled with abused slaves. Then there was Maurice and Millicent Freeman, siblings, who owned 500 acres south on the Mississippi. They were regular buyers and sellers on the slave market. One of their main businesses was raising slaves for sale, breeding them for the market. They bought well-bred, husky, and pretty people, and mated them."

Annalise summarized. "I've written down Corby Pitcock, the Grahams, Thomas Boatman, Alfie Myron, and the Freemans. Anyone else?"

"I'll review my records. I can probably triple your list. Get back to me in a few days. I do admire what you're doing. I'll help anyway I can. Keep me up to date. There may be a good story at the end."

That afternoon, Jefferson and Annalise reviewed the list.

"This gives us a start. It sounds as if St. Louis was depraved," she said.

"What do you think about the list you have?"

"Mama was beautiful. The Freemans would have been attracted to her, for breeding, or whatever. Thomas Boatman might have seen her as a bed-warmer. Corby Pitcock had the means to buy slaves by the boatload."

"Tomorrow, I'll ride down to the Jefferson Barracks. That will use up most of the day. You go to the river and the cotton exchange. Part of the exchange ran slave auctions too. We'll meet back here between four and six o'clock. You won't get lost?"

"No," she said somewhat testily. "I can ask directions."

She was waiting outside of the cotton exchange when the doors opened. She walked into what looked like an office, and up to a bespectacled man at the desk.

"Sir, I was wondering if you can help me."

"What is it," he replied curtly, but changed his manner when he looked up to see the attractive young girl dressed in men's clothing with a slouch hat perched on the back of her head. "Yes, little lady, how can I help?"

"Well, Sir," she smiled broadly at him, "I'm looking for a cotton farmer named Corby Pitcock. He's got a farm near here. I was hoping you could tell me where it is."

"Your family up there, Miss?"

"Oh, no Sir." She hated it in the musty, dark office, and she despised the way he was looking at her. "Well, I'm not sure. I think so."

"You from around here somewheres?"

"No. I'm heading west to Kansas. My husband and I need to see him before we leave."

Kansas. That sounded good. She wasn't sure where any of that answer had come from. Probably from Jefferson's plans. The mention of "my husband" was to change the man's attitude toward her.

"Well, ma'am, I know Mr. Pitcock well. His spread is up in Lincoln County, 'bout twenty miles north of here. Brings us a good crop every year."

"That is wonderful news. Can you tell me how to get there?"

"It's kind of an isolated place. Nothing much near it. Hey, I can draw you a map."

"You are so kind."

She walked out with his scribbling. It was not yet 9 am, and she had a lead. Now what? The river, asking questions about Boatman and the Freemans? She couldn't waste an entire day waiting for Jefferson to get back. She would try the other names tomorrow. She'd ride to Pitcock's. What could happen? Besides, she had the little Navy pistol tucked in her waistband under the coat.

In the early afternoon, Annalise turned her mare onto a long lane which led to a collection of impressive buildings in the distance. Immediately she noticed that the Pitcock plantation was not what she had expected. More wealth than she had imagined. Fields of new cotton stretched in every direction save one, a fenced field where a hundred or more horses were grazing. She had encountered some difficulty finding the place, set on a range of hills above a plain, stretching to the horizon on all sides. She would be noticed, she knew, a solitary rider, long before she got close to the area with buildings.

As she neared the house, she saw a row of shacks and a population of black faces. Slavery had been abolished for three years, but she couldn't counter the thought that they were still slaves. Men with rifles in the crooks of their arms seemed to be stationed at intervals.

The main house was sizable, with tall pillars supporting the front porch. A man was standing on the porch watching her ride up. She'd play it with a combination of naivete and a smile.

"Good afternoon, Sir. Are you Mr. Pitcock?"

He leered at her. He was an ugly man with small eyes, floppy ears, and close-cropped hair.

"Hell no, I ain't Pitcock. Who's askin'?"

"My name is O'Neill. I'm looking for someone. Maybe Mr. Pitcock can help me."

"You by yourself, lady?"

There was an insinuation of evil about the man. He leaned against a pillar and raised an eyebrow. His eyes were all over her.

"No, not really. I've come from Jefferson Barracks. They told me how to get here. My husband will be here soon. He's right behind me."

His expression changed. Maybe he believed all of this. Maybe not.

"Mr. Pitcock. Why would he want to talk to you?"

"Lieutenant Murphy said that I should mention his name to you."

"Never heared of him." No wonder. She had made the name up.

"May I see Mr. Pitcock?"

He looked at her for a moment, and walked into the house.

When he returned, he was following another man, thin and well-dressed with blonde hair slicked back from his forehead, probably in his late forties.

"I'm Pitcock. You wanted to see me."

"Thank you, Mr. Pitcock." She dismounted and walked onto the porch. "I'm looking for a former slave. She's got some information about my family. The folks at Jefferson Barracks thought that you might be able to help. She may have worked for you."

"Lots of farms and slaves around here once. Why me?"

"Your name came up in conversations . Seems they have a lot of respect for you." She felt the Navy revolver pressing against her back.

"Who is this slave?"

"Her name is Missy. Missy Ollimore. She lived in Cincinnati years ago. She'd be somewhere in her forties. Tall, pretty woman."

His eyes widened. "Don't know her. She never worked here."

"Are you sure? She was reported to be in this area."

"By who?"

"Friends of hers. Former slaves."

"No. I don't know her."

"Lieutenant Murphy thought that I should talk to some of the workers here. Maybe they came across her sometime."

"Murphy?"

"Yes. From the Jefferson Barracks."

He looked at the other man. "Luther, you remember any Missy?"

"Nope." The man was jolted out of some reverie, intent on ogling her.

"That is not good news." She put on her most crestfallen look. She knew that she was on to something. She hoped that she was a better liar than they were.

"Sorry to have bothered you. Thanks for your time." She walked to her mare and mounted. "Good day."

They were still watching her, she knew, as she started back up the lane. She glanced back. They were gone. She turned her mare toward the row of shacks. A black woman was shuffling between two small barns, out of sight of the house.

"Excuse me. May I talk to you?"

The woman looked horrified.

"Please don't be afraid. I'm a friend. I just want to ask you something. Please."

She dismounted. The woman hadn't moved.

"I am the daughter of Missy Ollimore. Do you know her?"

The woman looked away. "Missy. Po' Missy."

Annalise's heart jumped. "You know her? You know Missy?"

"Missy. She gone."

"Gone? She left here?"

"No. Missy be dead for several years."

Annalise was suddenly dizzy, stunned.

"She was here? What happened?"

"You be Annalise?"

"Yes ! Yes! Please tell me."

"Missy, she talk about her Annalise. She loved you, chile."

Annalise felt tears welling in her eyes. She needed to sit down.

"Missy, she be the bedwarmer for Mastuh Corby. Hated it. Tried to run away. Dem bloodhounds, dey catch her. Mastuh Corby and Mastuh Luther, dey beat her near to death. She gets better 'n' Mastuh Corby, he come for her. Takes her to be a bedwarmer agin. We don't see her fuh a long time. One mawnin', Mastuh Luther say we got to bury her. House slaves say they heared her screamin' fum Mastuh Luther's room the night befo'."

"No. No!" The shock was being replaced by a terrible fury.

"Buried her near de stream. You wants to see it?"

Annalise followed the woman to an area with several makeshift wooden headstones. On one, someone had scratched the name "Misy."

Annalise sank to her knees, gently touching the marker. She remained that way for several minutes.

"Why…why didn't someone say something to the authorities? When you were set free, why did you stay here?"

"Set free? What you sayin', girl? We not free."

"Slavery is over. It has been for three years. There was a war that ended it."

It was too much for the woman to process. She stared at Annalise, turned, and walked away.

At last, after ten haunting years, the mystery was over. Annalise had found her mother.

She stayed at the grave, sitting cross-legged in front of it, crying freely. Then for a few minutes, she talked to her mother. Two riders appeared behind her before she had time to react.

"Had to get nosy, didn't you?" Pitcock said from his horse.

"You animal. You unspeakable animal. You killed her," Annalise spat at him, rising from the ground.

"She was a slave. Besides, Luther did it. Seems she didn't like him as well as she liked me. Ain't that so, Luther?" Pitcock grinned.

"Don't matter none, Mr. Pitcock. Got what I wanted from her, more than a few times."

Annalise reached for the revolver, and began to level it at Pitcock. Luther, at close range, kicked it from her hand.

"Seems we got a problem, Luther."

"You're in big trouble." Annalise recognized the need to settle down. "There'll be people here soon to help me. You'll have to answer for killing her, and for still keeping slaves. Some judge will be glad to put you away."

Pitcock laughed. "Who you kidding? That was bullshit about a husband and the military. Lieutenant Murphy? You're here by yourself. Why you so excited about this anyway?"

"Missy Ollimore was a free woman. She was my mother."

"Really? That makes you black too. Don't much look like it. What do you think. Luther? She make a good bedwarmer?"

"Let me have her, Mr. Pitcock. Let me have her."

"Maybe we'll share her. See if she's as good as her mother."

Annalise turned to run. If she could just get to her horse. Luther maneuvered his horse in front of her, blocking the way.

"You stay away from me! If I get a chance, I'll kill you both."

“Looks like we got to tame her, Luther. Lock her in the room above the shed. If she tries to get away, shoot her. By the way, girlie, no judge will put me away. You think they’d take the word of a black woman?”

Jefferson was deeply troubled when she didn’t return to the hotel. He waited calmly until after dark. He had news for her, wherever she was.

“Pitcock?” the officer at Jefferson Barracks had told him, after he had recited the editor’s list. “Yes, Colonel Chase, I know of him. He’s up in Lincoln County, maybe 40 miles from here. Pretty unsavory character, the way I hear it. Think he stole the land he’s on, 25 years ago, or so. No proof though. He was under suspicion for a murder in St. Louis, a horse trader. Again, not enough proof. Mainly, he’s one of the most powerful men in eastern Missouri.”

“Colonel, I’ve got to find him.”

“I’d be happy to give you directions. You may not remember me. I was with Custer’s cavalry. Saw a lot of you in the war. You, sir, were a hero. Didn’t have the same thought about General Custer.”

The colonel showed him a military map of the St. Charles area. Pitcock’s place was on a lunate-shaped piece of land, bordered on the north and east by bends in the Mississippi River. Several miles south was the Missouri River. To the west was an expanse of territory.

“Can you get there from the south? How much of a barrier is the Missouri River?”

“It’s a wide river, Colonel Chase. You can’t cross it without a boat, or a ferry. Used to be ferries at these two points,” he explained, pointing to locations below Pitcock’s. “Otherwise Pitcock himself would be cut off.”

“What sort of terrain there?”

“Plains, flood plains, probably. Rich soil. A few hills. Scattered forests. Some elevation, or he couldn’t farm there. It’s just south and around the corner from this area, the Lincoln County hills, sort of untamed. There’s another river up there, the Quivre. Runs almost north and south.”

So he had a mental picture of the Pitcock spread. The officer had offered to send an escort with him, if he wanted one.

“As I explained, I’m with a girl, looking for her mother. Let me talk it over with her. Thank you, sir.”

“My best thought is that you ought to look over Pitcock’s before the others. “

She wasn’t coming back. Tomorrow, he’d retrace her steps, from where? The cotton exchange, that’s where she was going. He prepared for a restless night.

He was early to the cotton exchange, and found the same squirrely man that Analise had talked to.

“Woman came in here yesterday. Pretty. Long black hair. Dressed in a jacket and pants. You remember her?”

“Who wants to know?”

“I’m a friend of hers. Can’t find her. You remember her?”

“You think we’re in charge of missing persons here?”

"No. I'd just like to know if you talked to her."

"And what if I did?"

Jefferson smiled and walked around the desk. He bent over, with his face inches away from the man.

"I'm asking some easy questions here, easy to answer. But you keep asking me questions back. One of us is going to have to start answering. Unless you want to end up under this desk, I figure that would be you. Did you talk to her?" Jefferson had not raised his voice, but the man understood that he was getting angered.

"Jesus, mister. Yes, I talked to her. She asked about Corby Pitcock."

"What did you tell her?"

"Told her how to get to his place."

"When was that? What time?"

"Dunno. What do you think I am, a clock?"

Jefferson stared hard at him.

"Maybe nine in the morning."

"She ask about anyone else?"

"No."

"Thanks for the information. Nice visiting with you. Maybe the next time I visit, I'll answer your questions."

"Bastard," the man uttered quietly, as Jefferson left the building.

Jefferson paused outside the door. So she had found out where Pitcock was. She had ridden up there. Maybe she got lost. Maybe she had found a place to stay last night after she left the Pitcock farm. Maybe she had even found her mother, and was spending time with her. Too unlikely. According to his Aunt Maribel, Missy would not have stayed away from Cincinnati, if she still had any freedom.

No. Military training had taught him to imagine the worst, and plan for it. Annalise was in trouble. He'd have to go after her. He mounted Storm at the instant that the dark clouds above began a spring storm.

He returned to the hotel, loaded the pack horse, and checked out.

"Leaving early, Sir? Miss O'Neill too?"

"Yes. We've got an emergency in Mississippi. We'll be heading south in the morning."

Before he rode out, he dropped his pistols into two large holsters, and strapped them on, one on each side, after fully loading both. Then he stopped at a merchandise store and bought a second slicker, one for Annalise. The rain gave no indication of lessening.

Getting to Pitcock's was a challenge. The rain was relentless. When he reached the appointed spot for the Missouri ferry, there was a bell, which he rang. There was no response. The operator was obviously on the north side. He rang the bell again. And again. He saw a man on the far side. He barely heard the man's "Hallo! No ferry today. Rainin' too hard. Come back if'n it stops!"

"Gotta cross now! Give you twenty dollars if you come for me!"

Twenty dollars was two month's pay for the operator. He hustled across to Jefferson, two teen-aged boys helping him pole the large flatboat, secured to a sagging rope between trees on each side. "Don't usually do this, mister."

"I know. I'm grateful. "I'll give you another ten if we get across safely." He was joking, but given the condition of the boat, there was some substance to it.

"Yes sir! Hey mister…"

"Yes?"

"Horses are extra."

Jefferson laughed. "OK. Get all of us across for forty dollars. By the way, did you have a passenger yesterday, a girl?"

"Yes sir! A pretty thing. Ferried her for a dollar. Mighta been all she had. Woulda took her across for free, ya know? She was might pretty. Mighty pretty." He winked at Jefferson.

"Did she ask you directions?"

"Wal, yes she did. Wanted to get to Pitcock's place, several mile fum here."

"What did you tell her?"

"Tole her to follow the old road up over them hills. After mebbe 30 minutes, look for a long lane on her right, leadin' back to a bunch of buildings. The only farm up that way."

"She didn't return later?"

"Nope. I'da membered. She was might pretty. Even told her I'd take her back for free."

"Do you know Corby Pitcock?"

"Wal, he sometimes uses my boat here. Unfriendly fella. Kinda mean-lookin'. Don't much cotton to him. Hope you ain't a friend of his."

"No. I'm not a friend of his."

Jefferson rode past the farm lane, continuing several miles farther west. He saw a heavy grove of trees, and rode into it, where he tied the pack horse to a tree. The area was isolated. There'd be no traffic past the spot, particularly in the heavy rain. If there was going to be a need for a quick getaway, he couldn't be bothered by having to lead a pack horse.

"OK. Little girl," he said as the stroked her nose, "you rest here. Eat some of this grass. I'll be back for you."

Later , he stood at the top of the lane, the entrance to the Pitcock Farm. There were fences everywhere. The lane was the only way onto or off of the property. Not good. That narrowed the possible escape options. The rain had turned into an ally. There was almost no activity in front of him. A piece of property this large probably had a lot of ranch hands. On a dry day, there would be no chance to arrive unnoticed or unchallenged. He squinted to the distance. Numerous shacks were clustered to the right about halfway down the lane, unimpressive, run-down. Probably slave quarters once, he thought. Or maybe they still were. He'd lead Storm down the lane to the shacks, duck into that area, and look things over.

He turned into the area in front of the first shack, and stopped short. In front of him, head down, bedraggled, was Annalise's mare, still saddled, huddling against the side of a building.

"Mr. Pitcock. Ain't no way to work today. Whole day wasted." Luther said.

Pitcock didn't even look up, nor answer. Luther bothered him sometimes. Constant chatter. But the man was loyal. Loathsome to look at, unpredictable, but loyal. Pitcock used him as a sort of guard and enforcer. That had earned Luther a room in the main house, the scene of nightly grunting and groaning and occasional screaming. Luther never spent a night without company, slave girls, sometimes young slave boys, some as young as twelve years old. He ravaged them in every demented way, kept them a few nights, and then looked for replacements. There were fifty-some chattels on the property; Pitcock added to the total at his whim, often just satisfy his lust, or Luther's. The slaves feared Luther much more than they feared the cruel master. Above the kitchen was the room of the other Pitcock boarder, a thin, scarred man missing an eye from a Civil War mishap. His name was Muley, a nickname earned from his expertise with horses and mules. The Pitcock farm was a hideout for him. He was a wanted man in several states, and was even more proficient in the arts of persuasion and termination than Luther. Muley was the overseer of the farm, rarely left it, content to exercise a malevolent presence within the safe confines. Pitcock paid them well, in comfort, in food, and in money.

"The men are in the bunkhouse, drinkin' and playin' cards. Seen Muley headed there. Anythin' I should be doin'?"

"Well I might suggest that you stop bothering me." Pitcock's voice always sounded as if he had a mouthful of food, garbled and sometimes indistinct.

"What are we goin' to do with that girl, boss?"

"I haven't decided."

"She could get you…us… in big trouble."

"How, Luther? Just how? She came here trespassing, and pulled a gun on me. Them slaves we got rid of, including her mother, who can prove how they died? Shouldn't be a law against that anyway."

"What about her tellin' the authorities we still keepin' slaves?"

"I don't expect any trouble from anyone. Them slaves are here because they want to be. Isn't that right?"

"Could they stick us in jail? Fine us?"

"Never heard of a white man being jailed because a colored complained."

"But it be different now, boss, after the war 'n' everything."

"Listen. The reason we're keeping her is that she came here all uppity and pulled a gun on me. And she's black, Luther, for Christsakes! She needs a lesson. If we can't tame her, we'll just get rid of her. In any case, I won't let her call attention to us out here."

"She likely told someone she was comin' here."

"So what? We haven't seen anyone. And if somebody does show up, we ain't seen her."

"Boss…"

Pitcock looked at him. He knew what was coming. "Boss, I ain't got nothin' to do right now. How 'bout I go up there and teach her a lesson now?"

"She's a handful, Luther. Think you can handle her?"

Luther rubbed his crotch. "Oh, yes. I can handle her. Gawd, you see that tight little ass." He bolted for the door.

"Don't kill her. I might want to teach her a lesson too."

Annalise struggled against the ropes. Her wrists were tied to the bed, too tightly. The rope around her upper body hindered movement. She looked around the room, desperate for something that would help her escape. The sharp edge of a tool. Her legs were still free.

They had led her up a flight of stairs from the outside. It was a storage area, maybe 15 feet square. The room was dark, except that numerous separations between boards let in some gray light from outside. She heard the driving rain, then thunder.

She had struggled initially, until Luther delivered a sharp punch to her jaw. That ached, and she knew that it was swollen.

So dumb, coming here by herself. She wondered if he would come to her rescue. Possible. He would retrace her steps, probably find out about Pitcock from the clerk at the cotton exchange. But what if he did come? Pitcock's farm was like a fortress. From what she had seen, he probably had fifteen men or so, and they were all armed. Jefferson would be outnumbered. They would both die here, on the farm where her mother had died.

She would have to get free somehow, before he got to the farm, find her horse, and ride away. They would come after her, and there was the slow ferry to contend with. She'd ride the other direction. But she had to get free first, and then somehow get through the locked shed door.

She looked around the bare room. She was on a large, rickety bed of some kind. The room was certainly used to bed or torment unwilling slave girls. Maybe even her mother. There was a small round table with a lantern, wooden boxes in the corner.

Then she heard steps tromping noisily up the stairs outside, heavy breathing as someone fumbled with the lock.

Luther.

Jefferson looked around. Nobody. The rain pelted him. Maybe he should knock on the door of one of the shacks. If there were slaves, he might find a friend. A broken porch blocked his way. He almost didn't see the man sitting on a stool, a sad-faced man, watching him quietly, motionless.

"Hello, friend."

The man said nothing.

"Will you talk to me?"

"You's gwine tell me to go out in da fields in dis rain, bossman?"

"I don't work here. I'm not a friend of your bosses. I'm looking for a girl. She might have come here yesterday. Did you see her?"

"You a friend of Missy's daughter?"

"Yes, and I'm worried about her. You saw her?"

"Seen her. She be in big trouble wif the Mastuh."

"Where is she?"

She come here. Lulan take her to Missy's grave place. Mastuh catched up wif her. Locked her in de shed."

"The shed? Show me."

"Yes, I gonna do dat. 'Bout time someone gets it on da Mastuh. He mean, a devil."

The man led Jefferson to the line of cabins nearest the shed, and pointed across a clearing.

"She be up dere. De top floor. 'Spect she be locked in."

Jefferson estimated the distance to the shed to be about 100 yards. In turn, the shed and barns were about that same distance from the main house. From behind the house at some distance, he heard muffled voices and laughter. That'll be the bunkhouse, he thought.

He'd leave the horses at that spot. If he could get Annalise and bring her to the horses, they could mount and ride away quickly with a head start on any pursuers. He was about to dash across the clearing to the shack, when a man emerged from the main house, and trotted toward the shed. He waited. The man fiddled with the shed door, cursed loudly, and kicked at the door. He settled down and began to try to open the lock again. He succeeded and walked inside, leaving the door slightly ajar. Jefferson waited again. Nobody else was coming. This is it, he thought.

He sprinted to the steps, drawing the pistol from his right holster. Slowly he began to climb.

He heard a man's voice, "You bitch!" There was a loud thump and then a whimper. Annalise. He reached the top step and opened the door. In a split second, he took in the scene. The man stood with his back to him, his pants around his ankles. Annalise was in the corner on a bed. Her pants were down to her knees, and the man was pulling at them. Her hands were tied to the headboard of the bed. The man had a knife in his left hand.

"What the hell!" the man screamed as Jefferson strode toward him.

The butt of Jefferson's pistol crunched against the man's head. He fell senseless, his hands still on Annalise.

"Jefferson!" she cried.

"We've got to get out of here," he said as he retrieved the man's knife and cut the ropes from her.

He cut the last strand just as her eyes widened. "Look out!"

In the doorway was Corby Pitcock with a pistol pointed at Jefferson's back. Jefferson dropped and turned, as he had done so many times in the military. Pitcock's shot went wildly into the back wall.

Jefferson's shot destroyed Pitcock's knee. The rancher lost his balance, falling backward, dropping his pistol, and skidding down the steps to the ground, where he lay still.

Jefferson grabbed the waist of her pants and pulled them up for her. "Those shots will bring company. Let's go. The horses are by the slave cabins."

As she passed the prone body of Pitcock at the foot of the steps, she kicked him viciously in the face. "That's for my mother," she hissed. They ran to the horses, and were soon breaking out of the rows of shacks, and turning up the lane. A man on a horse was starting to chase them up the lane, firing wildly. Jefferson's shot knocked him from the saddle.

"Go right up here. Don't slow down !" he yelled at her.

The two raced west until they came to the grove of trees. "The pack horse is here," he explained. He unhitched the animal.

"Which way?" she asked.

"They'll be right behind us. Probably expect us to cut south. We'll go northwest, that way, and try to lose them in the forests up there." He reached in his saddlebag, and pulled out the extra slicker.

"Should have given this to you back there. Didn't plan very well."

"Jefferson… Jefferson…" was all she could say.

Luther stood up groggily and leaned on the handrail to descend the steps. He bent over Pitcock, who was alternately screaming and shouting directions.

"My knee! That sonuvabitch! Muley, get after them. Take everyone. Catch up to them at the ferries. Bring back their bodies! Oh, God, my leg!"

"Boss, you may bleed to death. Your nose looks funny, kinda crooked."

"You stupid bastard ! Ride to O'Fallon. Get a doctor back here!"

"Can't see too well, boss. He put a dent in my head."

"Then get me a horse. I'll ride there myself. Swear to God, they'll pay for this, if I have to chase them to China."

They ran the horses hard until dark. Jefferson pulled up. "Rain's stopping. Let's rest the horses. We need to settle down too. No fire tonight. With this rain, we're leaving tracks. If they're tracking us, they'll ride to the fire."

"I don't know if they can track us. We haven't ridden in a straight line for four hours. You know where we are?"

"No idea at all," he teased. "We'll let the sun rescue us tomorrow."

Later, she asked, "What do we do now?"

"Here's the problem. If we ride back to St. Louis, they'll be waiting for us. If they lose us out here, that's where they'll go, especially to the boats. They're probably waiting at the ferry now. Did you say anything to the man at the ferry?"

"No. Just said that I was from the East. Idle conversation."

"Good, that'll reinforce their focus on St. Louis."

"Jefferson. I can't think. My mother's dead." She began to cry.

"I know, Annalise. I'm sorry."

He moved over to where she sat, and put his arm around her. She sobbed into his chest. He pulled the blanket around both of them.

"Jefferson, thank you."

Soon she was asleep.

He stood and moved to the horses. He stopped in front of the mare, and whispered, "Thanks for waiting for her." He had words for the other two. To the pack horse, "Samantha, I left you alone. You're such a sweetheart. I'll never do that again, little girl."

As always, he spent time with Storm, and the horse's ears perked up, as they always did. "You're still my hero, Stormie. We did some good things today. You are such a good horse."

He returned to lean against the stump. He closed his eyes. He was wet and cold and tired. He'd have to reason this out by himself. Tomorrow, they'd head west. It was the safest direction.

****

The door to Sheriff Siworth's office opened, and a man stuck his head inside. Siworth had been sheriff of Abilene for four months, and while the raucous little city hadn't quieted much, at least his "No Guns" rule was having some effect. He had announced the rule back in January: if you ride into Abilene, check your gun in the Sheriff's office. No exceptions.

Siworth was in his early fifties, a tired-looking man with a handlebar moustache. He often looked bewildered by his lot, and in truth, he led a lonely existence. His deputy, Stash, the only local who would take the job, was good with his guns and mostly dependable, except when he was drunk; that was most nights.

Together, they controlled inebriated cowboys. Wielding the only guns in town, they were able to bluff their way through most altercations. Nights were still noisy, especially when cowboys from cattle drives were in town. There was a semblance of order. The Committee was satisfied, if not pleased.

"Hi ! How's it going?" the man said, and then he entered the small office.

"Can I do something for you?" Siworth answered. He didn't get up from his desk. He noticed that the man, a hard-bitten looking sort, grinning broadly, still had his pistols, one stuck into his pants, another in a low-slung holster, butt forward on his left hip.

"Well, I'll tell you, yes you can. C'mon in, J.T." A second man wandered in behind the stranger, a red-haired man bearing some resemblance, a little thinner, a little taller.

"We're sort of new in town. Thought we'd come in and chew the fat, introduce ourselves."

"I see. But I am a little busy here."

"We won't take up your time, partner. My name's Lester Dooley. This here's my brother, J.T. He don't say much. Kinda ugly, ain't he?"

Siworth ignored the comment. "I see you are both armed. We have a rule here in Abilene. You're going to have to check them pistols with me."

"Well, you see sheriff, that's what we want to talk about," the blond man said, and he walked around the desk.

Siworth was immediately uncomfortable. He started to get up. At that moment Lester drew his gun, pushed Siworth back into his chair, and stuck the pistol hard against Siworth's nose.

"You see, sheriff, you ain't getting' our guns. Right, J.T.?"

The redhead answered with an inane giggle. "Right, Lester."

"You ain't man enough to take them from us, and you see, partner, we're kinda used to them. We'[d feel buck naked without 'em, right J.T.?"

"But we have a law," Siworth protested. He knew that he was in trouble.

"Naw…J.T., he says he has a law. You are a funny man, Sheriff. Now be careful how you answer this: can my ugly brother and I keep our guns in the town?" He pressed on his pistol harder, smashing Siworth's nose almost flat. At the same time he cocked the hammer of the pistol.

"Yesh…yesh…"

Lester holstered his gun. He reached down and grabbed Siworth's. "I believe we're goin' to check your gun." He put it in his belt.

The sheriff rubbed his nose. His eyes were watering.

"Mighty nice of you, Sheriff, givin' us your gun."

Siworth grunted.

"We're goin' to say goodbye now, Sheriff. I hope you have a very nice day." He walked to the door, turned, and winked at Siworth. "Hey, J.T., this is a right friendly town."

"Yeah, Lester, a friendly town."

The door shut behind them. Siworth jumped to his feet. The door re-opened. Lester stuck his head in.

"Silly of me, partner, I forgot to tell you. If we see you in town after tomorrow afternoon, we're goin' to blow your head off. Better find another town. Bye now."

Siworth started shaking. With his eye on the door, he reached to his chest and removed the star. He threw it on the desk.

Early the next morning, he was spotted riding out of town in a hurry on a fully loaded horse. The town never saw him again. Nobody ever saw Stash again either, though he was reported to be in Texas somewhere. Another report had him buried east of town in a large field.

****

Jefferson ducked underwater, stood, and shook the water from his hair. A roaring campfire blazed just over the hill. That's where he had left Annalise. The night was cool, but clear. A full moon shown in the west Missouri night, and crowned the sky from horizon to horizon. He had found the spot in the Blackwater River, a wide curve bending into a half-S with calm shallow water close to the bank. The dip served as a bath, as well as a swim. He rubbed the chunk of soap on his upper body, producing a grainy foam.

They had found and begun to follow the Missouri River several days ago as it meandered west, sometimes dropping, sometimes flowing uphill. Joshua had written the previous year that it was the best overland marker to Kansas.

After the first uncomfortable night, they had ridden hard the next day, staying well north of the Missouri River. If Pitcock's men had been looking for them to the west, that group probably would have stuck close to the Missouri.

Annalise was somewhat catatonic, still overwhelmed by the discovery at Pitcock's. She barely spoke, and followed him meekly as they rode. He gave her the privacy of her thoughts, and they pressed west. Soon they would have to discuss her next course of action. He could put her on a steamboat at some juncture, or a stagecoach heading east. She wasn't ready for that yet.

A breakthrough occurred on the fourth night. Again he held her while she slept, but it was a fitful sleep, and it kept him awake.

"Annalise, you want to talk?"

"Jefferson, I guess I've known for some time that she was dead. But I can't accept the way it happened."

"I understand. That was a difficult thing to deal with."

"I've got to get over it. I've got to begin a normal life. I'll never forget her."

"Are you ready to head back east?"

"No. I don't think so. Not yet. Where are we?"

"We're well into Missouri, maybe ten days from Joshua's."

"I just don't know." She began to cry again.

"We should be clear of Pitcock's men. They would have given up by now."

"I just don't want to be alone."

"I agree. Why don't we just keep going? We can talk about it later. One thing to consider…steamboats on the Missouri go both directions. We could put you on one heading east, but that would take you back to the St. Louis area. I'm not in favor of that, unless I'm with you. The other possibility is to get on a steamboat going west. That would make this trip easier for you."

"No. let's keep riding."

He understood. A steamboat would have been too sedentary for her, too calm. She would have too much time to reflect on her mother, and the chaos of the time at Pitcock's.

He held her again, and she was quiet. He kissed the top of her head, an impulse. Why did I do that, he wondered. She sighed. Asleep. Good. She snuggled closer in the blanket they shared.

The next afternoon, they pulled up across the river from a busy port on the south side of the Missouri. "If my information's correct, that's Jefferson City."

"Jefferson City, Jefferson Barracks, Jefferson Chase. Are you trying to impress me?"

"Is it working?"

"At least it's easy to remember names. Is this the Jefferson River?"

"Let's ferry across. We both need a warm bath, a hot meal, and soft beds."

And fresh clothes for both of them. Before they adjourned to separate rooms, he showed her the money belt strapped to his leg. "If something happens to me, make sure to grab this. Fair amount of money in here. Some rolled up in shirts in Samantha's packs too."

They left early the next morning, after a hearty breakfast.

"Maybe it's too early for the ferry," she said.

"Doesn't matter. We're going to stay on the south side of the river now. Man at the stable explained a short cut away from the river when it bends north. It'll save us a half-day of riding, to Kansas City."

The day's journey cut over some small forested hills, which they rode across, and some plains, where they dismounted and walked the horses for long distances.

"Jefferson, Do you think we killed any of them?"

"Pitcock groaned when you kicked him; he's probably OK, except he'll never walk the same again. The big guy in the room. I don't think I hit him hard enough to finish him. The rider, I'm not sure."

"I hate all of them, but I'd rather see them punished by law than dead."

"Yeah."

"Thanks for the date last night."

"That was a date?"

"Sure. A nice meal. You listened to me. You took me back to my room and held the door for me."

"I think I can do better than that," he said, a flippant remark that hinted at intimacy. He regretted saying it.

"Thanks for letting me talk last night. I guess I needed to. I hope I didn't bore you."

She hadn't. For several hours, she had told him of the early years on the plantation, traveling to the unknown with her mother, Levi Coffin, the O'Neill family, schools, the horror of the past ten years.

He had encouraged it, asking questions, responding, commiserating. She was grateful, and it seemed, in a more positive mood today.

"Two things I want to say," she stopped and looked at him as she spoke. "One is, if I never see you again after Abilene, I'll remember these last few days. I'm glad that I got to know you. I owe you so much. I like you a lot. I'll never forget you."

"Annnalise, I wish all of this had been easier on you. I'm thankful that you have resolution." He paused. "I like you a lot, too." He began walking again.

"And, you've been a perfect gentleman, along with being a good listener."

That had been easy. She was a mesmerizing conversationalist. Her memories, her descriptions, those parts where she revealed her feelings. He had been a rapt listener, in part because she was so interesting. The other part, well he couldn't think about that now.

"So, what is the second thing?"

"The what?"

"You said that you wanted to say two things."

"Yes, The second thing is, that you've let me do the talking. I don't know that much about you. I want to find out everything I can in the next four or five days. Your Aunt Maribel is so complimentary about your family. Will you share some of that with me?"

"Four or five days of that? You'll ride away screaming."

She giggled. "The war, Jefferson. How awful was it?"

"Worse than I can explain. Worse than you could imagine. I saw so much death, so much tragedy, so much inhumanity. But it had to be fought. It had to be fought, even though it more or less destroyed our family."

"How?"

"We were separated geographically and philosophically. My brother Jonathan was killed. My brother Joshua was badly wounded, and spent the balance of the war at a desk. My father had too much heartbreak to deal with. It made him an old man, and he died before it was over. Sort of an inglorious way for a great man to live his last years."

"Your mother?"

"She was extraordinary, the most amazing woman I've ever known. Intelligent, cultured, nurturing, fun. She died two years before the war."

"They both contributed to what you are today."

"In so many ways. Father was always prodding us to think. Got us all interested in reading. One room of the house had loaded bookshelves on two sides. And there were always a few stacks on the floor."

"I guess we have that in common. I had a book in my hands from the age of eight to the age of fourteen. I've been too distracted the last few years. I'll get back to it."

"Best thing you can do. What did you read?"

"Anything. Books on travel, places with mountains and snow. Books on great men. History. For a year or so, I read everything I could find on birds."

"Birds?" he grinned.

"Birds," she answered. She was grinning too. "What did you read?"

"Father had a lot of book, novels, by great authors. The problem with reading those was that he always expected us to explain the subtleties. It was always easier on us to read picture books."

She laughed.

"What else?"

"Books about the outdoors. How to survive. How to respect the wilderness. Books on horses. Books on birds." He looked sideways at her. She laughed again.

"You love horses, don't you?"

"Whatever I do with the rest of my life will involve horses in some way."

The banter continued for several miles. They mounted and continued the journey, which demonstrably increased in difficulty. They were forced to contend with steep foothills choked with underbrush. Often they retraced their route when they came upon a precipice atop a sheer drop of several hundred feet, or a wall of stone that was impossible to climb or to skirt. At times the forest canopy darkened their path to the point where the sun was useless as a directional guide. They heard various animals running from them through the brush, unidentifiable due to the foliage. For long miles they led the horses up steep inclines followed immediately by harrowing descents at near impossible angles. They both fell several times, although the horses kept their footing.

"Some short cut," Jefferson mumbled, the first time she had seen him frustrated. "You having second thoughts about Kansas?"

"This is an adventure. As long as we don't get lost, or maybe more lost," she smiled.

"Well put. As long as we keep going west, we'll hit a river. The man back in Jefferson City, bless his black heart, gave me several of them to use as reference points."

"Any of thosc thc Amazon?"

"I think he said one was the River Styx."

"Well, based on the last five or six hours, we must be close to that."

The end of the next day had brought them here to the Blackwater River. They had ridden through a morning rain, somewhat protected by the forest. When the rain cleared, the weather turned sultry, too warm and too humid. They had ridden until late afternoon; the breeze generated by moving somewhat relieved the discomfort. They rode up to a wide, body of water, banked by small hillocks.

"This would be the Blackwater River. We'll water the horses, eat something, and get into the river," he said.

The trail meal was surprisingly quiet, even awkward. The easy conversation was missing something. A tension of unexplained origin was palpable. Both seemed lost in thought. Each caught the other staring.

Jefferson broke the spell. "If I can find that bar of soap, I'll take a bath in the river. You could feed the fire until I get back. Then you can go, if you want."

He walked over the crest of the hill hiding the river bank from their camp. At the water's edge, he disrobed, stacking his clothes in a neat pile.

She sat by the fire for a few minutes, then got up and walked to the hill's crest. He was in the water, standing to his waist. She saw the pile of clothes. He was obviously naked. Reacting rather than thinking, she walked to the river's edge, and began taking off her clothes. He hadn't seen hcr yet. He was standing facing downstream. He ducked underwater again, and when he stood up, he saw her. She was in the water, walking toward him, wearing nothing. When she reached him, she put her arms around his neck, and tilted her head back. Their first kiss lasted for several moments.

"Annalise…"

"It's OK, Jefferson. It's OK."

****

Rose Chase knew it was coming. She had heard the news late the day before, and was sure that Joshua had too.

He came downstairs to the store. It was her day to open, but that was still a half-hour away.

"Rosie, we have to talk."

"About what, Honey?"

"Siworth resigned and left town. Nobody knows where Stash is."

"Maybe he's investigating someone or something."

"No. Siworth's badge was on his desk. He's gone. Even if Stash comes back, I don't think he's sheriff material."

"So what are you thinking, Honey?"

"I've got an appointment this morning to talk to the committee. Doc Rosbottom came by last night. You were cooking dinner upstairs."

"Joshua, I'm afraid of this conversation."

"Rosie, we were so close to getting control of this town, and Sullivan Siworth wasn't even a good sheriff."

"Honey, is it our business to solve this?"

"I think it has to be. We're sort of committed to living here. We've got a lot invested in this store and this town's future."

"So you're going to be the next sheriff?"

"I'm thinking about it. I need your opinion."

"Why you, Joshua?"

"I think that I could be fair, and consistent. I can manage guns better than most men. It's not something I want to do. It may be something I have to do."

"So, you're thinking of saying yes?"

"I thought about it all night. Couldn't sleep. We were going to hire more help for the store anyway."

"Joshua Chase. You are my heart, my entire existence. If something happened to you, I couldn't bear it. I could get angry about this, but there's something you should know before you make a decision."

"What is it, Rosie?"

"I saw Doc Rosbottom yesterday too, just after noon. He examined me."

Joshua raised his eyebrows. "Rosie…Sweetheart, are you OK?"

"I'm great Honey. I'm pregnant."

****

Just before daybreak, she woke him with kisses to his cheek and forehead.

"Annalise?"

"Yes. Yes."

Afterward, resting her head on his chest, she asked, "I'm not sure what to say. Is this…what's happened…is it important?"

"What do you mean?"

"I'll never regret any of this. How do you feel about it?"

He rolled over to face her. "For several days now, I've begun to understand something. I've become very fond of you, Annalise. More than anyone before."

She gasped, almost inaudibly. "But you realize, you know…I was a slave. I'm…"

He interrupted, "Don't say it. It doesn't matter. I haven't even thought about it."

"Jefferson. I am fond of you too. I was worried about…what you might think. This is the first time I've ever…been with a man."

"I know. I guess that I better tell you something."

"What?" she raised on one elbow, somewhat fearful of what he'd say.

"My friends, my closest friends, call me Jeff."

"OK, Jefferson. I can do that." He laughed at her, and pulled her closer.

Annalise was content to let him ride ahead on that afternoon. She studied him from a few feet behind, not just his broad shoulders and the easy way he rode, but she was also evaluating and admiring everything she knew about him. A life-changing event had occurred the previous night, and again on that morning, something that she would remember forever, whatever happened to her, to him, to them. What was she doing here, on this long journey to a strange place, toward people that she didn't know? She had acquiesced when he began heading west because she had to be with someone who realized the enormous emotional circumstances that had occurred at Pitcock's, and because in her condition, she couldn't make decisions. That had been perfect therapy for her. Now she wanted to be with him, and she would follow him all of the way to Abilene. She was still furious at the events of her mother's death. Her life as a daughter, with a blood relative, had ended years ago, and she had been sad for a long time. Maybe someday, she'd return to that awful place, claim her mother, bury her in a happier place. Whatever Abilene offered, she would return to Herman and Maribel in a short time.

She wondered if all of this was somehow preordained. Maybe this adventure with him was meant to happen. Maybe her whole life was pointed to meeting him. The accumulated thoughts caused her to smile. She was still smiling when he looked back at her.

"What are you thinking about, Annalise?"

"I think you know," she replied coyly.

The land they were crossing had changed to rolling hills and scattered forests. The sun was eclipsed by cloud masses that rushed frenetically across the sky, a surrealistic sight that neither had seen before.

Then he began doing a strange thing. He would slow up and peer intently to his right, then resume the canter. She caught up to him as he slowed again. He looked past her.

"Jefferson, is something the matter?"

"Probably nothing. There are two riders just out of sight over there. They're behind that hill a few hundred yards. They were following us a few minutes ago, now they're staying even with us."

She saw nothing. "Pitcock's men?"

"No. Pitcock's men wouldn't come this far. Like I said, it's probably nothing."

Sensitized by his cavalry experience, he's overreacting to something I can't even see, she thought.

A short time later, they approached a range of foothills. On a rising slope ahead of them was another woods, substantial and thick. They rode into the new dimension, covered by a canopy of oaks and hickory trees. He stopped and signaled her to do the same.

He was whispering. "Wait here. Don't follow me. Don't start up the hill. I'll come back for you."

"Jefferson?" She was whispering too.

"Don't worry. Those two riders galloped ahead of us a few minutes ago, and headed this way. I'm a little curious."

"Where are you going?"

"If anything happens that you don't understand, leave Samantha here and gallop back toward the Blackwater. Ride away from the sun as fast as Rags will go. Find a hiding place there. I'll come for you later."

"I should be scared?"

He smiled at her. "No, I'll probably look foolish when this is over."

He rode Storm over to her, leaned across and kissed her, and was gone.

He rode south, arced toward the west, and then walked Storm northward far past the top of the incline where they had stopped. He dismounted and pulled out a revolver, and walked stealthily, stopping every few feet to listen.

He heard it, a low voice and a scuffling of feet on the forest floor.

Then he saw them, 100 feet ahead, two hulks leaning against white oaks another 100 feet apart. Both had longarms leveled in the direction that he and Annalise would have come.

He inched toward the closest man, studying him as he approached, choosing carefully the spots where he would next step. The closest man was tall and thin, scruffy-looking, unshaven, clothed in tattered vestiges of a threadbare shirt and pants.

"See anythin', Doo?" the scruffy man whispered hoarsely.

Jefferson stepped behind a tree. The other man would look his way to answer.

"Naw. Nuthin'. They be here directly. Prolly restin' down there. Mebbe foolin' around. They gots to come this way."

"'Member, shoot that sonuvabitch soon's you see him. Then we start pokin' her in every hole she got. We be screwin' soon."

"Nice lookin' horses from what I seen."

"Alright, Doo. You pleasure them horses. I'll do the woman."

Doo grunted a laugh. Silently, Jefferson walked up behind the scruffy man, and placed the barrel of his revolver against the man's neck just as he started to speak.

"Sumthin' ain't right, Doo. They shoulda rode up by now…Jesus!"

"Unless you're hunting squirrels, you'd better drop that rifle," Jefferson commanded.

The man jumped and spun around, swinging the rifle. Jefferson clubbed him on the temple with the barrel of his pistol. The man groaned and fell to the ground.

The other man, Doo, turned to the commotion, and then charged, firing a shot that clunked into a tree ten feet away from Jefferson.

Jefferson walked toward him and shot, hitting him in the lower leg, as he intended. Doo dropped his weapon as he screamed and grabbed at his leg.

Jefferson turned back to the scruffy man's rifle, and swung it against a tree, shattering it. Then he walked to Doo's dropped rifle and grabbed it off of the ground. He turned as he heard a growl. The scruffy man was stumbling toward him, a pathetic charge from a man blinded by rage, and from the blood flowing from the left side of his face. He raised his arms and curled his fingers as he neared Jefferson.

Using the rifle as a club, Jefferson swung, catching the man full force in the groin. The man grabbed his crotch, screeched, and rolled onto the ground in agony.

Jefferson stood over him briefly, then smashed Doo's rifle against another tree.

From the crest of the incline, Jefferson shouted her name. "Annalise!" He listened as a faint echo bounced off of distant trees. No answer. He couldn't see past the trees to where he had left her, a half-mile away. She would have been confused, scared by the two shots. It was probable that she had followed his directive and galloped away. If she didn't appear soon, he would have to chase her down.

He caught a flash of movement down the slope, and then he saw her, tentatively walking Rags toward him, pulling the pack horse. He called her name again, and waved his arms. "It's safe!"

"Jefferson, I heard shots."

"Our new friends here were planning a surprise for us. That one over there, holding his leg, is Doo. This one holding onto his manhood is, well, I don't know his name, most likely Mary or Victoria, after what just happened to him."

Emboldened by the thought that Jefferson would not harm him further with the woman present, Doo broke in.

"That there's Walter."

"Shut up, Doo!" Walter snarled. Then he turned his head and vomited.

"Take off your shoes, gentlemen," Jefferson ordered. Both men hesitated.

"You was trespassin' on our land. We was just funnin'."

"From the looks of you, Doo, you don't own much of anything, and your idea of fun is a bit misguided," Jefferson answered.

"You go to hell," Walter choked.

"Walter, what language. I guess our friendship's over. Take off your shoes unless you want to die here."

Both men struggled to remove their shoes. The effort caused Walter to lean backward, and again he vomited. Jefferson retrieved the shoes, and threw them one by one into thick brush far down the incline.

"We're going to take your horses with us. You'll find them somewhere five or ten miles west of here, although I'm sure that they'd be glad to get rid of you."

"Mister, we'll die out here!"

"Yes, Walter, that's possible. You're both mean enough to survive, but if you follow us, if I ever see either of you again, I'll shoot your face off."

****

The room was not fancy. In fact it was very ordinary, furnished with two beds, two chairs, a small dresser, a spittoon, a slop jar and a small closet. It was all that Lester and J.T. Dooley required, because it served as a hideout. The two were wanted on a variety of charges, including the murders of lawmen in Tennessee in 1848.

The room was on the second floor of a bawdy house which sat in the middle of the confusion of buildings that offered flesh and temptation to the gentry of Abilene. The sign on the front of the establishment read "The Red Rose." The owner was a pudgy man with greasy hair named John Wicks, himself a fugitive from mischief, which included stealing horses and robbery. Wicks changed names as often as most men changed clothes. He was know in Missouri as "William Johnson," in Mississippi as "John Williams," and in Illinois s "Bill Carson."

At the insistence of Lester Dooley, Wicks gave the brothers the rooms free of charge. Further, Dooley had stated, "We want your wimmen to be good to us, if you know what I mean." Wicks, with forced bravado, had protested. Lester stuck a pistol into the fat man's belly, and said, "Fine, partner. Then I'll just kill you and take over the whorehouse." From that inauspicious beginning, Wicks and the Dooleys became friends of a sort. The Dooleys served as muscle for the Red Rose, in case inebriated cowboys became belligerent. The brothers used the anonymity of the location as a staging area for forays into Missouri and Nebraska. "Listen boys," Wicks had said, "you can have any of my ladies whenever. Just don't beat them up. If'n I lose a couple of them, might as well shut down the biz'ness."

Lester knew the arrangement was temporary. He told J.T., "Few more years of hittin' mebbe some banks, a few stagecoaches, we'll light out for Californey or Oregon with enough money to do anythin'. Won't need to hole up here no more."

Wicks employed nine ladies, the oldest in her forties, the youngest barely sixteen. There were no real beauties. One was black, another Chinese. All were unfortunates without families or prospects. "Got anyhin' you want except squaws," Wicks boasted. He personally let the doves alone, except when he was hiring them. His interest was in very young girls, a fact that he hid from everyone, lest he be ostracized or worse by his own profession.

Lester's personal favorite among the ladies was sixteen-year old Myra, a sad-looking waif with doe eyes and a thin, girlish figure. She felt no affection for him, however. He disgusted her, but she had no recourse except to service him any time of the day or night. He was insatiable. J.T. played no favorites, even forcing the aged cook into his bed at various times.

The arrangement was perfect for the Dooleys. The law didn't much come to that side of the railroad tracks, and over on the Abilene town side, the law was always inadequate at best. Lester had recently driven off the sheriff of the moment, and he had been replaced by a lawman in name only. Lester decided after that incident to lay low, to not call attention to himself and his brother. It was confining, but it was safe. Between sporadic explorations into neighboring states to relieve boredom and to relieve miners and bankers of their payrolls, the two contented themselves with their unwilling harem, a wealth of alcohol, and bashing in the heads of unruly patrons of the Red Rose.

****

Kansas City became a stopover. Abilene was just 100 miles away, and Jefferson noted that a couple of days together, out of the saddle, would verify recent revelations and sort out emotions.

They checked into the Broadway, a new hotel near Third Street, after Jefferson had demonstrated gallantry once again.

"Should I get two rooms?"

"Two rooms, Jefferson? Why?"

"Well, my preference is one room, with a small bed. I'm just not sure about your thoughts on the matter."

"You are such a gentleman. One room is perfect. A small bed is perfect."

"Tonight, we're going to find the most expensive meal in town. Tomorrow we're going to sleep late."

Sitting in the hotel restaurant with candlelight playing across the dim room, fancy white tablecloths, and a menu heavy with beef, she asked a question which puzzled him.

"Jefferson, where are we going?"

"To Abilene."

"That isn't what I mean. Of course we're going to Abilene. What's going to happen to us after that?"

"Will you stay with me?"

"I'm not sure what that means."

"I'm not sure either. I do know that you're important to me. I don't want to lose you."

Her voice caught. "I was hoping you'd say that."

"You're beautiful, Annalise."

"I do love you." It was a whisper.

"Annalise, we've only known each other three weeks. A lot has happened. Extraordinary stuff. Whatever we feel may just be the result of the danger we've been through."

"Maybe. It has been a blur. I think that we've had divine help. With all of the days on trails, there have only been two bad weather days. This is spring, after all. But more than that, you've saved my life three times. A part of me belongs to you."

"That's good news. It's a good trade-off," he smiled.

"Abilene is a good idea. We can get to know each other better. It could be that without big and ugly people threatening us, we're mismatched." She smiled back.

"Yes. We've had our share of big and ugly people," he laughed.

"I don't know anything about Abilene. I know your brother's there. How is this going to work?"

"You'll love him. He's the hero in the family."

"Like you."

"No, he's smarter, braver, gentler. Handsomer."

"That assessment shows your humility. You are my hero. But what will I do? Where will we stay?"

"You'll want to go back to Cincinnati to see Maribel and Herman."

"Not for a while. When I go, I'd want you to go with me."

"When we get to Abilene, you can stay with Joshua and Rose. They live above their business. Apparently, it's a big area. Rose's father has work for me on his ranch. It's close to town, about 15 miles. I can stay out there. We'll see each other often; I'll make sure of that."

"You'll court me?"

"I've already started." Her hands were folded on the table in front of her. He reached across and held them.

"I told Joshua that I'd stay with him for a couple of months," he continued," I don't have firm plans beyond that. Oregon, maybe. I'd like to raise horses. Does that interest you?"

"If you're there, it does."

"I don't have a clear idea of Abilene. Maybe that's a place to settle."

"Jefferson, I need to do two things before we leave Kansas City. I need to post a letter to Aunt Maribel, to tell her about Mamma. Then I need to send a letter to authorities somewhere in St. Louis to tell them that Corby Pitcock is still keeping slaves. I'm not sure who should get it."

"We'll send it to the officer at the Jefferson Barracks. He'll send it on to the appropriate authorities."

"Can we do that tomorrow, Honey?"

The last word took him by surprise. This was a girl who had refused to talk to him two weeks ago. Now she was the most important person in his life. Hearing that word spoken so naturally was a minor epiphany.

Suddenly the restaurant was too crowded. Too noisy.

"I'll pay the bill. Let's go to our room."

The couple rode up to a large two-story building one block south of Texas Street, the main street of Abilene. They had just ridden for some distance just south of the stockyards, teeming with cattle and activity, even though it was early May. "Interesting," Jefferson had said, "every cow in Kansas is in town.'

There was a fetid animal odor, a stench that circled in the wind, and the braying and complaining of thousands of cows. Dust hung thick in the air and lines of railroad cars filled tracks to the east, waiting for cargo. A ride of a few minutes took them into the city.

A gunshot echoed from another street. It was clear that cowboys from several ranches were in town. There was activity on the wooden walkways and in the street, a surge of people moving, in and out of stores, back and forth to cross the broad street. Annalise drew a whistle from a ragged man leaning against a hitching post. Many people, the great percentage of them male, paid scant attention to the two on horseback, weaving slowly through them.

Annalise noticed the buildings, some hastily constructed, vying for attention with more modern impressive stores. She counted three saloons in the first two blocks, and the massive Drover's Cottage Hotel at the end of the street. Blended into a kaleidoscope of cowboy shirts and chaps, boots clomping against wood, were men in fine shirts, ties, and polished shoes. Women bustled about, almost all on the protective arms of men. Strings of horses were tied to every available hitching post.

Jefferson made a sharp left turn at the Alamo Bar, and a block later pulled up in front of a large painted window, *Chase General Merchandise.* A wide front porch covered by a sturdy roof ran the width of the building. The store was the most impressive structure he had yet seen, freshly painted. Large sacks of flour and feed were stacked on opposite sides of a large double door, standing open.

Jefferson dismounted and moved to help Annalise. He heard a familiar voice from inside the store. "Darn it, Weasel. Put that back." Jefferson climbed onto the porch just as a little man, dirty and disheveled, burst from the doorway, "Weasel, come back here!" As the man rushed past, Jefferson grabbed him by the back of his pants and the collar of his shirt, and lifted him into a horizontal position two feet above the ground. A large tin of tobacco dropped from his hands. A handsome man came through the door, and broke into a wide grin.

"Jeff!"

"I've got a present for you here, Joshua."

"Jozwah, I weren't stealin' that there tobaccy. Brought it out here to see it better, swear to ya."

"Jeffie, meet Weasel. Sometimes he forgets to pay me."

Jefferson looked down. "Mr. Weasel, glad to meet you." He lowered the man to the ground and walked to his brother. They exchanged a hearty embrace, patting each other loudly on their backs.

"Hi, Joshua." Jefferson hadn't seen his brother for over a year. He hadn't changed. He looked a bit heavier, but the smile which had disappeared during the war years was back.

"Rosie, come on out! Jeffie's here!" Then he noticed the dark-haired girl standing next to her horse and was confused.

"Joshua, this is Annalise. She's the love of my life."

"Jeff, I didn't realize that you were…Sorry, Annalise, I'm so happy to meet you."

Annalise extended her hand. The brother was as she'd imagined, tall and good looking, with a definite facial resemblance to Jefferson, except for a neat beard.

"It's a long story, brother. We'll catch you up later," Jefferson said.

A beautiful blonde lady came through the door. She was young and so pretty that she seemed out of place in a cow town. She is elegant, Jefferson thought.

"Rosie, my brother Jefferson."

He offered his hand. She brushed past it, hugging him. "Jefferson!"

"Rose, this is Annalise."

Again there was confusion. Rose covered it quickly. "Annalise, I'm happy to meet you!"

"Rose, I've heard so much about you." Another embrace was shared.

"Jeffie, let's take the saddle bags and packs inside. The stable's out back. Rosie will get you two something to drink. The horses look thirsty too."

Jefferson turned to Weasel, sitting cross-legged on the ground holding the tobacco tin against his chest. "Mr. Weasel, sorry if I roughed you up. I'll buy that tobacco for you."

Weasel grinned, a completely toothless effort. "I 'preciate that. I do." He scrambled to his feet and hopped away.

"He won't forget you, Jeffie."

"He looked kind of needy."

"He hangs around town. Nobody knows where he lives or sleeps. He's in the store every day, trying to make off with something. I usually make a lot of noise at him, but basically we let him get away with it. He never tries to take anything expensive."

"Weasel."

"Nobody knows his real name. He's a spectral sort, harmless though. The other day he brought Rose a handful of prairie flowers. He must have walked half the day collecting them."

They walked the horses around the building. "Little brother, she is quite a woman. Are you serious?"

"Getting that way."

"After you're settled, I'll take you to see Catharine, and little Jeremiah."

"She's here?"

"She's here. Interesting lady. I like her. She's got a thousand questions about Jonathan."

They walked into the stable and passed a fine carriage.

"Nice," said Jefferson.

"A wedding gift from her parents," Joshua explained.

"That reminds me. I'm a gift behind."

"Don't worry about that. The best present is having you here, and I'm guessing that cost you plenty."

"Yes, it did, in many ways."

"Sounds like an interesting journey."

"Joshua, are you keeping something from me? Didn't I notice something about Rose?"

"We're going to have a baby. Some time this winter." He was smiling broadly. "I was going to tell you at supper."

"Wonderful, Joshua. You both happy about that?"

"Thrilled. Having a baby with that woman will be the best thing I've ever done."

Joshua suddenly got a serious look on his face. "Jefferson, I need to tell you this, and not in front of Annalise. We may have a problem developing."

"You and Rose?"

"No. Certainly not. We're still on our honeymoon." He loosened the cinch on the pack horse. "The Osage tribe is on the warpath west of here. They're trying to drive off settlement in the Solomon River Valley."

"How close is that?"

"Right now, they're over a hundred miles away." Joshua walked over to Annalise's mare, wrestled with the saddle, and pulled it free. "But they're heading this way."

"How big a force?"

"We don't know numbers. It could be the whole nation, for the stir they're causing. According to reports, they're killing men and taking the women."

"You think that they'd attack Abilene?"

"Don't know. People here are getting nervous. It's happened before."

"You have a larger population, twice or three times more than they could muster, I'd guess."

"Right now, there is no plan. You can't be sure about gamblers, transients, and cattle buyers. How many of them would hang around if the threat increased? How many would take up arms? The effect right now is that drovers are reluctant to bring in herds from the west. At worst, the threat is to the cattle market this spring and summer."

"We saw evidence of a lot of cattle here now, as we rode in."

"Mostly from the south and eastern Kansas. Rose's father has already delivered a herd, but he's only 15 miles away. Most everyone gets here in mid to late summer, particularly the drives from Texas."

"Mr. Brody is west of here?"

"Yes. If the Osage came this far, they'd go after him. I'm worried. Rose is worried."

"Her father?"

"He's taking it in stride. There isn't much that bothers him."

"Is he prepared?"

"He has only ten full-time people, but several of them are good with guns. Two of them are experts on Indians. Two of them are Indians. He's got an arsenal of guns. It would take a good-sized party to get to him. He'd come in here long before that. But, Jeff, here's my point. You'll be out there."

"Joshua, what's your best guess about this?"

Joshua poured three feed bags. "The government will throw some cavalry out here. It depends on how far the Osage have come by then."

Jefferson led Storm into a stall.

"In any case, you're here. I don't know what you'd find if you came out here in July. Welcome to Kansas."

Whit Brody was keeping tabs on the Osage tribe. He sent Herkimer Grimes and Big to scout the area west of the ranch twice. Later, Herk went out for two weeks by himself. The report was that the Osage seemed to be losing interest in their raid. They were still coming east, but at a snail's pace. Their stock of hostages was hindering progress. They were meeting more resistance from mobilized settlers. They were achieving little, and in Herk's words, "There ain't that many of them."

"It's goin' to die out, Whit. They'll never come this far," Herk had predicted.

The old Indian fighter was right. The tribesmen returned to their lands three days short of Abilene.

By that time, the odyssey of the trip west by Annalise and Jefferson had been told. On their first night, the two regaled their hosts with their adventure. Jefferson glossed over the details, but the story was fleshed out by Annalise, who prompted the narrative toward Jefferson' s heroics. At the end, well toward morning, Joshua and Rose sat transfixed, overwhelmed.

"Wow, brother," Joshua commented.

"Annalise knows about her mother now, and we're here. Those are the two most important details."

Rose stood and walked to Annalise, hugging her. "You two can stay here as long as you want. I'm so sorry about your mother."

"We're grateful. If you don't get tired of us, we'll stay a few weeks," Jefferson said.

"And then what?" Joshua probed.

"We're not sure yet. Maybe farther west. Maybe back to Cincinnati to see the O'Neills."

"Listen, Jefferson. This beautiful lady is going to give me a child in November. You missed the wedding. I won't let you miss the birth."

"Joshua, that's half a year."

"Im pulling big brother rank on you. You will stay, at least that long. I'm afraid that I'm going to insist."

Jefferson looked at Annalise. "We'll need something to keep busy."

"We'll solve that. You'll be at the ranch. He needs another horse trainer and wrangler. You can stay here or out there. It's an hour to the ranch. We'd love to have Annalise stay here and work in the store. We're understaffed too, and the next four months are the most hectic. This upstairs is so big, we'll never get in each other's way. Regardless of living arrangements, you can still see each other three or four days a week, all day on weekends."

"Joshua, give us a day or two to decide. We've been improvising, making decisions on the run for weeks. Something this important will take consideration."

Before they turned in that night, Annalise offered her opinion. "I've lost my mother. Your brother is all you have left. I will stay with you in Abilene for as long as you want, years, if we decide to. You'll get to work with horses. Rose will be a sweet companion for me, Joshua too. Whatever you decide is fine with me."

****

Maribel O'Neill saw the postmark , and the notation at the top of the envelope, *Annalise, Kansas City, Missouri.* Kansas City? Clear across the state from St. Louis. She found something, Maribel thought. Posted 10 days ago.

Herman was in the yard, sitting in the afternoon sun and watching William work the flower bed. She rushed to his side with the envelope still unopened, and sat on the grass next to the chair. "Herman, a letter from Annalise!" Herman turned to her and smiled the crooked smile, interest in his eyes.

William turned around. "Your daughter? She find something?" William had been the gardener at the other house, a kind old man who cajoled the girls into helping him pull weeds. He remembered the terrible days when Missy disappeared, and he had seen the joy disappear from the little girl. Maribel still called on him to tend to the new yard, although it was too small to support much of a display, and William had stopped the serious pursuit of gardening years ago. He was much more just a friend helping out, rather than an employee. She paid him with several meals and a small stipend, and he came twice a week.

Maribel removed the letter and began reading aloud. The two men listened.

Dearest Maribel and Herman,

So much has happened. We found Mamma. She is buried in a slaves' graveyard north of St. Louis.

"Oh!" Maribel's hand went to her mouth.

A man named Corby Pitcock took her. Sadly she became his bedwarmer. I don't know details about her kidnapping, but I was told that several years ago, one of his ranch hands beat her to death. There is no question. I saw her grave, and talked to those who knew her.

Maribel paused. Tears filled her eyes. Herman lowered his head. After a few minutes, she continued.

Corby Pitcock knew that I would cause trouble because he still keeps slaves, so he locked me in an outbuilding. The ranch hand who killed mother was trying to hurt me when Jefferson broke in. He knocked out the ranch hand and shot Pitcock and another hand who tried to stop us. We rode away and feared that Pitcock's men would chase us. We were cut off from returning to St. Louis. Jefferson decided that I should ride west with him. He said that after a time, he will put me on a riverboat back to Ohio.

It took us almost seven days to get here, to Kansas City. We will go on to Abilene, Kansas in a few days.

This is what I must tell you now. Jefferson is the kindest, most considerate, most intelligent man I've ever known. He held me and comforted me the nights after I found out about mother. He makes me laugh. I think that I may have found my Prince Charming.

I questioned him about my mixed race. He told me that it doesn't matter.

I have lost my mother, and am now somewhat at peace with that. I suppose I always knew that there would be no happy ending.

I also found a wonderful companion and friend, possibly much more than a friend.

We will stay in Abilene for a while where I will live with his brother and his wife while he visits them. After that, I don't know. He has mentioned us settling somewhere together.

So, after all of these years, we know. Poor Mama. I will never get past the anger and the injustice, but you two gave me such a wonderful life. I owe so much to you.

I wanted you to know these things. I pray that I will see you soon.

With deep affection,

Annalise.

Maribel folded the letter and put it in her lap. She closed her eyes.

"Thank you, God. Thank you."

****

The attendance at the House of Worship increased each Sunday. The congregants filled three-fourths of the seats on a bad weather day, and fairly filled the room in the sunshine. Twice a month, weather permitting, a contingent from the Brody Ranch attended, always minus Herk, Big, and Simeon, who stayed behind "to mind the place," notwithstanding their expressed aversions to supplication and worship. Bird and Charlie Fox also opted out, cautious about what kind of reception they'd receive in a "white man's church."

The Brody group then retired to the Chase store for a Sunday dinner prepared by Rose, Annalise, and Catharine before retiring back to the spread.

Jack Bertrand looked forward to Sunday mornings, but not for holy direction. He studied the pretty red-haired lady, the inn-keeper, Catharine, a war widow. She had occasionally accompanied Rose and Annalise on visits to the ranch, where he had the opportunity to speak to her twice, although those conversations had consisted only of "Pleased to meet you, Ma'am," and "Beautiful morning, Ma'am." Hardly the stuff of incisive interaction.

Jack was not a naivete when it came to women. He had experienced love of different types when he was a teen-ager, before he came to his Aunt Margaret's. Too, he had made good use of his annual "vacations" to St. Louis or Kansas City, cultivating friendships with several ladies of the night, and also with some respectable store clerks and such. This creature, Catharine, seemed unattainable, however, and managing any protracted conversation was impossible on Sundays, crowded and hectic as they were.

Another strong interest in the opposite sex occurred secretly at those services. Minnie, Catharine's housekeeper, was fascinated by the large black man, Lige, who attended with the Brody group. One morning she had passed him in the aisle, and smiled as openly as she could. He had averted his eyes.

The two instances of unrequited love were neither noticed nor suspected by the others.

Jonah Brooks, fond of all of his flock, particularly the rancher Brody, always noticed the three ladies in the back pew, Myra, Clara, and Phoebe, from across the railroad tracks. They were faithful attendees, and he saw that the sad young Myra sang the hymns with volume and gusto.

Within weeks of that observation, Jonah and Bear Woman organized a choir, or rather, recruited it. It consisted of Myra; Catharine Chase; Mr. Carver, the baker; and Mr. and Mrs.Beamish—he was a barber in Abilene. A prudish type, Mrs. Powers, with obvious musical talent, declined when she discovered that Myra, the prostitute, would be involved. Some said that Dr. Hank Rosbottom could play several musical instruments and sing too, but he also declined to participate.

The five, bolstered by the trilling soprano of Bear Woman, were soon a weekly feature of the services. Myra gradually became somewhat accepted by the church membership, although some in the congregation looked away during the paeans. One morning the group received a loud ovation. Jonah himself disregarded the sacrilege by joining in on the applause.

Jack Bertrand had an unobstructed view of Catharine Chase on the choir stage.

A relationship of a different ilk developed more along the lines of an uneasy truce. For almost two years, since she had treated his infected arm, and attacked him with unfettered wrath, Bird and Herkimer had kept their distances from each other. The sum totals of their communication had been silent nods. Over time a grudging respect had developed. She had to admit that he was a tireless worker, often completing a load of tasks and then helping in other areas. Nor had he demonstrated the surliness and apparent evil that she had inferred since his arrival. He was even trying to overcome what she termed "attitude" by occasionally showing up for meals in the kitchen. He had overstayed one evening to help Caroline with the clean-up, to the astonishment of the other hands. Caroline had interpreted that as maybe a developing interest in her, which was dispelled by subsequent indifference.

Herk had become aware that the ranch was Bird's life. She put in long hours, the first to rise in the morning, the last to adjourn to her cabin at night. She didn't make mistakes. She was complimentary toward her most diligent employees, and always rolled up her sleeves to assist in some task that was stuttered or delayed. He often wondered what she'd look like in a dress, cleaned up. Her life had created lines on her face and a sometimes sour demeanor, but in a rugged sort of way, she was attractive.

One Sunday morning in July, when most of the ranch personnel had left for church, Bird was cooking a large breakfast for Charlie Fox, the only time she had to do housekeeping activities. She glanced down the hill to the shack, and there was Herk, sitting in front busying himself with a knife and a stick, carving, but more than anything, just sitting and looking into the distance.

On a whim, she said to Charlie, "I'm going to make a plate for Mr. Grimes. Will you take it to him?"

"Are you sure, Mother?"

"Of course. I know that he hasn't eaten today. We've got plenty."

"What about Simeon? He's probably hungry too. And Big?"

"Saw them ride out an hour ago, going fishing."

Charlie balanced two plates and a coffee cup in his arms and started down the hill.

"Mr. Grimes, my mother thought you might like some breakfast."

Herk looked at the boy warily, and took the plates, setting them next to his chair. "You sure they're not poison, boy?" A smirk played across his face.

"No, Mr. Grimes, it's good food."

"Much obliged," Herk said as he raised the cup of coffee.

Bird watched the exchange from her window, saw Charlie coming back, and then saw the gunfighter, looking at her window, tip his hat. He knew that she was watching him. Later, she found the plates and the cup on her front porch, clean. Laid across them was a single wildflower.

****

July 11 of 1868 broke sunny and hot, just as Whit had hoped. Good weather was crucial; this couldn't be rescheduled. It depended on too many people.

The first mass baptism for the faithful of the House of Worship would occur at 2 pm. Over twenty people, including fifteen of his own, would commit to the teachings of the Reverend Jonah Brooks in the waters of the Solomon River. Whit was a nervous host, not because of the rite, but because of the event that would follow it, food, fellowship, and music, if Doc Rosbottom showed up. He had walked the eastern bank of the Solomon with Jonah Brooks and located a large pool, perhaps three feet deep, eddying gently into a solid bank. Even with a muddy, unstable bottom, the river, at summer depth, would play its part.

Whit was not a pious type. In fact, he understood that he and several other celebrants –Joshua, Jefferson, Jack, Catharine, probably Caroline, and some from Abilene --would participate largely out of deference to Reverend Brooks, and to the wishes of the more scriptural of the other participants. Margaret was excited; that was enough for him to care.

At two o'clock the entire group walked animatedly to the appointed spot, a sun-dappled half-mile from the ranch house.. Doc Rosbottom had showed up in the company of a fiddle, a banjo, and a mandolin. The Abilene gathering led by the wagon of Brooks, which contained Cleetus, Bear Woman, and Myra, arrived shortly after, sixty strong.

One by one, the baptismal initiates waded in to Jonah, attended by Cleetus and Bear Woman. Margaret was first, followed by Rose, Joshua, and Whit. After each ceremony, shouts of "Congratulations!" and a few "Hallelujahs!" were heard. Jefferson took the hand of Annalise and led her in to the ritual pool, standing nearby until she emerged, dark hair plastered down her back, a beatific smile on her face. Then he was eased back into the water until Jonah pronounced the benediction.

Catharine carried Jeremiah to the spot, and just before submersion, the young boy asked his mother, "Am I going to drown?' Lige, Noah, Elon, Jack, Caroline, Minnie, and surprisingly, Doc Rosbottom were next. Twelve members of the congregation followed. Last, the waiflike figure of Myra the prostitute waded to the Reverend. When she surfaced, she was crying.

Jack watched Catharine at the party that followed. It seemed that she danced every dance. He would build courage and walk toward her before each song, and she would be intercepted by some gentleman or another from the congregation.

Doc and Simeon played without breaks for over two hours until Whit recued them.

"Lots of food here. Let's work on that for a while and give these men a break." Then he whispered to Doc, "I've got some drinks that might interest you. Follow me." He led Doc into the front room, and went to the kitchen for a bottle of unopened whiskey and two glasses. He walked back to rejoin Hank. "I hid this. Didn't want to upset the Reverend, so I…" He stopped. Doc was standing in front of the fireplace, his head bowed, his shoulders shaking in strong emotion.

"Doc, what is it?"

"This painting. Where did you get it?" He pulled a handkerchief from his back pocket and blew his nose into it.

He was pointing to a large framed picture above the mantel, a pleasant view of a cabin on the banks of a river, backlit by a bright sun, the reflection sparkling on dark green foliage. At its bottom right was a signature, *A. Chiasson.*

"I took Margaret and Rose to New Orleans a few years back. Saw this picture in an art store. Had to have it."

"The artist, Angeline. She was my wife."

"Doc…" He didn't know what to say. "Your wife? Chiasson?"

"Her maiden name. We were married fifteen years. She passed away, in the bayou."

"Doc, it's beautiful. She was a great artist. I'm sorry."

"I'm fine. You honor her by hanging it in this wonderful house." He turned away.

"Can you tell me about her?" Whit poured two small glasses half full. Doc downed his in one long swallow.

"Gentle. Caring. An angel. My whole life. I still think about her first thing in the morning, last thing at night. When she passed on, the music did too. I haven't played much for a lot of years."

"Well, Doc. You should. I don't know the story, but you could celebrate your life together with your music. Her paintings live on. Your music should too." He refilled Rosbottom's glass.

"I had to think long and hard about playing today. I did it for you, and for the Reverend."

"It's a great gift, Doc. I'm grateful. Thank you." He hugged the old doctor awkwardly around his shoulders.

When the music resumed, Hank Rosbottom sang and played a solo, a moving song that he introduced as "My Cher, Angeline." The entire group of revelers stopped what they were doing to listen. His voice broke several times. At the end, led by Whit, the crowd applauded long and loud.

The last of the Abilene crowd left just before dark, counting on a half-moon to light their ways back. In the glow of candles and torches, Whit surveyed the aftermath. Margaret stepped onto the porch. "We'll clean up tomorrow, Maggie. Won't be going in to church. We had enough saving and carrying on today."

"Caroline's already in bed. Most everyone else too, I'd guess."

"You know, Maggie, this worked because of you and Caroline."

"And Rose and Annalise and Catharine and Bird."

"Let's sit. I had a thought a while ago. Do you think we ought to get some help for Caroline? She's not getting any younger. She's still cooking twelve large meals a week, helping you with the house, helping Simeon in the garden. Doing laundry every week for the hands. It's gotta be wearing her down?"

"You're right. We can we do, hire another cook?"

"No. The whole ranch would complain if she's not cooking. I'd say hire someone who can sew and do laundry, I suppose."

"Will you ask in town?"

"Nope. I've got an idea. That poor little girl, Myra. It seems as if she's trying to shed her life of sin. I think we could help her out. Get her out of the town. Improve her life."

Of course, Margaret thought. Myra. My husband is going to save another soul. "That's an inspired thought, Whit."

"Are you kidding me, Maggie?"

"Does one kid a saint?"

He laughed. "Herk and Big missed the fun again."

"Whit, that isn't who they are. They don't have the make-up for religion."

"Or for fun, it seems."

"It's not a problem, Whit. Let's go to bed."

****

"Problem. Coupla' hunnerd longhorns grazing our pastures, over east."

Whit stood and wiped the perspiration from his forehead. Elon paused midway through a swing. Whit dropped the horse's front leg, the horseshoe dropping heavily to the ground. Elon had no target for his nail.

"Longhorns? How the hell did they get there, Big?"

"Figure a herd was camped west of town, waitin' for buyers. Grazed out the land. Came to our land cause the pastures looked better. Fence is down."

"They came right through it?"

"Looks like someone cut it intentional. Most of the posts are still in the ground."

"Any of our cattle grazing with them?"

"A few. Tried to run off the longhorns. Too many. Herkimer's still out there tryin'."

"Where are they exactly?"

"North of our trail in. South of the line shack."

Whit's thought was not about losing a grazing area. Disease. Texas fever. The insidious plague that longhorns were suspected of spreading. That was a huge concern.

"Jack," he yelled toward the corral. "Come here!" He grabbed a cloth and wiped his hands. "Elon, smithing's done for today. Go find everyone. Lige is in the cornfield. Bring them here pronto!"

Not good at all. Several longhorn herds had been turned back to Texas. It was July and the disease had already claimed hundreds of northern cattle as the longhorns began arriving from Texas for sale.

Whit hurried to the house, then called back toward Elon. "Have everybody saddle up. Noah's going to need another horse; that was his we were shoeing."

Within minutes, he exited the house wearing a holstered pistol, and carrying a rifle. Big had already transmitted the news to the other hands. "Listen folks. I don't know what we'll be getting into, but you should all be armed," Whit instructed.

"You expecting trouble?" Bird asked.

"Big thinks the fence was cut. You see any brand, Big?"

"An "S" on its side."

Jefferson eased Storm along in the middle of the pack for several miles. It was Big's show. He and Herk had been on patrol when the spotted the invading herd. Jefferson heard the rancher exclaim "Dammit!" as they rode down a coulee toward a long pasture field. Longhorns were everywhere. Herk was riding along the edge, funneling strays back to the main body. He rode up to Whit. "Blasted Texas cattle. Can't budge them. They must be starved."

"What do you think, Herk? Stampede them?"

"That's our best bet. Can't get too close, if they're carrying ticks. The busted fence is up that way." He pointed east. The sun was nearing noon. "Keep moving. There may be ticks on the ground. They'll go after horses too."

"Spread out. When we're in position, we'll fire some shots to get them moving. We'll drive them back through the fence," Whit ordered.

"Uncle Whit, we drive them through the fence and leave, they'll just come back. "

"You're right. We've got to herd them back to wherever the drovers are camped. If the fence is cut, we'll have a few words with them. Herk, I'm going to need you in front of them, tracking them back to camp."

Herk rode on ahead.

As they rode to positions, Whit caught up to Jefferson and slowed. "You ever do anything like this?"

"I'll be fine, Mr. Brody."

"Yes, I knew you would be."

Whit then yelled ahead, "Bird, take Charlie and Elon. Cut out our cattle. Don't drive them too far. They may be infected." The foreman and her charges began to separate the integrated Brody cows and moved them in the other direction.

Within ten minutes, the invading herd was moving at a brisk pace toward the fence line. Whit surveyed the damaged fence as the longhorns rumbled through. To himself, he muttered, "It's been cut. Three places. Wires are the same length. Fence posts are still upright."

Herk led the group in a northeasterly direction as they cleared the fence, and they began to pass clusters of other longhorns. Herk pointed to two outriders who had spotted the movement and ridden away north. "Look at them skedaddle. I'd say they're guilty," Whit called to Jack.

Lige and Noah began to collect the small herds they passed. Far in the distance some thirty minutes later, Whit saw a few scattered tents and what was probably a chuckwagon. "They ain't slowin' down," Big shouted. Up ahead the first of the several hundred longhorns ran through several tents before they started milling.

A cowboy intercepted Whit's group as Herk circled back. "What the hell you doin'? Driving our herd through our camp?"

Whit rode up to him. "We're bringing them home. You the boss?"

"Hell no. That'd be Mr. Simpkins, from El Paso. He ain't gonna like this." The cowboy was so agitated that his horse picked it up and began to prance in circles.

"Where would I find him?"

Big saw a gang of Texas cowboys riding hard, bearing down on them from the area of the tents. He counted eleven. Some had already drawn pistols.

"Figger he's comin' out now. You men are in big trouble."

"Who's in charge here?" a middle-aged man with a crooked nose demanded, as his riders slowed in an angry semi-circle.

Jefferson edged Storm around them, and wedged in next to a man waving a gun. Herk moved his horse slowly around to the flank. Big rode up to the group and stopped.

"Holster your guns. We've got a major complaint with you people," Whit said calmly. "I'm Whit Brody. My ranch is a few miles that direction."

The leader's face relaxed. "Brody? I've heard of you. Cattle buyers think you're God." He turned in the saddle. "Put them guns away, men." He turned back to Whit. "I'm Simpkins of the Lazy S, from Texas."

"Mr. Simpkins, your cattle were on our land grazing. Our fence was cut. What do you know about that?"

The Texan's smile disappeared. "You crazy? We didn't cut no fences. You drove our cattle right into our camp! You another sonuvabitch who don't like us bringin' our longhorns to Abilene?"

"If you're telling me the truth, I'd suggest that you talk to your outriders, Mr. Simpkins. Either something is going on that you don't know about, or you're a liar… in which case we've got a big problem." Herk's gun was out. Big's rifle pointed at Simpkins. Noah's gun was unholstered too. "Easy, men," Whit called out. "Nobody fire. We don't want a shoot out."

"You're rustlers and bushwhackers," Simpkins snorted.

"I'd suggest that you listen to me, Mr. Simpkins. If your men show firearms, a lot of you won't be returning to Texas."

"You bluffin'?" He saw the look on Herk's face. "Lissen, Brody. What the hell do you want? You ain't none too hospitable."

"A herd of cattle known to carry disease was turned loose on my ranch, mingled with my herd. And they were driven through a cut fence."

"Far as I know, you are fixin' to roust us."

"We don't care about your longhorns. Or you."

"Can't tell longhorns where to graze," Simpkins backed off. "Maybe they trampled the damn fence. If'n they did, I'd tell you I'm sorry."

Simpkins realized that the rancher was not only angry, but he was also persistent. He hesitated. "Smokey, who was ridin' out yestidday?"

"That'd be Waco and them Mexicans, Mr. Simpkins. "

"They still out there?"

"The Mexs are. Waco, he's right behind you."

Simpkins turned his horse to face a weathered man, the cowboy who had first challenged Whit. "Waco, you cut that fence? If'n you did, you'd best own up to it."

"Mr. Simpkins, them cows grazed out the meadow. Been here 'most a week. Them buyers ain't showed up yet. Had to get the longhorns to good grass, the other side of the fence. Seen water over there too. Didn't see no other cows. Moved them over a coupla days ago. Didn't mean no harm."

"No harm! You damn idiot. We don't do things that way. Oughta shoot you right here."

"Figgered we'd be gone in three days. Wouldn't make no difference."

"Quiet! Jes' be quiet! " He turned back to Whit. "Mr. Brody, it 'pears we did cut your fence. Powerful sorry. We be over there tomorrow to fix it. We'll find materials in Abilene."

"Not necessary," Whit answered. "We'll have it mended before noon. Make sure no more of your longhorns get through. Any of your cattle sick?

"No. You can't tell with them longhorns though. I hope not. They'se good animals, Mr. Brody. Don't deserve no bad reputation."

"We've had a couple of infected herds from south Texas come through. Good luck to you, sir. Have a good sale." Whit turned his horse and rode away.

As the Brody group topped a rise obscuring the Texans, Jack rode up next to his uncle. "Did you believe him?"

"Some men are good liars, Jack. I find it hard to believe that his herd was starving, and he didn't know it. He gave the order to cut the fence, in my opinion. Desperate man, I'd guess."

Whit led the men through the hole in the fence and stopped. The others circled around.

"What are the chances that we've got ticks now?"

"Several things, Mr. Brody," Herk offered. "The first is that not all longhorns are infected. Most of that is from south Texas. Second, taking a chance that they're not is risky. We could lose a lot of cows."

"Jefferson, you went to animal school. What do you know about ticks?"

"The first one on a host feeds on its blood. That infects the host. Then the tick drops its progeny on the ground. They begin to wait for another host. They're already carriers."

"How long will they survive without finding a host?"

"A couple of months, or until the first hard freeze."

"So, if they're here, they'll be a problem until some time in October?"

Jefferson nodded gravely.

"Well, you know what we have to do," Herk said. It was not a question.

"We've got to destroy the cows that grazed with the longhorns. And we've got to keep the rest of the herd away from the eastern side…for three months," Whit said.

"That's a long time, Uncle Whit. After we kill the cattle, we'd have to get rid of the ticks, if they're here. Do you think we're overreacting?"

Whit's eyes narrowed. "Fire. Will fire work, Jefferson?"

"If we scorch the area thoroughly, it can't hurt. It will get rid of most of the ticks, and honestly, there wouldn't be that many anyway. The problems start if they find hosts and start to multiply. Burning off the grass will keep the cattle away, because there'll be nothing to feed on."

"It'll burn all of the carcasses too," Big added.

"What about the areas that are already grazed down, Herk?" Jack asked.

"Ain't many areas down to bare earth. Grass is long now. Fire will keep goin'."

Whit was thinking aloud. "Black powder. That will get the fire started. Joshua carries that at the store. There are some trees out there to keep the fire going. It's pretty dry now."

"Every pioneer in the middle states used controlled fires to clear land, and to burn out stumps," Jefferson offered. "If we start it southwest of the area, the wind will blow it where we want it."

"Yeah. And the area isn't that large anyway. Couple of square miles," Jack offered.

Directly, Bird, Charlie Fox, and Elon joined the group. "What's happened?" Bird asked.

"We're going to shoot the cows you've been herding, and set fire to that field. We may have disease out there."

"Shoot the herd?"

"How many did you round up?"

"Fifty or so. Most of the herd is in the north fields."

"So we lose fifty head and some grazing area. We'll survive this. It's the safest course."

Texas fever, sometimes called red water fever, was a fear of all ranchers, except those who raised longhorn cattle. The strain most disruptive to cattlemen seemed to be spread exclusively by the longhorns taken to stockyards from Texas. The longhorns had developed an immunity, but other breeds, it was devastating, killing over 90 percent of those cattle afflicted. The deaths were devastating as they occurred, ending in severe dissolution and pain so excruciating that dying cattle bawled and screamed before they succumbed.

By the 1850's stockyards in several states had banned Texas livestock. When Abilene opened its stockyards, longhorns were welcomed, and drovers using the Chisholm Trail moved cattle by the thousands to Kansas.

The disease persisted. At certain points in Indian Territory, grazing lands were leased by the tribes to white cattlemen. Lands shared by different breeds produced epic incidents of the disease. Early theories suggested that longhorns, with their voracious appetites, ate poisonous plants as part of their diets. If spores from their wastes were inhaled or eaten by other cattle, death was imminent.

By the early 1860's, another thought gained credibility. The disease was spread by an agent: ticks. All it took to infect a cow was proximity to infected or immune cattle. Sharing common grazing lands was a causative factor.

After the tick had infected the host, the disease progressed quickly. Within days, emaciation became apparent, and then the final stages would be hours away.

Whit watched his field burn away. His hands had surrounded the fifty victims the day before, and shot each cow, regardless of apparent health or age. The procedure was difficult. The riders' horses had balked and reared at the gunshots. The small herd had briefly stampeded, and the slaughter was accomplished on the move. The effect was ghastly. Toward the end, the last victims seemed to sense the inevitable. Jefferson found himself sighting his shots between brown eyes seemingly begging for pity. The ride back to the ranch was eerily quiet. Excluded from the execution, Lige, Bird, Charlie, and Elon kept the main herd away from the scene. Groups would attend to them throughout the night in four-hour shifts.

Controlling the fire was little challenge. The summer wind fanned the flames, and the fire swirled in a northeasternly direction. The tall, dry prairie grass was a fuel which advanced the flames quickly, and they burned evenly and hot.

Losing the grazing area wasn't a catastrophe. In the spring of 1869, Whit knew, new sprigs of grass would appear, fed by the rich soil which would benefit from the nutrition of ashes. The loss of cattle was minor. Less than 2% of his herd was destroyed. But this was a step backward; he wasn't used to those. Since the mammoth tornado which had destroyed both of his parents and the cotton farm so many years ago, his life had been one of prudent decisions and giant leaps forward.

What bothered him most was not the Texas cattlemen who had perpetrated the near tragedy. They were just like him, trying to achieve maximum results, striving to stay on top of the continuum. Even the one named Waco, who had stupidly crossed the barriers of decorum, was trying to assure success for his people.

No, it was the system that rankled him. It ignored danger and calamity for financial gain. Longhorns were always a potential disaster, yet they were the centerpiece of the Abilene economy. He would address that soon, in some way.

He gathered his hands on the northern side of the burn as the fire ebbed.

"We lost some fenceposts, but actually you folks made this happen the right way. We may never know if there were ticks in there, but we guaranteed that there aren't many now. You think the fire worked, Jefferson?"

"I'd say it was a good effort. Burning the grass off was the important part. The cattle won't be attracted over here. Any ticks we missed won't find hosts before winter."

"Let's head back. We'll mend the fences in a couple of days. You're all off tonight and tomorrow. Go fishing. Take a long nap. Thank you all. Better check your horses for ticks."

Annalise, Jefferson thought. I'm going to Abilene.

****

Eight riders stopped at the edge of the southern Illinois woods and studied the large farmhouse several hundred feet ahead. The night was quiet, and sinister in its moonless aspect. They would need the torches for several reasons.

"Light in the downstairs window. They's still up," one of the riders remarked.

"Don't see no dogs," another said.

"Oscar, it's so blamed dark. Could be a whole pack of them. We'd never know."

"Don't hear none, nohow."

The large man snorted. "Should be four people in there. The two whelps should be abed, I'm thinkin'."

"There be money in there too?"

"Man's name is Carey. Big hero. An officer, they say. 'Member, we ain't jist scarin' him. Folks say he's plenty rich, a farmer. Should be a passel of greenbacks in there somewheres."

"Let's get at it," another man said.

"Light them torches. Pull on them hoods."

The eight trotted up to the house and scattered at the front porch. They dismounted and charged to the front door. Unlocked. Unbolted. They rushed inside, screeching and howling. The farmer and his wife were sitting at a table near the fireplace. He instantly knew the truth. So did she. "Oh, no. No!" she sobbed.

The leader of the raiders walked to the farmer, who stood with his arms protectively around his wife, a pleasant-faced, buxom woman. The farmer tried a bluff. "You men get on out of here. My men will hear the commotion!"

The large man slapped him hard across his cheek with the military gloves he carried in his hand. "Ain't no workers that stay out here. Already checked that." He stood face-to-face with the farmer. "Lieutenant Carey, I charge you with the murders of women and children, and with crimes agin soldiers of the Confederate States of America."

The man's dark hood, a grotesque, poorly-stitched cloth with two large eyeholes and a breathing hole, flapped when he talked. None of the other raiders had spoken yet.

Desperate, the farmer continued his defiance. "The war's been over for almost three years. There is no reason to do this."

Two of the hooded men grabbed his arms from behind. "Shut your damn mouth!" the large man shouted, and slapped him in the face again. The wife suppressed a scream, a muffled sound that sounded as a squeal. "Wal, looky here. The man done hung his officer's saber over his fireplace. Newton, you be getting' it down." Two sobbing youngsters were pushed into the room, a boy who appeared to be not yet ten, and a frail-looking girl, probably two years older.

"Ripe little thing, aincha?" the man named Oscar said to the girl, as she scrambled to her mother's side.

"Leave them alone. Your argument's with me," the farmer pleaded.

"Now, dammit, Lieutenant Carey, you're getting me riled here. I'll tell you what. We be fair to soldiers. We gonna kill you outside. Ain't no man should be killed in his home," the large man said.

"I'm not a lieutenant anymore. I did what I had to do in the war, like you did. I'm just a family man, a farmer."

"Yeah. A man what hangs his saber that he killed innocent folks with, over his fireplace. Take them all outside."

In the front yard the large man got on his horse, assuming a theatrical position of authority. Oscar slammed the hilt of the saber against the farmer's head, knocking him to the ground. The farmer sprawled, and then rose to his knees.

"Any last words, Lieutenant?"

Silence.

"Dexter, you think this man is sorry? Make him say he's sorry."

"You sorry, Lieutenant?" Dexter howled. Carey raised his head, clearly unsure of a response that would save his family.

"Apologize, you bastard," Dexter demanded, unholstering his pistol and pressing the barrel into the cheek of the farmer. Then he pulled the pistol back, and slammed it into Carey's forehead. The farmer groaned and pitched forward from his knees.

"Didn't hear nothin' yet, Dexter. Bring over his missus."

"No! No! I'm sorry ! I'm sorry!"

"Sorry for what? Bein' a Republican? Sorry for gloatin' over the war? Sorry for settin' the darkies free? Ain't said nuthin' yet," Oscar growled.

"You was an officer in the Illinois infantry. You got plenty to be sorry about," the mounted man interrupted.

"It was a bad time for all of us," Carey said.

"You killed Southern gentlemen!" Oscar kicked him. The farmer rolled onto his back in agony.

"You see, Lieutenant Carey, the war ain't over." The man on horseback began to lecture. He was leaning forward on his saddle horn. "None of us here surrendered. You didn't win nuthin'!"

The farmer tried to stand again. He would do anything, say anything to save his family. Courage was folly. He glanced toward the porch, seen dimly through blood running from his forehead, and the flickering torch light. A hooded man held his wife from behind, obviously enjoying her struggles. His daughter was pressed against the front door, small and frightened, where another hooded man was groping her.

"Hey, boy ! You a man too? Git out here and lay next to your father," the mounted man called.

"Please, sir. No," Carey whispered.

The boy hesitated, then walked to the spot where his father stood, shoulders slumped.

"Both of you'uns lay on down."

Carey obeyed, but he had a sudden awareness that none of his family would survive this. He suddenly stood and turned toward Oscar. "See you in hell," Oscar crowed, and buried the saber in Carey's chest. The wife screamed. The daughter was already on her back on the porch, with a raider roughly tearing at her underclothes.

"You men got 30 minutes to do whatever you want to the women, then kill 'em. Take the boy's head off with the saber. Newton, you and Slick go inside and find the money. Take anything you want. We're burnin' everything in 30 minutes."

"Aw, Bravo, I was wantin' some of that farmer's wife," Newton said.

"Next time, Newton. Next time. There's plenty of bluecoats and wimmin between here and Kansas."

****

Such was their level of propriety, and of gratitude, that Jefferson and Annalise didn't share a bedroom on the weekends that she visited the ranch. In an awkward conversation, Whit gave his permission, even supported "intimate relations." Jefferson declined, explaining that as an unmarried couple, they would be taking advantage of the Brody hospitality. Annalise repeated that decision to Rose. "Someday we'll be together. We're just grateful that your parents let us spend time together out there." Rose suspected that the two were lovers, probably lusty and affectionate partners. She had witnessed adoring looks and intimate conversations between them. They were certainly getting together somewhere, somehow. It was none of her business.

Whit was fond of the new couple, telling Margaret, "I've only seen one other fella in my life that compares to Jefferson. That would be his brother. Amazing boys, those two. Annalise is all woman. Smart as a whip, so beautiful. Somebody raised her right, you know?"

"Yes, Whit. Reminds me of our daughter, don't you think?"

That was perceptive. In four months, the two girls had become good friends, a pairing that seemed to energize both. Annalise, mindful of the need for Joshua and Rose to expand their own relationship, vacated her second story bedroom in the store to spend two nights a week as Catharine's guest at the boarding house, initiating another close friendship. In effect, all three were filling voids in each other's lives, adding virtual sisters and confidantes. Jefferson noticed that Annalise was animated and felicitous, having cast off the pall and suspicious nature that had dominated her personality when they had first met. He credited Rose and the Brodys as the causes, forgetting that he was the real architect.

Joshua had recently added another dimension to Annalise's life.

"I've got an idea. Rose agrees. We're going to convert part of the store to a library."

"Joshua, a library?"

"Abilene could use some culture. We'll clear out the west wall, put in shelves, buy some books, ask for donations. Someone who understands literature and loves reading could make it work."

"Who would that be?"

"You."

"A librarian? Of course I'd love that. But there is work to be done in the store."

"Annalise, there won't be a run on the books. The three of us can still take care of the business. You could pay attention to the library too. Rose will help with that."

"We'll be selling books?"

"Some, but I envision it as a place where people can borrow books to read, and then bring them back. That won't cost them anything."

By late September, the store owned over 300 volumes, half of which were loaned out at any given time. Joshua added to the ambiance, adding chairs to an area inside the arc of the shelves to create a reading space. Weasel, the unpredictable little town dosser, brought in stacks of books several days a week, basking in Annalise's enthusiasm for his contributions."

"I hope he's not stealing them," Rose commented.

"Well, I think it's safe to say that they're not from his personal library," Joshua said.

"Bless his heart. He says that he's going door to door," Annalise offered.

"We just don't know if those doors are open or locked," Joshua laughed.

Unpacking one box, Annalise picked up a thin, worn book. "Rose, look at this." She held the book up, the title page facing Rose: *Herkimer Grimes, Rider of the Texas Plains.*

"Herkimer Grimes. Our Herkimer Grimes?"

"I heard my father talking about those books. There is an entire series about Mr. Grimes. Who wrote it?"

"It's on the spine. Robert Gerdon."

The two looked at the primitive artwork on the cover, a drawn picture of a heavily-muscled Texas Ranger with two pistols exploding from his hands, clean-shaven, a large hat perched on the back of his head.

"It's obvious that the artist never met the man," Annalise commented.

"According to my father, neither did the author. He wrote the entire series from New York."

A week earlier, a thin man had stumbled off of an incoming stagecoach two blocks away. He had pulled back a tan duster and began to brush off the bottom of rumpled, pin-striped trousers while he waited for his large valise to be unloaded from the coach top.

Robert Gerdon was certain that Herkimer Grimes was nearby somewhere, no farther than a few miles from where he stood. Too many of his sources had repeated the same information, that the gunfighter was in eastern Kansas, possibly around Topeka. The Topeka man he had questioned told him, "No, he's not around here, or I'd know about it. If I were you, I'd try Abilene."

Gerdon needed to find him. In a creative morass, he had not produced a Herkimer Grimes novel for some time. He had pitched the idea of a Grimes biography, authentic and accurate, to a hesitant publisher Sawyer, and had received a go-ahead, complete with funds to finance his search.

He picked up the valise, and walked into the small stagecoach office. "Excuse me," he approached the man behind the counter, "I'm looking for cattle ranches around here. I thought that I'd do some buying on site. Where would you suggest I start?"

The employee eyed the sincere-looking man, overdressed in the humidity of September. "If'n I was you, I'd head out to the Brody place, a click to the west. Biggest ranch for miles. Prime cattle. Fine horses."

"Thank you. And where can I look for lodging?"

"Drover's Cottage, out to the edge of town thataway. Big hotel. Kinda' noisy. Usually not full this time of year. Usually full all summer though."

"How about boarding houses?"

The man brightened. "Several. Real good one is runned by a lady named Chase. Pretty lady. Mighty easy on the eyes, if'n you know what I mean. Think she may be kin to Brody. Not sure of that. I'd surely try that place. Mizz Chase, she sings in the church choir. Hear there's good food there for boarders."

Gerdon didn't know it at the time, but he had two critical pieces of information. The employee was rambling, talking about what a fine church the Reverend Something ran. Gerdon stood politely, not really listening, but continuing to nod. If Grimes was tending cattle again as he had done years before in Nebraska, the Brody ranch was a logical place to begin his search. So now he had a possible location, and also a boarding house proprietor who knew the ranch owner well. Not much to go on, but at least it was a start.

"Have to tell you Mister, most of the ranches, they done been here with their cows. You here at a bad time. Brody may not have much stock left."

"That's fine. I'm doing research for the future."

"What's your name, mister?"

"Robert. Robert Sawyer…Gillespie, from…Chicago."

****

Besides being an inveterate shoplifter, expert housebreaker, and full-time irritant, Weasel was nosy and malodorous, and therefore collected few advocates among the citizens of Abilene. He was either the brunt of harassment, or ostracized to the point of being ignored or avoided by all except the spiritual leaders of the House of Worship although—truth be told—they counted their hymnals, sconces, firewood, chairs and benches after he had attended services, and by the owners and their friends at the Chase store. He shadowed Annalise almost daily, wheezing and making guttural noises in his throat. She felt no real threat, and there was none. He was proud to tell anyone that "Jozwah Chase is my friend," and he was in awe of "Jeffson, the brudder of Jozwah." Rose, of course, was held in his highest regard.

Somebody told the story of how Weasel had stopped a falling timber with his head in a forgotten mine years ago in a forgotten ore field. "Is there anywhere we can pen him up," an uncharitable resident had once suggested. Another had answered, "That wouldn't be fair to the pigs."

An attempt to guess his age would have been no more than a stab at numbers. He was wizened enough to be in his sixties, or he could have been a well-worn forty-something. Nobody remembered when he had come to Abilene, whether he had family, nor how or where he slept, although those conditions caused a plenitude of ribald or ungenerous opinions. Some likened him to a ghost, or worse, considered him an unconsecrated hex.

Were it not for Joshua, the little man would have been wearing frayed and septic clothing. Joshua gave him samples from the articles of men's apparel in the store, and Weasel wore them until they were an embarrassment. Joshua also gave him lectures. "Weasel, you are a good man. It isn't good to take things that don't belong to you. Good men don't steal."

Weasel would listen, his lower lip quivering, and invariably answer, "I'm powerful sorry, Jozwah." Also invariably, he would soon sneak crackers or jerky or candy under his soiled coat and quickly exit the store.

One afternoon Joshua heard a commotion out on the street. Rose reported the source.

"Joshua, they're whipping Weasel. They're hurting him, honey. It's Uriah Cobb."

Cobb was a homesteader from the eastern edge of Abilene, a rotund red-faced man with a legendary temper. He was not a law-breaker; he was simply an unhappy man, sharing a homesteader plot with two other men.

Weasel was on his knees crawling frantically when Josh ran out of the store. There were three men surrounding him. One was cracking a whip, allowing each lash to hit flesh somewhere. Another man, laughing heartily, was kicking at him, directing him back toward the man with the whip. The third man was just watching, but laughing even harder than his friend. Weasel was sobbing, but making no sound.

Joshua grabbed the wrist of the whip wielder, and stopped his arm.

"Can't say much for your courage, Mister Cobb. What are you doing?"

"None of your damn business," the man said, and jerked to free his arm. Josh had it too tightly.

"Yes, it is my business. Three of you. One man unable to defend himself. It is my business. Drop this whip and get out of here."

"This old bastard was fixin' to steal my horse," the man snapped over his shoulder.

"Which horse is yours?"

"That 'un over there."

"Can't imagine anyone stealing that horse. You ever feed him, Mister Cobb?"

"Lissen, storekeeper, let go of my hand. Let's see what kind of man you really are."

A crowd had formed a semi-circle around them. Josh had tried to avoid this escalation in the encounter, but it had gone too far. He took his hand away. Inside, Rose grabbed the shotgun from behind the counter, and walked to the door.

"I'm gonna beat your ass, storekeep," Cobb snarled.

The man threw the first punch, a heavy blow that struck Joshua on the shoulder as he sidestepped. Off balance, he fended off the next swing with his forearm, stepped up, and swung his fist into the man's midsection. A loud "Uuumph!" belched from his mouth. He wrapped his arms around Joshua, holding him face to face, and spit in his face. Then, stepping back, he slapped Joshua over his ear.

Joshua threw three punches in a bit over a second, a straight jab to Cobb's chin, another blow to his belly, an uppercut to his jaw that rendered him unconscious even before he fell to the ground. The kicking man jumped on Joshua's back, and jerked his head back. "You're a dead man, storekeep!" he yelled. Joshua twisted and fell back, landing on the man. The kicker grunted and rolled away. Joshua lifted the man up by his collar, and raised his knee into the man's chin, disabling him. Peripherally, Joshua saw the third man reaching for a pistol in his belt.

From the doorway, came an assertive voice, "Fight's over! You pull out that gun, and I'll splatter you all over the street," Rose shouted.

The third man hesitated. He wasn't going to gunfight with a crazy pregnant woman. He shook his two fallen buddies, and soon they were groggily following him up the street.

Cobb yelled back as the three reached their horses. "You're gonna pay for this, Chase!"

Joshua turned to the crowd. "Why don't you all find something to do besides watching an old man get beat up?" The chastened crowd broke up and slinked away.

"Weasel, come on inside. We need a glass of water," Joshua said, helping him up.

He passed his wife in the doorway. "Honey. 'I'll splatter you all over the street?' I'm married to a wild woman."

His grin settled her, as it always did. "I couldn't let them mess up that handsome face," she replied. She laid the shotgun against the door jamb, and kissed him.

When Weasel left an hour later, the two noticed that a bag of flour was missing.

****

Robert Sawyer Gillespie, he couldn't be Gerdon again for a while, roused himself from a deep sleep after a short night, adjusted glasses over his swollen eyes, and picked up the notes, his plan, scribbled the night before. He stumbled upon rising, caught himself on the night table, and walked the notepad to the window and better light.

Buy a camera, get Sawyer's permission later…buy photography plates…check out book on photography at Chase's…no book, wait for Kansas City…buy book on birds and animals…memorize it…Catharine. If no, Rose…binoculars good…another book on food preparation…buy Western clothing…buy second-hand wagon…must buy two horses cheap.

Too many *"buys"* on the list, but it didn't matter. Sawyer had fronted him a small fortune, although he'd agreed to pay it all back when his book sold.

His plan had been born on Monday morning as he'd sat in the Chase store scanning a book. He had cultivated both Catharine and Rose in his short time in Abilene, revealing very little about himself, but being courteous to them, and as omnipresent at both the store and the boarding house as he could manage. He had simply said that he was seeking a small fortune and interest in a large variety of opportunities. After years of unreturned letters, he knew that Herkimer Grimes had no patience for him, and pursuing his objective would have to be accomplished in a circumspect manner. Thus, the new moniker, Gillespie.

The genesis of his plan had been Annalise's enthusiastic description of a singular experience from her weekend at the ranch. She had ridden to the north line shack with Jefferson, a getaway for the two, an odyssey of twelve intimate hours. As they rode over a hill between grazing cattle, Jefferson had slowed Storm and pointed to the sky. Soaring far above them, far from its native habitat, was a bald eagle.

"It was so majestic," she enthused to Joshua and Rose. Nearby, perusing a book was Gerdon/Gillespie. "It was almost a reverent moment. It was gliding effortlessly, framed by the bluest sky in months."

"Annalise, I love you. You make ordinary things magical," Rose laughed.

"Not so ordinary, Honey," Joshua remarked. "Typically they're mountain birds. There's obviously a lot of small game on the ranch, plenty of fish in the Solomon. He was hundreds of miles from his normal home."

That's it, thought Gerdon. Through a note-scribbling afternoon and well into the night, he theorized and speculated, and was satisfied with the result, a near-foolproof scheme to get access to the Brody Ranch, to get close to Grimes, and to remain above suspicion. Heck, he might even benefit financially by another arm of the plan.

He was almost certain that Grimes was a ranch hand. He had heard conversations from the three referring to "Mr. Grimes."

It would take weeks to be ready. The preparation was complicated and time-consuming. In the meantime, he would continue to be a man of mystery, and to befriend further the two women who were the keys to his success. Herkimer Grimes, he thought, if you're out there, I've got you.

****

"What do you think, Jonah? Is it worth a try?"

He splashed his lure near a sapling bent over into the pond.

"Certainly. I appreciate your charity. In fact, it's an encouraging thought. If you're sure that you want to do it, if Margaret's of the same thought." He talked throughout the successful landing of another pan fish, large and shining in the afternoon sun.

The preacher is an uncanny fisherman, Whit thought. "Margaret agrees that it would help us out, and maybe straighten out the girl's life," Whit responded.

"What do you think, Cleetus?" Jonah asked.

The squat man answered as he labored over a snarl of his fishing line, an uncommon occurrence. He was the equal of the other two in fishing ability. He was nearing disgust with his predicament, but inscrutable as always.

"It's a good idea. Wicks isn't going to like it."

"Wicks?" Whit asked.

"He runs the house where she works. Disagreeable man," Jonah answered.

"Will he cause trouble?"

"I'm sure that he will. He's not happy that three of his girls are attending church. Sent me a message once through Clara. He doesn't want Myra in the choir. Said that he was ready to do something about it."

"What happened?"

"Nothing so far. I told Myra to let me know if he did anything to her."

"Darn it! Sorry, Jonah." Whit was hung up on a naked branch of the sapling, hidden underwater. "That's a good bait. Guess I'll have to wade in there." He began to remove his pants, and then tested the water. "None too warm," he commented.

"Whit, 'darn it' is an appropriate comment," Jonah laughed. "I would hope that would be my response. I am not offended, nor is God."

Whit tentatively waded to the sapling. The water sloshed around his waist.

"She'd have a nice bedroom to herself. Privacy. We've got books she could read, horses to ride, sewing, if she wanted to do that. Might even teach her how to fish, and shoot a gun." Whit bent over into the water, and flicked his lure clear of the branch.

"And you'd have her cook a few meals and tend to the house?"

"Mostly. Caroline is getting up in years a bit. She's got a lot of work to do. Margaret too. And we've got that big house with only three of us in it. I'd pay her more than she's making now, I'd wager."

"Your other hands would be kind to her."

"You bet. You know most of them. They're good people. Been through a lot. They'd make her feel part of a family." Whit sat on the bank in the sun, drying off.

"I heartily endorse this idea. I will broach it to her. Cleetus and I will get her moved."

"You think she'll do it?"

"She's a scared little girl. Doesn't know much else than selling her body. I think that I can sell it to her." Another strike. Another successful fish.

The three men had made the fishing excursions part of a routine. Every other Friday, Jonah and Cleetus would arrive after noon, and Whit would take them to the little lake, tied by a lazy stream to the Solomon River, wooded and quiet, two miles north of the ranch buildings. This might be the final outing of the year. Winter was in the offing.

Suddenly, Cleetus pointed to the sky. "Look at that! An eagle. A bald eagle, I'd guess."

"That's Jefferson's and Annalise's eagle. They saw him first. Don't know what he's doing around here. Seen him several times the last few weeks. Think maybe I'll call this Eagle Lake," Whit offered.

Fishing stopped as they watched the giant bird circle above them.

"He's found a home," Jonah rejoined. "Maybe that's a good omen for Myra."

****

October, 1868

Dear Mother Maribel,

How are you? I miss you.

Life in Abilene is interesting. I don't know how much longer we'll be here, but each day seems to bring a discovery, a joy, some new adventure. When our plans are settled, I will come to Cincinnati before we relocate. Jefferson, Joshua, and the wonderful Brody family are enjoying each other. Their time together now is precious.

Abilene continues to grow. There is a rudimentary school, but no newspaper. I miss that. Joshua's store is now surrounded by new buildings. As I've written, Joshua and Rose are expecting a baby next month. She is very pregnant, but still so beautiful. Her mother will move in with us in two weeks, and stay until the baby is born.

Jefferson is well, and thriving at the Brody ranch. We see each other three or four times a week. He is the most exciting man I know, so much knowledge, so many interests. He is much more than I deserve.

Several weekends ago we were riding along the Solomon River. In front of us at the top of a hill, a white wolf loped across our path, suspicious and frightened of us.

A white wolf! Then he disappeared. Mr. Brody explained later that a white wolf is rare, and that since he was alone, he was probably an outcast from the pack, fending for himself.

Wildlife of many types roams along the river and in the woods and pastures of the ranch. Occasionally, someone sees our eagle.

Sunsets here are wonderful, layers of red and purple. October is starting dry and somewhat hot. Autumn is not as colorful as along the Ohio River, because of fewer trees.

Little Jeremiah is growing and healthy. Jefferson says that if you visualize Jonathan as a child, you will have an accurate image of his son. Catharine is teaching him at home, but plans to start sending him to school next spring. She is a good mother. There is no photographer in town, or we would send you a picture.

I have told Rose and Catharine of my amazing parents, and of your kindness and wisdom. As the family's matriarch, you should meet them, but I have no idea how that can happen. Rose has asked if she can write to you. I told her that you'd like that.

Tell me about my sisters Deidre and Portia. Pass on my love to them.

I think constantly of my father. Poor Herman. I love him so. I hope that he is well. You two mean so much to me.

Until I see you, much love.

Your daughter, Annalise

****

In the span of twelve hours in November, three changes of relative importance occurred in the life of Whit Brody. Two revealed his charitable nature. The other moved him to strong emotion.

During a busy morning, Jonah and Cleetus had moved Myra to the ranch. She would willingly accept the new arrangement, helping Caroline. The plans were somewhat detoured when she told Margaret that she didn't know how to cook.

"Well," Whit had said, "there's still plenty of housework to do."

As Jonah and Whit unloaded her few possessions from the wagon, Whit questioned the minister. "Did you have any trouble moving her out?"

"Some," Jonah replied. "Mr. Wicks glared at us the entire time. He had a few choice words for Myra every time she passed him. I asked her to wait in the wagon. Then the girl named Clara tried to go out to say goodbye, and Wicks slammed her into a wall. I had to give him a little sermon."

"The Reverend told him that God might forgive him for battering a woman, but that he would stomp the man to eternity if he ever touched another woman," Cleetus reported through a smile.

"I've heard that he has two bodyguards at that house. Any trouble with them?"

"None. We didn't even see them," Jonah answered.

A skinny fellow with earnest eyes and a somewhat unorthodox wardrobe had ridden to the ranch in the early afternoon, awkwardly dismounting from a bulky, nervous horse, as ungainly as its rider.

As he moved toward Brody, the rancher was bemused by the flat-crowned gray hat with an outlandishly wide brim, the shiny black boots, and the multicolored coat with sleeves that didn't quite reach the wrists of its owner.

A stiff November breeze gusted around them. A mist that was not quite snow settled on them.

"Mr. Brody, is it? I've seen you in church. Mrs. Catharine Chase said that you would be expecting me today, I believe," the man said. "My name is Robert Sawyer Gillespie."

Whit extended his hand, and was mildly surprised by the strong grip of the stranger. "Mr. Gillespie, let's go have a talk in the house. There'll be some hot coffee in there."

Gillespie followed the rancher, towing the old horse.

"Elon," Whit yelled to a hand near what must have been a blacksmith's building next to a sizable corral, "Come get Mr. Gillespie's horse!"

Gillespie saw a young man trotting up, freckled and friendly looking. It was not an aging gunfighter.

Gillespie made quick and countless observations that he would convert to notes later. He had ridden up skirting a small pond, and seen a community of buildings. He counted at least five barns scattered in a wide semi-circle behind an impressive whitewashed house with four chimneys. Farther up on the opposite hillock to the west were a long one-story building with smoke rising from it, a comfortable cabin, and a shack with curtains hanging in its lone window. He assumed that all three were living quarters for the ranch hands.

Whit led the man inside to a room with a large picture hanging above an active fireplace.

"Caroline," he called to the back of the house, "May we have some coffee please, two cups?" He took off his coat and fit it to the back of a straight chair in the corner, pointed to the sofa, and then sat in a soft chair. He crossed his feet at the ankles, clasping his hands in front of him. He had not removed his hat, an indication to Gillespie that it would not be a lengthy conversation.

"So what's on your mind, Mr. Gillespie? Catharine said that you want to take some pictures."

Gillespie cleared his throat and began a carefully rehearsed spiel. "Mr. Brody, I'm assembling photographs and stories for a book, a record of the wildlife and the people of Kansas. I've already secured a publisher for it in New York. I need a place to use as a base. I can't spread out far enough from town. I would like to propose an arrangement, since your ranch is out here, and it is so large. It would put me in touch with natural picture sites."

"What kind of arrangement?"

"Well, sir, I am a man of modest means, at least until the book is sold. If you'd be so kind as to permit me room and board, I would offer my services to you as an employee."

"Services?"

"I would do whatever you need. I served as a cook in the recent war. I can garden. I could learn to work with livestock. I will do that gladly for no wages. I'd just ask for four days a week to explore and to take pictures."

A plump woman entered the room with two steaming cups on a tray.

"Thank you, Caroline. Mr. Gillespie, this is the best housekeeper on the frontier. My wife is in Abilene awaiting our first grandchild."

Gillespie rose, nodded at Caroline, and accepted the coffee. "Ma'am." She smiled at him.

"How long will this venture of yours take?"

"Possibly a few months."

"I'm willing to make this deal with you, with two conditions. One is that you'll have to stay in the bunkhouse.

"Fine with me. Are most of your men in there?"

"Some are." He paused to taste the coffee. "Second, you can take pictures of all of the animals you want. People? You'll have to take those away from here. We've got people on the ranch who value their privacy."

That's it, Gillespie thought. He is here.

Whit continued. "You mind working for a woman? You just met Caroline. Our foreman is a woman too."

"Not at all."

"You have a lot of equipment?"

"Yes, I do. I've got a Wolcott camera, plates, tripods, chemicals, paper. Not too much personal stuff though. I've got a buckboard in Abilene. Two horses."

"You can store some stuff in the closest barn, behind the house. The rest of it in the bunkhouse. There's a small interior room in the barn, empty now. You can make it as dark or light as you want, but it won't be warm in there until spring. Then I'd say, talk to Caroline about one of the smaller storerooms in the kitchen. We could move some stuff around. That might be best for finishing your pictures."

"Fine, Mr. Brody."

"Your chemicals safe?"

"Yes, Mr. Brody. They're no problem at all. Some odor, not much."

"You think that you could cook for 16-18 people, twice a day, on weekends?"

"Easily, sir."

Whit celebrated the answer. He had wanted to relieve Caroline. Myra wasn't the answer to the cooking part. Suddenly a solution had fallen into his lap, and it wasn't going to cost him anything. "Might ask you to clean stables, feed the animals, take the ladies in to Abilene, maybe on Wednesdays. You'd still have four days a week to do your picture taking."

I did it, Gerdon/Gillespie thought as he rode away. He bought the story. There was no remorse for all of the fiction, all of the truth-bending. He had researched and memorized all of the story for weeks. He did have a camera, purchased in Kansas City, complete with instructions provided by the merchant. He was passable in everything from setting up to clicking to development of the raw picture. It was a used camera. Eventually it would break down for him. That didn't matter. It covered his scheme. If Brody had pried more, he would have been ready. Who did you serve with in the war?

What were some of your postings? How does one develop pictures? Where did you grow up in Chicago? He could have answered them all. What types of wildlife will you look for? Yep, he could've answered that too. All fabrication was for the greater good. His good. He would have months of access to Herkimer Grimes.

As Gillespie rode back to Abilene, Rose Chase felt the first sharp pain of contractions at dusk. "Joshua, I'm about to change your life, Sweetheart. I think this is it."

He rushed to her side and grabbed her hand. "Honey?" She nodded at him.

From the kitchen came loud giggles from Annalise and Margaret, sharing some observation or another. "Mom Brody! Annalise!" he called back. "I think we've got something happening!"

As they entered the room Joshua rushed past them, carrying his coat. "I'm going for Doc Rosbottom."

"Joshua, dear, it may be too early. Did the pains just start?"

"Mother, I think it's time. I'm getting more contractions, close together."

"Joshua," Annalise said as she grabbed his arm, "You stay with Rose. I'll get him."

"No, Annalise. It's cold, it's dark, and it's Abilene. I'm going."

She protested, "It's time for people to stop treating me as fragile. It's less than ten minutes to his office. I am going." She moved to the door to the first level.

"Annalise, you go. Wear a coat. Saddle up my horse. Be careful." Joshua backed down.

"See what I mean?" Annalise winked at Margaret. She grabbed his coat from his arms, and was gone

Rose felt another pain. "Oh…my…gosh. This one hurts!"

Margaret had a pot of water boiling when Rosbottom and Annalise returned.

"Rose, you doin' alright?" the doctor inquired.

"Yes. If it weren't for the pain, I'd be having fun."

"Your water broke yet?"

"Yes. I'm ready. If you're ready, I'm certain the baby is ready. Ouch!"

Jacob Brody Chase was born at 9:15 pm.

It would be early the next day before Whit got the news, courtesy of a galloping Joshua before daybreak. He then turned his horse back to town.

Whit slapped his hat against his leg, and whooped "Wahoo!" so loud it carried up to the bunkhouse.

"What the hell was that?" a drowsy Big asked.

Jack opened the door and saw the rancher skipping in small circles on the porch of his house. "This is just a guess," he said, "but I'd say we have a baby. Hey, Jefferson ! You're an uncle again!"

CHAPTER TWENTY-NINE

1869

At first, Caroline was miffed that she had to relinquish her kitchen two days a week to the Easterner. Myra was one thing. The haunted girl was proving to be a thorough housecleaner, freeing Margaret, who had already developed hobbies, and reducing Caroline's workload. Caroline liked Myra. With no children of her own, she began fostering a motherly attitude toward the young prostitute. The girl was reclusive, but the addition of another person had broadened the purposes of all three.

Gillespie was another matter. He had appropriated her kitchen two days a week, disrupting her routine, exhausting ingredients, and creating menus too elaborate for ranch fare. It wouldn't last forever, she told herself. Besides, Mr. Brody wanted it that way. Two days a week with no responsibilities was almost too much. She wandered the big house on weekends, looking for diversions. She relished the Sundays when the group rode into Abilene, but winter had curtailed that for weeks.

Gillespie was in a delirious cycle of successes. He had met his fictional hero two days after moving into the bunkhouse. Whit had led him to the little shack and introduced him to Herk. Gillespie was speechless. The mysterious man was older than he'd imagined, somewhat stooped, with clear eyes that seemed to be evaluating him. Neither spoke a word to the other. Gillespie's hand was swallowed by Herk's in a brief, strong handshake. Gillespie recovered enough to make quick observations…small scar over the left eye…unshaven…moustache which hides his mouth…clean clothes…no sign of firearms…graying. Gillespie barely heard Whit's description of him after they left, "Hard worker, but he likes to be alone."

The young blacksmith, Elon, an outgoing, happy spirit of a man with a speech impediment, had shared what he knew about Herk one day in the bunkhouse. Gillespie had triggered it, "Interesting group of people out here. That man who lives alone is different though."

"He used to b-b-be a Texas Ranger. We hear he was b-born s-somewheres in the Texas p-p-panhandle. Think his dad was s-s-scalped or s-something. D-don't have n-n-n-no family."

"He looks like a sad man."

"Yessir. He k-keeps to himself. Seen him once with his s-s-shirt off. All gristle and muscle. Don't look his age. 'Spect he's in his s-s-sixties."

The living quarters in the bunkhouse suited Gillespie, ten small individual rooms with curtains on the front of each for a modicum of privacy. He was on the south side in an arrangement that started with Lige, then Noah, then his room. He was next to Jefferson, and then came the Indian boy. Opposite was Big, a prodigious snorer. The next room was a storeroom for personal items, crates of clothes, guns, a buffer for those who tossed and turned while Big snorted and rasped. Simeon, Elon, and Jack completed that side. At each end, a pot-bellied stove kept the building warm, and was usually stoked by the early risers, Jefferson and Simeon. An empty bunk bed sat in the middle of the west end for future employees. Two long tables with chairs separated the two sides. Each end had a washroom, and each also had a window and a door to the outside.

Gillespie considered the inhabitants. Who seemed most likely to spill information about the secretive Grimes? Elon, certainly, and the wizened Simeon, who was an inveterate talker.

Not the affable war hero Jefferson; he had not been at the ranch long. Not Whit's nephew Jack who was pleasant, but probably too clever to be lured into a revealing conversation. Big was a possibility. He had ridden with Herk. Gillespie could cultivate him. Charlie Fox and Lige didn't say much. Possibly Noah.

He noticed a healthy camaraderie among his bunk mates. Every Thursday night, Jefferson and Jack started a poker game, with pebbles as chips. Losers had to clean the outhouses for a week, or groom the winners' horses. Winners got first dibs on the washrooms.

Last Thursday, Big and Lige were the only two left in one hand, and kept raising each other until Big called. Lige laid down two aces. Big turned over three fives, stunning Lige, and then raked all of the pebbles in front of himself. Lige stared at him for a long moment, and then blurted out, "You big dummy." Big began laughing so hard he lost his breath. Then laughter filled the room. Even Lige began chuckling.

Gillespie had watched Noah teasing Simeon relentlessly. Charlie Fox, a winner one night, pumped his fist in the air and smiled broadly.

Gillespie finally scored a coup for himself in February. On a frigid afternoon, he asked Whit to assemble everyone, dressed as if for church, in the front parlor.

"What's he doing, Whit?" Margaret asked.

"It's a surprise, Maggie. He told me. I think you'll enjoy yourself."

Before the contingent from Abilene arrived, Gillespie set his tripod and camera in front of the fireplace. He made several trips to the kitchen, and carried back loads of photographic plates. Reluctantly, Herk and Big knocked on the front door at the last minute. Perfect, Gillespie noted.

"This is what I'm going to do for you, folks. You've all been kind to me, so I'm going to take portraits of all of you today. I'll develop them and print them for you. They're for you, not for me. In two weeks or so, I'll give you all of the printed pictures. Any of you ever have your picture taken?"

Joshua and Jefferson had, in the military. Rose had, in college. No one else raised a hand.

"It'll be quick enough. With these new cameras, all you have to do is sit still for a few seconds. We'll start with the boss and his pretty wife."

As the afternoon wore on, he assembled groups, Joshua and Rose with their baby, Jefferson and Annalise, the bunkhouse group, Charlie and Bird, the men, the women, Joshua and Jefferson and their women, Whit and Margaret and their grandson, Catharine and Jeremiah.

"I've got eight plates left. Any requests? Big, who do you want your picture with?"

"Herkimer, I suppose."

Gillespie counted. That would be two of Herkimer. Good. "Put your hats on."

"Lige, how about you?"

"Noah and Simeon."

"Jefferson," Annalise whispered, "Mother Maribel would love one of all of us. The Chases, the girls, and the two kids." It was suggested and taken, as was one of the Brody's and Jack, another of Caroline and Myra."

"What about you, Mr. Gillespie? You're part of the family too," Whit asked.

"I can teach someone to take one shot. I'd like a picture with Mr. Brody." He couldn't think fast enough to include himself in a picture with Herkimer. Better to play it safe anyway.

"Before we break up, I'd like to show you what I shot last week." He slid a print out of a cloth envelope.

It was the white wolf at the crest of a hill, no more than thirty feet away. It was looking straight at the camera, ears alert, with a prairie dog in its mouth.

"I'll be damned," Whit said, slightly astonished.

Two weeks later to the day, Gillespie produced the results. Joshua had brought a box of picture frames from the store, and Gillespie spread the photos on the dining room table, each on top of a picture frame.

"If you're in it, go ahead and take it," Gillespie said. His own stash was already printed and hidden.

"Whit and I would like maybe six or eight of these," Margaret said. "We'll hang a group of them on the wall here."

In the aftermath, amid expressions of gratitude, Gillespie assumed the mantle of a warm and generous friend, far from his previous station of strange interloper. Things were certainly looking up.

****

March 14, 1869
Cincinnati, Ohio

My Darling Daughter,

I received the wonderful picture yesterday. You and Jefferson are such a handsome couple. I am also grateful that the picture included Joshua and his beautiful bride and their son, and also Catharine and my other grand-nephew, Jeremiah. Now I can put faces to names.

You all look so healthy and happy. In regards to health, getting old is a bore. Herman is no better, no worse. His eyes brightened when he saw the picture, but he has been so depressed by the gray Ohio winter. I am tired all of the time, and have had a recent loss of weight, and of appetite. My doctor has said that it is only a consequence of aging. Oh, to be thirty again, or forty, or fifty.

We have guests much of the time, Herman's old colleagues from the university, and friends from the old neighborhood. I'm sure that you remember the Sloans, the Schmidts, the Wayovers, and the Montgomerys. Deidre will bring our grandchildren for a visit next month. She sends her love to you. Life is still good, despite the ravages of the calendar.

Dear William, our loyal gardener, has elaborate plans for our summer garden. We look forward to that. We also look forward to your letters, so descriptive and interesting.

The old lady paused. She was having another cold sweat, and that pain in her legs. She'd finish the letter later, and mail it the next day. She picked up the picture, and focused on Jefferson and Annalise, staring again at the pretty girl standing behind the seated cowboy, wide smiles on both faces, his hand reaching up to touch hers, which rested on his broad shoulder.

She was suddenly dizzy, emotion from seeing her loved ones, she thought.

****

"I was going to send Herkimer and Big to the north line shack for a few days. Noah noticed that the fence posts are leaning for a long stretch, and the fence is sagging. Should be a three day job. Thing is, Big's got a stomach misery, can't keep anything down. Can we spare anyone else?" Bird explained.

"Fence has to be fixed. We could lose a lot of stock up there. I'll go."

"No, Mr. Brody, no. I think that I have a solution."

Herk was ready to leave. The large buckboard was already loaded with bales of wire and a stack of new fence posts. Mr. Brody had said that he'd find a hand, what, thirty minutes ago? Brody appeared in the barn door. "I got your help, Herkimer."

Following him in, a large bag on her shoulders, was the foreman.

Herk's eyes narrowed. "Bird."

"That going to be a problem for you?" Whit asked.

"No. don't think so. Could be a problem for her." Whit could tell that even behind thick moustache, Herk was smiling, sort of.

Bird had been trying for a long time to move from despising the gunfighter toward liking him, or maybe just tolerating him. In a perverse way, he fascinated her. Was he a dangerous, immoral killer, or just a lonely man with an inflated reputation? He had killed uncountable Indians, that was fact, but most were hostile, relentless tormentors of white men. He had been a hired gun in a range war; she didn't know details. He had expressed a hatred of "all redskins," but for years, she had felt that way about the unseen white men who had lied to her tribal family. Her dislike of him, approaching disgust and fear, had tempered as she watched his reliable and consistent ranch work. Her son liked him.

Several days together could be a disaster, or a revelation. She'd find out.

"Remember," Whit was saying, "you can either come back each night, or stay at the line shack. If you stay out there, we'll send another wagon out each morning with more wire, and some vittles."

He was certain that he'd see them coming back each dusk. "I may have made a mistake, Margaret," he said after the two had left, "I sent Bird with Herkimer to mend the north fence."

"Whit they're both good people. They won't kill each other," she laughed.

"I'm not so sure about that," he answered.

"You've got a fine boy." Herk broke the icy silence that had dominated their first two hours together.

The suddenness of the comment both surprised and pleased her.

"Thank you, Mr. Grimes. He seems to like you."

Ma'am, you've been callin' me Mr. Grimes since I come here. Ain't too comfortable since you're my boss."

"And what do you call me besides 'ma'am?"

"I suppose that's true."

Silence again. Maybe her comment had been too harsh.

"You happy, Herkimer?"

"Not much to be happy about."

"What would make you happy?" she asked, as she dragged another bale off of the wagon.

"Dunno. Guess a man needs a good woman. Maybe some young uns."

"You've never had a good woman?"

"One, years ago. Little Mexican girl. Drove her off. Too much Rangerin'. Left me for another man."

"No others?"

"Lots of women.. None that I'd want to share my life."

She heard sadness in the comment.

"How about you?" Herkimer asked, diverting the conversation away from himself.

"One wonderful man, Charlie's father. A lot of men who were cruel to me."

There were now long pauses in the fence repair. She didn't mind.

"They turn you against all men?"

"Not at all." She wondered if she had conveyed that impression to him. "There have been some good men in my life, kind and gentle men. None ever went beyond friendship."

"Too bad, ma'am. Seems you offer a lot. A man would be lucky to…" He didn't finish the thought. Bird knew why. The topic was too personal. Herk wasn't going there, never would. She had a brief flashback to Rides With Fire. He too had been obstinate, unapproachable when they first met. Not that there were any other parallels between the two men.

****

It had not been a good year for Corby Pitcock. He hobbled on his one good leg. The other, minus a functional kneecap, wouldn't bend, nor support his weight. When he sat, it stuck out in front of him, useless and pathetic. A cane was his only connection to mobility. He suffered the indignity of having to be boosted onto his saddle. When he rode, he tilted to the left, putting weight to his good leg to keep from tottering.

A year earlier, he had still been recuperating from the attack by the tall young man and the girl that he'd tried to enslave, when a group of cavalrymen had descended, ordering him to show them his ranch, and evaluating his work force, sent they told him, after receiving a letter from a woman named Annalise Ollimore. It was plain to the officers that his employees were still in bondage three years after the Great War had freed them.

"They ain't slaves. They can leave whenever they please. I treat them well," he had protested, despite mounting evidence that he had ignored the new order of the country.

"Mr. Pitcock, I am offended by what you're doing here, sir. You will immediately set these people free, and you will give all of them monies to begin a new life." An officer ordered.

"By what authority?"

"Mr . Pitcock, everyone of us in this company is a veteran of the war. We've got a lot of bad memories. If I were you, I'd comply with this order. Then we'll deal with the charge of murder."

"Never killed nobody. Slave peoples are fragile. Lot of them just died."

"We'll see what they say about that."

The troop camped in his front yard for two weeks, monitoring the manumission process; wagons transported the enfranchised to St. Louis.

"We'll be leaving tomorrow, Pitcock. We will involve the civil authorities in the matter of extreme cruelty and murder. Might include rape in the charges."

Pitcock spat. He knew that the investigation was over. Black people had little credibility in the court system. Most of his slaves were illiterate. Many were still afraid. Even the Ollimore girl was black. Who would believe any of them?

Whatever happened to his immediate future might involve fines. He had already lost his work force. That was bad enough. He would get harassed by the legal system for a while, for the nuisance of it.

After seven months, the issue suddenly dropped away. It had cost him a small fortune. He had to pay wages to attract itinerant workers from St. Louis. He could not easily recoup his financial losses. Some people didn't want to do business with him.

He considered selling the farm. Yes, he'd move to Arkansas somewhere.

So Pitcock's obsession with the pair who had caused his comeuppance increased markedly.

"Whatever happens, when this is over," he had told Luther, "we'll find those two. We will cause the worst days of their lives. We will give them more pain than they could ever imagine.

"She's a sweet young thing. Give me some time with her, boss. I'll do her every way afore I kill her."

"Didn't go so well for you the last time you tried that. Them slaves with her mother was picked up in Cincinnati. Seems like a good place to start. Ollimore's not a common name."

"We goin' boss?"

"Yes, we can afford to mosey around. This time next year, we'll have 'em found and punished…dead."

As he spoke, hc drummed his fingers absent-mindedly on his shattered kneecap.

"First though, we'll be moving to Arkansas. We'll tell everyone we're going east. We'll get away from this hell here. Doesn't matter. We sell this, we'll have plenty to start somewhere else where nobody knows us. Might even pick up some darkies, like old times. You can come along or stay here. Doesn't matter to me."

Losing the farm was inevitablc, he'd guessed that months before. That thought made him hate the slave girl and her companion even more.

****

Herkimer and Bird worked in symbiotic ease, almost rhythmic precision, until evening, covering almost half of the dilapidated span.

"Mr. Grimes, we've done well. Let's stop for the day."

Herk nodded.

"We can either head back, and return tomorrow, or use the line shack. We stay, we'll be eating in an hour, and get a good sleep," Bird added.

"We're running out of wire," Herk answered.

"Mr. Brody'll bring us another load tomorrow, if we don't return tonight. Posts too."

"Well then, if it's all the same to you, I'd stay out here. Line shack's over the hill a piece. "Sides, got a catch in my back. Can get to bed early, sleep it out tonight."

"You're agreeable to stay out here, then?"

"Don't get some coffee soon, don't think I'll survive anyways." He was smiling.

Two hours later, Herk was snoring loudly on a blanket, an empty coffee cup on the floor beside him. Bird sat at a small table, eating alone and watching him. The man had not eaten since that morning. He had not complained nor slowed all day, accomplishing what two men might. There was no sloth in Herkimer Grimes. And a "catch" in his back. She'd slow the pace tomorrow, quit earlier.

A morning rain awakened them after daylight. "We overslept, Mr. Grimes."

Herk got to his feet, a bit unsteady, and opened the door of the shack. "Purty good rain out there. Can't work in that." He closed the door, and rummaged through his saddle bag for matches.

"Don't look like it'll settle in. Sky's clear to the west," he mumbled.

"How's your back, Mr. Grimes?"

"It's fine, ma'am."

"You don't have to be a hero. I'd guess it's still bothering you some."

"It'll loosen. Happens every morning". Getting old."

"Well, you work like you're twenty. I expect that's why."

"You did everythin' I did."

"Yes, but I'm still a young girl," she teased.

"Yes, ma'am." He was smiling, she knew.

By noon, they were back on the line, dealing with mud and an occasional sprinkle. Shortly after, they saw the promised wagon in the distance, slowly bumping toward them.

"Nice work here," Whit observed, "Figured the rain'd keep you in today. Everything OK?"

"Seems to be. Haven't seen any cows up here. Probably haven't lost any," Bird answered.

"Didn't think you'd get this far in a day."

"I've got a mean boss," Herkimer said. "Won't let me stop to sleep or eat."

Was he joking? It was hard to tell with Herkimer. Of course he was. Bird was laughing.

"Caroline sent along some grub. I'd eat it soon. Those two boxes up front."

Thirty minutes later with the bales dumped at intervals along the line, Whit was on his way back, driving the first wagon.

"Herkimer. We'll work toward those trees, and take a break."

"Fine with me." He was mildly startled , but pleased. She had called him by his name.

The sky cleared, and a full sun dried the area. They sat under the canopy of a large tree.

"A beautiful tree. Don't remember noticing it before."

"Best part of Kansas. You could ride all day in the west Texas, and never see a tree."

"You didn't like Texas?" she asked.

"Not much. Bad memories. Too much killin.' Too much hate."

"I'm sure you made a difference."

"Dunno. Never shot nobody that didn't deserve it. It was just a bad time."

"Colorado, Herkimer. You ever see Colorado?"

"Rode through parts of it."

"It's unbelievable. Makes a person feel small."

"You fixin' to go back some day?"

"Never. My worst memories are there. Same as you and Texas. Anyway, the land asks too much of a person."

"You'll stay with Brody?"

"I love the ranch. Only place I've ever felt needed. Perfect place for Chula too."

"Chula?"

"Charlies's Indian name?"

"What's your Indian name?"

"Pachallhppuwa Tuchena. It means 'three doves.'"

"I like 'Bird' better."

She had a flashback to Stephan Butler, the kind old man who had saved her life. He had said the same thing. Of course, there were no other similarities between the two.

"Herkimer, look." She pointed to a dark thunderhead, consuming the entire horizon to the southwest.

"There's a lot of rain in that one. Gonna be one of those days."

They worked feverishly for less than an hour, and then surrendered to the storm, which was intensifying.

Back at the line shack, Herkimer tethered the wagon's horses, and his own, under the lean-to. Bird started coffee. Both were soaked.

"We've got to get dry clothes. We can wrap in blankets. Start a fire. Dry these," she said, shivering.

Got some dry clothes in my saddlebags. A couple of extra shirts. One would cover you up."

He pulled a faded work shirt out of the bag, and handed it to her. He began to build a fire in the rugged fireplace, his back turned to her. She didn't take her eyes off of him while she changed, a distrust which bothered her, but that she felt was necessary.

"Done. Your turn, Herkimer."

He stood up and turned. The shirt covered her to just above her knees. At once he was nervous, and somewhat aroused. He had never seen her, never imagined her in this way.

He pulled off his shirt and walked past her. As he did, she reached out and touched his shoulder. Why did I do that, she thought. Stupid. That was stupid.

He kept walking. In the corner, he changed. She quickly wrapped a blanket around her legs and sat at the table.

The room was suffused with tension. They sat, quietly drinking coffee. She was too embarrassed to speak. Why did I do that? I didn't want anything to happen.

He avoided looking at her, and finally announced, "Think I'll take a nap, ma'am."

"Yes. Yes. A nap. A good idea,"

Soon he was asleep, the now familiar snoring in concert with the drumming of rain on the roof.

She lay on her back in another corner, unable to sleep.

****

They sat alone in the living room above the store. Joshua and Rose, retired for the night, were trying to be quiet in their bedroom, but now and then, a soft gasp or a shifting of the headboard betrayed their best efforts to conceal their activity. When that occurred, Annalise giggled quietly, and Jefferson smiled.

"You think we ought to move on soon?"

She sat in his lap with her head against his shoulder, his hand covering hers on her lap. The question caused her to sit up.

"Jefferson, you're not happy here?"

"No, it's not that. You've been patient. We've been here a year, and we were only going to stay a few months. Maybe it's time for a change."

"I'm ready when you are. But you should know that I'm content here, for as long as we stay. We're in the bosom of a warm family, surrounded by friends. It is comfortable."

"Joshua and Rose are frustrated with the lawlessness. I think they're positioning to sell the store, and move to Oregon. I'd guess they'll leave in a year or so. Joshua asked if we'd go with them. I've got a feeling that Rose's parents will leave soon after."

"The Brodys? Leave the ranch? Leave Abilene?"

"Whit promised Margaret that they'd live out their lives with their grandchildren."

"I'm shocked. He is Abilene."

"No, he's just the best part of it. Abilene's identity now is violence and greed. It's not safe for ladies to be out after dark. And it's getting crowded."

She leaned down and kissed him on the lips, a gesture which became a lengthy, passionate interval, her hands caressing his face, his hand lightly massaging her leg.

She turned serious. "I have a request."

"Anything," he said.

"Mother and Father O'Neill. Neither is in good health. They dedicated so much of their lives to me. Before we move farther west, I need to see them again, spend time with them, get their blessing on our plans. Can I do that?"

"Of course. I'll go with you."

"I was hoping you'd say that."

"I'll stay for the cattle drive and the horse sales. We can leave in May, stay in Cincinnati for a couple of months, and then come back. We could leave for Oregon next spring."

"Perfect."

No mention of a wedding. She wouldn't bring it up, ever. All of his plans included the word "we". That was good enough.

Horses were a small part of the Brody empire, but a profitable one.

At any given time, there were no more than a few hundred on hand, tamed and trained by Jack and Jefferson, pampered and shoed by Elon.

Abilene did not particularly cater to horse trading, but over the years, Whit had secured contracts with the military, the stagecoach line, the railroad, and scattered ranches in Nebraska and Kansas to provide well-fed and well-mannered horses. His original herds were mustangs gleaned from the plains of western Kansas and Oklahoma, some secured in trades with the Indians. Those were expanded by buying excursions to cities and ranches in a five-state area.

When Jack arrived from Mississippi, the venture grew and prospered. His nephew had a talent for managing and breeding horses. Elon had added expertise in smithing, and a gentle nature. The Chase brothers later were godsends, both expertise in breaking and care, both with a reverence for horses.

The ranch hands always had exceptional mounts, given to them by Whit, with the provision that they receive constant and appropriate care. Even Margaret and Caroline had cow ponies, which Elon tended. One barn, north and east of the house, was solely for those horses, and their fenced grazing area was separated from those of the main herd and the cattle.

Whit insisted that his employee's horses be given names, a subtle way to encourage bonding and care. Margaret named hers Spirit. Big's was called John J., after his former Ranger boss. Charlie's was Fire, named for his father. Jack rode Tornado. Noah, manumitted from slavery years before, opted for Freedom. Caroline picked Cookie.

The prize of the stables was Storm, ridden in by Jefferson a year earlier. Whit called him "the most beautiful horse I've ever seen, almost regal, that one."

North of the employees' horse barn, and connected to it by an oversized corral was the largest barn on the property, built to protect the general horse population during the winter months. Sales occurred in the spring, and in October.

The May 1869 round-ups and drives of both horses and cattle coincided. The cattle were mostly secluded in the western fields, awaiting buyers and inspections from Abilienc. The Brody staff would then drive them the short distances to the stockyards.

The horses, groomed and well-fed, would be driven to collection points in Nebraska, Iowa, and along the Mississippi River, a somewhat more time-consuming procedure. Whit considered shipping them by train, but had not yet attempted it.

Both undertakings were ahead of schedule by the end of the first week of May in 1869, but plans were disrupted by an unfortunate and prophetic accident.

A horse was down in the corral, just before breakfast on May 9, a fearful condition because of the constant spectre of disease.

Jefferson vaulted the rails and made his way to the afflicted animal. He bent over the horse and stoked his neck. "Hey boy. Don't feel so good today?"

The horse stopped his snorting, and one great eye focused on Jefferson. His muzzle was warm and moist. There were no outward signs of disease, no evidence of injury. Jefferson gently probed the horse's chest, and stopped at the slightly distended stomach.

Jefferson stood, and called over to Jack. "He's eaten something that didn't agree with him, I'd guess. I think he's got a pretty good stomach ache."

"Blockage?" Jack yelled back.

"Don't know. Don't think so."

The horse, comforted, suddenly struggled to get to his feet, a sudden, awkward movement that carried its full weight against Jefferson's right leg. It's balance gone, the horse crashed up Jefferson's leg, which was trapped by a boot which didn't yield.

The horse rolled over on top of Jefferson, who emitted a loud "oomph," and struggled to its feet.

"Jefferson! Jefferson! You OK?" Jack was quickly next to him.

Jefferson grimaced from his back, both hands on an area above his ankle. "I'm OK. I think my leg is broken."

"Don't move. We'll carry you out of there."

"I can get up…"

"You've got a break, and that horse rolled over you. Stay down!" He began yelling names, "Whit! Lige! Elon! Help!" Elon ran up from the barn."

"He's hurt, Elon. Broken leg. Maybe more. Go ring the dinner bell."

"Jack, let me up. I can hobble out of here." Even as he spoke, he felt nauseated. Beads of perspiration dotted his forehead.

"Nope. Don't want to make it worse."

The bell's incessant ringing brought Whit out of the house. Lige and Big trotted down the hill from the bunkhouse, Charlie close behind. "Horse fell on his leg," Jack explained.

"You think it's broken, son?" Whit asked as he knelt next to Jefferson.

"Good chance." Jefferson felt detached from the group as he fought to stay conscious.

"Horse rolled over him too," Jack said.

"My fault. Not the horse's. Poor guy was scared." Jefferson mumbled through clenched teeth.

"Big. Run over to the equipment barn. Bust up a barrel or a crate. Need about four pieces of wood. Charlie, go get some towels or sheets from your mother. Elon, hitch up the flat bed wagon, and bring it over here. I'm going to run him into Doc Rosbottom."

"Mr. Brody, get me to my feet. I can ride to Abilene."

"No sir. Not gonna do it that way."

The group of women from the house rushed to the scene.

"Whit…" Margaret's sentence was unfinished. Jefferson lay still.

"Better hurry folks! Looks like he's passed out. Elon, you ride ahead. Find Rosbottom. Ride to the store and tell Joshua and Annalise. We'll meet you at Rosbottom's."

Whit drove Jefferson slowly, avoiding ruts and bumps. A hastily constructed splint was tied to Jefferson's leg, a blanket wrapped around him. Jack cradled him in his arms, a pillow from somewhere tucked under his head. Big rode alongside.

A small crowd was gathered at the office of the doctor as the wagon came into view at the head of the street. Annalise pulled up her skirt and sprinted toward it.

"Jefferson, Honey…" she said, as she ran alongside the wagon. She could see the color had drained from his face.

"Might be hurt bad. Came to a while ago. Said he was having trouble breathing," Jack advised.

He was carefully unloaded, and carried gently into the small office by Whit, Joshua, Big, and Jack.

"He daid? Oh, Jesus, he daid?" Weasel had appeared from somewhere.

"I can let you in now." Rosbottom announced to a group over an hour later. "He's awake."

Jefferson was propped up on Rosbottom's rickety examination table. Annalise crossed quickly to him. "Jefferson. I was so scared." She kissed him on his forehead.

"I did a dumb thing. Annalise. Forgot the first rule about a downed horse…give him room."

She turned to Rosbottom. "Doc?"

"Broken leg right above his ankle. Didn't get displaced. Two, maybe three cracked ribs, from what I can tell. He's not spittin' up blood, so I'd say that there's no internal damage. Leg should heal up by itself, couple of months. Ribs'll be fine in a few weeks. His head received a good blow from something, maybe a hoof. That worries me some. To sum up, he'll have to stay quiet for two-three months. He'll have pain for some time. May have a bit of a limp afterwards."

"Doc, Annalise and I are going east in two weeks. I'll use a crutch."

"You'd better postpone that trip. I'd advise against it. Fact is, as your doctor, I'd say that you'd better stay flat on your back for a couple of weeks."

"Jeffie, you can stay with us. It'd be silly to chance another wagon ride," Joshua offered.

"Son , I can get you back to the ranch safely, I believe. You can move into the big house. Margaret, Caroline, and Myra'll probably fight to take care of you," Whit said.

In the end, the decision was that he'd stay at Josh and Rose's, with Annalise as his nurse. Someone from the ranch would bring in his clothes and personal items.

"Mr. Brody. I'm sorry. You've got round-ups and drives coming up. I picked a bad time to get careless."

"Jefferson, that could have happened to anybody," Jack interrupted.

A week later, another decision was made. Annalise was reading to him, sitting on the edge of the bed they shared. He stopped her.

"Annalise, you can go to Cincinnati alone."

"I won't leave you. We'll go in the autumn. I'll write Maribel."

"Maribel and Herman may not be around in the fall. From her letters and Diedre's, it's obvious that she's not well. I'll come when I can."

"No Jefferson. I won't leave you."

In the end, he convinced her.

"Go from the stagecoach directly to the hotel in St. Louis. Board the side-wheeler as early as you can. Pitcock won't be looking for us any more. Does that scare you?"

"Of course not. I've survived worse than a few days of travel."

The next Monday morning she was aboard a rocking Concord stagecoach, depressed that she wouldn't see him for weeks. She didn't know that circumstances would stretch that to a far more uncomfortable several months, with altered conditions in both of their lives.

She was on a riverboat, which just as it turned east from the Mississippi River to the Ohio River, crossed virtual paths with a telegram message heading to Abilene.

dearest annalise stop Mother passed last pm stop we're devastated stop don't know what your plans are stop love deidre.

****

The roundups of May and the subsequent sales were a considerable success. Whit realized close to $40,000. More than a third of that was split equally among his employees. Caroline and Myra received full shares, as did Gillespie, who managed his first round-up and drive with some trepidation. Jefferson, still recuperating, also got a full share, which he initially refused. "I wasn't there when you needed me." But Whit insisted. "We wouldn't have those fine horses to sell without you, son." The horse selling crew of Jack, Herk, and Charlie had returned from their third drive three days before the cattle were herded to Abilene.

After the cattle were penned, and the money transacted, the entire Brody assemblage walked to the Western wear store of Jacob Karotofsky, a sprawling emporium new to Abilene, and bought armloads of boots, Levi's shirts, and hats-Stetsons- from the loaded shelves of the German immigrant.

The Stetsons were the most valued purchases. Karotofsky carried a large selection, shipped from Philadelphia, where they were made by John B. Stetson and his employees. The first Stetsons had been produced at the end of the Civil War, exclusively for cowboys.

The purchases were loaded into the back of a farm wagon, presided over by Simeon, and driven behind the cattle drive expressively for this purpose. The Brody crew then returned to the ranch, a cattle drive completed in slightly more than half a day.

Instead of riding back, Jack broke off and rode to the Chase Place, the boarding house of Catharine Chase. He fairly galloped the few blocks, and was greeted at the door by Minnie.

"Yas suh? You be Mr. Jack."

"I am. Mr. Brody sent me to do some work for Mrs. Chase."

"She be expectin' you, Mr. Jack."

Minnie led him into the front parlor, and disappeared into the back of the house. Minutes later, Catharine walked into the room.

"Good afternoon, Jack. How did the drive go?"

As always. He was stunned. She wore a simple blue dress. Ringlets of auburn hair framed her face, a top knot somewhat askew. She was wiping her hands on a white towel. He was intimidated by her beauty, and as always, he was confused as to what to say to her. He silently cursed the effect that she had on him.

"Ma'am. It went well. Nothing much can happen on a twelve-mile drive."

"I'm so grateful to Mr. Brody and you for this. Will you have a cup of coffee? Or tea?"

"Yes, Ma'am. A cup of coffee would be nice."

He followed her to the kitchen, fumbling with his new Stetson.

"Sit at the table, Jack. Minnie, we'll need two cups of coffee. I'll be right back."

He sat and sipped at the coffee until she came back. He could swear that her hair was neater, more tightly coiffed than minutes before. She carried some rolled up papers.

"What did Mr. Brody tell you?"

"He said that you wanted to add a porch area to the back of the house."

"My boarders need a place to gather, especially in warm weather. I'd like to expand the back of the house, make it a sitting area, another place to eat, or an area just to sit and talk."

She unrolled and flattened the roll of papers, revealing intricate drawings of her concept. He smelled perfume of some sort as he stood next to her, but focused on the sketches.

"I've got timbers and cut wood stacked in the back yard, tools and nails. Can you do this?"

"Yes ma'am. Start tomorrow. Should be maybe a two-three week job, depending on the weather."

"I've got a small, extra room upstairs. You'll stay here?"

"I suppose so. Looks like maybe a two-man job. Mr. Brody told me to bring Lige, if I needed him. Looks like I might."

"That's fine. But you may have to sleep in the same room."

"We're in a bunkhouse together now."

"We'll give you all of your meals. I'd like to pay you."

"No ma'am. Mr. Brody says you're family."

He and Lige were back at daylight the next morning. Each carried a valise of clothes. The door was opened again by Minnie, who looked intently at Lige as the smells of breakfast drifted past them.

"Mawning, Mr. Jack. Mrs. Chase be in the kitchen. Says you can eat with us. Be ready soon. This be Mr. Lige? I be Minnie." She was smiling.

Lige nodded at her.

They sat in the parlor as a group of boarders filed past at intervals. Each nodded at Jack, and gave Lige a quick, cursory glance. An expensive-looking wall clock showed 7:00.

Minnie re-appeared, again paying visual deference to Lige. "Mizz Chase says to show you your room. It be upstairs, back corner."

Jack didn't see Catharine until breakfast was served, a copious collection of eggs, ham, fresh bread, and juices. She entered the dining room cosmetically ready for the day.

"Jack, I hope you have an appetite."

"Yes, ma'am." He could think of no other rejoinder, nothing clever.

"Good morning, Lige. I'm so grateful that you're part of this." She extended her hand, which Lige took tentatively, averting his eyes.

"These two men are going to build us a sitting room, ladies and gentlemen. This is Jack," she touched his arm, "and this is Lige. They're from the Brody ranch."

There were fourteen chairs crammed around the long table.

She introduced the boarders quickly, names that he wouldn't remember. One dapper man circled the table to shake their hands. Lige had not looked up yet.

He had counted eight bedroom doors upstairs. A couple of original rooms, he guessed, had been subdivided to create that number. There were eight boarders. An elderly couple, attentive to each other, were obviously together. Catharine and Minnie probably had separate bedrooms somewhere on the first floor. The house, built several years ago, had been bought and converted hastily into a boarding house. If Jack remembered correctly, Catharine had pulled that off in mere weeks. It was immaculate inside, and well-appointed. A handsome young boy flitted into the room. Jeremiah, Catharine's son. He sat next to his mother.

Jack watched the lively rapport among the boarders. Catharine sat at one end of the table, and deftly orchestrated the conversation. The older couple, the Talbots, responded openly and freely, as did the dapper man, a livestock buyer. Two widows of indeterminate age, a young clerk, and a gracious but opinionated lady named Priscilla Kamack completed the group.

All but the dapper man appeared to be permanent boarders. Jack thought several faces were familiar, probably from his infrequent attendance at Jonah Brook's House of Worship.

****

Dearest Jefferson,

All is so sad here. I arrived in time for Mother Maribel's funeral, a truly somber occasion attended by many people. It is quiet now. Portia and Deidre and their families have returned to their homes.

Sweet Herman is distraught beyond words. He has retreated both mentally and physically. He tears easily and often, and I must force him to eat. He requires much care.

I must stay here and tend to him. We decided we will not consign him to a facility. That would completely break him. His doctor informed us that he will probably not survive long without his soul mate.

Portia talked about hiring a private nurse, but I believe that someone from his family should be with him.

So, my Jefferson, I will remain with him for as long as he needs me. He sacrificed so much for me, and is the only father I've ever known.

I miss you so very much. When you heal, perhaps you can come here. I will live for that day. Are you being a good patient? Tell Rose and Joshua how much I miss them. I will write them as I can.

Portia and Deidre can't leave their families, but they have promised to relieve me here for two months so that I can come to Abilene later this year.

I must close. Dr. Webb's carriage has pulled up out front. He is a wonderful man, very attentive to Herman. He makes calls here several times a week.

Write when you can.

All my love,

Annalise

****

Catharine watched him surreptitiously from the kitchen window. He was in the back yard, securing a wall frame to a rope, preparing to lift the section into place by hoisting the piece over a secure beam. Tornado stood at the other end of the rope. Jack would nudge him gently soon, and the horse would pull away, lifting the frame into place. When it was upright, Jack and Lige would edge it into place, and nail it at various points.

The foundation was in place. This was the third and final wall piece.

Jack was efficient, skilled, confident. For that matter, so was Lige. They worked mainly without conversation, and took no breaks, except for meals.

She permitted herself to imagine Jack as a bed partner, and smiled privately at the thought. Lusty imaginings were nothing new to her. Jonathan had awakened and nurtured a strong libido in her years before. Abilene had not sustained it, barren of any men who stimulated desire, except for her brothers-in-law.

Why had she not noticed him before? He had been a quiet appurtenance, an attendant personality to her interactions with the Brody group. Rose had once teased her, "I think my cousin Jack is sweet on you." Her response had been, "Which one is he?" She had quickly dismissed the notion.

In the past days at the boarders' meals, he had participated actively in the mealtime conversations, demonstrating both a lively intelligence and a quiet wit. He unfailingly pulled out the chairs of the women nearest him, as they sat or left. Miss Kamack, thin and pale and stiff, flirted with him incessantly. Poor Lige had not yet uttered a word, except "Thank you ma'am" when Minnie filled his plate.

Countless men throughout Catharine's life had initially impressed her, and then had become nonentities as weaknesses and frailties became evident. All except for Jonathan. He and Jack Bertrand seemed to be doing it opposite ways.

The contradiction of a rugged physique and eyeglasses was attractive to her, as was his reticence and awkwardness in conversation with her. She had begun to cultivate the latter.

Some nights he walked down to the merchandise store to visit Joshua and Jefferson. Rose called him "the third brother." Most of the time he retired just after nightfall.

What would it be like to ruffle his thick brown hair, or to feel his strong arms around her? She was amused at the thought, and as no surprise, somewhat aroused.

****

"I'm going to take Noah to Abilene today, look over the building progress at Catharine's," Whit announced at breakfast. "If you want to go, you could spend a few hours with our grandson, maybe do some shopping. I can take the wagon."

"See Jacob?" Margaret mused. "That's the real reason you're going, isn't it?"

"Big part of it," he answered. "We haven't seen him for a while. I figure maybe Noah and I can give Jack and Lige a hand today. It's a pretty day, Maggie."

"Maybe Caroline would like to go. We could take her and Myra."

"Not a good idea for Myra to show up in Abilene yet. She'd probably love to be in charge here for a day. Gillespie can cook today."

"Caroline and I will ride our ponies. You won't need the wagon."

"Don't know. You're a good shopper. We can do both." He hugged her.

"By all means, take the wagon," she said, and kissed him on the cheek.

"Give me two hours to settle things here."

"Do you suppose Bird would want to go?"

"Not likely. She told me that she'll miss dinner tonight. Said she's cooking a meal for Herkimer."

"Whit?"

"I know. Will wonders never cease."

The familiar trail to Abilene was dazzling that morning. A light breeze blew against the riders, and the sky was untainted by clouds. The horses, swept up in the temperate conditions, were frisky. Almost to the Brody gate, Whit noticed four strangers approaching. One drove a buckboard, with a passenger; the other two were mounted. Whit slowed his wagon, and signaled his companions to stop. He waited as the wagon came closer. He saw no firearms. The approaching wagon was carelessly loaded, full of possessions.

"May I help you gentlemen?"

"Who you be?" the man driving the wagon answered. He squinted at Whit through one eye. The other was dull and clouded, obviously of no use to the man.

Whit looked them over. Next to the old man on the seat was a younger, fat man, taking up most of the seat. The riders were obviously related to the old man, thin and rumpled with tobacco stained beards. The old man was staring at him, mouth open. He was missing most of his front teeth.

"I'm Brody. I own this spread. You got business with me?"

"Don't figger so. Just havin' a look-see."

Noah rode up next to Whit, his hand resting lightly on his holster.

"Your wagon's loaded. You looking for a place to settle?" Whit asked.

"Might jist be doin' that," the old man responded. "Nice blackie you got there."

"That's mighty harsh, mister. This is private land in every direction."

"Wal, my boys was jist tellin' me that we found a home. Believe we'll find us a place to settle."

"Right now you're trespassing. I think you'd better turn around and ride out."

"You ain't none too friendly, Brody. We be goin' when we ready to be goin'." The two on horseback snickered at the remark. The fat boy shifted in his seat, a vacuous grin on his face.

Whit was struggling to hold on to his temper. "There is still free government land 100 miles north of here, if you're looking to homestead."

"Naw. Too far away. You got plenty of land here."

"This is a livestock ranch. Again, you'd better ride out."

"Now Brody, you makin' my sons angry. We like this here area. We're gonna pick out a nice spot."

"What is your name?" Whit asked.

"We be the Kaynes. That matter to you?"

Whit pulled his gun. Noah did the same.

"Mr. Kaynes, let me say this. If you don't turn around now, my friend and I will bust up your wagon, and shove it piece by piece up your sorry asses."

"You kiddin' me Brody? Two old men gonna drive us off?"

The four studied the odds for a moment. "Boys, let's go. Tellin' you this, Brody. We be back." He nodded toward the women. "We come back, may get some of them wimmin. They be old, but pretty nice, boys."

"If you come back, my men will turn you into scarecrows for our cornfield." Whit was shouting.

The Kaynes clan turned and rode back toward the east, past the Brody property line. Whit and his company followed, far behind.

"Noah, keep your gun handy. If they slow up or stop, we'll postpone this trip. We'll ride back to the ranch, and I'll pick up Herkimer and Big. "

"Whit," Margaret said, "those are pathetic, unfortunate men. You think you were too hard on them?"

"Maggie, they were on our land. You want them as neighbors?"

"I suppose not. You're cute when you're angry."

Several miles ahead, the Kaynes turned south. They were soon out of sight.

"Mistuh Brody, where you suppose they goin'?"

"Don't know Noah, probably to squat along the river. It's obvious that they don't intend to leave the area."

As soon as the Brody group had cleared the horizon, Elon Pack had left the smithy building and walked to the house.

She had seen him coming. She knew that he would. She stepped out of the back door to greet him.

"Miss Myra, I…" She threw her arms around his neck and kissed him, knocking off his hat. He pressed her against the door, continuing the embrace, and kissed her harder. She pulled him inside and pressed his hand to her chest. "So glad you came."

"Just wanted to see you alone, t-t-to explain 'bout the other night."

"That was wonderful."

"Don't seem r-right. I t-t-took advantage of you."

"I let you. Why you feeling bad?"

The months with the Brodys had been good to her. She had gained weight. She never wore make-up anymore. Her cheeks were ruddier, and the sun had delivered to her face almost as many freckles as he had. She would never be beautiful, but she was decidedly feminine, nicely rounded. She smiled often, and had not touched alcohol since she had come to the ranch. She spent hours brushing her hair, so that it was no longer frizzy, nor unhygienic. She pulled it back with an assortment of ribbons given to her by Caroline. Margaret had gotten her a new wardrobe.

"Just don't seem right, b-b-but it was n-nice."

"You already know you wasn't the first. Ain't real proud of that." She pulled away, and walked to the mess table. "I let you do it because I like you."

"You s'pose anybody k-knows?"

"I told Miss Caroline that I fancied you soon after I come here."

"You did?"

"You sorry we did it?"

"No. N-n-no. Just don't want you thinkin' b-bad of me."

The night in question had begun when Whit approached her before supper.

"Myra, everyone here has a horse. It's time you got one. We've got extra saddles and such in the barn. After supper tonight, go down to the stable and pick out a horse. Elon will help you out.

She was excited, grateful on many levels. "Thank you, Mr. Brody," she whispered. She was beaming.

Elon had prepared for her by missing supper, herding a dozen horses culled from a herd grazing nearby. They mingled quietly in the corral.

"All of these are gentle. S-s-some are around t-two-three years old," he had explained. "Them t-t-two over there are smaller than the rest. You can prob'ly see that."

She fixed on a light palomino, one of only three in the entire herd, and the smallest in the corral.

"That one. Yes. That one," she indicated.

"G-g-g-good choice, Miss Myra. He's a real nice horse." He entered the corral, and walked the palomino over to her. It nuzzled her arm.

"Listen. Coupla hours before dark. You w-want to ride him?"

"I'm not good on a horse. You want to help me?"

"Of course." He saddled the palomino, boosted her on somewhat awkwardly, and led them around the corral. She was unsteady.

"Miss Myra. Mr. Brody says you got t-to name him afore he's y-y-yours."

"Sunshine. Yes, Sunshine. He's so shiny."

"We got some t-time afore dark. You wanna take him for a short r-r-ride?"

"Ain't really dressed for it. Yes. That would be nice, if we don't go fast."

They cantered the horses north. Initially she held on to the saddle horn. Elon convinced her to use the reins, and soon a slow gallop boosted her confidence.

In a field several miles north of the ranch house, she slowed to a walk.

"You w-w-wanna rest a m-minute?"

She nodded.

He dismounted, and started to help her down, but she caught her shoe on the stirrup and fell fully into his arms. They both fell to the ground.

"Oh, I'm sorry. Sorry," she said as she turned toward him, their faces inches apart.

He kissed her rather brusquely, thought better of it, and pulled away. "Ma'am, I…"

She pulled him back and kissed him. The embrace continued, and then they were disrobing frantically. Soon she was astride him, breathing hard, moving against him with expertise gleaned from years of pleasuring horny cowboys. He closed his eyes, trying to sustain the moment, and then exhaled loudly as spasms from both of them peaked and subsided.

"Elon, that was nice," she told him.

"We b-b-better get b-back. It'll be dark soon."

Neither spoke on the trot back to the ranch. He took her reins and started for the barn.

"Goodnight, Elon, thank you," she called back to him.

"Goodnight, Ma'am."

****

Death was a constant presence in Abilene. It was an eventuality which would occur with some certitude between the ages of 35 and 55.

Many circumstances dictated that: the harsh living conditions, the separation from contemporary medical facilities, pestilence and disease, the prevalence of men and women with short tempers, alcoholism, and an inordinately high incidence of suicide from desperation and failed dreams.

Three factions benefitted from that, the doctors and ministers who tried to forestall it, and the undertakers, who profited from it.

Eleven doctors plied their trades in Abilene by 1869, ranging from untrained pretenders to former medical staff members from the Civil War to knowledgeable practitioners who read and researched voraciously to keep abreast of the latest theories and practices.

Of the latter group, two were prominent, Dr. Hank Rosbottom, a relative newcomer; and Dr. Jerome Beedle, a young man from the East who practiced in the country on the road to Topeka. Both were comfortable with their stations, but often, a large percentage of their patients couldn't pay for services rendered.

The main undertaking business was Schmidt-Muller on Spruce Street, run by three immigrants from Germany, Gunter Schmidt, and the Muller brothers Han and Josef. The brothers doubled as cabinet makers of great skill, so when a casket was needed, they could quickly produce an attractive, sturdy wood product, which could cost its buyer anywhere from six to seventy dollars. The company also offered an ornate black hearse with windows, pulled by the same two horses used to pull the wagon filled with corpses from a gunfight.

Schmidt-Muller was paid $3 per victim by the city to clean up after gunfights, and to remove indigent bodies found randomly and constantly, and unidentified victims of some tragedy. For that amount, the victim was taken to a paupers' cemetery east of town, and unceremoniously buried in a cheap casket in whatever he was wearing when he expired. Burials occurred as soon as possible after death. None of the Germans was proficient in the relatively new practice of embalming.

Churches were scattered around the area, some denominational to serve various cultures, and some like the House of Worship, which welcomed all congregants. The bulk of Abilene residents were not churchgoers, so attendance at most churches was scant and sporadic, until some small catastrophe, such as the drought of 1868, prompted a conversation with God.

Reverend Jonah Brooks had a substantial following, however, and had attained an iconic and heroic status among his congregants. Cleetus and Bear Woman were accorded the same admiration. How many souls had the three saved in their short time in Abilene? How many suicides prevented? How many soiled doves had found some semblance of self respect?

Those numbers continued to grow. So did the deaths in the Kansas community.

****

The fishing excursions had grown in scope in recent months, sometimes involving trips far up the Solomon River, or to tributaries of the Kaw. Doc Rosbottom was a regular. Jonah brought Cleetus, and the group from the ranch usually included Whit, Noah, Lige, Big, and Charlie Fox. Sometimes, old Simeon tagged along, although his energy was demonstrably slowing, his endurance eroding.

The trips occurred in mid-week, every five weeks or so, and had expanded to two-day affairs, overnights. Rosbottom drove his wagon, loaded with equipment, food, blankets, poles and lures, and rain gear.

Jonah was the most competent of the anglers, followed by Cleetus, but fellowship ruled the trips.

By firelight on the night of the most recent trip, Doc broke out his banjo. At daybreak Whit and Rosbottom stood on a bank above an eddy, casting around Jonah, who had waded into the flow, fly-casting. They were along the bank of a fast-flowing, cold stream, a tributary of a tributary. Farther downstream, the other five were scattered along the water.

"You're a lucky man, Whit," Doc said.

"How so, Doc?"

"Well look what you've gathered here, an Indian, three black men, a Texas Ranger, a minister, and a broken down doctor. Everybody enjoying each other. You're the reason."

It seemed a poignant comment from a lonely man.

Whit quickly deflected it. "No, Doc. You're the lucky one. Everything you do helps someone. There's something almost Biblical about a doctor who treats half his patients without pay."

"Then again, look at the Reverend. He's the luckiest. Best fisherman here because the Lord is on his side," Doc rejoined.

Jonah called over his shoulder, "From what's happening this morning, I'd say that the Lord is on the fishes' side."

"While we're praising each other, look what's happening downstream. Charlie Fox is fishing the stream dry," Whit pointed out.

"That boy is one of your best projects, Whit. Good-natured. Respectful," Doc said.

"The credit for that goes to his mother," Whit explained. "She's a fine lady, a survivor."

"Without you, where would any of your hands be?" Jonah called over.

"They're all survivors. They'd be fine," Whit replied.

"I hope the Lord puts a big fish on your line for being humble," Rosbottom said. "Can you make that happen, Jonah?"

"The Lord helps those who help themselves," Jonah responded. "Whit's got to put his hook closer to that brush pile over there."

There was a long silence. Big moved closer to the group, hoping to change his fortunes.

"How do you feel about Abilene?" Whit asked.

"To be honest. I'm concerned. At last count there were fifty-seven saloons, almost all of them offering gambling and sins of the flesh. More people coming every day. Too much violence," Jonah answered.

"Why'd you ask, Whit. You figuring on pulling up stakes?"

"Nothing's forever, Doc. It has crossed my mind. A couple of good lawmen and some honest judges would make a difference."

"Give the sheriff's job to Herkimer Grimes. Deputize Joshua, Jefferson, and Big. The town would be clean in two hours," Rosbottom offered.

Big grunted.

Whit smiled. "Herkimer's through with that. Big too. The other two have plans which don't include Abilene. I heard that two lawmen from St. Louis are coming in soon to look over the job."

"Heat of the day. Full sun on the water. The fish aren't biting," Jonah said as he sloshed to the bank.

"It is getting warm. That pool of water over there is beginning to look inviting," Rosbottom mentioned.

An hour later, the entire group basked in the sun, drying off.

"Did you have a good year, Whit? The cattle drive and all?" Jonah asked.

"Not bad. It was a good year, despite losing those cows last year."

"Losing cows?"

"Yeah. Texas fever scare. Had to shoot some of our own."

"Texas fever. Longhorns," Cleetus said.

"Exactly. It could have been bad. Some of our stock was exposed to a large herd of longhorns. We need some new rules."

"Ban the longhorns?" Jonah asked.

"They'd never do that. That's the attraction in Abilene. The Texas ranchers don't have many other options. I've had some talks with the buyer's group. They won't change anything, although they did promise to separate the longhorns. Different buying areas. Different stockyards. Different train cars."

"Won't that help?"

"In theory. You can separate the cattle. That doesn't mean you can separate the ticks."

"Let me ask. If infected longhorns are shipped east, butchered, is the meat tainted? Aren't people at risk?" Doc asked.

"Possibly. There's no definite word on that. The danger is that other breeds will get sick on the way, and die. Entire rail cars could arrive in Chicago with dead cargo. I've heard that it happens," Whit offered.

"Cleetus, we got enough fish for a meal?" Rosbottom asked.

Cleetus stood. “If we do, it’s because of Charlie Fox. Nobody else doing much today.”

“Big. How you doing? What’s the problem?” Doc asked.

“Too much palaver. We gonna talk, or we gonna fish? If we want meat for lunch, we goin’ to have to eat Doc’s horse.”

****

June. 6

My darling Annalise,

I received your latest letter yesterday, and gave your inclusion to Rose to her. I hope you got her letter last week. Mine too.

The leg is healing nicely. I’ve been walking around, after a fashion, with a crutch. Doc feels that the cast can some off at the end of the month. I won’t be running any footraces for a while, though. Meanwhile, Jacob has learned to walk. Joshua is on a buying trip, so I’m a fill-in father and babysitter while Rose minds the store. The little guy is becoming a handful. When he settles for a nap, I’ve been managing your library. Everyone asks about you. Weasel is particularly upset by your absence.

You asked about your eagle. Nobody’s seen him for several months. I’d guess that he was a young one, off on a bachelor trip before settling down as a family man. By now he’s probably chasing female eagles all over the Rocky Mountains.

There was a brawl in the Alamo Saloon two nights ago. Two cowboys got into a fight over a bar girl. They both pulled out firearms and killed each other. The Texas drives should be over in three weeks, so there should be a modicum of peace for a while.

Jack and Lige just finished putting up a closed porch at Catharine’s. It looks real nice. I miss you. Annalise. I’m thinking that I’ll be cleared to come to Cincinnati in a few weeks.

Much love,

Jefferson

****

Several questions along the waterfront were all that it took. Corby Pitcock, posing as a newspaper writer, asked them after convincing dock workers that he was doing a series on slavery.

“There was an incident here about ten years ago. A black female was kidnapped from here. Her daughter looked for her. I believe the slave’s name was Ollimore. Do you remember anything about the incident?”

The third dockworker remembered. “I was asked ‘bout that several years ago. Seem to ‘member the family was maybe called O’Neill. Don’t know much more. I’d ask them fellas in the cargo shack, if’n it was me.”

“O’Neill,” Pitcock repeated to a little man with a folder, a pencil stuck behind his ear.

"Oh, yessir. Been in Cincinnati 'most twenty year. Remember that well. Got a good mem'ry. That's be Herman O'Neill that owned her. Story got a lot of play for years. Believe he was a perfessor over to the medical school."

"Excellent, my good man. What is your name? I'll use it in a story."

The man eagerly gave up his name while Pitcock pretended to write it down.

"And how do I get to the medical school?"

Armed with directions, Pitcock rented a carriage and gave the reins to Muley. Luther rode a separate horse rented from the livery.

Arrived at the college, Pitcock changed persona. He was looking for a long-lost cousin he said, a professor, Herman O'Neill, but he had no idea of his whereabouts. "Our mothers were sisters. Haven't seen old Herman for thirty years. I really want to surprise him. My mother told me on her deathbed that Herman taught here."

A clerk informed, "Yes, I know of him. Poor soul. He's afflicted. He hasn't presided here in years. He lives over on the west side, I believe. If you ask the administration people, they could probably find an address for forwarding mail. Think his wife passed on recently. Big story in the papers."

"I'll do that. You've been a big help. I can't thank you enough."

"Didja get anything?" Luther asked, as Pitcock limped to the carriage.

"Just everything. The old man's the key. May have to persuade him to give up where she is."

Muley parked the carriage a good distance from the bungalow, and the three observed an old man stooping over a flower garden in the front yard.

"That him?" Luther asked.

"Now how the hell should I know that? Just shut up and watch."

There was no sign of other people.

"That must be O'Neill. Muley, those two young ones never saw you. Get up there, and find out what's going on," Pitcock commanded.

"What kin I ask him?"

"Jesus, man. Use your head. Tell him you like his damn garden."

"Mister O'Neill?" Muley addressed the white-haired gardener, who was hovering over a bed of red and white flowers of some kind. The man looked up.

"No, I ain't him. Name's William. I tend to his gardens."

"Is Mr. O'Neill home?"

"He's inside, but he ain't doin' well. What's your bizness with him?"

"Oh, nothing much. I be lookin' at this house and them beautiful flowers. Wondering if Mr. O'Neill be interested in sellin'."

William had a fleeting moment of suspicion. The man before him was disheveled, certainly not a man of means. He didn't look like a homeowner.

"Don't think he be selling right away. Pretty sick. Won't be movin'."

"Mebbe I can talk to Mrs. O'Neill."

"Ain't one. She died a few weeks back."

"Mr. O'Neill is takin' care of hisself?"

"Nope. Miss Annalise been takin' good care of him."

"I see. A relative, I suppose."

"Nope. Miss Annalise come here from Kansas somewheres. Came alone. Mr. Jefferson, he still in Kansas."

"You must be a good help too."

"Nope. Don't live here. Just come by every now and then to do some gardening, sometimes some shopping."

This stupid old man is telling me everything, Muley thought.

"Well, I've got my eye on this place. Got a large family. Hankerin' to move them into a nice house like this one. I can pay cash money for it."

"Spect you oughta ask again in a few months. Mr. O'Neill 'pears to be failin'. Wanna give me your name?"

"No. I'll check back late in the summer."

Muley was cackling as he returned to the carriage. "What be the name of the girl who sent that letter to the authorities back at our trial, Boss?"

"Annalise Ollimore."

"Annalise. That's it! She be in there all by herself, takin' care of old O'Neill. He's sickly. That feller is just the gardener; don't live here.."

"The big guy who shot me. What about him?"

"The gardener say he be in Kansas someplace."

"Get in. We'll wait until dark."

He'd have his revenge soon.

Annalise folded the letter from Jefferson, finished reading it for the third or fourth time. She laid it on the dining room table. In the lengthy routine of getting Herman to bed, of reading to him, of holding his hand, and singing quietly until he was asleep, she realized that she had again neglected her own supper. She had changed into billowing nightshirt, one of Herman's. The next two hours would be hers. She would prepare something simple and write to Jefferson.

If only Herman could hold on until Jefferson came east. There were signs that he would. In the past week, he seemed more alert. He was eating better, and brightened considerably when there were house guests. Her rewards were an occasional crooked smile, and an obvious tenderness in his eyes when he looked at her.

A noise, a bump of some sort against the back of the house, got her attention, and she turned that direction just as the front door crashed open, its small window shattering. The door bounced hard against the entrance wall.

To her horror, she saw the hulk of the man from Pitcock's, the ugly, primitive man who had tried to rape her, standing in the frame. She turned quickly, and collided with a skinny man coming from the back. He threw a violent fist into her jaw, and she fell backward, landing hard, dazed.

Reflexively she pulled her nightshirt down, rolled over, and leaped to her feet. Not fast enough. Luther wrapped her in a bear hug from behind, and wrestled her around to face the smashed front door.

Standing in the doorway, leering and smug, was Corby Pitcock.

"Well, look at this. What you got there, Luther? This the slave who cost me my leg, my plantation?"

Pitcock limped in and swung his cane into her left knee. Annalise crumpled and screamed.

"Close that door, Muley. Don't want to wake the neighbors. Lift her back up, Luther."

Luther pulled her back up by her hair. Pitcock slapped her hard enough to bring blood to her mouth, and she fell away from Luther, who kicked her in the chest as she bounced off of a chair.

"Let's have a look-see. Pull off her nightgown."

Annalise knew that she'd have to fight back, as hard and as long as she could. They meant to kill her. As Luther grabbed the hem of the nightshirt and tugged at it, she kicked out in an arc, kicking him in the crotch.

"Yeeow! You bitch!" Luther howled, and pushed her down, straddling her chest. "Bitch! Bitch! Bitch!" He growled, punctuating each word with a punch to her face, which snapped her head from side to side. She lay still, barely conscious, as he ripped off her nightshirt.

"Look at that, Muley. Fine piece of woman. Go ahead Luther. Get you some," Pitcock said. "Give us a show." He sat in Herman's large chair by the fire.

Luther dropped his pants and spread her legs. He raped her for several minutes, groaning and groveling until he moaned his release.

"Muley, you next?"

"S'pose so, Boss." The skinny man cackled and squealed as he climbed atop her and pumped furiously. He was still wearing his hat and shirt and boots, and Pitcock found that hilarious. The laughing stopped when Pitcock heard a noise from behind a closed door. The old man. "Luther, check out that room. Bring the old guy in here."

"Muley, splash some water on her. Wake her up. I want to talk to her. Put her in that chair over there."

"Aincha goin' to do her, Boss?"

"Not after you two spoiled the meat," Pitcock answered.

Annalise struggled back to consciousness, a hazy, fragile state, in time to feel excruciating pain as Pitcock sliced the left side of her face with a knife.

"Goin' to start peelin' your face off, little lady, unless you answer me. Where is your boyfriend."

Jefferson. She wouldn't tell. Whatever they did to her. Her situation was hopeless. She would protect him.

"Boss, over here on the table. Found a letter. Thinkin' it be from a Jefferson. Heared the gardener say his name."

"Bring it here." Pitcock circled the chair to take the letter. She saw a chance. She jumped up unsteadily and lunged for the door. She made it to the door, but her head seemed to explode as Pitcock's cane, swung erratically, crashed into the back of it. She grabbed at the doorknob, slid to the floor, and lay still.

"Boss, you done killed her."

"Gimme the damn letter." He scanned it quickly. "Doesn't mention no town name. Here. Talks about an Alamo Saloon. That's it. Large Kansas town with an Alamo Saloon. Cattle drives. That narrows it down. Where's the envelope?"

"Been lookin'. Can't find it."

Minutes passed as Pitcock and Muley searched for the envelope, which certainly had a postmarked city written on it.

"Where the hell is Luther? Luther, get out here! Gotta go now before someone investigates the noise over here."

Luther came back into the room, and checked Annalise sprawled on the floor, unmoving. "If'n she ain't dead, she close."

"What about the old man?"

"Think he be a dummy, Boss. Didn't make a sound."

"You killed him?"

"Won't do us no harm."

The faint sound of horse hooves caught Pitcock's attention. He limped to a front window. The rider had passed. "C'mon. We're leaving now!"

Dr. Phillipi Webb slowed his carriage in front of the O'Neill house. He had told Annalise that he'd check on Herman on his way to Good Sam. It was a bit early, just past seven am, he guessed.

Checking on the professor was his duty. Seeing her was a bonus. He was smitten with the raven-haired, lithe Annalise. Smart, beyond beautiful. He knew that she was somewhat fond of him too. The trouble was that she often talked of her fiancé, Jefferson Chase of Abilene, Kansas, a hero of the Great War. Several days ago, she had hugged him when he left after examining Mr. O"Neill. He would bide his time. She would be in Cincinnati for a while.

Strange. The front door of the O'Neill house stood partially open. He approached warily, and pushed tentatively on the door. "Hello?" The door was stopped by something behind it. He pushed harder, and it slid a bit more open. Then he saw blood on the floor. Scattered drops. He peeked behind the door and gasped. Bile rose in his throat. Annalise was lying on her side, unclothed, a wound across her face. Dried blood covered her face, partially obscuring eyes which were grotesquely swollen shut. He quickly knelt and felt for a pulse. It was faint, much too slow and feeble. She was alive, barely, he knew.

Herman. Webb walked straight to the bedroom. Careful he thought, I might not be alone in here. The room was dim, but he saw what he feared. Herman was on the floor on his back, a pillow hiding his face. Webb knew before he checked. The old man was dead, apparently smothered. There was no pulse, no heartbeat, no respiration.

"My God!" The sound involuntarily escaped. He was stunned. His focus then was on her. He'd have to transport her immediately to Good Samaritan Hospital. He grabbed a blanket from Herman's bed, and gently wrapped her in it, then carried her at a trot to his carriage, calling to a man he saw in the adjoining yard, "Get word to the police! There's been a murder in there!"

Jefferson handed the telegram to Rose, unable to speak.

"No, Jefferson, no!" She repeated the phrase as she read and reread the small missive.

terrible tragedy stop herman dead stop annalise critical stop come at once stop good samaritan hospital stop doctor phillipi webb stop

Rose embraced him, tears flowing freely.

"Rosie, please go get Doc Rosbottom. Tell him to bring his saw."

Pitcock and his cronies stayed in their rooms on the steamboat back to the West. "Don't want anyone to see us. We've already been seen by the dockworkers, the college folks, the gardener, the livery people. The law will know too much. They won't look for us in Arkansas, maybe never."

"Boss," Luther had asked, "Why didn't we lay low in Cincinnati, and wait for the big guy to show up?"

"Because, you idiot, you killed a man. For all we know, the girl's dead too. Two murders. It isn't like getting rid of slave people. A few months from now, we'll head out to Kansas. We'll get him there. Not much law out that way."

"Boss, what if the girl's still alive. What if she tells the law?"

"Been thinking about that. We should've finished the job with her. She's probably dead. If she is still alive, it's her word against ours, and nobody knows where we are now, anyway. Arkansas. They'd be looking for us in St. Louis. No other witnesses. We were never in Cincinnati. Never used our real names anywhere we were. Besides, she's had a grudge against us anyway. You know what, Luther? It feels good!"

Phillipi Webb contemplated the young man in front of him. He seemed composed. What would one expect from a war hero facing a crisis? But he was grim-faced and markedly concerned.

"Dr. Webb, I'm grateful that you can fill me in. I came straight from the riverfront. I don't know anything except what was in your telegram."

"I knew your name and Abilene from Miss Ollimore. Shall we sit down?"

"I want to see Annalise."

"Mr. Chase, she's hanging on, but nothing is certain. She lost a lot of blood. She was beaten severely."

"Where is she?"

"Prepare yourself for the worst. She's in a room down the hall. We've got staff with her around the clock."

"Is she alert?"

Webb shook his head no. "Walk with me." He guided Jefferson toward a hallway. "She's in a coma. She's not responding at all. That concerns me. She's held her own for a few days recently, but some of the damage to her head may be irreversible. She may pull through, but it's uncertain if she will be the girl you knew."

He noticed that Jefferson was limping. "Are you alright, Mr. Chase?"

"I'm fine. Does anyone know who did this? I'm assuming that the same thing happened to Professor O'Neill. Where did it happen?"

"It occurred in the O'Neill home, late at night. Professor O'Neill was smothered. And no, I'm afraid that no one knows anything. I discovered the tragedy, and for a while the police suspected me. When we determined that it happened around 9:00 in the evening, they let me go. I was here, delivering a baby at nine o'clock." They were in a hallway, hushed and sterile. A nurse looked up from a desk as they passed, and then averted her eyes.

"So you discovered them?"

"I was making a call on Mr. O'Neill." He stopped outside of a door, slightly ajar. "Before we go in, brace yourself. We're addressing the worst of her injuries. She has a broken jaw, a broken nose, and a severe injury to her knee. Her face was slashed with some type of knife. The head injury is serious, but the brain doesn't appear to be swollen. And, sir, I must tell you, she was brutalized, raped, possibly several times."

Jefferson turned his head away. "Let's go in," he muttered.

He followed the doctor into a dark room. A thin, stern-looking nurse stood from a bedside chair as they entered. In the dim light from a flickering candle, and a shaft of light from the hallway, he saw her. Her head was wrapped in dressings. Her eyes were closed,

swollen shut. A device of some kind was clamped on both sides of her head, immobilizing her. Her leg was elevated to a stirrup. One side of her face was covered by a lumpy bandage. Jefferson stopped.

"She is breathing effectively. The nose will heal. So will her jaw. We can't do much about her cheek; she will have a scar. Our concern is how much her brain suffered."

Jefferson wasn't listening to the description. At that moment, he was taken aback by the visual nightmare before him. He crossed to the bed, and lightly touched her arm. "Annalise, it's Jefferson. I'm here, sweetheart. I love you."

There was no response.

****

A tension was beginning to occupy him, a pervasive feeling that disturbed his sleep and soured his mood. He was getting nowhere. Several letters from the East were stacked unopened on a carton in his bunkhouse room. He knew what was in them, harsh reprimands from Sawyer, threats to stop the funding and to abandon the project.

Gillespie/Gerdon had no new information on Herkimer Grimes. Not that his sources were uncooperative. They simply didn't know more than they had already revealed, and what he did have was mostly hearsay. Western legend. Anecdotal garbage. Big was tight lipped, and no help. If he didn't luck onto some fount of biographical information soon, he would have to go to Grimes himself. That wouldn't go well. That failing, he could resort to his imagination again. Sawyer would never know. How about a romance between Grimes and the Indian foreman? Grimes hatred of Indians was well-known. That would have literary appeal, although in real life, it would never happen. It would be great drama, irony on a large scale. Gunplay of some sort was mandatory, the aging warrior strapping on his holster for some heroic purpose. Maybe he'd substitute Herkimer for Whit Brody's struggle through the blizzard years ago, an oft-repeated part of the ranch lore.

There was risk in all of that, but Gillespie was running out of options. He was already out of time.

At least his alter ego was still intact. His photographic record of the area was expanding. He had stumbled onto unique wildlife pictures so regularly that his cover story was becoming his abiding interest. Sawyer might be impressed. Maybe he'd publish another "picture book." Maybe his own station was one of a photo-chronicler.

If he continued his Grimes plan, fictional fantasy, Sawyer would discover the ruse eventually. He would sue for the return of the project funds. Gillespie would be ruined, financially and professionally.

Yet he had no clear plan on how to solve his problem.

****

In his first week in Cincinnati, Jefferson left her bedside only rarely. He visited the graves of his aunt and uncle. He secured a hotel room that he never used. He asked questions at the Cincinnati Police Department.

Scattered pieces of information had surfaced. William, the O'Neill gardener, told of a strange man with a scar who had asked questions on the day of the assault. A clerk at the medical college reported that a purported cousin of Herman's had that same day asked for his address. The description of the two men was different, a skinny man, and a well-dressed man who walked with a cane.

"We think it may be a random crime, maybe planned after the newspaper reports on the death of Mrs. O'Neill," the police investigator told Jefferson. "If I may talk indelicately, the girl may have been an attraction to somebody, pretty and all."

Jefferson grimaced.

"We know that robbery was not a motive. The daughter, Deidre, told us that it didn't appear that anything of value was missing," the official continued.

"I hope this case has high priority," Jefferson said.

"The highest. Your uncle was an academic legend in the community. We are stumped at the present time."

" The girl. She is a remarkable lady. Don't lose sight of that. There were two victims," Jefferson said testily.

"Of course, Mr. Chase."

"Will you inform me if anything else turns up?"

"Where are you staying?"

"I'll be at Good Samaritan Hospital. You can get a message to me through Dr. Phillipi Webb." Jefferson turned to go.

"Mr. Chase, may I ask you something? Are you related to Salmon P. Chase?"

"The politician?"

"One of my heroes. Almost became President. He's from here, you know. Met him once."

"No. No relation."

Jefferson had missed Herman's funeral by a day, and had missed seeing Portia and Deidre, who had departed the morning of the day he arrived. Both would return in the week ahead, to begin to settle the affairs of their father, and to help monitor the care of Annalise. That would begin a vigil next to the battered girl, still non-responsive, still clinging to life.

His cousins having returned, the hospital room became the center of memories for the sisters, as they told Jefferson stories of the young Annalise, precocious and animated, and of her beautiful, courageous mother.

"Nothing was too much of a challenge to either of them," Portia recalled. "Annalise was a tree climber, a reader of books, a collector of information. Missy learned to read and write in mere months. Annalise was her teacher."

"I remember hearing them sing together. There was beautiful music coming out of that cottage. They were so content, so happy…until Missy disappeared," Deidre said.

The two were pleasant and pretty. They had lost so much in the past months, and they were trying to buoy his spirits. Portia had Maribel's carriage and confidence. Deidre reminded him of Herman, astute and kind. Over the following days and long nights, they listened as he recounted the details of courtship, honoring Annalise's involvement more than his own.

The sisters left Cincinnati ten days later, without any resolution. Their father's killer or killers still remained unidentified. Annalise had not rallied. Jefferson dashed off a note to Joshua.

My Dear Brother and Sister-in-law,

There is no news. Dr. Webb informed me that if Annalise recovers, she may be seriously impaired for life. She is still in a coma.

There are no suspects and no leads. I am certain that the deed was done by two men or more. Annalise is so spirited that a single attacker would have had his hands full.

Her color has returned. Her face is healing. The bruises have disappeared. Her beauty is returning, but she has not come back yet.

I will stay here as long as I need to, as long as it takes. If that becomes years, so be it.

Be well, my loved ones. Kiss Jacob for me.

I love you both. Jefferson

She fought through a confusing web of pain, confusion, and constraint, focused on a pattern of afternoon light spread across the face of a man sleeping in a chair a few feet away. She whispered his name, he looked like Jefferson, and then stopped. Somewhere in the scrambled reorganization of rational thought, she assumed that she was dreaming. She blinked the one eye that was available to her, a puzzlement. A persistent ache, which spread from the back of her head and radiated down her shoulders and arms, distracted her, drowning her revived consciousness in a confluence of pain and fear. She closed her eye, blinking again against mounting anxiety and visual signals that made no sense. She tried to rally, to sort through information. That was Jefferson in the chair, she decided. He could explain this.

She whispered his name again, a hoarse sound framed as a question. "Jefferson?"

He jerked awake and moved quickly to her side. "Annalise, it's Jefferson. I'm here."

"Jefferson…what happened? Where are we?"

"An accident. There was an accident, Annalise."

She faded from consciousness and was still. He sprinted from the room to find Dr. Webb.

Rose paused, holding the telegram to her chest. It had arrived minutes ago, delivered by a running agent, fairly out of breath.

"Saw it…was from…Mister Jefferson. Figured…you'd want it…right away."

Rose knew that tragic news usually came by telegram. She couldn't read it.

She would wait for Joshua, who was loading a wagon at the depot. She folded the telegram in half, and laid it on a work table. She was trembling.

****

Part charade, part curiosity, Robert Sawyer Gillespie/Gerdon set the tripod on a flat spot at the edge of the northeast woods. Now he would wait, too much waiting, until some form of fauna appeared. Anything. Any size. Of course, the white wolf would make the day a success, but in preparation for this day, he had employed no stealth, little cover, and no technique for hiding himself.

Recently he had brought kitchen waste with him, and fashioned a primitive lure for whatever creature was emboldened enough to ignore a human presence. Not today. His only concession to diligence was a canvas tarpaulin, draped from the wagon behind him to sticks above the camera in front of him. The horse was unhitched, grazing on a knoll nearby.

He sat cross-legged on a blanket spread under the canopy, and extracted a pad of paper and a pencil from his vest. If nothing happened in a few hours, he would find a herd of the Brody cattle, and look for shots of interest. He had a large collection of pictures of the Brody cattle.

An hour into his half-hearted surveillance, he had a sudden feeling that he was not alone. He dismissed it. The Kansas wind was blowing vigorously, and his makeshift tent was fluttering loudly. The hot summer wind was both refreshing and oppressive.

He heard a whinny from the direction of the knoll, then another. It sounded as if the wagon horse was restless, maybe bored.

Or scared! That thought coincided with a sudden bulky weight on his back, which collapsed the canopy and the camera, and sent him tumbling. Tangled in the heavy weight of the canvas, he felt a sharp pain in an exposed leg, as something tore at it with a snarl. He kicked hard at the intruder with his other leg, panicked when it had no effect, and jerked the cover from his head, the screaming of the wagon horse in the background.

He saw the attacker. The white wolf.

The wolf leaped forward toward the photographer's face and neck. Desperate, Gerdon tried to wrap the canvas around the wolf, instead trapping his own right arm in the tangle of canvas.

Gerdon rolled away from the yellowed eyes and putrid breath. Bits of froth scattered from the wolf's mouth as it pounced on Gerdon, and sank his fangs into the man's neck. Summoning frantic energy, Gerdon rolled again and yelled, a tactic which froze the wolf. Gerdon scrambled to his knees and pulled the canvas away from his body.

Briefly, the two faced each other from a ten foot distance, the man panting, the wolf's head lowered. A hideous grin pulled back from shiny fangs which glistened with blood.

Gerdon's mind raced. Whit's rifle was in the wagon. The wolf was between him and the wagon. He kept his eyes on the wolf, knowing that if he looked away, it would attack again.

In the tenuous stand-off, Gerdon noticed that the wolf was emaciated, much more bedraggled than the proud figure in pictures that he had taken.

He got it. The wolf was rabid.

The demented wolf would persist, he knew. Predictable behavior would not occur.

Gerdon knew that he would probably die.

****

"Gone ! Dammit! When?" John Wicks was furious. The bawdy house owner had just discovered that two more of his doves had defected the night before, following several cowboys from Texas, who had flashed thick wads of greenbacks during a night of wild revelry. Wick's cheeks were bright red, his eyes twitched. "What in hell is goin' on!"

He stomped toward his piano player, a timid ex-slave named Tickles.

"Why dint you stop 'em? Why dint you wake me?"

Spittle flew into Tickles' face. He began to back away. He knew that he was about to get slapped, or worse.

"Afore I knowed it dey be gone. Tole me they be goin' to St. Louie. Say you tell 'em to have a vacation. That be three in de mawnin'. Thought it be sumpin' fishy. Check they rooms dis mawnin'. Dey be cleaned out, 'cept for de curtains."

Two more gone. Beginning with Myra, then Clara, several months ago, he had lost six of his whores. Business was bad. He now had five women, one of them pregnant, three of them middle-aged chubby locals with body odor and non-existent lovemaking skills. Why was it happening? He had fancied up the bordello recently, hired Tickles to liven up the waiting room, and taken on a chef of sorts for their meals. Sure, he sometimes beat on them, and ordered all of them to be compliant with the insistent and deviate desires of the two Dooley brothers. But that was part of business.

It was not just his whorehouse that was suffering defections. Throughout the district girls were abandoning their employers, striking out for new territory, or giving up their jobs to look for husbands. As always, there was no pressure from the law, and there were more clients than ever, from the cattle drives.

The one constant in many of the lives of the vanishing prostitutes was church. The Reverend Jonah Brooks.

He tip-toed up to the second floor door of the room that the Dooleys shared. They didn't like to be disturbed before noon, but he needed to talk.

A naked Lester answered the door. "What the hell, Wicks?" Lester turned away and went back to his bed, leaving the door open. Wicks stepped into the unkempt room.

"Wicks, get someone up here this afternoon. Beds ain't been changed for a month. Beginning to stink in here. When you leave send up Dinah Sue for J.T. He needs some pokin' to wake up," Lester ordered.

"Can't. Dinah Sue left, early this mornin', with Wilma."

"Gone where?" J.T. asked, raising to one elbow.

"Quit. Sneaked off last night."

"That's bad. Them two was good at pleasurin'," J.T. offered.

" Yes. Best two earners we had. Young. Clean."

"So, whatcha goin' to do about it? Just bitch?" Lester said.

"We's not to blame."

"How you get them whores in the first place?"

"First wagonload just came to Abilene, lookin' for a place to whore. I got most of them. Made a coupla trips to Kansas City. Brought back some new ones."

"Wicks, you ever think 'bout takin' some away from the other houses here?"

"I'd hafta pay more. Have a large base of cowboys."

"Yeah, or just tell 'em to get their asses over here. This talk is boring me. I don't give a fart 'bout this place, but it's a good hideout, and you had plenty of wimmin. You'd better leave for Kansas City in the next few days, and bring some more back. Time you get back, me an' J.T. have some ladies here from down the street."

"Don't kill nobody, Lester."

"Can't promise you that, partner."

"Now, there is one other thing, boys."

"Make it fast."

"Well," Wicks began, "there be a lot of whores from the street, worshippin' every Sunday down to the House of Worship."

"Why don't you stop it then? You supposed to have control over your whores, anyway," Lester said, reaching for a shirt on the floor.

"Been lettin' mine go to keep the townsfolk off our backs. Didn't seem to be no problem."

"You stupid man. What you think Jonah Brooks be teachin' them over there? How to suck a man dry?"

"No."

"They'se getting' told they'se special. That they'se disappointin' God. Then the damn townspeople support him and act kindly toward the whores. Never seen the like anywheres I've been. Look at Myra. Why you let her go out to that Brody place?"

"I had no choice. Brooks came demanding. You two weren't here."

"You gotta get your manhood back, Wicks. Think of somethin' to get back at the church."

"Well, you could burn the church down. You could kill Brooks. You could go get Myra back."

"J.T., he be thinkin' now. 'Cept he keeps usin' the word 'you'."

J.T. chuckled.

"Burn the church. That would be good. Killin' Brooks, not so much. Don't have to worry about the law here, but I wouldn't want to get the laws from Kansas City interested in us. Some of the laws in some places still be lookin' for me." Wicks was thinking out loud. "Fetchin' Myra back would be good too, 'cept they got folks who can shoot out to the ranch. I'll think this over."

"Let's kill the black man Cleetus, and his squaw," J.T. responded.

"Kill his squaw? Hell. The church goes out of bizness, she be here whorin' for us," Lester joked.

J.T. laughed.

"You two willin' to do some of these things?" Wicks asked.

"We ain't no fraidy cat like you," J.T. responded.

"Wouldn't spend too much time figgerin' what to do. Things get worse, you be hirin' pigs and cows as your whores," Lester said.

J.T. laughed again, pounding on his bed.

"I'll leave for Kansas City in two days. Don't do nothin' till I get back," Wicks said as he left.

****

The telegram from two days earlier lay on the kitchen table. It was so startling that Rose had reread it many times, and had it memorized.

dear family stop annalise regained consciousness stop said to send her love to you stop webb says the recovery will take months stop she is still in great pain stop I love you stop Jefferson stop.

She was on her way to the ranch to carry the news. Business was slow. Joshua was watching Jacob.

The day was oppressive. Heavy moisture hung in the air under a red hot sun. She was perspiring freely as she reined in at the big house.

"Rose! Honey, what is it?" Margaret said as she came onto the porch. "Is something wrong? Is it Annalise?" She was wiping her hands on the hem of her apron.

"It's Annalise, Mother. She's awakened. She seems to be fine."

"Thank goodness, oh thank goodness! I've been praying for her. We need some good news."

"Why? What's happened?"

"A tragedy, Honey. We lost Mr. Gillespie."

"What?"

"C'mon inside. Caroline will get you some water." Rose wrapped the reins around the hitching post and followed her mother inside.

They were soon joined by Whit. "I saw your horse in front, Rosie. Is anything wrong?"

"Annalise is conscious, Daddy. The crisis is passed."

"Wonderful ! Wonderful!" She thought she saw a tear forming at the corner of his cyc.

"Jefferson said that the recovery will be slow, but she's alive."

"Anything else? Have they caught the attackers?"

"It was just a telegram, so there weren't details. What about Mr. Gillespie?"

"I'll get you a drink, Sweetie. Your father can tell you."

"Mr. Gillespie? He's gone?"

"He's dead, Rosie. Mangled. Herkimer found him yesterday. He saw some vultures circling, and thought it might be dead livestock. He found the body, what was left of it, up by the north woods, ten feet away from the wagon and the rifle."

"That's terrible. What was it, a bear? Wolves?"

"Well, Herkimer followed signs blood and such. Found the white wolf dying up by the north fence. Finished it off. Seems as if it was rabid."

"That poor man."

"The shape he was in, we had to bury him as soon as possible. Didn't even send for Reverend Brooks. Was going to send Jack in with the news to you this afternoon."

"You buried him here?"

"He's up on the hill, next to Lem and old Hank. Elon's carving a marker."

Whit sat in his chair by the fireplace. "There's more, Honey. Jack and Elon went through Gillespie's belongings in the bunkhouse last night, trying to find family contact information back East. They came across letters and receipts in the name of Robert Gerdon."

"That name sounds familiar."

"He was the author of the Herkimer Grimes western books."

"Gillespie was Gerdon?"

"It appears so. They found a stack of papers with information about Herkimer. Gerdon was writing another story about Herkimer. He was here trying to gather facts, I'd guess."

"I can tell that you're really bothered by this, Daddy."

"He was a good man, even though he was telling us stories. Good photographer, good cook, smart man, generous. I'll miss him. Nobody should die like that."

The next day Caroline and Myra sorted through Gerdon's collection of photos. Whit packed them and included a note about Gerdon. He sent the package to the only address they could find, a Mr. Sawyer in New York City.

****

Herkimer Grimes had the dream so often that he couldn't escape it when he woke. The featured player was Bird, but the plot never dealt with romance. Instead he saw her holding the severed head of a settler's baby or driving a lance into the midsection of James Lewis, his slain friend from the Regulator-Moderator days. A scene might develop with her riding over a young boy, or standing proud with a war whoop and a scalp.

The unnerving part always came before he startled awake, shaking. She moved toward him wearing no clothes, blood covering her face and arms, undulating rather than walking. Worse, he couldn't move. He had no power to run, no ability to draw his pistol, no will to resist what she would do to him.

Some days, after a particularly stark episode, the memory would affect his interaction with her in real life. He would avoid her, respond curtly if she began a conversation. He began to refuse her dinner invitations. There was a lesson in those dreams, he was certain. He would never discuss it with her. It was too dark. He was too private.

Of course, he could escape it all. He could leave the Brody ranch, strike out another time to a new life in a new location. But he was fatigued with roving. He was getting old. He had developed an abiding affection for Whit Brody. The only friend of his adult life, Big, was there, as were young Jack, and the Chase brothers, and the doting housekeeper, Caroline. He felt strangely honored that Lige and Charlie Fox considered him with awe and too much respect. Life on the ranch made sense. It was uncomplicated.

He was doing routine work, replacing several slats in the horse barn, kicked out by one of its occupants during a thunderstorm.

He didn't know that she was behind him, hadn't heard her walk up.

"Herkimer, you want some help with that?" Bird asked.

"Nope." He began hammering without turning around. She waited until several nails were in place.

"Everyone else is busy this morning. I can give you a hand."

"Don't want help." There was no emotion on his face or in his words.

"Fine," she said and walked away.

Damn him. She considered him a good friend, a kindred spirit, a fellow survivor. She didn't know what he considered her. She was weary of his moodiness, his introspective nature. She was wasting her time trying to cultivate him, even though respect and trust was all that she wanted. She realized that she was inordinately angry by this last encounter. She expected too much of him, as if the two were on an unorthodox trail to a serious relationship.

Ridiculous.

****

Annalise had more good days than bad ones by the end of August. At her best she was talkative, attentive, and somewhat animated. Other days a cloud of depression silenced her, and brought on long sequences of staring and weeping.

She was frustrated that she had no memory of the night her stepfather was killed. So were the police, to the point that they had stopped several weeks of gentle questioning.

Jefferson held her hand while he told her stories of the war, and described Vermont and his boyhood in vivid detail. He bathed her, and massaged muscles that had not been used for weeks.

Her beauty had returned in many ways. The scar on her cheek was visible; it would always be. Close inspection revealed an imperfect nose, and her jaw had not yet fully aligned in its healing, but her dark eyes were clear and luminescent again, and when she smiled, she was stunning. She had a healthy appetite, and had gained back most of the weight she had lost. The stirrup had been removed from her leg.

Jefferson resigned himself to the thought that no one would ever be punished for the crime. She had probably not known the intruders anyway. He was beginning to believe the police theory, that she had been selected for a night of inhuman sexual activity by a group that knew she was alone with a feeble old man. Herman was killed because he was a witness. The intruders probably thought that she would die too, slowly bleeding to death alone.

On one of her morose days, she had sobbed to him. "I'm so sorry. I have ruined the lives of everyone I love. Mother. Maribel. Herman. You. Especially you. You could be in Oregon now."

"Annalise, I'm where I'm supposed to be. Where I need to be. Where I want to be. Kansas or Oregon or Vermont, no place would satisfy me unless you are there too."

She turned away to hide her tears.

"We need to get out of this room for a while," he said, grabbing a blanket and bending over her.

"Where are we going? I can't walk yet."

"I'll carry you. We're going out to the sunshine."

"I may be too weak to sit up for long."

"I'll hold you."

He wrapped her in the blanket, lifted her, and approached the nurses' desk in the hallway. "Any chairs on the back lawn?" he asked.

"Well, yes, Mr. Chase. Does Dr. Webb know what you're doing?"

"No, ma'am, but I'm sure that he'd approve."

For two hours, he cradled her in his lap while they sat in the dappled shade from a large tree. For the first time in two months, she felt a breeze, saw birds, and felt occasional flashes of sun cross her face.

****

"They're back, Margaret. I knew they would be. They've moved into the line shack on the east side. Charlie Fox saw them this morning."

"Who's back, Whit?"

"The squatters. The Kaynes."

"What are you going to do?'

"Run them off. This afternoon."

She had rarely seen him so agitated .

"Whit, somebody may get hurt."

"Maggie, they made threats, poked fun at Noah, tried to intimidate us, and made a comment about you. We let this happen, they'll be taking over a part of the ranch. We're going to drive them off."

Whit called together Herkimer, Big, Jack, Lige, Charlie Fox, and Noah, and the seven rode to the east line. Whit stopped them a half-mile away.

"No. gunplay, unless they force it. They'll see seven of us, so they may not want a fight. If they resist, we'll burn their stuff."

They saw four figures, alerted to their approach, scatter in front of the line shack. The old man and the fat son stood in front by their wagon. The other two ducked into the shack. Whit noticed two of his cows tied to a nearby tree.

"Howdy, Brody," the old man said, "mighty kind of you to let us use this house. It suits us just fine."

"Mr. Kaynes, I don't remember inviting you. You seem to be trespassing again."

"We ain't hurtin' nobody. This old shack ain't much, anyways."

"Since we built it and use it, since it's on our property, I'm going to ask you to move on. I'll give you ten minutes to leave."

"Listen Brody. You got plenty of land. We ain't got no place to be. Anyways, heared you come in here and hornswoggled the gov'mint into land meant for homesteaders. We takin' it back, like it's s'posed to be."

"That was years ago, and the government made out quite nicely. I overpaid for it. There was plenty of land left for homesteading. There still is. And, by the way, what do you intend to do with those cows over there?"

"Ain't right. Them cows, we just tied them to that tree."

"I've enjoyed our conversation, Mr. Kaynes. You now have eight minutes to leave."

"I don't reckon, we be leaving."

Herkimer was uneasy. He saw the fat son glance toward the window on the front of the shack. He walked his horse away from the group, peering toward the window. He pulled his pistol.

"Where's that there man goin'?" the old man yelled.

Suddenly there was a roar and a flash from the window. Shotgun pellets kicked up the ground in front of Whit. The old man and his fat son jumped behind the wagon. Whit saw pistols in their hands.

Herkimer fired once into the shack's darkness, and there was a scream from inside. Big quickly dismounted and fired a shot toward the wagon. Everyone in the Brody party showed weapons. The shack door opened. The careless son stumbled out and collapsed in the dirt. The other brother followed with his hands up, stepping over his brother.

Old Man Kaynes dropped his weapon and hobbled to the side of his crumpled son. "He's daid ! You done kilt him!"

"Jack, check him out," Whit ordered.

"He isn't dead, Uncle Whit. Shot in the arm. Bleeding a lot," Jack called from the ground.

"This is how it's going to go, Mr. Kaynes. You three clear the shack of your stuff. You dawdle and your son may bleed to death. You leave anything, we'll burn it. We're going to take you to town."

Whit walked into the sheriff's office after dropping the wounded son at Doc Rosbottom's with Big to supervise. He got a surprise,

"Mr. Jessup, you're the sheriff?" Jessup was a cashier at the bank.

"Yes, Mr. Brody, I am. Ain't even got a deputy today. He's off sick. Who are these men?"

"These men have trespassed twice on ranch property. Took two of our cows. We went today to move them on, and one of them shot at us. We shot back and wounded him. He's at Rosbottom's."

"Trespassin', huh. Mr. Brody, can I talk to you outside?"

Whit left Jack and Noah with the Kaynes, and stepped outside.

"Mr. Brody, trespassing ain't murder or bank robbin'. We ain't got a place to put them. Holding cell in back has got a couple of drunks. Let's make this simple. I don't even want to be doin' this job. Somebody's got to make it look like we got law in this place. Town's still lookin' for a lawman, so's I can get out of here. Them St. Louie men left town; didn't want to be the law."

"Do this for me, Mr. Jessup. Give them a good scare for a while. We'll leave town. Tell them you're giving them a break, if they stay off of my property. Then turn them loose."

"Mr. Brody, I can do that."

So much for appropriate justice, Whit thought.

Two hours later, the Kaynes family was back on the streets of Abilene.

****

"Y-y-you want to m-m-marry up?" Elon asked Myra as they lay together in a north pasture. Evening rides were their escape from the ranch, and usually ended with a frantic session of lovemaking wherever they dismounted.

Unclothed, Myra was busy trying to rouse him for a second bout. She stopped and shifted around until they were face to face.

"You want to marry with me, Elon?"

"We like each other p-plenty. But we n-n-never been in a bed together cep'n once. The pleasurin' is good, but we need a p-p-place together. Figure we get hitched, we can do this every n-n-n-night. Sides, we can't do this w-when the weather g-g-gets cold."

"You figger we'll be leavin' the ranch?"

"No. Thinkin' Mr. Brody be happy about it. Thinkin' he let us build a small p-p-place on the hill, next to Bird. If'n you'd drather not…"

"We'd keep our work here?"

"We can d-do that unless w-we decide to m-move on. Coupla years."

"You know what I was. Been with a lot of men around Abilene."

"Don't matter none."

"It ain't just the pleasurin' with us? We can have a family? Be a family?"

"I love you Myra. If we m-m-move on, we kin go far away. Always a need for smithin'."

"You'll tell Mr. Brody?"

"No. I'll hafta ask Mr. Brody if'n I work up the nerve."

"I'll go with you."

"Nope. He's the c-c-closest thing to a father you got. Hafta g-get his p-p-p-permission. It's a man's thing to do."

"You waitin' on an answer from me, Elon?"

He was quiet.

"I'm sayin' yes, for shore. Yes, I'll marry with you!"

He rolled on top of her. This time it lasted longer, and was much more tender.

****

In 1869 the first professional baseball team was formed. The Cincinnati Red Stockings paid players to play baseball, and the team toured, competing against non-professional squads from New York, New Jersey, the New England states, and the Deep South.

They also played a collection of home contests on a manicured field on the near west side of the city.

Harry Wright was the organizer, owner, manager, and centerfielder. He was a transplant from the East, and in his mid-thirties was a formidable athlete. He lured his brother, George, into a contract for $1,400, and the younger Wright became the team's star. A marvelously gifted former cricket player, he was the shortstop.

The available funds for salaries were modest at best, so the ten members kept their day jobs. On the roster were an engraver, an insurance man, a bookkeeper, and a piano maker. They completely dominated opponents, and were unbeaten in over sixty games when they prepared for a home game in September.

"We're doing something different today, Annalise. I played some rounders during the war, baseball. The best team in the country is here in Cincinnati, and they're playing this afternoon. I rented a carriage. We'll take a picnic lunch, and go watch a few endings. We'll be in the sun. You might enjoy it."

"If you like it, Jefferson, I'll like it."

The parked the carriage in left field foul territory near the foul line. By game time, carriages, chairs and tethered horses lined the entire field. She was attentive to the action on the field. "So what is the idea here, the purpose?" she asked.

"If you have a bat in your hands, you hit the ball. If you're on the other team, you catch the ball," he explained, a simplistic description that he delivered with a smile.

"That sounds really complicated," she countered with a raised eyebrow.

"I played on and off for three years with my unit. It was a diversion from the battle. I didn't much get into the details."

"Were you good?" she asked as the agile George Wright leaped to snag a hard-hit ball.

"I had fun."

He did explain the intricacies that he remembered as the game progressed, another one-sided victory for Cincinnati.

"Do ladies play this game?"

"Never saw that happen. Some day maybe. Are you interested?"

"Sure. Jefferson, I was tree-climber."

Another subject was on her mind, one that they hadn't addressed yet. "Dr. Webb is going to release me next week. Have you thought about that?"

"Yes."

"When will we go back to Kansas?"

"Dr. Webb doesn't want you to do anything for six weeks. We'll see how you are in November. Meantime, we'll stay in a hotel downtown."

"Herman's house hasn't been sold yet. We can stay there."

"I don't want you back in that house, ever."

"I don't remember anything from that night. Back in that house, I may remember something helpful."

"Whoever is responsible is still out there somewhere."

"Jefferson. What happened to me…Has that changed the way you feel about me? Be honest. I'll understand. I'm not the same person."

"I almost lost you. I can't imagine the horror of that. You're stuck with me. And you are the same person. Your spirit is back. Your beauty is back. We will move away from what happened."

She squeezed his arm as he moved the carriage away from the field.

****

Wicks was only gone two weeks. He returned to Abilene driving a wagonload of six women. Six women and girls, between the ages of 13 and 30, wore low bodices and ample make-up, and in an orchestrated procedure, he drove them down Texas Street instead of directly to his bawdy house. They were a noisy and profane collection. One, a buxom brunette, stood and repeatedly bared her breasts.

Of course, Wicks, even given his predilection for underaged girls, had sampled them on his stay In Kansas City, all except the thirteen-year old, whom he planned to install in his own bedroom until she had mastered all of the tricks of prostitution. There were a few pretty faces under the excess of powder and rouge, and there were several nationalities in the group.

He had promised all of them substantial wealth and healthy business. While he would renege on the first promise, he knew that the second one would materialize, despite the fact that the cattle drives were almost completed for the year. Men stopped and looked with lascivious interest as the wagon moved through the center of town.

Finally he reined up in front of his house.

"Don't look like he said," one plump woman whispered to her wagon mates. "None too fancy, you ask me."

"Esme, lot of hungry lookin' men back there in town. Betcha bizzness be good. And this be the biggest house in view, I swear it," another added.

"Unload your stuff. You're lookin' at home and money," Wicks yelled back at them.

He pushed open the front door and stopped. The parlor was a forlorn mess, some furniture overturned, empty bottles on the floor, items of food everywhere. Tickles was asleep, or passed out, in a corner. A naked woman he had not seen before was curled on a couch, her arm across ponderous breasts.

Wicks walked over to Tickles and kicked him hard.

"Wake up, you worthless bastard," he screamed. His female cargo stood just inside the door, uncertain of what to do next. Wicks reached down and slapped the old piano player as hard as he could, and spittle flew from the black man's mouth.

"Mistuh Wicks, why you beatin' on me?" Tickles said as he scrambled to his feet.

"What in hell's goin' on here?"

"Weren't me, Mistuh Wicks, No suh." Tickles cowered. "It be Mistuh Lester and J.T. Come in last week with some new ho's. Dey been havin' a party since. Drunk mos' of your likker. Tickles, he can't stop them."

Wicks took the steps to the second floor two at a time, and pounded on the brothers' door. He didn't wait for them to answer, charging red-faced inside.

Each of the brothers was curled around a woman. Lester opened one eye. "Wicks, you back?"

"Yes, I'm back ! What the hell have you done to my house?"

"J.T., you awake?" Lester muttered, without facing Wicks.

"Yup."

"Get out of bed, and throw Wicks out of here."

"You want I should shoot him, Lester?"

"If'n you want."

Wicks settled down. "Lester, you made a mess of this house."

A frowzy, mussed head of hair appeared above an attractive face next to Lester. "Who's he?"

"It's your new boss, Mary. Wicks, say hello to your new money-maker. She can go all night."

Wicks ignored him. "Who's goin' to clean up this house?"

"You bring back whores?"

"Yes. Six of them."

"Well, get them busy then. Now, get out of here before J.T. shoots you."

Wicks heard laughter as he closed the door.

The three new women, he learned later, were stolen by Lester from other houses in the district. Wicks now had a stable of nine new faces and bodies. The remnants of his former prostitutes had been summarily kicked out by Lester.

Business-wise he was far better off, and he had his thirteen-year old, who had the physical attributes of a young boy.

His increasing problem was Lester. J.T. was just a nuisance, a stupid man.

Lester scared him.

****

On a humid October afternoon, Simeon Whittaker passed away in his fields.

Lige found his body, still clinging to a scythe, lying face down across a row of browning corn stalks.

The big man had lifted him and carried him gently down the hill to the main area.

Whit rushed to the area from the maintenance barn.

"He be daid, Mistuh Whit. Simeon be daid."

Whit knelt next to the body listening for breathing. "How'd it happen, Lige?"

"Dunno. Missed him. Went lookin'. Found him in de cornfield."

Margaret came through the front door, followed by Caroline.

"He's dead, Maggie."

"Poor old man. Said his chest was hurting at breakfast," Caroline said softly.

"Caroline," Whit said, "go fetch a blanket. A nice one." He closed the lifeless eyes, and folded the gnarled hands across his chest. "Bird, no more work for today. Jack, will you ride to Abilene? Ask Reverend Brooks to ride out here. Better tell Joshua and Rose. And Doc Rosbottom; they played a lot of music together."

"Whit, does he have family?" Margaret asked.

"Never heard him say. Any of you ever hear him mention anyone? Lige?"

"No, suh. Talked 'bout times long ago. Never 'bout people."

"He was sort of a mystery. I hope he enjoyed his years here."

"He was happy here, Whit. I'm sure of it."

"Mistuh, Whit. I be digging the grave," Lige said.

"Thanks, Lige. Put it on the hill overlooking his gardens, down a piece from Lem and Gillespie. Will somebody help him?"

Several hands went up.

Two days later, Margaret found Whit sitting pensively in the large chair opposite the fireplace. It was the middle of the afternoon.

"Whit, what is it? Don't you feel well, Honey?"

"I'm fine, Maggie."

"No, you're not. Is something bothering you? Simeon?" She sat across from him on the divan.

"I've been uneasy for a while now. I have a feeling that something bad is going to happen. Something that will change our lives. Something I can't control."

"Whit, if this is about Simeon, he had a good life here. He was an old man."

"I suppose I'm feeling a bit mortal. Winter's coming up. That always scares me, since that blizzard in '56. We're getting older too, Maggie. We've had a good life, but we keep getting reminders about how fragile and how unfair it can be. Lem…Simeon…Gillespie… almost Annalise too."

"Whit, my darling, we're in a location and a period in history that makes life tenuous. You're a good man, one of the finest anywhere. But you can only control this ranch, and some of the people on it."

"That may not be enough, if the wrong things happen."

"What could they be?"

"Abilene's out of control. We took in the Kaynes for a variety of crimes, and they were free in two hours. The town survived another cattle drive season, barely. Some bad types of people keep showing up. I got no response about the Texas fever problem. Rosie may be leaving soon. We've got to decide about going west or staying here."

"There's no rush to that."

"Maggie, we may be down to our last ten years or so."

"Whit. No. There'll be more. You are depressed."

"Right now, I've got to replace Simeon. He was amazing out there in the fields."

"You'll do that. You've got an uncanny knack for seeing what people are capable of. You'll find someone."

Whit got quiet.

"You've built a sanctuary out here, Whit, a wonderful life for a lot of people.

Don't worry about a new hire."

"You're right, Maggie. You know, you're my compass."

She smiled. "You're feeling down today. I can help with that. You want to follow me upstairs?"

"Maggie, it's the middle of the afternoon."

"Whit Brody. That never stopped you before."

He was quickly out of the chair.

****

Hata Sing Wu, a small bald man with a constant grin and enormous energy, had more than filled the shoes of the deceased Simeon. Somewhere in his early fifties, he had come to the Brody ranch as the new gardener.

He had been an Oriental casualty of layoffs after railroad building labor was no longer needed. He then earned wages cleaning the Cowboy Bar on an Abilene back street. Stranded in Abilene, he and his wife and their daughter, Miyama, managed to survive, but his fortunes kept ebbing. His wife, a tiny woman, had succumbed during a fever three years ago. He had sold his horse to afford her funeral.

Miyama had grown into an attractive young lady of twenty, challenged by the English language, ogled by the gentry of Abilene. Hata knew that prostitution might present itself as an option to her, so vulnerable was their financial status. He couldn't permit that to happen.

He had been a regular in the Chase store for years, stubbornly refusing charity. Joshua recommended him to Whit after Simeon died.

"Will you come to work for me, Mr. Wu?" Whit asked.

"Will work hard for you, Brody-san."

"Can you grow things? Vegetables? Flowers?"

"Oh, yes. As a boy, yes. Also fix things, lift things, clean things."

"I'll pay you well. Can you start next week?"

"Oh, yes," Wu said with a deep bow, "Will walk to your home Monday."

"Walk?"

Hata lowered his eyes. "No horse. No wagon."

Whit had laughed. "Mr. Wu, one of my men will come and pick you up in a wagon. Will you be on this porch, Monday, mid-morning, with your things?"

"Don't have much, Brody-san. Two small beds, table. Few chairs. Rugs. Clothes."

"Well, Mr. Wu. You can sell your beds and other furniture, if you wish. We're going to take care of those things for you."

"Have another problem, Brody-san. Girl child. Daughter…Miyama. Cannot leave her. Cannot."

"How old is Miyama?"

"Twenty of the years. Just."

"Mr. Wu, she can come too. We'll find something for her to do."

Back at the ranch, Whit found Margaret in the kitchen with Caroline.

"You two will laugh at this. I just hired a little Oriental man to take Simeon's place. Joshua's recommendation. He's bringing his twenty-year old daughter."

"Whit…" Margaret looked at him and then rolled her eyes at Caroling. "Whatever will we do with her?"

"Don't have that clear yet. He can stay in the bunkhouse. We could put her in with Bird. I'll give Bird extra wages to look after her. As to work, she can clean the bunkhouse. Clean the stables. Help her father and Lige in the gardens."

"Whit, it's becoming Brodyville out here. You're the Mayor of Brodyville."

The three of them laughed for a long time.

****

Abilene in mid-November was not attractive, bleak and somewhat deserted and cold. Raw winds blew fiercely against clapboard, and whisked shingles off of roofs. The five-month clamor of trail drives and transient cowboys was over. The otherwise growing population kept merchants solvent. Gamblers and ne'er-do-wells still arrived sporadically.

Some things didn't change. Moral decline and criminal activity still ruled the day. But new mayor Theodore Henry was installed in office, so there was hope for change. Without rambunctious cowboys there was a level of tolerance. Abilene caught its collective breath.

Annalise actually welcomed the dire surroundings as the stagecoach wobbled and bounced along Texas Street. The only family she had was here.

"You OK, Sweetheart?" Jefferson asked, relaxing his grip on her hand. A sleeping man in a business suit sitting opposite started awake, cleared his throat, and mumbled. "We here?"

"Jefferson, there's a crowd ahead of us. I wonder if there's been trouble."

"It wouldn't surprise me," he said sotto voce.

Then as the coach slowed, she saw familiar faces… Rose, Joshua, Margaret, Bird, Catharine, Jack, Noah, Big, Caroline. She saw a grinning Herkimer, the first time she had seen him less than dour. Even Weasel, hovering on the edge of the group was there, and Jonah Brooks, Elon, and Bear Women. Whit stood almost in the path of the coach, as it rocked to a stop.

"Jefferson…Jefferson." She was crying.

"Welcome home, Annalise."

Whit jerked open the stagecoach door. "About time you two came back."

Annalise leaned into him as she alighted awkwardly, and then she was in the arms of Rose. Both sobbed through an overlong hug, little Jacob in the middle.

"What in hell is all this?" the sleeping man wondered aloud, poking his head out of the window. "She someone important?"

"Very important," Jefferson answered, as he left the coach.

"Joshua," Annalise spoke hoarsely as he kissed her on the cheek, "How did you know we'd be on this coach?"

"We didn't. We just assumed it would be today. Jefferson sent a few telegrams. If you hadn't come today, we'd all be back here again tomorrow."

One by one, she hugged each of them, a lengthy process which bothered no one. Jefferson went through the same gauntlet.

"Glad you're back, Anna-lisa," an emotional Weasel squeaked.

"Mr. Weasel, my book buddy. I missed you." She kissed him, which caused him to back away, embarrassed and cackling.

"God bless you, honey." Bear Woman said.

"And you, Bear Woman, I've missed your beautiful voice."

Catharine embraced both Annalise and Jefferson eagerly, and grabbing Jeremiah's hand, moved slightly away from the group, the better to watch Jack. She hadn't seen him for weeks, and she was confused by the fact that she missed him, desperately. What is going on here, she thought. He's so quiet and introverted, the opposite of Jonathan. But he was smart and polite and competent. A relationship with him would be different from the passionate years with Jonathan. She was ready for something like that, maybe. She would certainly sleep with him, but that seemed unlikely if she waited for him to initiate it. He had approached her timidly a while ago, and had muttered, "Miss Catharine. How are you?" She had put one hand on his shoulder and said effusively, "Jack I'm so glad to see you. I've missed you." He had mumbled something like. "Yes Ma'am. Me too…" and had removed his hat. Whatever else that may have been exchanged was lost, as the stagecoach was sighted at the end of the street.

"Listen now," Whit called after a while. "We can't stand around all day, kissing a pretty woman. Doc's bringing his fiddle out to the ranch. Caroline's been fixing vittles for two days, and Myra's tending them now. Joshua's got a man to watch the store. If Annalise doesn't mind another hour in a wagon, let's all meet at the ranch for a fitting party.

Joshua pulled Jefferson aside. "Brother, I've got something to show you. Before we leave for the ranch, let's take a walk.

On the way, Joshua spoke. “Jeffie, I don’t know your plans, but Rose and I feel that Annalise should be with you on at the ranch. Plenty of people there to help take care of her.”

“That’s what I thought,” Jefferson replied, “but I didn’t want to appear ungrateful to you and Rose.”

“It’s Whit and Margaret’s idea too. We’ve already moved her belongings from the store out to the ranch. It won’t be forever. Rose and I will probably move west early next summer. You still up for that?”

“Certainly. Annalise too.”

Joshua led him around the store. “There’s another friend who’ll be glad to see you.”

Standing tethered to a post behind the store was the majestic Storm, ears pricked, standing erect and motionless as the two came into view.

“Stormie…” Jefferson managed, as he crossed the few yards to his horse.

Joshua was certain that the horse was smiling.

****

Cleetus listened intently as Bear Woman soared through vocal embellishments to an old Christmas song. His wife’s voice was so melodic and soothing that it made him sleepy. But he dare not nod off; she was singing to him. She finished with a long note that seemed to surround him.

“Honey Bear, that’s so purty. Yessir, the church folks’ll be cryin’ Sunday.”

“Cleetus, it’s a song of joy. Not tryin’ to make someone cry…” Her voice trailed off. She was diverted by a flickering off of the window behind him.

“What is it, Bea?” He reacted to the quizzical look on her face.

“A light. Strange light out there.”

He turned and leaped to his feet.

“Oh no! The church! The church is on fire!”

He grabbed his shotgun from the wall, and thrust an arm through a parka from a pole in the corner.

“Run into town, Bea. Make noise. Some church folks live above their stores. Wake them up. Tell them to bring buckets. Blankets too. Gotta hurry, Bea. Flames already lickin’ up the sides!”

She was out the door behind him. Why was he carrying a shotgun?

The fire was set by someone, he thought as he rushed to the growing conflagration. No other explanation. Maybe they’re still around, admiring their work. He was caught between caution, and a mandate to hurry, to do something to save the church.

He slowed as he reached the building. The church was probably already too far gone. Heat resonated from the wall in front of him. Fingers of flames reached toward the roof. He tore off his coat, and frantically beat at the wall in front of him. Maybe there was a chance, if Bea brought help in the next few minutes. The nearby well was close enough and full enough; he’d have to break up a layer of surface ice.

He turned toward the well, and stared into the barrel of a revolver, inches from his head.

“Hey, how’s it goin’?”

Those were the last words he'd ever hear.

Bear Woman screamed through the streets. Lights came on in second-story windows, and a small flurry of activity developed behind her. She hopped onto the porch of the Chase store, and beat furiously on the door. She saw a form moving around inside, carrying a lantern.

"Bear Woman," Joshua said, "What is it?"

"The church, Mr. Joshua. The church is burning!"

He raced up the stairs, pulled on a pair of boots, grabbed a rifle, and his coat.

"Bear Woman!" He called to her. She was already up the street. "Help me with some buckets on your way back." He ducked back inside, grabbed a large stack of pails from a shelf, left some on the front porch, and sprinted to the west.

The fire lit the cold night sky and reflected off of the faces of a small group in furious activity as Joshua approached. He knew immediately that the buckets wouldn't be needed. The flames were flashing around the highest points of the building. The front of the building had collapsed.

Several men were huddled toward the back of the church. Some were kneeling.

"Joshua, you'd better have a look at this!"

Joshua saw a figure on his back on the ground. He recognized the man as Cleetus, even though the side of his head was missing.

On that Sunday, two weeks before Christmas, Cleetus Wilburn was buried, after a gravesite service, on the hill leading to the cabin above the charred remains of the House of Worship.

Sobs of the attendees were audible, mourning not only the demise of a friend, but also of the church, a somber backdrop to the ceremony.

Bear Woman insisted on singing, "for him," and managed a quiet rendition of "Amazing Grace" on the cold, sunny morning. Jonah stood next to her with his arm supportively around her waist. She then sat on a chair next to the casket, stoic and still.

Jonah delivered the eulogy, part of which was an impromptu, angry diatribe on the dark souls of many men. Several times his voice cracked. He would look down at a Bible held in his hands and find the will to continue. He ended on a personal note. A long tribute to "a fine brother, a giant of a human being, a servant to the Almighty, consumed by goodness and the love of a sainted wife."

As the earth was shoveled over the casket, Jonah walked a few feet away, and turned away from the group, his chin on his chest. Whit walked to him, put his arm around the taller man's shoulder, and stood quietly with him. The large crowd started to disperse.

"Jonah, we are all better for having known him. He was a hero to all of us," Whit said.

"Sometimes God gets confused. Cleetus dedicated his life to Him. How could this happen?"

"We can't blame this on God. Someone evil among us will have to pay for it."

"Well, Whit, as usual the law hasn't embraced the shooting, or the fire."

Whit didn't respond.

"I don't know how to comfort Bear Woman," Jonah said. "She wants to stay here, to continue His work with me, but I don't want her in that cabin alone. I can't take her in with me. The church folks wouldn't understand."

"Were you thinking about leaving Abilene?"

"No."

"I don't know your plans for church and services and such, but we can find room for Bear Woman at the ranch, at least until more is known. She'd be around good people." As he spoke, he wondered about what he had just offered. At that moment, he wasn't sure how the ranch could accommodate another female. Caroline, Myra, Annalise. There was no bedroom left. That would fill the house. Catharine's boarding house ? No. There was no vacancy there. Bird's cabin? No. Miyama was already sharing that. He'd figure it out later.

"How are you, Jonah?"

"I'm fighting demons. God cannot be happy with me. This wasn't a random act. Somebody wanted to get to me. Cleetus was in the wrong place at the wrong time."

"I'll give you some men, if you want to rebuild."

"No, I want the ashes to stay for a while. I want to keep my anger. I'm considering asking Joshua to let me use his store for Sunday services, but I don't want him burned out too."

The group from the ranch stood waiting for Whit some thirty feet away.

"Where is Bear Woman staying now?" Jonah asked.

"In her cabin. I've been there too, with a rifle at the ready. I just can't keep doing that. I need to get her settled."

They joined the Brody group and walked down the hill into town.

Four men watched from an alley. "Gawd, Pa. Looky there. The whole bunch from the Brody ranch is in town. We coulda rode out there and burned 'em out."

"We'll git our chance, son. We'll git our chance," Pa Kaynes answered. The other three squatters grinned.

Joshua and Rose welcomed the House of Worship to their store.

"Of course, Reverend Brooks. Some of the faithful will have to sit on boxes and barrels, maybe some on the floor. We'll make it work for you."

"Thank you, Joshua. Very generous."

"You should know that come May, maybe during the summer, we'll probably be moving west."

"You'll be selling the building?"

"Sometime soon."

"Well, we'll honor God in the interim."

Joshua was uncomfortable. Jonah's eyes usually met another's in conversation, friendly, kind, vibrant, alert. On that day, they were vacant, and he turned them away through most of their talk.

CHAPTER THIRTY

1870

As 1870 began, there were nine men and six women at the long table in the Brody kitchen. Whit and Margaret usually joined them. The kitchen staff had grown too, to meet the culinary demands of the group. Annalise and Bear Woman and Miyama occasionally joined Caroline and Myra in the preparation of meals.

Dinners in particular had become notable. Caroline had mandated that all hands change from work clothes before the dinner hour. She gave mealtime lectures on proper etiquette, and insisted that thanks of some cultural nature be given on a rotating schedule. Even the quiet ones--Lige, Miyama, Charlie Fox and Herk—took their turns. Birthdays were celebrated with much ado; for those that didn't recall their specific date of birth, Caroline assigned them one. Every other Friday night, Whit put a pay envelope under every plate.

Conversation was easy. When Margaret or Caroline detected reticence, she directed questions toward the silent party.

Hata, Miyama, and Bear Woman were assigned horses. Miyama had very limited experience on horseback, so Whit asked Charlie Fox to give her lessons.

"Charlie Fox? Those two will never say anything to each other. Why not Elon?" Margaret had asked.

"Maggie, you know what happened when Elon gave lessons to Myra. I'm sure that Myra would be uncomfortable if Elon was teaching another woman."

"Well, that's a good decision, Dear. Myra told me something today. She's pregnant."

"They got married in, what, October? They didn't waste time. That's great. We need some little guys around here."

"They moved into that new cabin when it was just a frame with a roof. They had to stay intimate to stay warm."

****

Minnie was puzzled. Where was her mistress? She hadn't seen Catharine since lunch, several hours ago. Taking a long nap? She never did that. Maybe ailing?

Jeremiah was doing lessons in the kitchen. She called out, "Mizz Chase?" No answer. Perhaps she had gone out while Minnie was cleaning second floor rooms. She had been going to the Chase store more frequently lately. She had even braved the snow to "pick up something" that morning. When she left, she always announced it to Minnie.

For a long time now, she considered Catharine more than her employer. Of similar ages, Minnie thought of Catharine as a benevolent friend. She worked hard to please Catharine, and not just for a generous paycheck.

Minnie's needs were minimal. She saved virtually every penny. For what purpose, she didn't know yet. She loved Catharine, and Jeremiah even more. The boarders treated her well, often with gifts.

Of course, a man was still missing from her life. She had earlier fixated on the young clerk from Karotofsky's western store. If he were willing, she'd let him do anything to her. He was white, so nothing would come of it, but if he wanted to bed her, she'd participate eagerly.

She was aging, but she was still passably pretty and pleased that her body was still trim. She had flirted briefly with the clerk, once cleaning his room while he was still in it, planning her movements, bending over when she knew he was watching, brushing against him once. She was being too brazen. Mizz Catharine wouldn't approve.

That Lige out at the Brody ranch. He was so big. But he was so shy that she never heard him speak more than a few words. She had an opportunity at him when he and Mr. Jack had been building the addition. She had earned brief smiles when she served him seconds at meals. One day she was alone with him in the kitchen. He was devouring cookies that she had made for him. She had boldly walked over to him and sat on his lap. "Anythin' else I kin do for you, Mister Lige," she had said huskily, her face inches from his.

He began choking and abruptly stood, discharging her to a sitting position on the floor. "No, ma'am," he gasped between heaving coughs, and hurried from the room.

But she knew. In the brief moment on his lap, she had felt his excitement. Some day. Maybe.

"Mizz Catharine gotta be sick. Better check on her," she said to herself.

She walked down the hallway to Catharine's room, and stood close to the door. She heard nothing.

She quietly turned the latch and peeked in. There was motion of some kind reflected in a dressing mirror. She eased the door open to get a better view from the mirror.

Jack was on top of Catharine. Both were naked. Her legs circled his waist. Catharine's eyes were closed. The bed was creaking rhythmically. Clothes were strewn on the floor.

Minnie quickly pulled the door closed.

"Oh, Lordy," she whispered, and scampered back down the hall.

****

January was particularly brutal. Snow fell in substantial amounts for two weeks, and temperatures hovered around zero-degrees. Except for tending to livestock, ranch life took a holiday. Everyone worked mornings and took afternoons off. Card games and afternoon naps proliferated. Occasionally, Whit, Jack and Big made their way through drifts to Abilene for supplies.

"March, Maggie. Can't wait for March so we can be a ranch again. Boredom's not good. Not productive. Not good for morale."

"Whit, you may be missing some details. Haven't you noticed that Jack is eager to go to town with you? Herk is helping Bird every day re-doing her cabin. Charlie has been spending hours with Miyama grooming her horse; Jefferson and Annalise spend every afternoon together. We never see Elon and Myra. I think that there's a lot of productive, maybe reproductive, activity," she laughed.

He paused for a minute. "Of course I've noticed those things. Some of them."

"Dear, you don't have to entertain these people. We've been through harsh winters before. The inactivity is good. I get to see more of you, even when you're a grouch."

Jacob sat on his Uncle Jefferson's knee, crushing two wooden figures together, a mock battle between two "gwizzwy beahs." Sitting next to them, Annalise thought he'll be such a good father, if we get to that. She was desperate to find out if the brutal attack in Cincinnati would interfere with her conceiving or carrying a baby, Jefferson's baby. She and Jefferson were intimate frequently, but nothing had happened. Not that she wanted it to, yet. She did want to nurture, to continue the family line, to honor her mother with a free generation. If not, being with Jefferson would be enough.

Joshua and Rose sat opposite them, holding hands as usual. It was Saturday night and the four were enjoying an overnight in the large apartment above the store. Jefferson and Annalise had slogged through melting snow to spend the weekend.

"Here's an interesting thought," Joshua was saying, "In May of last year, the Union Pacific and the Central Pacific joined their railroad lines in Utah. It is possible to take a train from New York City to the Pacific Ocean, and points between."

"I've heard that," Jefferson replied. "You could cross the country in less than a week."

"Joshua told me that if we board in Nebraska, we can be in California in four days. The wagon train takes five months," Rose offered.

"Where in California?" Annalise asked.

"Sacramento. Here's my point. Would you two consider making California our destination? I've been checking on it for a while. The weather's more stable than Oregon's. It's more accessible. It has everything from mountains to hills to plains, and the ocean too, depending on where we'd settle," Joshua said.

"California is fine with me. We had considered Oregon because of the trail, and the wagon trains. We're looking for climate and land, wherever we go."

"Here's what I'm thinking. Jefferson and I could take the train from Nebraska to California, look things over, buy land, hire builders, and be back here in a month," Joshua added."

"That sounds good. That gives us all of the decisions to make, however. The girls won't have much of a say," Jefferson mentioned.

Annalise laughed. "Jefferson, we agree on most everything. I don't see anything wrong with that plan, except that I'll miss you terribly for a month." She kissed him on the cheek.

"I changed my thought to California months ago," Joshua said. "You two could still head for Oregon, but we'd be 600 miles apart."

"Being close to you and Rose and Jacob is a priority for us," Jefferson replied.

"The other good thing about the train is that we could visit back and forth with my folks and the people at the ranch… if we move."

"Rosie, darling, are you having second thoughts about leaving Kansas?" Jefferson asked.

"Of course not. Kansas is all that I've ever known, but there are limited possibilities in Abilene." She glanced back at Joshua.

"I know what she's thinking. I've been balancing staying here with the advantages of starting over somewhere else too. I wouldn't want to raise a family in Abilene, the way it is now. But being close to the Brodys has been wonderful," Annalise said.

Rose crossed to the couch and lifted a sleepy Jacob off of Jefferson's lap.

"There was a lot of uncertainty with the original plan, taking an arduous trek on a wagon train to a place we've never seen, and then foraging for comfort while we try to get settled," Joshua said, as Rose lay Jacob in his arms.

"It was going to be an adventure. It probably would have taken two years to get completely settled. The railroad changes everything," Jefferson added.

"I hope you two don't think that I'm manipulating things for my own interests. But in a way, I am. Our life continues to change. Tell them, Rosie."

"Tell them?" Rose blushed. "My wonderful husband and I are going to be parents again. Sometime in late May. I'm pregnant. We haven't told anyone."

"Rose!" Annalise exclaimed, rushing to hug her, "That's wonderful!"

"Congratulations, brother ! Why the secret?"

"We had to have this conversation with you first. We certainly couldn't be part of a wagon train to Oregon, for maybe two years. If the railroad and California was agreeable to you, then we could leave this year, in early autumn. But we didn't want to influence your plans with the baby news."

"I guess it's time for another announcement," Jefferson said. "I couldn't start a new life with unfinished business. I have asked Annalise to marry me, and for some reason she accepted."

Rose put her hands to her face. "What incredible news! When?"

"We talked about a late March wedding. We wanted to do it here, in front of everyone, before we left for Oregon," Annalise answered.

"With the new plans, there's no rush. A warm weather wedding in June or July would be better," Jefferson offered.

"This is great. I wondered when my brother would ask you. I'm glad that he finally summoned his courage."

There was a short silence as everyone digested the news. Rose started giggling, then Annalise, and finally there was full-throated laughter from the two men.

Over coffee, far into the night, the four formulated a tentative plan. Joshua and Jefferson would leave for California in April. The wedding would occur in early August, three months after Rose's delivery; she insisted on the nuptial date, saying, "I want to be able to help, well after the baby is born. My sister is getting married."

The move to California would begin in late August.

****

Joseph McCoy and Abilene finally had a man.

McCoy, intent on promoting Abilene as a safe cow town, involved himself in every area of the community's well-being. His lingering problem continued to be law enforcement. Finally, he had an applicant, perhaps not capable of long-term success, but at least a capable stopgap.

Hastings Foley, a former Northern officer in the Civil War, had most recently been a drifter. He had applied for the job as sheriff , and had been approved.

He was a prematurely gray haired man in his early forties, a native of Indiana, who had gone from being a successful pre-War haberdasher in Indianapolis to becoming a storied but battle weary officer. After the war he had failed in a succession of jobs in a strange odyssey of wandering west.

Privately he traced the genesis of his transformation to army duty. He had signed on to the 21st Indiana Infantry at the onset of hostilities, along with his brother and his three closest friends. Soon after, his unit became the First Regiment Heavy Artillery, which became known as the "Jackass Regiment."

Thus began a series of journeys, long marches, and deprivation as the unit was assigned to New Orleans, western Louisiana, Texas, and Alabama. The stretch in Louisiana was fraught with biting insects, heat, alligators, isolation, and disease. Foley, a quiet, intelligent, personable man, rose quickly up the ranks, and was respected and admired.

But the Jackass Regiment lost 320 men and three officers to disease caused by poor water, spoiled food, and mosquitos. Among them were Foley's brother and two of his friends. In battles, seven more officers were casualties, because they had to ride skirmish lines on their horses, affording the only real human targets. Foley became a colonel, and held on to his emotional stability until the war ended.

Post-war he tried a variety of jobs to earn a living, fireman, bank teller, and even a stint as a police officer. The sale of his haberdashery business had given him the means to move on, but that occupation was forever behind him. He needed to find a place to forget the war, so he became a vagabond, and the longer that lasted, the more he lost his focus.

He arrived in Abilene in November of 1869 looking for a challenge, or more appropriately, a niche. He met Joshua Chase in his store, and after a lengthy conversation with a fellow colonel, he noted that there was no law officer in the town. Joshua advised him to talk to Joseph McCoy. It took McCoy two months to present him to Mayor Theodore Henry, prompted eventually by the murder of Cleetus Wilburn.

Foley hired two deputies, "Snarf" Farnes, a former shotgun rider for the stagecoach line, and Clint Prudhomme, a security officer from the stockyards.

McCoy and Henry considered Foley and his deputies as temporary. Interviews with dozens of other applicants from around the country would pay off in time, they reasoned. Hopefully the three could at least neutralize crime until a proper lawman was hired.

Meanwhile the new sheriff revived the "check your firearms" law, and posted that on all avenues of ingress to Abilene. He patrolled the area across the tracks. One of the three lawmen was always on duty, and the detention cells and the holding shack hosted a variety of miscreants. District judges had full dockets when they rotated to Abilene.

****

Bravo Wright and his murderous horde had ridden in zig-zag patterns in a four-year rampage through Iowa, Nebraska, Missouri, Illinois, and Tennessee, destroying property and lives.

These disciples of Bloody Bill Anderson were bridging a gap between the end of the Civil War and the start of a new one, in which the embattled South would rise up and this time be triumphant.

One of their aims was to reduce the opposition. They sought to embarrass and to slaughter former Union officers and soldiers, to create fear, and to eliminate entire families. In the process, they looted and pillaged, leaving no witnesses.

They would ride separately into small communities, scout the area, blend in for a while, and then strike somewhere in the middle of the night. There was no geographical pattern, and no deadlines for their work. They might lay low for a few months, "bivouac" Bravo called it, and then strike somewhere twice in a week.

Newton, a particularly vicious member, cut notches in a leather strap, and announced at the beginning of 1870 that their victims numbered 17 former Union officers, thirty-one family members, and 12 former slaves, sixty victims who would never take up arms against, or protest, the New South.

Of course, their accumulated wealth grew exponentially. Some was secreted away in a gang retreat in Iowa. Someday soon they would recover it, and wait in Mexico until they could finance their own cavalry unit in the next war.

Bravo was beginning to feel the onset of middle age. He had developed a considerable paunch, and there were three of his seven subordinates who were older than he. What he wanted was a big strike somewhere, in some unprotected area, a passel of slain veterans, and a bank job to increase the gang's wealth.

He was a wanted man, but content that no one knew his face. He knew that his name was out there, Newton's too probably. The authorities certainly were familiar with the name of these avengers. The gang was wanted and hunted throughout the Midwest, and eventually their motives became clear, hence the name "Border Ruffians," the moniker used formerly by Bill Anderson and Archie Clement. It was a name that Bravo perpetrated by leaving badly misspelled notes at the murder sites. Bloody Bill would have approved. Quantrill too.

They had long ago dispelled of the leather masks. They weren't necessary. No one survived the massacres to describe them.

Bravo's immediate plan was to head for Falls City, Nebraska, well known for its pre-war status as an Underground Railroad haven. He would mock that by finding darkies of any gender or age in that community, and then summarily hanging them.

Then, sometime in April, he would lead his men into Abilene, Kansas.

****

Annalise sat upright in her bed. She wanted to scream, had to scream, but the room was dark and the house was dark. She wouldn't disturb other people.

She calmed a bit, and reviewed the collection of fitful images that she had just dreamed, a tornadic battering of faces and voices and noises and pain.

To be sure, it was a nightmare, but so realistic that she shivered in her lonely bedroom, covered in cold perspiration.

She turned and put her feet on the floor, and sat that way for a long time, absorbing parts of the frightful experience. Snippets of memory began to break in, scattered incidents at first, and they began to coalesce into sequences…a smashed door, a knife, a pain in her head, a memory so real that she gasped aloud.

The voices started to blend into recognizable sentences, evil, demanding, threatening. She recognized one, then another. She saw an ugly scarred face, unknown to her. It came closer to hers, and she relived the pain of forced penetration. Bile rose in her throat. She swallowed hard. She stood and walked weakly to her window. A gleaming half moon reflecting off of the snow restored serenity to the moment, a beautiful, tangible presentation in the confusion.

She leaned against the window frame. Tears began to form and slide down her cheeks. She replayed the grotesque scenario, trying to force a narrative.

She got back into bed. She knew that she wouldn't fall back to sleep, and realistically she was afraid to. She would continue to organize her thoughts, decide how to assess the distorted phantasms.

A brutish fat face began to take on identity. It belonged to Corby Pitcock's henchman, Luther. An impeccably dressed man, that was Pitcock.

But what to make of it? Perhaps she was substituting them into the villainous experience in Cincinnati. Perhaps the nightmare was a ghoulish substitution of evil for evil. More than likely this was a conglomerate gathering from the two darkest incidents in her recent life, as if they had cascaded together into her subconscious.

Until she was clearer, until she had substantial proof of any connection, she wouldn't tell anyone about what had just happened to her, not even Jefferson.

****

Abilene was slowly changing. Sheriff Hastings Foley and his deputies seemed to have control of the city, but it was only early March. The real test would be in May, June, and July, when the cowboys of the West brought their cattle and their mischief back.

Mayor Henry wasn't convinced. "After all, " he said, "how much crime can occur with a foot of snow on the ground?"

The constant nuisance was Uriah Cobb, the tormenter of Weasel months before. He was a sometime drunk and a fulltime complainer with a volcanic temper, "the sourest man I ever seen," according to deputy Clint Prudhomme.

Cobb blamed Abilene for his failure to make a success of his homestead plot. "Town has ruined me," he growled from a holding cell one morning. "Uppity people, stupid laws. Some day I'll get back at all of youse," he had told Prudhomme.

He had a strong dislike of Joshua Chase, who had bested him in the street fight. "I'll get my revenge," he told the few people who could tolerate his company. He seemed to be all talk and bluff, and only crossed the line when he was fortified with alcohol. Sheriff Foley sensed a threat, however. "Keep an eye on him," he told his deputies. "If a man like that runs out of words, he may do something extreme."

"Trouble is, Sheriff," Farnes had mentioned, "he seems to be in town all of the time these days."

By Foley's new edicts, bars and saloons, gambling houses, and whorehouses had to close by 1 am daily, and all day on Sundays. None could open until 2 pm. When two establishments resisted, he closed them. He and the deputies loaded a wagon with their alcohol assets, and smashed them in a nearby field.

"I don't like what you're doing," he had told Wicks, "but you can do business as long as you follow the rules. If you ignore the new laws, we'll burn you down."

"He's bluffin'," Lester had told Wicks. "We'll pay him a visit. Mebbe finish him off."

"No. Don't do that, for Chrissake! The damn town be drivin' us out. This'll sort out when the cattle drives start again. Don't draw attention to us. Bad enough you killed the black man at the church."

"Ain't nobody can trace that to us."

"Don't make no sense to take a chance. Even when we open late and close early, we be makin' as much as when the cows are in town."

"None of the whores be goin' to church, neither."

"If they was, you'd hafta burn out that store."

"Damn preacher. Damn sheriff. Some day, we take care of both of them."

****

Weasel always celebrated the Marches of his life. Through blind luck and simple-minded persistence, he had survived all of the winters of his adult years, although some of those were tenuous. He had no place of his own. Never had really, although most of the decades were fuzzy in his mind.

He had an animal-like instinct for survival, abetted by abandoned shacks, protected alleyways, neglected barns and stables, and crawl spaces.

He owned little more than the clothes he wore. When the shirts, coats, pants and shoes of the moment wore out, he supplemented his wardrobe by snatching drying articles off of clotheslines. He fended off hunger by taking whatever he could off of the shelves of trading posts and general stores, or by begging at the backdoors of whatever town he was in.

He had only a dim recollection of his life before the accident. He didn't remember much of the accident either, but he did know that it caused the headaches that never really left him. He couldn't recall the frontier towns that he had wandered through. A few maybe. Certainly he recalled some that had run him off, or had abused him in many ways. Kindness was rare on the frontier.

That Jozwah over to the general store, and his woman, Rose, now they were fine people. Jozwah gave him clothes sometimes. Rose made him an occasional meal. And the big man, Jeffson, he was nice, and so was the book lady, Anna-lisa. They were the reason he was still in Abilene. He avoided most other people, wary of what they might do to him.

His was the existence of an apparition, constantly moving around, unpredictable. He observed people and listened surreptitiously to what they discussed, protective measures to avoid confrontations, embarrassments, and pain.

The clomping of boots on the wooden walkway on Texas Street roused him from sleep. The sun was high. He had overslept in the narrow alley. It took him a while to stand. Aging muscles protested, and he was light-headed. He jammed the too-small hat on his head, and lifted the ragged blanket from the ground, stuffing it into a bag that contained an old firearm and a tin of crackers that he's taken from the Chase store the day before. The little man with the addled brain and the shuffling gait would soon become the centerpiece in a denouement of the criminal pestilence that plagued Abilene.

Today? Well, he'd tell Jozwah the important thing he'd heard days before. But what was it? Maybe he'd remember. Maybe not.

****

A skein of mild March days drew Hata, Lige, and Big into the fields. The three took turns on two plows, each drawn by a sturdy mule.

As usual, Hata Wu had started well before the others, jumping up from the breakfast table to hitch the equipment.

Whit called after him, "Hata, have another cup of coffee. We don't have to do all of the plowing this week, let alone today."

"Brody-san, honorable father once said 'be the first to the field and the last to bed,' " and he was gone.

"Bless his heart, " said Annalise, "Yesterday I was basking in the sun on the front porch, reading a book. He came by and said, 'Aha! A book is like a garden held in your hands.' What a beautiful sentiment."

Jack laughed. "Several weeks ago, with snow on the ground, he was putting axle grease on all of our wagon wheels. I mentioned something about being prepared. He told me, 'You must always dig the well before you are thirsty.'"

"Apropos of nothing, he once told me, 'To know the road ahead, you must ask the ones coming back.' I missed the point on that one, but it sounded like good advice," Whit said.

"Pearls of wisdom," Caroline added, stoking the fireplace, "One morning in here, I was complaining about getting old, slowing down. It was before any of you had come in. He smiled at me and said, 'Be not afraid of going slowly, Be afraid of standing still.'"

"Which is good advice for all of us today," Whit said, getting up from the table.

The room began to empty. Caroline, Bear Woman, Myra, and Annalise worked efficiently. "Annalise, sit here with me for a moment," Margaret said from the table.

They sat adjacent to each other at a corner of the large table.

"Jefferson and Joshua are leaving in a few weeks, dear?"

"Yes, Mrs. Brody."

"Are you comfortable with all of the plans?"

"Yes, completely, although it will be difficult to leave you. You and Mr. Brody, are you comfortable with the plans?" Annalise asked, after noticing a pensiveness in Margaret's voice.

"We'll miss you, and Rose, and little Jacob, and the boys. But Mr. Brody brightened up with the moving plans when he realized that we can reach you out there in the space of a week, whenever we're invited. I doubt that we'd have ever seen you again if we had to count on a wagon train, or some long trip by boats."

"We can easily come back here for visits too."

"Mr. Brody is not ready to leave the ranch permanently, whatever he says." She reached out and covered Annalise's hands with her own. "We'll always hold you in our hearts. We've only known you for two years, but we consider you our second child. Rose thinks of you as her sister. You know that."

"I've had three mothers in my life. Wonderful, kind, intelligent women. In that regard, I've been blessed."

"This is what I want to say. You and Jefferson will never be alone. Mr. Brody and I want to know how we can help you with the move. Is there anything you need? Money?"

"No money, please, Mrs. Brody. Jefferson still has over half of his inheritance, most of his severance pay, and every penny of his wages here. I still have some of mine. We'll make it work."

"Well, we want to do something for a wedding present. You really don't have much, do you, Dear?"

"Starting out a marriage with few possessions is probably the best way. We'll appreciate things more when they come."

"I'm going to ask something of you, Annalise."

"Yes. Anything."

"I'd be honored if you'd call me Mother Brody."

Annalise's voice broke as she whispered, "Yes. Yes. I would love that."

In the fields that morning, one of the mules came up lame. Lige unhitched him, and led him slowly down to Elon.

Big, frustrated, wrestled the unhitched plow to a furrow. "Wastin' time here," he growled.

Using his bulk he pushed against the plow, barely scraping a few feet of dirt. He pushed again and again. The spring soil didn't yield much.

Hata slowed his mule and watched.

"Big-san. Won't work without mule. Man with one chopstick go hungry."

Big chuckled to himself. Good one. If he got a chance, he'd bring that up at some breakfast.

****

The fee for crossing the country to Sacramento in third class, or emigrant, was $40. Third class offered no amenities. Cars were cramped and crowded, filled with people crossing to new lives. The Chase brothers would have tolerated the wooden seats and the people just to have saved money. The problem with that was that the emigrant trains took twice as long to make the journey, frequently stopping or being shunted to sidings to let the express trains pass.

So they spent twice as much for the quick crossing, modified some by the shorter trip from Nebraska to California. Their first class accommodations included privacy and soft seats which turned down into sleeping berths, and fresh linens.

"Joshua, this makes sense doesn't it, the move?"

"Jefferson, it's getting late for second thoughts."

"No. For Annalise and me, it's a natural progression. Neither of us has parents or close relatives. Any move only affects us. We could go anywhere."

"So, you're talking about me."

"Somewhat. You have 100 friends in Abilene, a successful business, the Brodys, the respect of the community."

"Rose and I had this talk last year. What we don't have is safety, schools for Jacob, culture, and solitude. Abilene is no better after four years, and the nature of its business will always be rowdy and intrusive. We're not moving for an adventure; we're moving for a better life."

"How will your plans change if Sacramento is a mistake?"

"If it is, we'll wait a year and find another destination. The thing is that moving west means moving all of the way west. The Indian problems won't be easily solved, and they will consume all of the territory from Kansas to California. We can easily go east."

"Back to Vermont?"

"That's a possibility."

"Joshua, we grew up in the best possible place, but what we're doing now is like a progressive game. Start in Vermont. Face west. Step by step, event by event, follow the sun to the conclusion of the game."

"What about Annalise, Jefferson? Can she carry this off physically?"

"I'm sure of it. Two days before we left, she was in the flower gardens, attacking them with a scythe and a hoe for most of the day. Her spirit is back. The limp is gone. She has an appetite. I hope Sacramento will wipe away everything that she's been through."

On a twenty-year run of prosperity and circumstance, Sacramento in 1870 was a city of over 12,000 residents, sprawled comfortably along the Sacramento and American rivers.

Its status as the terminus of several prominent modes of migration and communication fueled the growth. Over the years, wagon trains to California ended there, as did a stagecoach line, the Pony Express, the telegraph line, and the transcontinental railroad.

First attracted by two gold strikes in the foothills within 50 miles of the settlement, and by protection offered by nearby Fort Sutter, settlers began to arrive in large numbers in the 1850's.

In 1854, after several location changes around the state, the state capital was moved to Sacramento, generating another influx of immigration. Construction of the state capitol building began in 1860. Two respected newspapers served the city; *The Sacramento Union* first appeared in 1851, and in 1866 counted Mark Twain among its feature writers. *The Sacramento Bee* began publishing in 1858.

It had survived two disastrous floods, The last one, in 1854, caused a massive reconstruction project in affected areas. Protective walls were built, and buildings were elevated in place. As Sacramento spread north, south, and east, mansions and fine homes appeared throughout the area. Outlying land became valuable to an infant wine industry, eventually extending north and far south throughout the valley.

All was not perfect. A rapidly expanding Chinese population was abused. Laws were passed to curtail the growth of a Chinatown section. Asian immigrants were scorned. Social rejects, they banded together, and more than a few ugly incidents resulted.

April 19, 1870

My Dearest Wife,

Rosie, today I purchased our future, a large brick house on six acres in the northwest quadrant of Sacramento. It is everything we've discussed, roomy with a large front porch, and a modicum of privacy. It is within blocks of a thriving, clean business district. Given your wonderful ability to produce children, it has five bedrooms.

The entire expanse of land is well-kept with several mature trees. The house sits back on the property at the end of a tree-lined lane. Behind it are a sizable shed and a small barn.

Also, I've found a nice little building five blocks south, which could serve as a smaller version of our store, if we decide to do that. There is a nice school just to the east.

On the train ride, which was a pleasant experience, I explained to Jefferson my dream of running for political office. Whether that would entail local or state service, Sacramento is an appropriate place to begin it. After a bit, he looked sideways at me and said, "Governor Chase. I like it."

He did not return to the hotel tonight. I suspect that he is somewhere under the stars, hopefully camping on his future home. He was going to look over footage to the north, along the Sacramento River.

The lawyer we retained upon arrival is respected and a valuable source of information. His name is Walter McNelly, and his sources have provided us with all of our leads on properties. We have contracted him to manage our affairs here, after we return to Abilene.

I'm hopeful that Reverend Brooks and Bear Woman have been a help to you. It's nice that they are staying with you and helping in the store while I'm away.

Be well, my Rose. The next portion of our life will be full of laughter and contentment. I promise you.

I miss you terribly. Kiss our son for me.

Affectionately, Joshua

****

The two Ruffians lay in the darkness of their room in the Drover's Cottage, waiting for sleep.

"The Chase Place. What is that, Bravo? Them brothers own a boarding house?"

"No. I asked that strange fella. He says they ain't related. Woman runs the place."

"Too bad. We coulda got to her, made them brothers come to us."

"Thought of that, Newton, after I learned 'bout that place. But they'se allus people in there. Full house. And that one deppity, he lives there. Ain't related nohow, from what that Weasel said."

"That ain't but a block away from the store, and they ain't related? Mebbe that stanky idiot don't know."

"He ain't been wrong about nuthin' else. Told me everything he knew. None too bright, but he knows a bunch 'bout them Chase brothers."

"He ain't gonna say nothin' about you askin' them questions, is he?"

"You kiddin' me? He prob'ly forgot he talked to me already. Tell you what, if we gets a chance, we'll finish him off anyhow."

"Don't know if'n I'll help with that, Bravo," Newton laughed. "Wouldn't want to catch nuthin' from him."

"Hell. We get them Chase boys, we'll make him a Ruffian too."

"You kiddin' aincha, boss?"

Wright was silent.

"Rest of the gang be comin' in tomorrow?"

"They be here in two groups, morning and afternoon. We'll meet 'em east of town. Send them in to places to stay. Long as no one sees us all together."

"Then we do that other thing?"

"Yep. Then we do that other thing."

****

April 20, 1870

My Annalise,

A dense fog surrounded me this morning as I awoke on the crest of a small hill on the west side of the Sacramento River.

I spent the night there with Storm, curled under a valley oak tree of considerable size. A steady breeze and spikes of sunshine dispersed the fog, and I was looking at undulating hills with a view of small mountains on the horizon.

During the afternoon yesterday, I saw ducks over the river, a cooper's hawk, swifts, a covey of quail, and what I think was an osprey nesting in another oak near the river. The call of a mourning dove was the first sound that I heard this morning. There were trees around me, more than in Kansas, fewer than in Vermont.

Enough teasing. I will purchase the property this afternoon, a few more than sixty acres, 20-some miles north of Sacramento. The area is dotted with vineyards and other orchards. The soil is remarkably fertile. We will be 15 miles south of a settlement with several stores.

There is a house on the property, not exactly what we wanted, but it is sturdy. It is two rooms over two rooms and a kitchen. We can decide later whether to build what we want, or add to the existing house. I haven't seen inside yet. It was locked. There is also a barn. The owner was going to grow grapes, but some family tragedy forced him to sell. There is plenty of room for gardens.

The asking price is a bit steep, but we can afford it and a nice-sized stable. Affording horse stock of size will be a problem at first, and we'll need a fence in good time.

I am back in Sacramento as I write this. After purchasing the tract this afternoon, my business will almost be complete. Joshua has already bought a nice house in northern Sacramento. We will probably board a train east in the next few days, and be back in Abilene by the 30th.

The most exciting feature of the land is that I'll be sharing it with you. I can picture our children romping on the verdant hills, watched over by the most beautiful mother in the world.

I love you,

Jefferson

Annalise read the letter to Margaret.

"What a wonderful letter, and good news. The descriptions. It's funny, but Whit used some like that to describe this land to me years ago," Margaret said. "It was even better than what he said. I wish that for you."

"The 30th? That's only four days from now," Annalise said. "They're on the train now."

****

Even in the morning rain scavengers circled the lifeless body, gliding closer with each swoop. A full complement of the birds would soon settle and compete with each other in a ravenous orgy.

The homesteader expected to see a downed cow, or the carcass of a wolf or wild horse at the center of activity. He reined in his horse twenty feet away, and the vultures' naked heads came to attention as they alighted.

"Go on, now ! Git away!" the man yelled. He reached for his rifle, and fired a shot into the air, and the birds squawked and screamed as they flew wildly away from the noise.

The man paused. The carcass was a human body on its back, twisted away from him. A puddle of rain around it splashed water as the rain increased, washing away blood.

Must have happened during the night sometime, before the rain, the man surmised. Murder. He looked around to make sure that he was alone out there, and then dismounted, pulling the slicker tighter around himself.

"Damn!" he said aloud. He recognized the victim. He knelt, but knew that the man was beyond help. He could do nothing. It was four miles to town. He examined the victim without touching him, counting bullet wounds in both arms, the chest, and to the side of the head. Patches of cloth were missing from around the knees. They had been shot away too, he guessed.

"What a mess. Best ride into Abilene, tell somebody. Bring 'em back out here," he muttered to himself. He failed to see a slip of paper jammed into a pocket of the dead man's shirt, getting soaked by the downpour.

The low rattle of thunder sounded in the distance. Maybe the thunder would keep the birds away until he returned with help. He mounted and galloped to Abilene.

Twenty minutes later, he burst through a door and announced to a man wearing a star, "He's daid! Sheriff Foley's been kilt!"

To further recruit trail drives to Abilene, Joseph McCoy had again hired men to circulate fliers throughout the Texas cattle country. Competition with other cow towns was getting keen. He was attuned to anything which might disturb his ventures, and so he had summoned Mayor Theodore Henry to the Drover's Hotel the day after Foley's death.

"Thanks for coming, Theodore. A cup of coffee?"

"Joseph, I need something stronger. Much stronger."

McCoy escorted him to a small office off of the lobby. They sat in overstuffed chairs.

"Theodore, what do you know?"

"Well, I know that both deputies turned in their badges. We've got no law. I also know that we're dealing with a murderous group called the Border Ruffians. They might be murdering more people. It's not good."

"Border Ruffians? Wasn't that a vigilante group of Southerners during the war? How do you know about them?"

"There was a note stuck in Foley's shirt. It's over at the sheriff's office. Here, I wrote down the words." He pulled a folded piece of paper from his pocket, and handed it to McCoy. "You'll have to get past the spelling."

McCoy took the paper.

Unyun filth. The south will rize agin. Bye Kansas. Of to Misuri. Bordor Ruffins.

"And, Joseph, this wanted poster was hung in Foley's office."

$1,000 REWARD
For information on the Border Ruffians.
Cowards responsible for the
Deaths of over 20 former
Union officers
In Illinois, Kentucky, Missouri
They are
Possibly eight or more
Former confederates
May include Bravo Wright
And Rollie Newton

"Theodore, aren't the Feds involved in this?"

"Yes. There is a concentrated manhunt, I hear. Trouble is no one knows where they are. There are no witnesses. Only a few notes like this one."

"Well, the note says that they're heading to Missouri, if I read it correctly."

"Think about it, Joseph. Foley was a Union officer, but not well known. If their motive is to murder high ranking Union officers, who is more important than the Chase brothers? One was an advisor to President Lincoln; the other was the hero of Brandy Station and a friend of General Custer."

"Have you told them?"

"No. They're in California for a spell. Didn't want to tell Joshua's wife, get her all upset. She's pregnant and all."

"Christ, Theodore. The Ruffians would be new faces in town. Easy to spot."

"Joseph, there's 200 new faces in town every couple of weeks."

"So, what are you going to do about this? Something happens to those two brothers, every newspaper in the country will have a story."

"Problem is, there's maybe eight of them. Anybody we hire is going to be outnumbered. Sent a telegraph to the governor. Also, do you remember Tom Smith, 'Bear River' Smith? We talked to him about being sheriff. City marshal in Wyoming. He wanted too much money to come here."

"Yes, I remember the name. He settled some kind of dispute in Bear River, Wyoming."

"Yes, well, he's the sheriff now in Kit Carson, Colorado. I telegraphed him too, offered him whatever he wants to come here. Told him to get back to us."

"It'll take him a while to get here, and that's only if he wants the job. What are you going to do in the meantime? I've got a lot at stake here, Theodore."

"I'll talk to them deputies. See if they'll hang around until Smith gets here. Offer them double their wages."

"How will you pay them?"

"Damned if I know."

"Well, Theodore. You'd better get on this. The first thing you've got to do is to let the Chase brothers know about it. And the town. Make some more of the wanted posters. Put them up around Abilene. If the Ruffians are still here, maybe we can scare them away."

****

The Chase brothers rode up to the store on May 2 covered in Kansas dust, all California business concluded. They had ridden in shirt sleeves since early morning, rain gear and coats stowed away in saddlebags.

Rose saw them coming up First Street from the large windows of the storefront. "Reverend Brooks, they're here!" she shouted, as she ran through the front door.

"Joshua, honey ! I expected you two days ago." He dismounted, and she jumped into him enthusiastically, almost knocking him over.

"Hi, Rosie." They embraced, and the greeting kiss turned into a long moment of affection.

Jefferson chuckled as he hitched Storm to the post. "Nice show you're putting on, folks."

"Hi Jefferson! I missed you too." Rose exclaimed, and went to hug him. "Are you two hungry? Thirsty?"

"Thirsty," Joshua said. "Let's go inside. Rosie, you're waddling, but it's pretty waddling." He patted her stomach.

"Yes, Honey. I am very, very pregnant."

Jonah appeared in the doorway. "The prodigal sons are back."

"Reverend Brooks, it's good to see you," Joshua said as he shook hands with the minister. "Rose, where's my son?"

"He's taking a nap with Bear Woman. We'll let him sleep a while. We have some things to talk about."

"Good things?"

She softened. "Good and not so good."

"Listen, I'll head out to the ranch now," Jefferson offered.

"No, please, Jeffie. Not yet. The news concerns you too." She led them through the door. "We've been busy in here this morning. I would have been lost without Reverend Brooks."

Jefferson sat on a barrel just inside the door. Joshua followed his wife behind the counter, and Jonah stood a few feet away.

"You two suddenly look a bit glum. Tell us the good news first," Jefferson said.

"OK," Rose responded. "Here's the best of it. Elon and Myra had their baby last week. A boy they named Isaiah. He was a few weeks early, but healthy."

"Wonderful," Joshua exclaimed. "that is good news."

"Secondly, still under good news…you'd better sit down for this, Joshua. Catharine and Jack are going to get married."

Jefferson's head snapped up. Joshua simply responded, "What?"

"I know. It surprised me too. According to her, she asked him. They've been serious for several months. Jack had been spending a lot of time at the boarding house."

"Well, I'm somewhat stunned. I've never even seen them together," Joshua mused.

"Seems like a good match," Jefferson said.

"She asked Reverend Brooks to marry them. Nobody else knows about it. She won't tell anyone else until she talks to you two. She wants your approval. Because of Jonathan, she needs you to bless the union."

"I think it's great," Jefferson offered.

"She needs you to tell her that."

"Is that all of the good news, Honey?"

Rose looked at the minister. "Reverend Brooks?"

"No way to tell it except straight out," Jonah asserted. "The bad news is that Sheriff Foley was murdered a few days ago."

The room was suddenly quiet.

Jonah continued. "They found his body north of town, riddled with gunshots."

"Who did it?" Joshua snapped.

"No idea. According to talk, a note was found in his shirt pocket. A group called the Border Ruffians is taking credit. Mayor Henry wants to talk to you two as soon as possible. You need to see him now."

"Why, Jonah?" Jefferson asked. "You think he wants us to put on badges?"

"Unlikely. Farnes and Prudhomme are sticking around for a while. Henry mentioned yesterday that he's hiring a lawman from Colorado named Bear River Smith."

"Services for Foley?"

"Two days ago. We buried him up near Cleetus. No next of kin."

"Jefferson, can you hang around for a few minutes? We can go talk to Henry now."

"Sure, Joshua."

Jonah interrupted. "I'll go with you."

The three walked out onto the Abilene street.

"Keep walking, but listen to me," Jonah said in a low voice. "Henry talked to me, but he didn't want Rose to know these things. The Border Ruffians are a group of Southern sympathizers, They have killed over twenty Union officers in the past few years. Maybe more. They don't just kill their victims; they torture them first, and then they kill family members, including children. It looks like they're here now. You two would be prime targets. Their note said that they're heading to Missouri, but Henry thinks they'll stick around to get to you."

"The war's been over for five years," Jefferson said.

"Apparently they're involved in a lot more than revenge. Family possessions and money stashes have come up missing. They've been involved in several bank robberies."

"Anything else?"

"There's not too much information about them. The authorities say that they're the remnants of the Border Ruffians who rode with Quantrill and Bloody Bill Anderson. Remember them?"

"They were a major concern for President Lincoln. Southern renegades," Joshua said.

"Exactly," Jonah responded. "They used to number 400 men. They seem to be down to eight now."

"Any names?" Jefferson asked.

"Two. The last full Ruffian group was led by two men named Archie Clement and Bravo Wright. Clement was killed several years ago. Bravo Wright is unaccounted for. A man named Rollie Newton may be involved too."

"Reverend Brooks, you would seem to be a target too. Your involvement in helping slaves escape is well known," Jefferson suggested.

"I've thought about that. The two of you have to be more vigilant though."

"What do you think, Joshua?" Jefferson asked.

"I don't think that waiting for something to happen is wise. I'd say that we get aggressive. Talk to people around town. Look for people we don't recognize. The worst thing would be to change our lives, to hide out somewhere. I'm not concerned for me. I am worried about Rose and Jacob."

"I think that you two should move out to the ranch for a while. Bear Woman and I can mind the store."

"Jonah, I went through four years of dealing with people who wanted to kill me. Joshua did too, before he was wounded. Compared to that, this is nothing."

"I understand. I'd say that we move Rose, Bear Woman, and Jacob out to the ranch. I'll stay here in the store with you."

"Me too," Jefferson said.

"Let's just not underestimate them. They've been doing this for several years and they haven't been caught," Jonah reminded them.

"Rose can't ride in her condition. We'll need a wagon from the ranch. I'll tell Doc Rosbottom tomorrow that his patient will be 15 miles farther away."

"Tell him the whole story. He's a good man. He can keep his eyes and ears open," Jefferson offered.

"Something else. I don't know how important it is. The past three weeks, while you were away, I began noticing a man hanging out virtually every day across the street. Rose saw him too. She told me it was Uriah Cobb, a man you had a run-in with two years ago. He mostly just stands there watching the store every day," Jonah explained.

"He was rousting Weasel. It was just an altercation, over in a hurry, several punches thrown," Joshua recalled. "If he shows up again, I'll have a talk with him."

"On top of that, the men who killed Cleetus are still out there, whoever they are," Jonah added.

"Abilene…" Jefferson added.

They had stopped to talk along Texas Street, well out of view from the store.

But several other pairs of eyes watched them intently.

"Nobody," Whit Brody said, "in my care is going to be at risk until this thing is settled. We don't even know what we're dealing with. These assassins have a record of killing family members."

The trail drive crews would be cut in half. No horses would be involved, and strangely, Whit grinned broadly whenever that subject came up.

The day was Friday, the first Friday of the month, the designated day for picking up supplies in town. Whit asked Big, Charlie Fox, and Jack to go with him. That will give Jack some time with Catharine, he thought.

Catharine. How safe was she? She was a Chase too. She was always surrounded by people at the boarding house, it was on a busy street, Deputy Prudhomme had taken a room there, and she flatly refused to leave. Case closed.

Several precautions were in place, but were they enough? The eight Ruffians were clever and adept with firearms, if they were still in the area.

In Abilene, the Chase store was on alert, although daily customers didn't notice. There were always three men circulating inside during the busy hours, working, but suspicious of new faces. At other times, Doc Rosbottom joined them, posting a note on his office door that he could be found at the store. Deputy Farnes checked in every few hours.

Very late on Thursday night, shadows produced by a full moon had moved around in front of the store. On watch, Jefferson woke the others. Joshua joined him at the front windows; Jonah and Doc went to the rear entrance. Then Joshua spotted the source of the apparitions. Weasel was setting up on the front porch.

"Weasel, come in here. You can stay inside tonight."

"Thanky, Jozwah. Didn't want the ugly man to getcha."

"The ugly man?"

"Yessir. Heared him tellin' some men they was goin' to kill the Chase boys sometime soon. Same ugly man was askin' me 'bout you some time ago."

"Would you recognize him if you saw him again?"

"If I seed him agin."

"How many men was he talking to, Weasel?" Jefferson asked.

"Didn't count. Six, mebbe seven. Mebbe five."

"How about the others? Did you get a look at them?"

"Some. They was a tall man, a short man with long hair, a fat man." From years of protecting himself, Weasel was adept, after a fashion, at noting and remembering those who were a threat to him. "Pretty dark when I heared them. Some light from the barbershop winder."

"They were in front of the barbershop?" Jonah asked.

"Nosir, Reveren'. Behind it. They was behind it."

"Weasel, what were you doing there?"

"Fixin' to get some shut-eye. Stayin' there tonight. They come up close to where I was. Stayed quiet. They never did see me. Heared one called Bravo."

"It sounds as if the Ruffians are not in Missouri," Jefferson said.

Across town, Bravo Wright and Newton were asleep in the Drover's Cottage. The other six, divided into two groups, were in a boarding house and the Frontier Hotel, also asleep.

Several hours earlier, the eight had met in a dark place north of Texas Street.

"Bravo, there be posts on us all over town."

"Don't matter at all. They be lookin' for eight men. We's never together."

"Your name and Newton's are on the posts."

"Bravo Wright ain't my name. I be David Anderson, far as anyone knows."

"Bravo, cain't get to them brothers. Protected by gunslingers ever' night. In the store ever' day," Oscar said.

"We ain't gonna get them yet. We just wait a while. Ain't ready to rob the bank yet, nohow."

"How long, you figger?"

"Trail drives fixin' to pick up. Town will be crazy. Mebbe two weeks, mebbe three."

"We gonna get them Chase boys afore that?"

"We get them Chase boys whenever we can. Sooner the better. They be makin' a mistake soon."

"Joshua Chase. Jefferson Chase. You be dead soon."

"Dex, we gonna make them hurt so bad, they be beggin' us to kill them."

Behind an outhouse twenty feet away, Weasel heard every word.

Over morning coffee, Joshua outlined a plan.

"So how do you figure to do this, Joshua?" Jonah asked.

"Mr. Brody is coming in for supplies today. When he gets here, he can watch the store with you. Jefferson and I will go out on the streets with Weasel."

"I should go with you two," Jonah responded.

"Joshua, Mr. Brody will bring some other people with him. They can stay here. Reverend Brooks will be helpful, if there's a confrontation," Jefferson suggested.

Whit pulled the wagon in front of the store just before noon. Soon after, Joshua, Jefferson, and Jonah exited the store with Weasel.

They walked the streets for over an hour with no sightings. It was an overcast, balmy day.

"Seems that most people would be out on a day like this," Jefferson said.

"Bars'll be open in a while," Jonah noted.

"Let's walk up toward the Drover's," Joshua said.

Suddenly, Weasel stopped.

"That's one of them! That! And the other man too!"

"You sure, Weasel?" Jefferson asked.

"Yessir. Yessir! Fer sure."

A fat scowling man, was crossing the street in front of them. Next to him was a short man with hair to his shoulders, bowlegged and skinny.

"Wait here. They have to walk past us. Just stand here. Follow my lead. Weasel, disappear for a while," Jefferson stated.

The two were almost upon them when the fat man spotted the threesome. He stopped briefly, paused, and then grabbed the short man by the elbow, and they continued.

Jefferson stood in their way. "Morning, gentlemen." He put his hands on his hips and smiled at them. Joshua tipped his hat. The two strangers walked around them, obviously on edge.

"C'mon, let's follow them," Jefferson said.

Without discretion, Jefferson and the others walked brazenly ten steps behind, hands on their holsters. "Hey, Bravo!" Joshua yelled. Both men stopped.

"Dammit, Dex. Them's the Chases. They followin' us!"

"Dammit! Dammit! How they know us? What they doin'? Let's cross the street."

They crossed. The three followed.

"Still there, Oscar. Think they be on to us?"

"Pears so, mebbe. Why they don't stop us?"

"We gonna go to the Drover's. Talk to Bravo about this."

Behind them, Joshua said, "That's probably enough. Two killers. They got off easy. But we gave them something to think about."

"Couldn't do much more. We're working on the word of Weasel. I don't think that would hold up in court," Jefferson mentioned.

"They're guilty. They were acting mighty peculiar. They stopped when Joshua yelled 'Bravo'. One of them is Bravo, or they're both working for him. I think we ought to let the deputies in on this before we go back to your store." Jonah added.

At that moment, Whit and Charlie Fox were in the wagon bed stacking supplies carried to them by Big.

"We're about finished here," Whit said. "The boys should…"

A gunshot broke the mid-afternoon quiet. Whit spun around in time to see Charlie topple off of the wagon. Big's pistol was out of his holster in an instant as he scoured the street. Whit jumped from the wagon, and knelt protectively over Charlie, who was holding his right shoulder.

"Lie still, son." He saw blood seeping around a hole in the upper shirt sleeve. He pulled at the material, exposing the wound.

Big moved to the center of the street. He saw nobody. Holstering his pistol, he returned to the wagon.

"Mr. Brody?"

"Looks like it went into muscle here. Probably went clean through. We need Doc Rosbottom."

"Be right back."

Footsteps behind him, running.

Whit pulled his pistol, and saw Weasel.

"Seed 'im. Seed 'im, Mister Whit. Old man, look like he have one eye. Over there, cross the street. Seed 'im shoot! Four of them!"

"Where's Joshua, and the others?"

"Made me leave. Found 'em two men. Meetin' them here. Seed the old man what shot."

"Old man?"

"Ole hat pulled down on his face too. Looked old."

"It wasn't the Ruffians." Whit told Joshua minutes later, "it was Old Man Kaynes, the squatter. He wasn't aiming for Charlie. He was trying to get me."

"Want to look for him?"

"Nope. Charlie's OK. The shot went through. We'll wait for Rosbottom to finish with him, then head back to the ranch. "I'll be back, probably Monday."

"We found two of the Ruffians. We're almost certain of that. We know where to find them. They went to the Drover's."

"What are you going to do?"

"They know we're onto something. We'll close the store on Sunday. Jonah says no church. We'll see if we can flush them out again. We didn't see the other six."

"This town is out of control. Be careful, Joshua."

"Here's a note to Rose, Sir, if you don't mind delivering it."

****

Muley was chosen for the task, because no one involved had seen his face two years before in Missouri.

He entered the Chase store early. Corby Pitcock and Luther stayed well out of sight up the street.

"Mawnin'," he said to the man behind the counter, a tall, older man. "I be lookin' for a man named Jefferson. Don't know much else about him. Somebody up the street thought I might find him in here. Big fella. Young. Seen him a few years ago in Cincinnati. I was a friend of the gardener who worked for his folks. Pulled into Abilene a few days ago. Heared he might be here afore I left Cincinnati. His uncle was a fine man. A perfesser, I believe. Afflicted man. Know where I can find this Jefferson fella?"

"Why are you looking for him?" Jonah asked.

"Don't know nobody else here. Thought maybe he'd have a lead on work around here. A man's gotta eat."

"What is his uncle's name?"

"O'Neill. He be dead now, I figger."

"Nobody here by that name."

"No. No. He ain't a O'Neill. If'n I 'member, his name is Chase.

"The gardener, you say. What is his name?"

"We called him 'Bud.' Never knew his given name."

"If I run into him, I'll tell him you're looking for him. What's your name?"

"It be Jackson. Carl Jackson."

Muley had exhausted his knowledge of anything related to Cincinnati, information gleaned from quizzing the gardener, then murdering the O'Neill uncle. The letter found by Pitcock had been signed "Jefferson," and it had related to a Kansas saloon in a cow town. A man up the street had mentioned "Chase" as a possible last name an hour ago.

But this man was suspicious, asking him things that he could answer, but he was uncomfortable. Time to leave. He had his answer anyway.

"Thanks, Mister. Tell him I was here."

That is no friend of Jefferson's, Jonah thought, and certainly no friend of a college professor. Jefferson was upstairs, but Jonah hadn't summoned him for the visitor, based on other current situations. He followed the man onto the front porch, and watched him stroll away. Far down the street, he was joined by a man walking with a cane, and a stooped, bigger man. He said that he didn't know anyone here, Jonah remembered.

Jonah Brooks noticed the restlessness of his two companions.

"Why don't you two ride out to the ranch this morning? It should be safe enough, if you leave now, and come back in the early afternoon. I can tell you're missing two ladies, and besides that you're making me nervous."

"You're comfortable with being alone in the store?"

"No problem."

They rode out of town at a canter, and increased that to a gallop several miles out of town. Both horses, quiet for a week, seemed to relish the workout.

The run of warm weather had continued, and later, Jefferson and Annalise walked up the slope to the little cemetery.

"We don't need any more graves up here," Annalise said.

He stopped to kiss her.

"Jefferson, I've been so worried."

"Thanks to Weasel, we've identified two of the vigilantes. We also have a good notion as to who shot Charlie. This could be over soon."

"With guns?"

"Probably."

"Isn't there another way to do it?"

"I don't know how. Think of it this way. It'll be more dangerous than a picnic, and less dangerous than a stampede."

"Jefferson, that doesn't help."

"Let's sit under that tree." He guided her to a shady spot and sat next to her.

"I need to tell you this. A strange man came into the store yesterday, and talked to Reverend Brooks. He was rambling on about Cincinnati. Said he knew Herman. Do you remember a Carl Jackson?"

"Herman knew everybody. That name isn't familiar."

"Did your gardener have a nickname?"

"Just William. That's all we ever called him."

"He was apparently with two other men who stayed outside. This Carl Jackson was a thin man with a scar, and bad teeth."

"No. I don't know."

"Jonah described one of the men who waited outside. Said he was husky and dark, clumsy looking."

Something began to bother her, a thought that wouldn't complete. "No."

"The other seemed to be middle-aged, well dressed and walked with a cane."

Her eyes widened, and she gasped.

"Annalise. What is it?" He reached for her. She was quietly sobbing.

She forced the tears to stop. "The night of the attack. I've been having dreams about it. Each time that it happens, there is more information. I haven't been sure that it was more than a nightmare. But each time, the same people are after me. The man with the cane. The cane. Suddenly I remember what happened. Vividly. The cane, of course."

"Annalise?"

"I know who killed Herman. Who attacked me." She began to cry again. "It was Corby Pitcock."

"From the plantation?"

"Yes. Yes! The large man Jonah described, that was Luther, the one you knocked out. The scarred man…he raped me that night. It was them, Jefferson. I'm sure of it. No doubt at all. It was them. Corby Pitcock!"

"And they're in Abilene," Jefferson said quietly.

"Annalise, we've got to share this with Joshua and Whit. It increases the danger in town and complicates whatever we do now. I don't want you to have to talk about it again. I'll tell them."

"No, please. I have to do it."

"Do you want to do it now?"

"Yes. But can we include Rose and Margaret? They're my family now."

The room was dramatically quiet, save for the soft, steady voice of Annalise. Her bedroom was the chosen location, away from the bustle of the house. Rose sat next to her on the bed, one arm around her shoulders.

Whit cleared his throat as the narration ended, a half-hour of definitive description, containing segments that were clear for the first time…the knife…Jefferson's letter…the cane, swung against her head…the smashed front door. "Annalise, you're a remarkable woman. I'm sorry that you had to endure all of that, and that you had to relive it for us."

"We love you so much, Annalise," Margaret's voice broke.

"This is another layer of danger. They're in Abilene. They can only be here to get to Jefferson," Joshua remarked.

"Pitcock is crippled because of me. He's probably lost his plantation or a lot of money in the past two years," Jefferson said. "The attack on Annalise, and their questioning to Jonah about me are both indications that they're after revenge.

"What can we do?" Rose asked.

"They have to answer for atrocities that go back years. Annalise's mother. Herman. I'm going after them," Jefferson asserted.

"No, son. Not by yourself. We're going to do this with you. Herk and Big and I will ride with you and Joshua," Whit stated.

Margaret started. "I've got a say in this. The people whom I love most dearly will be at risk. Why don't you all come out here while you're reasoning it out? It's safe out here."

"I'd say no to that, Mrs. Brody," Jefferson responded. "That would put everyone here in danger. We don't want to hide from these people. Our running from this makes them stronger."

"With Jonah, we'd be six. If you count the Kaynes, there might be fifteen of them, at least eight of them good with guns. We'll have to find a way to separate them," Whit offered.

"Mr. Brody, they won't be together. We'd probably need to go after the Ruffians first, then the three who attacked Annalise. The Kaynes are toothless nuisances. I'd say we go after them last. We can probably count on Farnes and Prudhomme to help, if we can find them," Joshua said.

"I'm going with you," Annalise stated.

"No. You're not. I don't want to worry about you. I know that you've got a stake in this, Sweetheart, but it's going to get hot," Jefferson countered.

"Jack, Daddy, take Jack. Catharine's in town; he'll want to be there. Noah and Lige are good with guns," Rose said.

"If we're all in town, this ranch is unprotected," Whit interrupted.

"Whit, every woman out here can use a gun. Bird is as good as some of you."

"No, Maggie. What about Myra? Bear Woman? Miyama? Caroline? I doubt if any of them have even held a gun."

"My God, Daddy. What have we come to?"

"We have no choice, Rosie. We have no choice."

There was a gentle rapping at the door. Caroline peeked in. "Reverend Brooks just rode in. Doc Rosbottom is with him. He needs to see you."

Jonah explained that he had closed the store early. The man named Carl Jackson had spent the afternoon across the street from the store, watching. "Something strange about that. I didn't want Jefferson and Joshua to ride back into some surprise. He could be a Border Ruffian. I didn't see the other two."

"No, they're not Ruffians. Sit down, Jonah. We've got a lot to tell you," Whit said.

An hour later, all of the men gathered around the large table in the bunkhouse. Whit explained what he knew, and a proposed plan for the next day. "My thought is that we have to go after them. They're not going to go away."

Herkimer's expression changed markedly.

"Let me get this straight," he said. "Six of us are goin' up against fifteen men, most of whom we won't recognize or don't know. That it?"

"Yes, Herkimer. It is."

"Sounds about right. I'm in."

"Me too," Big snorted.

"Think about it, Herkimer. You two don't have a stake in this."

"The hell you say," Herkimer answered, "We're family."

Whit swallowed hard. The room got quiet.

"Ammunition, boys. It ain't going to be over quick. Make sure you got plenty of ammo," Herk asserted.

"Could be that we won't see any of them tomorrow," Jonah said.

"If not, we'll go back Monday. Tuesday, if we have to. Jack, I need you in charge of things here, in case we get busy, and someone rides out to cause problems."

****

In a room on the top floor of the Drover's Cottage, eight men held a council of war.

"Thought we wasn't s'posed to be together."

"We's past that," Bravo Wright replied. "Somethin's goin' on. Dex and Oscar got tailed by them Chase boys. Don't know why they was tailin' them."

"How'd they know anythin'? We ain't been careless. Don't nobody know why we're here," a man remarked.

"Mebbe that loco man what I was talkin' to, mebbe he said somethin'. When they found the note on the sheriff, the old man give us away."

"They don't know nothin' for sure. If'n they did, they'd come after us," Newton said.

"Been wonderin'. Why they tail Oscar and Dex if the old man said somethin'? He never even seen them two." Bravo added.

"Mebbe it's them wanted posters. They'se every where."

"Nope it ain't them. No pictures. No, they know somethin'. They'se onto us. They got us in their sights. We're changin' plans. All of us goin' to stick together from now on. There's eight of us. Only three of them were tailin' these two. There ain't no law in town, leastwise any that can handle eight of us. Most they can put together is two. Them Chase boys start tailin' us again, we open up on them, then hightail it out of town. Them three ain't laws nohow."

"What if they're waitin' for help from the authorities, a posse?"

"If'n we see men ride into town, we just ride away. Forget the bank."

"Mebbe we should ride out now, Bravo."

"Newton, you turnin' yellow belly on me? Getting' them Chases'll get the attention of every Rebel man in the country. We be heroes. Too good to pass up. We see them Chases after us, we shoot 'em. We'll figger out the bank later."

"Another thing, boss," Oscar noted, "they called out your name. Bravo. That's somethin' to worry about."

"Then you worry 'bout that, Oscar!" Bravo roared. "Ain't going to cost me no sleep. You six check into the Drover's tonight. Tomorrow, we'll all go out onto the street and see what happens."

Far into the night, lanterns and candles burned in the bedrooms of the ranch. Whispered endearments and nervous conversation competed for time. Joshua asked Rose to bring Jacob into their bed, and Bird heard the words, "You're special to me," from Herkimer, somewhat short of "I love you," but she considered the source.

Annalise's mind was busy making plans for the next day, plans so terrifying that she could not speak them. She abandoned those thoughts when Jefferson came to her.

In the master's bedroom, Margaret sought to diffuse her tense husband.

"Whit, maybe they've left town. Maybe you won't see them."

"We've got to make it happen tomorrow, Maggie. There are three groups of them. They wouldn't all leave town."

"This wouldn't just go away, would it?"

"No."

"You'll be with good men. Just be careful. Except for the brothers, you're all old men," she said, patting his cheek.

"I'm not worried about me. Our family will take some hits tomorrow. Nothing will ever bc the same."

Several hours before, Whit had gathered everyone in the front room, describing all scenarios, and distributing firearms and ammunition to everyone. There were quick lessons on usage. His collection cabinets were empty when he finished.

"Take care of each other tomorrow," he had told them. "We should be back here well before dark. You here at the ranch stay vigilant. Listen to Jack. No one is to come into town. Tomorrow we'll do what we have to do. God be with all of you."

At daybreak, without breakfast, six men saddled their horses, and Doc hitched his carriage.

"Doc," Whit said, "You don't have to do this. You can stay out here."

"No, Whit. All of you are the closest thing to kin that I've had…for a long time. I'm going."

"Herkimer," Jefferson asked. "Any thoughts?"

"Yeah. You put those fifteen men together, they don't make one good Comanche. Let's get it over with."

The six rode abreast on the lane away from the ranch. Doc followed behind.

Minutes after they were out of sight, Annalise, fully dressed, ran to the stable and began to saddle Rags.

"Annalise," Bird called from behind her, "What are you doing?"

"The man I love is going to Abilene. The men who killed my mother and step-father are in Abilene. I need to be in Abilene." She swung up into the saddle.

"Why did I know that you'd do this? I can't talk you out of it, can I?"

"No. It's time for me to take control again. I have to go,"

"Then wait a minute. I'm going with you. I've got a man in Abilene too."

"What?"

"Never mind. Let's go before someone tries to talk us out of it. You have your pistol?"

"Tucked into my pants. Ammunition in my pockets."

"Wait until I get saddled up."

"Bravo?"

"No. We ain't gonna be scared down. What do you think? Hide in our hotel? There was only three men, two of them Chases. I hope they come today. If'n we gun them down, who can blame us? They been after us. They ain't lawmen."

"We gonna be here all day?"

Eight Ruffians were in front of the Ussery Farm Supply Store, lounging. Bravo and Newton were on the bench in front, the other six standing or sitting casually next to them. The street was quiet. None of the stores was open on Sunday, and the walkers who came by them were the homeless, or families on their ways to one of the three small churches on the east side.

"If they show up, what we gonna do?"

"Nothing, Dex. Nothing. They come with their guns out, we gonna shoot. If'n they just out watchin' us, we just sit here."

Two men sat on the step to the supply front door. "We mind our business, and don't jump outa our skin, we gonna git our chance at them. Mebbe not today. But soon." Bravo spit into the street. "Now, boys, be friendly to these people." He tipped his hat to a young girl walking with her parents. "Mawnin' little lady."

Her father pushed her ahead, away from them.

The seven men rode into the west end of Abilene, and crossed the bridge over the creek. Weasel suddenly appeared out of nowhere and flagged them down a short distance from the Chase store.

"Jozwah. I seen them! Three men. I couldn't do nuthin'. Sorry, Jozwah."

"What are you talking about?"

"They busted up your place. Last night after dark."

Joshua rode quickly to First Street. The store's front windows were destroyed. He saw that from a half-block away. Large shards of glass were strewn on the front porch. He dismounted as the others came up behind him. He stepped through the front door with his gun drawn.

Barrels were overturned. Boxes and crates were scattered. The serving counter was pushed over, as were rows of shelves.

"Jozwah, it were a man with a cane. Two others."

"Pitcock," Jefferson said.

"Weasel," Joshua asked, "did you tell the deputies?"

"They gone, Jozwah. Left for good. Left their badges on the desk. They gone."

"Joshua, you know where Mayor Henry lives?" Whit asked.

"Big house, about a half-mile northwest, out Cedar Street. Why?"

"We're going to get deputized," Whit responded.

Disheveled, Henry answered the insistent knocking on his front door. A large dog stuck his nose out and growled.

"Yes, got word that the deputies pulled out. Seems they were threatened by those two brothers from Wicks' whorehouse. The Dooleys. Bad people, but they haven't broken any laws here," Henry advised.

"Can you deputize all of us? We're going to clean up the town today," Whit said.

"On the Lord's Day? This can wait until tomorrow."

"Listen, Mr. Mayor. We've got a minister with us, and I'm sure he blesses what we're about to do. One way or another, this is going to get messy, but we're going to do it."

"Wait here," Henry responded. When he returned, he handed a paper to Whit. "U.S. marshal showed up yesterday afternoon. Gave me this." It was a wanted poster for Bravo Wright, with a sketch of the Ruffian included. "Don't know if it'll help."

"U.S. marshal was in town?"

"Yes. Wasn't much help though. Said there was no proof that the Ruffians were here. Governor sent him. I had nothing to tell him. Law enforcement is committed to Missouri. Said to contact him immediately if something came up."

"Something did come up," Whit said. "They're here. We found two of them yesterday."

"You'll wait until I send him a telegram?"

"No, we won't, Mr. Henry. You send your message, but we're going to end this today."

Six horses were hitched in front of the Chase store. Doc, still in his carriage, waited for instructions.

"Herkimer, you've done this sort of thing before. What do you suggest?" Whit asked.

"I'd say we walk up Texas Street, in the street, with guns pulled. Doc can drive up the street maybe 100 feet ahead, just like he's riding through town on a Sunday morning. Doc, keep your eyes peeled on the spaces between buildings. You see anything suspicious, hold up your hand on that side."

"I've never seen any of these men. How will I know?"

"You see anybody in the alleys or spaces, let us know. Anybody. The first shot, you head for cover. You got a firearm?"

"A shotgun, right here."

"Have to tell you, Whit. Gunplay is good. We just arrest them, I don't know where we put fifteen men."

"Jefferson and I are targets. Maybe we ought to walk apart from the rest of you," Joshua suggested.

"We stay together, side by side. Everybody loaded up?"

The other five nodded.

"When the shooting starts, find cover. Don't shoot it out from the street," Herkimer warned.

"Jonah said it last night. We may not see any of them," Whit said. "Everybody ready ? Big?"

"Done this before."

Doc started his carriage onto Texas Street. The other six followed, Herkimer slightly to the left side, flanked by Whit and Big. Jonah was on the right, with Jefferson to his left, and Joshua on the building side.

The procession started up Texas Street. A couple passed on Whit's side. "Folks, there's going to be some shooting directly. Better take cover," Whit advised.

Small collections of Abilene citizens were strolling, riding, or congregated along the street. Most understood that trouble was imminent, with six men with guns drawn walking resolutely up the street. The street began to clear.

Up ahead, Doc sat upright, and raised his right arm above the carriage hood. Jonah and Joshua turned to that side as they came to an alley. False alarm. Two older men, obviously hung over, stumbled toward them. "Stay back in there," Jonah growled.

Jefferson saw them first, eight men in front of the farm supply. He saw the fat man among them. "The Ruffians, up ahead on the left," he said, loud enough for the others to hear.

"Keep walking," Herkimer said.

Bird and Annalise rode up to the Chase store cautiously., noticing the destruction and the six tethered horses.

"We're not that far behind them, a half-hour at most. Where are they?" Bird asked.

"They've got to be on foot on Texas Street," Annalise offered.

Up First Street just past the Town Stables, Pitcock looked at Muley. "Well look at that. I guess we didn't kill her."

"You was right. We coulda shot it out with them six men. Waitin' here was smart." Luther was smiling.

"You want I should take a shot at them?" Muley asked.

"Too far away, but a shot will get them off those horses. Yeah, Muley, take a shot."

"May bring back them six men. Can't shoot it out with all of them, boss," Luther said.

"They were on foot. Left several minutes ago. I don't know," Pitcock replied.

Then they heard a gun fire far down Texas Street. Then several more. "Muley, take your shot. Sounds like those six are going to be busy."

Annalise spun her mare at the sound of the distant shot. Muley's shot glanced harmlessly off of the building behind them. Immediately both women were off of their horses. Both disappeared into the store through the broken front window, as their horses trotted away up First Street.

"Boss, they're back. There's six of them comin' this way. They got their guns out! Must be the law!"

"I see 'em, dammit! Don't look good, boys. Get ready," Bravo said in a nervous voice.

"What you think? What you think!"

"I think we're gonna do some shootin'!"

There was a flurry of activity on the small porch. Newton pulled his pistol, and fired a shot at the advancing group.

Instantly there was a salvo back from all six. From seventy-five feet away, nothing hit its mark. A man in front of the store was in the act of turning around his large wagon. The gunfire panicked him. He sprang from the jump seat and sprinted to cover, leaving the wagon sideways in the street, horses rearing.

Doc Rosbottom turned his carriage hard to the right, and drove into a gap between buildings.

Bravo, Newton, and Dex ran into the street to the cover of the wagon. Their five companions ran for the corner of the farm supply building.

Thirty yards away, Jefferson and Jonah broke for a watering trough in front of them. Joshua took cover in a recessed doorway. On the other side of the street, Herkimer and Big walked toward the building's safety in no hurry, each shooting with two pistols. Whit was pressed against a doorway.

Gunfire which sounded as if it were one long burst followed. Windows broke, and smoke already hung in the air, drifting north.

The five Ruffians at the farm supply were undecided. Three made a break for the wagon. Oscar was only feet from protection when Jefferson gunned him down.

"Big, them other two may circle behind them buildings. Head 'em off," Herkimer yelled. Big trotted down the side yard and turned just as a Ruffian appeared in front of him. Big fired off four shots in quick succession, and the Ruffian crumpled. Behind the felled Ruffian, the second one appeared, running toward Big, and firing wildly.

The Ruffian continued to charge and then suddenly stiffened and fell, at the same time that his last bullet thumped into Big's chest. Big stumbled and dropped his pistols, then he was on his knees. Blood began to run from his mouth, drenching his shirt front. He pitched forward.

"Pa, Look at that. The whole Brody group is here, it 'pears."

From a vantage point well behind the battle, Old Man Kaynes saw it too.

"Git to the horses. We gonna ride out and burn us a ranch!"

Whit turned around, a reflexive check, and noticed a man walking up behind the three on the other side. A shotgun was leveled toward Joshua.

"Joshua ! Behind you !" As the warning ended, Whit poured a volley of shots toward the stalker. Several hit the target, and the man fell, rolled over once and was still.

Joshua pivoted toward the commotion behind him. "Uriah Cobb," he said to himself, "You just couldn't leave it alone."

The movement had exposed Whit, and he felt a searing pain in his foot. He fell back against the building and began to reload.

"J.T! There's a gunfight over in town! Heard it start. Jist checked it out. Herkimer Grimes, the famous gunfighter, is in it. The preacher man, he's in it too!" Lester yelled at his brother in the Wicks bordello. "C'mon now, we gonna have some fun!"

"Yessir, Lester, we gonna have some fun." J.T. quickly pulled on clothing and grabbed a rifle from the corner, and his holster. "Where we be goin'?"

"Just over on Texas Street. C'mon!"

Bullets skidded across the dusty street.

"Dex ! Get around behind 'em!" Bravo yelled.

Dex suddenly ran for a building gap on the south side, to circle behind Joshua and Jefferson.

"I've got him," Jefferson called as he moved quickly between buildings.

"They'll try to get behind us," Bird said. "There's more than one."

"I'll go to the back door," Annalise answered.

A staccato burst of shots came from the street side. "That's cover fire. They're sending someone to the back," Bird warned.

Annalise hurried to the back door. Bird saw a skinny man running toward the front of the store, and across in front of it. She had no shot. The six hitched horses were in the way.

Arrived in the back room, Annalise saw Pitcock and Luther skulking near Joshua's shed. A feeling of revulsion overtook her. They were coming toward the back door. She waited until she saw a shadow beyond the door's small window, and fired her pistol three times at the window and door. She heard a loud exclamation.

Bird called from the front room, "Annalise ! How many?"

"Two ! I shot through the door as they tried to open it."

"Stay there!" There was a shot from the front room.

Annalise waited. She moved to the side to get a different bead on the window, if they tried to return fire or come through.

From outside, "Annalise, it's Bird. You can come out. They're gone."

Annalise stepped out, noticing a splatter of blood on the step.

"You must have gotten one of them, Annalise. They've gone around the building."

"I heard you shoot just now."

"Stupid man rushed the store when he heard your shots. Ran into my bullet. Heard him scream."

Lester and J.T. edged between the Longhorn Saloon and a gambling house, and watched the ongoing battle.

"What we gonna do, Lester?"

"Now jist hang on, J.T."

On the street in front of them, the incessant gunfire slowed down. Reloading was furious, but ammunition was exhausting.

Whit noticed movement several buildings down on the opposite side. It was Doc Rosbottom, positioning for a shot on the four Ruffians behind the wagon. He was directly in front of the Longhorn Saloon without cover.

"Doc," he yelled, "Be careful! That's far enough!"

At the east end, Jefferson saw Dex come out behind a building. Dex turned toward him and, surprised, shot quickly and badly, well over the head of Jefferson. Jefferson calmly shot him in the upper chest. Turning back, Jefferson had a view of First Street. Over there was a horse, running free.

It was Annalise's mare, Rags. He heard several shots from somewhere on First Street. He made a quick calculation. The two men who disappeared with Big minutes ago, hadn't shown up back in the fight. If Big got them, there were only four Ruffians left, all behind the wagon. He ran back to the street. "Joshua," he called, "Annalise is here. I saw her horse. She's in trouble !"

"Go!" Joshua yelled back.

Then Jefferson was running toward First Street.

"To hell with this!" Herkimer said. He stepped into the street. With a pistol roaring from each hand, he walked toward the wagon.

"I'll be damned," Whit said to himself.

A Herkimer shot thudded into the forehead of a Ruffian. His hat flew off, and he slid down the side of the wagon.

"That's him, J.T.! That's Herkimer Grimes ! Watch this!"

Lester walked into the street between the wagon and Herkimer with his hands high above his head. The shooting stopped momentarily from both sides. He stopped fifteen feet in front of Herkimer, and his hands dropped to his pistol butts.

"Hi, how's it goin'?"

Herkimer stopped. "Who are you?" he growled.

"I'm going to kill you Grimes. I'm your worst nightmare." Lester was grinning.

"Not even close," Herkimer replied, and shot Lester in the chest.

Lester's eyes opened wide for a brief moment. Then he fell dead.

Herkimer's attention returned to the wagon.

A primal scream came from the alley. J.T. charged the scene with his rifle aimed at Herkimer. Ten feet away, Doc Rosbottom pulled the trigger of his shotgun, and scored a hit on J.T., who twisted and fired a wild shot as he went down.

The shot struck Doc.

J.T. had enough left to scramble to his knees, pull his pistol, and aim again at Doc. Jonah dispatched him with two rapid shots.

Annalise and Bird moved carefully around the building, on the same path Pitcock and Luther had used moments before. They came out on First Street. Nothing.

"They're in the Town Stables, Annalise. The door is wide open."

"They must be in trouble. There were six horses here to get away on. I'm going in."

"No. Too dangerous. Let's wait for help."

The gunfire from Texas Street continued.

"Sounds as if that will be going on for a while. These three may not even be in the stable. We've got to check," Annalise argued. "We could be waiting outside of an empty building."

"You're a stubborn girl."

"They killed two people that I loved. And they…you know."

"Give me a minute to get behind them. The back door. Just be careful. If they're in there, two of them are wounded."

Annalise waited, out of the line of fire from inside the building. She slowly walked up to the open double door. So dark in there. It would take time after she got inside to get used to the darkness. Should she go in?

She ran through the doors and ducked quickly to the left. Islands of reflected light from the open door and small windows high on the wall revealed several horses on both sides of the stable's length. The back doors were closed and that end was dark. She listened. A horse to her right bumped against a side wall. She almost shot.

There was nervous pawing somewhere ahead. Somewhere in the darkness.

She edged along the stalls on the left. Where was Bird? The back doors were still shut, probably locked. Bird would come in behind her, from the front. A horse whinnied loudly as she passed it, startling her again.

She didn't see the cane that came crashing down on her shoulders.

Herkimer continued toward the wagon. He shot a Ruffian who stood to pull bullets from his ammunition belt.

"Boss! We got to get out! We got to run!" Newton stood and bellowed at Bravo Wright.

Herkimer's next shot thudded into the head of Newton. But Herkimer was finished. Both of his pistols clicked. Empty. Bravo took his shot and it spun Herk around. He fell backward.

Then Bravo realized that he was alone. Steadily advancing on him were Whit, Joshua, and Jonah. He put his pistol against his temple and pulled the trigger.

The street was suddenly very quiet.

Pitcock, his left arm shattered by the shots through the door of the store, had swung the cane at Annalise with all of the strength he could muster with his other arm.

She rolled away, unhurt, but her pistol was somewhere in the darkness. Pitcock stood over her. A gun had replaced the cane, and she heard the click of the hammer being cocked.

There was a shot from behind her. Bird. The charge tore into Pitcock's upper leg, well above his good knee. He dropped the gun and grabbed his leg, and fell to the floor.

A large shadow crashed heavily into Bird. Luther had her pinned with his hands on her throat. Annalise picked up the cane, and swung it hard into Luther's face with enough force to send him rolling off of Bird.

"You ain't got no guns now. That cane ain't gonna stop me," Luther said, as he got to his feet. He swiped at blood running from his nose.

"Kill them, Luther," Pitcock moaned, as he fought to stay conscious.

"That cane ain't gonna stop me, boss."

"But I will," a voice sounded from near the front door.

"Jefferson!"

"Jefferson, there's another one in here somewhere," Bird called.

Muley's voice quavered from the locked back door. "Don't shoot. I been shot. Can't see nuthin'."

"Throw your gun out here. Crawl out where we can see you!" Jefferson ordered.

"Can't see nuthin'. Shot in the face."

Muley's pistol skidded to Jefferson's feet. He handed it to Annalise. The skinny man followed, scrambling on all fours. Even in the faint light, Jefferson could see the scarred face smeared with blood. Bird's shot on the porch had probably grazed his head or his cheek.

"If either of these two moves, kill them both," Jefferson told Annalise. He unbuckled his holster belt and tossed it to Bird. "I don't know your name, fat boy, but let's see how you do against another man, instead of women."

Jefferson walked to him and slapped him twice. "C'mon. Pretend that I'm a little girl."

Luther's expression changed. His eyebrows furrowed and his vacant expression became a snarl. He charged and grabbed Jefferson and they fell to the floor. Jefferson pulled him to his feet. Holding him by the collar of his shirt, he threw a punch to the ample midsection. Luther ooomphed, and then took a fist to his face, and there were suddenly teeth loose in his mouth.

Luther countered with a wild roundhouse, which Jefferson ducked. He floored Luther with a fist to his nose.

Groggy, Luther stood again. Jefferson's legendary control disappeared. This hulk of a man had killed his uncle and raped his beloved on a floor littered with glass and blood. He pushed Luther to the back wall of an empty stall. The wall held him up while Jefferson punished him.

Luther was already unconscious when the final punches were thrown. Jefferson finished, and pushed the fat man into the horse excrement in the stall.

"Is everybody good?" Jefferson asked.

"This man over here," Bird answered next to Pitcock, " he's not so good."

Pitcock was slowly bleeding out. The wound to his upper leg was severe, and he was speaking gibberish through pale lips. "Can't blame me. You ruined me. I lost everything because of you."

Jefferson ignored him, and looked to Annalise. She was standing mute over the fallen Luther, the pistol raised and pointed at his head. "Mother…" she whispered.

She slumped and the pistol was lowered. "I can't do it."

She began to shake, and then she was in Jefferson's arms.

Pitcock's moaning became less audible.

"Jefferson, all of the shooting up the street…" Bird asked.

"We ran into the Ruffians. Four of them and an interloper were down when I saw Rags running free. I've got to go back." He took his gun belt from Bird.

"I'm going with you," Bird asserted.

"Me too,' Annalise said.

"No time to argue about that. Stay here until I come back. Keep your guns on these three. Shoot if you have to."

"Won't be three. This man's dead." Bird pointed at Pitcock.

Jefferson raced across the street to Storm, and was gone.

Joshua rushed to Rosbottom. "Doc?"

The doctor was sitting up, propped against the wall of the Longhorn saloon.

"He got me pretty good, Joshua." His voice was halting and weak.

"You hang on. I'm going to help you. Stay awake, Doc. You've got to talk me through this."

"You've got to stop the bleeding, Joshua."

Joshua pulled Doc's shirt up. The wound was in his belly, a gaping hole. Joshua pulled off his own shirt, balled it, and pressed it against the wound.

Whit called up to Herkimer, "You alright, Herk?"

"Yeah, I'm fine. Shoulder. Better check on them Ruffians. Look for Big." Whit stood, unsteadily. He felt wetness in his boot. "Jonah, see if you can find Big."

Jonah saw Big as soon as he circled the farm supply store. He knew as he approached the body that Big was gone. He lay on his side, his eyes open wide. The two Ruffians lay still near each other. He returned to the street. "Big didn't make it. He took two Ruffians with him," he announced to Whit.

"Gotta be another Ruffian behind the saloon. Maybe Jefferson too," Whit called back. He unfolded the wanted poster that Henry had given him, and approached the wagon, limping noticeably. The face on the paper matched the first Ruffian he checked, the last man standing, the one who had ended his own life.

"Well, Mr. Bravo Wright, your war is over now," he said.

Jefferson rode up and quickly dismounted. "Son, where have you been?" Whit asked.

"The three from Missouri. They were shooting it out with Annalise and Bird."

"The girls came into town?"

"They're here. Pitcock is dead. The other two are under control. What happened here?"

"Big's dead. Three of us wounded. Ruffians are all dead."

Several feet away, Jonah examined J.T. Dooley. Dooley's eyes fluttered open, and he saw the minister. "Damn you!" He coughed twice. "Leastways, we kilt your black boy."

Cleetus. The Dooleys had killed him back in December, and had burned the church, probably at the behest of Wicks.

"Wicks. He put you up to it?"

J.T.'s eyes rolled back, and he shivered, and then he stopped.

Doc watched Joshua minister to him, as if he were far away.

Then, starkly clear, he had a vision. He wasn't slumped against a building. He was on the bank of a beautiful expanse of water shaded by tall trees. He had a fishing pole in his hands. To his right was a crudely crafted boat, and sitting inside was a beautiful dark-haired lady, dressed in white and beckoning to him.

A crutch lay up on the bank behind her.

He smiled at her. She smiled back. He put down his pole and walked to the pirogue. She extended her hand to help him in.

He grabbed an oar and pushed them off. And he poled toward the sunset.

"Doc's dead," Joshua said.

Elon had scanned the horizon all morning, looking for movement or dust clouds, or whayever else would give notice that someone was coming. He was several hundred yards inside the Brody gate, somewhat hidden by a hillock. His horse was tied to a nearby tree.

The women and Hata Wu were inside the main house, each assigned to a window on the ground level. Lige and Noah crouched at opposite ends of the large valley. Jack was on his horse, riding the crest of the slope nearest the river, and then across the north end above the crops and cemetery. Charlie Fox rode back and forth a mile to the north-east, ready for a race back to the house if he saw anyone. Miyama was in Caroline's room upstairs watching Jacob and Isaiah.

Elon tipped his hat back. Staying alert was becoming a problem. Little Isaiah had a bad night. Myra was out of sorts. He had not enjoyed much sleep the night before, and the sun was encouraging a quick nap. The lane he was assigned to was the main ingress to the house and buildings. Nobody sneaking onto the property would come that way, he reasoned. Too obvious.

He lay back against the grass and looked up at a massive white cloud rolling across the sky. His eyes blinked and closed.

He awoke suddenly sometime later, and was looking up at another cloud. And then the cloud was obscured by a darkness, a blur.

Old Man Kaynes slit his throat.

"Pa, you done kilt him!"

"Don't matter none. One less to worry about."

The four then rode farther up the lane, left their horses, and advanced slowly on the ranch house, crossing the wide expanse of flat land in front, using trees as cover.

"Ain't likin' this, Pa. Too quiet."

"Hush your mouth. Get the top off that can. We get to the house, you run along the porch spillin' that kerosene. I be right behind you, lightin' it. Then we do the back. Calvin, you two keep us covered. After this, we burn the big barn."

"Gotta be some people here somewheres, Pa."

Pa Kaynes spit. "Women. That Injun we winged. The black man. They'se prob'ly somewhere with their cows. They show up, we shoot 'em. Then we skedaddle."

"Long way to the horses, Pa, if'n we have to run."

"Son, they done shot you once already. Tried to lock us up. When we seen them in town at that funeral, they was mostly women. This be our chance."

"Wait until dark?"

"Hell no. Them others might be back by then. We doin' it now!"

"Somebody see us, Pa, the whole bunch be after us."

"We be long gone afore that. Ain't gonna stay in Abilene nohow."

They moved forward, the old man and the son carrying the can leading the way. Steps behind, the fat Kaynes whispered to Calvin. "This be crazy. Pa gonna git us all kilt."

"Dunno. Don't see nobody."

Kaynes walked the last hundred feet brazenly. His sons hopped behind.

Twenty feet from the porch, they were startled by Margaret, who yelled from the front door, "That's far enough! Stop where you are!"

"Pa?"

Kaynes was suddenly uncertain, but he had come too far. He pulled a pistol from his belt and shot at the front door. Instantly there was gunfire from the front windows. Kaynes leaped onto the porch.

"Git pourin', son!" the old man ordered.

The son tipped the container and kerosene splashed onto the porch floor. Kaynes scratched a match.

Noah, coming from around the porch, shot for the son but hit the can, and the oil spilled on the father and his lighted match. There was a bright puff and the old man was on fire. His shrieking confused the son and he leaped off of the porch and shot at Noah. The other two sons looked for a way to escape.

Old Man Kaynes was consumed by flames. Lige and Charlie galloped up quickly from the east, pistols drawn.

The front door jumped open. Margaret and Rose fired their shotguns. The son was hit and partially disabled, but he aimed his gun at Margaret. Jack suddenly appeared at the west end of the porch and shot once. The young Kaynes staggered around briefly, his pistol dangling from his finger, and slumped over five feet from his dying father. His last view was of Caroline, Rose, Margaret, Bear Woman, Hata Wu, and Myra lined up on the porch, pointing their weapons at the other two brothers.

The brothers were in a bind, and panic ruled the day. They both fired a round toward the porch. Lige shot Calvin from horseback at close range. The fat son turned to run. Eight guns went off at once. The fat son stood up straight, and fell.

"Any more?" Jack called.

"Jack…water…" Rose said, pointing at the old man.

"Too late for him." A growing flame caught his attention. "We'd better douse that fire on the porch."

"Where's Elon?" Myra asked.

Bird reined Whit's horse up close to Herkimer and Whit, propped up in front of the Longhorn Saloon. She dismounted and ran next to them.

"Herkimer, you're shot."

"Ain't much, really. Seen worse. What are you doing in town?"

"I came to help Annalise. Mr. Brody, you hit too?"

"Took one in the foot. We're waiting for Doctor Beedle. Someone went for him."

Curious townspeople milled in the street, checking bodies and damage to nearby buildings.

"Big's dead, Bird. Doc Rosbottom too." Herk said. She lowered her head.

"Where's Jefferson? He went back to collect you." Whit asked.

"That's him coming there," she pointed.

Heads turned to see Jefferson, astride Storm, pushing a bloodied fat man up the street. Behind him, Annalise, on Big's horse, pulled Joshua's horse carrying a man strapped across the saddle.

"They're the ones who killed her mother and stepfather, and raped her," Bird explained. "The third one's dead."

"That's everyone except the Kaynes," Whit observed. "I wonder where they are."

"Under a rock somewhere," Herkimer said.

Walking up to the group, Jonah responded tersely, "No, that's not everyone." He was loading his pistol. Then he was striding toward Whit's horse. "I need to borrow your horse, Whit. I'll be back directly."

The townspeople began to drag the scattered bodies to the boardwalk in front of the bank. "Joshua, don't let them stack Doc and Big with those others. We'll take care of them," Whit yelled.

A photographer set up his tripod and began taking pictures. "Eleven of them," Whit noted. "My god."

"Hope the undertakers show up soon. Don't like what's happening," Bird observed. She sat next to Herkimer.

Wicks had seen the Dooley brothers leave earlier. Then he had heard the faint sound of gunfire. Maybe they got shot, he thought. That was fine with him. It was only a matter of time before Lester would take over the whorehouse, maybe even shoot him. Lester had already commandeered the 13-year old, using her for his own pleasure, refusing to let Wicks install her downstairs. More than that, the other whores were listening to Lester, disrespecting him. He had thought that he could kill Lester, shoot him in bed or something, but then he'd have to deal with the idiot, J.T. No way he could get both of them.

There was a pounding on the front door. Who the hell would be making that racket on a Sunday afternoon?

"We ain't open!" he yelled, and then the door swung open in pieces.

The minister was in the front parlor with him.

"Mr. Wicks, if you move, you're a dead man." He walked to the second floor stairway, and fired his pistol into the ceiling. The sound reverberated through the house.

"Listen to me ladies, and Tickles, or whatever your name is! Get down here now!" He fired his pistol again. Tickles slowly walked down the stairs with his hands up, then Esme, then several others.

"You've got ten minutes to get your stuff together, and get into the street. If you don't, you'll burn with this house."

"Reverend Brooks," Wicks stuttered, "What are you doin'?"

"We just shot down your gunslingers, Wicks. Before one died, he said that you ordered them to kill Cleetus and burn the church." It was only a half-truth, but it worked.

"That ain't true. I knew they was going to burn the church. I didn't tell them to kill nobody."

"You sent them to burn the church?" Jonah aimed his pistol at Wicks.

"Yes. Yes. But I didn't tell them to kill nobody."

"Five minutes, ladies!" Jonah called upstairs.

Soon the string of ladies scurried down the steps, all carrying valises and sacks.

"You'd better all get away from this building. I don't care where you go. Find another house. Get out of town. Somebody, you," he ordered Esme, "take care of the little girl."

"But we's church-goers, Reverend," Esme protested.

"Get out!"

He and Wicks were alone.

"Take off all of your clothes, Wicks."

"You go to hell!"

Jonah fired a shot which barely missed Wick's foot. He immediately began disrobing.

"Now, spill all of the lamps on the floor, then get me some matches." He followed Wicks to a back room.

"Reverend, let's talk about this. I'd be glad to pay you, anything."

"Mr. Wicks, this is about fire for fire."

Wicks slowly began to empty the kerosene from the lamps.

"Strike the matches. Throw them on the floor."

Wicks, whimpering, followed the instructions. Fires began to build throughout the bottom level.

"Can I get my money?"

"No, Mr. Wicks. It's dirty money. It can burn with the house."

Wicks thought frantically. Could he stop this somehow?

"We're going to leave now. You'd better find some clothes somewhere and get out of town. If I see you in Abilene after tomorrow, I'll shoot you." Jonah punctuated the thought by shooting the mirror behind the bar. Wicks hurried out the front door.

In less than fifteen minutes, the fire was roaring. By that time, Jonah was riding Whit's borrowed horse back to town.

CHAPTER THIRTY-ONE
AFTERMATH

Spring became summer in Kansas, and there were burials and celebrations. There was change, and there was closure.

Big and Elon were buried in the little cemetery on the hill. To perpetuate the area, Whit ordered headstones for all of the graves, including one for Doc Rosbottom. With no kin, he was buried in the same area, in a casket which also contained his banjo and fiddle.

Myra Pack was inconsolable, and for weeks, Miyama tended to little Isaiah.

The danger over, Bear Woman moved back to the cabin she had shared with Cleetus.

Work commenced on a house near the big pond. Given time off by Whit, Jack did most of the work, occasionally joined by Noah or Lige. Catharine rode out daily to help as she could.

The survivors of May 8, Muley and Luther, were taken by wagon to district court, where letters from Jefferson, Annalise, Whit, Mayor Henry, Margaret, and Jonah were read to the officiate. The judge in question, impressed by the defeat of the Ruffians, showed no mercy nor spent appreciable time in his decision. If the Abilene heroes declared these men murderers, so be it. The two killers were promptly found guilty of various murders, and were soon hanged, in what would be viewed as an appropriate miscarriage of justice.

On June 4, Rose gave birth to a healthy girl named after her father's affectionate name for her mother, Maggie.

That same day, Tom "Bear River" Smith was sworn in as police chief of Abilene. One of his first duties was to tame two wild cowboys, Big Hank Hawkins and Wyoming Frank. He arrested them, and they resisted. Despite being outweighed and outnumbered, Smith soundly beat the two into submission in front of a large crowd, and banished them from Abilene. It was immediately clear that this ex-boxer from New York City would not become a peace officer who relied solely on his guns. On his beautiful saddle horse Silverheels, he became an almost mythic symbol of a new order in the cow town. There was relative quiet during the cattle drives. In July, there was not a single miscreant and no untoward incidents. Even more remarkable was the fact that he did it alone; there was no police force, no deputies.

In late June, Joshua surprised Jonah.

"Reverend Brooks, will you still hold services here after we move to California?"

"I doubt that the new owner will be as generous as you have been. We'll hold services outside until the weather changes."

"Well, I've had a thought. You're not going to rebuild on that site, are you?"

"I don't have the energy, or the money."

"Then sell that property, minus the cemetery. Whatever you get for it will be the cost of this store for you."

"What? Your store is worth much more than that."

"Rose and I have talked it over. We want to do it. We don't need that much money."

"Joshua, I don't know what to say."

"We both admire and respect you. You have made as much of a difference here as anybody. You're a good man."

Jonah was still.

"You can convert the bottom level to a full-time church, and live on the second floor like we did. You are going to stay in Abilene?"

"Yes. There are so many lost souls here. Bear Woman wants to stay near Cleetus. I won't leave her."

"Then it's done."

****

For two days, Miyama, Caroline, Rose, and Margaret collected blue lobelia, blue hearts, and prairie phlox from the east fields, and fashioned bridesmaids' bouquets and table decorations.

By wagon, Whit picked up a four-man band which had arrived by train from Kansas City, and housed them in the bunkhouse. Jack and Joshua disappeared for hours on some mysterious project. Catharine worked to alter Rose's wedding dress, which Rose had insisted that Annalise wear. Two chefs were brought in from Abilene, so that Caroline could be a guest, not a cook. Jefferson and Charlie Fox cleaned out the large barn, in case the August weather didn't cooperate.

"Whit, you're still limping," Margaret mentioned one night.

"I suppose I always will to some extent. Looking back to May, I wonder sometimes if it was worth it. We lost three good men. Things changed. Too much."

"We haven't talked much about that terrible time. But you had to do it."

"It seems unfair that you could live your life trying to do the best for everyone, obeying the law, and you end up sacrificing everything out of anger and fear."

"Whit, Abilene is a better place because of that day."

"Maggie, our people faced death, saw death, caused death. They are different people now."

"I think you're looking at it the wrong way. There were resolutions. Doc Rosbottom. He was doing something that he wanted to do, something that bound him to a group he loved, after so many years of loneliness and pain. The threat of a violent death followed Big throughout his life, and when he chose to go with you, he knew what the outcome might be. Every person who contributed that day was doing it out of love for you, or out of a need to correct an injustice."

"I keep wondering if there might have been a better way to handle things."

"You were dealing with fifteen murderers. Fifteen heathens who had no respect for human life. There couldn't have been a different outcome."

"It's been haunting me, Maggie."

"I know, dear. But you have to get past it. Tomorrow, the 'father of the bride' should have a smile on his face."

Annalise, wearing a garland of Deptford pinks, smiled on the arm of Whit, and then beamed throughout the late afternoon ceremony, much of which was a testimony to her heritage and her courage, delivered by a solemn and emotional Jonah.

Midway through a reading, Jefferson caught her eye, and silently bade her to look up. There in the blueness, flying majestically, was a bald eagle.

"Ours?" she mouthed.

He shook his head no, and quietly answered, "But it's a good sign."

Afterward, the band and a photographer from Abilene earned their money. Torches illuminated a large area in the front yard. Margaret approached Whit, sitting at a table and watching the dancers.

He grabbed her hand. "Maggie, are you having a good time, darlin'?"

"Yes, if you'll get up and dance with me again. What are you doing?"

"Watching Herk and Bird dance. Probably the first time ever for him. They've been laughing the entire time."

"Little Jeremiah and Caroline, did you see them dancing? Charlie and Miyama?"

"There are smiles everywhere. We needed this."

"I hope Myra is enjoying herself. I'm worried about her. She told me this morning that she might be leaving soon. Too many memories here."

"The order of business now is for me to get up and dance again on my gimpy foot with the prettiest woman here."

Several minutes later, he told her, "It's time."

He asked for quiet from the crowd.

"I'm glad that all you folks from town hung around past dark. We've got a surprise for you later. After a bad spring for most of us, we needed this joyous occasion, the joining of two souls whom we dearly love. Jefferson and Annalise will leave in three weeks to begin a new life as the owners of a horse ranch in California.

"I can't bring out our wedding present for them. It would get too messy out here. Soon after they arrive in California, Margaret and I will ship twenty of our best horses to them by train." The assemblage applauded loudly.

"Now I know that Jefferson won't let those horses run free. We contacted his business manager in California, a Mr. McNelly, in June. Everyone here at the ranch chipped in and we bought a fence for their property. We got word last week that it is completed."

Jefferson rose to respond.

"Sit down, brother," Joshua said. "Rose and I couldn't believe that two persons so attracted to each other wouldn't soon have a large family. Lawyer McNelly is overseeing the addition of two rooms to your new house, one on each end. One can be a library, if you choose, and the other an extra bedroom for when folks from Abilene come to visit. So, you two will have a library. What else could you possibly need?"

Jefferson stood again. "Annalise and I are overwhelmed. Several years ago, we showed up here, running from a terrible experience in St. Louis. I knew only my brother, who, I have to tell you, is my hero. What we gathered in a short time was a family, a wonderful collection of people. Each of you—all of you—are special to us, and always will be. Thank you so much."

Annalise stood next to her husband.

"It will be difficult to get through this without crying. Despite tragic circumstances in my life, I am the most fortunate person in the universe. I have the most incredible husband, two wonderful step-parents, two sisters—Rose and Catharine—whom I love so dearly, a brother-in-law who is a hero to all of us, and all of you, who are not just friends, but instead the most inspirational family members imaginable." She paused and swallowed. "I have enormous feelings for all of you. Thank you for everything."

Whit took over again. "Now, folks, turn your chairs to face north. That way. And be patient for a moment or two."

A few minutes later, a series of percussive explosions resounded in the darkness, and the night sky filled with bursts of red, yellow, blue, and green.

For the first time in history, fireworks lit up the Kansas plains.

"Whit?" Mayor Henry said through the echoing explosions.

"Joshua ordered them. British explosives. Color's a new thing. Copper and something called strontium and such. They hauled in a wagonload of them."

On the hill above the gardens, Joshua, Hata Wu, and Jack lit long fuses with torches and matches, and multi-colored showers resonated high above the ground.

"We sneaked them in yesterday. Hata Wu's done this before with Oriental fireworks. We were up there until dark, this morning too, laying them out. Had a hard time hiding it from Jefferson and Annalise," Whit continued in a shout barely audible above the din.

"Dangerous?"

"Shouldn't be. Some of the fuses are twenty feet long. Like setting off dynamite."

For twenty minutes, gasps and exclamations from the wedding guests followed each display. There was raucous cheering as they concluded.

****

On Wednesday, November 2, 1870, Bear River Smith attempted to serve a warrant on Andrew McConnell and Moses Miles, wanted in connection with the murder of John Shea.

A gunfight ensued, and Bear River Smith was wounded. As he tried to recover, Moses Miles picked up an axe and decapitated him.

He was replaced in the office of police chief by James Butler "Wild Bill" Hickock.

ACKNOWLEDGMENTS

In developing a time line, for expanding my knowledge of pertinent history, and for comprehensive facts, these sources were invaluable.

The Old West Series, Time-Life Books, 1974

The Civil War Series, Time-Life Books, 1984

Age of the Gunfighter, Joseph Rosa, Salamander Books, 1993

Life History of the United States Series, Time-Life Books, 1964

The American Frontier, William C. Davis, Salamander Books, 2002

The Civil War, Tom Robotham, JG Press, 1992

The Old West Quiz and Fact Book, Rod Gragg, Promontory Press, 1986

The Native Americans, the Indigenous People of North America, Colin Taylor and William C. Sturdivant, Salamander Books, 1991

Encyclopedia of Western Lawmen and Outlaws, Jay Robert Nash, De Capo Press, 1992

The American Heritage New History of the Civil War, Bruce Catton, Penguin Books, 1999

First of the Kansas Cow Towns, George Cushman, the Kansas Historical Society, August, 1940

To confirm facts and for supplemental information, I depended on these books and websites.

A Glimpse of Texas Past, Jeffrey Robenalt, Saga of a Texas Ranger

War in the Redlands, Skipper Steely, Kindle edition

Custer, Jeffrey D. Wert, Simon and Schuster, 1996

The Taos Revolt, Adam James Jones, wordpress.com

The Roar and the Silence, Ronald M. James, Wilbur Shepperoth Series in History and Humanities

Abilene History, Jim Gray, The Kansas Cowboy

Cloudsplitter, Russell Banks, Harper Flamingo, 1998

www.nativelanguages.org/Choctaw.htm

www.choctaw_nation.com

www.thefurtrapper.com/rendezvous_sites

www.onhealth.com/leprosy/article.htm

chemistry.about.com/od/historyofchemistry/a/fireworks

Finally, I found Wikipedia helpful in chasing down lesser incidents, and in providing additional links. Subjects that needed further exploration included Archie Clements, Sacramento, Jermain Loguen, the Natchez Tornado, the Jerry Rescue, the Saluda steamship, the Kansas Land Rush, the Natchez Trace, the Dakota War of 1862, Topeka, and for additional information on Abilene, and the Jackass Regiment.

Historical fiction is a unique genre, almost an oxymoron. Facts sometimes suffer to accommodate characters. For example, Herk, Big, and Flapjack were obviously not at the Texas Ranger's Hibbons Rescue; J.J. Tumlinson was.

There was never a Brody Ranch west of Abilene, nor a Chase homestead above Lake Champlain. At times geography is altered to serve the narrative.

History itself is sometimes an elusive entity. The author found several different versions of the founding of the Comstock Lode and Virginia City, and finally settled on an amalgam of those stories. Also, history can't seem tp decide on "Clement" or "Clements" as the surname of the Confederate raider. His gravestone says "Clements." Historical accounts leave off the final "s."

The great John Jakes was able to feature history, and fit his fictional characters into niches that didn't disturb the factual comtinuum. For us novices, that is a monumental undertaking.

In any case, the author has built this narrative on the premise that actual historical events influence the characters –both fictional and non-fictional, and has attempted to present those events as authentically as possible.

Don Ross